MARK TWAIN

ROUGHING IT

THE MARK TWAIN LIBRARY

The Library offers for the first time popular editions of Mark Twain's best works just as he wanted them to be read. These moderately priced volumes, faithfully reproduced from the California scholarly editions and printed on acid-free paper, are expertly annotated and include all the original illustrations that Mark Twain commissioned and enjoyed.

"Huck waited for no particulars. He sprang away and sped down the hill as fast as his legs could carry him."

—THE ADVENTURES OF TOM SAWYER

Contributing Editors for This Volume

Richard Bucci

Victor Fischer

Michael B. Frank

Kenneth M. Sanderson

Samuel L. Clemens in 1863 (above) and 1872.
Mark Twain Papers, The Bancroft Library (CU-MARK).

The Miner's Dream.

MARK TWAIN

ROUGHING IT

ILLUSTRATED BY TRUE WILLIAMS,
EDWARD F. MULLEN, AND OTHERS

Editors
Harriet Elinor Smith and Edgar Marquess Branch

Associate Editors
Lin Salamo and Robert Pack Browning

A publication of the
Mark Twain Project of The Bancroft Library

University of California Press
Berkeley Los Angeles London

The text of this Mark Twain Library edition of *Roughing It* is identical with the text of the scholarly edition of *Roughing It*, edited by Harriet Elinor Smith and Edgar Marquess Branch (University of California Press, 1993). It was established in accord with the standards of the Center for Scholarly Editions (CSE). Editorial work was supported by a generous grant from the L. J. Skaggs and Mary C. Skaggs Foundation and by matching funds from the National Endowment for the Humanities, an independent federal agency.

University of California Press, one of the most distinguished university presses in the United States, enriches lives around the world by advancing scholarship in the humanities, social sciences, and natural sciences. Its activities are supported by the UC Press Foundation and by philanthropic contributions from individuals and institutions. For more information, visit www.ucpress.edu.

University of California Press
Berkeley and Los Angeles, California

University of California Press, Ltd.
London, England

Library of Congress
Cataloging-in-Publication Data

Twain, Mark, 1835–1910.
Roughing it / Mark Twain ; illustrated by True Williams, Edward F. Mullen, and others ; editors, Harriet Elinor Smith and Edgar Marquess Branch ; associate editors, Lin Salamo and Robert Pack Browning.
p. cm.—(The Mark Twain library)
"A publication of the Mark Twain Project of the Bancroft Library."
Includes bibliographical references (p.).
ISBN 978-0-520-26817-3 (pbk. : alk. paper)
1. Twain, Mark, 1835–1910—Journeys—West (U.S.) 2. Authors, American—19th century—Journeys—West (U.S.) 3. West (U.S.)—Description and travel. I. Smith, Harriet Elinor. II. Branch, Edgar Marquess, 1913–. III. Bancroft Library. IV. Title. V. Series: Twain, Mark, 1835–1910. Mark Twain Library.
PS1318.A1 1996 818′.403 95-30007
[B]

19 18 17 16 15 14 13 12 11 10
10 9 8 7 6 5 4 3 2 1

The Mark Twain Library is designed by Steve Renick.

The text of this Mark Twain Library edition of
Roughing It
is drawn from the Mark Twain Project's complete edition of
The Works and Papers of Mark Twain.
Editorial work for this volume has been supported by a grant to
The Friends of The Bancroft Library from the

L. J. SKAGGS AND MARY C. SKAGGS FOUNDATION

and by matching funds from the
NATIONAL ENDOWMENT FOR THE HUMANITIES,
an independent federal agency.

Without such generous support, these editions could
not have been produced.

CONTENTS

LIST OF ILLUSTRATIONS
BY
FAY & COX
5 NASSAU ST.
N.Y.

FOREWORD

Like most of Mark Twain's best work, *Roughing It* is largely autobiographical, as its preface explains: "This book is merely a personal narrative, and not a pretentious history or a philosophical dissertation. It is a record of several years of variegated vagabondizing. . . . Still, there is information in the volume; information concerning an interesting episode in the history of the Far West, about which no books have been written by persons who were on the ground in person." *Roughing It* recreates a six-year period from Clemens's early life, beginning in the summer of 1861, when the Civil War had interrupted (and, as it turned out, terminated) Clemens's career as a Mississippi River steamboat pilot. His brother, Orion, had just been appointed secretary of Nevada Territory, where a mining boom had infected nearly everyone with "silver fever." Clemens eagerly accepted the chance to accompany him to Nevada, using his own savings to pay both stagecoach fares for the trip across the continent. The opening chapters of the book describe this arduous but exhilarating journey, and these are followed by anecdotal but essentially accurate accounts of Clemens's adventures as a prospector and miner, then as a journalist in Nevada, California, and the Sandwich Islands, and finally as a lecturer in 1866. But *Roughing It* is also partly fiction—what has been aptly called an "imaginative interpretation" of Clemens's experience in the West. His "personal narrative" ingeniously combines reminiscence and factual reporting with anecdotes and tall tales, many told in the "vigorous new vernacular" of the West. Several of these are so successful that they are often reprinted as separate sketches: the Great Land-Slide Case (chapter 34); Buck Fanshaw's funeral (chapter 47); the Genuine Mexican Plug (chapter 24); Bemis and the buffalo (chapter 7); and Dick Baker's sagacious cat, Tom Quartz (chapter 61).

It was in the West that Clemens found and eventually accepted his vocation as a humorist. The experiences described in *Roughing It* illuminate how the freedom and spontaneity of the frontier helped him to develop as a writer, encouraging him to experiment and cultivate a distinctive style. Although he considered writing a book about the West as early as 1864, he did not in fact begin on it until after he had published the immensely successful *Innocents Abroad* (1869). In July 1870 he signed a contract to provide his subscription publisher with a 600-page book—and although the topic was not specified, he soon confided to his brother that he proposed to "do up Nevada & Cal., beginning with the trip across the country in the stage. Have you a memorandum of the route we took—or the names of any of the Stations we stopped at? Do you remember any of the scenes, names, incidents or adventures of the coach trip?" Orion did indeed have such a memorandum, and Clemens found it (and other similar notes) an essential stimulant for his imagination: "Incidents are better, any time, than dry history," he explained.

Although Clemens began to make use of Orion's memorandum in late August and early September 1870, a series of personal crises, combined with a mysterious "lapse of facility" in writing, effectively postponed any significant progress on the book until the following March. The episodic nature of his narrative enabled Clemens to explore virtually any subject that occurred to him, and to add (or delete) chapters without much affecting the continuity of his story. It also permitted him to incorporate revised versions of sketches he had previously published in newspapers—for example, a series of western reminiscences that had appeared originally in the Buffalo *Express*. Having fallen behind schedule, he began submitting chapters to his publisher long before he had completed his book—something he had not done before, and refrained from doing with any later book. As a consequence, he found himself radically altering the early chapters even after they had been set in type. And more than once he was obliged to add chapters, after he thought his book was complete, in order to make it as long as the announced 600 pages. It was not until July 1871, for instance, that he decided to add "4 or 5 chapters" about the Sandwich Islands, but under the necessity of making the book longer he eventually devoted *fifteen* chapters to describing his 1866 experiences there, eleven of them based on letters he had first published in the Sacramento *Union*. And the appendixes were probably not added until the book was nearly ready to print, with the result that the final one bears only a dubious relationship to his subject. Some of the late additions were by no means so perfunctory, however. While putting the final touches on his manuscript he added a "splendid chapter" to the "middle of the book"—probably Jim Blaine's rambling story of his grandfather's old ram (chapter 53).

The publication of *Roughing It* was formally announced on 29 February 1872. It was the first of Mark Twain's books to be published "simultaneously" in England, a strategy designed to ensure a valid British copyright in the absence of international copyright protection. The book was not widely reviewed, a result of Clemens's own policy: fearing the book "would be considered pretty poor stuff," he declined to send complimentary copies to the newspapers. But his fear was not realized: on the whole it was well received, and sold more than 75,000 copies within a year of publication. William Dean Howells praised the "grotesque exaggeration and broad irony" of Clemens's account of western life, calling them "conjecturably the truest colors that could have been used, for all existence there must have looked like an extravagant joke, the humor of which was only deepened by its nether-side of tragedy." And Charles Dudley Warner noted, "Behind the mask of the story-teller is the satirist, whose head is always clear, who is not imposed on by shams, who hates all pretension, and who uses his humor, which is often extravagant, to make pretension and false dignity ridiculous." Warner also defended Clemens's controversial use of slang, calling it the "*argot* that was current in the mining regions," and asserting that the "description of the life there would be entirely imperfect if it had been left out." The vernacular style of *Roughing It* often seems surprisingly fresh to modern readers, an effect of Clemens's remarkable prescience about his native tongue: many of the words objected to as "slang" in 1872 have outlived their detractors and become part of our everyday language.

Although readers have long been entertained by *Roughing It,* it has gradually become part of all serious study of American culture. Students of history have come to rely on it for accurate information about the period, and it has played a major role in shaping the myth of the "wild West," especially as perpetuated in countless novels, films, and television programs. No examination of American popular culture would be complete without Mark Twain's imaginative reminiscence of what it was like to be "on the ground in person."

Harriet Elinor Smith

MARK TWAIN

ROUGHING IT

TO
CALVIN H. HIGBIE,
Of California,
An Honest Man, a Genial Comrade, and a Steadfast Friend,
THIS BOOK IS INSCRIBED
By the Author,
In Memory of the Curious Time
When We Two
WERE MILLIONAIRES FOR TEN DAYS.

PREFATORY

This book is merely a personal narrative, and not a pretentious history or a philosophical dissertation. It is a record of several years of variegated vagabondizing, and its object is rather to help the resting reader while away an idle hour than afflict him with metaphysics, or goad him with science. Still, there is information in the volume; information concerning an interesting episode in the history of the Far West, about which no books have been written by persons who were on the ground in person, and saw the happenings of the time with their own eyes. I allude to the rise, growth and culmination of the silver-mining fever in Nevada—a curious episode, in some respects; the only one, of its peculiar kind, that has occurred in the land; and the only one, indeed, that is likely to occur in it.

Yes, take it all around, there is quite a good deal of information in the book. I regret this very much; but really it could not be helped: information appears to stew out of me naturally, like the precious ottar of roses out of the otter. Sometimes it has seemed to me that I would give worlds if I could retain my facts; but it cannot be. The more I caulk up the sources, and the tighter I get, the more I leak wisdom. Therefore, I can only claim indulgence at the hands of the reader, not justification.

THE AUTHOR.

CHAPTER 1

My brother had just been appointed Secretary of Nevada Territory—an office of such majesty that it concentrated in itself the duties and dignities of Treasurer, Comptroller, Secretary of State, and Acting Governor in the Governor's absence. A salary of eighteen hundred dollars a year and the title of "Mr. Secretary," gave to the great position an air of wild and imposing grandeur. I was young and ignorant, and I envied my brother. I coveted his distinction and his financial splendor, but particularly and especially the

ENVIOUS CONTEMPLATIONS.

long, strange journey he was going to make, and the curious new world he was going to explore. He was going to travel! I never had been away from home, and that word "travel" had a seductive charm for me. Pretty soon he would be hundreds and hundreds of miles away on the great plains and deserts, and among the mountains of the Far West, and would see buffaloes and Indians, and prairie dogs, and antelopes, and have all kinds of adventures, and maybe get hanged or scalped, and have ever such a fine time, and write home and tell us all about it, and be a hero. And he would see the gold mines and the silver mines, and maybe go about of an afternoon when his work was done, and pick up two or three pailfuls of shining slugs, and nuggets of gold and silver on the hillside. And by and by he would become very rich, and return home by sea, and be able to talk as calmly about San Francisco and the ocean, and "the Isthmus" as if it was nothing of any consequence to have seen those marvels face to face. What I suffered in contemplating his happiness, pen cannot describe. And so, when he offered me, in cold blood, the sublime position of private secretary under him, it appeared to me that the heavens and the earth passed away, and the firmament was rolled together as a scroll! I had nothing more to desire. My contentment was complete. At the end of an hour or two I was ready for the journey. Not much packing up was necessary, because we were going in the overland stage from the Missouri frontier to Nevada, and passengers were only allowed a small quantity of baggage apiece. There was no Pacific railroad in those fine times of ten or twelve years ago—not a single rail of it.

I only proposed to stay in Nevada three months—I had no thought of staying longer than that. I meant to see all I could that was new and strange, and then hurry home to business. I little thought that I would not see the end of that three-month pleasure excursion for six or seven uncommonly long years!

I dreamed all night about Indians, deserts, and silver bars, and in due time, next day, we took shipping at the St. Louis wharf on board a steamboat bound up the Missouri river.

We were six days going from St. Louis to "St. Joe"—a trip that was so dull, and sleepy, and eventless that it has left no more impression on my memory than if its duration had been six minutes instead of that many days. No record is left in my mind, now, concerning it, but a confused jumble of savage-looking snags, which we deliberately walked over with one wheel or the other; and of reefs which we butted and butted, and then retired from and

INNOCENT DREAMS.

climbed over in some softer place; and of sand-bars which we roosted on occasionally, and rested, and then got out our crutches and sparred over. In fact, the boat might almost as well have gone to St. Joe by land, for she was walking most of the time, anyhow—climbing over reefs and clambering over snags patiently and laboriously all day long. The captain said she was a "bully" boat, and all she wanted was more "shear" and a bigger wheel. I thought she wanted a pair of stilts, but I had the deep sagacity not to say so.

CHAPTER 2

THE first thing we did on that glad evening that landed us at St. Joseph was to hunt up the stage-office, and pay a hundred and fifty dollars apiece for tickets per overland coach to Carson City, Nevada.

The next morning, bright and early, we took a hasty breakfast, and hurried to the starting-place. Then an inconvenience presented itself which we had not properly appreciated before, namely, that one cannot make a heavy traveling trunk stand for twenty-five pounds of baggage—because it weighs a good deal more. But that was all we could take—twenty-five pounds each. So we had to snatch our trunks open, and make a selection in a good deal of a hurry. We put our lawful twenty-five pounds apiece all in one valise, and shipped the trunks back to St. Louis again. It was a sad parting, for now we had no swallow-tail coats and white kid gloves to wear at Pawnee receptions in the Rocky Mountains, and no stove-pipe hats nor patent-leather boots, nor anything else necessary to make life calm and peaceful. We were reduced to a war-footing. Each of us put on a rough, heavy suit of clothing, woolen army shirt and "stogy" boots included; and into the valise we crowded a few white shirts, some underclothing and such things. My brother, the Secretary, took along about four pounds of U. S. statutes and six pounds of Unabridged Dictionary; for we did not know—poor in-

LIGHT TRAVELING ORDER.

nocents—that such things could be bought in San Francisco on one day and received in Carson City the next. I was armed to the teeth with a pitiful little Smith & Wesson's seven-shooter, which carried a ball like a homœopathic pill, and it took the whole seven to make a dose for an adult. But I thought it was grand. It appeared to me to be a dangerous weapon. It only had one fault—you could not hit anything with it. One of our "conductors" practiced awhile on a cow with it, and as long as she stood still and behaved herself she was safe; but as soon as she went to moving about, and he got to shooting at other things, she came to grief. The Secretary had a small-sized Colt's revolver strapped around him for protection against the Indians, and to guard against accidents he carried it uncapped. Mr. George Bemis was dismally formidable. George Bemis was our fellow-traveler. We had never seen him before. He wore in his belt an old original "Allen" revolver, such as irreverent people called a "pepper-box." Simply drawing the trigger back, cocked and fired the pistol. As the trigger came back, the hammer would begin to rise and the barrel to turn over, and presently down would drop the hammer, and away would speed the ball. To aim along the turning barrel and hit the thing aimed at was a feat which was probably never done with an "Allen" in the world. But George's was a reliable weapon, nevertheless, because, as one of the stage-drivers afterward said, "If she didn't get what she went after, she would fetch something else." And so she did. She went after a deuce of spades nailed against a tree, once, and fetched a mule standing about thirty yards to the left of it. Bemis did not want the mule; but the owner came out with a double-barreled shotgun and persuaded him to buy it, anyhow. It was a cheerful weapon—the "Allen." Sometimes all its six barrels would go off at once, and then there was no safe place in all the region round about, but behind it.

THE "ALLEN."

We took two or three blankets for protection against frosty weather in the mountains. In the matter of luxuries we were modest—we took none along but some pipes and five pounds of smok-

INDUCEMENTS TO PURCHASE.

ing tobacco. We had two large canteens to carry water in, between stations on the Plains, and we also took with us a little shot-bag of silver coin for daily expenses in the way of breakfasts and dinners.

By eight o'clock everything was ready, and we were on the other side of the river. We jumped into the stage, the driver cracked his whip, and we bowled away and left "the States" behind us. It was a superb summer morning, and all the landscape was brilliant with sunshine. There was a freshness and breeziness, too, and an exhilarating sense of emancipation from all sorts of cares and responsibilities, that almost made us feel that the years we had spent in the close, hot city, toiling and slaving, had been wasted and thrown away. We were spinning along through Kansas, and in the course of an hour and a half we were fairly abroad on the great Plains. Just here the land was rolling—a grand sweep of regular elevations and depressions as far as the eye could reach—like the stately heave and swell of the ocean's bosom after a storm. And everywhere were cornfields, accenting with squares of deeper green, this limitless expanse of grassy land. But presently this sea upon dry ground was to lose its "rolling" character and stretch away for seven hundred miles as level as a floor!

Our coach was a great swinging and swaying stage, of the most sumptuous description—an imposing cradle on wheels. It was drawn by six handsome horses, and by the side of the driver sat the "conductor," the legitimate captain of the craft; for it was his business to take charge and care of the mails, baggage, express matter, and passengers. We three were the only passengers, this trip. We sat on the back seat, inside. About all the rest of the coach was full of mail-bags—for we had three days' delayed mails with us. Almost touching our knees, a perpendicular wall of mail matter rose up to the roof. There was a great pile of it strapped on top of the stage, and both the fore and hind boots were full. We had twenty-seven hundred pounds of it aboard, the driver said—"a little for Brigham, and Carson, and 'Frisco, but the heft of it for the Injuns, which is powerful troublesome 'thout they get plenty of truck to read." But as he just then got up a fearful convulsion of his countenance which was suggestive of a wink being swallowed by an earthquake, we guessed that his remark was intended to be facetious, and to mean that we would unload the most of our mail matter somewhere on the Plains and leave it to the Indians, or whosoever wanted it.

THE FACETIOUS DRIVER.

We changed horses every ten miles, all day long, and fairly flew over the hard, level road. We jumped out and stretched our legs every time the coach stopped, and so the night found us still vivacious and unfatigued.

After supper a woman got in, who lived about fifty miles further on, and we three had to take turns at sitting outside with the driver and conductor. Apparently she was not a talkative woman. She would sit there in the gathering twilight and fasten her steadfast

PLEASING NEWS.

eyes on a mosquito rooting into her arm, and slowly she would raise her other hand till she had got his range, and then she would launch a slap at him that would have jolted a cow; and after that she would sit and contemplate the corpse with tranquil satisfaction—for she never missed her mosquito; she was a dead shot at short range. She never removed a carcase, but left them there for bait. I sat by this grim Sphynx and watched her kill thirty or forty mosquitoes—watched her, and waited for her to say something, but she never did. So I finally opened the conversation myself. I said:

THE SPHYNX.

"The mosquitoes are pretty bad, about here, madam."

"You bet!"

"What did I understand you to say, madam?"

"You BET!"

Then she cheered up, and faced around and said:

"Danged if I didn't begin to think you fellers was deef and dumb. I did, b' gosh. Here I've sot, and sot, and sot, a bust'n muskeeters and wonderin' what was ailin' ye. Fust I thot you was deef and dumb, then I thot you was sick or crazy, or suthin', and then by and by I begin to reckon you was a passel of sickly fools that couldn't think of nothing to say. Wher'd ye come from?"

The Sphynx was a Sphynx no more! The fountains of her great deep were broken up, and she rained the nine parts of speech forty days and forty nights, metaphorically speaking, and buried us under a desolating deluge of trivial gossip that left not a crag or pinnacle of rejoinder projecting above the tossing waste of dislocated grammar and decomposed pronunciation!

How we suffered, suffered, suffered! She went on, hour after hour, till I was sorry I ever opened the mosquito question and gave her a start. She never did stop again until she got to her journey's end toward daylight; and then she stirred us up as she was leaving the stage (for we were nodding, by that time), and said:

"Now you git out at Cottonwood, you fellers, and lay over a couple o' days, and I'll be along some time to-night, and if I can do ye any good by edgin' in a word now and then, I'm right thar. Folks 'll tell you 't I've always ben kind o' offish and partic'lar for a gal that's raised in the woods, and I *am*, with the rag-tag and bob-tail, and a gal *has* to be, if she wants to *be* anything, but when people comes along which is my equals, I reckon I'm a pretty sociable heifer after all."

We resolved not to "lay by at Cottonwood."

CHAPTER 3

About an hour and a half before daylight we were bowling along smoothly over the road—so smoothly that our cradle only rocked in a gentle, lulling way, that was gradually soothing us to sleep, and dulling our consciousness—when something gave away under us! We were dimly aware of it, but indifferent to it. The coach stopped. We heard the driver and conductor talking together outside, and rummaging for a lantern, and swearing because they could not find it—but we had no interest in whatever had happened, and it only added to our comfort to think of those people out there at work in the murky night, and we snug in our nest with the curtains drawn. But presently, by the sounds, there seemed to be an examination going on, and then the driver's voice said:

"By George, the thoroughbrace is broke!"

This startled me broad awake—as an undefined sense of calamity is always apt to do. I said to myself: "Now, a thoroughbrace is probably part of a horse; and doubtless a vital part, too, from the dismay in the driver's voice. Leg, maybe—and yet how could he break his leg waltzing along such a road as this? No, it can't be his leg. That is impossible, unless he was reaching for the driver. Now, what can be the thoroughbrace of a horse, I wonder? Well, whatever comes, I shall not air my ignorance in this crowd, anyway."

Just then the conductor's face appeared at a lifted curtain, and his lantern glared in on us and our wall of mail matter. He said:

"Gents, you'll have to turn out a spell. Thoroughbrace is broke."

We climbed out into a chill drizzle, and felt ever so homeless and dreary. When I found that the thing they called a "thoroughbrace" was the massive combination of belts and springs which the coach rocks itself in, I said to the driver:

"I never saw a thoroughbrace used up like that, before, that I can remember. How did it happen?"

"Why, it happened by trying to make one coach carry three days' mail—that's how it happened," said he. "And right here is the very direction which is wrote on all the newspaper-bags which was to be put out for the Injuns for to keep 'em quiet. It's most uncommon lucky, becuz it's so nation dark I should 'a' gone by unbeknowns if that air thoroughbrace hadn't broke."

I knew that he was in labor with another of those winks of his, though I could not see his face, because he was bent down at work; and wishing him a safe delivery, I turned to and helped the rest get out the mail-sacks. It made a great pyramid by the roadside when it was all out. When they had mended the thoroughbrace we filled the two boots again, but put no mail on top, and only half as much inside as there was before. The conductor bent all the seat-backs down, and then filled the coach just half full of mail-bags from end to end. We objected loudly to this, for it left us no seats. But the conductor was wiser than we, and said a bed was better than seats, and moreover, this plan would protect his thoroughbraces. We never wanted any seats after that. The lazy bed was infinitely preferable. I had many an exciting day, subsequently, lying on it reading the statutes and the Dictionary, and wondering how the characters would turn out.

The conductor said he would send back a guard from the next station to take charge of the abandoned mail-bags, and we drove on.

It was now just dawn; and as we stretched our cramped legs full length on the mail-sacks, and gazed out through the windows across the wide wastes of greensward clad in cool, powdery mist, to where there was an expectant look in the eastern horizon, our perfect enjoyment took the form of a tranquil and contented ecstasy. The stage whirled along at a spanking gait, the breeze flapping curtains and suspended coats in a most exhilarating way; the cradle swayed and swung luxuriously, the pattering of the horses' hoofs, the cracking of the driver's whip, and his "Hi-yi! g'lang!" were music; the spinning ground and the waltzing trees appeared to give us a mute hurrah as we went by, and then slack up and look after us with interest, or envy, or something; and as we lay and smoked the pipe of peace and compared all this luxury with the years of tiresome city life that had gone before it, we felt that there was only one complete and satisfying happiness in the world, and we had found it.

After breakfast, at some station whose name I have forgotten, we three climbed up on the seat behind the driver, and let the conductor have our bed for a nap. And by and by, when the sun made me drowsy, I lay down on my face on top of the coach, grasping the slender iron railing, and slept for an hour or more. That will give one an appreciable idea of those matchless roads. Instinct will make a sleeping man grip a fast hold of the railing when the stage jolts, but when it only swings and sways, no grip is necessary. Overland drivers and conductors used to sit in their places and sleep thirty or forty minutes at a time, on good roads, while spinning along at the rate of eight or ten miles an hour. I saw them do it, often. There was no danger about it; a sleeping man *will* seize the irons in time when the coach jolts. These men were hard worked, and it was not possible for them to stay awake all the time.

By and by we passed through Marysville, and over the Big Blue and Little Sandy; thence about a mile, and entered Nebraska. About a mile further on, we came to the Big Sandy—one hundred and eighty miles from St. Joseph.

As the sun was going down, we saw the first specimen of an animal known familiarly over two thousand miles of mountain and desert—from Kansas clear to the Pacific Ocean—as the "jackass rabbit." He is well named. He is just like any other rabbit, except that he is from one-third to twice as large, has longer legs in proportion to his size, and has the most preposterous ears that ever were mounted on any creature *but* a jackass. When he is sitting quiet, thinking about his sins, or is absent-minded or unapprehensive of danger, his majestic ears project above him conspicuously; but the breaking of a twig will scare him nearly to death, and then he tilts his ears back

MEDITATION.

gently and starts for home. All you can see, then, for the next minute, is his long gray form stretched out straight and "streaking it" through the low sage-brush, head erect, eyes right, and ears just canted a little to the rear, but showing you where the animal is, all the time, the same as if he carried a jib. Now and then he makes a marvelous spring with his long legs, high over the stunted sage-brush, and scores a leap that would make a horse envious. Presently he comes down to a long, graceful "lope," and shortly he mysteriously disappears. He has crouched behind a sage-bush, and will sit there and listen and tremble until you get within six feet of him, when he will get under way again. But one must shoot at this creature once, if he wishes to see him throw his heart into his heels, and do the best he knows how. He is frightened clear

ON BUSINESS.

through, now, and he lays his long ears down on his back, straightens himself out like a yard-stick every spring he makes, and scatters miles behind him with an easy indifference that is enchanting.

Our party made this specimen "hump himself," as the conductor said. The Secretary started him with a shot from the Colt; I commenced spitting at him with my weapon; and all in the same instant the old "Allen's" whole broadside let go with a rattling crash, and it is not putting it too strong to say that the rabbit was frantic! He dropped his ears, set up his tail, and left for San Francisco at a speed which can only be described as a flash and a vanish! Long after he was out of sight we could hear him whiz.

I do not remember where we first came across "sage-brush," but as I have been speaking of it I may as well describe it. This is easily done, for if the reader can imagine a gnarled and venerable live oak tree reduced to a little shrub two feet high, with its rough bark, its foliage, its twisted boughs, all complete, he can picture the "sage-brush" exactly. Often, on lazy afternoons in the mountains, I have lain on the ground with my face under a sage-bush, and entertained myself with fancying that the gnats among its foliage were lilliputian birds, and that the ants marching and countermarching

AUTHOR AS GULLIVER.

about its base were lilliputian flocks and herds, and myself some vast loafer from Brobdingnag waiting to catch a little citizen and eat him.

It is an imposing monarch of the forest in exquisite miniature, is the "sage-brush." Its foliage is a grayish green, and gives that tint to desert and mountain. It smells like our domestic sage, and "sage-tea" made from it tastes like the sage-tea which all boys are so well acquainted with. The sage-brush is a singularly hardy plant, and grows right in the midst of deep sand, and among barren rocks, where nothing else in the vegetable world would try to grow, except "bunch-grass."* The sage-bushes grow from three to six or seven feet apart, all over the mountains and deserts of the Far West, clear to the borders of California. There is not a tree of any kind in the deserts, for hundreds of miles—there is no vegetation at all in a regular desert, except the sage-brush and its cousin the "grease-wood," which is so much like the sage-brush that the difference amounts to little. Camp-fires and hot suppers in the deserts would be impossible but for the friendly sage-brush. Its trunk is as large as a boy's wrist (and from that up to a man's arm), and its crooked branches are half as large as its trunk—all good, sound, hard wood, very like oak.

When a party camps, the first thing to be done is to cut sage-brush; and in a few minutes there is an opulent pile of it ready for use. A hole a foot wide, two feet deep, and two feet long, is dug, and sage-brush chopped up and burned in it till it is full to the brim with glowing coals. Then the cooking begins, and there is no smoke, and consequently no swearing. Such a fire will keep all night, with very little replenishing; and it makes a very sociable camp-fire, and one around which the most impossible reminiscences sound plausible, instructive, and profoundly entertaining.

Sage-brush is very fair fuel, but as a vegetable it is a distinguished failure. Nothing can abide the taste of it but the jackass and his illegitimate child the mule. But their testimony to its nutritiousness is worth nothing, for they will eat pine knots, or anthracite coal, or brass filings, or lead pipe, or old bottles, or anything that comes handy, and then go off looking as grateful as if they had had oysters for dinner. Mules and donkeys and camels have appetites that anything will relieve temporarily, but nothing satisfy. In Syria, once, at the head-waters of the Jordan, a camel took charge of my overcoat while the tents were being pitched, and examined it with a critical eye, all over, with as much interest as if

*"Bunch-grass" grows on the bleak mountain sides of Nevada and neighboring Territories, and offers excellent feed for stock, even in the dead of winter, wherever the snow is blown aside and exposes it; notwithstanding its unpromising home, bunch-grass is a better and more nutritious diet for cattle and horses than almost any other hay or grass that is known—so stock-men say.

A tough statement.

he had an idea of getting one made like it; and then, after he was done figuring on it as an article of apparel, he began to contemplate it as an article of diet. He put his foot on it, and lifted one of the sleeves out with his teeth, and chewed and chewed at it, gradually taking it in, and all the while opening and closing his eyes in a kind of religious ecstasy, as if he had never tasted anything as good as an overcoat before, in his life. Then he smacked his lips once or twice, and reached after the other sleeve. Next he tried the velvet collar, and smiled a smile of such contentment that it was plain to see that he regarded that as the daintiest thing about an overcoat. The tails went next, along with some percussion caps and cough candy, and some fig-paste from Constantinople. And then my newspaper correspondence dropped out, and he took a chance in that—manuscript letters written for the home papers. But he was treading on dangerous ground, now. He began to come across solid wisdom in those documents that was rather weighty on his stomach; and occasionally he would take a joke that would shake him up till it loosened his teeth; it was getting to be perilous times with him, but he held his grip with good courage and hopefully, till at last he began to stumble on statements that not even a camel could swallow with impunity. He began to gag and gasp, and his eyes to stand out, and his forelegs to spread, and in about a quarter of a minute he fell over as stiff as a carpenter's work-bench, and died a death of indescribable agony. I went and pulled the manuscript out of his mouth, and found that the sensitive creature had choked to death on one of the mildest and gentlest statements of fact that I ever laid before a trusting public.

I was about to say, when diverted from my subject, that occasionally one finds sage-bushes five or six feet high, and with a spread of branch and foliage in proportion, but two or two and a half feet is the usual height.

CHAPTER 4

As the sun went down and the evening chill came on, we made preparation for bed. We stirred up the hard leather letter-sacks, and the knotty canvas bags of printed matter (knotty and uneven because of projecting ends and corners of magazines, boxes and books). We stirred them up and redisposed them in such a way as to make our bed as level as possible. And we *did* improve it, too, though after all our work it had an upheaved and billowy look about it, like a little piece of a stormy sea. Next we hunted up our boots from odd nooks among the mail-bags where they had settled, and put them on. Then we got down our coats, vests, pantaloons and heavy woolen shirts, from the arm-loops where they had been swinging all day, and clothed ourselves in them—for, there being no ladies either at the stations or in the coach, and the weather being hot, we had looked to our comfort by stripping to our underclothing, at nine o'clock in the morning. All things being now ready, we stowed the uneasy Dictionary where it would lie as quiet as possible, and placed the water canteens and pistols where we could find them in the dark. Then we smoked a final pipe, and swapped a final yarn; after which, we put the pipes, tobacco and bag of coin in snug holes and caves among the mail-bags, and then fastened down the coach curtains all around, and made the place as "dark as the inside of a cow," as the conductor phrased it in his picturesque way. It was certainly as dark as any place could be—nothing was even dimly visible in it. And finally, we rolled ourselves up like silk-worms, each person in his own blanket, and sank peacefully to sleep.

Whenever the stage stopped to change horses, we would wake up, and try to recollect where we were—and succeed—and in a minute or two the stage would be off again, and we likewise. We began to get into country, now, threaded here and there with little streams. These had high, steep banks on each side, and every time we flew down one bank and scrambled up the other, our party inside got mixed somewhat. First we would all be down in a pile at the forward end of the stage, nearly in a sitting posture, and in a second we would shoot to the other end, and stand on our heads. And we would sprawl and kick, too, and ward off ends and corners of mail-bags that came lumbering over us and about us; and as the dust rose from the tumult, we would all sneeze in chorus, and the majority of us would grumble, and probably say some hasty thing, like: "Take your elbow out of my ribs!—can't you quit crowding?"

Every time we avalanched from one end of the stage to the other, the Unabridged Dictionary would come too; and every time it came it damaged somebody. One trip it "barked" the Secretary's elbow; the next trip it hurt me in the stomach, and the third it tilted Bemis's nose up till he could look down his nostrils—he said. The

THIRD TRIP OF THE UNABRIDGED.

pistols and coin soon settled to the bottom, but the pipes, pipestems, tobacco and canteens clattered and floundered after the Dictionary every time it made an assault on us, and aided and abetted the book by spilling tobacco in our eyes, and water down our backs.

Still, all things considered, it was a very comfortable night. It wore gradually away, and when at last a cold gray light was visible through the puckers and chinks in the curtains, we yawned and stretched with satisfaction, shed our cocoons, and felt that we had slept as much as was necessary. By and by, as the sun rose up and warmed the world, we pulled off our clothes and got ready for breakfast. We were just pleasantly in time, for five minutes afterward the driver sent the weird music of his bugle winding over the grassy solitudes, and presently we detected a low hut or two in the distance. Then the rattling of the coach, the clatter of our six horses' hoofs, and the driver's crisp commands, awoke to a louder and stronger emphasis, and we went sweeping down on the station at our smartest speed. It was fascinating—that old overland stage-coaching.

We jumped out in undress uniform. The driver tossed his gathered reins out on the ground, gaped and stretched complacently, drew off his heavy buckskin gloves with great deliberation and insufferable dignity—taking not the slightest notice of a dozen solicitous inquiries after his health, and humbly facetious and flattering accostings, and obsequious tenders of service, from five or six hairy and half-civilized station-keepers and hostlers who were nimbly unhitching our steeds and bringing the fresh team out of the stables—for in the eyes of the stage-driver of that day, station-keepers and hostlers were a sort of good enough low creatures, useful in their place, and helping to make up a world, but not the kind of beings which a person of distinction could afford to concern himself with; while, on the contrary, in the eyes of the station-keeper and the hostler, the stage-driver was a hero—a great and shining dignitary, the world's favorite son, the envy of the people, the observed of the nations. When they spoke to him they received his insolent silence meekly, and as being the natural and proper conduct of so great a man; when he opened his lips they all hung on his words with admiration (he never honored a particular individual with a remark, but addressed it with a broad generality to the horses, the stables, the surrounding country *and* the human underlings); when he discharged a facetious insulting personality at a hostler, that hostler was happy for the day; when he uttered his one jest—old as the hills, coarse, profane, witless, and inflicted on the same audience, in the same language, every time his coach drove up there—the varlets roared, and slapped their thighs, and swore it was the best thing they'd ever heard in all their lives. And how they would fly around when he wanted a basin of water, a gourd of the same, or a light for his pipe!—but they would instantly insult a passenger if he so far forgot himself as to crave a favor at their hands. They could do that sort of insolence as well as the driver they copied it from—for, let it be borne in mind, the overland driver had but little less contempt for his passengers than he had for his hostlers.

The hostlers and station-keepers treated the really powerful *conductor* of the coach merely with the best of what was their idea of civility, but the *driver* was the only being they bowed down to and worshipped. How admiringly they would gaze up at him in his high seat as he gloved himself with lingering deliberation, while some happy hostler held the bunch of reins aloft, and waited patiently for him to take it! And how they would bombard him with glorifying ejaculations as he cracked his long whip and went careering away.

The station buildings were long, low huts, made of sun-dried, mud-colored bricks, laid up without mortar (*adobes*, the Spaniards call these bricks, and Americans shorten it to "'dobies"). The roofs, which had no slant to them worth speaking of, were thatched and then sodded or covered with a thick layer of earth, and from this sprung a pretty rank growth of weeds and grass. It was the first time we had ever seen a man's front yard on top of his house. The buildings consisted of barns, stable-room for twelve or fifteen horses, and a hut for an eating-room for passengers. This latter had bunks in it for the station-keeper and a hostler or two. You could rest your elbow on its eaves, and you had to bend in order to get in at the door. In place of a window there was a square hole about large enough for a man to crawl through, but this had no glass in it. There was no flooring, but the ground was packed hard. There was no stove, but the fire-place served all needful purposes. There were no shelves, no cupboards, no closets. In a corner stood an open sack of flour, and nestling against its base were a couple of black and venerable tin coffee-pots, a tin teapot, a little bag of salt, and a side of bacon.

By the door of the station-keeper's den, outside, was a tin washbasin, on the ground. Near it was a pail of water and a piece of yellow bar soap, and from the eaves hung a hoary blue woolen shirt, significantly—but this latter was the station-keeper's private towel, and only two persons in all the party might venture to use it—the stage-driver and the conductor. The latter would not, from a sense of decency; the former would not, because he did not choose to encourage the advances of a station-keeper. We had towels—in the valise; they might as well have been in Sodom and Gomorrah. We (and the conductor) used our handkerchiefs, and the driver his pantaloons and sleeves. By the door, inside, was fastened a small old-fashioned looking-glass frame, with two little fragments of the original mirror lodged down in one corner of it. This arrangement afforded a pleasant double-barreled portrait of you when you looked into it, with one-half of your head set up a couple of inches above the other half. From the glass frame hung the half of a comb by a string—but if I had to describe that patriarch or die, I believe I would order some sample coffins. It had come down from Esau and Samson, and had been accumulating hair ever since—along with certain impurities. In one corner of the room stood three or four rifles and muskets, together with horns and pouches of ammunition. The station-men wore pantaloons of coarse, country-woven stuff, and into the seat and the inside of the legs were sewed ample additions of buckskin, to do duty in place of leggings, when the man rode horseback—so the pants were half dull blue and half yellow, and unspeakably picturesque. The pants were stuffed into the tops of

A POWERFUL GLASS.

AN HEIRLOOM.

high boots, the heels whereof were armed with great Spanish spurs, whose little iron clogs and chains jingled with every step. The man wore a huge beard and mustachios, an old slouch hat, a blue woolen shirt, no suspenders, no vest, no coat—in a leathern sheath in his belt, a great long "navy" revolver (slung on right side, hammer to the front), and projecting from his boot a horn-handled bowie knife. The furniture of the hut was neither gorgeous nor much in the way. The rocking-chairs and sofas were not present, and never had been, but they were represented by two three-legged stools, a pine-board bench four feet long, and two empty candle-boxes. The table was a greasy board on stilts, and the table-cloth and napkins had not come—and they were not looking for them, either. A battered tin platter, a knife and fork, and a tin pint cup, were at each man's place, and the driver had a queensware saucer that had seen better days. Of course this duke sat at the head of the table. There was one isolated piece of table furniture that bore about it a touching air of grandeur in misfortune. This was the caster. It was German silver, and crippled and rusty, but it was so preposterously out of place there that it was suggestive of a tattered exiled king among barbarians, and the majesty of its native position compelled respect even in its degradation. There

OUR LANDLORD.

DIGNIFIED EXILE.

was only one cruet left, and that was a stopperless, fly-specked, broken-necked thing, with two inches of vinegar in it, and a dozen preserved flies with their heels up and looking sorry they had invested there.

The station-keeper up-ended a disk of last week's bread, of the shape and size of an old-time cheese, and carved some slabs from it which were as good as Nicolson pavement, and tenderer.

He sliced off a piece of bacon for each man, but only the experienced old hands made out to eat it, for it was condemned army bacon which the United States would not feed to its soldiers in the forts, and the stage company had bought it cheap for the sustenance of their passengers and employés. We may have found this condemned army bacon further out on the plains than the section I am locating it in, but we *found* it—there is no gainsaying that.

Then he poured for us a beverage which he called *"Slumgullion,"* and it is hard to think he was not inspired when he named it.

DRINKING SLUMGULLION.

It really pretended to be tea, but there was too much dish-rag, and sand, and old bacon-rind in it to deceive the intelligent traveler. He had no sugar and no milk—not even a spoon to stir the ingredients with.

We could not eat the bread or the meat, nor drink the "slumgullion." And when I looked at that melancholy vinegar-cruet, I thought of the anecdote (a very, very old one, even at that day) of the traveler who sat down to a table which had nothing on it but a mackerel and a pot of mustard. He asked the landlord if this was all. The landlord said:

"*All!* Why, thunder and lightning, I should think there was mackerel enough there for six."

"But I don't like mackerel."

"Oh—then help yourself to the mustard."

In other days I had considered it a good, a very good, anecdote, but there was a dismal plausibility about it, here, that took all the humor out of it.

Our breakfast was before us, but our teeth were idle.

I tasted and smelt, and said I would take coffee, I believed. The station-boss stopped dead still, and glared at me speechless. At last, when he came to, he turned away and said, as one who communes with himself upon a matter too vast to grasp:

"*Coffee!* Well, if that don't go clean ahead of me, I'm d—d!"

A JOKE WITHOUT CREAM.

We could not eat, and there was no conversation among the hostlers and herdsmen—we all sat at the same board. At least there was no conversation further than a single hurried request, now and then, from one employé to another. It was always in the same form, and always gruffly friendly. Its western freshness and novelty startled me, at first, and interested me; but it presently grew monotonous, and lost its charm. It was:

"Pass the bread, you son of a skunk!" No, I forget—skunk was not the word; it seems to me it was still stronger than that; I know it was, in fact, but it is gone from my memory, apparently. However, it is no matter—probably it was too strong for print, anyway. It is the landmark in my memory which tells me where I first encountered the vigorous new vernacular of the occidental plains and mountains.

We gave up the breakfast, and paid our dollar apiece and went back to our mail-bag bed in the coach, and found comfort in our pipes. Right here we suffered the first diminution of our princely state. We left our six fine horses and took six mules in their place. But they were wild Mexican fellows, and a man had to stand at the head of each of them and hold him fast while the driver gloved and got himself ready. And when at last he grasped the reins and gave the word, the men sprung suddenly away from the mules' heads and the coach shot from the station as if it had issued from a cannon. How the frantic animals did scamper! It was a fierce and furious gallop—and the gait never altered for a moment till we reeled off ten or twelve miles and swept up to the next collection of little station-huts and stables.

So we flew along all day. At 2 P.M. the belt of timber that fringes the North Platte and marks its windings through the vast level floor of the Plains came in sight. At 4 P.M. we crossed a branch of the river, and at 5 P.M. we crossed the Platte itself, and landed at Fort Kearny, *fifty-six hours out from St. Joe*—THREE HUNDRED MILES!

Now that was stage-coaching on the great overland, ten or twelve years ago, when perhaps not more than ten men in America, all told, expected to live to see a railroad follow that route to the Pacific. But the railroad is there, now, and it pictures a thousand odd comparisons and contrasts in my mind to read the following sketch, in the New York *Times*, of a recent trip over almost the very ground I have been describing. I can scarcely comprehend the new state of things:

ACROSS THE CONTINENT.

At 4:20 P. M., Sunday, we rolled out of the station at Omaha and started westward on our long jaunt. A couple of hours out, dinner was announced—an "event" to those of us who had yet to experience what it is to eat in one of PULLMAN'S hotels on wheels; so stepping into the car next forward of our sleeping palace, we found ourselves in the dining car. It was a revelation to us, that first dinner on Sunday; and though we con-

PULLMAN CAR DINING-SALOON.

tinued to dine for four days, and had as many breakfasts and suppers, our whole party never ceased to admire the perfection of the arrangements and the marvelous results achieved. Upon tables covered with snowy linen and garnished with services of solid silver, Ethiop waiters, flitting about in spotless white, placed as by magic a repast at which DELMONICO himself could have had no occasion to blush; and indeed in some respects it would be hard for that distinguished *chef* to match our *menu;* for, in addition to all that ordinarily makes up a first-chop dinner, had we not our antelope steak, (the gourmet who has not experienced *this*—bah! what does he know of the feast of fat things?) our delicious mountain brook-trout, our choice fruits and berries, and, sauce piquante and unpurchase-able, our sweet-scented appetite-compelling air of the prairies? You may depend upon it, we all did justice to the good things; and, as we washed them down with bumpers of sparkling Krug, while we sped along at the rate of thirty miles an hour, agreed it was the *fastest* living we had ever experienced. (We beat that, however, two days afterward, when we made *twenty-seven miles in twenty-seven minutes,* while our Champagne glasses filled to the brim spilled not a drop!) After dinner we repaired to our drawing-room car, and, as it was Sabbath eve, intoned some of the grand old hymns—"Praise God from whom," &c.; "Shining Shore," "Coronation," &c.—the voices of the men singers and of the women singers blending sweetly in the evening air, while our train, with its great, glaring

Polyphemus eye, lighting up long vistas of prairie, rushed into the night and the Wild. Then to bed in luxurious couches, where we slept the sleep of the just, and only awoke the next morning, (Monday,) at 8 o'clock, to find ourselves at the crossing of the North Platte, 300 miles from Omaha—*fifteen hours and forty minutes out.*

CHAPTER 5

ANOTHER night of alternate tranquillity and turmoil. But morning came, by and by. It was another glad awakening to fresh breezes, vast expanses of level greensward, bright sunlight, an impressive solitude utterly without visible human beings or human habitations, and an atmosphere of such amazing magnifying properties that trees that seemed close at hand were more than three miles away. We resumed undress uniform, climbed a-top of the

OUR MORNING RIDE.

flying coach, dangled our legs over the side, shouted occasionally at our frantic mules, merely to see them lay their ears back and scamper faster, tied our hats on to keep our hair from blowing away, and leveled an outlook over the world-wide carpet about us for things new and strange to gaze at. Even at this day it thrills me through and through to think of the life, the gladness and the wild

PRAIRIE DOGS.

sense of freedom that used to make the blood dance in my veins on those fine overland mornings!

Along about an hour after breakfast we saw the first prairie-dog villages, the first antelope, and the first wolf. If I remember rightly, this latter was the regular *cayote* (pronounced ky-*o*-te) of the farther deserts. And if it *was*, he was not a pretty creature or respectable either, for I got well acquainted with his race afterward, and can speak with confidence. The cayote is a long, slim, sick and sorry-looking skeleton, with a gray wolf-skin stretched over it, a tolerably bushy tail that forever sags down with a despairing

A CAYOTE.

expression of forsakenness and misery, a furtive and evil eye, and a long, sharp face, with slightly lifted lip and exposed teeth. He has a general slinking expression all over. The cayote is a living, breathing allegory of Want. He is *always* hungry. He is always poor, out of luck and friendless. The meanest creatures despise him, and even the fleas would desert him for a velocipede. He is so spiritless and cowardly that even while his exposed teeth are pretending a threat, the rest of his face is apologizing for it. And he is *so* homely!—so scrawny, and ribby, and coarse-haired, and pitiful. When he sees you he lifts his lip and lets a flash of his teeth out, and then turns a little out of the course he was pursuing, depresses his head a bit, and strikes a long, soft-footed trot through the sage-brush, glancing over his shoulder at you, from time to time, till he is about out of easy pistol range, and then he stops and takes a deliberate survey of you; he will trot fifty yards and stop again—another fifty and stop again; and finally the gray of his gliding body blends with the gray of the sage-brush, and he disappears. All this is when you make no demonstration against him; but if you do, he develops a livelier interest in his journey, and instantly electrifies his heels and puts such a deal of real estate between himself and your weapon, that by the time you have raised the hammer you see that you need a minie rifle, and by the time you have got him in line you need a rifled cannon, and by the time you have "drawn a bead" on him you see well enough that nothing but an unusually long-winded streak of lightning could reach him where he is now. But if you start a swift-footed dog after him, you will enjoy it ever so much—especially if it is a dog that has a good opinion of himself, and has been brought up to think he knows something about speed. The cayote will go swinging gently off on that deceitful trot of his, and every little while he will smile a fraudful smile over his shoulder that will fill that dog entirely full of encouragement and worldly ambition, and make him lay his head still lower to the ground, and stretch his neck further to the front, and pant more fiercely, and stick his tail out straighter behind, and move his furious legs with a yet wilder frenzy, and leave a broader and broader, and higher and denser cloud of desert sand smoking behind, and marking his long wake across the level plain! And all this time the dog is only a short twenty feet behind the cayote, and to save the soul of him he cannot understand why it is that he cannot get perceptibly closer; and he begins to get aggravated, and it makes him madder and madder to see how gently the cayote glides along and never pants or sweats or ceases to smile; and he grows still more and more incensed to see how shamefully he has been taken in by an entire stranger, and what an ignoble swindle that long, calm, soft-footed trot is; and next he notices that he is getting fagged, and that the cayote actually has to slacken speed a little to keep from running away from him—and *then* that town-dog is mad in earnest, and he begins to strain and weep and swear, and paw the sand higher than ever, and reach for the cayote with concentrated and desperate energy. This "spurt" finds him six feet behind the gliding enemy, and two miles from his friends. And then, in the instant that a wild new hope is lighting up his face, the cayote turns and smiles blandly upon him once more, and with a something about it which seems to say: "Well, I shall have to tear myself away from you, bub—business is business, and it will not do for me to be fooling along this way all day"—and forthwith there is a rushing sound, and the sudden splitting of a long crack through the atmosphere, and behold that dog is solitary and alone in the midst of a vast solitude!

It makes his head swim. He stops, and looks all around; climbs the nearest sand-mound, and gazes into the distance; shakes his head reflectively, and then, without a word, he turns and jogs along back to his train, and takes up a humble position under the hindmost wagon, and feels unspeakably mean, and looks ashamed, and hangs his tail at half-mast for a week. And for as much as a year after that, whenever there is a great hue and cry after a cayote, that dog will merely glance in that direction without emotion, and apparently observe to himself, "I believe I do not wish any of the pie."

The cayote lives chiefly in the most desolate and forbidding deserts, along with the lizard, the jackass rabbit and the raven, and gets an uncertain and precarious living, and earns it. He seems to subsist almost wholly on the carcases of oxen, mules and horses that have dropped out of emigrant trains and died, and upon windfalls of carrion, and occasional legacies of offal bequeathed to him by white men who have been opulent enough to have something better to butcher than condemned army bacon. He will eat anything in the world that his first cousins, the desert-frequenting tribes of Indians will, and they will eat anything they can bite. It is a curious fact that these latter are the only creatures known to history who will eat nitro-glycerine and ask for more if they survive.

The cayote of the deserts beyond the Rocky Mountains has a peculiarly hard time of it, owing to the fact that his relations, the Indians, are just as apt to be the first to detect a seductive scent on the desert breeze, and follow the fragrance to the late ox it emanated from, as he is himself; and when this occurs he has to content himself with sitting off at a lit-

SHOWING RESPECT TO RELATIVES.

tle distance watching those people strip off and dig out everything edible, and walk off with it. Then he and the waiting ravens explore the skeleton and polish the bones. It is considered that the cayote, and the obscene bird, and the Indian of the desert, testify their blood kinship with each other in that they live together in the waste places of the earth on terms of perfect confidence and friendship, while hating all other creatures and yearning to assist at their funerals. He does not mind going a hundred miles to breakfast, and a hundred and fifty to dinner, because he is sure to have three or four days between meals, and he can just as well be traveling and looking at the scenery as lying around doing nothing and adding to the burdens of his parents.

We soon learned to recognize the sharp, vicious bark of the cayote as it came across the murky plain at night to disturb our dreams among the mail-sacks; and remembering his forlorn aspect and his hard fortune, made shift to wish him the blessed novelty of a long day's good luck and a limitless larder the morrow.

CHAPTER 6

OUR new conductor (just shipped) had been without sleep for twenty hours. Such a thing was very frequent. From St. Joseph, Missouri, to Sacramento, California, by stage-coach, was nearly nineteen hundred miles, and the trip was often made in fifteen days (the cars do it in four and a half, now), but the time specified in the mail contracts, and required by the schedule, was eighteen or nineteen days, if I remember rightly. This was to make fair allowance for winter storms and snows, and other unavoidable causes of detention. The stage company had everything under strict discipline and good system. Over each two hundred and fifty miles of road they placed an agent or superintendent, and invested him with great authority. His beat or jurisdiction of two hundred and fifty miles was called a "division." He purchased horses, mules, harness, and food for men and beasts, and distributed these things among his stage stations, from time to time, according to his judgment of what each station needed. He erected station buildings and dug wells. He attended to the paying of the station-keepers, hostlers, drivers and blacksmiths, and discharged them whenever he chose. He was a very, very great man in his "division"—a kind of Grand Mogul, a Sultan of the Indies, in whose presence common men were modest of speech and manner, and in the glare of whose greatness even the dazzling stage-driver dwindled to a penny dip. There were about eight of these kings, all told, on the overland route.

Next in rank and importance to the division-agent came the "conductor." His beat was the same length as the agent's—two hundred and fifty miles. He sat with the driver, and (when necessary) rode that fearful distance, night and day, without other rest or sleep than what he could get perched thus on top of the flying vehicle. Think of it! He had absolute charge of the mails, express matter, passengers and stage-coach, until he delivered them to the next conductor, and got his receipt for them. Consequently he had to be a man of intelligence, decision and considerable executive ability. He was usually a quiet, pleasant man, who attended closely to his duties, and was a good deal of a gentleman. It was not absolutely necessary that the division-agent should be a gentleman, and occasionally he wasn't. But he was always a general in administrative ability, and a bulldog in courage and determination—otherwise the chieftainship over the lawless underlings of the overland service would never in any instance have been to him anything but an equivalent for a month of insolence and distress and a bullet and a coffin at the end of it. There were about sixteen or eighteen conductors on the overland, for there was a daily stage each way, and a conductor on every stage.

THE CONDUCTOR.

Next in *real* and official rank and importance, *after* the conductor, came my delight, the driver—next in real but not in *apparent* importance—for we have seen that in the eyes of the common herd the driver was to the conductor as an admiral is to the captain of the flag-ship. The driver's beat was pretty long, and his sleeping-time at the stations pretty short, sometimes; and so, but for the grandeur of his position his would have been a sorry life, as well as a hard and a wearing one. We took a new driver every day or every night (for they drove backwards and forwards over the same piece of road all the time), and therefore we never got as well acquainted with them as we did with the conductors; and besides, they would have been above being familiar with such rubbish as passengers, anyhow, as a general thing. Still, we were always eager to get a sight of each and every new driver as soon as the watch changed, for each and every day we were either anxious to get rid of an unpleasant one, or loath to part with a driver we had learned to like and had come to be sociable and friendly with. And so the first question we asked the conductor whenever we got to where we were to exchange drivers, was always, "Which is him?" The grammar was faulty, maybe, but we could not know, then, that it would go into a book some day. As long as everything went smoothly, the overland driver was well enough situated, but if a fellow driver got sick suddenly it made trouble, for the coach *must* go on, and so the potentate who was about to climb down and take a luxurious rest after his long night's siege in the midst of wind and rain and darkness, had to stay where he was and do the sick man's work. Once, in the Rocky Mountains, when I found a driver sound asleep on the box, and the mules going at the usual break-neck pace, the conductor said never mind him, there was no danger, and he was doing double duty—had driven seventy-five miles on one coach, and was now going back over it on this without rest or sleep. A hundred and fifty miles of holding back of six vindictive mules and keeping them from climbing the trees! It sounds incredible, but I remember the statement well enough.

The station-keepers, hostlers, etc., were low, rough characters, as already described; and from western Nebraska to Nevada a considerable sprinkling of them might be fairly set down as outlaws—fugitives from justice, criminals whose best security was a section of country which was without law and without even the pretense of it. When the "division-agent" issued an order to one of these parties he did it with the full understanding that he might have to enforce it with a navy six-shooter, and so he always went "fixed" to make things go along smoothly. Now and then a division-agent was really obliged to shoot a hostler through the head to teach him some simple matter that he could have taught him with a club if his circumstances and surroundings had been different. But they were snappy, able men, those division-agents, and when they tried to teach a subordinate anything, that subordinate generally "got it through his head."

A great portion of this vast machinery—these hundreds of men and coaches, and thousands of mules and horses—was in the hands of Mr. Ben Holladay. All the western half of the business was in his

THE SUPERINTENDENT AS A TEACHER.

hands. This reminds me of an incident of Palestine travel which is pertinent here, and so I will transfer it just in the language in which I find it set down in my Holy Land note-book:

No doubt everybody has heard of Ben Holladay—a man of prodigious energy, who used to send mails and passengers flying across the continent in his overland stage-coaches like a very whirlwind—two thousand long miles in fifteen days and a half, by the watch! But this fragment of history is not about Ben Holladay, but about a young New York boy by the name of Jack, who traveled with our small party of pilgrims in the Holy Land (and who had traveled to California in Mr. Holladay's overland coaches three years before, and had by no means forgotten it or lost his gushing admiration of Mr. H.) Aged nineteen. Jack was a good boy—a good-hearted and always well-meaning boy, who had been reared in the city of New York, and although he was bright and knew a great many useful things, his Scriptural education had been a good deal neglected—to such a degree, indeed, that all Holy Land history was fresh and new to him, and all Bible names mysteries that had never disturbed his virgin ear. Also in our party was an elderly pilgrim who was the reverse of Jack, in that he was learned in the Scriptures and an enthusiast concerning them. He was our encyclopedia, and we were never tired of listening to his speeches, nor he of making them. He never passed a celebrated locality, from Bashan to Bethlehem, without illuminating it with an oration. One day, when camped near the ruins of Jericho, he burst forth with something like this:

"Jack, do you see that range of mountains over yonder that bounds the Jordan valley? The mountains of Moab, Jack! Think of it, my boy—the actual mountains of Moab—renowned in Scripture history! We are actually standing face to face with those illustrious crags and peaks—and for all we know" [dropping his voice impressively], *"our eyes may be resting at this very moment upon the spot* WHERE LIES THE MYSTERIOUS GRAVE OF MOSES! Think of it, Jack!"

JACK AND THE ELDERLY PILGRIM.

"Moses *who?*" [falling inflection].

"Moses *who!* Jack, you ought to be ashamed of yourself—you ought to be ashamed of such criminal ignorance. Why, Moses, the great guide, soldier, poet, lawgiver of ancient Israel! Jack, from this spot where we stand, to Egypt, stretches a fearful desert three hundred miles in extent—and across that desert that wonderful man brought the children of Israel!—guiding them with unfailing sagacity for forty years over the sandy desolation and among the obstructing rocks and hills, and landed them at last, safe and sound, within sight of this very spot; and where we now stand they entered the Promised Land with anthems of rejoicing! It was a wonderful, wonderful thing to do, Jack! Think of it!"

"Forty years? Only three hundred miles? Humph! Ben Holladay would have fetched them through in thirty-six hours!"

The boy meant no harm. He did not know that he had said anything that was wrong or irreverent. And so no one scolded him or felt offended with him—and nobody *could* but some ungenerous spirit incapable of excusing the heedless blunders of a boy.

At noon on the fifth day out, we arrived at the "Crossing of the South Platte," *alias* "Julesburg," *alias* "Overland City," four hundred and seventy miles from St. Joseph—the strangest, quaintest, funniest frontier town that our untraveled eyes had ever stared at and been astonished with.

CHAPTER 7

It did seem strange enough to see a town again after what appeared to us such a long acquaintance with deep, still, almost lifeless and houseless solitude! We tumbled out into the busy street feeling like meteoric people crumbled off the corner of some other world, and wakened up suddenly in this. For an hour we took as much interest in Overland City as if we had never seen a town before. The reason we had an hour to spare was because we had to change our stage (for a less sumptuous affair, called a "mud-wagon") and transfer our freight of mails.

Presently we got under way again. We came to the shallow, yellow, muddy South Platte, with its low banks and its scattering flat sand-bars and pigmy islands—a melancholy stream straggling through the centre of the enormous flat plain, and only saved from being impossible to find with the naked eye by its sentinel rank of scattering trees standing on either bank. The Platte was "up," they said—which made me wish I could see it when it was down, if it could look any sicker and sorrier. They said it was a dangerous stream to cross, now, because its quicksands were liable to swallow up horses, coach and passengers if an attempt was made to ford it. But the mails had to go, and we made the attempt. Once or twice in midstream the wheels sunk into the yielding sands so threateningly that we half believed we had dreaded and avoided the sea all our lives to be shipwrecked in a "mud-wagon" in the middle of a desert at last. But we dragged through and sped away toward the setting sun.

Next morning, just before dawn, when about five hundred and fifty miles from St. Joseph, our mud-wagon broke down. We were to be delayed five or six hours, and therefore we took horses, by invitation, and joined a party who were just starting on a buffalo hunt. It was noble sport galloping over the plain in the dewy freshness of the morning, but our part of the hunt ended in disaster and disgrace, for a wounded buffalo bull chased the passenger Bemis nearly two miles, and then he forsook his horse and took to a lone tree. He was very sullen about the matter for some twenty-four hours, but at last he began to soften little by little, and finally he said:

CROSSING THE PLATTE.

"Well, it was not funny, and there was no sense in those gawks making themselves so facetious over it. I tell you I was angry in earnest for a while. I should have shot that long gangly lubber they called Hank, if I could have done it without crippling six or seven other people—but of course I couldn't, the old 'Allen's' so confounded comprehensive. I wish those loafers had been up in the tree; they wouldn't have wanted to laugh so. If I had had a horse worth a cent—but no, the minute he saw that buffalo bull wheel on him and give a bellow, he raised straight up in the air and stood on his heels. The saddle began to slip, and I took him round the neck and laid close to him, and began to pray. Then he came down and stood up on the other end awhile, and the bull actually stopped pawing sand and bellowing to contemplate the inhuman spectacle. Then the bull made a pass at him and uttered a bellow that sounded perfectly frightful, it was so close to me, and that seemed to literally prostrate my horse's reason, and make a

AN INHUMAN SPECTACLE.

raving distracted maniac of him, and I wish I may die if he didn't stand on his head for a quarter of a minute and shed tears. He was absolutely out of his mind—he was, as sure as truth itself, and he really didn't know what he was doing. Then the bull came charging at us, and my horse dropped down on all fours and took a fresh start—and then for the next ten minutes he would actually throw one hand-spring after another so fast that the bull began to get unsettled, too, and didn't know where to start in—and so he stood there sneezing, and shoveling dust over his back, and bellowing every now and then, and thinking he had got a fifteen-hundred-dollar circus horse for breakfast, certain. Well, I was first out on his neck—the horse's, not the bull's—and then underneath, and next on his rump, and sometimes head up, and sometimes heels—but I tell you it seemed solemn and awful to be ripping and tearing and carrying on so in the presence of death, as you might say. Pretty soon the bull made a snatch for us and brought away some of my horse's tail (I suppose, but do not know, being pretty busy at the time), but *something* made him hungry for solitude and suggested to him to get up and hunt for it. And then you ought to have seen

A NEW DEPARTURE.

that spider-legged old skeleton go! and you ought to have seen the bull cut out after him, too—head down, tongue out, tail up, bellowing like everything, and actually mowing down the weeds, and tearing up the earth, and boosting up the sand like a whirlwind! By George, it was a hot race! I and the saddle were back on the rump, and I had the bridle in my teeth and holding on to the pommel with both hands. First we left the dogs behind; then we passed a jackass rabbit; then we overtook a cayote, and were gaining on an antelope when the rotten girth let go and threw me about thirty yards off to the left, and as the saddle went down over the horse's rump he gave it a lift with his heels that sent it more than four hundred yards up in the air, I wish I may die in a minute if he didn't. I fell at the foot of the only solitary tree there was in nine counties adjacent (as any creature could see with the naked eye), and the next second I had hold of the bark with four sets of nails and my teeth, and the next second after that I was astraddle of the main limb and blaspheming my luck in a way that made my breath smell of brimstone. I *had* the bull, now, if he did not think of *one* thing. But that one thing I dreaded. I dreaded it very seriously. There was a possibility that the bull might not think of it, but there were greater chances that he would. I made up my mind what I would do in case he did. It was a little over forty feet to the ground from where I sat. I cautiously unwound the lariat from the pommel of my saddle—"

"Your *saddle?* Did you take your saddle up in the tree with you?"

"Take it up in the tree with me? Why, how you talk. Of course I didn't. No man could do that. It *fell* in the tree when it came down."

"Oh—exactly."

"Certainly. I unwound the lariat, and fastened one end of it to the limb. It was the very best green raw-hide, and capable of sustaining tons. I made a slip-noose in the other end, and then hung it down to see the length. It reached down twenty-two feet—half way to the ground. I then loaded every barrel of the Allen with a double charge. I felt satisfied. I said to myself, if he never thinks of that one thing that I dread, all right—but if he does, all right anyhow—I am fixed for him. But don't you know that the very thing a man dreads is the thing that always happens? Indeed it is so. I watched the bull, now, with anxiety—anxiety which no one can conceive of who has not been in such a situation and felt that at any moment death might come. Presently a thought came into the bull's eye. I knew it! said I—if my nerve fails now, I am lost. Sure enough, it was just as I had dreaded, he started in to climb the tree—"

"What, the bull?"

"Of course—who else?"

"But a bull can't climb a tree."

"He can't, can't he? Since you know so much about it, did you ever see a bull try?"

"No! I never dreamt of such a thing."

"Well, then, what is the use of your talking that way, then? Because you never saw a thing done, is that any reason why it can't be done?"

"Well, all right—go on. What did you do?"

"The bull started up, and got along well for about ten feet, then slipped and slid back. I breathed easier. He tried it again—got up a little higher—slipped again. But he came at it once more, and this time he was careful. He got gradually higher and higher, and my spirits went down more and more. Up he came—an inch at a time—with his eyes hot, and his tongue hanging out. Higher and higher—hitched his foot over the stump of a limb, and looked up, as much as to say, 'You are my meat, friend.' Up again—higher and higher, and getting more excited the closer he got. He was within ten feet of me! I took a long breath,—and then said I, 'It is now or never.' I had the coil of the lariat all ready; I paid it out slowly, till it hung right over his head; all of a sudden I let go of the slack, and

SUSPENDED OPERATIONS.

the slip-noose fell fairly round his neck! Quicker than lightning I out with the Allen and let him have it in the face. It was an awful roar, and must have scared the bull out of his senses. When the smoke cleared away, there he was, dangling in the air, twenty foot from the ground, and going out of one convulsion into another faster than you could count! I didn't stop to count, anyhow—I shinned down the tree and shot for home."

"Bemis, is all that true, just as you have stated it?"

"I wish I may rot in my tracks and die the death of a dog if it isn't."

"Well, we can't refuse to believe it, and we don't. But if there were some proofs—"

"Proofs! Did I bring back my lariat?"

"No."

"Did I bring back my horse?"

"No."

"Did you ever see the bull again?"

"No."

"Well, then, what more do you want? I never saw anybody as particular as you are about a little thing like that."

I made up my mind that if this man was not a liar he only missed it by the skin of his teeth. This episode reminds me of an incident of my brief sojourn in Siam, years afterward. The European citizens of a town in the neighborhood of Bangkok had a prodigy among them by the name of Eckert, an Englishman—a person famous for the number, ingenuity and imposing magnitude of his lies. They were always repeating his most celebrated falsehoods, and always trying to "draw him out" before strangers; but they seldom succeeded. Twice he was invited to the house where I was visiting, but nothing could seduce him into a specimen lie. One day a planter named Bascom, an influential man, and a proud and sometimes irascible one, invited me to ride over with him and call on Eckert. As we jogged along, said he:

"Now, do you know where the fault lies? It lies in putting Eckert on his guard. The minute the boys go to pumping at Eckert he knows perfectly well what they are after, and of course he shuts up his shell. Anybody might know he would. But when we get there, we must play him finer than that. Let him shape the conversation to suit himself—let him drop it or change it whenever he wants to. Let him see that nobody is trying to draw him out. Just let him have his own way. He will soon forget himself and begin to grind out lies like a mill. Don't get impatient—just keep quiet, and let me play him. I will make him lie. It does seem to me that the boys must be blind to overlook such an obvious and simple trick as that."

Eckert received us heartily—a pleasant-spoken, gentle-mannered creature. We sat in the veranda an hour, sipping English ale, and talking about the king, and the sacred white elephant, the Sleeping Idol, and all manner of things; and I noticed that my comrade never led the conversation himself or shaped it, but simply followed Eckert's lead, and betrayed no solicitude and no anxiety about anything. The effect was shortly perceptible. Eckert began to grow communicative; he grew more and more at his ease, and more and more talkative and sociable. Another hour passed in the same way, and then all of a sudden Eckert said:

A WONDERFUL LIE.

"Oh, by the way! I came near forgetting. I have got a thing here to astonish you. Such a thing as neither you nor any other man ever heard of—I've got a cat that will eat cocoanut! Common green cocoanut—and not only eat the meat, but drink the milk. It is so—I'll swear to it."

A quick glance from Bascom—a glance that I understood—then:

"Why, bless my soul, I never heard of such a thing. Man, it is impossible."

"I knew you would say it. I'll fetch the cat."

He went in the house. Bascom said:

"There—what did I tell you? Now, that is the way to handle Eckert. You see, I have petted him along patiently, and put his suspicions to sleep. I am glad we came. You tell the boys about it when you go back. Cat eat a cocoanut—oh, my! Now, that is just his way, exactly—he will tell the absurdest lie, and trust to luck to get out of it again. Cat eat a cocoanut—the innocent fool!"

Eckert approached with his cat, sure enough.

Bascom smiled. Said he:

"I'll hold the cat—you bring a cocoanut."

Eckert split one open, and chopped up some pieces. Bascom smuggled a wink to me, and proffered a slice of the fruit to puss. She snatched it, swallowed it ravenously, and asked for more!

We rode our two miles in silence, and wide apart. At least I was silent, though Bascom cuffed his horse and cursed him a good deal, notwithstanding the horse was behaving well enough. When I branched off homeward, Bascom said:

"Keep the horse till morning. And—you need not speak of this —— foolishness to the boys."

CHAPTER 8

In a little while all interest was taken up in stretching our necks and watching for the "pony-rider"—the fleet messenger who sped across the continent from St. Joe to Sacramento, carrying letters nineteen hundred miles in eight days! Think of that for perishable horse and human flesh and blood to do! The pony-rider was usually a little bit of a man, brim full of spirit and endurance. No matter what time of the day or night his watch came on, and no matter whether it was winter or summer, raining, snowing, hailing, or sleeting, or whether his "beat" was a level straight road or a crazy trail over mountain crags and precipices, or whether it led through peaceful regions or regions that swarmed with hostile Indians, he must be always ready to leap into the saddle and be off like the wind! There was no idling-time for a pony-rider on duty. He rode fifty miles without stopping, by daylight, moonlight, starlight, or through the blackness of darkness—just as it happened. He rode a splendid horse that was born for a racer and fed and lodged like a gentleman; kept him at his utmost speed for ten miles, and then, as he came crashing up to the station where stood two men holding fast a fresh, impatient steed, the transfer of rider and mail-bag was made in the twinkling of an eye, and away flew the eager pair and were out of sight before the spectator could get hardly the ghost of a look. Both rider and horse went "flying light." The rider's dress was thin and fitted close; he wore a "roundabout" and a skull-cap, and tucked his pantaloons into his boot-tops like a race-rider. He carried no arms—he carried nothing that was not absolutely necessary, for even the postage on his literary freight was worth *two dollars an ounce.* He got but little frivolous correspondence to carry—his bag had business letters in it, mostly. His horse was stripped of all unnecessary weight, too. He wore a little wafer of a racing-saddle, and no visible blanket. He wore light shoes, or none at all. The little flat mail-pockets strapped under the rider's thighs would each hold about the bulk of a child's primer. They held many and many an important business chapter and newspaper letter, but these were written on paper as airy and thin as gold-leaf, nearly, and thus bulk and weight were economized. The stage-coach traveled about a hundred to a hundred and twenty-five miles a day (twenty-four hours), the pony-rider about two hundred and fifty. There were about eighty pony-riders in the saddle all the time, night and day, stretching in a long, scattering procession from Missouri to California, forty flying eastward and forty toward the west, and among them making four hundred gallant horses earn a stirring livelihood and see a deal of scenery every single day in the year.

"HERE HE COMES!"

We had had a consuming desire, from the beginning, to see a pony-rider, but somehow or other all that passed us and all that met us managed to streak by in the night, and so we heard only a whiz and a hail, and the swift phantom of the desert was gone before we could get our heads out of the windows. But now we were expecting one along every moment, and would see him in broad daylight. Presently the driver exclaims:

"HERE HE COMES!"

Every neck is stretched further, and every eye strained wider. Away across the endless dead level of the prairie a black speck appears against the sky, and it is plain that it moves. Well, I should think so! In a second or two it becomes a horse and rider, rising and falling, rising and falling—sweeping toward us nearer and nearer—growing more and more distinct, more and more sharply defined—nearer and still nearer, and the flutter of the hoofs comes faintly to the ear—another instant a whoop and a hurrah from our upper deck, a wave of the rider's hand, but no reply, and man and horse burst past our excited faces, and go winging away like a belated fragment of a storm!

So sudden is it all, and so like a flash of unreal fancy, that but for the flake of white foam left quivering and perishing on a mail-sack

CHANGING HORSES.

after the vision had flashed by and disappeared, we might have doubted whether we had seen any actual horse and man at all, maybe.

We rattled through Scott's Bluffs Pass, by and by. It was along here somewhere that we first came across genuine and unmistakable alkali water in the road, and we cordially hailed it as a first-class curiosity, and a thing to be mentioned with eclat in letters to the ignorant at home. This water gave the road a soapy appearance, and in many places the ground looked as if it had been whitewashed. I think the strange alkali water excited us as much as any wonder we had come upon yet, and I know we felt very complacent and conceited, and better satisfied with life after we had added it to our list of things which *we* had seen and some other people had not. In a small way we were the same sort of simpletons as those who climb unnecessarily the perilous peaks of Mont Blanc and the Matterhorn, and derive no pleasure from it except the reflection that it isn't a common experience. But once in a while one of those parties trips and comes darting down the long mountain crags in a sitting posture, making the crusted snow smoke behind him, flitting from bench to bench, and from terrace to terrace, jarring the earth where he strikes, and still glancing and flitting on again, sticking an iceberg into himself every now and then, and tearing his clothes, snatching at things to save himself, taking hold of trees and fetching them along with him, roots and all, starting little rocks now and then, then big boulders, then acres of ice and snow and patches of forest, gathering and still gathering as he goes, adding and still adding to his massed and sweeping grandeur as he

RIDING THE AVALANCHE.

nears a three-thousand-foot precipice, till at last he waves his hat magnificently and rides into eternity on the back of a raging and tossing avalanche!

This is all very fine, but let us not be carried away by excitement, but ask calmly, how does this person feel about it in his cooler moments next day, with six or seven thousand feet of snow and stuff on top of him?

We crossed the sand hills near the scene of the Indian mail robbery and massacre of 1856, wherein the driver and conductor perished, and also all the passengers but one, it was supposed; but this must have been a mistake, for at different times afterward on the Pacific coast I was personally acquainted with a hundred and thirty-three or four people who were wounded during that massacre, and barely escaped with their lives. There was no doubt of the truth of it—I had it from their own lips. One of these parties told me that he kept coming across arrow-heads in his system for nearly seven years after the massacre; and another of them told me that he was stuck so literally full of arrows that after the Indians were gone and he could raise up and examine himself, he could not restrain his tears, for his clothes were completely ruined.

The most trustworthy tradition avers, however, that only one man, a person named Babbitt, survived the massacre, and he was desperately wounded. He dragged himself on his hands and knee (for one leg was broken) to a station several miles away. He did it during portions of two nights, lying concealed one day and part of another, and for more than forty hours suffering unimaginable anguish from hunger, thirst and bodily pain. The Indians robbed the coach of everything it contained, including quite an amount of treasure.

CHAPTER 9

We passed Fort Laramie in the night, and on the seventh morning out we found ourselves in the Black Hills, with Laramie Peak at our elbow (apparently) looming vast and solitary—a deep, dark, rich indigo blue in hue, so portentously did the old colossus frown under his beetling brows of storm-cloud. He was thirty or forty miles away, in reality, but he only seemed removed a little beyond the low ridge at our right. We breakfasted at Horseshoe station, six hundred and seventy-six miles out from St. Joseph. We had now reached a hostile Indian country, and during the afternoon we passed La Prele station, and enjoyed great discomfort all the time we were in the neighborhood, being aware that many of the trees we dashed by at arm's length concealed a lurking Indian or two. During the preceding night an ambushed savage had sent a bullet through the pony-rider's jacket, but he had ridden on, just the same, because pony-riders were not allowed to stop and inquire into such things except when killed. As long as they had life enough left in them they had to stick to the horse and ride, even if the Indians had been waiting for them a week, and were entirely out of patience. About two hours and a half before we arrived at La Prele station, the keeper in charge of it had fired four times at an Indian, but he said with an injured air that the Indian had "skipped around so's to spile everything—and ammunition's blamed skurse, too." The most natural inference conveyed by his manner of speaking was, that in "skipping around," the Indian had taken an unfair advantage. The coach we were in had a neat hole through its front—a reminiscence of its last trip through this region. The bullet that made it wounded the driver slightly, but he did not mind it much. He said the place to keep a man "huffy" was down on the Southern Overland, among the Apaches, before the company moved the stage-line up on the northern route. He said the

Apaches used to annoy him all the time down there, and that he came as near as anything to starving to death in the midst of abundance, because they kept him so leaky with bullet holes that he "couldn't hold his vittles." This person's statements were not generally believed.

We shut the blinds down very tightly that first night in the hostile Indian country, and lay on our arms. We slept on them some,

INDIAN COUNTRY.

but most of the time we only lay on them. We did not talk much, but kept quiet and listened. It was an inky-black night, and occasionally rainy. We were among woods and rocks, hills and gorges—so shut in, in fact, that when we peeped through a chink in a curtain, we could discern nothing. The driver and conductor on top were still, too, or only spoke at long intervals, in low tones, as is the way of men in the midst of invisible dangers. We listened to rain-drops pattering on the roof; and the grinding of the wheels through the muddy gravel; and the low wailing of the wind; and all the time we had that absurd sense upon us, inseparable from travel at night in a close-curtained vehicle, the sense of remaining perfectly still in one place, notwithstanding the jolting and swaying of the vehicle, the trampling of the horses, and the grinding of the wheels. We listened a long time, with intent faculties and bated breath; every time one of us would relax, and draw a long sigh of relief and start to say something, a comrade would be sure to utter a sudden "Hark!" and instantly the experimenter was rigid and listening again. So the tiresome minutes and decades of minutes dragged away, until at last our tense forms filmed over with a dulled consciousness, and we slept, if one might call such a condition by so strong a name—for it was a sleep set with a hair-trigger. It was a sleep seething and teeming with a weird and distressful confusion of shreds and fag-ends of dreams—a sleep that was a chaos. Presently, dreams and sleep and the sullen hush of the night were startled by a ringing report, and cloven by *such* a long, wild, agonizing shriek! Then we heard—ten steps from the stage—

"Help! help! help!" [It was our driver's voice.]

"Kill him! Kill him like a dog!"

"I'm being murdered! Will no man lend me a pistol?"

"Look out! head him off! head him off!"

[Two pistol shots; a confusion of voices and the trampling of many feet, as if a crowd were closing and surging together around some object; several heavy, dull blows, as with a club; a voice that said appealingly, "Don't, gentlemen, please don't—I'm a dead man!" Then a fainter groan, and another blow, and away sped the stage into the darkness, and left the grisly mystery behind us.]

What a startle it was! Eight seconds would amply cover the time it occupied—maybe even five would do it. We only had time to plunge at a curtain and unbuckle and unbutton part of it in an awkward and hindering flurry, when our whip cracked sharply overhead, and we went rumbling and thundering away, down a mountain "grade."

We fed on that mystery the rest of the night—what was left of it, for it was waning fast. It had to remain a present mystery, for all we could get from the conductor in answer to our hails was something that sounded, through the clatter of the wheels, like "Tell you in the morning!"

So we lit our pipes and opened the corner of a curtain for a chimney, and lay there in the dark, listening to each other's story of how he first felt and how many thousand Indians he first thought had hurled themselves upon us, and what his remembrance of the subsequent sounds was, and the order of their occurrence. And we theorized, too, but there was never a theory that would account for our driver's voice being out there, nor yet account for his Indian murderers talking such good English, if they *were* Indians.

So we chatted and smoked the rest of the night comfortably away, our boding anxiety being somehow marvelously dissipated by the real presence of something to be anxious *about*.

We never did get much satisfaction about that dark occurrence. All that we could make out of the odds and ends of the information we gathered in the morning, was that the disturbance occurred at a station; that we changed drivers there, and that the driver that got off there had been talking roughly about some of the outlaws that infested the region ("for there wasn't a man around there but had a price on his head and didn't dare show himself in the settlements," the conductor said); he had talked roughly about these characters, and ought to have "drove up there with his pistol cocked and ready on the seat alongside of him, and begun business himself, because any softy would know they would be laying for him."

That was all we could gather, and we could see that neither the conductor nor the new driver were much concerned about the matter. They plainly had little respect for a man who would deliver offensive opinions of people and then be so simple as to come into their presence unprepared to "back his judgment," as they pleasantly phrased the killing of any fellow-being who did not like said opinions. And likewise they plainly had a contempt for the man's poor discretion in venturing to rouse the wrath of such utterly reckless wild beasts as those outlaws—and the conductor added:

"I tell you it's as much as Slade himself wants to do!"

This remark created an entire revolution in my curiosity. I cared nothing now about the Indians, and even lost interest in the murdered driver. There was such magic in that name, SLADE! Day or night, now, I stood always ready to drop any subject in hand, to listen to something new about Slade and his ghastly exploits. Even before we got to Overland City, we had begun to hear about Slade and his "division" (for he was a "division-agent") on the Overland;

and from the hour we had left Overland City we had heard drivers and conductors talk about only three things—"Californy," the Nevada silver mines, and this desperado Slade. And a deal the most of the talk was about Slade. We had gradually come to have a realizing sense of the fact that Slade was a man whose heart and hands and soul were steeped in the blood of offenders against his dignity; a man who awfully avenged all injuries, affronts, insults or slights, of whatever kind—on the spot if he could, years afterward if lack of earlier opportunity compelled it; a man whose hate tortured him day and night till vengeance appeased it—and not an ordinary vengeance either, but his enemy's absolute death—nothing less; a man whose face would light up with a terrible joy when he surprised a foe and had him at a disadvantage. A high and efficient servant of the Overland, an outlaw among outlaws and yet their relentless scourge, Slade was at once the most bloody, the most dangerous and the most valuable citizen that inhabited the savage fastnesses of the mountains.

CHAPTER 10

Really and truly, two-thirds of the talk of drivers and conductors had been about this man Slade, ever since the day before we reached Julesburg. In order that the eastern reader may have a clear conception of what a Rocky Mountain desperado is, in his highest state of development, I will reduce all this mass of overland gossip to one straightforward narrative, and present it in the following shape:

Slade was born in Illinois, of good parentage. At about twenty-six years of age he killed a man in a quarrel and fled the country. At St. Joseph, Missouri, he joined one of the early California-bound emigrant trains, and was given the post of train-master. One day on the plains he had an angry dispute with one of his wagon-drivers, and both drew their revolvers. But the driver was the quicker artist, and had his weapon cocked first. So Slade said it was a pity to waste life on so small a matter, and proposed that the pistols be thrown on the ground and the quarrel settled by a fist-fight. The unsuspecting driver agreed, and threw down his pistol—whereupon Slade laughed at his simplicity, and shot him dead!

He made his escape, and lived a wild life for a while, dividing his time between fighting Indians and avoiding an Illinois sheriff, who had been sent to arrest him for his first murder. It is said that in one Indian battle he killed three savages with his own hand, and afterward cut their ears off and sent them, with his compliments, to the chief of the tribe.

Slade soon gained a name for fearless resolution, and this was sufficient merit to procure for him the important post of overland division-agent at Julesburg, in place of Mr. Jules, removed. For some time previously, the company's horses had been frequently stolen, and the coaches delayed, by gangs of outlaws, who were wont to laugh at the idea of any man's having the temerity to resent such outrages. Slade resented them promptly. The outlaws soon found that the new agent was a man who did not fear anything that breathed the breath of life. He made short work of all

A PROPOSED FIST-FIGHT.

offenders. The result was that delays ceased, the company's property was let alone, and no matter what happened or who suffered, Slade's coaches went through, every time! True, in order to bring about this wholesome change, Slade had to kill several men—some say three, others say four, and others six—but the world was the richer for their loss. The first prominent difficulty he had was with the ex-agent Jules, who bore the reputation of being a reckless and desperate man himself. Jules hated Slade for supplanting him,

FROM BEHIND THE DOOR.

and a good fair occasion for a fight was all he was waiting for. By and by Slade dared to employ a man whom Jules had once discharged. Next, Slade seized a team of stage-horses which he accused Jules of having driven off and hidden somewhere for his own use. War was declared, and for a day or two the two men walked warily about the streets, seeking each other, Jules armed with a double-barreled shotgun, and Slade with his history-creating revolver. Finally, as Slade stepped into a store, Jules poured the contents of his gun into him from behind the door. Slade was pluck, and Jules got several bad pistol wounds in return. Then both men fell, and were carried to their respective lodgings, both swearing that better aim should do deadlier work next time. Both were bedridden a long time, but Jules got on his feet first, and gathering his possessions together, packed them on a couple of mules, and fled to the Rocky Mountains to gather strength in safety against the day of reckoning. For many months he was not seen or heard of, and was gradually dropped out of the remembrance of all save Slade himself. But Slade was not the man to forget him. On the contrary, common report said that Slade kept a reward standing for his capture, dead or alive!

After a while, seeing that Slade's energetic administration had restored peace and order to one of the worst divisions of the road, the overland stage company transferred him to the Rocky Ridge division in the Rocky Mountains, to see if he could perform a like miracle there. It was the very paradise of outlaws and desperadoes. There was absolutely no semblance of law there. Violence was the rule. Force was the only recognized authority. The commonest misunderstandings were settled on the spot with the revolver or the knife. Murders were done in open day, and with sparkling frequency, and nobody thought of inquiring into them. It was considered that the parties who did the killing had their private reasons for it; for other people to meddle would have been looked upon as indelicate. After a murder, all that Rocky Mountain etiquette required of a spectator was, that he should help the gentleman bury his game—otherwise his churlishness would surely be remembered against him the first time he killed a man himself and needed a neighborly turn in interring him.

Slade took up his residence sweetly and peacefully in the midst of this hive of horse-thieves and assassins, and the very first time one of them aired his insolent swaggerings in his presence he shot him dead! He began a raid on the outlaws, and in a singularly short space of time he had completely stopped their depredations on the stage stock, recovered a large number of stolen horses, killed several of the worst desperadoes of the district, and gained such a dread ascendancy over the rest that they respected him, admired him, feared him, obeyed him! He wrought the same marvelous change in the ways of the community that had marked his administration at Overland City. He captured two men who had stolen overland stock, and with his own hands he hanged them. He was supreme judge in his district, and he was jury and executioner likewise—and not only in the case of offenses against his employers, but against passing emigrants as well. On one occasion some emigrants had their stock lost or stolen, and told Slade, who chanced to visit their camp. With a single companion he rode to a ranch, the owners of which he suspected, and opening the door, commenced firing, killing three, and wounding the fourth.

SLADE AS EXECUTIONER.

From a bloodthirstily interesting little Montana book* I take this paragraph:

> While on the road, Slade held absolute sway. He would ride down to a station, get into a quarrel, turn the house out of windows, and maltreat the occupants most cruelly. The unfortunates had no means of redress, and were compelled to recuperate as best they could. On one of these occasions, it is said, he killed the father of the fine little half-breed boy, Jemmy, whom he adopted, and who lived with his widow after his execution. Stories of Slade's hanging men, and of innumerable assaults, shootings, stabbings and beatings, in which he was a principal actor, form part of the legends of the stage line. As for minor quarrels and shootings, it is absolutely certain that a minute history of Slade's life would be one long record of such practices.

Slade was a matchless marksman with a navy revolver. The legends say that one morning at Rocky Ridge, when he was feeling comfortable, he saw a man approaching who had offended him some days before—observe the fine memory he had for matters like that—and, "Gentlemen," said Slade, drawing, "it is a good twenty-yard shot—I'll clip the third button on his coat!" Which he

*"The Vigilantes of Montana," by Prof. Thos. J. Dimsdale.

did. The bystanders all admired it. And they all attended the funeral, too.

On one occasion a man who kept a little whisky-shelf at the station did something which angered Slade—and went and made his will. A day or two afterward Slade came in and called for some brandy. The man reached under the counter (ostensibly to get a bottle—possibly to get something else), but Slade smiled upon him that peculiarly bland and satisfied smile of his which the neighbors had long ago learned to recognize as a death-warrant in

AN UNPLEASANT VIEW.

disguise, and told him "none of that!—pass out the high-priced article." So the poor barkeeper had to turn his back and get the high-priced brandy from the shelf; and when he faced around again he was looking into the muzzle of Slade's pistol. "And the next instant," added my informant, impressively, "he was one of the deadest men that ever lived."

The stage-drivers and conductors told us that sometimes Slade would leave a hated enemy wholly unmolested, unnoticed and unmentioned, for weeks together—had done it once or twice at any rate. And some said they believed he did it in order to lull the victims into unwatchfulness, so that he could get the advantage of them, and others said they believed he saved up an enemy that way, just as a school-boy saves up a cake, and made the pleasure go as far as it would by gloating over the anticipation. One of these cases was that of a Frenchman who had offended Slade. To the surprise of everybody Slade did not kill him on the spot, but let him alone for a considerable time. Finally, however, he went to the Frenchman's house very late one night, knocked, and when his enemy opened the door, shot him dead—pushed the corpse inside the door with his foot, set the house on fire and burned up the dead man, his widow and three children! I heard this story from several different people, and they evidently believed what they were saying. It may be true, and it may not. "Give a dog a bad name," etc.

Slade was captured, once, by a party of men who intended to lynch him. They disarmed him, and shut him up in a strong log house, and placed a guard over him. He prevailed on his captors to send for his wife, so that he might have a last interview with her. She was a brave, loving, spirited woman. She jumped on a horse and rode for life and death. When she arrived they let her in without searching her, and before the door could be closed she whipped out a couple of revolvers, and she and her lord marched forth defying the party. And then, under a brisk fire, they mounted double and galloped away unharmed!

In the fulness of time Slade's myrmidons captured his ancient enemy Jules, whom they found in a well-chosen hiding-place in the remote fastnesses of the mountains, gaining a precarious livelihood with his rifle. They brought him to Rocky Ridge, bound hand and foot, and deposited him in the middle of the cattle-yard with his back against a post. It is said that the pleasure that lit Slade's face when he heard of it was something fearful to contemplate. He examined his enemy to see that he was securely tied, and then went to bed, content to wait till morning before enjoying the luxury of killing him. Jules spent the night in the cattle-yard, and it is a region where warm nights are never known. In the morning Slade practiced on him with his revolver, nipping the flesh here and there, and occasionally clipping off a finger, while Jules begged him to kill him outright and put him out of his misery. Finally Slade reloaded, and walking up close to his victim, made some characteristic remarks and then dispatched him. The body lay there half a day, nobody venturing to touch it without orders, and then Slade detailed a party and assisted at the burial himself. But he first cut off the dead man's ears and put them in his vest pocket, where he carried them for some time with great satisfaction. That is the story as I have frequently heard it told and seen it in print in California newspapers. It is doubtless correct in all essential particulars.

In due time we rattled up to a stage station, and sat down to breakfast with a half-savage, half-civilized company of armed and bearded mountaineers, ranchmen and station employés. The most gentlemanly-appearing, quiet and affable officer we had yet found along the road in the Overland Company's service was the person who sat at the head of the table, at my elbow. Never youth stared and shivered as I did when I heard them call him SLADE!

Here was romance, and I sitting face to face with it!—looking upon it—touching it—hobnobbing with it, as it were! Here, right by my side, was the actual ogre who, in fights and brawls and various ways, *had taken the lives of twenty-six human beings,* or all men lied about him! I suppose I was the proudest stripling that ever traveled to see strange lands and wonderful people.

He was so friendly and so gentle-spoken that I warmed to him in spite of his awful history. It was hardly possible to realize that this pleasant person was the pitiless scourge of the outlaws, the rawhead-and-bloody-bones the nursing mothers of the mountains terrified their children with. And to this day I can remember nothing remarkable about Slade except that his face was rather broad across the cheek bones, and that the cheek bones were low and the lips peculiarly thin and straight. But that was enough to leave something of an effect upon me, for since then I seldom see a face possessing those characteristics without fancying that the owner of it is a dangerous man.

The coffee ran out. At least it was reduced to one tin-cupful, and Slade was about to take it when he saw that my cup was empty. He politely offered to fill it, but although I wanted it, I politely declined. I was afraid he had not killed anybody that morning, and might be needing diversion. But still with firm politeness he insisted on filling my cup, and said I had traveled all night and better deserved it than he—and while he talked he placidly poured the

UNAPPRECIATED POLITENESS.

fluid, to the last drop. I thanked him and drank it, but it gave me no comfort, for I could not feel sure that he would not be sorry, presently, that he had given it away, and proceed to kill me to distract his thoughts from the loss. But nothing of the kind occurred. We left him with only twenty-six dead people to account for, and I felt a tranquil satisfaction in the thought that in so judiciously taking care of No. 1 at that breakfast-table I had pleasantly escaped being No. 27. Slade came out to the coach and saw us off, first ordering certain reärrangements of the mail-bags for our comfort, and then we took leave of him, satisfied that we should hear of him again, some day, and wondering in what connection.

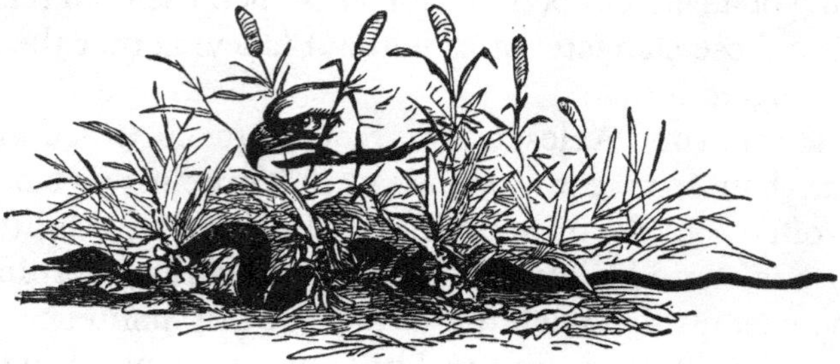

CHAPTER 11

AND sure enough, two or three years afterward, we did hear of him again. News came to the Pacific coast that the Vigilance Committee in Montana (whither Slade had removed from Rocky Ridge) had hanged him. I find an account of the affair in the thrilling little book I quoted a paragraph from in the last chapter—"The Vigilantes of Montana; being a Reliable Account of the Capture, Trial and Execution of Henry Plummer's Notorious Road Agent Band: By Prof. Thos. J. Dimsdale, Virginia City, M. T." Mr. Dimsdale's chapter is well worth reading, as a specimen of how the people of the frontier deal with criminals when the courts of law prove inefficient. Mr. Dimsdale makes two remarks about Slade, both of which are accurately descriptive, and one of which is exceedingly picturesque: "Those who saw him in his natural state only, would pronounce him to be a kind husband, a most hospitable host and a courteous gentleman; on the contrary, those who met him when maddened with liquor and surrounded by a gang of armed roughs, would pronounce him a fiend incarnate." And this: "From Fort Kearny, west, he was feared *a great deal more than the Almighty.*" For compactness, simplicity and vigor of expression, I will "back" that sentence against anything in literature. Mr. Dimsdale's narrative is as follows. In all places where italics occur, they are mine:

After the execution of the five men, on the 14th of January, the Vigilantes considered that their work was nearly ended. They had freed the country from highwaymen and murderers to a great extent, and they determined that, in the absence of the regular civil authority, they would establish a People's Court, where all offenders should be tried by Judge and Jury. This was the nearest approach to social order that the circumstances permitted, and, though strict legal authority was wanting, yet the people were firmly determined to maintain its efficiency, and to enforce its decrees. It may here be mentioned that the overt act which was the last round on the fatal ladder leading to the scaffold on which Slade perished, *was the tearing in pieces and stamping upon a writ of this court, followed by his arrest of the Judge, Alex. Davis, by authority of a presented Derringer, and with his own hands.*

J. A. Slade was himself, we have been informed, a Vigilanter; he openly boasted of it, and said he knew all that they knew. He was never accused, or even suspected of either murder or robbery, committed in this Territory, (the latter crime was never laid to his charge, in any place;) but that he had killed several men in other localities, was notorious, and his bad reputation in this respect was a most powerful argument in determining his fate, when he was finally arrested for the offense above mentioned. On returning from Milk River he became more and more addicted to drinking; until at last, it was a common feat for him and his friends to "take the town." He and a couple of his dependants might often be seen on one horse, galloping through the streets, shouting and yelling, firing revolvers, etc. On many occasions he would ride his horse into stores; break up bars; toss the scales out of doors, and use most insulting language to parties present. Just previous to the day of his arrest, he had given a fearful beating to one of his followers; but such was his influence over them that the man wept bitterly at the gallows, and begged for his life with all his power. *It had become quite common, when Slade was on a spree, for the shopkeepers and citizens to close the stores and put out all the lights;* being fearful of some outrage at his hands. For his wanton destruction of goods and furniture, he was always ready to pay, when sober if he had money; but there were not a few who regarded payment as small satisfaction for the outrage, and these men were his personal enemies.

From time to time, Slade received warnings from men that he well knew would not deceive him, of the certain end of his conduct. There was not a moment, for weeks previous to his arrest, in which the public did not expect to hear of some bloody outrage. The dread of his very name, and the presence of the armed band of hangers-on, who followed him alone prevented a resistance, which must certainly have ended in the instant murder or mutilation of the opposing party.

Slade was frequently arrested by order of the court whose organization we have described, and had treated it with respect by paying one or two fines, and promising to pay the rest when he had money; but in the transaction that occurred at this crisis, he forgot even this caution, and goaded by passion and the hatred of restraint, he sprang into the embrace of death.

Slade had been drunk and "cutting up" all night. He and his companions had made the town a perfect hell. In the morning, J. M. Fox, the Sheriff, met him, arrested him, took him into court, and commenced reading a warrant that he had for his arrest, by way of arraignment. He became uncontrollably furious, and *seizing the writ, he tore it up, threw it on the ground and stamped upon it.* The clicking of the locks of his companions' revolvers was instantly heard and a crisis was expected. The Sheriff did not attempt his retention; but being at least as prudent as he was valiant, he succumbed, leaving Slade the *master of the situation and the conqueror and ruler of the courts, law and law-makers.* This was a declaration of war, and

SLADE IN COURT.

was so accepted. The Vigilance Committee now felt that the question of social order and the preponderance of the law abiding citizens had then and there to be decided. They knew the character of Slade, and they were well aware that they must submit to his rule without murmur, or else that he must be dealt with in such fashion as would prevent his being able to wreak his vengeance on the Committee, who could never have hoped to live in the Territory secure from outrage or death, and who could never leave it without encountering his friends, whom his victory would have emboldened and stimulated to a pitch that would have rendered them reckless of consequences. The day previous, he had ridden into Dorris' store, and on being requested to leave, he drew his revolver and threatened to kill the gentleman who spoke to him. Another saloon he had led his horse into, and buying a bottle of wine, he tried to make the animal drink it. This was not considered an uncommon performance, as he had often entered saloons, and commenced firing at the lamps, causing a wild stampede.

A leading member of the committee met Slade, and informed him in the quiet earnest manner of one who feels the importance of what he is saying: "Slade, get your horse at once, and go home, or there will be ——— to pay." Slade started and took a long look with his dark and piercing eyes, at the gentleman— "what do you mean?" said he. "You have no right to ask me what I mean," was the quiet reply, "get your horse at once, and remember what I tell you." After a short pause he promised to do so, and actually got into the saddle; but, being still intoxicated, he began calling aloud to one after another of his friends, and, at last seemed to have forgotten the warning he had received and became again uproarious, shouting the name of a well known courtezan in company with those of two men whom he considered heads of the Committee, as a sort of challenge; perhaps, however, as a simple act of bravado. It seems probable that the intimation of personal danger he had received had not been forgotten entirely; though fatally for him, he took a foolish way of showing his remembrance of it. He sought out Alexander Davis, the Judge of the Court, and drawing a cocked Derringer, he presented it at his head, and told him that he should hold him as a hostage for his own safety. As the Judge stood perfectly quiet, and offered no resistance to his captor, no further outrage followed on this score. Previous to this, on account of the critical state of affairs, the Committee had met, and at last resolved to arrest him. His execution had not been agreed upon, and, at that time, would have been negatived, most assuredly. A messenger rode down to Nevada to inform the leading men of what was on hand, as it was desirable to show that there was a feeling of unanimity on the subject, all along the gulch.

The miners turned out almost en masse, leaving their work and forming in solid column, about six hundred strong, armed to the teeth, they marched up to Virginia. The leader of the body well knew the temper of his men, on the subject. He spurred on ahead of them, and hastily calling a meeting of the Executive, he told them plainly that the miners meant "business," and that, if they came up, they would not stand in the street to be shot down by Slade's friends; but that they would take him and hang him. The meeting was small, as the Virginia men were loath to act at all. This momentous announcement of the feeling of the Lower Town was made to a cluster of men, who were deliberating behind a wagon, at the rear of a store on Main street.

The Committee were most unwilling to proceed to extremities. All the duty they had ever performed seemed as nothing to the task before them; but they had to decide, and that quickly. It was finally agreed that if the whole body of the miners were of the opinion that he should be hanged, that the Committee left it in their hands to deal with him. Off, at hot speed, rode the leader of the Nevada men to join his command.

Slade had found out what was intended, and the news sobered him instantly. He went into P. S. Pfouts' store, where Davis was, and apologized for his conduct, saying that he would take it all back.

The head of the column now wheeled into Wallace street and marched up at quick time. Halting in front of the store, the executive officer of the Committee stepped forward and arrested Slade, who was at once informed of his doom, and inquiry was made as to whether he had any business to settle. Several parties spoke to him on the subject; but to all such inquiries he turned a deaf ear, being entirely absorbed in the terrifying reflections on his own awful position. He never ceased his entreaties for life, and to see his dear wife. The unfortunate lady referred to, between whom and Slade there existed a warm affection, was at this time living at their Ranch on the Madison. She was possessed of considerable personal attractions; tall, well-formed, of graceful carriage, pleasing manners, and was, withal, an accomplished horsewoman.

A messenger from Slade rode at full speed to inform her of her husband's arrest. In an instant she was in the saddle, and with all the energy that love and despair could lend to an ardent temperament and a strong physique, she urged her fleet charger over the twelve miles of rough and rocky ground that intervened between her and the object of her passionate devotion.

Meanwhile a party of volunteers had made the necessary preparations for the execution, in the valley traversed by the branch. Beneath the site of Pfouts and Russell's stone building there was a corral, the gate-posts of which were strong and high. Across the top was laid a beam, to which the rope was fastened, and a dry-goods box served for the platform. To this place Slade was marched, surrounded by a guard, composing the best armed and most numerous force that has ever appeared in Montana Territory.

The doomed man had so exhausted himself by tears, prayers and lamentations, that he had scarcely strength left to stand under the fatal beam. He repeatedly exclaimed, "my God! my God! must I die? Oh, my dear wife!"

On the return of the fatigue party, they encountered some friends of Slade, staunch and reliable citizens and members of the Committee, but who were personally attached to the condemned. On hearing of his sentence, one of them, a stout-hearted man, pulled out his handkerchief and walked away, weeping like a child. Slade still begged to see his wife, most piteously, and it seemed hard to deny his request; but the bloody consequences that were sure to follow the inevitable attempt at a rescue, that her presence and entreaties would have certainly incited, forbade the granting of his request. Several gentlemen were sent for to see him, in his last moments, one of whom, (Judge Davis) made a short address to the people; but in such low tones as to be inaudible, save to a few in his immediate vicinity. One of his friends, after exhausting his powers of entreaty, threw off his coat and declared that the prisoner could not be hanged until he himself was killed. A hundred guns were instantly leveled at him; whereupon he turned and fled; but, being brought back, he was compelled to resume his coat, and to give a promise of future peaceable demeanor.

Scarcely a leading man in Virginia could be found, though numbers of the citizens joined the ranks of the guard when the arrest was made. All lamented the stern necessity which dictated the execution.

Everything being ready, the command was given, "Men, do your duty," and the box being instantly slipped from beneath his feet, he died almost instantaneously.

The body was cut down and carried to the Virginia Hotel, where,

A WIFE'S LAMENTATION.

in a darkened room, it was scarcely laid out, when the unfortunate and bereaved companion of the deceased arrived, at headlong speed, to find that all was over, and that she was a widow. Her grief and heart-piercing cries were terrible evidences of the depth of her attachment for her lost husband, and a considerable period elapsed before she could regain the command of her excited feelings.

There is something about the desperado-nature that is wholly unaccountable—at least it looks unaccountable. It is this. The true desperado is gifted with splendid courage, and yet he will take the most infamous advantage of his enemy; armed and free, he will stand up before a host and fight until he is shot all to pieces, and yet when he is under the gallows and helpless he will cry and plead like a child. Words are cheap, and it is easy to call Slade a coward (all executed men who do not "die game" are promptly called cowards by unreflecting people), and when we read of Slade that he "had so exhausted himself by tears, prayers and lamentations, that he had scarcely strength left to stand under the fatal beam," the disgraceful word suggests itself in a moment—yet in frequently defying and inviting the vengeance of banded Rocky Mountain cut-throats by shooting down their comrades and leaders, and never offering to hide or fly, Slade showed that he was a man of peerless bravery. No coward would dare that. Many a notorious coward, many a chicken-livered poltroon, coarse, brutal, degraded, has made his dying speech without a quaver in his voice and been swung into eternity with what looked like the calmest fortitude, and so we are justified in believing, from the low intellect of such a creature, that it was not *moral* courage that enabled him to do it. Then, if moral courage is not the requisite quality, what could it have been that this stout-hearted Slade lacked?—this bloody, desperate, kindly-mannered, urbane gentleman, who never hesitated to warn his most ruffianly enemies that he would kill them whenever or wherever he came across them next! I think it is a conundrum worth investigating.

CHAPTER 12

Just beyond the breakfast-station we overtook a Mormon emigrant train of thirty-three wagons; and tramping wearily along and driving their herd of loose cows, were dozens of coarse-clad and sad-looking men, women and children, who had walked as they were walking now, day after day for eight lingering weeks, and in that time had compassed the distance our stage had come in *eight days and three hours*—seven hundred and ninety-eight miles! They were dusty and uncombed, hatless, bonnetless and ragged, and they did look so tired!

After breakfast, we bathed in Horse Creek, a (previously) limpid, sparkling stream—an appreciated luxury, for it was very seldom that our furious coach halted long enough for an indulgence of that kind. We changed horses ten or twelve times in every twenty-four hours—changed mules, rather—six mules—and did it nearly every time in *four minutes.* It was lively work. As our coach rattled up to each station six harnessed mules stepped gayly from the stable; and in the twinkling of an eye, almost, the old team was out, and the new one in and we off and away again.

During the afternoon we passed Sweetwater Creek, Independence Rock, Devil's Gate and the Devil's Gap. The latter were wild specimens of rugged scenery, and full of interest—*we were in the heart of the Rocky Mountains, now.* And we also passed by "Alkali" or "Soda Lake," and we woke up to the fact that our journey had stretched a long way across the world when the driver said that the Mormons often came there from Great Salt Lake City to haul away saleratus. He said that a few days gone by they had shoveled up enough pure saleratus from the ground (it was a *dry* lake) to load two wagons, and that when they got these two wagon loads of a drug that cost them nothing, to Salt Lake, they could sell it for twenty-five cents a pound.

In the night we sailed by a most notable curiosity, and one we had been hearing a good deal about for a day or two, and were suffering to see. This was what might be called a natural ice-house. It was August, now, and sweltering weather in the daytime, yet at one of the stations the men could scrape the soil on the hillside under the lee of a range of boulders, and at a depth of six inches cut out pure blocks of ice—hard, compactly frozen, and clear as crystal!

Toward dawn we got under way again, and presently as we sat with raised curtains enjoying our early-morning smoke and contemplating the first splendor of the rising sun as it swept down the long array of mountain peaks, flushing and gilding crag after crag and summit after summit, as if the invisible Creator reviewed his gray veterans and they saluted with a smile, we hove in sight of South Pass City. The hotel-keeper, the postmaster, the blacksmith, the mayor, the constable, the city marshal and the principal citizen and property holder, all came out and greeted us cheerily, and we gave him good-day. He gave us a little Indian news, and a little Rocky Mountain news, and we gave him some Plains information in return. He then retired to his lonely grandeur and we climbed on up among the bristling peaks and the ragged clouds. South Pass City consisted of four log cabins, one of which was unfinished, and the gentleman with all those offices and titles was the chiefest of the ten citizens of the place. Think of hotel-keeper, postmaster, blacksmith, mayor, constable, city marshal and principal citizen all condensed into one person and crammed into one skin. Bemis said he was "a perfect Allen's revolver of dignities." And he said that if he were to die as postmaster, or as blacksmith, or as postmaster and blacksmith both, the people might stand it; but if he were to die all over, it would be a frightful loss to the community.

Two miles beyond South Pass City we saw for the first time that mysterious marvel which all western untraveled boys have heard of and fully believe in, but are sure to be astounded at when they see it with their own eyes, nevertheless—banks of snow in dead summer time. We were now far up toward the sky, and knew all the time that we must presently encounter lofty summits clad in the "eternal snow" which was so commonplace a matter of mention in books, and yet when I did see it glittering in the sun on stately

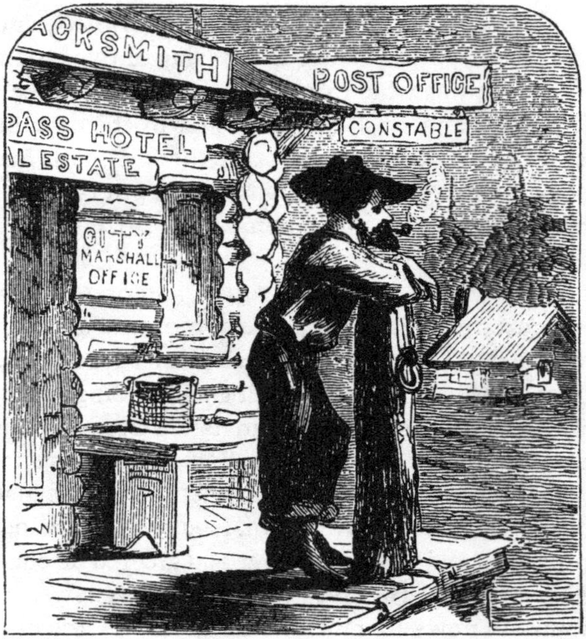

THE CONCENTRATED INHABITANT.

domes in the distance and knew the month was August and that my coat was hanging up because it was too warm to wear it, I was full as much amazed as if I never had heard of snow in August before. Truly, "seeing is believing"—and many a man lives a long life through, *thinking* he believes certain universally received and well established things, and yet never suspects that if he were confronted by those things once, he would discover that he did not *really* believe them before, but only thought he believed them.

In a little while quite a number of peaks swung into view with long claws of glittering snow clasping them; and with here and there, in the shade, down the mountain side, a little solitary patch of snow looking no larger than a lady's pocket-handkerchief, but being in reality as large as a "public square."

And now, at last, we were fairly in the renowned SOUTH PASS, and whirling gayly along high above the common world. We were perched upon the extreme summit of the great range of the Rocky Mountains, toward which we had been climbing, patiently climb-

THE SOUTH PASS.

ing, ceaselessly climbing, for days and nights together—and about us was gathered a convention of Nature's kings that stood ten, twelve, and even thirteen thousand feet high—grand old fellows who would have to stoop to see Mount Washington, in the twilight. We were in such an airy elevation above the creeping populations of the earth, that now and then when the obstructing crags stood out of the way it seemed that we could look around and abroad and contemplate the whole great globe, with its dissolving views of mountains, seas and continents stretching away through the mystery of the summer haze.

As a general thing the Pass was more suggestive of a valley than a suspension bridge in the clouds—but it strongly suggested the latter at one spot. At that place the upper third of one or two majestic purple domes projected above our level on either hand and gave us a sense of a hidden great deep of mountains and plains and valleys down about their bases which we fancied we might see if we could step to the edge and look over. These Sultans of the fastnesses were turbaned with tumbled volumes of cloud, which shredded away from time to time and drifted off fringed and torn, trailing their continents of shadow after them; and catching presently on an intercepting peak, wrapped it about and brooded there—then shredded away again and left the purple peak, as they had left the purple domes, downy and white with new-laid snow. In passing, these monstrous rags of cloud hung low and swept along right over the spectator's head, swinging their tatters so nearly in his face that his impulse was to shrink when they came closest. In the one place I speak of, one could look below him upon a world of diminishing crags and cañons leading down, down, and away to a vague plain with a thread in it which was a road, and bunches of feathers in it which were trees,—a pretty picture sleeping in the sunlight—but with a darkness stealing over it and glooming its features deeper and deeper under the frown of a coming storm; and then, while no film or shadow marred the noon brightness of his high perch, he could watch the tempest break forth down there and see the lightnings leap from crag to crag and the sheeted rain drive along the cañon-sides, and hear the thunders peal and crash and roar. We had this spectacle; a familiar one to many, but to us a novelty.

We bowled along cheerily, and presently, at the very summit (though it had been all summit to us, and all equally level, for half an hour or more), we came to a spring which spent its water through two outlets and sent it in opposite directions. The conductor said that one of those streams which we were looking at, was just starting on a journey westward to the Gulf of California and the Pacific Ocean, through hundreds and even thousands of miles of desert solitudes. He said that the other was just leaving its home among the snow-peaks on a similar journey eastward—and we knew that long after we should have forgotten the simple rivulet it would still be plodding its patient way down the mountain sides, and cañon-beds, and between the banks of the Yellowstone; and by and by would join the broad Missouri and flow through unknown plains and deserts and unvisited wildernesses; and add a long and troubled pilgrimage among snags and wrecks and sand-bars; and enter the Mississippi, touch the wharves of St. Louis and still drift on, traversing shoals and rocky channels, then endless chains of bottomless and ample bends, walled with unbroken forests, then mysterious byways and secret passages among woody islands, then the chained bends again, bordered with wide levels of shining sugar-cane in place of the sombre forests; then by New Orleans and still other chains of bends—and finally, after two long months of daily and nightly harassment, excitement, enjoyment, adventure, and awful peril of parched throats, pumps and evaporation, pass the Gulf and enter into its rest upon the bosom of the tropic sea, never to look upon its snow-peaks again or regret them.

THE PARTED STREAM.

I freighted a leaf with a mental message for the friends at home, and dropped it in the stream. But I put no stamp on it and it was held for postage somewhere.

On the summit we overtook an emigrant train of many wagons, many tired men and women, and many a disgusted sheep and cow. In the wofully dusty horseman in charge of the expedition I recognized John ——. Of all persons in the world to meet on top of the Rocky Mountains thousands of miles from home, he was the last one I should have looked for. We were school-boys together and warm friends for years. But a boyish prank of mine had disruptured this friendship and it had never been renewed. The act of which I speak was this. I had been accustomed to visit occasionally an editor whose room was in the third story of a building and overlooked the street. One day this editor gave me a watermelon which I made preparations to devour on the spot, but chancing to look out of the window, I saw John standing directly under it and an irresistible desire came upon me to drop the melon on his head, which I immediately did. I was the loser, for it spoiled the melon, and John never forgave me and we dropped all intercourse and parted, but now met again under these circumstances.

IT SPOILED THE MELON.

We recognized each other simultaneously, and hands were grasped as warmly as if no coldness had ever existed between us, and no allusion was made to any. All animosities were buried and the simple fact of meeting a familiar face in that isolated spot so far from home, was sufficient to make us forget all things but pleasant ones, and we parted again with sincere "good-byes" and "God bless you" from both.

We had been climbing up the long shoulders of the Rocky Mountains for many tedious hours—we started *down* them, now. And we went spinning away at a round rate too.

We left the snowy Wind River Mountains and Uinta Mountains behind, and sped away, always through splendid scenery but occasionally through long ranks of white skeletons of mules and oxen—monuments of the huge emigration of other days—and here and there were up-ended boards or small piles of stones which

GIVEN OVER TO THE CAYOTE AND THE RAVEN.

the driver said marked the resting-place of more precious remains. It was the loneliest land for a grave! A land given over to the cayote and the raven—which is but another name for desolation and utter solitude. On damp, murky nights, these scattered skeletons gave forth a soft, hideous glow, like very faint spots of moonlight starring the vague desert. It was because of the phosphorus in the bones. But no scientific explanation could keep a body from shivering when he drifted by one of those ghostly lights and knew that a skull held it.

At midnight it began to rain, and I never saw anything like it—indeed, I did not even see this, for it was too dark. We fastened down the curtains and even caulked them with clothing, but the rain streamed in in twenty places, notwithstanding. There was no escape. If one moved his feet out of a stream, he brought his body under one; and if he moved his body he caught one somewhere else. If he struggled out of the drenched blankets and sat up, he was bound to get one down the back of his neck. Meantime the stage was wandering about a plain with gaping gullies in it, for the driver could not see an inch before his face nor keep the road, and the storm pelted so pitilessly that there was no keeping the horses still. With the first abatement the conductor turned out with lanterns to look for the road, and the first dash he made was into a chasm about fourteen feet deep, his lantern following like a meteor. As soon as he touched bottom he sang out frantically:

"Don't come here!"

To which the driver, who was looking over the precipice where he had disappeared, replied, with an injured air: "Think I'm a dam fool?"

"DON'T COME HERE!"

"THINK I'M A DAM FOOL?"

The conductor was more than an hour finding the road—a matter which showed us how far we had wandered and what chances we had been taking. He traced our wheel-tracks to the imminent verge of danger, in two places. I have always been glad that we were not killed that night. I do not know any particular reason, but I have always been glad.

In the morning, the tenth day out, we crossed Green river, a fine, large, limpid stream—stuck in it, with the water just up to the top of our mail-bed, and waited till extra teams were put on to haul us up the steep bank. But it was nice cool water, and besides it could not find any fresh place on us to wet.

At the Green river station we had breakfast—hot biscuits, fresh antelope steaks, and coffee—the only decent meal we tasted between the United States and Great Salt Lake City, and the only one we were ever really thankful for. Think of the monotonous execrableness of the thirty that went before it, to leave this one simple breakfast looming up in my memory like a shot-tower after all these years have gone by!

At 5 P.M. we reached Fort Bridger, one hundred and seventeen miles from the South Pass, and one thousand and twenty-five miles from St. Joseph. Fifty-two miles further on, near the head of Echo Cañon, we met sixty U. S. soldiers from Camp Floyd. The day before, they had fired upon three hundred or four hundred Indians, whom they supposed gathered together for no good purpose. In the fight that had ensued, four Indians were captured, and the main body chased four miles, but nobody killed. This looked like business. We had a notion to get out and join the sixty soldiers, but upon reflecting that there were four hundred of the Indians, we concluded to go on and join the Indians.

Echo Cañon is twenty miles long. It was like a long, smooth, narrow street, with a gradual descending grade, and shut in by enormous perpendicular walls of coarse conglomerate, four hundred feet high in many places, and turreted like mediæval castles. This was the most faultless piece of road in the mountains, and the driver said he would "let his team out." He did, and if the Pacific express trains whiz through there now any faster than we did then in the stage-coach, I envy the passengers the exhilaration of it. We fairly seemed to pick up our wheels and fly—and the mail matter was lifted up free from everything and held in solution! I am not given to exaggeration, and when I say a thing I mean it.

However, time presses. At four in the afternoon we arrived on the summit of Big Mountain, fifteen miles from Salt Lake City, when all the world was glorified with the setting sun, and the most stupendous panorama of mountain peaks yet encountered burst on our sight. We looked out upon this sublime spectacle from under the arch of a brilliant rainbow! Even the overland stage-driver stopped his horses and gazed!

Half an hour or an hour later, we changed horses, and took supper with a Mormon "Destroying Angel." "Destroying Angels," as I understand it, are Latter-Day Saints who are set apart by the church to conduct permanent disappearances of obnoxious citizens. I had heard a deal about these Mormon Destroying Angels and the dark and bloody deeds they had done, and when I entered this one's house I had my shudder all ready. But alas for all our romances, he was nothing but a loud, profane, offensive, old blackguard! He was murderous enough, possibly, to fill the bill of a Destroyer, but would you have *any* kind of an Angel devoid of

THE "DESTROYING ANGEL."

dignity? Could you abide an Angel in an unclean shirt and no suspenders? Could you respect an Angel with a horse-laugh and a swagger like a buccaneer?

There were other blackguards present—comrades of this one. And there was one person that looked like a gentleman—Heber C. Kimball's son, tall and well made, and thirty years old, perhaps. A lot of slatternly women flitted hither and thither in a hurry, with coffee-pots, plates of bread, and other appurtenances to supper, and these were said to be the wives of the Angel—or some of them, at least. And of course they were; for if they had been hired "help" they would not have let an angel from above storm and swear at them as he did, let alone one from the place this one hailed from.

This was our first experience of the western "peculiar institution," and it was not very prepossessing. We did not tarry long to observe it, but hurried on to the home of the Latter-Day Saints, the stronghold of the prophets, the capital of the only absolute monarch in America—Great Salt Lake City. As the night closed in we took sanctuary in the Salt Lake House and unpacked our baggage.

CHAPTER 13

WE had a fine supper, of the freshest meats and fowls and vegetables—a great variety and as great abundance. We walked about the streets some, afterward, and glanced in at shops and stores; and there was fascination in surreptitiously staring at every creature we took to be a Mormon. This was fairy-land to us, to all intents and purposes—a land of enchantment, and goblins, and awful mystery. We felt a curiosity to ask every child how many mothers it had, and if it could tell them apart; and we experienced a thrill every time a dwelling-house door opened and shut as we passed, disclosing a glimpse of human heads and backs and shoulders—for we so longed to have a good satisfying look at a Mormon family in all its comprehensive ampleness, disposed in the customary concentric rings of its home circle.

By and by the Acting Governor of the Territory introduced us to other "Gentiles," and we spent a sociable hour with them. "Gentiles" are people who are not Mormons. Our fellow-passenger, Bemis, took care of himself, during this part of the evening, and did not make an overpowering success of it, either, for he came into our room in the hotel about eleven o'clock, full of cheerfulness, and talking loosely, disjointedly and indiscriminately, and every now and then tugging out a ragged word by the roots that had more hiccups than syllables in it. This, together with his hanging his coat on the floor on one side of a chair, and his vest on the floor on the other side, and piling his pants on the floor just in front of the same chair, and then contemplating the general result with superstitious awe, and finally pronouncing it "too many for *him*" and going to bed with his boots on, led us to fear that something he had eaten had not agreed with him.

But we knew afterward that it was something he had been drinking. It was the exclusively Mormon refresher, "valley tan." Valley tan (or, at least, one form of valley tan) is a kind of whisky, or first cousin to it; is of Mormon invention and manufactured only in Utah. Tradition says it is made of (imported) fire and brimstone. If

EFFECTS OF "VALLEY TAN."

I remember rightly no public drinking saloons were allowed in the kingdom by Brigham Young, and no private drinking permitted among the faithful, except they confined themselves to "valley tan."

Next day we strolled about everywhere through the broad, straight, level streets, and enjoyed the pleasant strangeness of a city of fifteen thousand inhabitants with no loafers perceptible in it; and no visible drunkards or noisy people; a limpid stream rippling and dancing through every street in place of a filthy gutter; block after block of trim dwellings, built of "frame" and sunburned brick—a great thriving orchard and garden behind every one of them, apparently—branches from the street stream winding and sparkling among the garden beds and fruit trees—and a grand general air of neatness, repair, thrift and comfort, around and about and over the whole. And everywhere were workshops, factories, and all manner of industries; and intent faces and busy hands were to be seen wherever one looked; and in one's ears was the ceaseless clink of hammers, the buzz of trade and the contented hum of drums and fly-wheels.

The armorial crest of my own State consisted of two dissolute bears holding up the head of a dead and gone cask between them and making the pertinent remark, "UNITED, WE STAND—(HIC!)—DIVIDED, WE FALL." It was always too figurative for the author of

ONE CREST.

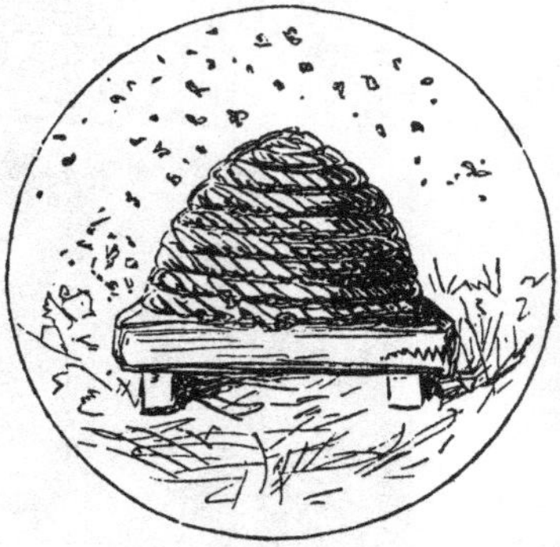

THE OTHER.

this book. But the Mormon crest was easy. And it was simple, unostentatious, and fitted like a glove. It was a representation of a GOLDEN BEEHIVE, with the bees all at work!

The city lies in the edge of a level plain as broad as the State of Connecticut, and crouches close down to the ground under a curving wall of mighty mountains whose heads are hidden in the clouds, and whose shoulders bear relics of the snows of winter all the summer long. Seen from one of these dizzy heights, twelve or fifteen miles off, Great Salt Lake City is toned down and diminished till it is suggestive of a child's toy-village reposing under the majestic protection of the Chinese wall.

On some of those mountains, to the southwest, it had been raining every day for two weeks, but not a drop had fallen in the city. And on hot days in late spring and early autumn the citizens could quit fanning and growling and go out and cool off by looking at the luxury of a glorious snow-storm going on in the mountains. They could enjoy it at a distance, at those seasons, every day, though no snow would fall in their streets, or anywhere near them.

Salt Lake City was healthy—an extremely healthy city. They declared there was only one physician in the place and he was arrested every week regularly and held to answer under the vagrant act for having "no visible means of support." [They always give you

THE VAGRANT.

a good substantial article of truth in Salt Lake, and good measure and good weight, too. Very often, if you wished to weigh one of their airiest little commonplace statements you would want the hay scales.]

We desired to visit the famous inland sea, the American "Dead Sea," the great Salt Lake—seventeen miles, horseback, from the city—for we had dreamed about it, and thought about it, and talked about it, and yearned to see it, all the first part of our trip; but now when it was only arm's length away it had suddenly lost nearly every bit of its interest. And so we put it off, in a sort of general way, till next day—and that was the last we ever thought of it. We dined with some hospitable Gentiles; and visited the foundation of the prodigious temple; and talked long with that shrewd Connecticut Yankee, Heber C. Kimball (since deceased), a saint of

high degree and a mighty man of commerce. We saw the "Tithing-House," and the "Lion House," and I do not know or remember how many more church and government buildings of various kinds and curious names. We flitted hither and thither and enjoyed every hour, and picked up a great deal of useful information and entertaining nonsense, and went to bed at night satisfied.

The second day, we made the acquaintance of Mr. Street (since deceased) and put on white shirts and went and paid a state visit to the king. He seemed a quiet, kindly, easy-mannered, dignified, self-possessed old gentleman of fifty-five or sixty, and had a gentle craft in his eye that probably belonged there. He was very simply dressed and was just taking off a straw hat as we entered. He talked about Utah, and the Indians, and Nevada, and general American matters and questions, with our Secretary and certain government officials who came with us. But he never paid any attention to me,

notwithstanding I made several attempts to "draw him out" on Federal politics and his high-handed attitude toward Congress. I thought some of the things I said were rather fine. But he merely looked around at me, at distant intervals, something as I have seen a benignant old cat look around to see which kitten was meddling with her tail. By and by I subsided into an indignant silence, and so sat until the end, hot and flushed, and execrating him in my heart for an ignorant savage. But he was calm. His conversation with those gentlemen flowed on as sweetly and peacefully and musically as any summer brook. When the audience was ended and we were retiring from the presence, he put his hand on my head, beamed down on me in an admiring way and said to my brother:

"Ah—your child, I presume? Boy, or girl?"

CHAPTER 14

Mr. Street was very busy with his telegraphic matters—and considering that he had eight or nine hundred miles of rugged, snowy, uninhabited mountains, and waterless, treeless, melancholy deserts to traverse with his wire, it was natural and needful that he should be as busy as possible. He could not go comfortably along and cut his poles by the roadside, either, but they had to be hauled by ox teams across those exhausting deserts—and it was two days' journey from water to water, in one or two of them. Mr. Street's contract was a vast work, every way one looked at it; and yet to comprehend what the vague words "eight hundred miles of rugged mountains and dismal deserts" mean, one must go over the ground in person—pen and ink descriptions cannot convey the dreary reality to the reader. And after all, Mr. S.'s mightiest difficulty turned out to be one which he had never taken into the account at all. Unto Mormons he had sub-let the hardest and heaviest half of his great undertaking, and all of a sudden they concluded that they were going to make little or nothing, and so they tranquilly threw their poles overboard in mountain or desert, just as it happened when they took the notion, and drove home and went about their customary business! They were under written contract to Mr. Street, but they did not care anything for that. They said they would "admire" to see a "Gentile" force a Mormon to fulfil a losing contract in Utah! And they made themselves very merry over the matter. Street said—for it was he that told us these things:

"I was in dismay. I was under heavy bonds to complete my contract in a given time, and this disaster looked very much like ruin.

It was an astounding thing; it was such a wholly unlooked-for difficulty, that I was entirely nonplussed. I am a business man—have always been a business man—do not know anything *but* business—and so you can imagine how like being struck by lightning it was to find myself in a country where *written contracts were worthless!*—that main security, that sheet-anchor, that absolute necessity, of business. My confidence left me. There was no use in making new contracts—that was plain. I talked with first one prominent citizen and then another. They all sympathized with me, first rate, but they did not know how to help me. But at last a Gentile said, 'Go to Brigham Young!—these small fry cannot do you any good.' I did not think much of the idea, for if the *law* could not help me, what could an individual do who had not even anything to do with either making the laws or executing them? He might be a very good patriarch of a church and preacher in its tabernacle, but something sterner than religion and moral suasion was needed to handle a hundred refractory, half-civilized subcontractors. But what was a man to do? I thought if Mr. Young could not do anything else, he might probably be able to give me some advice and a valuable hint or two, and so I went straight to him and laid the whole case before him. He said very little, but he showed strong interest all the way through. He examined all the papers in detail, and whenever there seemed anything like a hitch, either in the papers or my statement, he would go back and take up the thread and follow it patiently out to an intelligent and satisfactory result. Then he made a list of the contractors' names. Finally he said:

"'Mr. Street, this is all perfectly plain. These contracts are strictly and legally drawn, and are duly signed and certified. These men manifestly entered into them with their eyes open. I see no fault or flaw anywhere.'

"Then Mr. Young turned to a man waiting at the other end of the room and said: 'Take this list of names to So-and-so, and tell him to have these men here at such-and-such an hour.'

"They were there, to the minute. So was I. Mr. Young asked

them a number of questions, and their answers made my statement good. Then he said to them:

"'You signed these contracts and assumed these obligations of your own free will and accord?'

"'Yes.'

"'Then carry them out to the letter, if it makes paupers of you! Go!'

"And they *did* go, too! They are strung across the deserts now, working like bees. And I never hear a word out of them. There is a batch of governors, and judges, and other officials here, shipped

THE CONTRACTORS BEFORE THE KING.

from Washington, and they maintain the semblance of a republican form of government—but the petrified truth is that Utah is an absolute monarchy and Brigham Young is king!"

Mr. Street was a fine man, and I believe his story. I knew him well during several years afterward in San Francisco.

Our stay in Salt Lake City amounted to only two days, and therefore we had no time to make the customary inquisition into the workings of polygamy and get up the usual statistics and deductions preparatory to calling the attention of the nation at large once more to the matter. I had the will to do it. With the gushing self-sufficiency of youth I was feverish to plunge in headlong and achieve a great reform here—until I saw the Mormon women.

I WAS TOUCHED.

Then I was touched. My heart was wiser than my head. It warmed toward these poor, ungainly and pathetically "homely" creatures, and as I turned to hide the generous moisture in my eyes, I said, "No—the man that marries one of them has done an act of Christian charity which entitles him to the kindly applause of mankind, not their harsh censure—and the man that marries sixty of them has done a deed of open-handed generosity so sublime that the nations should stand uncovered in his presence and worship in silence."*

*For a brief sketch of Mormon history, and the noted Mountain Meadows massacre, see Appendices A and B.

CHAPTER 15

It is a luscious country for thrilling evening stories about assassinations of intractable Gentiles. I cannot easily conceive of anything more cosy than the night in Salt Lake which we spent in a Gentile den, smoking pipes and listening to tales of how Burton galloped in among the pleading and defenceless "Morrisites" and shot them down, men and women, like so many dogs. And how Bill Hickman, a Destroying Angel, shot Drown and Arnold dead for bringing suit against him for a debt. And how Porter Rockwell did this and that dreadful thing. And how heedless people often come to Utah and make remarks about Brigham, or polygamy, or some other sacred matter, and the very next morning at daylight such parties are sure to be found lying up some back alley, contentedly waiting for the hearse.

And the next most interesting thing is to sit and listen to these Gentiles talk about polygamy; and how some portly old frog of an elder, or a bishop, marries a girl—likes her, marries her sister—likes her, marries another sister—likes her, takes another—likes her, marries her mother—likes her, marries her father, grandfather, great grandfather, and then comes back hungry and asks for more. And how the pert young thing of eleven will chance to be the favorite wife and her own venerable grandmother have to rank away down toward D 4 in their mutual husband's esteem, and have to sleep in the kitchen, as like as not. And how this dreadful sort of thing, this hiving together in one foul nest of mother and daughters, and the making a young daughter superior to her own mother in rank and authority, are things which Mormon women submit to because their religion teaches them that the more wives a man has on earth, and the more children he rears, the higher the place they will all have in the world to come—and the warmer, maybe, though they do not seem to say anything about that.

According to these Gentile friends of ours, Brigham Young's harem contains twenty or thirty wives. They said that some of

FAVORITE WIFE AND D 4.

them had grown old and gone out of active service, but were comfortably housed and cared for in the hennery—or the Lion House, as it is strangely named. Along with each wife were her children—fifty altogether. The house was perfectly quiet and orderly, when the children were still. They all took their meals in one room, and a happy and homelike sight it was pronounced to be. None of our party got an opportunity to take dinner with Mr. Young, but a Gentile by the name of Johnson professed to have enjoyed a sociable breakfast in the Lion House. He gave a preposterous account of the "calling of the roll," and other preliminaries, and the carnage that ensued when the buckwheat cakes came in. But he embellished rather too much. He said that Mr. Young told him several smart sayings of certain of his "two-year-olds," observing with some pride that for many years he had been the heaviest contributor in that line to one of the eastern magazines; and then he wanted to show Mr. Johnson one of the pets that had said the last good thing, but he could not find the child. He searched the faces of the children in detail, but could not decide which one it was. Finally he gave it up with a sigh and said:

"I thought I would know the little cub again but I don't." Mr. Johnson said further, that Mr. Young observed that life was a sad,

NEEDED MARKING.

sad thing—"because the joy of every new marriage a man contracted was so apt to be blighted by the inopportune funeral of a less recent bride." And Mr. Johnson said that while he and Mr. Young were pleasantly conversing in private, one of the Mrs. Youngs came in and demanded a breast-pin, remarking that she had found out that he had been giving a breast-pin to No. 6, and *she,* for one, did not propose to let this partiality go on without making a satisfactory amount of trouble about it. Mr. Young reminded her that there was a stranger present. Mrs. Young said that if the state of things inside the house was not agreeable to the stranger, he could find room outside. Mr. Young promised the breast-pin, and she went away. But in a minute or two another Mrs.

Young came in and demanded a breast-pin. Mr. Young began a remonstrance, but Mrs. Young cut him short. She said No. 6 had got one, and No. 11 was promised one, and it was "no use for him to try to impose on her—she hoped she knew her rights." He gave his promise, and she went. And presently three Mrs. Youngs entered in a body and opened on their husband a tempest of tears, abuse, and entreaty. They had heard all about No. 6, No. 11, and No. 14. Three more breast-pins were promised. They were hardly gone when nine more Mrs. Youngs filed into the presence, and a new tempest burst forth and raged round about the prophet and his guest. Nine breast-pins were promised, and the weird sisters filed out again. And in came eleven more, weeping and wailing and gnashing their teeth. Eleven promised breast-pins purchased peace once more.

"That is a specimen," said Mr. Young. "You see how it is. You see what a life I lead. A man *can't* be wise all the time. In a heedless moment I gave my darling No. 6—excuse my calling her thus, as her other name has escaped me for the moment—a breast-pin. It was only worth twenty-five dollars—that is, *apparently* that was its whole cost—but its ultimate cost was inevitably bound to be a good deal more. You yourself have seen it climb up to six hundred and fifty dollars—and alas, even that is not the end! For I have wives all over this Territory of Utah. I have dozens of wives whose *numbers,* even, I do not know without looking in the family Bible. They are scattered far and wide among the mountains and valleys of my realm. And mark you, every solitary one of them will hear of this wretched breast-pin, and every last one of them will have one or die. No. 6's breast-pin will cost me twenty-five hundred dollars before I see the end of it. And these creatures will compare these pins together, and if one is a shade finer than the rest, they will all be thrown on my hands, and I will have to order a new lot to keep peace in the family. Sir, you probably did not know it, but all the time you were present with my children your every movement was watched by vigilant servitors of mine. If you had offered to give a child a dime, or a stick of candy, or any trifle of the kind, you would have been snatched out of the house instantly, provided it could be done before your gift left your hand. Otherwise it would be absolutely necessary for you to make an exactly similar gift to all my children—and knowing by experience the importance of the thing, I would have stood by and seen to it myself that you did it, and did it thoroughly. Once a gentleman gave one of my children a tin whistle—a veritable invention of Satan, sir, and one which I have an unspeakable horror of, and so would you if you had eighty or ninety children in your house. But the deed was done—the man escaped. I knew what the result was going to be, and I thirsted for vengeance. I ordered out a flock of Destroying Angels, and they hunted the man far into the fastnesses of the Nevada mountains. But they never caught him. I am not cruel, sir—I am not vindictive except when sorely outraged—but if I had caught him, sir, so help me Joseph Smith, I would have locked him into the nursery till the brats whistled him to death! By the slaughtered body of St. Parley Pratt (whom God assoil!) there was never anything on this earth like it! *I* knew who gave the whistle to the child, but I could not make those jealous mothers believe me. They believed *I* did it, and the result was just what any man of reflection could have foreseen: I had to order a hundred and ten whistles—I think we had a hundred and ten children in the house then, but some of them are off at college now—I had to order a hundred and ten of those shrieking things, and I wish I may never speak another word if we didn't have to talk on our fingers entirely, from that time forth until the children got tired of the whistles. And if ever another man gives a whistle to a child of mine and I get my hands on him, I will hang him higher than Haman! That is the word with the bark on it! Shade of Nephi! *You* don't know anything about married life. I am rich, and everybody knows it. I am benevolent, and everybody takes advantage of it. I have a strong fatherly instinct and all the foundlings are foisted on me. Every time a woman wants to do well by her darling, she puzzles her brain to cipher out some scheme for getting it into my hands. Why, sir, a woman came here once with a child of a curious lifeless sort of complexion (and so had the woman), and swore that the child was mine and she my wife—that I had married her at such-and-such a time in such-and-such a place, but she had forgotten her number, and of course I could not remember her name. Well, sir, she called my attention to the fact that the child looked like me, and really it did seem to resemble me—a common thing in the Territory—and, to cut the story short, I put it in my nursery, and she left. And by the ghost of Orson Hyde, when they came to wash the paint off that child it was an Injun! Bless my soul, you don't know anything about married life.

A REMARKABLE RESEMBLANCE.

It is a perfect dog's life, sir—a perfect dog's life. You can't economize. It isn't possible. I have tried keeping one set of bridal attire for all occasions. But it is of no use. First you'll marry a combination of calico and consumption that's as thin as a rail, and next you'll get a creature that's nothing more than the dropsy in disguise, and then you've got to eke out that bridal dress with an old balloon. That is the way it goes. And think of the wash-bill—(excuse these tears)—nine hundred and eighty-four pieces a week! No, sir, there is no such a thing as economy in a family like mine. Why, just the one item of cradles—think of it! And vermifuge! Soothing syrup! Teething rings! And 'papa's watches' for the babies to play with! And things to scratch the furniture with! And lucifer matches for them to eat, and pieces of glass to cut themselves with! The item of glass alone would support *your* family, I venture to say, sir. Let me scrimp and squeeze all I can, I still can't get ahead as fast as I feel I ought to, with my opportunities. Bless you, sir, at a time when I had seventy-two wives in this house, I groaned under the pressure of keeping thousands of dollars tied up in seventy-two bedsteads when the money ought to have been out at interest; and I just sold out the whole stock, sir, at a sacrifice, and built a bedstead seven feet long and ninety-six feet wide. But it was a failure, sir. I could *not* sleep. It appeared to me that the whole seventy-two women snored at once. The roar was deafening. And then the danger of it! That was what I was looking at. They would all draw in their breath at once, and you could actually see the walls of the house suck in—and then they would all exhale their breath at once, and you could see the walls swell out, and strain, and hear the rafters crack, and the shingles grind together. My friend, take an old man's advice, and *don't* encumber yourself with a large family—mind, I tell you, don't do it. In a small family, and in a small family only, you will find that comfort and that peace of mind which are the best at last of the blessings this world is able to afford us, and for the lack of which no accumulation of wealth, and no acquisition of fame, power, and greatness

THE FAMILY BEDSTEAD.

can ever compensate us. Take my word for it, ten or eleven wives is all you need—never go over it."

Some instinct or other made me set this Johnson down as being unreliable. And yet he was a very entertaining person, and I doubt if some of the information he gave us could have been acquired from any other source. He was a pleasant contrast to those reticent Mormons.

CHAPTER 16

All men have heard of the Mormon Bible, but few except the "elect" have seen it, or, at least, taken the trouble to read it. I brought away a copy from Salt Lake. The book is a curiosity to me, it is such a pretentious affair, and yet so "slow," so sleepy; such an insipid mess of inspiration. It is chloroform in print. If Joseph Smith composed this book, the act was a miracle—keeping awake while he did it was, at any rate. If he, according to tradition, merely translated it from certain ancient and mysteriously-engraved plates of copper, which he declares he found under a stone, in an out-of-the-way locality, the work of translating was equally a miracle, for the same reason.

The book seems to be merely a prosy detail of imaginary history, with the Old Testament for a model; followed by a tedious plagiarism of the New Testament. The author labored to give his words and phrases the quaint, old-fashioned sound and structure of our King James's translation of the Scriptures; and the result is a mongrel—half modern glibness, and half ancient simplicity and gravity. The latter is awkward and constrained; the former natural, but grotesque by the contrast. Whenever he found his speech growing too modern—which was about every sentence or two—he ladled in a few such Scriptural phrases as "exceeding sore," "and it came to pass," etc., and made things satisfactory again. "And it came to pass" was his pet. If he had left that out, his Bible would have been only a pamphlet.

The title-page reads as follows:

The Book of Mormon: an account written by the Hand of Mormon, upon Plates taken from the Plates of Nephi.

Wherefore it is an abridgment of the record of the people of Nephi, and also of the Lamanites; written to the Lamanites, who are a remnant of the House of Israel; and also to Jew and Gentile: written by way of commandment, and also by the spirit of prophecy and of revelation. Written and sealed up, and hid up unto the Lord, that they might not be destroyed; to come forth by the gift and power of God unto the interpretation thereof: sealed by the hand of Moroni, and hid up unto the Lord, to come forth in due time by the way of Gentile; the interpretation thereof by the gift of God. An abridgment taken from the Book of Ether also; which is a record of the people of Jared; who were scattered at the time the Lord confounded the language of the people when they were building a tower to get to Heaven.

"Hid up" is good. And so is "wherefore"—though why "wherefore?" Any other word would have answered as well—though in truth it would not have sounded so Scriptural.

Next comes

THE TESTIMONY OF THREE WITNESSES.

Be it known unto all nations, kindreds, tongues, and people unto whom this work shall come, that we, through the grace of God the Father, and our Lord Jesus Christ, have seen the plates which contain this record, which is a record of the people of Nephi, and also of the Lamanites, their brethren, and also of the people of Jared, who came from the tower of which hath been spoken; and we also know that they have been translated by the gift and power of God, for his voice hath declared it unto us; wherefore we know of a surety that the work is true. And we also testify that we have seen the engravings which are upon the plates; and they have been shewn unto us by the power of God, and not of man. And we declare with words of soberness, that an angel of God came down from heaven, and he brought and laid before our eyes, that we beheld and saw the plates, and the engravings thereon; and we know that it is by the grace of God the Father, and our Lord Jesus Christ, that we beheld and bear record that these things are true; and it is marvellous in our eyes, nevertheless the voice of the Lord commanded us that we should bear record of it; wherefore, to be obedient unto the commandments of God, we bear testimony of these things. And we know that if we are faithful in Christ, we shall rid our garments of the blood of all men, and be found spotless before the judgment-seat of Christ, and shall dwell with him eternally in the heavens. And the honour be to the Father, and to the Son, and to the Holy Ghost, which is one God. Amen.

OLIVER COWDERY,
DAVID WHITMER,
MARTIN HARRIS.

Some people have to have a world of evidence before they can come anywhere in the neighborhood of believing anything; but for me, when a man tells me that he has "seen the engravings which are upon the plates," and not only that, but an angel was there at the time, and saw him see them, and probably took his receipt for it, I am very far on the road to conviction, no matter whether I ever heard of that man before or not, and even if I do not know the name of the angel, or his nationality either.

Next is this:

AND ALSO THE TESTIMONY OF EIGHT WITNESSES.

Be it known unto all nations, kindreds, tongues, and people unto whom this work shall come, that Joseph Smith, Jun., the translator of this work, has shewn unto us the plates of which hath been spoken, which have the appearance of gold; and as many of the leaves as the said Smith has translated, we did handle with our hands; and we also saw the engravings thereon, all of which has the appearance of ancient work, and of curious workmanship. And this we bear record with words of soberness, that the said Smith has shewn unto us, for we have seen and hefted, and know of a surety that the said Smith has got the plates of which we have spoken. And we give our names unto the world, to witness unto the world that which we have seen; and we lie not, God bearing witness of it.

CHRISTIAN WHITMER,
JACOB WHITMER,
PETER WHITMER, Jun.
JOHN WHITMER,
HIRAM PAGE,
JOSEPH SMITH, Sen.
HYRUM SMITH,
SAMUEL H. SMITH.

And when I am far on the road to conviction, and eight men, be they grammatical or otherwise, come forward and tell me that they have seen the plates too; and not only seen those plates but "hefted" them, I *am* convinced. I could not feel more satisfied and at rest if the entire Whitmer family had testified.

The Mormon Bible consists of fifteen "books"—being the books of Jacob, Enos, Jarom, Omni, Mosiah, Zeniff, Alma, Helaman, Ether, Moroni, two "books" of Mormon, and three of Nephi.

In the first book of Nephi is a plagiarism of the Old Testament, which gives an account of the exodus from Jerusalem of the "children of Lehi;" and it goes on to tell of their wanderings in the wilderness, during eight years, and their supernatural protection by one of their number, a party by the name of Nephi. They finally reached the land of "Bountiful," and camped by the sea. After they had remained there "for the space of many days"—which is more Scriptural than definite—Nephi was commanded from on high to build a ship wherein to "carry the people across the waters." He travestied Noah's ark—but he obeyed orders in the matter of the plan. He finished the ship *in a single day,* while his brethren stood by and made fun of it—and of him, too—"saying, our brother is a fool, for he thinketh that he can build a ship." They did not wait for the timbers to dry, but the whole tribe or nation sailed the next day. Then a bit of genuine nature cropped out, and is revealed by outspoken Nephi with Scriptural frankness—they all got on a spree! They, "and also their wives, began to make themselves merry, insomuch that they began to dance, and to sing, and to

THE MIRACULOUS COMPASS.

speak with much rudeness; yea, they were lifted up unto exceeding rudeness."

Nephi tried to stop these scandalous proceedings; but they tied him neck and heels, and went on with their lark. But observe how

Nephi the prophet circumvented them by the aid of the invisible powers:

> And it came to pass that after they had bound me, insomuch that I could not move, the compass, which had been prepared of the Lord, did cease to work; wherefore, they knew not whither they should steer the ship, insomuch that there arose a great storm, yea, a great and terrible tempest, and we were driven back upon the waters for the space of three days; and they began to be frightened exceedingly, lest they should be drowned in the sea; nevertheless they did not loose me. And on the fourth day, which we had been driven back, the tempest began to be exceeding sore.
>
> And it came to pass that we were about to be swallowed up in the depths of the sea.

Then they untied him.

> And it came to pass after they had loosed me, behold, I took the compass, and it did work whither I desired it. And it came to pass that I prayed unto the Lord; and after I had prayed, the winds did cease, and the storm did cease, and there was a great calm.

Equipped with their compass, these ancients appear to have had the advantage of Noah.

Their voyage was toward a "promised land"—the only name they give it. They reached it in safety.

Polygamy is a recent feature in the Mormon religion, and was added by Brigham Young after Joseph Smith's death. Before that, it was regarded as an "abomination." This verse from the Mormon Bible occurs in Chapter II. of the book of Jacob:

> For behold, thus saith the Lord, this people begin to wax in iniquity; they understand not the scriptures; for they seek to excuse themselves in committing whoredoms, because of the things which were written concerning David, and Solomon his son. Behold, David and Solomon truly had many wives and concubines, which thing was abominable before me, saith the Lord; wherefore, thus saith the Lord, I have led this people forth out of the land of Jerusalem, by the power of mine arm, that I might raise up unto me a righteous branch from the fruit of the loins of Joseph. Wherefore, I the Lord God, will not suffer that this people shall do like unto them of old.

However, the project failed—or at least the modern Mormon end of it—for Brigham "suffers" it. This verse is from the same chapter:

Behold, the Lamanites your brethren, whom ye hate, because of their filthiness and the cursings which hath come upon their skins, are more righteous than you; for they have not forgotten the commandment of the Lord, which was given unto our fathers, that they should have, save it were one wife; and concubines they should have none.

The following verse (from Chapter IX. of the book of Nephi) appears to contain information not familiar to everybody:

And now it came to pass that when Jesus had ascended into heaven, the multitude did disperse, and every man did take his wife and his children, and did return to his own home.

And it came to pass that on the morrow, when the multitude was gathered together, behold, Nephi and his brother whom he had raised from the dead, whose name was Timothy, and also his son, whose name was Jonas, and also Mathoni, and Mathonihah, his brother, and Kumen, and Kumenonhi, and Jeremiah, and Shemnon, and Jonas, and Zedekiah, and Isaiah; now these were the names of the disciples whom Jesus had chosen.

In order that the reader may observe how much more grandeur and picturesqueness (as seen by these Mormon twelve) accompanied one of the tenderest episodes in the life of our Savior than other eyes seem to have been aware of, I quote the following from the same "book"—Nephi:

And it came to pass that Jesus spake unto them, and bade them arise. And they arose from the earth, and he said unto them, blessed are ye because of your faith. And now behold, my joy is full. And when he had said these words, he wept, and the multitude bear record of it, and he took their little children, one by one, and blessed them, and prayed unto the Father for them. And when he had done this he wept again, and he spake unto the multitude, and saith unto them, behold your little ones. And as they looked to behold, they cast their eyes towards heaven, and they saw the heavens open, and they saw angels descending out of heaven as it were, in the midst of fire; and they came down and encircled those little ones about, and they were encircled about with fire; and the angels did minister unto them, and the multitude did see and hear and bear record; and they know that their record is true, for they all of them did see and hear, every man for himself; and they were in number about two thousand and five hundred souls; and they did consist of men, women, and children.

And what else would they be likely to consist of?

The book of Ether is an incomprehensible medley of "history," much of it relating to battles and sieges among peoples whom the reader has possibly never heard of; and who inhabited a country which is not set down in the geography. There was a King with the remarkable name of Coriantumr, and he warred with Shared, and Lib, and Shiz, and others, in the "plains of Heshlon;" and the "valley of Gilgal;" and the "wilderness of Akish;" and the "land of Moron;" and the "plains of Agosh;" and "Ogath," and "Ramah," and the "land of Corihor," and the "hill Comnor," by "the waters of Ripliancum," etc., etc., etc. "And it came to pass," after a deal of fighting, that Coriantumr, upon making calculation of his losses, found that "there had been slain two millions of mighty men, and also their wives and their children"—say 5,000,000 or 6,000,000 in all—"and he began to sorrow in his heart." Unquestionably it was time. So he wrote to Shiz, asking a cessation of hostilities, and offering to give up his kingdom to save his people. Shiz declined, except upon condition that Coriantumr would come and let him cut his head off first—a thing which Coriantumr would not do. Then there was more fighting for a season; then *four years* were devoted to gathering the forces for a final struggle—after which ensued a battle, which, I take it, is the most remarkable set forth in history,—except, perhaps, that of the Kilkenny cats, which it resembles in some respects. This is the account of the gathering and the battle:

7. And it came to pass that they did gather together all the people, upon all the face of the land, who had not been slain, save it was Ether. And it came to pass that Ether did behold all the doings of the people; and he beheld that the people who were for Coriantumr, were gathered together to the army of Coriantumr; and the people who were for Shiz, were gathered together to the army of Shiz; wherefore they were for the space of four years, gathering together the people, that they might get all who were upon the face of the land, and that they might receive all the strength which it was possible that they could receive. And it came to pass that when they were all gathered together, every one to the army which he would, with their wives and their children; both men, women, and children being armed with weapons of war, having shields, and breast-plates, and head-plates, and being clothed after the manner of war, they did march forth one against another, to battle; and they fought all that day, and conquered not. And it came to pass that when it was night they were weary, and retired to their camps; and after they had

retired to their camps, they took up a howling and a lamentation for the loss of the slain of their people; and so great were their cries, their howlings and lamentations, that it did rend the air exceedingly. And it came to pass that on the morrow they did go again to battle, and great and terrible was that day; nevertheless they conquered not, and when the night came again, they did rend the air with their cries, and their howlings, and their mournings, for the loss of the slain of their people.

8. And it came to pass that Coriantumr wrote again an epistle unto Shiz, desiring that he would not come again to battle, but that he would take the kingdom, and spare the lives of the people. But behold, the spirit of the Lord had ceased striving with them, and satan had full power over the hearts of the people, for they were given up unto the hardness of their hearts, and the blindness of their minds that they might be destroyed; wherefore they went again to battle. And it came to pass that they fought all that day, and when the night came they slept upon their swords; and on the morrow they fought even until the night came; and when the night came they were drunken with anger, even as a man who is drunken with wine; and they slept again upon their swords; and on the morrow they fought again; and when the night came they had all fallen by the sword save it were fifty and two of the people of Coriantumr, and sixty and nine of the people of Shiz. And it came to pass that they slept upon their swords that night, and on the morrow they fought again, and they contended in their mights with their swords, and with their shields, all that day; and when the night came there were thirty and two of the people of Shiz, and twenty and seven of the people of Coriantumr.

9. And it came to pass that they ate and slept, and prepared for death on the morrow. And they were large and mighty men, as to the strength of men. And it came to pass that they fought for the space of three hours, and they fainted with the loss of blood. And it came to pass that when the men of Coriantumr had received sufficient strength, that they could walk, they were about to flee for their lives, but behold, Shiz arose, and also his men, and he swore in his wrath that he would slay Coriantumr, or he would perish by the sword; wherefore he did pursue them, and on the morrow he did overtake them; and they fought again with the sword. And it came to pass that when they had all fallen by the sword, save it were Coriantumr and Shiz, behold Shiz had fainted with loss of blood. And it came to pass that when Coriantumr had leaned upon his sword, that he rested a little, he smote off the head of Shiz. And it came to pass that after he had smote off the head of Shiz, that Shiz raised upon his hands and fell; and after that he had struggled for breath, he died. And it came to pass that Coriantumr fell to the earth, and became as if he had no life. And the Lord spake unto Ether, and said unto him, go forth. And he went forth, and beheld that the words of the Lord had all been fulfilled; and he finished his record; and the hundredth part I have not written.

It seems a pity he did not finish, for after all his dreary former chapters of commonplace, he stopped just as he was in danger of becoming interesting.

The Mormon Bible is rather stupid and tiresome to read, but there is nothing vicious in its teachings. Its code of morals is unobjectionable—it is "smouched"* from the New Testament and no credit given.

---

*Milton.

CHAPTER 17

At the end of our two days' sojourn, we left Great Salt Lake City hearty and well fed and happy—physically superb but not so very much wiser, as regards the "Mormon question," than we were when we arrived, perhaps. We had a deal more "information" than we had before, of course, but we did not know what portion of it was reliable and what was not—for it all came from acquaintances of a day—strangers, strictly speaking. We were told, for instance, that the dreadful "Mountain Meadows massacre" was the work of the Indians entirely, and that the Gentiles had meanly tried to fasten it upon the Mormons; we were told, likewise, that the Indians were to blame, partly, and partly the Mormons; and we were told,

THREE SIDES TO A QUESTION.

likewise, and just as positively, that the Mormons were almost if not wholly and completely responsible for that most treacherous and pitiless butchery. We got the story in all these different shapes, but it was not till several years afterward that Mrs. Waite's book, "The Mormon Prophet," came out with Judge Cradlebaugh's trial of the accused parties in it and revealed the truth that the latter version was the correct one and that the Mormons *were* the assassins. All our "information" had three sides to it, and so I gave up the idea that I could settle the "Mormon question" in two days. Still I have seen newspaper correspondents do it in one.

I left Great Salt Lake a good deal confused as to what state of things existed there—and sometimes even questioning in my own mind whether a state of things existed there at all or not. But presently I remembered with a lightening sense of relief that we had learned two or three trivial things there which we could be certain of; and so the two days were not wholly lost. For instance, we had learned that we were at last in a pioneer land, in absolute and tangible reality. The high prices charged for trifles were eloquent of

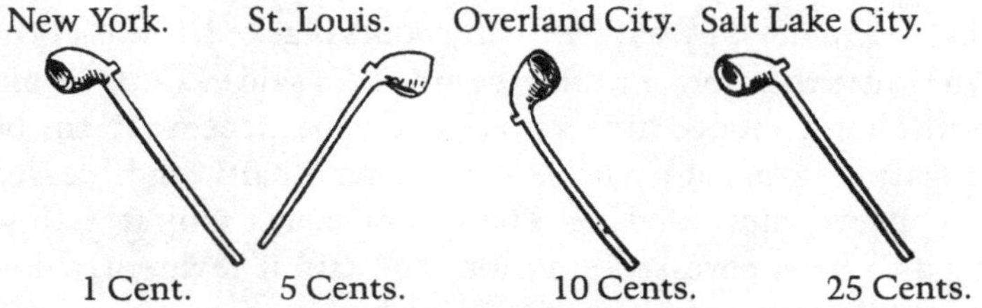

RESULT OF HIGH FREIGHTS.

high freights and bewildering distances of freightage. In the east, in those days, the smallest moneyed denomination was a penny and it represented the smallest purchasable quantity of any commodity. West of Cincinnati the smallest coin in use was the silver five-cent piece and no smaller quantity of an article could be bought than "five cents' worth." In Overland City the lowest coin appeared to be the ten-cent piece; but in Salt Lake there did not seem to be any money in circulation smaller than a quarter, or any smaller quantity purchasable of any commodity than twenty-five cents' worth. We had always been used to half dimes and "five cents' worth" as the minimum of financial negotiations; but in Salt Lake if one wanted a cigar, it was a quarter; if he wanted a chalk pipe, it was a quarter; if he wanted a peach, or a candle, or a newspaper, or a shave, or a little Gentile whisky to rub on his corns to arrest indigestion and keep him from having the toothache, twenty-five cents was the price, every time. When we looked at the shot-bag of silver, now and then, we seemed to be wasting our substance in riotous living, but if we referred to the expense account we could see that we had not been doing anything of the kind. But people easily get reconciled to big money and big prices, and fond and vain of both—it is a descent to little coins and cheap prices that is hardest to bear and slowest to take hold upon one's toleration. After a month's acquaintance with the twenty-five-cent minimum, the average human being is ready to blush every time he thinks of his despicable five-cent days. How sunburnt with blushes I used to get in gaudy Nevada, every time I thought of my first financial experience in Salt Lake. It was on this wise (which is a favorite expression of great authors, and a very neat one, too, but I never hear anybody *say* on this wise when they are talking). A young half-breed with a complexion like a yellow-jacket asked me if I would have my boots blacked. It was at the Salt Lake House the morning after we arrived. I said yes, and he blacked them. Then I handed him a silver five-cent piece, with the benevolent air of a person who is conferring wealth and blessedness upon poverty and suffering. The yellow-jacket took it with what I judged to be suppressed emotion, and laid it reverently down in the middle of his broad hand. Then he began to contemplate it, much as a philosopher contemplates a gnat's ear in the ample field of his microscope. Several mountaineers, teamsters, stage-drivers, etc., drew near and dropped into the tableau and fell to surveying the money with that attractive indifference to formality which is noticeable in the hardy pioneer. Presently the yellow-jacket handed the half dime back to me and told me I ought to keep my money in my pocket-book instead of in my soul, and then I wouldn't get it cramped and shriveled up so!

What a roar of vulgar laughter there was! I destroyed the mongrel reptile on the spot, but I smiled and smiled all the time I was detaching his scalp, for the remark he made *was* good for an "Injun."

Yes, we had learned in Salt Lake to be charged great prices without letting the inward shudder appear on the surface—for even already we had overheard and noted the tenor of conversations among drivers, conductors, and hostlers, and finally among citizens of Salt Lake, until we were well aware that these superior beings despised "emigrants." We permitted no tell-tale shudders and winces in our countenances, for we wanted to seem pioneers, or Mormons, half-breeds, teamsters, stage-drivers, Mountain

A SHRIVELED QUARTER.

Meadows assassins—anything in the world that the plains and Utah respected and admired—but we were wretchedly ashamed of being "emigrants," and sorry enough that we had white shirts and could not swear in the presence of ladies without looking the other way.

And many a time in Nevada, afterward, we had occasion to remember with humiliation that we were "emigrants," and consequently a low and inferior sort of creatures. Perhaps the reader has visited Utah, Nevada, or California, even in these latter days, and while communing with himself upon the sorrowful banishment of those countries from what he considers "the world," has had his wings clipped by finding that *he* is the one to be pitied, and that there are entire populations around him ready and willing to do it for him—yea, who are complacently doing it for him already, wherever he steps his foot. Poor thing, they are making fun of his hat; and the cut of his New York coat; and his conscientiousness about his grammar; and his feeble profanity; and his consumingly ludicrous ignorance of ores, shafts, tunnels, and other things

AN OBJECT OF PITY.

which he never saw before, and never felt enough interest in to read about. And all the time that he is thinking what a sad fate it is to be exiled to that far country, that lonely land, the citizens around him are looking down on him with a blighting compassion because he is an "emigrant" instead of that proudest and blessedest creature that exists on all the earth, a "FORTY-NINER."

The accustomed coach life began again, now, and by midnight it almost seemed as if we never had been out of our snuggery among the mail-sacks at all. We had made one alteration, however. We had provided enough bread, boiled ham and hard boiled eggs to last double the six hundred miles of staging we had still to do.

And it was comfort in those succeeding days to sit up and contemplate the majestic panorama of mountains and valleys spread out below us and eat ham and hard boiled eggs while our spiritual natures reveled alternately in rainbows, thunderstorms, and peerless sunsets. Nothing helps scenery like ham and eggs. Ham and eggs, and after these a pipe—an old, rank, delicious pipe—ham and eggs and scenery, a "down grade," a flying coach, a fragrant pipe and a contented heart—these make happiness. It is what all the ages have struggled for.

CHAPTER 18

At eight in the morning we reached the remnant and ruin of what had been the important military station of "Camp Floyd," some forty-five or fifty miles from Salt Lake City. At 4 P.M. we had doubled our distance and were ninety or a hundred miles from Salt Lake. And now we entered upon one of that species of deserts whose concentrated hideousness shames the diffused and diluted horrors of Sahara—an "*alkali*" desert. For sixty-eight miles there was but one break in it. I do not remember that this was really a break; indeed it seems to me that it was nothing but a watering depot *in the midst* of the stretch of sixty-eight miles. If my memory serves me, there was no well or spring at this place, but the water was hauled there by mule and ox teams from the further side of the desert. There was a stage station there. It was forty-five miles from the beginning of the desert, and twenty-three from the end of it.

We plowed and dragged and groped along, the whole livelong night, and at the end of this uncomfortable twelve hours we finished the forty-five-mile part of the desert and got to the stage station where the imported water was. The sun was just rising. It was easy enough to cross a desert in the night while we were asleep; and it was pleasant to reflect, in the morning, that we in actual person *had* encountered an absolute desert and could always speak knowingly of deserts in presence of the ignorant thenceforward. And it was pleasant also to reflect that this was not an obscure, back country desert, but a very celebrated one, the metropolis itself, as you may say. All this was very well and very comfortable and satisfactory—but now we were to cross a desert in *daylight.* This was fine—novel—romantic—dramatically adventurous—

this, indeed, was worth living for, worth traveling for! We would write home all about it.

This enthusiasm, this stern thirst for adventure, wilted under the sultry August sun and did not last above one hour. One poor little hour—and then we were ashamed that we had "gushed" so. The poetry was all in the anticipation—there is none in the reality. Imagine a vast, waveless ocean stricken dead and turned to ashes; imagine this solemn waste tufted with ash-dusted sage-bushes; imagine the lifeless silence and solitude that belong to such a place; imagine a coach, creeping like a bug through the midst of this shoreless level, and sending up tumbled volumes of dust as if it were a bug that went by steam; imagine this aching monotony of toiling and plowing kept up hour after hour, and the shore still as far away as ever, apparently; imagine team, driver, coach and passengers so deeply coated with ashes that they are all one colorless color; imagine ash-drifts roosting above moustaches and eyebrows like snow accumulations on boughs and bushes. This is the reality of it.

The sun beats down with dead, blistering, relentless malignity; the perspiration is welling from every pore in man and beast, but scarcely a sign of it finds its way to the surface—it is absorbed before it gets there; there is not the faintest breath of air stirring; there is not a merciful shred of cloud in all the brilliant firmament; there is not a living creature visible in any direction whither one searches the blank level that stretches its monotonous miles on every hand; there is not a sound—not a sigh—not a whisper—not a buzz, or a whir of wings, or distant pipe of bird—not even a sob from the lost souls that doubtless people that dead air. And so the occasional sneezing of the resting mules, and the champing of the bits, grate harshly on the grim stillness, not dissipating the spell but accenting it and making one feel more lonesome and forsaken than before.

The mules, under violent swearing, coaxing and whip-cracking, would make at stated intervals a "spurt," and drag the coach a hundred or maybe two hundred yards, stirring up a billowy cloud of dust that rolled back, enveloping the vehicle to the wheel-tops or higher, and making it seem afloat in a fog. Then a rest followed, with the usual sneezing and bit-champing. Then another "spurt" of a hundred yards and another rest at the end of it. All day long we kept this up, without water for the mules and without ever changing the team. At least we kept it up ten hours, which, I take it, is a day, and a pretty honest one, in an alkali desert. It was from four in the morning till two in the afternoon. And it was so hot! and so close! and our water canteens went dry in the middle of the day and we got so thirsty! It was so stupid and tiresome and dull! and the tedious hours did lag and drag and limp along with such a cruel deliberation! It was so trying to give one's watch a good long undisturbed spell and then take it out and find that it had been fooling away the time and not trying to get ahead any! The alkali dust cut through our lips, it persecuted our eyes, it ate through the delicate membranes and made our noses bleed and *kept* them bleeding—and truly and seriously the romance all faded far away and disappeared, and left the desert trip nothing but a harsh reality—a thirsty, sweltering, longing, hateful reality!

Two miles and a quarter an hour for ten hours—that was what we accomplished. It was hard to bring the comprehension away down to such a snail-pace as that, when we had been used to making eight and ten miles an hour. When we reached the station on the farther verge of the desert, we were glad, for the first time, that the Dictionary was along, because we never could have found language to tell how glad we were, in any sort of dictionary but an unabridged one with pictures in it. But there could not have been found in a whole library of dictionaries language sufficient to tell how tired those mules were after their twenty-three-mile pull. To try to give the reader an idea of how *thirsty* they were, would be to "gild refined gold or paint the lily."

Somehow, now that it is there, the quotation does not seem to fit—but no matter, let it stay, anyhow. I think it is a graceful and attractive thing, and therefore have tried time and time again to work it in where it *would* fit, but could not succeed. These efforts have kept my mind distracted and ill at ease, and made my narrative seem broken and disjointed, in places. Under these circumstances it seems to me best to leave it in, as above, since this will afford at least a temporary respite from the wear and tear of trying to "lead up" to this really apt and beautiful quotation.

CHAPTER 19

On the morning of the sixteenth day out from St. Joseph we arrived at the entrance of Rocky Cañon, two hundred and fifty miles from Salt Lake. It was along in this wild country somewhere, and far from any habitation of white men, except the stage stations, that we came across the wretchedest type of mankind I have ever seen, up to this writing. I refer to the Goshoot Indians. From what we could see and all we could learn, they are very considerably inferior to even the despised Digger Indians of California; inferior to all races of savages on our continent; inferior to even the Terra del Fuegans; inferior to the Hottentots, and actually inferior in some respects to the Kytches of Africa. Indeed, I have been obliged to

GOSHOOT INDIANS HANGING AROUND STATIONS.

look the bulky volumes of Wood's "Uncivilized Races of Men" clear through in order to find a savage tribe degraded enough to take rank with the Goshoots. I find but one people fairly open to that shameful verdict. It is the Bosjesmans (Bushmen) of South Africa. Such of the Goshoots as we saw, along the road and hanging about the stations, were small, lean, "scrawny" creatures; in complexion a dull black like the ordinary American negro; their faces and hands bearing dirt which they had been hoarding and accumulating for months, years, and even generations, according to the age of the proprietor; a silent, sneaking, treacherous looking race; taking note of everything, covertly, like all the other "Noble Red Men" that we (do not) read about, and betraying no sign in their countenances; indolent, everlastingly patient and tireless, like all other Indians; prideless beggars—for if the beggar instinct were left out of an Indian he would not "go," any more than a clock without a pendulum; hungry, always hungry, and yet never refusing anything that a hog would eat, though often eating what a hog would decline; hunters, but having no higher ambition than to kill and eat jackass rabbits, crickets and grasshoppers, and embezzle carrion from the buzzards and cayotes; savages who, when asked if they have the common Indian belief in a Great Spirit show a something which almost amounts to emotion, thinking whisky is referred to; a thin, scattering race of almost naked black children, these Goshoots are, who produce nothing at all, and have no villages, and no gatherings together into strictly defined tribal communities—a people whose only shelter is a rag cast on a bush to keep off a portion of the snow, and yet who inhabit one of the most rocky, wintry, repulsive wastes that our country or any other can exhibit.

The Bushmen and our Goshoots are manifestly descended from the self-same gorilla, or kangaroo, or Norway rat, whichever animal-Adam the Darwinians trace them to.

One would as soon expect the rabbits to fight as the Goshoots, and yet they used to live off the offal and refuse of the stations a few months and then come some dark night when no mischief was expected, and burn down the buildings and kill the men from ambush as they rushed out. And once, in the night, they attacked the stage-coach when a District Judge, of Nevada Territory, was the only passenger, and with their first volley of arrows (and a bullet or two) they riddled the stage curtains, wounded a horse or two and mortally wounded the driver. The latter was full of pluck, and so was his passenger. At the driver's call Judge Mott swung himself out, clambered to the box and seized the reins of the team, and away they plunged, through the racing mob of skeletons and under

THE DRIVE FOR LIFE.

a hurtling storm of missiles. The stricken driver had sunk down on the boot as soon as he was wounded, but had held on to the reins and said he would manage to keep hold of them until relieved. And after they were taken from his relaxing grasp, he lay with his head between Judge Mott's feet, and tranquilly gave directions about the road; he said he believed he could live till the miscreants were outrun and left behind, and that if he managed that, the main difficulty would be at an end, and then if the Judge drove so and so (giving directions about bad places in the road, and general course) he would reach the next station without trouble. The Judge distanced the enemy and at last rattled up to the station and knew that the night's perils were done; but there was no comrade-in-arms for him to rejoice with, for the soldierly driver was dead.

Let us forget that we have been saying harsh things about the Overland drivers, now. The disgust which the Goshoots gave me, a disciple of Cooper and a worshipper of the Red Man—even of the scholarly savages in the "Last of the Mohicans" who are fittingly associated with backwoodsmen who divide each sentence into two equal parts: one part critically grammatical, refined and choice of language, and the other part just such an attempt to talk like a hunter or a mountaineer, as a Broadway clerk might make after eating an edition of Emerson Bennett's works and studying frontier life at the Bowery Theatre a couple of weeks—I say that the nausea which the Goshoots gave me, an Indian worshipper, set me to examining authorities, to see if perchance I had been overestimating the Red Man while viewing him through the mellow moonshine of romance. The revelations that came were disenchanting. It was curious to see how quickly the paint and tinsel fell away from him and left him treacherous, filthy and repulsive—and how quickly the evidences accumulated that wherever one finds an Indian tribe he has only found Goshoots more or less modified by circumstances and surroundings—but Goshoots, after all. They deserve pity, poor creatures; and they can have mine—at this distance. Nearer by, they never get anybody's.

There is an impression abroad that the Baltimore and Washington Railroad Company and many of its employés are Goshoots; but it is an error. There is only a plausible resemblance, which, while it is apt enough to mislead the ignorant, cannot deceive parties who have contemplated both tribes. But seriously, it was not only poor wit, but very wrong to start the report referred to above; for however innocent the motive may have been, the necessary effect was to injure the reputation of a class who have a hard enough time of it in the pitiless deserts of the Rocky Mountains, Heaven knows! If we cannot find it in our hearts to give those poor naked creatures our Christian sympathy and compassion, in God's name let us at least not throw mud at them.

CHAPTER 20

On the seventeenth day we passed the highest mountain peaks we had yet seen, and although the day was very warm the night that followed upon its heels was wintry cold and blankets were next to useless.

On the eighteenth day we encountered the eastward-bound telegraph-constructors at Reese river station and sent a message to his Excellency Gov. Nye at Carson City (distant one hundred and fifty-six miles).

On the nineteenth day we crossed the Great American Desert—forty memorable miles of bottomless sand, into which the coach wheels sunk from six inches to a foot. We worked our passage most of the way across. That is to say, we got out and walked. It was a dreary pull and a long and thirsty one, for we had no water. From one extremity of this desert to the other, the road was white with the bones of oxen and horses. It would hardly be an exaggeration to say that we could have walked the forty miles and set our feet on a bone at every step! The desert was one prodigious graveyard. And the log-chains, wagon tyres, and rotting wrecks of vehicles were almost as thick as the bones. I think we saw log-chains enough rusting there in the desert, to reach across any State in the Union. Do not these relics suggest something of an idea of the fearful suffering and privation the early emigrants to California endured?

At the border of the desert lies Carson Lake, or the "Sink" of the Carson, a shallow, melancholy sheet of water some eighty or a hundred miles in circumference. Carson river empties into it and is lost—sinks mysteriously into the earth and never appears in the light of the sun again—for the lake has no outlet whatever.

There are several rivers in Nevada, and they all have this mysterious fate. They end in various lakes or "sinks," and that is the last of them. Carson Lake, Humboldt Lake, Walker Lake, Mono Lake, are all great sheets of water without any visible outlet. Water is always flowing into them; none is ever seen to flow out of them, and yet they remain always level full, neither receding nor overflowing. What they do with their surplus is only known to the Creator.

On the western verge of the desert we halted a moment at Ragtown. It consisted of one log house and is not set down on the map.

This reminds me of a circumstance. Just after we left Julesburg, on the Platte, I was sitting with the driver, and he said:

"I can tell you a most laughable thing indeed, if you would like to listen to it. Horace Greeley went over this road once. When he was leaving Carson City he told the driver, Hank Monk, that he

GREELEY'S RIDE.

had an engagement to lecture at Placerville and was very anxious to go through quick. Hank Monk cracked his whip and started off at an awful pace. The coach bounced up and down in such a terrific way that it jolted the buttons all off of Horace's coat, and finally shot his head clean through the roof of the stage, and then he yelled at Hank Monk and begged him to go easier—said he warn't in as much of a hurry as he was a while ago. But Hank Monk said, 'Keep your seat, Horace, and I'll get you there on time!'—and you bet you he did, too, what was left of him!"

A day or two after that we picked up a Denver man at the cross roads, and he told us a good deal about the country and the Gregory Diggings. He seemed a very entertaining person and a man well posted in the affairs of Colorado. By and by he remarked:

"I can tell you a most laughable thing indeed, if you would like to listen to it. Horace Greeley went over this road once. When he was leaving Carson City he told the driver, Hank Monk, that he had an engagement to lecture at Placerville and was very anxious to go through quick. Hank Monk cracked his whip and started off at an awful pace. The coach bounced up and down in such a terrific way that it jolted the buttons all off of Horace's coat, and finally shot his head clean through the roof of the stage, and then he yelled at Hank Monk and begged him to go easier—said he warn't in as much of a hurry as he was a while ago. But Hank Monk said, 'Keep your seat, Horace, and I'll get you there on time!'—and you bet you he did, too, what was left of him!"

At Fort Bridger, some days after this, we took on board a cavalry sergeant, a very proper and soldierly person indeed. From no other man during the whole journey, did we gather such a store of concise and well-arranged military information. It was surprising to find in the desolate wilds of our country a man so thoroughly acquainted with everything useful to know in his line of life, and yet of such inferior rank and unpretentious bearing. For as much as three hours we listened to him with unabated interest. Finally he got upon the subject of trans-continental travel, and presently said:

"I can tell you a most laughable thing indeed, if you would like to listen to it. Horace Greeley went over this road once. When he was leaving Carson City he told the driver, Hank Monk, that he had an engagement to lecture at Placerville and was very anxious to go through quick. Hank Monk cracked his whip and started off at an awful pace. The coach bounced up and down in such a terrific way that it jolted the buttons all off of Horace's coat, and finally shot his head clean through the roof of the stage, and then he yelled at Hank Monk and begged him to go easier—said he warn't in as much of a hurry as he was a while ago. But Hank Monk said, 'Keep your seat, Horace, and I'll get you there on time!'—and you bet you he did, too, what was left of him!"

When we were eight hours out from Salt Lake City a Mormon preacher got in with us at a way station—a gentle, soft-spoken, kindly man, and one whom any stranger would warm to at first sight. I can never forget the pathos that was in his voice as he told, in simple language, the story of his people's wanderings and unpitied sufferings. No pulpit eloquence was ever so moving and so beautiful as this outcast's picture of the first Mormon pilgrimage across the plains, struggling sorrowfully onward to the land of its banishment and marking its desolate way with graves and watering it with tears. His words so wrought upon us that it was a relief to us all when the conversation drifted into a more cheerful channel and the natural features of the curious country we were in came under treatment. One matter after another was pleasantly discussed, and at length the stranger said:

"I can tell you a most laughable thing indeed, if you would like to listen to it. Horace Greeley went over this road once. When he was leaving Carson City he told the driver, Hank Monk, that he had an engagement to lecture at Placerville and was very anxious to go through quick. Hank Monk cracked his whip and started off at an awful pace. The coach bounced up and down in such a terrific way that it jolted the buttons all off of Horace's coat, and finally shot his head clean through the roof of the stage, and then he yelled at Hank Monk and begged him to go easier—said he warn't in as much of a hurry as he was a while ago. But Hank Monk said, 'Keep your seat, Horace, and I'll get you there on time!'—and you bet you he did, too, what was left of him!"

Ten miles out of Ragtown we found a poor wanderer who had lain down to die. He had walked as long as he could, but his limbs had failed him at last. Hunger and fatigue had conquered him. It would have been inhuman to leave him there. We paid his fare to

Carson and lifted him into the coach. It was some little time before he showed any very decided signs of life; but by dint of chafing him and pouring brandy between his lips we finally brought him to a languid consciousness. Then we fed him a little, and by and by he seemed to comprehend the situation and a grateful light softened his eye. We made his mail-sack bed as comfortable as possible, and constructed a pillow for him with our coats. He seemed very thankful. Then he looked up in our faces, and said in a feeble voice that had a tremble of honest emotion in it:

"Gentlemen, I know not who you are, but you have saved my life; and although I can never be able to repay you for it, I feel that I can at least make one hour of your long journey lighter. I take it you are strangers to this great thoroughfare, but I am entirely familiar with it. In this connection I can tell you a most laughable thing indeed, if you would like to listen to it. Horace Greeley—"

I said, impressively:

"Suffering stranger, proceed at your peril. You see in me the melancholy wreck of a once stalwart and magnificent manhood. What has brought me to this? That thing which you are about to tell.

BOTTLING AN ANECDOTE.

Gradually but surely, that tiresome old anecdote has sapped my strength, undermined my constitution, withered my life. Pity my helplessness. Spare me only just this once, and tell me about young George Washington and his little hatchet for a change."

We were saved. But not so the invalid. In trying to retain the anecdote in his system he strained himself and died in our arms.

I am aware, now, that I ought not to have asked of the sturdiest citizen of all that region, what I asked of that mere shadow of a man; for, after seven years' residence on the Pacific coast, I know that no passenger or driver on the Overland ever corked that anecdote in, when a stranger was by, and survived. Within a period of six years I crossed and recrossed the Sierras between Nevada and California thirteen times by stage and listened to that deathless incident four hundred and eighty-one or eighty-two times. I have the list somewhere. Drivers always told it, conductors told it, landlords told it, chance passengers told it, the very Chinamen and vagrant Indians recounted it. I have had the same driver tell it to me two or three times in the same afternoon. It has come to me in all the multitude of tongues that Babel bequeathed to earth, and flavored with whisky, brandy, beer, cologne, sozodont, tobacco, garlic, onions, grasshoppers—everything that has a fragrance to it through all the long list of things that are gorged or guzzled by the sons of men. I never have smelt any anecdote as often as I have smelt that one; never have smelt any anecdote that smelt so variegated as that one. And you never could learn to know it by its smell, because every time you thought you had learned the smell of it, it would turn up with a different smell. Bayard Taylor has written about this hoary anecdote, Richardson has published it; so have Jones, Smith, Johnson, Ross Browne, and every other correspondence-inditing being that ever set his foot upon the great overland road anywhere between Julesburg and San Francisco; and I have heard that it is in the Talmud. I have seen it in print in nine different foreign languages; I have been told that it is employed in the inquisition in Rome; and I now learn with regret that it is going to be set to music. I do not think that such things are right.

Stage-coaching on the Overland is no more, and stage-drivers are a race defunct. I wonder if they bequeathed that bald-headed anecdote to their successors, the railroad brakemen and conductors, and if these latter still persecute the helpless passenger with it until he concludes, as did many a tourist of other days, that the real grandeurs of the Pacific coast are not Yo Semite and the Big Trees, but Hank Monk and his adventure with Horace Greeley.*

---

*And what makes that worn anecdote the more aggravating, is, that the adventure it celebrates *never occurred.* If it were a good anecdote, that seeming demerit would be its chiefest virtue, for creative power belongs to greatness; but what ought to be done to a man who would wantonly contrive so flat a one as this? If *I* were to suggest what ought to be done to him, I should be called extravagant—but what does the thirteenth chapter of Daniel say? Aha!

CHAPTER 21

We were approaching the end of our long journey. It was the morning of the twentieth day. At noon we would reach Carson City, the capital of Nevada Territory. We were not glad, but sorry. It had been a fine pleasure trip; we had fed fat on wonders every day; we were now well accustomed to stage life, and very fond of it; so the idea of coming to a stand-still and settling down to a humdrum existence in a village was not agreeable, but on the contrary depressing.

Visibly our new home was a desert, walled in by barren, snow-clad mountains. There was not a tree in sight. There was no vegetation but the endless sage-brush and greasewood. All nature was gray with it. We were plowing through great deeps of powdery alkali dust that rose in thick clouds and floated across the plain like smoke from a burning house. We were coated with it like millers; so were the coach, the mules, the mail-bags, the driver—we and the sage-brush and the other scenery were all one monotonous color. Long trains of freight wagons in the distance enveloped in ascending masses of dust suggested pictures of prairies on fire. These teams and their masters were the only life we saw. Otherwise we moved in the midst of solitude, silence and desolation. Every twenty steps we passed the skeleton of some dead beast of burthen, with its dust-coated skin stretched tightly over its empty ribs. Frequently a solemn raven sat upon the skull or the hips and contemplated the passing coach with meditative serenity.

CONTEMPLATION.

By and by Carson City was pointed out to us. It nestled in the edge of a great plain and was a sufficient number of miles away to look like an assemblage of mere white spots in the shadow of a grim range of mountains overlooking it, whose summits seemed lifted clear out of companionship and consciousness of earthly things.

We arrived, disembarked, and the stage went on. It was a "wooden" town; its population two thousand souls. The main street consisted of four or five blocks of little white frame stores which were too high to sit down on, but not too high for various other purposes; in fact, hardly high enough. They were packed close together, side by side, as if room were scarce in that mighty plain. The sidewalk was of boards that were more or less loose and inclined to rattle when walked upon. In the middle of the town, opposite the stores, was the "plaza" which is native to all towns beyond the Rocky Mountains—a large, unfenced, level vacancy, with a liberty pole in it, and very useful as a place for public auctions, horse trades, and mass meetings, and likewise for teamsters to camp in. Two other sides of the plaza were faced by stores, offices and stables. The rest of Carson City was pretty scattering.

We were introduced to several citizens, at the stage-office and on the way up to the Governor's from the hotel—among others, to a Mr. Harris, who was on horseback; he began to say something, but interrupted himself with the remark:

"I'll have to get you to excuse me a minute; yonder is the witness that swore I helped to rob the California coach—a piece of impertinent intermeddling, sir, for I am not even acquainted with the man."

Then he rode over and began to rebuke the stranger with a six-shooter, and the stranger began to explain with another. When the pistols were emptied, the stranger resumed his work (mending a whip-lash), and Mr. Harris rode by with a polite nod, homeward bound, with a bullet through one of his lungs, and several in his hips; and from them issued little rivulets of blood that coursed down the horse's sides and made the animal look quite picturesque. I never saw Harris shoot a man after that but it recalled to mind that first day in Carson.

This was all we saw that day, for it was two o'clock, now, and according to custom the daily "Washoe Zephyr" set in; a soaring dust-drift about the size of the United States set up edgewise came with it, and the capital of Nevada Territory disappeared from view. Still, there were sights to be seen which were not wholly uninteresting to new comers; for the vast dust-cloud was thickly freckled with things strange to the upper air—things living and dead, that

THE WASHOE ZEPHYR.

flitted hither and thither, going and coming, appearing and disappearing among the rolling billows of dust—hats, chickens and parasols sailing in the remote heavens; blankets, tin signs, sage-brush and shingles a shade lower; door-mats and buffalo robes lower still; shovels and coal scuttles on the next grade; glass doors, cats and little children on the next; disrupted lumber yards, light buggies and wheelbarrows on the next; and down only thirty or forty feet above ground was a skurrying storm of emigrating roofs and vacant lots.

It was something to see that much. I could have seen more, if I could have kept the dust out of my eyes.

But seriously a Washoe wind is by no means a trifling matter. It blows flimsy houses down, lifts shingle roofs occasionally, rolls up tin ones like sheet music, now and then blows a stage-coach over and spills the passengers; and tradition says the reason there are so many bald people there, is, that the wind blows the hair off their heads while they are looking skyward after their hats. Carson streets seldom look inactive on summer afternoons, because there are so many citizens skipping around their escaping hats, like chambermaids trying to head off a spider.

The "Washoe Zephyr" (Washoe is a pet nickname for Nevada) is a peculiarly Scriptural wind, in that no man knoweth "whence it cometh." That is to say, where it *originates*. It comes right over the mountains from the west, but when one crosses the ridge he does not find any of it on the other side! It probably is manufactured on the mountain-top for the occasion, and starts from there. It is a pretty regular wind, in the summer time. Its office hours are from two in the afternoon till two the next morning; and anybody venturing abroad during those twelve hours needs to allow for the wind or he will bring up a mile or two to leeward of the point he is aiming at. And yet the first complaint a Washoe visitor to San Francisco makes, is that the sea winds blow so, there! There is a good deal of human nature in that.

THE GOVERNOR'S HOUSE.

We found the state palace of the Governor of Nevada Territory to consist of a white frame one-story house with two small rooms in it and a stanchion supported shed in front—for grandeur—it compelled the respect of the citizen and inspired the Indians with awe. The newly arrived Chief and Associate Justices of the Territory, and other machinery of the government, were domiciled with less splendor. They were boarding around privately, and had their offices in their bedrooms.

The Secretary and I took quarters in the "ranch" of a worthy French lady by the name of Bridget O'Flannigan, a camp follower of his Excellency the Governor. She had known him in his prosperity as commander-in-chief of the Metropolitan Police of New York, and she would not desert him in his adversity as Governor of Nevada. Our room was on the lower floor, facing the plaza, and when we had got our bed, a small table, two chairs, the government fire-proof safe, and the Unabridged Dictionary into it, there was still room enough left for a visitor—maybe two, but not without straining the walls. But the walls could stand it—at least the partitions could, for they consisted simply of one thickness of white "cotton domestic" stretched from corner to corner of the room. This was the rule in Carson—any other kind of partition

DARK DISCLOSURES.

was the rare exception. And if you stood in a dark room and your neighbors in the next had lights, the shadows on your canvas told queer secrets sometimes! Very often these partitions were made of old flour sacks basted together; and then the difference between the common herd and the aristocracy was, that the common herd had unornamented sacks, while the walls of the aristocrat were overpowering with rudimental fresco—*i. e.,* red and blue mill brands on the flour sacks. Occasionally, also, the better classes embellished their canvas by pasting pictures from *Harper's Weekly* on them. In many cases, too, the wealthy and the cultured rose to spittoons and other evidences of a sumptuous and luxurious taste.* We had a carpet and a genuine queensware washbowl. Consequently we were hated without reserve by the other tenants of the O'Flannigan "ranch." When we added a painted oil-cloth window curtain, we simply took our lives into our own hands. To prevent bloodshed I removed up stairs and took up quarters with the untitled plebeians in one of the fourteen white pine cot-bedsteads that stood in two long ranks in the one sole room of which the second story consisted.

THE IRISH BRIGADE.

*Washoe people take a joke so hard that I must explain that the above description was only the rule; there were many honorable exceptions in Carson—plastered ceilings and houses that had considerable furniture in them.—M. T.

It was a jolly company, the fourteen. They were principally voluntary camp followers of the Governor, who had joined his retinue by their own election at New York and San Francisco and came along, feeling that in the scuffle for little Territorial crumbs and offices they could not make their condition more precarious than it was, and might reasonably expect to make it better. They were popularly known as the "Irish Brigade," though there were only four or five Irishmen among all the Governor's retainers. His good-natured Excellency was much annoyed at the gossip his henchmen created—especially when there arose a rumor that they were paid assassins of his, brought along to quietly reduce the Democratic vote when desirable!

Mrs. O'Flannigan was boarding and lodging them at ten dollars a week apiece, and they were cheerfully giving their notes for it. They were perfectly satisfied, but Bridget presently found that notes that could not be discounted were but a feeble constitution for a Carson boarding house. So she began to harry the Governor to find employment for the "Brigade." Her importunities and theirs together drove him to a gentle desperation at last, and he finally summoned the Brigade to the presence. Then, said he:

"Gentlemen, I have planned a lucrative and useful service for you—a service which will provide you with recreation amid noble landscapes, and afford you never ceasing opportunities for enriching your minds by observation and study. I want you to survey a railroad from Carson City westward to a certain point! When the legislature meets I will have the necessary bill passed and the remuneration arranged."

"What, a railroad over the Sierra Nevada Mountains?"

"Well, then, survey it eastward to a certain point!"

RECREATION.

He converted them into surveyors, chain-bearers and so on, and turned them loose in the desert. It was "recreation" with a vengeance! Recreation on foot, lugging chains through sand and sagebrush, under a sultry sun and among cattle bones, cayotes and tarantulas. "Romantic adventure" could go no further. They surveyed very slowly, very deliberately, very carefully. They returned every night during the first week, dusty, footsore, tired, and hungry, but very jolly. They brought in great store of prodigious hairy spiders—tarantulas—and imprisoned them in covered tumblers up stairs in the "ranch." After the first week, they had to camp on the field, for they were getting well eastward. They made a good many inquiries as to the location of that indefinite "certain point," but got no information. At last, to a peculiarly urgent inquiry of "How far eastward?" Gov. Nye telegraphed back:

"To the Atlantic Ocean, blast you!—and then bridge it and go on!"

This brought back the dusty toilers, who sent in a report and ceased from their labors. The Governor was always comfortable about it; he said Mrs. O'Flannigan would hold him for the Brigade's board anyhow, and he intended to get what entertainment he could out of the boys; he said, with his old-time pleasant twinkle, that he meant to survey them into Utah and then telegraph Brigham to hang them for trespass!

The surveyors brought back more tarantulas with them, and so we had quite a menagerie arranged along the shelves of the room. Some of these spiders could straddle over a common saucer with their hairy, muscular legs, and when their feelings were hurt, or

THE TARANTULA.

their dignity offended, they were the wickedest-looking desperadoes the animal world can furnish. If their glass prison-houses were touched ever so lightly they were up and spoiling for a fight in a minute. Starchy?—proud? Indeed, they would take up a straw and pick their teeth like a member of Congress. There was as usual a furious "zephyr" blowing the first night of the Brigade's return, and about midnight the roof of an adjoining stable blew off, and a corner of it came crashing through the side of our ranch. There was a simultaneous awakening, and a tumultuous muster of the Brigade in the dark, and a general tumbling and sprawling over each other in the narrow aisle between the bed-rows. In the midst of the turmoil, Bob H—— sprung up out of a sound sleep, and knocked down a shelf with his head. Instantly he shouted:

"Turn out, boys—the tarantulas is loose!"

No warning ever sounded so dreadful. Nobody tried, any longer, to leave the room, lest he might step on a tarantula. Every man groped for a trunk or a bed, and jumped on it. Then followed the strangest silence—a silence of grisly suspense it was, too—waiting, expectancy, fear. It was as dark as pitch, and one had to imagine the spectacle of those fourteen scant-clad men roosting gingerly on trunks and beds, for not a thing could be seen. Then came occasional little interruptions of the silence, and one could recognize a man and tell his locality by his voice, or locate any other sound a sufferer made by his gropings or changes of position. The occasional voices were not given to much speaking—you simply heard a gentle ejaculation of "Ow!" followed by a solid thump, and you knew the gentleman had felt a hairy blanket or something touch his bare skin and had skipped from a bed to the floor. Another silence. Presently you would hear a gasping voice say:

"Su-su-something's crawling up the back of my neck!"

Every now and then you could hear a little subdued scramble and a sorrowful "O Lord!" and then you knew that somebody was getting away from something he took for a tarantula, and not losing any time about it, either. Directly a voice in the corner rang out wild and clear:

"I've got him! I've got him!" [Pause, and probable change of circumstances.] "No, he's got me! Oh, ain't they *never* going to fetch a lantern!"

The lantern came at that moment, in the hands of Mrs. O'Flannigan, whose anxiety to know the amount of damage done by the assaulting roof had not prevented her waiting a judicious interval, after getting out of bed and lighting up, to see if the wind was done, now, up stairs, or had a larger contract.

The landscape presented when the lantern flashed into the room was picturesque, and might have been funny to some people, but was not to us. Although we were perched so strangely upon boxes,

LIGHT THROWN ON THE SUBJECT.

trunks and beds, and so strangely attired, too, we were too earnestly distressed and too genuinely miserable to see any fun about it, and there was not the semblance of a smile anywhere visible. I know I am not capable of suffering more than I did during those few minutes of suspense in the dark, surrounded by those creeping, bloody-minded tarantulas. I had skipped from bed to bed and from box to box in a cold agony, and every time I touched anything that was furzy I fancied I felt the fangs. I had rather go to war than live that episode over again. Nobody was hurt. The man who thought a tarantula had "got him" was mistaken—only a crack in a box had caught his finger. Not one of those escaped tarantulas was ever seen again. There were ten or twelve of them. We took candles and hunted the place high and low for them, but with no success. Did we go back to bed then? We did nothing of the kind. Money could not have persuaded us to do it. We sat up the rest of the night playing cribbage and keeping a sharp lookout for the enemy.

CHAPTER 22

It was the end of August, and the skies were cloudless and the weather superb. In two or three weeks I had grown wonderfully fascinated with the curious new country, and concluded to put off my return to "the States" awhile. I had grown well accustomed to wearing a damaged slouch hat, blue woolen shirt, and pants crammed into boot-tops, and gloried in the absence of coat, vest and braces. I felt rowdyish and "bully," (as the historian Josephus phrases it, in his fine chapter upon the destruction of the Temple). It seemed to me that nothing could be so fine and so romantic. I had become an officer of the government, but that was for mere sublimity. The office was an unique sinecure. I had nothing to do and no salary. I was private secretary to his majesty the Secretary and there was not yet writing enough for two of us. So Johnny K—— and I devoted our time to amusement. He was the young son of an Ohio nabob and was out there for recreation. He got it. We had heard a world of talk about the marvelous beauty of Lake Tahoe, and finally curiosity drove us thither to see it. Three or four members of the Brigade had been there and located some timber lands on its shores and stored up a quantity of provisions in their camp. We strapped a couple of blankets on our shoulders and took an axe apiece and started—for we intended to take up a wood ranch or so ourselves and become wealthy. We were on foot. The reader will find it advantageous to go horseback. We were told that the distance was eleven miles. We tramped a long time on level ground, and then toiled laboriously up a mountain about a thousand miles high and looked over. No lake there. We descended on the other side, crossed the valley and toiled up another mountain three or four thousand miles high, apparently, and looked over again. No lake yet. We sat down tired and perspiring, and hired a couple of Chinamen to curse those people who had beguiled us.

Thus refreshed, we presently resumed the march with renewed vigor and determination. We plodded on, two or three hours longer, and at last the lake burst upon us—a noble sheet of blue water lifted six thousand three hundred feet above the level of the sea, and walled in by a rim of snow-clad mountain peaks that towered aloft full three thousand feet higher still! It was a vast oval, and one would have to use up eighty or a hundred good miles in traveling around it. As it lay there with the shadows of the mountains brilliantly photographed upon its still surface I thought it must surely be the fairest picture the whole earth affords.

We found the small skiff belonging to the Brigade boys, and without loss of time set out across a deep bend of the lake toward the landmarks that signified the locality of the camp. I got Johnny to row—not because I mind exertion myself, but because it makes me sick to ride backwards when I am at work. But I steered. A three-mile pull brought us to the camp just as the night fell, and we stepped ashore very tired and wolfishly hungry. In a "cache" among the rocks we found the provisions and the cooking utensils, and then, all fatigued as I was, I sat down on a boulder and superintended while Johnny gathered wood and cooked supper. Many a man who had gone through what I had, would have wanted to rest.

I STEERED.

It was a delicious supper—hot bread, fried bacon, and black coffee. It was a delicious solitude we were in, too. Three miles away was a saw-mill and some workmen, but there were not fifteen other human beings throughout the wide circumference of the lake. As the darkness closed down and the stars came out and spangled the great mirror with jewels, we smoked meditatively in the solemn hush and forgot our troubles and our pains. In due time we spread our blankets in the warm sand between two large boulders and soon fell asleep, careless of the procession of ants that passed in through rents in our clothing and explored our persons. Nothing could disturb the sleep that fettered us, for it had been fairly earned, and if our consciences had any sins on them they had to adjourn court for that night, anyway. The wind rose just as we were losing consciousness, and we were lulled to sleep by the beating of the surf upon the shore.

It is always very cold on that lake shore in the night, but we had plenty of blankets and were warm enough. We never moved a muscle all night, but waked at early dawn in the original positions, and got up at once, thoroughly refreshed, free from soreness, and brim full of friskiness. There is no end of wholesome medicine in such an experience. That morning we could have whipped ten such people as we were the day before—sick ones at any rate. But the world is slow, and people will go to "water cures" and "movement cures" and to foreign lands for health. Three months of camp life on Lake Tahoe would restore an Egyptian mummy to his pristine vigor, and give him an appetite like an alligator. I do not mean the oldest and driest mummies, of course, but the fresher ones. The air up there in the clouds is very pure and fine, bracing and delicious. And why shouldn't it be?—it is the same the angels breathe. I think that hardly any amount of fatigue can be gathered together that a man cannot sleep off in one night on the sand by its side. Not under a roof, but under the sky; it seldom or never rains there in the summer time. I know a man who went there to die. But he made a failure of it. He was a skeleton when he came, and could barely stand. He had no appetite, and did nothing but read tracts and reflect on the future. Three months later he was sleeping out of doors regularly, eating all he could hold, three times a day, and chasing game over mountains three thousand feet high for recreation. And he was a

THE INVALID.

skeleton no longer, but weighed part of a ton. This is no fancy sketch, but the truth. His disease was consumption. I confidently commend his experience to other skeletons.

THE RESTORED.

I superintended again, and as soon as we had eaten breakfast we got in the boat and skirted along the lake shore about three miles and disembarked. We liked the appearance of the place, and so we claimed some three hundred acres of it and stuck our "notices" on a tree. It was yellow pine timber land—a dense forest of trees a hundred feet high and from one to five feet through at the butt. It was necessary to fence our property or we could not hold it. That is to say, it was necessary to cut down trees here and there and make them fall in such a way as to form a sort of enclosure (with pretty wide gaps in it). We cut down three trees apiece, and found it such heart-breaking work that we decided to "rest our case" on those; if they held the property, well and good; if they didn't, let the property spill out through the gaps and go; it was no use to work ourselves to death merely to save a few acres of land. Next day we came back to build a house—for a house was also necessary, in order to hold the property. We decided to build a substantial log house and excite the envy of the Brigade boys; but by the time we had cut and trimmed the first log it seemed unnecessary to be so elaborate, and so we concluded to build it of saplings. However, two saplings, duly cut and trimmed, compelled recognition of the fact that

OUR HOUSE.

a still modester architecture would satisfy the law, and so we concluded to build a "brush" house. We devoted the next day to this work, but we did so much "sitting around" and discussing, that by the middle of the afternoon we had achieved only a half-way sort of affair which one of us had to watch while the other cut brush, lest if both turned our backs we might not be able to find it again, it had such a strong family resemblance to the surrounding vegetation. But we were satisfied with it.

We were land owners now, duly seized and possessed, and within the protection of the law. Therefore we decided to take up our residence on our own domain and enjoy that large sense of independence which only such an experience can bring. Late the next afternoon, after a good long rest, we sailed away from the Brigade camp with all the provisions and cooking utensils we could carry off—borrow is the more accurate word—and just as the night was falling we beached the boat at our own landing.

CHAPTER 23

If there is any life that is happier than the life we led on our timber ranch for the next two or three weeks, it must be a sort of life which I have not read of in books or experienced in person. We did not see a human being but ourselves during the time, or hear any sounds but those that were made by the wind and the waves, the sighing of the pines, and now and then the far-off thunder of an avalanche. The forest about us was dense and cool, the sky above us was cloudless and brilliant with sunshine, the broad lake before us was glassy and clear, or rippled and breezy, or black and storm-tossed, according to Nature's mood; and its circling border of mountain domes, clothed with forests, scarred with land-slides, cloven by cañons and valleys, and helmeted with glittering snow, fitly framed and finished the noble picture. The view was always fascinating, bewitching, entrancing. The eye was never tired of gazing, night or day, in calm or storm; it suffered but one grief, and that was that it could not look always, but must close sometimes in sleep.

We slept in the sand close to the water's edge, between two protecting boulders, which took care of the stormy night-winds for us. We never took any paregoric to make us sleep. At the first break of dawn we were always up and running foot-races to tone down excess of physical vigor and exuberance of spirits. That is, Johnny was—but I held his hat. While smoking the pipe of peace after breakfast we watched the sentinel peaks put on the glory of the sun, and followed the conquering light as it swept down among the shadows, and set the captive crags and forests free. We watched the tinted pictures grow and brighten upon the water till every little detail of forest, precipice and pinnacle was wrought in and finished, and the miracle of the enchanter complete. Then to "business."

That is, drifting around in the boat. We were on the north shore. There, the rocks on the bottom are sometimes gray, sometimes white. This gives the marvelous transparency of the water a fuller advantage than it has elsewhere on the lake. We usually pushed out a hundred yards or so from shore, and then lay down on the thwarts, in the sun, and let the boat drift by the hour whither it would. We seldom talked. It interrupted the Sabbath stillness, and marred the dreams the luxurious rest and indolence brought. The shore all along was indented with deep, curved bays and coves, bordered by narrow sand-beaches; and where the sand ended, the steep mountain sides rose right up aloft into space—rose up like a vast wall a little out of the perpendicular, and thickly wooded with tall pines.

AT BUSINESS.

So singularly clear was the water, that where it was only twenty or thirty feet deep the bottom was so perfectly distinct that the boat seemed floating in the air! Yes, where it was even *eighty* feet deep. Every little pebble was distinct, every speckled trout, every hand's-breadth of sand. Often, as we lay on our faces, a granite boulder, as large as a village church, would start out of the bottom apparently, and seem climbing up rapidly to the surface, till presently it threatened to touch our faces, and we could not resist the impulse to seize an oar and avert the danger. But the boat would float on, and the boulder descend again, and then we could see that when we had been exactly above it, it must still have been twenty or thirty feet below the surface. Down through the transparency of these great depths, the water was not *merely* transparent, but dazzlingly, brilliantly so. All objects seen through it had a bright, strong vividness, not only of outline, but of every minute detail, which they would not have had when seen simply through the same depth of atmosphere. So empty and airy did all spaces seem below us, and so strong was the sense of floating high aloft in mid-nothingness, that we called these boat-excursions "balloon-voyages."

We fished a good deal, but we did not average one fish a week. We could see trout by the thousand winging about in the emptiness under us, or sleeping in shoals on the bottom, but they would not bite—they could see the line too plainly, perhaps. We frequently selected the trout we wanted, and rested the bait patiently and persistently on the end of his nose at a depth of eighty feet, but he would only shake it off with an annoyed manner, and shift his position.

We bathed occasionally, but the water was rather chilly, for all it looked so sunny. Sometimes we rowed out to the "blue water," a mile or two from shore. It was as dead blue as indigo there, because of the immense depth. By official measurement the lake in its centre is one thousand five hundred and twenty-five feet deep!

Sometimes, on lazy afternoons, we lolled on the sand in camp, and smoked pipes and read some old well-worn novels. At night, by the camp-fire, we played euchre and seven-up to strengthen the mind—and played them with cards so greasy and defaced that only a whole summer's acquaintance with them could enable the student to tell the ace of clubs from the jack of diamonds.

We never slept in our "house." It never recurred to us, for one thing; and besides, it was built to hold the ground, and that was enough. We did not wish to strain it.

By and by our provisions began to run short, and we went back to the old camp and laid in a new supply. We were gone all day, and reached home again about nightfall, pretty tired and hungry. While Johnny was carrying the main bulk of the provisions up to our "house" for future use, I took the loaf of bread, some slices of bacon, and the coffee-pot, ashore, set them down by a tree, lit a fire, and went back to the boat to get the frying pan. While I was at this, I heard a shout from Johnny, and looking up I saw that my fire was galloping all over the premises!

Johnny was on the other side of it. He had to run through the flames to get to the lake shore, and then we stood helpless and watched the devastation.

The ground was deeply carpeted with dry pine-needles, and the fire touched them off as if they were gunpowder. It was wonderful to see with what fierce speed the tall sheet of flame traveled! My coffee-pot was gone, and everything with it. In a minute and a half

FIRE AT LAKE TAHOE.

the fire seized upon a dense growth of dry manzanita chaparral six or eight feet high, and then the roaring and popping and crackling was something terrific. We were driven to the boat by the intense heat, and there we remained, spell-bound.

Within half an hour all before us was a tossing, blinding tempest of flame! It went surging up adjacent ridges—surmounted them and disappeared in the cañons beyond—burst into view upon higher and farther ridges, presently—shed a grander illumination abroad, and dove again—flamed out again, directly, higher and still higher up the mountain side—threw out skirmishing parties of fire here and there, and sent them trailing their crimson spirals away among remote ramparts and ribs and gorges, till as far as the eye could reach the lofty mountain-fronts were webbed as it were with a tangled net-work of red lava streams. Away across the water the crags and domes were lit with a ruddy glare, and the firmament above was a reflected hell!

Every feature of the spectacle was repeated in the glowing mirror of the lake! Both pictures were sublime, both were beautiful; but that in the lake had a bewildering richness about it that enchanted the eye and held it with the stronger fascination.

We sat absorbed and motionless through four long hours. We never thought of supper, and never felt fatigue. But at eleven o'clock the conflagration had traveled beyond our range of vision, and then darkness stole down upon the landscape again.

Hunger asserted itself now, but there was nothing to eat. The provisions were all cooked, no doubt, but we did not go to see. We were homeless wanderers again, without any property. Our fence was gone, our house burned down; no insurance. Our pine forest was well scorched, the dead trees all burned up, and our broad acres of manzanita swept away. Our blankets were on our usual sand-bed, however, and so we lay down and went to sleep. The next morning we started back to the old camp, but while out a long way from shore, so great a storm came up that we dared not try to land. So I baled out the seas we shipped, and Johnny pulled heavily through the billows till we had reached a point three or four miles beyond the camp. The storm was increasing, and it became evident that it was better to take the hazard of beaching the boat than go down in a hundred fathoms of water; so we ran in, with tall whitecaps following, and I sat down in the stern-sheets and pointed her head on to the shore. The instant the bow struck, a wave came over the stern that washed crew and cargo ashore, and saved a deal of trouble. We shivered in the lee of a boulder all the rest of the day, and froze all the night through. In the morning the tempest had gone down, and we paddled down to the camp without any unnecessary delay. We were so starved that we ate up the rest of the Brigade's provisions, and then set out to Carson to tell them about it and ask their forgiveness. It was accorded, upon payment of damages.

We made many trips to the lake after that, and had many a hair-breadth escape and blood-curdling adventure which will never be recorded in any history.

CHAPTER 24

I RESOLVED to have a horse to ride. I had never seen such wild, free, magnificent horsemanship outside of a circus as these picturesquely-clad Mexicans, Californians and Mexicanized Americans displayed in Carson streets every day. How they rode! Leaning just gently forward out of the perpendicular, easy and nonchalant, with broad slouch-hat brim blown square up in front, and long *riata* swinging above the head, they swept through the town like the wind! The next minute they were only a sailing puff of dust on the far desert. If they trotted, they sat up gallantly and gracefully, and seemed part of the horse; did not go jiggering up and down after the silly Miss-Nancy fashion of the riding-schools. I had quickly learned to tell a horse from a cow, and was full of anxiety to learn more. I was resolved to buy a horse.

While the thought was rankling in my mind, the auctioneer came skurrying through the plaza on a black beast that had as many humps and corners on him as a dromedary, and was necessarily uncomely; but he was "going, going, at twenty-two!—horse, saddle and bridle at twenty-two dollars, gentlemen!" and I could hardly resist.

A man whom I did not know (he turned out to be the auctioneer's brother) noticed the wistful look in my eye, and observed that that was a very remarkable horse to be going at such a price; and added that the saddle alone was worth the money. It was a Spanish saddle, with ponderous *tapaderas,* and furnished with the ungainly sole-leather covering with the unspellable name. I said I had half a notion to bid. Then this keen-eyed person appeared to me to be "taking my measure;" but I dismissed the suspicion when he spoke, for his manner was full of guileless candor and truthfulness. Said he:

"I know that horse—know him well. You are a stranger, I take it, and so you might think he was an American horse, maybe, but I assure you he is not. He is nothing of the kind; but—excuse my speaking in a low voice, other people being near—he is, without the shadow of a doubt, a Genuine Mexican Plug!"

"YOU MIGHT THINK HE WAS AN AMERICAN HORSE."

I did not know what a Genuine Mexican Plug was, but there was something about this man's way of saying it, that made me swear inwardly that I would own a Genuine Mexican Plug, or die.

"Has he any other—er—advantages?" I inquired, suppressing what eagerness I could.

He hooked his forefinger in the pocket of my army-shirt, led me to one side, and breathed in my ear impressively these words:

"He can out-buck anything in America!"

"Going, going, going—at *twent–ty*-four dollars and a half, gen—"

"Twenty-seven!" I shouted, in a frenzy.

"And sold!" said the auctioneer, and passed over the Genuine Mexican Plug to me.

I could scarcely contain my exultation. I paid the money, and put the animal in a neighboring livery-stable to dine and rest himself.

In the afternoon I brought the creature into the plaza, and certain citizens held him by the head, and others by the tail, while I mounted him. As soon as they let go, he placed all his feet in a bunch together, lowered his back, and then suddenly arched it upward, and shot me straight into the air a matter of three or four feet! I came as straight down again, lit in the saddle, went instantly

UNEXPECTED ELEVATION.

up again, came down almost on the high pommel, shot up again, and came down on the horse's neck—all in the space of three or four seconds. Then he rose and stood almost straight up on his hind feet, and I, clasping his lean neck desperately, slid back into the saddle, and held on. He came down, and immediately hoisted his heels into the air, delivering a vicious kick at the sky, and stood on his forefeet. And then down he came once more, and began the original exercise of shooting me straight up again. The third time I went up I heard a stranger say:

"Oh, *don't* he buck, though!"

While I was up, somebody struck the horse a sounding thwack with a leathern strap, and when I arrived again the Genuine Mexican Plug was not there. A Californian youth chased him up and caught him, and asked if he might have a ride. I granted him that luxury. He mounted the Genuine, got lifted into the air once, but sent his spurs home as he descended, and the horse darted away like a telegram. He soared over three fences like a bird, and disappeared down the road toward the Washoe Valley.

I sat down on a stone, with a sigh, and by a natural impulse one of my hands sought my forehead, and the other the base of my stomach. I believe I never appreciated, till then, the poverty of the human machinery—for I still needed a hand or two to place elsewhere. Pen cannot describe how I was jolted up. Imagination cannot conceive how disjointed I was—how internally, externally and

UNIVERSALLY UNSETTLED.

universally I was unsettled, mixed up and ruptured. There was a sympathetic crowd around me, though.

One elderly-looking comforter said:

"Stranger, you've been taken in. Everybody in this camp knows that horse. Any child, any Injun, could have told you that he'd buck; he is the very worst devil to buck on the continent of America. You hear *me.* I'm Curry. *Old* Curry. Old *Abe* Curry. And moreover, he is a simon-pure, out-and-out, genuine d—d Mexican plug, and an uncommon mean one at that, too. Why, you turnip, if you had laid low and kept dark, there's chances to buy an *American* horse for mighty little more than you paid for that bloody old foreign relic."

I gave no sign; but I made up my mind that if the auctioneer's brother's funeral took place while I was in the Territory I would postpone all other recreations and attend it.

After a gallop of sixteen miles the Californian youth and the Genuine Mexican Plug came tearing into town again, shedding foam-flakes like the spume-spray that drives before a typhoon, and, with one final skip over a wheelbarrow and a Chinaman, cast anchor in front of the "ranch."

Such panting and blowing! Such spreading and contracting of the red equine nostrils, and glaring of the wild equine eye! But was the imperial beast subjugated? Indeed he was not. His lordship the Speaker of the House thought he was, and mounted him to go down to the Capitol; but the first dash the creature made was over

RIDING THE PLUG.

a pile of telegraph poles half as high as a church; and his time to the Capitol—one mile and three-quarters—remains unbeaten to this day. But then he took an advantage—he left out the mile, and only did the three-quarters. That is to say, he made a straight cut across lots, preferring fences and ditches to a crooked road; and when the Speaker got to the Capitol he said he had been in the air so much he felt as if he had made the trip on a comet.

In the evening the Speaker came home afoot for exercise, and got the Genuine towed back behind a quartz wagon. The next day I loaned the animal to the Clerk of the House to go down to the

WANTED EXERCISE.

Dana silver mine, six miles, and *he* walked back for exercise, and got the horse towed. Everybody I loaned him to always walked back; they never could get enough exercise any other way. Still, I continued to loan him to anybody who was willing to borrow him, my idea being to get him crippled, and throw him on the borrower's hands, or killed, and make the borrower pay for him. But somehow nothing ever happened to him. He took chances that no other horse ever took and survived, but he always came out safe. It was his daily habit to try experiments that had always before been considered impossible, but he always got through. Sometimes he miscalculated a little, and did not get his rider through intact, but *he* always got through himself. Of course I had tried to sell him; but that was a stretch of simplicity which met with little sympathy. The auctioneer stormed up and down the streets on him for four days, dispersing the populace, interrupting business, and destroying children, and never got a bid—at least never any but the eighteen-dollar one he hired a notoriously substanceless bummer to make. The people only smiled pleasantly, and restrained their desire to buy, if they had any. Then the auctioneer brought in his bill, and I withdrew the horse from the market. We tried to trade him off at private vendue next, offering him at a sacrifice for second-hand tombstones, old iron, temperance tracts—any kind of property. But holders were stiff, and we retired from the market again. I never tried to ride the horse any more. Walking was good enough exercise for a man like me, that had nothing the matter with him except ruptures, internal injuries, and such things. Finally I tried to *give* him away. But it was a failure. Parties said earthquakes were handy enough on the Pacific coast—they did not wish to own one. As a last resort I offered him to the Governor for the use of the "Brigade." His face lit up eagerly at first, but toned down again, and he said the thing would be too palpable.

Just then the livery-stable man brought in his bill for six weeks' keeping—stall-room for the horse, fifteen dollars; hay for the horse, two hundred and fifty! The Genuine Mexican Plug had eaten a ton of the article, and the man said he would have eaten a hundred if he had let him.

I will remark here, in all seriousness, that the regular price of hay during that year and a part of the next was really two hundred and fifty dollars a ton. During a part of the previous year it had sold at five hundred a ton, in gold, and during the winter before that there was such scarcity of the article that in several instances small quantities had brought eight hundred dollars a ton in coin!

The consequence might be guessed without my telling it: people turned their stock loose to starve, and before the spring arrived Carson and Eagle Valleys were almost literally carpeted with their carcases! Any old settler there will verify these statements.

I managed to pay the livery bill, and that same day I gave the Genuine Mexican Plug to a passing Arkansas emigrant whom fortune delivered into my hand. If this ever meets his eye, he will doubtless remember the donation.

Now whoever has had the luck to ride a real Mexican plug will recognize the animal depicted in this chapter, and hardly consider him exaggerated—but the uninitiated will feel justified in regarding his portrait as a fancy sketch, perhaps.

CHAPTER 25

Originally, Nevada was a part of Utah and was called Carson County; and a pretty large county it was, too. Certain of its valleys produced no end of hay, and this attracted small colonies of Mormon stock-raisers and farmers to them. A few orthodox Americans straggled in from California, but no love was lost between the two classes of colonists. There was little or no friendly intercourse; each party staid to itself. The Mormons were largely in the majority, and had the additional advantage of being peculiarly under the protection of the Mormon government of the Territory. Therefore they could afford to be distant, and even peremptory toward their neighbors. One of the traditions of Carson Valley illustrates the condition of things that prevailed at the time I speak of. The hired girl of one of the American families was Irish, and a Catholic; yet it was noted with surprise that she was the only person outside of the Mormon ring who could get favors from the Mormons. She asked kindnesses of them often, and always got them. It was a mystery to everybody. But one day as she was passing out at the door, a large bowie knife dropped from under her apron, and when her mistress asked for an explanation she observed that she was going out to "borry a wash-tub from the Mormons!"

In 1858 silver lodes were discovered in "Carson County," and then the aspect of things changed. Californians began to flock in, and the American element was soon in the majority. Allegiance to Brigham Young and Utah was renounced, and a temporary Territorial government for "Washoe" was instituted by the citizens. Gov. Roop was the first and only chief magistrate of it. In due course of time Congress passed a bill to organize "Nevada Territory," and President Lincoln sent out Gov. Nye to supplant Roop.

At this time the population of the Territory was about twelve or fifteen thousand, and rapidly increasing. Silver mines were being vigorously developed and silver mills erected. Business of all kinds was active and prosperous and growing more so day by day.

BORROWING MADE EASY.

The people were glad to have a legitimately constituted government, but did not particularly enjoy having strangers from distant States put in authority over them—a sentiment that was natural enough. They thought the officials should have been chosen from among themselves—from among prominent citizens who had earned a right to such promotion, and who would be in sympathy with the populace and likewise thoroughly acquainted with the needs of the Territory. They were right in viewing the matter thus, without doubt. The new officers were "emigrants," and that was no title to anybody's affection or admiration either.

The new government was received with considerable coolness. It was not only a foreign intruder, but a poor one. It was not even worth plucking—except by the smallest of small-fry office-seekers and such. Everybody knew that Congress had appropriated only twenty thousand dollars a year in greenbacks for its support—about money enough to run a quartz mill a month. And everybody knew, also, that the first year's money was still in Washington, and that the getting hold of it would be a tedious and difficult process. Carson City was too wary and too wise to open up a credit account with the imported bantling with anything like indecent haste.

There is something solemnly funny about the struggles of a new-born Territorial government to get a start in this world. Ours had a trying time of it. The Organic Act and the "instructions" from the State Department commanded that a legislature should be elected at such-and-such a time, and its sittings inaugurated at such-and-such a date. It was easy to get legislators, even at three dollars a day, although board was four dollars and fifty cents, for distinction has its charm in Nevada as well as elsewhere, and there were plenty of patriotic souls out of employment; but to get a legislative hall for them to meet in was another matter altogether. Carson blandly declined to give a room rent-free, or let one to the government on credit.

FREE RIDES.

But when Curry heard of the difficulty, he came forward, solitary and alone, and shouldered the Ship of State over the bar and got her afloat again. I refer to "Curry—*Old* Curry—Old *Abe* Curry." But for him the legislature would have been obliged to sit in the desert. He offered his large stone building just outside the capital limits, rent-free, and it was gladly accepted. Then he built a horse-railroad from town to the Capitol, and carried the legislators gratis. He also furnished pine benches and chairs for the legislature, and covered the floors with clean saw-dust by way of carpet and spittoon combined. But for Curry the government would have died in its tender infancy. A canvas partition to separate the Senate from the House of Representatives was put up by the Secretary, at a cost of three dollars and forty cents, but the United States declined to pay for it. Upon being reminded that the "instructions" permitted the payment of a liberal rent for a legislative hall, and that that money was saved to the country by Mr. Curry's generosity, the United States said that did not alter the matter, and the three dollars and forty cents would be subtracted from the Secretary's eighteen-hundred-dollar salary—and it *was!*

The matter of printing was from the beginning an interesting feature of the new government's difficulties. The Secretary was sworn to obey his volume of written "instructions," and these commanded him to do two certain things without fail, viz.:

1. Get the House and Senate journals printed; and,
2. For this work, pay one dollar and fifty cents per "thousand" for composition, and one dollar and fifty cents per "token" for press-work, in greenbacks.

It was easy to swear to do these two things, but it was entirely impossible to do more than one of them. When greenbacks had gone down to forty cents on the dollar, the prices regularly charged everybody by printing establishments were one dollar and fifty cents per "thousand" and one dollar and fifty cents per "token," in *gold.* The "instructions" commanded that the Secretary regard a paper dollar issued by the government as equal to any other dollar issued by the government. Hence the printing of the journals was discontinued. Then the United States sternly rebuked the Secretary for disregarding the "instructions," and warned him to correct his ways. Wherefore he got some printing done, forwarded the bill to Washington with full exhibits of the high prices of things in the Territory, and called attention to a printed market report wherein it would be observed that even hay was two hundred and fifty dollars a ton. The United States responded by subtracting the printing-bill from the Secretary's suffering salary—and moreover remarked with dense gravity that he would find nothing in his "instructions" requiring him to purchase hay!

Nothing in this world is palled in such impenetrable obscurity as a U. S. Treasury Comptroller's understanding. The very fires of the hereafter could get up nothing more than a fitful glimmer in it. In the days I speak of he never could be made to comprehend why it was that twenty thousand dollars would not go as far in Nevada, where all commodities ranged at an enormous figure, as it would in the other Territories, where exceeding cheapness was the rule. He was an officer who looked out for the little expenses all the time. The Secretary of the Territory kept his office in his bedroom, as I before remarked; and he charged the United States no rent, although his "instructions" provided for that item and he could have justly taken advantage of it (a thing which I would have done with more than lightning promptness if I had been Secretary myself). But the United States never applauded this devotion. Indeed, I think my country was ashamed to have so improvident a person in its employ.

Those "instructions" (we used to read a chapter from them every morning, as intellectual gymnastics, and a couple of chapters in Sunday school every Sabbath, for they treated of all subjects under the sun and had much valuable religious matter in them along with the other statistics) those "instructions" commanded that pen-knives, envelops, pens and writing-paper be furnished the members of the legislature. So the Secretary made the purchase and the distribution. The knives cost three dollars apiece. There was one too many, and the Secretary gave it to the Clerk of the House of Representatives. The United States said the Clerk of the House was not a "member" of the legislature, and took that three dollars out of the Secretary's salary, as usual.

White men charged three or four dollars a "load" for sawing up stove-wood. The Secretary was sagacious enough to know that the United States would never pay any such price as that; so he got an Indian to saw up a load of office wood at one dollar and a half. He made out the usual voucher, but signed no name to it—simply appended a note explaining that an Indian had done the work, and had done it in a very capable and satisfactory way, but could not sign the voucher owing to lack of ability in the necessary direction. The Secretary had to pay that dollar and a half. He thought the United States would admire both his economy and his honesty in getting the work done at half price and not putting a pretended Indian's signature to the voucher, but the United States did not see it in that light. The United States was too much accustomed to employing dollar-and-a-half thieves in all manner of official capacities to regard his explanation of the voucher as having any foundation in fact.

But the next time the Indian sawed wood for us I taught him to make a cross at the bottom of the voucher—it looked like a cross that had been drunk a year—and then I "witnessed" it and it went through all right. The United States never said a word. I was sorry

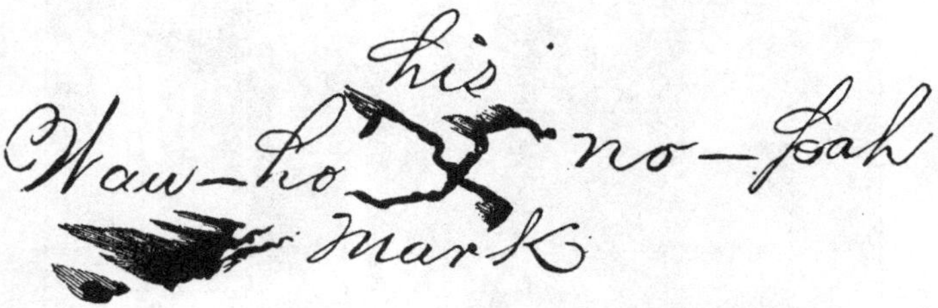

SATISFACTORY VOUCHER.

I had not made the voucher for a thousand loads of wood instead of one. The government of my country snubs honest simplicity but fondles artistic villainy, and I think I might have developed into a very capable pickpocket if I had remained in the public service a year or two.

That was a fine collection of sovereigns, that first Nevada legislature. They levied taxes to the amount of thirty or forty thousand dollars and ordered expenditures to the extent of about a million.

Yet they had their little periodical explosions of economy like all other bodies of the kind. A member proposed to save three dollars a day to the nation by dispensing with the Chaplain. And yet that short-sighted man needed the Chaplain more than any other member, perhaps, for he generally sat with his feet on his desk, eating raw turnips, during the morning prayer.

The legislature sat sixty days, and passed private toll-road fran-

NEEDS PRAYING FOR.

chises all the time. When they adjourned it was estimated that every citizen owned about three franchises, and it was believed that unless Congress gave the Territory another degree of longitude there would not be room enough to accommodate the toll-roads. The ends of them were hanging over the boundary line everywhere like a fringe.

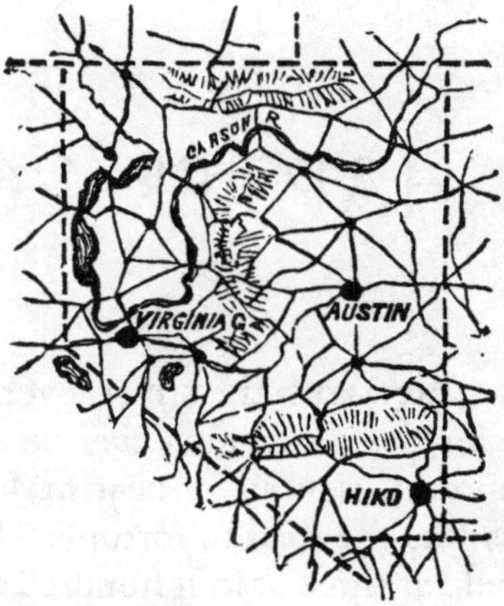

MAP OF TOLL-ROADS.

The fact is, the freighting business had grown to such important proportions that there was nearly as much excitement over suddenly acquired toll-road fortunes as over the wonderful silver mines.

CHAPTER 26

By and by I was smitten with the silver fever. "Prospecting parties" were leaving for the mountains every day, and discovering and taking possession of rich silver-bearing lodes and ledges of quartz. Plainly this was the road to fortune. The great "Gould & Curry" mine was held at three or four hundred dollars a foot when we arrived; but in two months it had sprung up to eight hundred. The "Ophir" had been worth only a mere trifle, a year gone by, and now it was selling at nearly *four thousand dollars a foot!* Not a mine could be named that had not experienced an astonishing advance in value within a short time. Everybody was talking about these marvels. Go where you would, you heard nothing else, from morning till far into the night. Tom So-and-so had sold out of the "Amanda Smith" for forty thousand dollars—hadn't a cent when he "took up" the ledge six months ago. John Jones had sold half his interest in the "Bald Eagle and Mary Ann" for sixty-five thousand dollars, gold coin, and gone to the States for his family. The widow Brewster had "struck it rich" in the "Golden Fleece" and sold ten feet for eighteen thousand dollars—hadn't money enough to buy a crape bonnet when Sing-Sing Tommy killed her husband at Baldy Johnson's wake last spring. The "Last Chance" had found a "clay casing" and knew they were "right on the ledge"—consequence, "feet" that went begging yesterday were worth a brick house apiece to-day, and seedy owners who could not get trusted for a drink at any bar in the country yesterday were roaring drunk on champagne to-day and had hosts of warm personal friends in a town where they had forgotten how to bow or shake hands from long-continued want of practice. Johnny Morgan, a common loafer, had gone to sleep in the gutter and waked up worth a hundred thousand dollars in consequence of the decision in the "Lady

Franklin and Rough and Ready" lawsuit. And so on—day in and day out the talk pelted our ears and the excitement waxed hotter and hotter around us.

I would have been more or less than human if I had not gone mad like the rest. Cart-loads of solid silver bricks, as large as pigs of lead, were arriving from the mills every day, and such sights as that

UNLOADING SILVER BRICKS.

gave substance to the wild talk about me. I succumbed and grew as frenzied as the craziest.

Every few days news would come of the discovery of a bran-new mining region; immediately the papers would teem with accounts of its richness, and away the surplus population would scamper to take possession. By the time I was fairly inoculated with the disease, "Esmeralda" had just had a run and "Humboldt" was beginning to shriek for attention. "Humboldt! Humboldt!" was the new cry, and straightway Humboldt, the newest of the new, the richest of the rich, the most marvelous of the marvelous discoveries in silver-land, was occupying two columns of the public prints to "Esmeralda's" one. I was just on the point of starting to Esmeralda, but turned with the tide and got ready for Humboldt. That the reader may see what moved me, and what would as surely have moved him had he been there, I insert here one of the newspaper letters of the day. It and several other letters from the same calm hand were the main means of converting me. I shall not garble the extract, but put it in just as it appeared in the *Daily Territorial Enterprise:*

But what about our mines? I shall be candid with you. I shall express an honest opinion, based upon a thorough examination. Humboldt county is the richest mineral region upon God's footstool. Each mountain range is gorged with the precious ores. Humboldt is the true Golconda.

The other day an assay of mere *croppings* yielded exceeding *four thousand dollars to the ton.* A week or two ago an assay of just such surface developments made returns of *seven thousand* dollars to the ton. Our mountains are full of rambling prospectors. Each day and almost every hour reveals new and more startling evidences of the profuse and intensified wealth of our favored county. The metal is not silver alone. There are distinct ledges of auriferous ore. A late discovery plainly evinces cinnabar. The coarser metals are in gross abundance. Lately evidences of bituminous coal have been detected. My theory has ever been that coal is a ligneous formation. I told Col. Whitman, in times past, that the neighborhood of Dayton (Nevada) betrayed no present or previous manifestations of a ligneous foundation, and that hence I had no confidence in his lauded coal mines. I repeated the same doctrine to the exultant coal discoverers of Humboldt. I talked with my friend Captain Burch on the subject. My pyrrhonism vanished upon his statement that in the very region referred to he had seen petrified trees of the length of two hundred feet. Then is the fact established that huge forests once cast their grim shadows over this remote section. I am firm in the coal faith. Have no fears of the mineral resources of Humboldt county. They are immense—incalculable.

Let me state one or two things which will help the reader to better comprehend certain items in the above. At this time, our near neighbor, Gold Hill, was the most successful silver mining locality in Nevada. It was from there that more than half the daily shipments of silver bricks came. "Very rich" (and scarce) Gold Hill ore yielded from a hundred to four hundred dollars to the ton; but the usual yield was only twenty to forty dollars per ton—that is to say, each hundred pounds of ore yielded from one dollar to two dollars. But the reader will perceive by the above extract, that in Humboldt from one-fourth to nearly half the mass was silver! That is to say, every one hundred pounds of the ore had from *two hundred* dollars up to about *three hundred and fifty* in it. Some days later this same correspondent wrote:

I have spoken of the vast and almost fabulous wealth of this region—it is incredible. The intestines of our mountains are gorged with precious ore to plethora. I have said that nature has so shaped our mountains as to furnish most excellent facilities for the working of our mines. I have also told you that the country about here is pregnant with the finest mill sites in the world. But what is the mining history of Humboldt? The Sheba mine is in the hands of energetic San Francisco capitalists. It would seem that the ore is combined with metals that render it difficult of reduction with our imperfect mountain machinery. The proprietors have combined the capital and labor hinted at in my exordium. They are toiling and probing. Their tunnel has reached the length of one hundred feet. From primal assays alone, coupled with the development of the mine and public confidence in the continuance of effort, the stock had reared itself to eight hundred dollars market value. I do not know that one ton of the ore has been converted into current metal. I do know that there are many lodes in this section that surpass the Sheba in primal assay value. Listen a moment to the calculations of the Sheba operators. They purpose transporting the ore concentrated to Europe. The conveyance from Star City (its locality) to Virginia City will cost seventy dollars per ton; from Virginia to San Francisco, forty dollars per ton; from thence to Liverpool, its destination, ten dollars per ton. Their idea is that its conglomerate metals will reimburse them their cost of original extraction, the price of transportation, and the expense of reduction, and that then a ton of the raw ore will net them

VIEW IN HUMBOLDT MOUNTAINS.

twelve hundred dollars. The estimate may be extravagant. Cut it in twain, and the product is enormous, far transcending any previous developments of our racy Territory.

A very common calculation is that many of our mines will yield five hundred dollars to the ton. Such fecundity throws the Gould & Curry, the Ophir and the Mexican, of your neighborhood, in the darkest shadow. I have given you the estimate of the value of a single developed mine. Its richness is indexed by its market valuation. The people of Humboldt county are *feet* crazy. As I write, our towns are near deserted. They look as languid as a consumptive girl. What has become of our sinewy and athletic fellow-citizens? They are coursing through ravines and over mountain tops. Their tracks are visible in every direction. Occasionally a horseman will dash among us. His steed betrays hard usage. He alights before his adobe dwelling, hastily exchanges courtesies with his townsmen, hurries to an assay office and from thence to the District Recorder's. In the morning, having renewed his provisional supplies, he is off again on his wild and unbeaten route. Why, the fellow numbers already his feet by the thousands. He is the horse-leech. He has the craving stomach of the shark or anaconda. He would conquer metallic worlds.

This was enough. The instant we had finished reading the above article, four of us decided to go to Humboldt. We commenced getting ready at once. And we also commenced upbraiding ourselves for not deciding sooner—for we were in terror lest all the rich mines would be found and secured before we got there, and we might have to put up with ledges that would not yield more than two or three hundred dollars a ton, maybe. An hour before, I would have felt opulent if I had owned ten feet in a Gold Hill mine whose ore produced twenty-five dollars to the ton; now I was already annoyed at the prospect of having to put up with mines the poorest of which would be a marvel in Gold Hill.

CHAPTER 27

HURRY, was the word! We wasted no time. Our party consisted of four persons—a blacksmith sixty years of age, two young lawyers, and myself. We bought a wagon and two miserable old horses. We put eighteen hundred pounds of provisions and mining tools in the wagon and drove out of Carson on a chilly December afternoon. The horses were so weak and old that we soon found that it would be better if one or two of us got out and walked. It was an improvement. Next, we found that it would be better if a third man got out. That was an improvement also. It was at this time that I volunteered to drive, although I had never driven a harnessed horse before and many a man in such a position would have felt fairly excused from such a responsibility. But in a little while it was found that it would be a fine thing if the driver got out and walked also. It was at this time that I resigned the position of driver, and never resumed it again. Within the hour, we found that it would not only be better, but was absolutely necessary, that we four, taking turns, two at a time, should put our hands against the end of

GOING TO HUMBOLDT.

the wagon and push it through the sand, leaving the feeble horses little to do but keep out of the way and hold up the tongue. Perhaps it is well for one to know his fate at first, and get reconciled to it. We had learned ours in one afternoon. It was plain that we had to walk through the sand and shove that wagon and those horses two hundred miles. So we accepted the situation, and from that time forth we never rode. More than that, we stood regular and nearly constant watches pushing up behind.

We made seven miles, and camped in the desert. Young Clagett (now member of Congress from Montana) unharnessed and fed and watered the horses; Oliphant and I cut sage-brush, built the fire and brought water to cook with; and old Mr. Ballou the blacksmith did the cooking. This division of labor, and this appointment, was adhered to throughout the journey. We had no tent, and so we slept under our blankets in the open plain. We were so tired that we slept soundly.

We were fifteen days making the trip—two hundred miles; thirteen, rather, for we lay by a couple of days, in one place, to let the horses rest. We could really have accomplished the journey in ten days if we had towed the horses behind the wagon, but we did not think of that until it was too late, and so went on shoving the horses and the wagon too when we might have saved half the labor. Parties who met us, occasionally, advised us to put the horses *in* the wagon, but Mr. Ballou, through whose iron-clad earnestness no sarcasm could pierce, said that that would not do, because the provisions were exposed and would suffer, the horses being "bituminous from long deprivation." The reader will excuse me from translating. What Mr. Ballou customarily meant, when he used a long word, was a secret between himself and his Maker. He was one of the best and kindest hearted men that ever graced a humble sphere of life. He was gentleness and simplicity itself—and unselfishness, too. Although he was more than twice as old as the eldest of us, he never gave himself any airs, privileges, or exemptions on that account. He did a *young* man's share of the work; and did his share of conversing and entertaining from the general stand-point of *any* age—not from the arrogant, overawing summit-height of sixty years. His one striking peculiarity was his Partingtonian fashion of loving and using big words *for their own sakes,* and independent of any bearing they might have upon the thought he was purposing to convey. He always let his ponderous syllables fall with an easy unconsciousness that left them wholly without offensiveness. In truth his air was so natural and so simple that one was always catching himself accepting his stately sentences as meaning something, when they really meant nothing in the world. If a word was long and grand and resonant, that was sufficient to win the old man's love, and he would drop that word into the most out-of-the-way place in a sentence or a subject, and be as pleased with it as if it were perfectly luminous with meaning.

We four always spread our common stock of blankets together on the frozen ground, and slept side by side; and finding that our foolish, long-legged hound pup had a deal of animal heat in him, Oliphant got to admitting him to the bed, between himself and

BALLOU'S BEDFELLOW.

Mr. Ballou, hugging the dog's warm back to his breast and finding great comfort in it. But in the night the pup would get stretchy and brace his feet against the old man's back and shove, grunting complacently the while; and now and then, being warm and snug, grateful and happy, he would paw the old man's back simply in excess of comfort; and at yet other times he would dream of the chase and in his sleep tug at the old man's back hair and bark in his ear. The old gentleman complained mildly about these familiarities, at last, and when he got through with his statement he said that such a dog as that was not a proper animal to admit to bed with tired men, because he was "so meretricious in his movements and so organic in his emotions." We turned the dog out.

It was a hard, wearing, toilsome journey, but it had its bright side; for after each day was done and our wolfish hunger appeased with a hot supper of fried bacon, bread, molasses and black coffee, the pipe-smoking, song-singing and yarn-spinning around the evening camp-fire in the still solitudes of the desert was a happy, care-free sort of recreation that seemed the very summit and culmination of earthly luxury. It is a kind of life that has a potent charm for all men, whether city or country-bred. We are descended from desert-lounging Arabs, and countless ages of growth toward perfect civilization have failed to root out of us the nomadic instinct. We all confess to a gratified thrill at the thought of "camping out."

PLEASURES OF CAMPING OUT.

Once we made twenty-five miles in a day, and once we made forty miles (through the Great American Desert), and ten miles beyond—fifty in all—in twenty-three hours, without halting to eat, drink or rest. To stretch out and go to sleep, even on stony and frozen ground, after pushing a wagon and two horses fifty miles, is a delight so supreme that for the moment it almost seems cheap at the price.

We camped two days in the neighborhood of the "Sink of the Humboldt." We tried to use the strong alkaline water of the Sink, but it would not answer. It was like drinking lye, and not weak lye, either. It left a taste in the mouth, bitter and every way execrable, and a burning in the stomach that was very uncomfortable. We put molasses in it, but that helped it very little; we added a pickle, yet the alkali was the prominent taste, and so it was unfit for drinking. The coffee we made of this water was the meanest compound man has yet invented. It was really viler to the taste than the uname-liorated water itself. Mr. Ballou, being the architect and builder of the beverage, felt constrained to endorse and uphold it, and so drank half a cup, by little sips, making shift to praise it faintly the while, but finally threw out the remainder, and said frankly it was "too technical for *him*."

But presently we found a spring of fresh water, convenient, and then, with nothing to mar our enjoyment, and no stragglers to interrupt it, we entered into our rest.

CHAPTER 28

After leaving the Sink, we traveled along the Humboldt river a little way. People accustomed to the monster mile-wide Mississippi, grow accustomed to associating the term "river" with a high degree of watery grandeur. Consequently, such people feel rather disappointed when they stand on the shores of the Humboldt or the Carson and find that a "river" in Nevada is a sickly rivulet which is just the counterpart of the Erie Canal in all respects save that the canal is twice as long and four times as deep. One of the pleasantest and most invigorating exercises one can contrive is to run and jump across the Humboldt river till he is overheated, and then drink it dry.

On the fifteenth day we completed our march of two hundred miles and entered Unionville, Humboldt County, in the midst of a driving snow-storm. Unionville consisted of eleven cabins and a liberty pole. Six of the cabins were strung along one side of a deep cañon, and the other five faced them. The rest of the landscape was made up of bleak mountain walls that rose so high into the sky from both sides of the cañon that the village was left, as it were, far down in the bottom of a crevice. It was always daylight on the mountain-tops a long time before the darkness lifted and revealed Unionville.

We built a small, rude cabin in the side of the crevice and roofed it with canvas, leaving a corner open to serve as a chimney, through which the cattle used to tumble occasionally, at night, and mash our furniture and interrupt our sleep. It was very cold weather and fuel was scarce. Indians brought brush and bushes several miles on their backs; and when we could catch a laden Indian it was well—and when we could not (which was the rule, not the exception), we shivered and bore it.

I confess, without shame, that I expected to find masses of silver lying all about the ground. I expected to see it glittering in the sun on the mountain summits. I said nothing about this, for some instinct told me that I might possibly have an exaggerated idea about it, and so if I betrayed my thought I might bring derision upon myself. Yet I was as perfectly satisfied in my own mind as I could be of anything, that I was going to gather up, in a day or two, or at furthest a week or two, silver enough to make me satisfactorily wealthy—and so my fancy was already busy with plans for spending this money. The first opportunity that offered, I sauntered carelessly away from the cabin, keeping an eye on the other boys, and stopping and contemplating the sky when they seemed to be observing me; but as soon as the coast was manifestly clear, I fled away as guiltily as a thief might have done and never halted till I was far beyond sight and call. Then I began my search with a feverish excitement that was brim full of expectation—almost of certainty. I crawled about the ground, seizing and examining bits of stone, blowing the dust from them or rubbing them on my clothes, and then peering at them with anxious hope. Presently I found a bright fragment and my heart bounded! I hid behind a boulder and polished it and scrutinized it with a nervous eagerness and a delight that was more pronounced than absolute certainty itself could have afforded. The more I examined the fragment the more I was convinced that I had found the door to fortune. I marked the spot and carried away my specimen. Up and down the rugged mountain side I searched, with always increasing interest and always augmenting gratitude that I had come to Humboldt and come in time. Of all the experiences of my life, this secret search among the hidden treasures of silver-land was the nearest to unmarred ecstasy. It was a delirious revel. By and by, in the bed of a shallow rivulet, I found a deposit of shining yellow scales, and my breath almost forsook me! A gold mine, and in my simplicity I had been content with vulgar silver! I was so excited that I half believed my overwrought imagination was deceiving me. Then a fear came upon me that people might be observing me and would guess my secret. Moved by this thought, I made a circuit of the place, and ascended a knoll to reconnoitre. Solitude. No creature was near. Then I returned to my mine, fortifying myself against possible disappointment, but my fears were groundless—the shining scales

THE SECRET SEARCH.

were still there. I set about scooping them out, and for an hour I toiled down the windings of the stream and robbed its bed. But at last the descending sun warned me to give up the quest, and I turned homeward laden with wealth. As I walked along I could not help smiling at the thought of my being so excited over my fragment of silver when a nobler metal was almost under my nose. In this little time the former had so fallen in my estimation that once or twice I was on the point of throwing it away.

The boys were as hungry as usual, but I could eat nothing. Neither could I talk. I was full of dreams and far away. Their conversation interrupted the flow of my fancy somewhat, and annoyed me a little, too. I despised the sordid and commonplace things they talked about. But as they proceeded, it began to amuse me. It grew to be rare fun to hear them planning their poor little economies and sighing over possible privations and distresses when a gold mine, all our own, lay within sight of the cabin and I could point it out at any moment. Smothered hilarity began to oppress me, presently. It was hard to resist the impulse to burst out with exultation and reveal everything; but I did resist. I said within myself that I would filter the great news through my lips calmly and be serene as a summer morning while I watched its effect in their faces. I said:

"Where have you all been?"

"Prospecting."

"What did you find?"

"Nothing."

"Nothing? What do you think of the country?"

"Can't tell, yet," said Mr. Ballou, who was an old gold miner, and had likewise had considerable experience among the silver mines.

"Well, haven't you formed any sort of opinion?"

"Yes, a sort of a one. It's fair enough here, maybe, but overrated. Seven-thousand-dollar ledges are scarce, though. That Sheba may be rich enough, but we don't own it; and besides, the rock is so full of base metals that all the science in the world can't work it. We'll not starve, here, but we'll not get rich, I'm afraid."

"So you think the prospect is pretty poor?"

"No name for it!"

"Well, we'd better go back, hadn't we?"

"Oh, not yet—of course not. We'll try it a riffle, first."

"Suppose, now—this is merely a supposition, you know—suppose you could find a ledge that would yield, say, a hundred and fifty dollars a ton—would that satisfy you?"

"Try us once!" from the whole party.

"Or suppose—merely a supposition, of course—suppose you were to find a ledge that would yield two thousand dollars a ton—would *that* satisfy you?"

"Here—what do you mean? What are you coming at? Is there some mystery behind all this?"

"Never mind. I am not saying anything. You know perfectly well there are no rich mines here—of course you do. Because you have been around and examined for yourselves. Anybody would know that, that had been around. But just for the sake of argument, suppose—in a kind of general way—suppose some person were to tell you that two-thousand-dollar ledges were simply contemptible—contemptible, understand—and that right yonder in sight of this very cabin there were piles of pure gold and pure silver—oceans of it—enough to make you all rich in twenty-four hours! Come!"

"I should say he was as crazy as a loon!" said old Ballou, but wild with excitement, nevertheless.

"Gentlemen," said I, "I don't say anything—*I* haven't been around, you know, and of course don't know anything—but all I ask of you is to cast your eye on *that*, for instance, and tell me what you think of it!" and I tossed my treasure before them.

"CAST YOUR EYE ON *THAT!*"

There was an eager scramble for it, and a closing of heads together over it under the candle-light. Then old Ballou said:

"Think of it? I think it is nothing but a lot of granite rubbish and nasty glittering mica that isn't worth ten cents an acre!"

So vanished my dream. So melted my wealth away. So toppled my airy castle to the earth and left me stricken and forlorn.

Moralizing, I observed, then, that "all that glitters is not gold."

Mr. Ballou said I could go further than that, and lay it up among my treasures of knowledge, that *nothing* that glitters is gold. So I learned then, once for all, that gold in its native state is but dull, unornamental stuff, and that only low-born metals excite the admiration of the ignorant with an ostentatious glitter. However, like the rest of the world, I still go on underrating men of gold and glorifying men of mica. Commonplace human nature cannot rise above that.

CHAPTER 29

TRUE knowledge of the nature of silver mining came fast enough. We went out "prospecting" with Mr. Ballou. We climbed the mountain sides, and clambered among sage-brush, rocks and snow till we were ready to drop with exhaustion, but found no silver—nor yet any gold. Day after day we did this. Now and then we came upon holes burrowed a few feet into the declivities and apparently abandoned; and now and then we found one or two listless men still burrowing. But there was no appearance of silver. These holes were the beginnings of tunnels, and the purpose was to drive them hundreds of feet into the mountain, and some day tap the hidden ledge where the silver was. Some day! It seemed far enough away, and very hopeless and dreary. Day after day we toiled, and climbed and searched, and we younger partners grew sicker and still sicker of the promiseless toil. At last we halted under a beetling rampart of rock which projected from the earth high upon the mountain. Mr. Ballou broke off some fragments with a hammer, and examined them long and attentively with a small eye-glass; threw them away and broke off more; said this rock was quartz, and quartz was the sort of rock that contained silver. *Contained* it! I had thought that at least it would be caked on the outside of it like a kind of veneering. He still broke off pieces and critically examined them, now and then wetting the piece with his tongue and applying the glass. At last he exclaimed:

"We've got it!"

We were full of anxiety in a moment. The rock was clean and white, where it was broken, and across it ran a ragged thread of blue. He said that that little thread had silver in it, mixed with base metals, such as lead and antimony, and other rubbish, and that there was a speck or two of gold visible. After a great deal of effort we managed to discern some little fine yellow specks, and judged that a couple of tons of them massed together might make a gold dollar, possibly. We were not jubilant, but Mr. Ballou said

"WE'VE GOT IT!"

there were worse ledges in the world than that. He saved what he called the "richest" piece of the rock, in order to determine its value by the process called the "fire-assay." Then we named the mine "Monarch of the Mountains" (modesty of nomenclature is not a prominent feature in the mines), and Mr. Ballou wrote out and stuck up the following "notice," preserving a copy to be entered upon the books in the mining recorder's office in the town.

NOTICE.

We the undersigned claim three claims, of three hundred feet each (and one for discovery), on this silver-bearing quartz lead or lode, extending north and south from this notice, with all its dips, spurs, and angles, variations and sinuosities, together with fifty feet of ground on either side for working the same.

We put our names to it and tried to feel that our fortunes were made. But when we talked the matter all over with Mr. Ballou, we felt depressed and dubious. He said that this surface quartz was not all there was of our mine; but that the wall or ledge of rock called the "Monarch of the Mountains," extended down hundreds and hundreds of feet into the earth—he illustrated by saying it was like a curb-stone, and maintained a nearly uniform thickness—say twenty feet—away down into the bowels of the earth, and was perfectly distinct from the casing rock on each side of it; and that it kept to itself, and maintained its distinctive character always, no matter how deep it extended into the earth or how far it stretched itself through and across the hills and valleys. He said it might be a mile deep and ten miles long, for all we knew; and that wherever we bored into it above ground or below, we would find gold and silver in it, but no gold or silver in the meaner rock it was cased between. And he said that down in the great depths of the ledge was its richness, and the deeper it went the richer it grew. Therefore, instead of working here on the surface, we must either bore down into the rock with a shaft till we came to where it was rich—say a hundred feet or so—or else we must go down into the valley and bore a long tunnel into the mountain side and tap the ledge far under the earth. To do either was plainly the labor of months; for we could blast and bore only a few feet a day—some five or six. But this was not all. He said that after we got the ore out it must be hauled in wagons to a distant silver mill, ground up, and the silver extracted by a tedious and costly process. Our fortune seemed a century away!

But we went to work. We decided to sink a shaft. So, for a week we climbed the mountain, laden with picks, drills, gads, crowbars, shovels, cans of blasting powder and coils of fuse and strove with might and main. At first the rock was broken and loose and we dug it up with picks and threw it out with shovels, and the hole progressed very well. But the rock became more compact, presently, and gads and crowbars came into play. But shortly nothing could make an impression but blasting powder. That was the weariest work! One of us held the iron drill in its place and another would strike with an eight-pound sledge—it was like driving nails on a

INCIPIENT MILLIONAIRES.

large scale. In the course of an hour or two the drill would reach a depth of two or three feet, making a hole a couple of inches in diameter. We would put in a charge of powder, insert half a yard of fuse, pour in sand and gravel and ram it down, then light the fuse and run. When the explosion came and the rocks and smoke shot into the air, we would go back and find about a bushel of that hard, rebellious quartz jolted out. Nothing more. One week of this satisfied me. I resigned. Clagett and Oliphant followed. Our shaft was only twelve feet deep. We decided that a tunnel was the thing we wanted.

So we went down the mountain side and worked a week; at the end of which time we had blasted a tunnel about deep enough to hide a hogshead in, and judged that about nine hundred feet more of it would reach the ledge. I resigned again, and the other boys only held out one day longer. We decided that a tunnel was not what we wanted. We wanted a ledge that was already "developed." There were none in the camp.

We dropped the "Monarch" for the time being.

Meantime the camp was filling up with people, and there was a constantly growing excitement about our Humboldt mines. We fell victims to the epidemic and strained every nerve to acquire more "feet." We prospected and took up new claims, put "notices" on them and gave them grandiloquent names. We traded some of our "feet" for "feet" in other people's claims. In a little while we owned largely in the "Gray Eagle," the "Columbiana," the "Branch Mint," the "Maria Jane," the "Universe," the "Root-Hog-or-Die," the "Samson and Delilah," the "Treasure Trove," the "Golconda," the "Sultana," the "Boomerang," the "Great Republic," the "Grand Mogul," and fifty other "mines" that had never been molested by a shovel or scratched with a pick. We had not less than thirty thousand "feet" apiece in the "richest mines on earth" as the frenzied cant phrased it—and were in debt to the butcher. We were stark mad with excitement—drunk with happiness—smothered under mountains of prospective wealth—arrogantly compassionate toward the plodding millions who knew not our marvelous cañon—but our credit was not good at the grocer's.

It was the strangest phase of life one can imagine. It was a beggars' revel. There was nothing doing in the district—no mining—no milling—no productive effort—no income—and not enough money in the entire camp to buy a corner lot in an eastern village, hardly; and yet a stranger would have supposed he was walking among bloated millionaires. Prospecting parties swarmed out of town with the first flush of dawn, and swarmed in again at nightfall laden with spoil—rocks. Nothing but rocks. Every man's pockets were full of them; the floor of his cabin was littered with them; they were disposed in labeled rows on his shelves.

CHAPTER 30

I MET men at every turn who owned from one thousand to thirty thousand "feet" in undeveloped silver mines, every single foot of which they believed would shortly be worth from fifty to a thousand dollars—and as often as any other way they were men who had not twenty-five dollars in the world. Every man you met had his new mine to boast of, and his "specimens" ready; and if the opportunity offered, he would infallibly back you into a corner and offer as a favor to *you,* not to *him,* to part with just a few feet in the "Golden Age," or the "Sarah Jane," or some other unknown stack of croppings, for money enough to get a "square meal" with, as the phrase went. And you were never to reveal that he had made you the offer at such a ruinous price, for it was only out of friendship for you that he was willing to make the sacrifice. Then he would fish a piece of rock out of his pocket, and after looking mysteriously around as if he feared he might be waylaid and robbed if caught with such wealth in his possession, he would dab the rock against his tongue, clap an eye-glass to it, and exclaim:

"Look at that! Right there in that red dirt! See it? See the specks of gold? And the streak of silver? That's from the 'Uncle Abe.' There's a hundred thousand tons like that in sight! Right in sight, mind you! And when we get down on it and the ledge comes in solid, it will be the richest thing in the world! Look at the assay! I don't want you to believe *me*—look at the assay!"

Then he would get out a greasy sheet of paper which showed that the portion of rock assayed had given evidence of containing silver and gold in the proportion of so many hundreds or thousands of dollars to the ton. I little knew, then, that the custom was to hunt out the *richest* piece of rock and get it assayed! Very often, that piece, the size of a filbert, was the only fragment in a ton that had a particle of metal in it—and yet the assay made it pretend to represent the average value of the ton of rubbish it came from!

"DO YOU SEE IT?"

On such a system of assaying as that, the Humboldt world had gone crazy. On the authority of such assays its newspaper correspondents were frothing about rock worth four and seven thousand dollars a ton!

And does the reader remember, a few pages back, the calculations, of a quoted correspondent, whereby the ore is to be mined and shipped all the way to England, the metals extracted, and the gold and silver contents received back by the miners as clear profit, the copper, antimony and other things in the ore being sufficient to pay all the expenses incurred? Everybody's head was full of such "calculations" as those—such raving insanity, rather. Few people took *work* into their calculations—or outlay of money either; except the work and expenditures of other people.

We never touched our tunnel or our shaft again. Why? Because we judged that we had learned the *real* secret of success in silver mining—which was, *not* to mine the silver ourselves by the sweat of our brows and the labor of our hands, but to *sell* the ledges to the dull slaves of toil and let them do the mining!

Before leaving Carson, the Secretary and I had purchased "feet" from various Esmeralda stragglers. We had expected immediate returns of bullion, but were only afflicted with regular and constant "assessments" instead—demands for money wherewith to develop the said mines. These assessments had grown so oppressive that it seemed necessary to look into the matter personally. Therefore I projected a pilgrimage to Carson and thence to Esmeralda. I bought a horse and started, in company with Mr. Ballou and a gentleman named Ollendorff, a Prussian—not the party who has inflicted so much suffering on the world with his wretched foreign grammars, with their interminable repetitions of questions which never have occurred and are never likely to occur in any conversation among human beings. We rode through a snow-storm for two or three days, and arrived at "Honey Lake Smith's," a sort of isolated inn on the Carson river. It was a two-story log house situated on a small knoll in the midst of the vast basin or desert through which the sickly Carson winds its melancholy way. Close to the house were the Overland stage stables, built of sun-dried bricks. There was not another building within several leagues of the place. Toward sunset about twenty hay wagons arrived and camped around the house and all the teamsters came in to supper—a very, very rough set. There were one or two Overland stage-drivers there, also, and half a dozen vagabonds and stragglers; consequently the house was well crowded.

We walked out, after supper, and visited a small Indian camp in the vicinity. The Indians were in a great hurry about something, and were packing up and getting away as fast as they could. In their broken English they said, "By'm-by, heap water!" and by the help of signs made us understand that in their opinion a flood was coming. The weather was perfectly clear, and this was not the rainy season. There was about a foot of water in the insignificant river—or maybe two feet; the stream was not wider than a back alley in a village, and its banks were scarcely higher than a man's head. So,

FAREWELL SWEET RIVER.

where was the flood to come from? We canvassed the subject awhile and then concluded it was a ruse, and that the Indians had some better reason for leaving in a hurry than fears of a flood in such an exceedingly dry time.

At seven in the evening we went to bed in the second story—with our clothes on, as usual, and all three in the same bed, for every available space on the floors, chairs, etc., was in request, and even then there was barely room for the housing of the inn's guests. An hour later we were awakened by a great turmoil, and springing out of bed we picked our way nimbly among the ranks of snoring teamsters on the floor and got to the front windows of the long room. A glance revealed a strange spectacle, under the moonlight. The crooked Carson was full to the brim, and its waters were raging and foaming in the wildest way—sweeping around the sharp bends at a furious speed, and bearing on their surface a chaos of logs, brush and all sorts of rubbish. A depression, where its bed had once been, in other times, was already filling, and in one or two places the water was beginning to wash over the main bank. Men were flying hither and thither, bringing cattle and wagons close up to the house, for the spot of high ground on which it stood extended only some thirty feet in front and about a hundred in the rear. Close to the old river bed just spoken of, stood a little log stable, and in this our horses were lodged. While we looked, the waters increased so fast in this place that in a few minutes a torrent was roaring by the little stable and its margin encroaching steadily on the logs. We suddenly realized that this flood was not a mere holiday spectacle, but meant damage—and not only to the small log stable but to the Overland buildings close to the main river, for the waves had now come ashore and were creeping about

THE RESCUE.

the foundations and invading the great hay-corral adjoining. We ran down and joined the crowd of excited men and frightened animals. We waded knee-deep into the log stable, unfastened the horses and waded out almost *waist*-deep, so fast the waters increased. Then the crowd rushed in a body to the hay-corral and began to tumble down the huge stacks of baled hay and roll the bales up on the high ground by the house. Meantime it was discovered that Owens, an overland driver, was missing, and a man ran to the large stable, and wading in, boot-top deep, discovered him asleep in his bed, awoke him, and waded out again. But Owens was drowsy and resumed his nap; but only for a minute or two, for presently he turned in his bed, his hand dropped over the side and came in contact with the cold water! It was up level with the mattrass! He waded out, breast-deep, almost, and the next moment the sunburned bricks melted down like sugar and the big building crumbled to a ruin and was washed away in a twinkling.

At eleven o'clock only the roof of the little log stable was out of water, and our inn was on an island in mid-ocean. As far as the eye could reach, in the moonlight, there was no desert visible, but only a level waste of shining water. The Indians were true prophets, but how did they get their information? I am not able to answer the question.

We remained cooped up eight days and nights with that curious crew. Swearing, drinking and card playing were the order of the day, and occasionally a fight was thrown in for variety. Dirt and vermin—but let us forget those features; their profusion is simply inconceivable—it is better that they remain so.

There were two men—however, this chapter is long enough.

CHAPTER 31

There were two men in the company who caused me particular discomfort. One was a little Swede, about twenty-five years old, who knew only one song, and he was forever singing it. By day we were all crowded into one small, stifling bar-room, and so there was no escaping this person's music. Through all the profanity, whisky-guzzling, "old sledge" and quarreling, his monotonous song meandered with never a variation in its tiresome sameness, and it seemed to me, at last, that I would be content to die, in order to be rid of the torture. The other man was a stalwart ruffian called "Arkansas," who carried two revolvers in his belt and a bowie knife projecting from his boot, and who was always drunk and always suffering for a fight. But he was so feared, that nobody would accommodate him. He would try all manner of little wary ruses to entrap somebody into an offensive remark, and his face would light up now and then when he fancied he was fairly on the scent of a fight, but invariably his victim would elude his toils and then he would show a disappointment that was almost pathetic. The landlord, Johnson, was a meek, well-meaning fellow, and Arkansas fastened on him early, as a promising subject, and

"MR. ARKANSAS."

gave him no rest day or night, for a while. On the fourth morning, Arkansas got drunk and sat himself down to wait for an opportunity. Presently Johnson came in, just comfortably sociable with whisky, and said:

"I reckon the Pennsylvania 'lection—"

Arkansas raised his finger impressively and Johnson stopped. Arkansas rose unsteadily and confronted him. Said he:

"Wha-what do you know a-about Pennsylvania? Answer me that. Wha-what do you know 'bout Pennsylvania?"

"I was only goin' to say—"

"You was only goin' to *say. You* was! You was only goin' to say—*what* was you goin' to say? That's it! That's what *I* want to know. *I* want to know wha-what you (*'ic*) what you know about Pennsylvania, since you're makin' yourself so d—d free. Answer me that!"

"Mr. Arkansas, if you'd only let me—"

"Who's a henderin' you? Don't you insinuate nothing agin me!—don't you do it. Don't you come in here bullyin' around, and cussin' and goin' on like a lunatic—don't you do it. 'Coz *I* won't *stand* it. If fight's what you want, out with it! I'm your man! Out with it!"

Said Johnson, backing into a corner, Arkansas following, menacingly:

"Why, *I* never said nothing, Mr. Arkansas. You don't give a man no chance. I was only goin' to say that Pennsylvania was goin' to have an election next week—that was all—that was everything I was goin' to say—I wish I may never stir if it wasn't."

"Well then why d'n't you say it? What did you come swellin' around that way for, and tryin' to raise trouble?"

"Why *I* didn't come swellin' around, Mr. Arkansas—I just—"

"I'm a liar am I! Ger-reat Cæsar's ghost—"

"Oh, please, Mr. Arkansas, I never meant such a thing as that, I wish I may die if I did. All the boys will tell you that I've always spoke well of you, and respected you more'n any man in the house. Ask Smith. Ain't it so, Smith? Didn't I say, no longer ago than last night, that for a man that was a gentleman *all* the time and every way you took him, give me Arkansas? I'll leave it to any gentleman here if them warn't the very words I used. Come, now, Mr. Arkansas, le's take a drink—le's shake hands and take a drink. Come up—everybody! It's my treat. Come up, Bill, Tom, Bob, Scotty—come up. I want you all to take a drink with me and Arkansas—*old* Arkansas, I call him—bully old Arkansas. Gimme your hand agin. Look at him, boys—just take a *look* at him. Thar stands the whitest man in America!—and the man that denies it has got to fight *me,* that's all. Gimme that old flipper agin!"

They embraced, with drunken affection on the landlord's part and unresponsive toleration on the part of Arkansas, who, bribed by a drink, was disappointed of his prey once more. But the foolish landlord was so happy to have escaped butchery, that he went on talking when he ought to have marched himself out of danger. The consequence was that Arkansas shortly began to glower upon him dangerously, and presently said:

"Lan'lord, will you p-please make that remark over agin if you please?"

"I was a sayin' to Scotty that my father was up'ards of eighty year old when he died."

"Was that *all* that you said?"

"Yes, that was all."

"Didn't say nothing but that?"

"No—nothing."

Then an uncomfortable silence.

Arkansas played with his glass a moment, lolling on his elbows on the counter. Then he meditatively scratched his left shin with his right boot, while the awkward silence continued. But presently he loafed away toward the stove, looking dissatisfied; roughly shouldered two or three men out of a comfortable position; occupied it himself, gave a sleeping dog a kick that sent him howling under a bench, then spread his long legs and his blanket-coat tails apart and proceeded to warm his back. In a little while he fell to grumbling to himself, and soon he slouched back to the bar and said:

"Lan'lord, what's your idea for rakin' up old personalities and blowin' about your father? Ain't this company agreeable to you? Ain't it? If this company ain't agreeable to you, p'r'aps we'd better leave. Is that your idea? Is that what you're coming at?"

"Why bless your soul, Arkansas, I warn't thinking of such a thing. My father and my mother—"

"Lan'lord, *don't* crowd a man! Don't do it. If nothing 'll do you but a disturbance, out with it like a man (*'ic*)—but *don't* rake up old bygones and fling 'em in the teeth of a passel of people that wants to be peaceable if they could git a chance. What's the matter with you this mornin', anyway? I never see a man carry on so."

"Arkansas, I reely didn't mean no harm, and I won't go on with it if it's onpleasant to you. I reckon my licker's got into my head, and what with the flood, and havin' so many to feed and look out for—"

"So *that's* what's a ranklin' in your heart, is it? You want us to leave do you? There's too many on us. You want us to pack up and swim. Is that it? Come!"

"Please be reasonable, Arkansas. Now *you* know that I ain't the man to—"

"Are you a threatenin' me? Are you? By George, the man don't live that can skeer me! Don't you try to come that game, my chicken—'cuz I can stand a good deal, but I won't stand that. Come out from behind that bar till I clean you! You want to drive us out, do you, you sneakin' underhanded hound! Come out from behind that bar! *I'll* learn you to bully and badger and browbeat a gentleman that's forever trying to befriend you and keep you out of trouble!"

"Please, Arkansas, please don't shoot! If there's got to be bloodshed—"

"Do you hear that, gentlemen? Do you hear him talk about bloodshed? So it's blood you want, is it, you ravin' desperado! You'd made up your mind to murder somebody this mornin'—I knowed it perfectly well. I'm the man, am I? It's me you're goin' to murder, is it? But you can't do it 'thout I get one chance first, you thievin' black-hearted, white-livered son of a nigger! Draw your weepon!"

With that, Arkansas began to shoot, and the landlord to clamber over benches, men and every sort of obstacle in a frantic desire to escape. In the midst of the wild hubbub the landlord crashed through a glass door, and as Arkansas charged after him the landlord's wife suddenly appeared in the doorway and confronted the desperado with a pair of scissors! Her fury was magnificent. With head erect and flashing eye she stood a moment and then advanced, with her weapon raised. The astonished ruffian hesitated, and then fell back a step. She followed. She backed him step by step into the middle of the bar-room, and then, while the wondering

AN ARMED ALLY.

crowd closed up and gazed, she gave him such another tongue-lashing as never a cowed and shamefaced braggart got before, perhaps! As she finished and retired victorious, a roar of applause shook the house, and every man ordered "drinks for the crowd" in one and the same breath.

The lesson was entirely sufficient. The reign of terror was over, and the Arkansas domination broken for good. During the rest of the season of island captivity, there was one man who sat apart in a state of permanent humiliation, never mixing in any quarrel or uttering a boast, and never resenting the insults the once cringing crew now constantly leveled at him, and that man was "Arkansas."

By the fifth or sixth morning the waters had subsided from the land, but the stream in the old river bed was still high and swift and there was no possibility of crossing it. On the eighth it was still too high for an entirely safe passage, but life in the inn had become next to insupportable by reason of the dirt, drunkenness, fighting, etc., and so we made an effort to get away. In the midst of a heavy snow-storm we embarked in a canoe, taking our saddles aboard

CROSSING THE FLOOD.

and towing our horses after us by their halters. The Prussian, Ollendorff, was in the bow, with a paddle, Ballou paddled in the middle, and I sat in the stern holding the halters. When the horses lost their footing and began to swim, Ollendorff got frightened, for there was great danger that the horses would make our aim uncertain, and it was plain that if we failed to land at a certain spot the current would throw us off and almost surely cast us into the main Carson, which was a boiling torrent, now. Such a catastrophe would be death, in all probability, for we would be swept to sea in the "Sink" or overturned and drowned. We warned Ollendorff to keep his wits about him and handle himself carefully, but it was useless; the moment the bow touched the bank, he made a spring and the canoe whirled upside down in ten-foot water. Ollendorff seized some brush and dragged himself ashore, but Ballou and I had to swim for it, encumbered with our overcoats. But we held on to the canoe, and although we were washed down nearly to the Carson, we managed to push the boat ashore and make a safe landing. We were cold and water-soaked, but safe. The horses made a landing, too, but our saddles were gone, of course. We tied the animals in the sage-brush and there they had to stay for twenty-four hours. We baled out the canoe and ferried over some food and blankets for them, but we slept one more night in the inn before making another venture on our journey.

The next morning it was still snowing furiously when we got away with our new stock of saddles and accoutrements. We mounted and started. The snow lay so deep on the ground that there was no sign of a road perceptible, and the snow-fall was so thick that we could not see more than a hundred yards ahead, else we could have guided our course by the mountain ranges. The case looked dubious, but Ollendorff said his instinct was as sensitive as any compass, and that he could "strike a bee-line" for Carson City and never diverge from it. He said that if he were to straggle a single point out of the true line his instinct would assail him like an outraged conscience. Consequently we dropped into his wake happy and content. For half an hour we poked along warily enough, but at the end of that time we came upon a fresh trail, and Ollendorff shouted proudly:

"I knew I was as dead certain as a compass, boys! Here we are, right in somebody's tracks that will hunt the way for us without any trouble. Let's hurry up and join company with the party."

So we put the horses into as much of a trot as the deep snow would allow, and before long it was evident that we were gaining on our predecessors, for the tracks grew more distinct. We hurried along, and at the end of an hour the tracks looked still newer and fresher—but what surprised us was, that the *number* of travelers in advance of us seemed to steadily increase. We wondered how so large a party came to be traveling at such a time and in such a solitude. Somebody suggested that it must be a company of soldiers from the fort, and so we accepted that solution and jogged along a little faster still, for they could not be far off now. But the tracks still multiplied, and we began to think the platoon of soldiers was miraculously expanding into a regiment—Ballou said they had already increased to five hundred! Presently he stopped his horse and said:

"Boys, these are our own tracks, and we've actually been circussing round and round in a circle for more than two hours, out here in this blind desert! By George this is perfectly hydraulic!"

ADVANCE IN A CIRCLE.

Then the old man waxed wroth and abusive. He called Ollendorff all manner of hard names—said he never saw such a lurid fool as he was, and ended with the peculiarly venomous opinion that he "did not know as much as a logarithm!"

We certainly had been following our own tracks. Ollendorff and his "mental compass" were in disgrace from that moment. After all our hard travel, here we were on the bank of the stream again, with the inn beyond dimly outlined through the driving snow-fall. While we were considering what to do, the young Swede landed from the canoe and took his pedestrian way Carson-wards, singing his same tiresome song about his "sister and his brother" and "the child in the grave with its mother," and in a short minute faded and disappeared in the white oblivion. He was never heard of again. He no doubt got bewildered and lost, and Fatigue delivered him over to Sleep and Sleep betrayed him to Death. Possibly he followed our treacherous tracks till he became exhausted and dropped.

THE SONGSTER.

Presently the Overland stage forded the now fast receding stream and started toward Carson on its first trip since the flood came. We hesitated no longer, now, but took up our march in its wake, and trotted merrily along, for we had good confidence in the driver's bump of locality. But our horses were no match for the fresh stage team. We were soon left out of sight; but it was no matter, for we had the deep ruts the wheels made for a guide. By this time it was three in the afternoon, and consequently it was not very long before night came—and not with a lingering twilight, but with a sudden shutting down like a cellar door, as is its habit in that country. The snow-fall was still as thick as ever, and of course we could not see fifteen steps before us; but all about us the white glare of the snow-bed enabled us to discern the smooth sugar-loaf mounds made by the covered sage-bushes, and just in front of us the two faint grooves which we knew were the steadily filling and slowly disappearing wheel-tracks.

Now those sage-bushes were all about the same height—three or four feet; they stood just about seven feet apart, all over the vast desert; each of them was a mere snow-mound, now; in *any* direction that you proceeded (the same as in a well laid out orchard) you would find yourself moving down a distinctly defined avenue, with a row of these snow-mounds on either side of it—an avenue the customary width of a road, nice and level in its breadth, and rising at the sides in the most natural way, by reason of the mounds. But we had not thought of this. Then imagine the chilly thrill that shot through us when it finally occurred to us, far in the night, that since the last faint trace of the wheel-tracks had long ago been buried from sight, we might now be wandering down a mere sage-brush avenue, miles away from the road and diverging further and further away from it all the time. Having a cake of ice slipped down one's back is placid comfort compared to it. There was a sudden leap and stir of blood that had been asleep for an hour, and as sudden a rousing of all the drowsing activities in our minds and bodies. We were alive and awake at once—and shaking and quaking with consternation, too. There was an instant halting and dismounting, a bending low and an anxious scanning of the road-bed. Useless, of course; for if a faint depression could not be discerned from an altitude of four or five feet above it, it certainly could not with one's nose nearly against it.

CHAPTER 32

We seemed to be in a road, but that was no proof. We tested this by walking off in various directions—the regular snow-mounds and the regular avenues between them convinced each man that *he* had found the true road, and that the others had found only false ones. Plainly the situation was desperate. We were cold and stiff and the horses were tired. We decided to build a sage-brush fire and camp out till morning. This was wise, because if we were wandering from the right road and the snow-storm continued another day our case would be the next thing to hopeless if we kept on.

All agreed that a camp-fire was what would come nearest to saving us, now, and so we set about building it. We could find no matches, and so we tried to make shift with the pistols. Not a man in the party had ever tried to do such a thing before, but not a man in the party doubted that it *could* be done, and without any trouble—because every man in the party had read about it in books many a time and had naturally come to believe it, with trusting simplicity, just as he had long ago accepted and believed *that other* common book-fraud about Indians and lost hunters making a fire by rubbing two dry sticks together.

We huddled together on our knees in the deep snow, and the horses put their noses together and bowed their patient heads over us; and while the feathery flakes eddied down and turned us into a group of white statuary, we proceeded with the momentous experiment. We broke twigs from a sage-bush and piled them on a little cleared place in the shelter of our bodies. In the course of ten or fifteen minutes all was ready, and then, while conversation ceased and our pulses beat low with anxious suspense, Ollendorff applied his revolver, pulled the trigger and blew the pile clear out of the county! It was the flattest failure that ever was.

This was distressing, but it paled before a greater horror—the horses were gone! I had been appointed to hold the bridles, but in my absorbing anxiety over the pistol experiment I had unconsciously dropped them and the released animals had walked off in

A FLAT FAILURE.

the storm. It was useless to try to follow them, for their footfalls could make no sound, and one could pass within two yards of the creatures and never see them. We gave them up without an effort at recovering them, and cursed the lying books that said horses would stay by their masters for protection and companionship in a distressful time like ours.

We were miserable enough, before; we felt still more forlorn, now. Patiently, but with blighted hope, we broke more sticks and piled them, and once more the Prussian shot them into annihilation. Plainly, to light a fire with a pistol was an art requiring practice and experience, and the middle of a desert at midnight in a snow-storm was not a good place or time for the acquiring of the accomplishment. We gave it up and tried the other. Each man took a couple of sticks and fell to chafing them together. At the end of half an hour we were thoroughly chilled, and so were the sticks. We bitterly execrated the Indians, the hunters and the books that had betrayed us with the silly device, and wondered dismally what was next to be done. At this critical moment Mr. Ballou fished out four matches from the rubbish of an overlooked pocket. To have found four gold bars would have seemed poor and cheap good luck

THE LAST MATCH.

compared to this. One cannot think how good a match looks under such circumstances—or how lovable and precious, and sacredly beautiful to the eye. This time we gathered sticks with high hopes; and when Mr. Ballou prepared to light the first match, there was an amount of interest centred upon him that pages of writing could not describe. The match burned hopefully a moment, and then went out. It could not have carried more regret with it if it had been a human life. The next match simply flashed and died. The wind puffed the third one out just as it was on the imminent verge of success. We gathered together closer than ever, and developed a solicitude that was rapt and painful, as Mr. Ballou scratched our last hope on his leg. It lit, burned blue and sickly, and then budded into a robust flame. Shading it with his hands, the old gentleman bent gradually down and every heart went with him—everybody, too, for that matter—and blood and breath stood still. The flame touched the sticks at last, took gradual hold upon them—hesitated—took a stronger hold—hesitated again—held its breath five heart-breaking seconds, then gave a sort of human gasp and went out.

Nobody said a word for several minutes. It was a solemn sort of silence; even the wind put on a stealthy, sinister quiet, and made no more noise than the falling flakes of snow. Finally a sad-voiced conversation began, and it was soon apparent that in each of our hearts lay the conviction that this was our last night with the living. I had so hoped that I was the only one who felt so. When the others calmly acknowledged their conviction, it sounded like the summons itself. Ollendorff said:

"Brothers, let us die together. And let us go without one hard feeling towards each other. Let us forget and forgive bygones. I know that you have felt hard towards me for turning over the canoe, and for knowing too much and leading you round and round in the snow—but I meant well; forgive me. I acknowledge freely that I have had hard feelings against Mr. Ballou for abusing me and calling me a logarithm, which is a thing I do not know what, but no doubt a thing considered disgraceful and unbecoming in America, and it has scarcely been out of my mind and has hurt me a great deal—but let it go; I forgive Mr. Ballou with all my heart, and—"

Poor Ollendorff broke down and the tears came. He was not alone, for I was crying too, and so was Mr. Ballou. Ollendorff got his voice again and forgave me for things I had done and said. Then he got out his bottle of whisky and said that whether he lived or died he would never touch another drop. He said he had given up all hope of life, and although ill-prepared, was ready to submit humbly to his fate; that he wished he could be spared a little longer, not for any selfish reason, but to make a thorough reform in his character, and by devoting himself to helping the poor, nursing the sick, and pleading with the people to guard themselves against the evils of intemperance, make his life a beneficent example to the young, and lay it down at last with the precious reflection that it had not been lived in vain. He ended by saying that his reform should begin at this moment, even here in the presence of death, since no longer time was to be vouchsafed wherein to prosecute it to men's help and benefit—and with that he threw away the bottle of whisky.

Mr. Ballou made remarks of similar purport, and began the reform he could not live to continue, by throwing away the ancient pack of cards that had solaced our captivity during the flood and made it bearable. He said he never gambled, but still was satisfied

DISCARDED VICES.

that the meddling with cards in any way was immoral and injurious, and no man could be wholly pure and blemishless without eschewing them. "And therefore," continued he, "in doing this act I already feel more in sympathy with that spiritual saturnalia necessary to entire and obsolete reform." These rolling syllables touched him as no intelligible eloquence could have done, and the old man sobbed with a mournfulness not unmingled with satisfaction.

My own remarks were of the same tenor as those of my comrades, and I know that the feelings that prompted them were heartfelt and sincere. We were all sincere, and all deeply moved and earnest, for we were in the presence of death and without hope. I threw away my pipe, and in doing it felt that at last I was free of a hated vice and one that had ridden me like a tyrant all my days. While I yet talked, the thought of the good I might have done in the world and the still greater good I might *now* do, with these new incentives and higher and better aims to guide me if I could only be spared a few years longer, overcame me and the tears came again. We put our arms about each other's necks and awaited the warning drowsiness that precedes death by freezing.

It came stealing over us presently, and then we bade each other a last farewell. A delicious dreaminess wrought its web about my yielding senses, while the snow-flakes wove a winding sheet about my conquered body. Oblivion came. The battle of life was done.

CHAPTER 33

I do not know how long I was in a state of forgetfulness, but it seemed an age. A vague consciousness grew upon me by degrees, and then came a gathering anguish of pain in my limbs and through all my body. I shuddered. The thought flitted through my brain, "this is death—this is the hereafter."

Then came a white upheaval at my side, and a voice said, with bitterness:

"Will some gentleman be so good as to kick me behind?"

It was Ballou—at least it was a towzled snow image in a sitting posture, with Ballou's voice.

I rose up, and there in the gray dawn, not fifteen steps from us, were the frame buildings of a stage station, and under a shed stood our still saddled and bridled horses!

An arched snow-drift broke up, now, and Ollendorff emerged from it, and the three of us sat and stared at the houses without speaking a word. We really had nothing to say. We were like the profane man who could not "do the subject justice," the whole situation was so painfully ridiculous and humiliating that words were tame and we did not know where to commence anyhow.

The joy in our hearts at our deliverance was poisoned; well-nigh dissipated, indeed. We presently began to grow pettish by degrees, and sullen; and then, angry at each other, angry at ourselves, angry at everything in general, we moodily dusted the snow from our clothing and in unsociable single file plowed our way to the horses, unsaddled them, and sought shelter in the station.

I have scarcely exaggerated a detail of this curious and absurd adventure. It occurred almost exactly as I have stated it. We actually went into camp in a snow-drift in a desert, at midnight in a storm, forlorn and hopeless, within fifteen steps of a comfortable inn.

For two hours we sat apart in the station and ruminated in dis-

CAMPING IN THE SNOW.

gust. The mystery was gone, now, and it was plain enough why the horses had deserted us. Without a doubt they were under that shed a quarter of a minute after they had left us, and they must have overheard and enjoyed all our confessions and lamentations.

After breakfast we felt better, and the zest of life soon came back. The world looked bright again, and existence was as dear to us as ever. Presently an uneasiness came over me—grew upon me—assailed me without ceasing. Alas, my regeneration was not complete—I wanted to smoke! I resisted with all my strength, but the flesh was weak. I wandered away alone and wrestled with myself an hour. I recalled my promises of reform and preached to myself persuasively, upbraidingly, exhaustively. But it was all vain, I shortly found myself sneaking among the snow-drifts hunting for my pipe. I discovered it after a considerable search, and crept away to hide myself and enjoy it. I remained behind the barn a good while, asking myself how I would feel if my braver, stronger, truer comrades should catch me in my degradation. At last I lit the pipe, and no human being can feel meaner and baser than I did then. I was ashamed of being in my own pitiful company. Still dreading discovery, I felt that perhaps the further side of the barn would be somewhat safer, and so I turned the corner. As I turned the one corner, smoking, Ollendorff turned the other with his bottle to his lips, and between us sat unconscious Ballou deep in a game of "solitaire" with the old greasy cards!

Absurdity could go no farther. We shook hands and agreed to say no more about "reform" and "examples to the rising generation."

The station we were at was at the verge of the Twenty-six-Mile Desert. If we had approached it half an hour earlier the night before, we must have heard men shouting there and firing pistols; for they were expecting some sheep drovers and their flocks and knew that they would infallibly get lost and wander out of reach of help unless guided by sounds. While we remained at the station, three of the drovers arrived, nearly exhausted with their wanderings, but two others of their party were never heard of afterward.

We reached Carson in due time, and took a rest. This rest, together with preparations for the journey to Esmeralda, kept us

IT WAS THUS WE MET.

there a week, and the delay gave us the opportunity to be present at the trial of the great land-slide case of Hyde *vs.* Morgan—an episode which is famous in Nevada to this day. After a word or two of necessary explanation, I will set down the history of this singular affair just as it transpired.

CHAPTER 34

THE mountains are very high and steep about Carson, Eagle and Washoe Valleys—very high and very steep, and so when the snow gets to melting off fast in the spring and the warm surface-earth begins to moisten and soften, the disastrous land-slides commence. The reader cannot know what a land-slide is, unless he has lived in that country and seen the whole side of a mountain taken off some fine morning and deposited down in the valley, leaving a vast, treeless, unsightly scar upon the mountain's front to keep the circumstance fresh in his memory all the years that he may go on living within seventy miles of that place.

Gen. Buncombe was shipped out to Nevada in the invoice of Territorial officers, to be U. S. Attorney. He considered himself a lawyer of parts, and he very much wanted an opportunity to manifest it—partly for the pure gratification of it and partly because his salary was Territorially meagre (which is a strong expression.) Now the older citizens of a new territory look down upon the rest of the world with a calm, benevolent compassion, as long as it keeps out of the way—when it gets in the way they snub it. Sometimes this latter takes the shape of a practical joke.

One morning Dick Hyde rode furiously up to Gen. Buncombe's door in Carson City and rushed into his presence without stopping to tie his horse. He seemed much excited. He told the General that he wanted him to conduct a suit for him and would pay him five hundred dollars if he achieved a victory. And then, with violent gestures and a world of profanity, he poured out his griefs. He said it was pretty well known that for some years he had been farming (or ranching as the more customary term is,) in Washoe District, and making a successful thing of it, and furthermore it was known that his ranch was situated just in the edge of the valley, and that

Tom Morgan owned a ranch immediately above it on the mountain side. And now the trouble was that one of those hated and dreaded land-slides had come and slid Morgan's ranch, fences, cabins, cattle, barns and everything down on top of *his* ranch and exactly covered up every single vestige of his property, to a depth of about thirty-eight feet. Morgan was in possession and refused to vacate the premises—said he was occupying his own cabin and not interfering with anybody else's—and said the cabin was standing on the same dirt and same ranch it had always stood on, and he would like to see anybody make him vacate.

TAKING POSSESSION.

"And when I reminded him," said Hyde, weeping, "that it was on top of my ranch and that he was trespassing, he had the infernal meanness to ask me why didn't I *stay* on my ranch and hold possession when I see him a coming! Why didn't I *stay* on it, the blathering lunatic—by George, when I heard that racket and looked up that hill it was just like the whole world was a ripping and a tearing down that mountain side—splinters, and cord-wood, thunder and lightning, hail and snow, odds and ends of hay stacks, and awful clouds of dust!—trees going end over end in the air, rocks as big as a house jumping 'bout a thousand feet high and busting into ten million pieces, cattle turned inside out and a coming head on with their tails hanging out between their teeth!—and in the midst of all that wrack and destruction sot that cussed Morgan on his gate-post, a wondering why I didn't *stay and hold possession!* Laws bless me, I just took one glimpse, General, and lit out'n the county in three jumps exactly.

"But what grinds me is that that Morgan hangs on there and won't move off'n that ranch—says it's his'n and he's going to keep it—likes it better'n he did when it was higher up the hill. Mad! Well, I've been so mad for two days I couldn't find my way to town—been wandering around in the brush in a starving condition—got anything here to drink, General? But I'm here *now,* and I'm a going to law. You hear *me!*"

Never in all the world, perhaps, were a man's feelings so outraged as were the General's. He said he had never heard of such high-handed conduct in all his life as this Morgan's. And he said there was no use in going to law—Morgan had no shadow of right to remain where he was—nobody in the wide world would uphold him in it, and no lawyer would take his case and no judge listen to it. Hyde said that right there was where he was mistaken—everybody in town sustained Morgan; Hal Brayton, a very smart lawyer, had taken his case; the courts being in vacation, it was to be tried before a referee, and ex-Governor Roop had already been appointed to that office and would open his court in a large public hall near the hotel at two that afternoon.

The General was amazed. He said he had suspected before that the people of that Territory were fools, and now he knew it. But he said rest easy, rest easy and collect the witnesses, for the victory was just as certain as if the conflict were already over. Hyde wiped away his tears and left.

At two in the afternoon referee Roop's court opened, and Roop appeared throned among his sheriffs, the witnesses, and spectators, and wearing upon his face a solemnity so awe-inspiring that some of his fellow-conspirators had misgivings that maybe he had not comprehended, after all, that this was merely a joke. An unearthly stillness prevailed, for at the slightest noise the judge uttered sternly the command:

"Order in the court!"

And the sheriffs promptly echoed it. Presently the General elbowed his way through the crowd of spectators, with his arms full of law-books, and on his ears fell an order from the judge which was the first respectful recognition of his high official dignity that had ever saluted them, and it trickled pleasantly through his whole system:

"Way for the United States Attorney!"

The witnesses were called—legislators, high government officers, ranchmen, miners, Indians, Chinamen, negroes. Three-fourths of them were called by the defendant Morgan, but no matter, their testimony invariably went in favor of the plaintiff Hyde. Each new witness only added new testimony to the absurdity of a man's claiming to own another man's property because his farm had slid down on top of it. Then the Morgan lawyers made their speeches, and seemed to make singularly weak ones—they did really nothing to help the Morgan cause. And now the General, with exultation in his face, got up and made an impassioned effort;

A GREAT EFFORT.

he pounded the table, he banged the law-books, he shouted, and roared, and howled, he quoted from everything and everybody, poetry, sarcasm, statistics, history, pathos, bathos, blasphemy, and wound up with a grand war-whoop for free speech, freedom of the press, free schools, the Glorious Bird of America and the principles of eternal justice! [Applause.]

When the General sat down, he did it with the conviction that if there was anything in good strong testimony, a great speech and believing and admiring countenances all around, Mr. Morgan's case was killed. Ex-Governor Roop leant his head upon his hand for some minutes, thinking, and the still audience waited for his decision. Then he got up and stood erect, with bended head, and thought again. Then he walked the floor with long, deliberate strides, his chin in his hand, and still the audience waited. At last he returned to his throne, seated himself, and began, impressively:

"Gentlemen, I feel the great responsibility that rests upon me this day. This is no ordinary case. On the contrary it is plain that it is the most solemn and awful that ever man was called upon to decide. Gentlemen, I have listened attentively to the evidence, and have perceived that the weight of it, the overwhelming weight of it, is in favor of the plaintiff Hyde. I have listened also to the remarks of counsel, with high interest—and especially will I commend the masterly and irrefutable logic of the distinguished gentleman who represents the plaintiff. But gentlemen, let us beware how we allow mere human testimony, human ingenuity in argument and human ideas of equity to influence us at a moment so solemn as this. Gentlemen, it ill becomes us, worms as we are, to meddle with the decrees of Heaven. It is plain to me that Heaven, in its inscrutable wisdom, has seen fit to move this defendant's ranch for a purpose. We are but creatures, and we must submit. If Heaven has chosen to favor the defendant Morgan in this marked and wonderful manner; and if Heaven, dissatisfied with the position of the Morgan ranch upon the mountain side, has chosen to remove it to a position more eligible and more advantageous for its owner, it ill becomes us, insects as we are, to question the legality of the act or inquire into the reasons that prompted it. No—Heaven created the ranches and it is Heaven's prerogative to reärrange them, to experiment with them, to shift them around at its pleasure. It is for us to submit, without repining. I warn you that

REÄRRANGING AND SHIFTING.

this thing which has happened is a thing with which the sacrilegious hands and brains and tongues of men must not meddle. Gentlemen, it is the verdict of this court that the plaintiff, Richard Hyde, has been deprived of his ranch by the visitation of God! And from this decision there is no appeal."

Buncombe seized his cargo of law-books and plunged out of the court room frantic with indignation. He pronounced Roop to be a miraculous fool, an inspired idiot. In all good faith he returned at night and remonstrated with Roop upon his extravagant decision, and implored him to walk the floor and think for half an hour, and see if he could not figure out some sort of modification of the verdict. Roop yielded at last and got up to walk. He walked two hours and a half, and at last his face lit up happily and he told Buncombe it had occurred to him that the ranch underneath the new Morgan ranch still belonged to Hyde, that his title to the ground was just as good as it had ever been, and therefore he was of opinion that Hyde had a right to dig it out from under there and—

The General never waited to hear the end of it. He was always an impatient and irascible man, that way. At the end of two months the fact that he had been played upon with a joke had managed to bore itself, like another Hoosac Tunnel, through the solid adamant of his understanding.

CHAPTER 35

WHEN we finally left for Esmeralda, horseback, we had an addition to the company in the person of Capt. John Nye, the Governor's brother. He had a good memory, and a tongue hung in the middle. This is a combination which gives immortality to conversation. Capt. John never suffered the talk to flag or falter once during the hundred and twenty miles of the journey. In addition to his conversational powers, he had one or two other endowments of a marked character. One was a singular "handiness" about doing anything and everything, from laying out a railroad or organizing a political party, down to sewing on buttons, shoeing a horse, or setting a broken leg, or a hen. Another was a spirit of accommodation that prompted him to take the needs, difficulties and perplexities of anybody and everybody upon his own shoulders at any and all times, and dispose of them with admirable facility and alacrity—hence he always managed to find vacant beds in crowded inns, and plenty to eat in the emptiest larders. And finally, wherever he met a man, woman or child, in camp, inn or desert, he either knew such parties personally or had been acquainted with a relative of the same. Such another traveling comrade was never seen before. I cannot forbear giving a specimen of the way in which he overcame difficulties. On the second day out, we arrived, very tired and hungry, at a poor little inn in the desert, and were told that the house was full, no provisions on hand, and neither hay nor barley to spare for the horses—we must move on. The rest of us wanted to hurry on while it was yet light, but Capt. John insisted on stopping awhile. We dismounted and entered. There was no welcome for us on any face. Capt. John began his blandishments, and within twenty minutes he had accomplished the following things, viz.: found old acquaintances in three teamsters; discovered that he used to go to school with the landlord's mother; recognized his wife as a lady whose life he had saved once in California, by stopping her runaway horse; mended a child's broken toy and won the favor of its mother, a guest of the inn; helped the hostler bleed a horse, and prescribed for another horse that had the "heaves;" treated the entire party three times at the landlord's bar; produced a later paper than anybody had seen for a week and sat himself down to read the news to a deeply interested audience. The result, summed up, was as follows: The hostler found plenty of feed for our horses; we had a trout supper, an exceedingly sociable time after it, good beds to sleep in, and a surprising breakfast in the morning—and when we left, we left lamented by all! Capt. John had some bad traits, but he had some uncommonly valuable ones to offset them with.

WE LEFT LAMENTED.

Esmeralda was in many respects another Humboldt, but in a little more forward state. The claims we had been paying assessments on were entirely worthless, and we threw them away. The principal one cropped out of the top of a knoll that was fourteen feet high, and the inspired Board of Directors were running a tunnel under that knoll to strike the ledge. The tunnel would have to be seventy feet long, and would then strike the ledge at the same depth that a *shaft* twelve feet deep would have reached! The Board were living on the "assessments." [N. B.—This hint comes too late for the enlightenment of New York silver miners; they have already learned all about this neat trick by experience.] The Board had no desire to strike the ledge, knowing that it was as barren of silver as a curb-stone. This reminiscence calls to mind Jim Townsend's tunnel. He had paid assessments on a mine called the "Daley" till he was well-nigh penniless. Finally an assessment was levied to run a tunnel two hundred and fifty feet on the Daley, and Townsend went up on the hill to look into matters. He found the Daley cropping out of the apex of an exceedingly sharp-pointed peak, and a couple of men up there "facing" the proposed tunnel. Townsend made a calculation. Then he said to the men:

"So you have taken a contract to run a tunnel into this hill two hundred and fifty feet to strike this ledge?"

"Yes, sir."

"Well, do you know that you have got one of the most expensive and arduous undertakings before you that was ever conceived by man?"

"Why no—how is that?"

"Because this hill is only twenty-five feet through from side to side; and so you have got to build two hundred and twenty-five feet of your tunnel on trestle-work!"

The ways of silver mining Boards are exceedingly dark and sinuous.

PICTURE OF TOWNSEND'S TUNNEL.

We took up various claims, and *commenced* shafts and tunnels on them, but never finished any of them. We had to do a certain amount of work on each to "hold" it, else other parties could seize our property after the expiration of ten days. We were always hunting up new claims and doing a little work on them and then waiting for a buyer—who never came. We never found any ore that would yield more than fifty dollars a ton; and as the mills charged fifty dollars a ton for *working* ore and extracting the silver, our pocket-money melted steadily away and none returned to take its place. We lived in a little cabin and cooked for ourselves; and altogether it was a hard life, though a hopeful one—for we never ceased to expect fortune and a customer to burst upon us some day.

At last, when flour reached a dollar a pound, and money could not be borrowed on the best security at less than *eight per cent a month* (I being without the security, too), I abandoned mining and went to milling. That is to say, I went to work as a common laborer in a quartz mill, at ten dollars a week and board.

CHAPTER 36

I HAD already learned how hard and long and dismal a task it is to burrow down into the bowels of the earth and get out the coveted ore; and now I learned that the burrowing was only half the work; and that to get the silver out of the ore was the dreary and laborious other half of it. We had to turn out at six in the morning and keep at it till dark. This mill was a six-stamp affair, driven by steam. Six tall, upright rods of iron, as large as a man's ankle, and heavily shod

QUARTZ MILL IN NEVADA.

with a mass of iron and steel at their lower ends, were framed together like a gate, and these rose and fell, one after the other, in a ponderous dance, in an iron box called a "battery." Each of these rods or stamps weighed six hundred pounds. One of us stood by the battery all day long, breaking up masses of silver-bearing rock with a sledge and shoveling it into the battery. The ceaseless dance of the stamps pulverized the rock to powder, and a stream of water that trickled into the battery turned it to a creamy paste. The minutest particles were driven through a fine wire screen which fitted close around the battery, and were washed into great tubs warmed by super-heated steam—amalgamating pans, they are called. The mass of pulp in the pans was kept constantly stirred up by revolving "mullers." A quantity of quicksilver was kept always in the battery, and this seized some of the liberated gold and silver particles and held on to them; quicksilver was shaken in a fine shower into the pans, also, about every half hour, through a buckskin sack. Quantities of coarse salt and sulphate of copper were added, from time to time, to assist the amalgamation by destroying base metals which coated the gold and silver and would not let it unite with the quicksilver. All these tiresome things we had to attend to constantly. Streams of dirty water flowed always from the pans and were carried off in broad wooden troughs to the ravine. One would not suppose that atoms of gold and silver would float on top of six inches of water, but they did; and in order to catch them, coarse blankets were laid in the troughs, and little obstructing "riffles" charged with quicksilver were placed here and there across the troughs also. These riffles had to be cleaned and the blankets washed out every evening, to get their precious accumulations—and after all this eternity of trouble one-third of the silver and gold in a ton of rock would find its way to the end of the troughs in the ravine at last and have to be worked over again some day. There is nothing so aggravating as silver milling. There never was any idle time in that mill. There was always something to do. It is a pity that Adam could not have gone straight out of Eden into a quartz mill, in order to understand the full force of his doom to "earn his bread by the sweat of his brow." Every now and then, during the day, we had to scoop some pulp out of the pans, and tediously "wash" it in a horn spoon—wash it little by little over the edge till at last nothing was left but some little dull globules of quicksilver in the bottom. If they were soft and yielding, the pan needed some salt or some sulphate of copper or some other chemical rubbish to assist digestion; if they were crisp to the touch and would retain a dint, they were freighted with all the silver and gold they could seize and hold, and consequently the pans needed a fresh charge of quicksilver. When there was nothing else to do, one could always "screen tailings." That is to say, he could shovel up the dried sand that had washed down to the ravine through the troughs and dash it against an upright wire screen to free it from

ANOTHER PROCESS OF AMALGAMATION.

pebbles and prepare it for working over. The process of amalgamation differed in the various mills, and this included changes in style of pans and other machinery, and a great diversity of opinion existed as to the best in use, but none of the methods employed, involved the principle of milling ore without "screening the tailings." Of all recreations in the world, screening tailings on a hot day, with a long-handled shovel, is the most undesirable.

At the end of the week the machinery was stopped and we "cleaned up." That is to say, we got the pulp out of the pans and batteries, and washed the mud patiently away till nothing was left but the long accumulating mass of quicksilver, with its imprisoned treasures. This we made into heavy, compact snow-balls, and piled them up in a bright, luxurious heap for inspection. Making these snow-balls cost me a fine gold ring—that and ignorance together; for the quicksilver invaded the ring with the same facility with which water saturates a sponge—separated its particles and the ring crumbled to pieces.

We put our pile of quicksilver balls into an iron retort that had a pipe leading from it to a pail of water, and then applied a roasting heat. The quicksilver turned to vapor, escaped through the pipe into the pail, and the water turned it into good wholesome quicksilver again. Quicksilver is very costly, and they never waste it. On opening the retort, there was our week's work—a lump of pure white, frosty looking silver, twice as large as a man's head. Perhaps a fifth of the mass was gold, but the color of it did not show—would not have shown if two-thirds of it had been gold. We melted it up and made a solid brick of it by pouring it into an iron brick-mould.

By such a tedious and laborious process were silver bricks obtained. This mill was but one of many others in operation at the time. The first one in Nevada was built at Egan Cañon and was a

FIRST QUARTZ MILL IN NEVADA.

small insignificant affair and compared most unfavorably with some of the immense establishments afterward located at Virginia City and elsewhere.

From our bricks a little corner was chipped off for the "fire-assay"—a method used to determine the proportions of gold, silver and base metals in the mass. This is an interesting process. The chip is hammered out as thin as paper and weighed on scales so fine and sensitive that if you weigh a two-inch scrap of paper on them and then write your name on the paper with a coarse, soft pencil and weigh it again, the scales will take marked notice of the addition. Then a little lead (also weighed) is rolled up with the flake of silver and the two are melted at a great heat in a small vessel called a cupel, made by compressing bone ashes into a cup-shape in a steel mould. The base metals oxydize and are absorbed with the lead into the pores of the cupel. A button or globule of perfectly pure gold and silver is left behind, and by weighing it and noting the loss, the assayer knows the proportion of base metal the brick contains. He has to separate the gold from the silver now. The button is hammered out flat and thin, put in the furnace and kept some time at a red heat; after cooling it off it is rolled up like a quill and heated in a glass vessel containing nitric acid; the acid dissolves the silver and leaves the gold pure and ready to be weighed on its own merits. Then salt water is poured into the vessel containing the dissolved silver and the silver returns to palpable form again and sinks to the bottom. Nothing now remains but to weigh it; then the proportions of the several metals contained in the brick are known, and the assayer stamps the value of the brick upon its surface.

The sagacious reader will know now, without being told, that the speculative miner, in getting a "fire-assay" made of a piece of rock from his mine (to help him sell the same), was not in the habit of picking out the least valuable fragment of rock on his dump-pile, but quite the contrary. I have seen men hunt over a pile of nearly worthless quartz for an hour, and at last find a little piece as large as a filbert, which was rich in gold and silver—and this was reserved for a fire-assay! Of course the fire-assay would demonstrate that a ton of such rock would yield hundreds of dollars—and on such assays many an utterly worthless mine was sold.

Assaying was a good business, and so some men engaged in it, occasionally, who were not strictly scientific and capable. One assayer got such rich results out of all specimens brought to him that in time he acquired almost a monopoly of the business. But like all men who achieve success, he became an object of envy and suspicion. The other assayers entered into a conspiracy against him, and let some prominent citizens into the secret in order to show that they meant fairly. Then they broke a little fragment off a carpenter's grindstone and got a stranger to take it to the popular scientist and get it assayed. In the course of an hour the result came—whereby it appeared that a ton of that rock would yield $1,284.40 in silver and $366.36 in gold!

A SLICE OF RICH ORE.

Due publication of the whole matter was made in the paper, and the popular assayer left town "between two days."

I will remark, in passing, that I only remained in the milling business one week. I told my employer I could not stay longer without an advance in my wages; that I liked quartz milling, indeed was infatuated with it; that I had never before grown so tenderly attached to an occupation in so short a time; that nothing, it seemed to me, gave such scope to intellectual activity as feeding a battery and screening tailings, and nothing so stimulated the moral attributes as retorting bullion and washing blankets—still, I felt constrained to ask an increase of salary.

He said he was paying me ten dollars a week, and thought it a good round sum. How much did I want?

I said about four hundred thousand dollars a month, and board, was about all I could reasonably ask, considering the hard times.

I was ordered off the premises! And yet, when I look back to those days and call to mind the exceeding hardness of the labor I performed in that mill, I only regret that I did not ask him seven hundred thousand.

Shortly after this I began to grow crazy, along with the rest of the population, about the mysterious and wonderful "cement mine," and to make preparations to take advantage of any opportunity that might offer to go and help hunt for it.

CHAPTER 37

It was somewhere in the neighborhood of Mono Lake that the marvelous Whiteman cement mine was supposed to lie. Every now and then it would be reported that Mr. W. had passed stealthily through Esmeralda at dead of night, in disguise, and then we would have a wild excitement—because he must be steering for his secret mine, and now was the time to follow him. In less than three hours after daylight all the horses and mules and donkeys in the vicinity would be bought, hired or stolen, and half the community would be off for the mountains, following in the wake of Whiteman. But W. would drift about through the mountain gorges for days together, in a purposeless sort of way, until the provisions of the miners ran out, and they would have to go back home. I have known it reported at eleven at night, in a large mining camp, that Whiteman had just passed through, and in two hours, the streets, so quiet before, would be swarming with men and animals. Every individual would be trying to be very secret, but yet venturing to whisper to just one neighbor that W. had passed through. And long before daylight—this in the dead of winter—the stampede would be complete, the camp deserted, and the whole population gone chasing after W.

The tradition was that in the early immigration, more than twenty years ago, three young Germans, brothers, who had survived an Indian massacre on the Plains, wandered on foot through the deserts, avoiding all trails and roads, and simply holding a westerly direction and hoping to find California before they starved or died of fatigue. And in a gorge in the mountains they sat down to rest one day, when one of them noticed a curious vein of cement running along the ground, shot full of lumps of dull yellow metal. They saw that it was gold, and that here was a fortune to be acquired in a single day. The vein was about as wide as a curbstone, and fully two-thirds of it was pure gold. Every pound of the wonderful cement was worth well-nigh two hundred dollars. Each of the brothers loaded himself with about twenty-five pounds of it, and then they covered up all traces of the vein, made a rude drawing of the locality and the principal landmarks in the vicinity, and started westward again. But troubles thickened about them. In their wanderings one brother fell and broke his leg, and the others were obliged to go on and leave him to die in the wilderness. Another, worn out and starving, gave up by and by, and lay down to die, but after two or three weeks of incredible hardships, the third reached the settlements of California exhausted, sick, and his mind deranged by his sufferings. He had thrown away all his cement but a few fragments, but these were sufficient to set everybody wild with excitement. However, he had had enough of the cement country, and nothing could induce him to lead a party thither. He was entirely content to work on a farm for wages. But he gave Whiteman his map, and described the cement region as well as he could, and thus transferred the curse to that gentleman—for when I had my one accidental glimpse of Mr. W. in Esmeralda, he had been hunting for the lost mine, in hunger and thirst, poverty and sickness, for twelve or thirteen years. Some people believed he had found it, but most people believed he had not. I saw a

THE SAVED BROTHER.

piece of cement as large as my fist which was said to have been given to Whiteman by the young German, and it was of a seductive nature. Lumps of virgin gold were as thick in it as raisins in a slice of fruit cake. The privilege of working such a mine one week would be sufficient for a man of reasonable desires.

A new partner of ours, a Mr. Higbie, knew Whiteman well by sight, and a friend of ours, a Mr. Van Dorn, was well acquainted with him, and not only that, but had Whiteman's promise that he should have a private hint in time to enable him to join the next cement expedition. Van Dorn had promised to extend the hint to us. One evening Higbie came in greatly excited, and said he felt certain he had recognized Whiteman, up town, disguised and in a pretended state of intoxication. In a little while Van Dorn arrived and confirmed the news; and so we gathered in our cabin and with heads close together arranged our plans in impressive whispers.

We were to leave town quietly, after midnight, in two or three small parties, so as not to attract attention, and meet at dawn on the "divide" overlooking Mono Lake, eight or nine miles distant. We were to make no noise after starting, and not speak above a whisper under any circumstances. It was believed that for once Whiteman's presence was unknown in the town and his expedition unsuspected. Our conclave broke up at nine o'clock, and we set about our preparations diligently and with profound secrecy. At eleven o'clock we saddled our horses, hitched them with their long *riatas* (or lassos), and then brought out a side of bacon, a sack of beans, a small sack of coffee, some sugar, a hundred pounds of flour in sacks, some tin cups and a coffee-pot, frying pan and some few other necessary articles. All these things were "packed" on the back of a led horse—and whoever has not been taught, by a Spanish adept, to pack an animal, let him never hope to do the thing by natural smartness. That is impossible. Higbie had had some experience, but was not perfect. He put on the pack saddle (a thing like a saw-buck), piled the property on it and then wound a rope all over and about it and under it, "every which way," taking a hitch in it every now and then, and occasionally surging back on it till the horse's sides sunk in and he gasped for breath—but every time the lashings grew tight in one place they loosened in another. We never did get the load tight all over, but we got it so that it would do, after a fashion, and then we started, in single file, close order, and without a word. It was a dark night. We kept the middle of the road, and proceeded in a slow walk past the rows of cabins, and whenever a miner came to his door I trembled for fear the light would shine on us and excite curiosity. But nothing happened. We began the long winding ascent of the cañon, toward the "divide," and presently the cabins began to grow infrequent, and the intervals between them wider and wider, and then I began to breathe tolerably freely and feel less like a thief and a murderer. I was in the rear, leading the pack horse. As the ascent grew steeper he grew proportionately less satisfied with his cargo, and began to pull back on his *riata* occasionally and delay progress. My comrades were passing out of sight in the gloom. I was getting anxious. I coaxed and bullied the pack horse till I presently got him into a trot, and then the tin cups and pans strung about his person frightened him and he ran. His *riata* was wound around the pommel of my saddle, and so, as he went by he dragged me from my horse and the two animals traveled briskly on without me. But I was not alone—the loosened cargo tumbled overboard from the pack horse and fell close to me. It was abreast of almost the last cabin. A miner came out and said:

"Hello!"

I was thirty steps from him, and knew he could not see me, it was so very dark in the shadow of the mountain. So I lay still. Another head appeared in the light of the cabin door, and presently the two men walked toward me. They stopped within ten steps of me, and one said:

" 'St! Listen."

I could not have been in a more distressed state if I had been escaping justice with a price on my head. Then the miners appeared to sit down on a boulder, though I could not see them distinctly enough to be very sure what they did. One said:

"I heard a noise, as plain as I ever heard anything. It seemed to be about there—"

A stone whizzed by my head. I flattened myself out in the dust like a postage stamp, and thought to myself if he mended his aim ever so little he would probably hear another noise. In my heart, now, I execrated secret expeditions. I promised myself that this

ON A SECRET EXPEDITION.

should be my last, though the Sierras were ribbed with cement veins. Then one of the men said:

"I'll tell you what! Welch knew what he was talking about when he said he saw Whiteman to-day. I heard horses—that was the noise. I am going down to Welch's, right away."

They left and I was glad. I did not care whither they went, so they went. I was willing they should visit Welch, and the sooner the better.

As soon as they closed their cabin door my comrades emerged from the gloom; they had caught the horses and were waiting for a clear coast again. We remounted the cargo on the pack horse and got under way, and as day broke we reached the "divide" and joined Van Dorn. Then we journeyed down into the valley of the lake, and feeling secure, we halted to cook breakfast, for we were tired and sleepy and hungry. Three hours later the rest of the population filed over the "divide" in a long procession, and drifted off out of sight around the borders of the lake!

Whether or not my accident had produced this result we never knew, but at least one thing was certain—the secret was out and Whiteman would not enter upon a search for the cement mine this time. We were filled with chagrin.

We held a council and decided to make the best of our misfortune and enjoy a week's holiday on the borders of the curious lake. Mono, it is sometimes called, and sometimes the "Dead Sea of California." It is one of the strangest freaks of Nature to be found in any land, but it is hardly ever mentioned in print and very seldom visited, because it lies away off the usual routes of travel and besides is so difficult to get at that only men content to endure the roughest life will consent to take upon themselves the discomforts of such a trip. On the morning of our second day, we traveled around to a remote and particularly wild spot on the borders of the lake, where a stream of fresh, ice-cold water entered it from the mountain side, and then we went regularly into camp. We hired a large boat and two shotguns from a lonely ranchman who lived some ten miles further on, and made ready for comfort and recreation. We soon got thoroughly acquainted with the lake and all its peculiarities.

MONO LAKE.

CHAPTER 38

Mono Lake lies in a lifeless, treeless, hideous desert, eight thousand feet above the level of the sea, and is guarded by mountains two thousand feet higher, whose summits are always clothed in clouds. This solemn, silent, sailless sea—this lonely tenant of the loneliest spot on earth—is little graced with the picturesque. It is an unpretending expanse of grayish water, about a hundred miles in circumference, with two islands in its centre, mere upheavals of rent and scorched and blistered lava, snowed over with gray banks and drifts of pumice stone and ashes, the winding sheet of the dead volcano, whose vast crater the lake has seized upon and occupied.

The lake is two hundred feet deep, and its sluggish waters are so strong with alkali that if you only dip the most hopelessly soiled garment into them once or twice, and wring it out, it will be found as clean as if it had been through the ablest of washerwomen's hands. While we camped there our laundry work was easy. We tied the week's washing astern of our boat, and sailed a quarter of a mile, and the job was complete, all to the wringing out. If we threw the water on our heads and gave them a rub or so, the white lather would pile up three inches high. This water is not good for bruised places and abrasions of the skin. We had a valuable dog. He had raw places on him. He had more raw places on him than sound ones. He was the rawest dog I almost ever saw. He jumped overboard one day to get away from the flies. But it was bad judgment. In his condition, it would have been just as comfortable to jump into the fire. The alkali water nipped him in all the raw places simultaneously, and he struck out for the shore with considerable interest. He yelped and barked and howled as he went—and by the time he got to the shore there was no bark to him—for he had barked the bark all out of his inside, and the alkali water had cleaned the bark all

RATHER SOAPY.

off his outside, and he probably wished he had never embarked in any such enterprise. He ran round and round in a circle, and pawed the earth and clawed the air, and threw double summersets, some-

A BARK UNDER FULL SAIL.

times backwards and sometimes forwards, in the most extraordinary manner. He was not a demonstrative dog, as a general thing, but rather of a grave and serious turn of mind, and I never saw him take so much interest in anything before. He finally struck out over the mountains, at a gait which we estimated at about two hundred and fifty miles an hour, and he is going yet. This was about nine years ago. We look for what is left of him along here every day.

A white man cannot drink the water of Mono Lake, for it is nearly pure lye. It is said that the Indians in the vicinity drink it sometimes, though. It is not improbable, for they are among the purest liars I ever saw. [There will be no additional charge for this joke, except to parties requiring an explanation of it. This joke has received high commendation from some of the ablest minds of the age.]

There are no fish in Mono Lake—no frogs, no snakes, no polly-wogs—nothing, in fact, that goes to make life desirable. Millions of wild ducks and sea-gulls swim about the surface, but no living thing exists *under* the surface, except a white feathery sort of worm, one-half an inch long, which looks like a bit of white thread frayed out at the sides. If you dip up a gallon of water, you will get about fifteen thousand of these. They give to the water a sort of grayish-white appearance. Then there is a fly, which looks something like our house fly. These settle on the beach to eat the worms that wash ashore—and any time, you can see there a belt of flies an inch deep and six feet wide, and this belt extends clear around the lake—a belt of flies one hundred miles long. If you throw a stone among them, they swarm up so thick that they look dense, like a cloud. You can hold them under water as long as you please—they do not mind it—they are only proud of it. When you let them go, they pop up to the surface as dry as a patent office report, and walk off as unconcernedly as if they had been educated especially with a view to affording instructive entertainment to man in that particular way. Providence leaves nothing to go by chance. All things have their uses and their part and proper place in Nature's economy: the ducks eat the flies—the flies eat the worms—the Indians eat all three—the wild-cats eat the Indians—the white folks eat the wild-cats—and thus all things are lovely.

Mono Lake is a hundred and fifty miles in a straight line from the ocean—and between it and the ocean are one or two ranges of mountains—yet thousands of sea-gulls go there every season to lay their eggs and rear their young. One would as soon expect to find sea-gulls in Kansas. And in this connection let us observe another instance of Nature's wisdom. The islands in the lake being merely huge masses of lava, coated over with ashes and pumice stone, and utterly innocent of vegetation or anything that would burn; and sea-gulls' eggs being entirely useless to anybody unless they be cooked, Nature has provided an unfailing spring of boiling water on the largest island, and you can put your eggs in there, and in four minutes you can boil them as hard as any statement I have made during the past fifteen years. Within ten feet of the boiling spring is a spring of pure cold water, sweet and wholesome. So, in that island you get your board and washing free of charge—and if nature had gone further and furnished a nice American hotel clerk who was crusty and disobliging, and didn't know anything about the time tables, or the railroad routes—or—anything—and was proud of it—I would not wish for a more desirable boarding house.

A MODEL BOARDING HOUSE.

Half a dozen little mountain brooks flow into Mono Lake, but *not a stream of any kind flows out of it.* It neither rises nor falls, apparently, and what it does with its surplus water is a dark and bloody mystery.

There are only two seasons in the region round about Mono Lake—and these are, the breaking up of one winter and the beginning of the next. More than once (in Esmeralda) I have seen a perfectly blistering morning open up with the thermometer at ninety degrees at eight o'clock, and seen the snow fall fourteen inches deep and that same identical thermometer go down to forty-four degrees under shelter, before nine o'clock at night. Under favorable circumstances it snows at least once in every single month in the year, in the little town of Mono. So uncertain is the climate in summer that a lady who goes out visiting cannot hope to be prepared for all emergencies unless she takes her fan under one arm and her snow shoes under the other. When they have a Fourth of July procession it generally snows on them, and they do say that as a general thing when a man calls for a brandy toddy there, the barkeeper chops it off with a hatchet and wraps it up in a paper, like maple sugar. And it is further reported that the old soakers haven't any teeth—wore them out eating gin cocktails and brandy punches. I do not endorse that statement—I simply give it for what it is worth—and it is worth—well, I should say, millions, to any man who can believe it without straining himself. But I do endorse the snow on the Fourth of July—because I know that to be true.

CHAPTER 39

About seven o'clock one blistering hot morning—for it was now dead summer time—Higbie and I took the boat and started on a voyage of discovery to the two islands. We had often longed to do this, but had been deterred by the fear of storms; for they were frequent, and severe enough to capsize an ordinary row-boat like ours without great difficulty—and once capsized, death would ensue in spite of the bravest swimming, for that venomous water would eat a man's eyes out like fire, and burn him out inside, too, if he shipped a sea. It was called twelve miles, straight out to the islands—a long pull and a warm one—but the morning was so quiet and sunny, and the lake so smooth and glassy and dead, that we could not resist the temptation. So we filled two large tin canteens with water (since we were not acquainted with the locality of the spring said to exist on the large island), and started. Higbie's brawny muscles gave the boat good speed, but by the time we reached our destination we judged that we had pulled nearer fifteen miles than twelve.

We landed on the big island and went ashore. We tried the water in the canteens, now, and found that the sun had spoiled it; it was so brackish that we could not drink it; so we poured it out and began a search for the spring—for thirst augments fast as soon as it is apparent that one has no means at hand of quenching it. The island was a long, moderately high hill of ashes—nothing but gray ashes and pumice stone, in which we sunk to our knees at every step—and all around the top was a forbidding wall of scorched and blasted rocks. When we reached the top and got within the wall, we found simply a shallow, far-reaching basin, carpeted with ashes, and here and there a patch of fine sand. In places, picturesque jets of steam shot up out of crevices, giving evidence that although this ancient crater had gone out of active business, there was still some fire left in its furnaces. Close to one of these jets of steam stood the

LIFE AMID DEATH.

only tree on the island—a small pine of most graceful shape and most faultless symmetry; its color was a brilliant green, for the steam drifted unceasingly through its branches and kept them always moist. It contrasted strangely enough, did this vigorous and beautiful outcast, with its dead and dismal surroundings. It was like a cheerful spirit in a mourning household.

We hunted for the spring everywhere, traversing the full length of the island (two or three miles), and crossing it twice—climbing ash-hills patiently, and then sliding down the other side in a sitting posture, plowing up smothering volumes of gray dust. But we found nothing but solitude, ashes and a heart-breaking silence. Finally we noticed that the wind had risen, and we forgot our thirst in a solicitude of greater importance; for, the lake being quiet, we had not taken pains about securing the boat. We hurried back to a point overlooking our landing place, and then—but mere words cannot describe our dismay—the boat was gone! The chances were that there was not another boat on the entire lake. The situation was not comfortable—in truth, to speak plainly, it was frightful. We were prisoners on a desolate island, in aggravating proximity to friends who were for the present helpless to aid us; and what was still more uncomfortable was the reflection that we had neither food nor water. But presently we sighted the boat. It was drifting along, leisurely, about fifty yards from shore, tossing in a foamy sea. It drifted, and continued to drift, but at the same safe distance from land, and we walked along abreast it and waited for fortune to favor us. At the end of an hour it approached a jutting cape, and Higbie ran ahead and posted himself on the utmost verge and prepared for the assault. If we failed there, there was no hope for us. It was driving gradually shoreward all the time, now; but whether it was driving fast enough to make the connection or not was the momentous question. When it got within thirty steps of Higbie I was so excited that I fancied I could hear my own heart beat. When, a little later, it dragged slowly along and seemed about to go by, only one little yard out of reach, it seemed as if my heart stood still; and when it was exactly abreast him and began to widen away, and he still standing like a watching statue, I knew my heart did stop. But

A JUMP FOR LIFE.

when he gave a great spring, the next instant, and lit fairly in the stern, I discharged a war-whoop that woke the solitudes!

But it dulled my enthusiasm, presently, when he told me he had not been caring whether the boat came within jumping distance or not, so that it passed within eight or ten yards of him, for he had made up his mind to shut his eyes and mouth and swim that trifling distance. Imbecile that I was, I had not thought of that. It was only a long swim that could be fatal.

The sea was running high and the storm increasing. It was growing late, too—three or four in the afternoon. Whether to venture toward the mainland or not, was a question of some moment. But we were so distressed by thirst that we decided to try it, and so Higbie fell to work and I took the steering-oar. When we had pulled a mile, laboriously, we were evidently in serious peril, for the storm had greatly augmented; the billows ran very high and were capped with foaming crests, the heavens were hung with black, and the wind blew with great fury. We would have gone back, now, but we did not dare to turn the boat around, because as soon as she got in the trough of the sea she would upset, of course. Our only hope lay in keeping her head on to the seas. It was hard work to do this, she plunged so, and so beat and belabored the billows with her rising and falling bows. Now and then one of Higbie's oars would trip on the top of a wave, and the other one would snatch the boat half around in spite of my cumbersome steering apparatus. We were drenched by the sprays constantly, and the boat occasionally shipped water. By and by, powerful as my comrade was, his great exertions began to tell on him, and he was anxious that I should change places with him till he could rest a little. But I told him this was impossible; for if the steering-oar were dropped a moment while we changed, the boat would slue around into the trough of the sea, capsize, and in less than five minutes we would have a hundred gallons of soap-suds in us and be eaten up so quickly that we could not even be present at our own inquest.

But things cannot last always. Just as the darkness shut down we came booming into port, head on. Higbie dropped his oars to hurrah—I dropped mine to help—the sea gave the boat a twist, and over she went!

The agony that alkali water inflicts on bruises, chafes and blistered hands, is unspeakable, and nothing but greasing all over will modify it—but we ate, drank and slept well, that night, notwithstanding.

In speaking of the peculiarities of Mono Lake, I ought to have mentioned that at intervals all around its shores stand picturesque turret-looking masses and clusters of a whitish, coarse-grained rock that resembles inferior mortar dried hard; and if one breaks off fragments of this rock he will find perfectly shaped and thoroughly petrified gulls' eggs deeply imbedded in the mass. How did they get there? I simply state the fact—for it is a fact—and leave the geological reader to crack the nut at his leisure and solve the problem after his own fashion.

At the end of a week we adjourned to the Sierras on a fishing excursion, and spent several days in camp under snowy Castle Peak, and fished successfully for trout in a bright, miniature lake whose surface was between ten and eleven thousand feet above the level of the sea; cooling ourselves during the hot August noons by sitting on snow banks ten feet deep, under whose sheltering edges *fine grass and dainty flowers flourished luxuriously;* and at night entertaining ourselves by almost freezing to death. Then we returned to Mono Lake, and finding that the cement excitement was over for the present, packed up and went back to Esmeralda. Mr. Ballou reconnoitred awhile, and not liking the prospect, set out alone for Humboldt.

About this time occurred a little incident which has always had a sort of interest to me, from the fact that it came so near "instigating" my funeral. At a time when an Indian attack had been expected, the citizens hid their gunpowder where it would be safe and yet convenient to hand when wanted. A neighbor of ours hid six cans of rifle powder in the bake-oven of an old discarded cooking stove which stood on the open ground near a frame out-house or shed, and from and after that day never thought of it again. We hired a half-tamed Indian to do some washing for us, and he took up quarters under the shed with his tub. The ancient stove reposed within six feet of him, and before his face. Finally it occurred to him that hot water would be better than cold, and he went out and fired up under that forgotten powder magazine and set on a kettle of water. Then he returned to his tub. I entered the shed presently and threw down some more clothes, and was about to speak to him when the stove blew up with a prodigious crash, and disappeared, leaving not a splinter behind. Fragments of it fell in the streets full two hundred yards away. Nearly a third of the shed roof over our heads was destroyed, and one of the stove lids, after cutting a small stanchion half in two in front of the Indian, whizzed between us and drove partly through the weather-boarding beyond. I was as white as a sheet and as weak as a kitten and speechless. But the Indian betrayed no trepidation, no distress, not even discomfort. He simply stopped washing, leaned forward and surveyed the clean, blank ground a moment, and then remarked:

"STOVE HEAP GONE!"

"Mph! Dam stove heap gone!"—and resumed his scrubbing as placidly as if it were an entirely customary thing for a stove to do. I will explain, that "heap" is "Injun-English" for "very much." The reader will perceive the exhaustive expressiveness of it in the present instance.

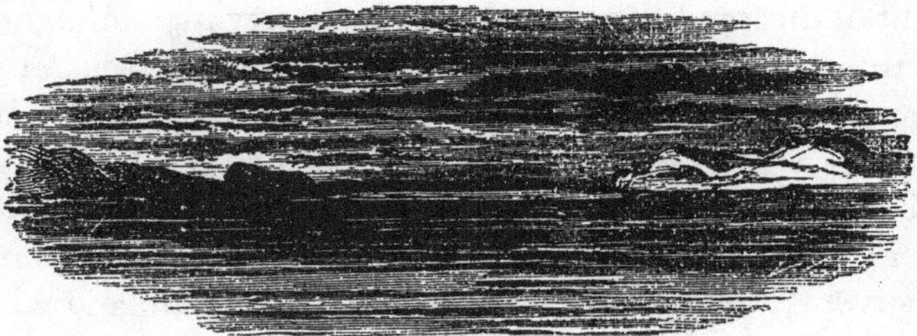

CHAPTER 40

I NOW come to a curious episode—the most curious, I think, that had yet accented my slothful, valueless, heedless career. Out of a hillside toward the upper end of the town, projected a wall of reddish looking quartz-croppings, the exposed comb of a silver-bearing ledge that extended deep down into the earth, of course. It was owned by a company entitled the "Wide West." There was a shaft sixty or seventy feet deep on the under side of the croppings, and everybody was acquainted with the rock that came from it—and tolerably rich rock it was, too, but nothing extraordinary. I will remark here, that although to the inexperienced stranger all the quartz of a particular "district" looks about alike, an old resident of the camp can take a glance at a mixed pile of rock, separate the fragments and tell you which mine each came from, as easily as a confectioner can separate and classify the various kinds and qualities of candy in a mixed heap of the article.

All at once the town was thrown into a state of extraordinary excitement. In mining parlance the Wide West had "struck it rich!" Everybody went to see the new developments, and for some days there was such a crowd of people about the Wide West shaft that a stranger would have supposed there was a mass meeting in session there. No other topic was discussed but the rich strike, and nobody thought or dreamed about anything else. Every man brought away a specimen, ground it up in a hand mortar, washed it out in his horn spoon, and glared speechless upon the marvelous result. It was not hard rock, but black, decomposed stuff which could be crumbled in the hand like a baked potato, and when spread out on a paper exhibited a thick sprinkling of gold and particles of "native" silver. Higbie brought a handful to the cabin, and when he had washed it out his amazement was beyond description. Wide

West stock soared skywards. It was said that repeated offers had been made for it at a thousand dollars a foot, and promptly refused. We have all had the "blues"—the mere sky-blues—but mine were indigo, now—because I did not own in the Wide West. The world seemed hollow to me, and existence a grief. I lost my appetite, and ceased to take an interest in anything. Still I had to stay, and listen to other people's rejoicings, because I had no money to get out of the camp with.

The Wide West company put a stop to the carrying away of "specimens," and well they might, for every handful of the ore was worth a sum of some consequence. To show the exceeding value of the ore, I will remark that a sixteen-hundred-pound parcel of it was sold, just as it lay, at the mouth of the shaft, at *one dollar a pound;* and the man who bought it "packed" it on mules a hundred and fifty or two hundred miles, over the mountains, to San Francisco, satisfied that it would yield at a rate that would richly compensate him for his trouble. The Wide West people also commanded their foreman to refuse any but their own operatives permission to enter the mine at any time or for any purpose. I kept up my "blue" meditations and Higbie kept up a deal of thinking, too, but of a different sort. He puzzled over the "rock," examined it with a glass, inspected it in different lights and from different points of view, and after each experiment delivered himself, in soliloquy, of one and the same unvarying opinion in the same unvarying formula:

"It is *not* Wide West rock!"

He said once or twice that he meant to have a look into the Wide West shaft if he got shot for it. I was wretched, and did not care whether he got a look into it or not. He failed that day, and tried again at night; failed again; got up at dawn and tried, and failed again. Then he lay in ambush in the sage-brush hour after hour, waiting for the two or three hands to adjourn to the shade of a boulder for dinner; made a start once, but was premature—one of the men came back for something; tried it again, but when almost at the mouth of the shaft, another of the men rose up from behind the boulder as if to reconnoitre, and he dropped on the ground and lay quiet; presently he crawled on his hands and knees to the mouth of the shaft, gave a quick glance around, then seized the rope and slid down the shaft. He disappeared in the gloom of a "side drift" just as a head appeared in the mouth of the shaft and somebody shouted "Hello!"—which he did not answer. He was not disturbed any more. An hour later he entered the cabin, hot, red, and ready to burst with smothered excitement, and exclaimed in a stage whisper:

"I knew it! We are rich! IT'S A BLIND LEAD!"

I thought the very earth reeled under me. Doubt—conviction—doubt again—exultation—hope, amazement, belief, unbelief—every emotion imaginable swept in wild procession through my heart and brain, and I could not speak a word. After a moment or two of this mental fury, I shook myself to rights, and said:

INTERVIEWING THE "WIDE WEST."

"Say it again!"

"It's a blind lead!"

"Cal., let's—let's burn the house—or kill somebody! Let's get out where there's room to hurrah! But what is the use? It is a hundred times too good to be true."

"It's a blind lead, for a million!—hanging wall—foot wall—clay casings—everything complete!" He swung his hat and gave three cheers, and I cast doubt to the winds and chimed in with a will. For I was worth a million dollars, and did not care "whether school kept or not!"

But perhaps I ought to explain. A "blind lead" is a lead or ledge that does not "crop out" above the surface. A miner does not know where to look for such leads, but they are often stumbled upon by accident in the course of driving a tunnel or sinking a shaft. Higbie knew the Wide West rock perfectly well, and the more he had examined the new developments the more he was satisfied that the

WORTH A MILLION.

ore could not have come from the Wide West vein. And so had it occurred to him alone, of all the camp, that there was a blind lead down in the shaft, and that even the Wide West people themselves did not suspect it. He was right. When he went down the shaft, he found that the blind lead held its independent way through the Wide West vein, cutting it diagonally, and that it was enclosed in its own well-defined casing-rocks and clay. Hence it was public property. Both leads being perfectly well defined, it was easy for any miner to see which one belonged to the Wide West and which did not.

We thought it well to have a strong friend, and therefore we brought the foreman of the Wide West to our cabin that night and revealed the great surprise to him. Higbie said:

"We are going to take possession of this blind lead, record it and establish ownership, and then forbid the Wide West company to take out any more of the rock. You cannot help your company in this matter—nobody can help them. I will go into the shaft with you and prove to your entire satisfaction that it *is* a blind lead. Now we propose to take you in with us, and claim the blind lead in our three names. What do you say?"

What could a man say who had an opportunity to simply stretch forth his hand and take possession of a fortune without risk of any kind and without wronging any one or attaching the least taint of dishonor to his name? He could only say, "Agreed."

The notice was put up that night, and duly spread upon the recorder's books before ten o'clock. We claimed two hundred feet each—six hundred feet in all—the smallest and compactest organization in the district, and the easiest to manage.

No one can be so thoughtless as to suppose that we slept, that night. Higbie and I went to bed at midnight, but it was only to lie broad awake and think, dream, scheme. The floorless, tumbledown cabin was a palace, the ragged gray blankets silk, the furni-

MILLIONAIRES LAYING PLANS.

ture rosewood and mahogany. Each new splendor that burst out of my visions of the future whirled me bodily over in bed or jerked me to a sitting posture just as if an electric battery had been applied to me. We shot fragments of conversation back and forth at each other. Once Higbie said:

"When are you going home—to the States?"

"To-morrow!"—with an evolution or two, ending with a sitting position. "Well—no—but next month, at furthest."

"We'll go in the same steamer."

"Agreed."

A pause.

"Steamer of the 10th?"

"Yes. No, the 1st."

"All right."

Another pause.

"Where are you going to live?" said Higbie.

"San Francisco."

"That's me!"

Pause.

"Too high—too much climbing"—from Higbie.

"What is?"

"I was thinking of Russian Hill—building a house up there."

"Too much climbing? Shan't you keep a carriage?"

"Of course. I forgot that."

Pause.

"Cal., what kind of a house are you going to build?"

"I was thinking about that. Three-story and an attic."

"But what *kind*?"

"Well, I don't hardly know. Brick, I suppose."

"Brick—bosh."

"Why? What is your idea?"

"Brown stone front—French plate glass—billiard-room off the dining-room—statuary and paintings—shrubbery and two-acre grass plat—greenhouse—iron dog on the front stoop—gray horses—landau, and a coachman with a bug on his hat!"

"By George!"

A long pause.

"Cal., when are you going to Europe?"

"Well—I hadn't thought of that. When are you?"

"In the spring."

"Going to be gone all summer?"

"All summer! I shall remain there three years."

"No—but are you in earnest?"

"Indeed I am."

"I will go along too."

"Why of course you will."

"What part of Europe shall you go to?"

"All parts. France, England, Germany—Spain, Italy, Switzerland, Syria, Greece, Palestine, Arabia, Persia, Egypt—all over—everywhere."

"I'm agreed."

"All right."

"Won't it be a swell trip!"

"We'll spend forty or fifty thousand dollars trying to make it one, anyway."

Another long pause.

"Higbie, we owe the butcher six dollars, and he has been threatening to stop our—"

"Hang the butcher!"

"Amen."

And so it went on. By three o'clock we found it was no use, and so we got up and played cribbage and smoked pipes till sunrise. It was my week to cook. I always hated cooking—now, I abhorred it.

The news was all over town. The former excitement was great—this one was greater still. I walked the streets serene and happy. Higbie said the foreman had been offered two hundred thousand dollars for his third of the mine. I said I would like to see myself selling for any such price. My ideas were lofty. My figure was a million. Still, I honestly believe that if I had been offered it, it would have had no other effect than to make me hold off for more.

I found abundant enjoyment in being rich. A man offered me a three-hundred-dollar horse, and wanted to take my simple, unendorsed note for it. That brought the most realizing sense I had yet had that I was actually rich, beyond shadow of doubt. It was followed by numerous other evidences of a similar nature—among which I may mention the fact of the butcher leaving us a double supply of meat and saying nothing about money.

By the laws of the district, the "locators" or claimants of a ledge were obliged to do a fair and reasonable amount of work on their new property within ten days after the date of the location, or the property was forfeited, and anybody could go and seize it that chose. So we determined to go to work the next day. About the middle of the afternoon, as I was coming out of the post office, I met a Mr. Gardiner, who told me that Capt. John Nye was lying dangerously ill at his place (the "Nine-Mile Ranch"), and that he

DANGEROUSLY SICK.

and his wife were not able to give him nearly as much care and attention as his case demanded. I said if he would wait for me a moment, I would go down and help in the sick room. I ran to the cabin to tell Higbie. He was not there, but I left a note on the table for him, and a few minutes later I left town in Gardiner's wagon.

CHAPTER 41

CAPT. NYE was very ill indeed, with spasmodic rheumatism. But the old gentleman was himself—which is to say, he was kind-hearted and agreeable when comfortable, but a singularly violent wild-cat when things did not go well. He would be smiling along pleasantly enough, when a sudden spasm of his disease would take him and he would go out of his smile into a perfect fury. He would groan and wail and howl with the anguish, and fill up the odd chinks with the most elaborate profanity that strong convictions and a fine fancy could contrive. With fair opportunity he could swear very well and handle his adjectives with considerable judgment; but when the spasm was on him it was painful to listen to him, he was so awkward. However, I had seen him nurse a sick man himself and put up patiently with the inconveniences of the situation, and consequently I was willing that he should have full license now that his own turn had come. He could not disturb me, with all his raving and ranting, for my mind had work on hand, and it labored on diligently, night and day, whether my hands were idle or employed. I was altering and amending the plans for my house, and thinking over the propriety of having the billiard-room in the attic, instead of on the same floor with the dining-room; also, I was trying to decide between green and blue for the upholstery of the drawing-room, for, although my preference was blue I feared it was a color that would be too easily damaged by dust and sunlight; likewise while I was content to put the coachman in a modest livery, I was uncertain about a footman—I needed one, and was even resolved to have one, but wished he could properly appear and perform his functions out of livery, for I somewhat dreaded so much show; and yet, inasmuch as my late grandfather had had a coachman and such things, but no liveries, I felt rather drawn to beat him;—or beat his ghost, at any rate; I was also systematizing the

European trip, and managed to get it all laid out, as to route and length of time to be devoted to it—everything, with one exception—namely, whether to cross the desert from Cairo to Jerusalem per camel, or go by sea to Beirut, and thence down through the country per caravan. Meantime I was writing to the friends at home every day, instructing them concerning all my plans and intentions, and directing them to look up a handsome homestead for my mother and agree upon a price for it against my coming, and also directing them to sell my share of the Tennessee land and tender the proceeds to the widows' and orphans' fund of the typographical union of which I had long been a member in good standing. [This Tennessee land had been in the possession of the family many years, and promised to confer high fortune upon us some day; it still promises it, but in a less violent way.]

When I had been nursing the Captain nine days he was somewhat better, but very feeble. During the afternoon we lifted him into a chair and gave him an alcoholic vapor bath, and then set about putting him on the bed again. We had to be exceedingly careful, for the least jar produced pain. Gardiner had his shoulders and I his legs; in an unfortunate moment I stumbled and the patient fell heavily on the bed in an agony of torture. I never heard a man swear so in my life. He raved like a maniac, and tried to snatch a revolver from the table—but I got it. He ordered me out of the house, and swore a world of oaths that he would kill me wherever he caught me when he got on his feet again. It was simply a passing fury, and meant nothing. I knew he would forget it in an hour, and maybe be sorry for it, too; but it angered me a little, at the moment. So much so, indeed, that I determined to go back to Esmeralda. I thought he was able to get along alone, now, since he was on the war path. I took supper, and as soon as the moon rose, began my nine-mile journey, on foot. Even millionaires needed no horses, in those days, for a mere nine-mile jaunt without baggage.

As I "raised the hill" overlooking the town, it lacked fifteen minutes of twelve. I glanced at the hill over beyond the cañon, and in the bright moonlight saw what appeared to be about half the population of the village massed on and around the Wide West croppings. My heart gave an exulting bound, and I said to myself, "They have made a new strike to-night—and struck it richer than ever, no doubt." I started over there, but gave it up. I said the "strike" would keep, and I had climbed hills enough for one night. I went on down through the town, and as I was passing a little German bakery, a woman ran out and begged me to come in and help her. She said her husband had a fit. I went in, and judged she was right—he appeared to have a hundred of them, compressed into one. Two Germans were there, trying to hold him, and not making much of a success of it. I ran up the street half a block or so and routed out a sleeping doctor, brought him down half dressed, and we four wrestled with the maniac, and doctored, drenched and bled him, for more than an hour, and the poor German woman did the crying. He grew quiet, now, and the doctor and I withdrew and left him to his friends.

It was a little after one o'clock. As I entered the cabin door, tired but jolly, the dingy light of a tallow candle revealed Higbie, sitting by the pine table gazing stupidly at my note, which he held in his fingers, and looking pale, old, and haggard. I halted, and looked at him. He looked at me, stolidly. I said:

"Higbie, what—what is it?"

"We're ruined—we didn't do the work—THE BLIND LEAD'S RELOCATED!"

It was enough. I sat down sick, grieved—broken-hearted, indeed. A minute before, I was rich and brim full of vanity; I was a pauper now, and very meek. We sat still an hour, busy with thought, busy with vain and useless self-upbraidings, busy with "Why *didn't* I do this, and why *didn't* I do that," but neither spoke a word. Then we dropped into mutual explanations, and the mystery was cleared away. It came out that Higbie had depended on me, as I had on him, and as both of us had on the foreman. The folly of it! It was the first time that ever staid and steadfast Higbie had left an important matter to chance or failed to be true to his full share of a responsibility.

But he had never seen my note till this moment, and this moment was the first time he had been in the cabin since the day he had seen me last. He, also, had left a note for me, on that same fatal afternoon—had ridden up on horseback, and looked through the window, and being in a hurry and not seeing me, had tossed the

WORTH NOTHING.

note into the cabin through a broken pane. Here it was, on the floor, where it had remained undisturbed for nine days:

> Don't fail to do the work before the ten days expire. W. has passed through and given me notice. I am to join him at Mono Lake, and we shall go on from there to-night. He says he will find it this time, sure. CAL.

"W." meant Whiteman, of course. That thrice accursed "cement!"

That was the way of it. An old miner, like Higbie, could no more withstand the fascination of a mysterious mining excitement like this "cement" foolishness, than he could refrain from eating when he was famishing. Higbie had been dreaming about the marvelous cement for months; and now, against his better judgment, he had gone off and "taken the chances" on my keeping secure a mine worth a million undiscovered cement veins. They had not been followed this time. His riding out of town in broad daylight was such a commonplace thing to do that it had not attracted any attention. He said they prosecuted their search in the fastnesses of the mountains during nine days, without success; they could not find the cement. Then a ghastly fear came over him that something might have happened to prevent the doing of the necessary work to hold the blind lead (though indeed he thought such a thing hardly possible), and forthwith he started home with all speed. He would have reached Esmeralda in time, but his horse broke down and he had to walk a great part of the distance. And so it happened that as he came into Esmeralda by one road, I entered it by another. His was the superior energy, however, for he went straight to the Wide West, instead of turning aside as I had done—and he arrived there about five or ten minutes too late! The "notice" was already up, the "relocation" of our mine completed beyond recall, and the crowd rapidly dispersing. He learned some facts before he left the ground. The foreman had not been seen about the streets since the night we had located the mine—a telegram had called him to California on a matter of life and death, it was said. At any rate he had done no work and the watchful eyes of the community were taking note of the fact. At midnight of this woful tenth day, the ledge would be "relocatable," and by eleven o'clock the hill was black with men prepared to do the relocating. That was the crowd I had seen when I fancied a new "strike" had been made—idiot that I was. [We three had the same right to relocate the lead that other people had, provided we were quick enough.] As midnight was announced, fourteen men, duly armed and ready to back their proceedings, put up their "notice" and proclaimed their ownership of the blind lead, under the new name of the "Johnson." But A. D. Allen our partner (the foreman) put in a sudden appearance about that time, with a cocked revolver in his hand, and said his name must be added to the list, or he would "thin out the Johnson company some." He was a manly, splendid, determined fellow, and known to be as good as his word, and therefore a compromise was effected. They put in his name for a hundred feet, reserving to themselves the customary two hundred feet each. Such was the history of the night's events, as Higbie gathered from a friend on the way home.

ENFORCING A COMPROMISE.

Higbie and I cleared out on a new mining excitement the next morning, glad to get away from the scene of our sufferings, and after a month or two of hardship and disappointment, returned to Esmeralda once more. Then we learned that the Wide West and the Johnson companies had consolidated; that the stock, thus united, comprised five thousand feet, or shares; that the foreman, apprehending tiresome litigation, and considering such a huge concern unwieldy, had sold his hundred feet for ninety thousand dollars in gold and gone home to the States to enjoy it. If the stock was worth such a gallant figure, with five thousand shares in the corporation, it makes me dizzy to think what it would have been worth with only our original six hundred in it. It was the difference between six hundred men owning a house and five thousand owning it. We would have been millionaires if we had only worked with pick and spade one little day on our property and so secured our ownership!

It reads like a wild fancy sketch, but the evidence of many witnesses, and likewise that of the official records of Esmeralda District, is easily obtainable in proof that it is a true history. I can always have it to say that I was absolutely and unquestionably worth a million dollars, once, for ten days.

A year ago my esteemed and in every way estimable old millionaire partner, Higbie, wrote me from an obscure little mining camp in California that after nine or ten years of buffetings and hard striving, he was at last in a position where he could command twenty-five hundred dollars, and said he meant to go into the fruit business in a modest way. How such a thought would have insulted him the night we lay in our cabin planning European trips and brown stone houses on Russian Hill!

CHAPTER 42

WHAT to do next?

It was a momentous question. I had gone out into the world to shift for myself, at the age of thirteen (for my father had endorsed for friends; and although he left us a sumptuous legacy of pride in his fine Virginian stock and its national distinction, I presently found that I could not live on that alone without occasional bread to wash it down with). I had gained a livelihood in various vocations, but had not dazzled anybody with my successes; still the list was before me, and the amplest liberty in the matter of choosing, provided I wanted to work—which I did not, after being so wealthy. I had once been a grocery clerk, for one day, but had consumed so much sugar in that time that I was relieved from further duty by the proprietor; said he wanted me outside, so that he could have my custom. I had studied law an entire week, and then given it up because it was so prosy and tiresome. I had engaged briefly in the study of blacksmithing, but wasted so much time trying to fix the bellows so that it would blow itself, that the master turned me adrift in disgrace, and told me I would come to no good. I had been a bookseller's clerk for a while, but the customers bothered me so much I could not read with any comfort, and so the proprietor gave me a furlough and forgot to put a limit to it. I had clerked in a drug store part of a summer, but my prescriptions were unlucky, and we appeared to sell more stomach pumps than soda water. So I had to go. I had made of myself a tolerable printer, under the impression that I would be another Franklin some day, but somehow had missed the connection thus far. There was no berth open in the Esmeralda *Union*, and besides I had always been such a slow compositor that I looked with envy upon the achievements of apprentices of two years' standing; and when I took a "take," foremen were in the habit of suggesting that it would be wanted "some time during the year." I was a good average St. Louis and New Orleans pilot and by no means ashamed of my abilities in that line; wages were two

ONE OF MY FAILURES.

hundred and fifty dollars a month and no board to pay, and I did long to stand behind a wheel again and never roam any more—but I had been making such an ass of myself lately in grandiloquent letters home about my blind lead and my European excursion that I did what many and many a poor disappointed miner had done before; said "It is all over with me now, and I will never go back home to be pitied—and snubbed." I had been a private secretary, a silver miner and a silver mill operative, and amounted to less than nothing in each, and now—

What to do next?

I yielded to Higbie's appeals and consented to try the mining once more. We climbed far up on the mountain side and went to work on a little rubbishy claim of ours that had a shaft on it eight feet deep. Higbie descended into it and worked bravely with his pick till he had loosened up a deal of rock and dirt and then I went down with a long-handled shovel (the most awkward invention yet contrived by man) to throw it out. You must brace the shovel forward with the side of your knee till it is full, and then, with a skilful toss, throw it backwards over your left shoulder. I made the toss and landed the mess just on the edge of the shaft and it all came back on my head and down the back of my neck. I never said a word, but climbed out and walked home. I inwardly resolved that I would starve before I would make a target of myself and shoot rubbish at it with a long-handled shovel. I sat down, in the cabin, and gave myself up to solid misery—so to speak. Now in pleasanter days I had amused myself with writing letters to the chief paper of the Territory, the Virginia *Daily Territorial Enterprise,* and had always been surprised when they appeared in print. My good opinion of the editors had steadily declined; for it seemed to me that they might have found something better to fill up with than my literature. I had found a letter in the post office as I came home from the hillside, and finally I opened it. Eureka! [I never did know what Eureka meant, but it seems to be as proper a word to heave in as any when no other that sounds pretty offers.] It was a deliberate offer to me of Twenty-Five Dollars a week to come up to Virginia and be city editor of the *Enterprise.*

TARGET SHOOTING.

I would have challenged the publisher in the "blind lead" days—I wanted to fall down and worship him, now. Twenty-Five Dollars a week—it looked like bloated luxury—a fortune—a sinful and lavish waste of money. But my transports cooled when I thought of my inexperience and consequent unfitness for the position—and straightway, on top of this, my long array of failures rose up before me. Yet if I refused this place I must presently become dependent upon somebody for my bread, a thing necessarily distasteful to a man who had never experienced such a humiliation since he was thirteen years old. Not much to be proud of, since it is so common—but then it was all I had to *be* proud of. So I was scared into being a city editor. I would have declined, otherwise. Necessity is the mother of "taking chances." I do not doubt that if, at that time, I had been offered a salary to translate the Talmud from the original Hebrew, I would have accepted—albeit with diffidence and some misgivings—and thrown as much variety into it as I could for the money.

I went up to Virginia and entered upon my new vocation. I was a rusty looking city editor, I am free to confess—coatless, slouch hat, blue woolen shirt, pantaloons stuffed into boot-tops, whiskered half down to the waist, and the universal navy revolver slung to my belt. But I secured a more Christian costume and discarded the revolver. I had never had occasion to kill anybody, nor ever felt a desire to do so, but had worn the thing in deference to popular sentiment, and in order that I might not, by its absence, be offensively conspicuous, and a subject of remark. But the other editors, and all the printers, carried revolvers. I asked the chief editor and proprietor (Mr. Goodman, I will call him, since it describes him as well as any name could do) for some instructions with regard to my duties, and he told me to go all over town and ask all sorts of people all sorts of questions, make notes of the information gained, and write them out for publication. And he added:

AS CITY EDITOR.

"Never say 'We learn' so-and-so, or 'It is reported,' or 'It is rumored,' or 'We understand' so-and-so, but go to headquarters and get the absolute facts, and then speak out and say 'It *is* so-and-so.' Otherwise, people will not put confidence in your news. Unassailable certainty is the thing that gives a newspaper the firmest and most valuable reputation."

It was the whole thing in a nut-shell; and to this day when I find a reporter commencing his article with "We understand," I gather a suspicion that he has not taken as much pains to inform himself as he ought to have done. I moralize well, but I did not always practice well when I was a city editor; I let fancy get the upper hand of fact too often when there was a dearth of news. I can never forget my first day's experience as a reporter. I wandered about town questioning everybody, boring everybody, and finding out that nobody knew anything. At the end of five hours my note-book was still barren. I spoke to Mr. Goodman. He said:

"Dan used to make a good thing out of the hay wagons in a dry time when there were no fires or inquests. Are there no hay wagons in from the Truckee? If there are, you might speak of the renewed activity and all that sort of thing, in the hay business, you know. It isn't sensational or exciting, but it fills up and looks business-like."

I canvassed the city again and found one wretched old hay truck dragging in from the country. But I made affluent use of it. I multi-

THE ENTIRE MARKET.

plied it by sixteen, brought it into town from sixteen different directions, made sixteen separate items out of it, and got up such another sweat about hay as Virginia City had never seen in the world before.

This was encouraging. Two nonpareil columns had to be filled, and I was getting along. Presently, when things began to look dismal again, a desperado killed a man in a saloon and joy returned once more. I never was so glad over any mere trifle before in my life. I said to the murderer:

"Sir, you are a stranger to me, but you have done me a kindness this day which I can never forget. If whole years of gratitude can be to you any slight compensation, they shall be yours. I was in trouble and you have relieved me nobly and at a time when all seemed dark and drear. Count me your friend from this time forth, for I am not a man to forget a favor."

A FRIEND INDEED.

If I did not really say that to him I at least felt a sort of itching desire to do it. I wrote up the murder with a hungry attention to details, and when it was finished experienced but one regret—namely, that they had not hanged my benefactor on the spot, so that I could work him up too.

Next I discovered some emigrant wagons going into camp on the plaza and found that they had lately come through the hostile Indian country and had fared rather roughly. I made the best of the item that the circumstances permitted, and felt that if I were not confined within rigid limits by the presence of the reporters of the other papers I could add particulars that would make the article much more interesting. However, I found one wagon that was going on to California, and made some judicious inquiries of the proprietor. When I learned, through his short and surly answers to my cross-questioning, that he was certainly going on and would not be in the city next day to make trouble, I got ahead of the other papers, for I took down his list of names and added his party to the killed and wounded. Having more scope here, I put this wagon through an Indian fight that to this day has no parallel in history.

My two columns were filled. When I read them over in the morning I felt that I had found my legitimate occupation at last. I reasoned within myself that news, and stirring news, too, was what a paper needed, and I felt that I was peculiarly endowed with the ability to furnish it. Mr. Goodman said that I was as good a reporter as Dan. I desired no higher commendation. With encouragement like that, I felt that I could take my pen and murder all the immigrants on the plains if need be and the interests of the paper demanded it.

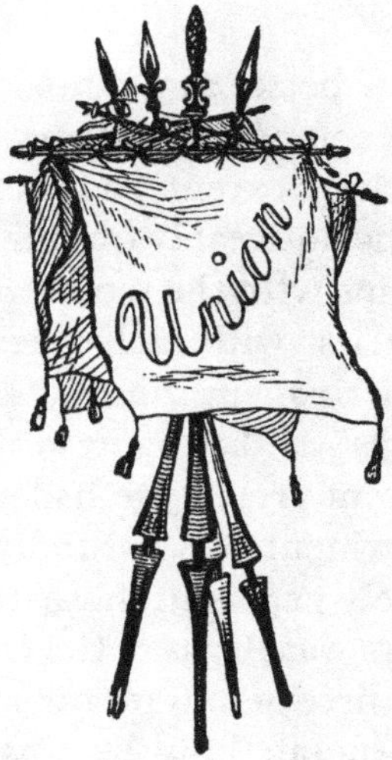

CHAPTER 43

HOWEVER, as I grew better acquainted with the business and learned the run of the sources of information I ceased to require the aid of fancy to any large extent, and became able to fill my columns without diverging noticeably from the domain of fact.

I struck up friendships with the reporters of the other journals, and we swapped "regulars" with each other and thus economized work. "Regulars" are permanent sources of news, like courts, bullion returns, "clean-ups" at the quartz mills, and inquests. Inasmuch as everybody went armed, we had an inquest about every day, and so this department was naturally set down among the "regulars." We had lively papers in those days. My great competitor among the reporters was Boggs of the *Union*. He was an excellent reporter. Once in three or four months he would get a little intoxicated, but as a general thing he was a wary and cautious drinker although always ready to tamper a little with the enemy. He had the advantage of me in one thing; he could get the monthly public school report and I could not, because the principal hated the *Enterprise*. One snowy night when the report was due, I started out sadly wondering how I was going to get it. Presently, a few steps up the almost deserted street I stumbled on Boggs and asked him where he was going.

"After the school report."

"I'll go along with you."

"No, *sir*. I'll excuse you."

"Just as you say."

A saloon-keeper's boy passed by with a steaming pitcher of hot punch, and Boggs snuffed the fragrance gratefully. He gazed fondly after the boy and saw him start up the *Enterprise* stairs. I said:

"I wish you could help me get that school business, but since you can't, I must run up to the *Union* office and see if I can get them to let me have a proof of it after they have set it up, though I don't begin to suppose they will. Good night."

"Hold on a minute. I don't mind getting the report and sitting around with the boys a little, while you copy it, if you're willing to drop down to the principal's with me."

"Now you talk like a rational being. Come along."

We plowed a couple of blocks through the snow, got the report and returned to our office. It was a short document and soon copied. Meantime Boggs helped himself to the punch. I gave the manuscript back to him and we started out to get an inquest, for we heard pistol shots near by. We got the particulars with little loss of time, for it was only an inferior sort of bar-room murder, and of little interest to the public, and then we separated. Away at three o'clock in the morning, when we had gone to press and were having a relaxing concert as usual—for some of the printers were good singers and others good performers on the guitar and on that atrocity the accordeon—the proprietor of the *Union* strode in and desired to know if anybody had heard anything of Boggs or the school report. We stated the case, and all turned out to help hunt for the delinquent. We found him standing on a table in a saloon, with an old tin lantern in one hand

AN EDUCATIONAL REPORT.

and the school report in the other, haranguing a gang of intoxicated Cornish miners on the iniquity of squandering the public moneys on education "when hundreds and hundreds of honest hard-working men are literally starving for whisky." [Riotous applause.] He had been assisting in a regal spree with those parties for hours. We dragged him away and put him to bed.

Of course there was no school report in the *Union,* and Boggs held me accountable, though I was innocent of any intention or desire to compass its absence from that paper and was as sorry as any one that the misfortune had occurred.

But we were perfectly friendly. The day that the school report was next due, the proprietor of the "Genesee" mine furnished us a buggy and asked us to go down and write something about the property—a very common request and one always gladly acceded to when people furnished buggies, for we were as fond of pleasure excursions as other people. In due time we arrived at the "mine"—nothing but a hole in the ground ninety feet deep, and no way of getting down into it but by holding on to a rope and being lowered with a windlass. The workmen had just gone off somewhere to dinner. I was not strong enough to lower Boggs's bulk; so I took an unlighted candle in my teeth, made a loop for my foot in the end of the rope, implored Boggs not to go to sleep or let the windlass get the start of him, and then swung out over the shaft. I reached the bottom muddy and bruised about the elbows, but safe. I lit the candle, made an examination of the rock, selected some specimens and shouted to Boggs to hoist away. No answer. Presently a head appeared in the circle of daylight away aloft, and a voice came down:

"Are you all set?"

"All set—hoist away."

"Are you comfortable?"

"Perfectly."

"Could you wait a little?"

"Oh certainly—no particular hurry."

"Well—good-bye."

"Why? Where are you going?"

"After the school report!"

And he did. I staid down there an hour, and surprised the workmen when they hauled up and found a man on the rope instead of a bucket of rock. I walked home, too—five miles—up hill. We had no school report next morning; but the *Union* had.

NO PARTICULAR HURRY.

Six months after my entry into journalism the grand "flush times" of Silverland began, and they continued with unabated splendor for three years. All difficulty about filling up the "local department" ceased, and the only trouble now was how to make the lengthened columns hold the world of incidents and happenings that came to our literary net every day. Virginia had grown to be the "livest" town, for its age and population, that America had ever produced. The sidewalks swarmed with people—to such an extent, indeed, that it was generally no easy matter to stem the human tide. The streets themselves were just as crowded with quartz wagons, freight teams and other vehicles. The procession was endless. So great was the pack, that buggies frequently had to wait half an hour for an opportunity to cross the principal street. Joy sat on every countenance, and there was a glad, almost fierce, intensity in every eye, that told of the money-getting schemes that were seething in every brain and the high hope that held sway in every heart. Money was as plenty as dust; every individual considered himself wealthy, and a melancholy countenance was nowhere to be seen. There were military companies, fire companies, brass bands, banks, hotels, theatres, "hurdy-gurdy houses," wide-open gambling palaces, political pow-wows, civic processions, street fights, murders, inquests, riots, a whisky mill every fifteen steps, a Board of Aldermen, a Mayor, a City Surveyor, a City Engineer, a Chief of the Fire Department, with First, Second and Third Assistants, a Chief of Police, City Marshal and a large police force, two Boards of Mining Brokers, a dozen breweries and half a dozen jails and station-houses in full operation, and some talk of building a church. The "flush times" were in magnificent flower! Large fireproof brick buildings were going up in the principal streets, and the wooden suburbs were spreading out in all directions. Town lots soared up to prices that were amazing.

The great "Comstock lode" stretched its opulent length straight through the town from north to south, and every mine on it was in diligent process of development. One of these mines alone employed six hundred and seventy-five men, and in the matter of elections the adage was, "as the 'Gould & Curry' goes, so goes the city." Laboring men's wages were four and six dollars a day, and they worked in three "shifts" or gangs, and the blasting and picking and shoveling went on without ceasing, night and day.

The "city" of Virginia roosted royally midway up the steep side of Mount Davidson, seven thousand two hundred feet above the level of the sea, and in the clear Nevada atmosphere was visible from a distance of fifty miles! It claimed a population of fifteen thousand to eighteen thousand, and all day long half of this little army swarmed the streets like bees and the other half swarmed among the drifts and tunnels of the "Comstock," hundreds of feet down in the earth directly under those same streets. Often we felt our chairs jar, and heard the faint boom of a blast down in the bowels of the earth under the office.

The mountain side was so steep that the entire town had a slant to it like a roof. Each street was a terrace, and from each to the next street below the descent was forty or fifty feet. The fronts of the houses were level with the street they faced, but their rear first floors were propped on lofty stilts; a man could stand at a rear first floor window of a C street house and look down the chimneys of the row of houses below him facing D street. It was a laborious climb, in that thin atmosphere, to ascend from D to A street, and you were panting and out of breath when you got there; but you could

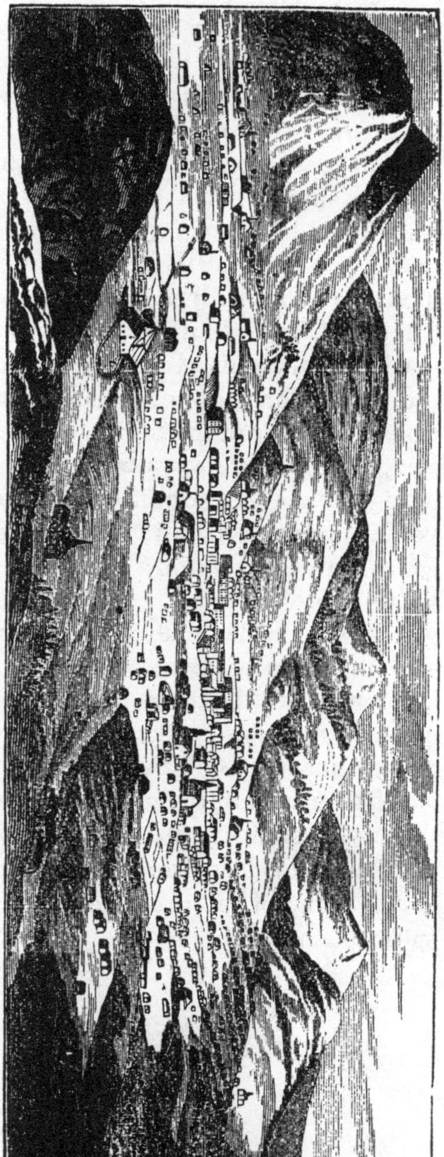

BIRD'S EYE VIEW OF VIRGINIA AND MOUNT DAVIDSON.

turn around and go down again like a house a-fire—so to speak. The atmosphere was so rarified, on account of the great altitude, that one's blood lay near the surface always, and the scratch of a pin was a disaster worth worrying about, for the chances were that a grievous erysipelas would ensue. But to offset this, the thin atmosphere seemed to carry healing to gunshot wounds, and therefore, to simply shoot your adversary through both lungs was a thing not likely to afford you any permanent satisfaction, for he would be nearly certain to be around looking for you within the month, and not with an opera glass, either.

From Virginia's airy situation one could look over a vast, far-reaching panorama of mountain ranges and deserts; and whether the day was bright or overcast, whether the sun was rising or setting, or flaming in the zenith, or whether night and the moon held sway, the spectacle was always impressive and beautiful. Over your head Mount Davidson lifted its gray dome, and before and below you a rugged cañon clove the battlemented hills, making a sombre gateway through which a soft-tinted desert was glimpsed, with the silver thread of a river winding through it, bordered with trees which many miles of distance diminished to a delicate fringe; and still further away the snowy mountains rose up and stretched their long barrier to the filmy horizon—far enough beyond a lake that burned in the desert like a fallen sun, though that, itself, lay fifty miles removed. Look from your window where you would, there was fascination in the picture. At rare intervals—but very rare—there were clouds in our skies, and then the setting sun would gild and flush and glorify this mighty expanse of scenery with a bewildering pomp of color that held the eye like a spell and moved the spirit like music.

CHAPTER 44

My salary was increased to forty dollars a week. But I seldom drew it. I had plenty of other resources, and what were two broad twenty-dollar gold pieces to a man who had his pockets full of such and a cumbersome abundance of bright half dollars besides? [Paper money has never come into use on the Pacific coast.] Reporting was lucrative, and every man in the town was lavish with his money and his "feet." The city and all the great mountain side were riddled with mining shafts. There were more mines than miners. True, not ten of these mines were yielding rock worth hauling to a mill, but everybody said, "Wait till the shaft gets down where the ledge comes in solid, and then you will see!" So nobody was discouraged. These were nearly all "wild cat" mines, and wholly worthless, but nobody believed it then. The "Ophir," the "Gould & Curry," the "Mexican," and other great mines on the Comstock lead in Virginia and Gold Hill were turning out huge piles of rich rock every day, and every man believed that his little wild cat claim was as good as any on the "main lead" and would infallibly be worth a thousand dollars a foot when he "got down where it came in solid." Poor fellow, he was blessedly blind to the fact that he never would see that day. So the thousand wild cat shafts burrowed deeper and deeper into the earth day by day, and all men were beside themselves with hope and happiness. How they labored, prophesied, exulted! Surely nothing like it was ever seen before since the world began. Every one of these wild cat mines—not mines, but holes in the ground over imaginary mines—was incorporated and had handsomely engraved "stock" and the stock was salable, too. It was bought and sold with a feverish avidity in the boards every day. You could go up on the mountain side, scratch around and find a ledge (there was no lack of them), put up a "notice" with a grandiloquent name in it, start a shaft, get your stock printed, and with nothing whatever to prove

A NEW MINE.

that your mine was worth a straw, you could put your stock on the market and sell out for hundreds and even thousands of dollars. To make money, and make it fast, was as easy as it was to eat your dinner. Every man owned "feet" in fifty different wild cat mines and considered his fortune made. Think of a city with not one solitary poor man in it! One would suppose that when month after month went by and still not a wild cat mine (by wild cat I mean, in general terms, *any* claim not located on the mother vein, *i. e.*, the "Comstock") yielded a ton of rock worth crushing, the people would begin to wonder if they were not putting too much faith in their prospective riches; but there was not a thought of such a thing. They burrowed away, bought and sold, and were happy.

New claims were taken up daily, and it was the friendly custom to run straight to the newspaper offices, give the reporters forty or fifty "feet," and get them to go and examine the mine and publish a notice of it. They did not care a fig what you said about the property so you said something. Consequently we generally said a word or two to the effect that the "indications" were good, or that the ledge was "six feet wide," or that the rock "resembled the Comstock" (and so it did—but as a general thing the resemblance was not startling enough to knock you down). If the rock was moderately promising, we followed the custom of the country, used strong adjectives and frothed at the mouth as if a very marvel in silver discoveries had transpired. If the mine was a "developed" one, and had no pay ore to show (and of course it hadn't), we praised the tunnel; said it was one of the most infatuating tunnels in the land; driveled and driveled about the tunnel till we ran entirely out of ecstasies—but never said a word about the rock. We would squander half a column of adulation on a shaft, or a new wire rope, or a dressed pine windlass, or a fascinating force pump, and close with a burst of admiration of the "gentlemanly and efficient Superintendent" of the mine—but never utter a whisper about the rock. And those people were always pleased, always satisfied. Occasionally we patched up and varnished our reputation for discrimination and stern, undeviating accuracy, by giving some old abandoned claim a blast that ought to have made its dry bones rattle—and then somebody would seize it and sell it on the fleeting notoriety thus conferred upon it.

There was *nothing* in the shape of a mining claim that was not salable. We received presents of "feet" every day. If we needed a hundred dollars or so, we sold some; if not, we hoarded it away, satisfied that it would ultimately be worth a thousand dollars a foot. I had a trunk about half full of "stock." When a claim made a stir in the market and went up to a high figure, I searched through my pile to see if I had any of its stock—and generally found it.

The prices rose and fell constantly; but still a fall disturbed us little, because a thousand dollars a foot was our figure, and so we were content to let it fluctuate as much as it pleased till it reached it. My pile of stock was not all given to me by people who wished their claims "noticed." At least half of it was given me by persons who had no thought of such a thing, and looked for nothing more than a simple verbal "thank you;" and you were not even obliged by law to furnish that. If you are coming up the street with a couple of baskets of apples in your hands, and you meet a friend, you naturally invite him to take a few. That describes the condition of things in Virginia in the "flush times." Every man had his pockets full of stock, and it was the actual *custom* of the country to part with small quantities of it to friends without the asking. Very often it was a good idea to close the transaction instantly, when a man offered a stock present to a friend, for the offer was only good and binding at that moment, and if the price went to a high figure shortly afterward the procrastination was a thing to be regretted. Mr. Stewart (Senator, now, from Nevada) one day told me he would give me twenty feet of "Justis" stock if I would walk over to his office. It was worth five or ten dollars a foot. I asked him to make the offer good for next day, as I was just going to dinner. He said he would not be in town; so I risked it and took my dinner instead of the stock. Within the week the price went up to seventy dollars and afterward to a hundred and fifty, but nothing could make that man yield. I suppose he sold that stock of mine and placed the guilty proceeds in his own pocket. [My revenge will be found in the accompanying portrait.] I met three friends one afternoon, who said they had been buying "Overman" stock at auction at eight dollars a foot. One said if I would come up to his office he would give me fifteen feet; another said he would add fifteen; the third said he would do the same. But I was going after an inquest and could not stop. A few weeks afterward they sold all their "Overman" at six hundred dollars a foot and generously came around to tell me about it—and also to urge me to accept of the next forty-five feet of it that people tried to force on me. These are actual facts, and I could make the list a long one and still confine

"TAKE A FEW?"

myself strictly to the truth. Many a time friends gave us as much as twenty-five feet of stock that was selling at twenty-five dollars a foot, and they thought no more of it than they would of offering a guest a cigar. These were "flush times" indeed! I thought they were going to last always, but somehow I never was much of a prophet.

PORTRAIT OF MR. STEWART.

To show what a wild spirit possessed the mining brain of the community, I will remark that "claims" were actually "located" in excavations for cellars, where the pick had exposed what seemed to be quartz veins—and not cellars in the suburbs, either, but in the very heart of the city; and forthwith stock would be issued and thrown on the market. It was small matter who the cellar belonged to—the "ledge" belonged to the finder, and unless the U. S. government interfered (inasmuch as the government holds the primary right to mines of the noble metals in Nevada—or at least did then), it was considered to be his privilege to work it. Imagine a stranger staking out a mining claim among the costly shrubbery in your front yard and calmly proceeding to lay waste the ground with pick and shovel and blasting powder! It has been often done in California. In the middle of one of the principal business streets of Virginia, a man "located" a mining claim and began a shaft on it. He gave me a hundred feet of the stock and I sold it for a fine suit of clothes because I was afraid somebody would fall down the shaft and sue for damages. I owned in another claim that was located in the middle of another street; and to show how absurd people can be, that "East India" stock (as it was called) sold briskly although there was an ancient tunnel running directly under the claim and any man could go into it and see that it did not cut a quartz ledge or anything that remotely resembled one.

One plan of acquiring sudden wealth was to "salt" a wild cat claim and sell out while the excitement was up. The process was

SELLING A MINE.

simple. The schemer located a worthless ledge, sunk a shaft on it, bought a wagon load of rich "Comstock" ore, dumped a portion of it into the shaft and piled the rest by its side, above ground. Then he showed the property to a simpleton and sold it to him at a high figure. Of course the wagon load of rich ore was all that the victim ever got out of his purchase. A most remarkable case of "salting" was that of the "North Ophir." It was claimed that this vein was a remote "extension" of the original "Ophir," a valuable mine on the "Comstock." For a few days everybody was talking about the rich developments in the North Ophir. It was said that it yielded perfectly pure silver in small, solid lumps. I went to the place with the owners, and found a shaft six or eight feet deep, in the bottom of which was a badly shattered vein of dull, yellowish, unpromising rock. One would as soon expect to find silver in a grindstone. We got out a pan of the rubbish and washed it in a puddle, and sure enough, among the sediment we found half a dozen black, bullet-looking pellets of unimpeachable "native" silver. Nobody had ever heard of such a thing before; science could not account for such a queer novelty. The stock rose to sixty-five dollars a foot, and at this figure the world-renowned tragedian, McKean Buchanan, bought a commanding interest and prepared to quit the stage once more—he was always doing that. And then it transpired that the mine had been "salted"—and not in any hackneyed way, either, but in a singularly bold, barefaced and peculiarly original and outrageous fashion. On one of the lumps of "native" silver was discovered the minted legend, "TED STATES OF," and then it was plainly apparent that the mine had been "salted" with melted half dollars! The lumps thus obtained had been blackened till they resembled native silver, and were then mixed with the shattered rock in the bottom of the shaft. It is literally true. Of course the price of the stock at once fell to nothing, and the tragedian was ruined. But for this calamity we might have lost McKean Buchanan from the stage.

CHAPTER 45

THE "flush times" held bravely on. Something over two years before, Mr. Goodman and another journeyman printer, had borrowed forty dollars and set out from San Francisco to try their fortunes in the new city of Virginia. They found the *Territorial Enterprise*, a poverty-stricken weekly journal, gasping for breath and likely to die. They bought it, type, fixtures, good-will and all, for a thousand dollars, on long time. The editorial sanctum, news-room, press-room, publication office, bed-chamber, parlor, and kitchen were all compressed into one apartment and it was a small one, too. The editors and printers slept on the floor, a Chinaman did their cooking, and the "imposing-stone" was the general dinner table. But now things were changed. The paper was a great daily, printed by steam; there were five editors and twenty-three compositors; the subscription price was sixteen dollars a year; the advertising rates were exorbitant, and the columns crowded. The paper was clearing from six to ten thousand dollars a month, and the "Enterprise Building" was finished and ready for occupation—a stately fire-proof brick. Every day from five all the way up to eleven columns of "live" advertisements were left out or crowded into spasmodic and irregular "supplements."

The "Gould & Curry" company were erecting a monster hundred-stamp mill at a cost that ultimately fell little short of a million dollars. Gould & Curry stock paid heavy dividends—a rare thing, and an experience confined to the dozen or fifteen claims located on the "main lead," the "Comstock." The Superintendent of the Gould & Curry lived, rent-free, in a fine house built and furnished by the company. He drove a fine pair of horses which were a present from the company, and his salary was twelve thousand dollars a year. The Superintendent of another of the great mines traveled in grand state, had a salary of twenty-eight thousand dollars a year, and in a lawsuit in after days claimed that he was to have had one per cent on the gross yield of the bullion likewise.

Money was wonderfully plenty. The trouble was, not how to get it,—but how to spend it, how to lavish it, get rid of it, squander it. And so it was a happy thing that just at this juncture the news came over the wires that a great U. S. Sanitary Commission had been formed and money was wanted for the relief of the wounded sailors and soldiers of the Union languishing in the eastern hospitals. Right on the heels of it came word that San Francisco had responded superbly before the telegram was half a day old. Virginia rose as one man! A Sanitary Committee was hurriedly organized, and its chairman mounted a vacant cart in C street and tried to make the clamorous multitude understand that the rest of the committee were flying hither and thither and working with all their might and main, and that if the town would only wait an hour, an office would be ready, books opened, and the Commission prepared to receive contributions. His voice was drowned and his information lost in a ceaseless roar of cheers, and demands that the money be received *now*—they swore they would not wait. The chairman pleaded and argued, but, deaf to all entreaty, men plowed their way through the throng and rained checks and gold coin into the cart and skurried away for more. Hands clutching money, were thrust aloft out of the jam by men who hoped this eloquent appeal would cleave a road their strugglings could not open. The very Chinamen and Indians caught the excitement and dashed their half dollars into the cart without knowing or caring what it was all about. Women plunged into the crowd, trimly attired, fought their way to the cart with their coin, and emerged again, by and by, with their apparel in a state of hopeless dilapidation. It was the wildest mob Virginia had ever seen and the most determined and ungovernable; and when at last it abated its fury and dispersed, it had not a penny in its pocket. To use its own phraseology, it came there "flush" and went away "busted."

After that, the Commission got itself into systematic working order, and for weeks the contributions flowed into its treasury in a generous stream. Individuals and all sorts of organizations levied upon themselves a regular weekly tax for the Sanitary fund, graduated according to their means, and there was not another grand

COULDN'T WAIT.

universal outburst till the famous "Sanitary Flour Sack" came our way. Its history is peculiar and interesting. A former schoolmate of mine, by the name of Reuel Gridley, was living at the little city of Austin, in the Reese river country, at this time, and was the Democratic candidate for mayor. He and the Republican candidate made an agreement that the defeated man should be publicly presented with a fifty-pound sack of flour by the successful one, and should carry it home on his shoulder. Gridley was defeated. The new mayor gave him the sack of flour, and he shouldered it and carried it a mile or two, from Lower Austin to his home in Upper Austin, attended by a band of music and the whole population. Arrived there, he said he did not need the flour, and asked what the people thought he had better do with it. A voice said:

"Sell it to the highest bidder, for the benefit of the Sanitary fund."

The suggestion was greeted with a round of applause, and Gridley mounted a dry-goods box and assumed the role of auctioneer. The bids went higher and higher, as the sympathies of the pioneers awoke and expanded, till at last the sack was knocked down to a mill man at two hundred and fifty dollars, and his check taken. He was asked where he would have the flour delivered, and he said:

"Nowhere—sell it again."

Now the cheers went up royally, and the multitude were fairly in the spirit of the thing. So Gridley stood there and shouted and perspired till the sun went down; and when the crowd dispersed he had sold the sack to three hundred different people, and had taken in eight thousand dollars in gold. And still the flour sack was in his possession.

The news came to Virginia, and a telegram went back:

"Fetch along your flour sack!"

Thirty-six hours afterward Gridley arrived, and an afternoon mass meeting was held in the Opera House, and the auction began. But the sack had come sooner than it was expected; the people were not thoroughly aroused, and the sale dragged. At nightfall only five thousand dollars had been secured, and there was a crestfallen feeling in the community. However, there was no disposition to let the matter rest here and acknowledge vanquishment at the hands of the village of Austin. Till late in the night the principal citizens were at work arranging the morrow's campaign, and when they went to bed they had no fears for the result. At eleven the next morning a procession of open carriages, attended by clamorous bands of music and adorned with a moving display of flags, filed along C street and was soon in danger of blockade by a huzzaing multitude of citizens. In the first carriage sat Gridley, with the flour sack in prominent view, the latter splendid with bright paint and gilt lettering; also in the same carriage sat the mayor and the recorder. The other carriages contained the Common Council, the editors and reporters, and other people of imposing consequence. The crowd pressed to the corner of C and Taylor streets, expecting the sale to begin there, but they were disappointed, and also unspeakably surprised; for the cavalcade moved on as if Virginia had ceased to be of importance, and took its way over the "divide," toward the small town of Gold Hill. Telegrams had gone ahead to Gold Hill, Silver City and Dayton, and those communities were at fever heat and rife for the

THE GREAT "FLOUR SACK" PROCESSION.

conflict. It was a very hot day, and wonderfully dusty. At the end of a short half hour we descended into Gold Hill with drums beating and colors flying, and enveloped in imposing clouds of dust. The whole population—men, women and children, Chinamen and Indians, were massed in the main street, all the flags in town were at the mast head, and the blare of the bands was drowned in cheers. Gridley stood up and asked who would make the first bid for the National Sanitary Flour Sack. Gen. W. said:

"The Yellow Jacket silver mining company offers a thousand dollars, coin!"

A tempest of applause followed. A telegram carried the news to Virginia, and fifteen minutes afterward that city's population was massed in the streets devouring the tidings—for it was part of the programme that the bulletin boards should do a good work that day. Every few minutes a new dispatch was bulletined from Gold Hill, and still the excitement grew. Telegrams began to return to us from Virginia beseeching Gridley to bring back the flour sack; but such was not the plan of the campaign. At the end of an hour Gold Hill's small population had paid a figure for the flour sack that awoke all the enthusiasm of Virginia when the grand total was displayed upon the bulletin boards. Then the Gridley cavalcade moved on, a giant refreshed with new lager beer and plenty of it—for the people brought it to the carriages without waiting to measure it—and within three hours more the expedition had carried Silver City and Dayton by storm and was on its way back covered with glory. Every move had been telegraphed and bulletined, and as the procession entered Virginia and filed down C street at half past eight in the evening the town was abroad in the thoroughfares, torches were glaring, flags flying, bands playing, cheer on cheer cleaving the air, and the city ready to surrender at discretion. The auction began, every bid was greeted with bursts of applause, and at the end of two hours and a half a population of fifteen thousand souls had paid in coin for a fifty-pound sack of flour a sum equal to forty thousand dollars in greenbacks! It was at a rate in the neighborhood of three dollars for each man, woman and child of the population. The grand total would have been twice as large, but the streets were very narrow, and hundreds who wanted to bid could not get within a block of the stand, and could not make themselves heard. These grew tired of waiting and many of them went home long before the auction was over. This was the greatest day Virginia ever saw, perhaps.

Gridley sold the sack in Carson City and several California towns; also in San Francisco. Then he took it east and sold it in one or two Atlantic cities, I think. I am not sure of that, but I know that he finally carried it to St. Louis, where a monster Sanitary Fair was being held, and after selling it there for a large sum and helping on the enthusiasm by displaying the portly silver bricks which Nevada's donation had produced, he had the flour baked up into small cakes and retailed them at high prices.

It was estimated that when the flour sack's mission was ended it had been sold for a grand total of a hundred and fifty thousand dollars in greenbacks! This is probably the only instance on record where common family flour brought three thousand dollars a pound in the public market.

It is due to Mr. Gridley's memory to mention that the expenses of his Sanitary flour sack expedition of fifteen thousand miles, going and returning, were paid in large part, if not entirely, out of his own pocket. The time he gave to it was not less than three months. Mr. Gridley was a soldier in the Mexican war and a pioneer Californian. He died at Stockton, California, in December, 1870, greatly regretted.

CHAPTER 46

THERE were nabobs in those days—in the "flush times," I mean. Every rich strike in the mines created one or two. I call to mind several of these. They were careless, easy-going fellows, as a general thing, and the community at large was as much benefited by their riches as they were themselves—possibly more, in some cases.

Two cousins, teamsters, did some hauling for a man, and had to take a small segregated portion of a silver mine in lieu of three hundred dollars cash. They gave an outsider a third to open the mine, and they went on teaming. But not long. Ten months afterward the mine was out of debt and paying each owner eight to ten thousand dollars a month—say a hundred thousand dollars a year.

A NABOB.

One of the earliest nabobs that Nevada was delivered of wore six thousand dollars' worth of diamonds in his bosom, and swore he was unhappy because he could not spend his money as fast as he made it.

Another Nevada nabob boasted an income that often reached sixteen thousand dollars a month; and he used to love to tell how he had worked in the very mine that yielded it, for five dollars a day, when he first came to the country.

The silver and sage-brush State has knowledge of another of these pets of fortune—lifted from actual poverty to affluence almost in a single night—who was able to offer a hundred thousand dollars for a position of high official distinction, shortly afterward, and did offer it—but failed to get it, his politics not being as sound as his bank account.

Then there was John Smith. He was a good, honest, kind-hearted soul, born and reared in the lower ranks of life, and miraculously ignorant. He drove a team, and owned a small ranch—a ranch that paid him a comfortable living, for although it yielded but little hay, what little it did yield was worth from two hundred and fifty to three hundred dollars in gold per ton in the market. Presently Smith traded a few acres of the ranch for a small undeveloped silver mine in Gold Hill. He opened the mine and built a little unpretending ten-stamp mill. Eighteen months afterward he retired from the hay business, for his mining income had reached a most comfortable figure. Some people said it was thirty thousand dollars a month, and others said it was sixty thousand dollars. Smith was very rich at any rate.

And then he went to Europe and traveled. And when he came back he was never tired of telling about the fine hogs he had seen in England, and the gorgeous sheep he had seen in Spain, and the fine cattle he had noticed in the vicinity of Rome. He was full of the wonders of the old world, and advised everybody to travel. He said a man never imagined what surprising things there were in the world till he had traveled.

One day, on board ship, the passengers made up a pool of five hundred dollars, which was to be the property of the man who should come nearest to guessing the run of the vessel for the next twenty-four hours. Next day, toward noon, the figures were all in the purser's hands in sealed envelops. Smith was serene and happy, for he had been bribing the engineer. But another party won the prize! Smith said:

"Here, that won't do! He guessed two miles wider of the mark than I did."

The purser said, "Mr. Smith, you missed it further than any man on board. We traveled two hundred and eight miles yesterday."

"Well, sir," said Smith, "that's just where I've got you, for I guessed two hundred and nine. If you'll look at my figgers again you'll find a 2 and two 0's, which stands for 200, don't it?—and after 'em you'll find a 9 (2009), which stands for two hundred and nine. I reckon I'll take that money, if you please."

The Gould & Curry claim comprised twelve hundred feet, and it all belonged originally to the two men whose names it bears. Mr. Curry owned two-thirds of it—and he said that he sold it out for twenty-five hundred dollars, in cash, and an old plug horse that ate up his market value in hay and barley in seventeen days by the watch. And he said that Gould sold out for a pair of second-hand government blankets and a bottle of whisky that killed nine men in three hours, and that an unoffending stranger that smelt the cork was disabled for life. Four years afterward the mine thus disposed of was worth in the San Francisco market seven million six hundred thousand dollars in gold coin.

In the early days a poverty-stricken Mexican who lived in a cañon directly back of Virginia City, had a stream of water as large as a man's wrist trickling from the hillside on his premises. The Ophir Company segregated a hundred feet of their mine and traded it to him for the stream of water. The hundred feet proved to be the richest part of the entire mine; four years after the swap, its market value (including its mill) was one million five hundred thousand dollars.

An individual who owned twenty feet in the Ophir mine before its great riches were revealed to men, traded it for a horse, and a very sorry-looking brute he was, too. A year or so afterward, when Ophir stock went up to three thousand dollars a foot, this man, who had not a cent, used to say he was the most startling example of magnificence and misery the world had ever seen—because he was able to ride a sixty-thousand-dollar horse—yet could not scrape up cash enough to buy a saddle, and was obliged to borrow one or ride bareback. He said if fortune were to give him another sixty-thousand-dollar horse it would ruin him.

A youth of nineteen, who was a telegraph operator in Virginia on a salary of a hundred dollars a month, and who, when he could not make out German names in the list of San Francisco steamer arrivals, used to ingeniously select and supply substitutes for them out of an old Berlin city directory, made himself rich by watching the mining telegrams that passed through his hands and buying and selling stocks accordingly, through a friend in San Francisco.

Once when a private dispatch was sent from Virginia announcing a rich strike in a prominent mine and advising that the matter be

MAGNIFICENCE AND MISERY.

kept secret till a large amount of the stock could be secured, he bought forty "feet" of the stock at twenty dollars a foot, and afterward sold half of it at eight hundred dollars a foot and the rest at double that figure. Within three months he was worth a hundred and fifty thousand dollars, and had resigned his telegraphic position.

Another telegraph operator who had been discharged by the company for divulging the secrets of the office, agreed with a moneyed man in San Francisco to furnish him the result of a great Virginia mining lawsuit within an hour after its private reception by the parties to it in San Francisco. For this he was to have a large percentage of the profits on purchases and sales made on it by his fellow-conspirator. So he went, disguised as a teamster, to a little wayside telegraph office in the mountains, got acquainted with the operator, and sat in the office day after day, smoking his pipe, complaining that his team was fagged out and unable to travel—and meantime listening to the dispatches as they passed clicking through the machine from Virginia. Finally the private dispatch announcing the result of the lawsuit sped over the wires, and as soon as he heard it he telegraphed his friend in San Francisco:

"Am tired waiting. Shall sell the team and go home."

It was the signal agreed upon. The word "waiting" left out, would have signified that the suit had gone the other way. The mock teamster's friend picked up a deal of the mining stock, at low figures, before the news became public, and a fortune was the result.

For a long time after one of the great Virginia mines had been incorporated, about fifty feet of the original location were still in the hands of a man who had never signed the incorporation papers. The stock became very valuable, and every effort was made to find this man, but he had disappeared. Once it was heard that he was in New York, and one or two speculators went east but failed to find him. Once the news came that he was in the Bermudas, and straightway a speculator or two hurried east and sailed for Bermuda—but he was not there. Finally he was heard of in Mexico, and a friend of his, a barkeeper on a salary, scraped together a little money and sought him out, bought his "feet" for a hundred dollars, returned and sold the property for seventy-five thousand dollars.

But why go on? The traditions of Silverland are filled with instances like these, and I would never get through enumerating them were I to attempt to do it. I only desired to give the reader an idea of a peculiarity of the "flush times" which I could not present so strikingly in any other way, and which some mention of was necessary to a realizing comprehension of the time and the country.

I was personally acquainted with the majority of the nabobs I have referred to, and so, for old acquaintance sake, I have shifted their occupations and experiences around in such a way as to keep the Pacific public from recognizing these once notorious men. No longer notorious, for the majority of them have drifted back into poverty and obscurity again.

In Nevada there used to be current the story of an adventure of two of her nabobs, which may or may not have occurred. I give it for what it is worth:

Col. Jim had seen somewhat of the world, and knew more or less of its ways; but Col. Jack was from the back settlements of the States, had led a life of arduous toil, and had never seen a city. These two, blessed with sudden wealth, projected a visit to New York,—Col. Jack to see the sights, and Col. Jim to guard his unsophistication from misfortune. They reached San Francisco in the night, and sailed in the morning. Arrived in New York, Col. Jack said:

"I've heard tell of carriages all my life, and now I mean to have a ride in one; I don't care what it costs. Come along."

They stepped out on the sidewalk, and Col. Jim called a stylish barouche. But Col. Jack said:

"*No,* sir! None of your cheap-John turn-outs for me. I'm here to have a good time, and money ain't any object. I mean to have the nobbiest rig that's going. Now here comes the very trick. Stop that yaller one with the pictures on it—don't you fret—I'll stand all the expenses myself."

So Col. Jim stopped an empty omnibus, and they got in. Said Col. Jack:

"Ain't it gay, though? Oh, no, I reckon not! Cushions, and windows, and pictures, till you can't rest. What would the boys say if they could see us cutting a swell like this in New York? By George, I wish they *could* see us."

Then he put his head out of the window, and shouted to the driver:

"Say, Johnny, this suits *me!*—suits yours truly, you bet you! I want this shebang all day. I'm *on* it, old man! Let 'em out! Make 'em go! We'll make it all right with *you,* sonny!"

The driver passed his hand through the strap-hole, and tapped for his fare—it was before the gongs came into common use. Col. Jack took the hand, and shook it cordially. He said:

"You twig me, old pard! All right between gents. Smell of *that,* and see how you like it!"

And he put a twenty-dollar gold piece in the driver's hand. After a moment the driver said he could not make change.

"Bother the change! Ride it out. Put it in your pocket."

Then to Col. Jim, with a sounding slap on his thigh:

"*Ain't* it style, though? Hanged if I don't hire this thing every day for a week."

A FRIENDLY DRIVER.

The omnibus stopped, and a young lady got in. Col. Jack stared a moment, then nudged Col. Jim with his elbow:

"Don't say a word," he whispered. "Let her ride, if she wants to. Gracious, there's room enough."

The young lady got out her porte-monnaie, and handed her fare to Col. Jack.

"What's this for?" said he.

"Give it to the driver, please."

"Take back your money, madam. We can't allow it. You're welcome to ride here as long as you please, but this shebang's chartered, and we can't let you pay a cent."

The girl shrunk into a corner, bewildered. An old lady with a basket climbed in, and proffered her fare.

"Excuse me," said Col. Jack. "You're perfectly welcome here, madam, but we can't allow you to pay. Set right down there, mum, and don't you be the least uneasy. Make yourself just as free as if you was in your own turn-out."

Within two minutes, three gentlemen, two fat women, and a couple of children, entered.

"Come right along, friends," said Col. Jack; "don't mind *us*. This is a free blow-out." Then he whispered to Col. Jim, "New York ain't no sociable place, I don't reckon—it ain't no *name* for it!"

He resisted every effort to pass fares to the driver, and made everybody cordially welcome. The situation dawned on the people, and they pocketed their money, and delivered themselves up to covert enjoyment of the episode. Half a dozen more passengers entered.

ASTONISHES THE NATIVES.

"Oh, there's *plenty* of room," said Col. Jack. "Walk right in, and make yourselves at home. A blow-out ain't worth anything *as* a blow-out, unless a body has company." Then in a whisper to Col. Jim: "But *ain't* these New Yorkers friendly? And ain't they cool about it, too? Icebergs ain't anywhere. I reckon they'd tackle a hearse, if it was going their way."

More passengers got in; more yet, and still more. Both seats were filled, and a file of men were standing up, holding on to the cleats overhead. Parties with baskets and bundles were climbing up on the roof. Half-suppressed laughter rippled up from all sides.

COL. JACK "WEAKENS."

"Well, for clean, cool, out-and-out cheek, if this don't bang anything that ever I saw, I'm an Injun!" whispered Col. Jack.

A Chinaman crowded his way in.

"I weaken!" said Col. Jack. "Hold on, driver! Keep your seats, ladies and gents. Just make yourselves free—everything's paid for. Driver, rustle these folks around as long as they're a mind to go—friends of ours, you know. Take them everywheres—and if you want more money, come to the St. Nicholas, and we'll make it all right. Pleasant journey to you, ladies and gents—go it just as long as you please—it shan't cost you a cent!"

The two comrades got out, and Col. Jack said:

"Jimmy, it's the sociablest place *I* ever saw. The Chinaman waltzed in as comfortable as anybody. If we'd staid awhile, I reckon we'd had some niggers. B' George, we'll have to barricade our doors to-night, or some of these ducks will be trying to sleep with us."

CHAPTER 47

Somebody has said that in order to know a community, one must observe the style of its funerals and know what manner of men they bury with most ceremony. I cannot say which class we buried with most eclat in our "flush times," the distinguished public benefactor or the distinguished rough—possibly the two chief grades or grand divisions of society honored their illustrious dead about equally; and hence, no doubt the philosopher I have quoted from would have needed to see two representative funerals in Virginia before forming his estimate of the people.

There was a grand time over Buck Fanshaw when he died. He was a representative citizen. He had "killed his man"—not in his own quarrel, it is true, but in defence of a stranger unfairly beset by numbers. He had kept a sumptuous saloon. He had been the proprietor of a dashing helpmeet whom he could have discarded without the formality of a divorce. He had held a high position in the fire department and been a very Warwick in politics. When he died there was great lamentation throughout the town, but especially in the vast bottom-stratum of society.

On the inquest it was shown that Buck Fanshaw, in the delirium of a wasting typhoid fever, had taken arsenic, shot himself through the body, cut his throat, and jumped out of a four-story window and broken his neck—and after due deliberation, the jury, sad and tearful, but with intelligence unblinded by its sorrow, brought in a verdict of death "by the visitation of God." What could the world do without juries?

Prodigious preparations were made for the funeral. All the vehicles in town were hired, all the saloons put in mourning, all the municipal and fire-company flags hung at half-mast, and all the firemen ordered to muster in uniform and bring their machines duly draped in black. Now—let us remark in parenthesis—as all the peoples of the earth had representative adventurers in the Silverland, and as each adventurer had brought the slang of his nation or his locality with him, the combination made the slang of Nevada the richest and the most infinitely varied and copious that had ever existed anywhere in the world, perhaps, except in the mines of California in the "early days." Slang was the language of Nevada. It was hard to preach a sermon without it, and be understood. Such phrases as "You bet!" "Oh, no, I reckon not!" "No Irish need apply," and a hundred others, became so common as to fall from the lips of a speaker unconsciously—and very often when they did not touch the subject under discussion and consequently failed to mean anything.

After Buck Fanshaw's inquest, a meeting of the short-haired brotherhood was held, for nothing can be done on the Pacific coast without a public meeting and an expression of sentiment. Regretful resolutions were passed and various committees appointed; among others, a committee of one was deputed to call on the minister, a fragile, gentle, spirituel new fledgling from an eastern theological seminary, and as yet unacquainted with the ways of the

COMMITTEEMAN AND MINISTER.

mines. The committeeman, "Scotty" Briggs, made his visit; and in after days it was worth something to hear the minister tell about it. Scotty was a stalwart rough, whose customary suit, when on weighty official business, like committee work, was a fire helmet, flaming red flannel shirt, patent-leather belt with spanner and revolver attached, coat hung over arm, and pants stuffed into boot-tops. He formed something of a contrast to the pale theological student. It is fair to say of Scotty, however, in passing, that he had a warm heart, and a strong love for his friends, and never entered into a quarrel when he could reasonably keep out of it. Indeed, it was commonly said that whenever one of Scotty's fights was investigated, it always turned out that it had originally been no affair of his, but that out of native goodheartedness he had dropped in of his own accord to help the man who was getting the worst of it. He and Buck Fanshaw were bosom friends, for years, and had often taken adventurous "pot luck" together. On one occasion, they had thrown off their coats and taken the weaker side in a fight among strangers, and after gaining a hard-earned victory, turned and found that the men they were helping had deserted early, and not only that, but had stolen their coats and made off with them! But to return to Scotty's visit to the minister. He was on a sorrowful mission, now, and his face was the picture of woe. Being admitted to the presence he sat down before the clergyman, placed his fire-hat on an unfinished manuscript sermon under the minister's nose, took from it a red silk handkerchief, wiped his brow and heaved a sigh of dismal impressiveness, explanatory of his business. He choked, and even shed tears; but with an effort he mastered his voice and said in lugubrious tones:

"Are you the duck that runs the gospel-mill next door?"

"Am I the—pardon me, I believe I do not understand?"

With another sigh and a half-sob, Scotty rejoined:

"Why you see we are in a bit of trouble, and the boys thought maybe you would give us a lift, if we'd tackle you—that is, if I've got the rights of it and you are the head clerk of the doxology-works next door."

"I am the shepherd in charge of the flock whose fold is next door."

"The which?"

"The spiritual adviser of the little company of believers whose sanctuary adjoins these premises."

Scotty scratched his head, reflected a moment, and then said:

"You ruther hold over me, pard. I reckon I can't call that hand. Ante and pass the buck."

"How? I beg pardon. What did I understand you to say?"

"Well, you've ruther got the bulge on me. Or maybe we've both got the bulge, somehow. You don't smoke me and I don't smoke you. You see, one of the boys has passed in his checks and we want to give him a good send-off, and so the thing I'm on now is to roust out somebody to jerk a little chin-music for us and waltz him through handsome."

"My friend, I seem to grow more and more bewildered. Your observations are wholly incomprehensible to me. Cannot you simplify them in some way? At first I thought perhaps I understood you, but I grope now. Would it not expedite matters if you restricted yourself to categorical statements of fact unencumbered with obstructing accumulations of metaphor and allegory?"

Another pause, and more reflection. Then, said Scotty:

"I'll have to pass, I judge."

"How?"

"You've raised me out, pard."

"I still fail to catch your meaning."

"Why, that last lead of yourn is too many for me—that's the idea. I can't neither trump nor follow suit."

The clergyman sank back in his chair perplexed. Scotty leaned his head on his hand and gave himself up to thought. Presently his face came up, sorrowful but confident.

"I've got it now, so's you can savvy," he said. "What we want is a gospel-sharp. See?"

"A what?"

"Gospel-sharp. Parson."

"Oh! Why did you not say so before? I am a clergyman—a parson."

"Now you talk! You see my blind and straddle it like a man. Put it there!"—extending a brawny paw, which closed over the minister's small hand and gave it a shake indicative of fraternal sympathy and fervent gratification.

"Now we're all right, pard. Let's start fresh. Don't you mind my snuffling a little—becuz we're in a power of trouble. You see, one of the boys has gone up the flume—"

"Gone where?"

"Up the flume—throwed up the sponge, you understand."

"Thrown up the sponge?"

"Yes—kicked the bucket—"

"Ah—has departed to that mysterious country from whose bourne no traveler returns."

"Return! I reckon not. Why pard, he's *dead!*"

"Yes, I understand."

"Oh, you do? Well I thought maybe you might be getting tangled some more. Yes, you see he's dead again—"

"*Again?* Why, has he ever been dead before?"

"Dead before? No! Do you reckon a man has got as many lives as a cat? But you bet you he's awful dead now, poor old boy, and I wish I'd never seen this day. I don't want no better friend than Buck Fanshaw. I knowed him by the back; and when I know a man and like him, I freeze to him—you hear *me.* Take him all round, pard, there never was a bullier man in the mines. No man ever knowed Buck Fanshaw to go back on a friend. But it's all up, you know, it's all up. It ain't no use. They've scooped him."

"Scooped him?"

"Yes—death has. Well, well, well, we've got to give him up. Yes indeed. It's a kind of a hard world, after all, *ain't* it? But pard, he was a rustler! You ought to seen him get started once. He was a bully boy with a glass eye! Just spit in his face and give him room according to his strength, and it was just beautiful to see him peel and go in. He was the worst son of a thief that ever drawed breath. Pard, he was *on* it! He was on it bigger than an Injun!"

"On it? On what?"

"On the shoot. On the shoulder. On the fight, you understand. *He* didn't give a continental for *any*body. *Beg* your pardon, friend, for coming so near saying a cuss-word—but you see I'm on an awful strain, in this palaver, on account of having to cramp down and draw everything so mild. But we've got to give him up. There ain't any getting around that, I don't reckon. Now if we can get you to help plant him—"

"Preach the funeral discourse? Assist at the obsequies?"

"Obs'quies is good. Yes. That's it—that's our little game. We are going to get the thing up regardless, you know. He was always nifty himself, and so you bet you his funeral ain't going to be no slouch—solid silver door-plate on his coffin, six plumes on the hearse, and a nigger on the box in a biled shirt and a plug hat—how's that for high? And we'll take care of *you*, pard. We'll fix you all right. There'll be a kerridge for you; and whatever you want, you just 'scape out and we'll 'tend to it. We've got a shebang fixed up for you to stand behind, in No. 1's house, and don't you be afraid. Just go in and toot your horn, if you don't sell a clam. Put Buck through as bully as you can, pard, for anybody that knowed him will tell you that he was one of the whitest men that was ever in the mines. You can't draw it too strong. He never could stand it to see things going wrong. He's done more to make this town quiet and peaceable than any man in it. I've seen him lick four Greasers in eleven minutes, myself. If a thing wanted regulating, *he* warn't

SCOTTY REGULATING MATTERS.

a man to go browsing around after somebody to do it, but he would prance in and regulate it himself. He warn't a Catholic. Scasely. He was down on 'em. His word was, 'No Irish need apply!' But it didn't make no difference about that when it came down to what a man's rights was—and so, when some roughs jumped the Catholic bone-yard and started in to stake out town lots in it he *went* for 'em! And he *cleaned* 'em, too! I was there, pard, and I seen it myself."

"That was very well indeed—at least the impulse was—whether the act was strictly defensible or not. Had deceased any religious convictions? That is to say, did he feel a dependence upon, or acknowledge allegiance to a higher power?"

More reflection.

"I reckon you've stumped me again, pard. Could you say it over once more, and say it slow?"

"Well, to simplify it somewhat, was he, or rather had he ever been connected with any organization sequestered from secular concerns and devoted to self-sacrifice in the interests of morality?"

"All down but nine—set 'em up on the other alley, pard."

"What did I understand you to say?"

"Why, you're most too many for me, you know. When you get in with your left I hunt grass every time. Every time you draw, you fill; but I don't seem to have any luck. Let's have a new deal."

"How? Begin again?"

"That's it."

"Very well. Was he a good man, and—"

"There—I see that; don't put up another chip till I look at my hand. A good man, says you? Pard, it ain't no name for it. He was the best man that ever—pard, you would have doted on that man. He could lam any galoot of his inches in America. It was him that put down the riot last election before it got a start; and everybody said he was the only man that could have done it. He waltzed in with a spanner in one hand and a trumpet in the other, and sent fourteen men home on a shutter in less than three minutes. He had that riot all broke up and prevented nice before anybody ever got a chance to strike a blow. He was always for peace, and he would *have* peace—he could not stand disturbances. Pard, he was a great loss to this town. It would please the boys if you could chip in something like that and do him justice. Here once when the Micks got to throwing stones through the Methodis' Sunday school windows, Buck Fanshaw, all of his own notion, shut up his saloon and took a couple of six-shooters and mounted guard over the Sunday school. Says he, 'No Irish need apply!' And they didn't. He was the bulliest man in the mountains, pard! He could run faster, jump higher, hit harder, and hold more tangle-foot whisky without spilling it than any man in seventeen counties. Put that in, pard—it'll please the boys more than anything you could say. And you can say, pard, that he never shook his mother."

"Never shook his mother?"

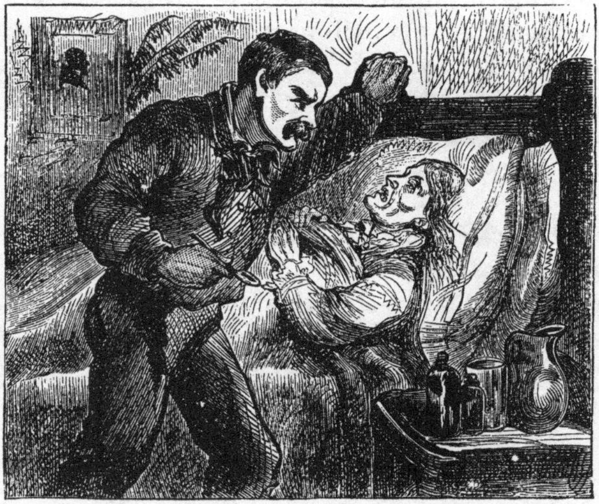

NEVER SHOOK HIS MOTHER.

"That's it—any of the boys will tell you so."

"Well, but why *should* he shake her?"

"That's what *I* say—but some people does."

"Not people of any repute?"

"Well, some that averages pretty so-so."

"In my opinion the man that would offer personal violence to his own mother, ought to—"

"Cheese it, pard; you've banked your ball clean outside the string. What I was a drivin' at, was, that he never *throwed off* on his mother—don't you see? No indeedy. He give her a house to live in, and town lots, and plenty of money; and he looked after her and took care of her all the time; and when she was down with the small-pox I'm d—d if he didn't set up nights and nuss her himself! *Beg* your pardon for saying it, but it hopped out too quick for yours truly. You've treated me like a gentleman, pard, and I ain't the man to hurt your feelings intentional. I think you're white. I think you're a square man, pard. I like you, and I'll lick any man that don't. I'll lick him till he can't tell himself from a last year's corpse! Put it *there!*" [Another fraternal hand-shake—and exit.]

The obsequies were all that "the boys" could desire. Such a marvel of funeral pomp had never been seen in Virginia. The plumed hearse, the dirge-breathing brass bands, the closed marts of business, the flags drooping at half-mast, the long, plodding procession of uniformed secret societies, military battalions and fire companies, draped engines, carriages of officials, and citizens in vehicles and on foot, attracted multitudes of spectators to the sidewalks, roofs and windows; and for years afterward, the degree of grandeur attained by any civic display in Virginia was determined by comparison with Buck Fanshaw's funeral.

Scotty Briggs, as a pall-bearer and a mourner, occupied a prominent place at the funeral, and when the sermon was finished and the last sentence of the prayer for the dead man's soul ascended, he responded, in a low voice, but with feeling:

"AMEN. No Irish need apply."

As the bulk of the response was without apparent relevancy, it was probably nothing more than a humble tribute to the memory of the friend that was gone; for, as Scotty had once said, it was "his word."

Scotty Briggs, in after days, achieved the distinction of becoming the only convert to religion that was ever gathered from the Virginia roughs; and it transpired that the man who had it in him

SCOTTY AS A SUNDAY SCHOOL TEACHER.

to espouse the quarrel of the weak out of inborn nobility of spirit was no mean timber whereof to construct a Christian. The making him one did not warp his generosity or diminish his courage; on the contrary it gave intelligent direction to the one and a broader field to the other. If his Sunday school class progressed faster than the other classes, was it matter for wonder? I think not. He talked to his pioneer small fry in a language they understood! It was my large privilege, a month before he died, to hear him tell the beautiful story of Joseph and his brethren to his class "without looking at the book." I leave it to the reader to fancy what it was like, as it fell, riddled with slang, from the lips of that grave, earnest teacher, and was listened to by his little learners with a consuming interest that showed that they were as unconscious as he was that any violence was being done to the sacred proprieties!

CHAPTER 48

THE first twenty-six graves in the Virginia cemetery were occupied by *murdered* men. So everybody said, so everybody believed, and so they will always say and believe. The reason why there was so much slaughtering done, was, that in a new mining district the rough element predominates, and a person is not respected until he has "killed his man." That was the very expression used.

If an unknown individual arrived, they did not inquire if he was capable, honest, industrious, but—had he killed his man? If he had not, he gravitated to his natural and proper position, that of a man of small consequence; if he had, the cordiality of his reception was graduated according to the number of his dead. It was tedious work struggling up to a position of influence with bloodless hands; but when a man came with the blood of half a dozen men on his soul, his worth was recognized at once and his acquaintance sought.

In Nevada, for a time, the lawyer, the editor, the banker, the chief desperado, the chief gambler, and the saloon-keeper, occupied the same level in society, and it was the highest. The cheapest and easiest way to become an influential man and be looked up to by the community at large, was to stand behind a bar, wear a cluster-diamond pin, and sell whisky. I am not sure but that the saloon-keeper held a shade higher rank than any other member of society. His opinion had weight. It was his privilege to say how the elections should go. No great movement could succeed without the countenance and direction of the saloon-keepers. It was a high favor when the chief saloon-keeper consented to serve in the legislature or the board of aldermen. Youthful ambition hardly aspired so much to the honors of the law, or the army and navy as to the dignity of proprietorship in a saloon.

To be a saloon-keeper and kill a man was to be illustrious. Hence the reader will not be surprised to learn that more than one man was killed in Nevada under hardly the pretext of provocation, so impatient was the slayer to achieve reputation and throw off the

THE MAN WHO HAD KILLED A DOZEN.

galling sense of being held in indifferent repute by his associates. I knew two youths who tried to "kill their men" for no other reason—and got killed themselves for their pains. "There goes the man that killed Bill Adams" was higher praise and a sweeter sound in the ears of this sort of people than any other speech that admiring lips could utter.

The men who murdered Virginia's original twenty-six cemetery-occupants were never punished. Why? Because Alfred the Great, when he invented trial by jury, and knew that he had admirably framed it to secure justice in his age of the world, was not aware that in the nineteenth century the condition of things would be so entirely changed that unless he rose from the grave and altered the jury plan to meet the emergency, it would prove the most ingenious and infallible agency for *defeating* justice that human wisdom could contrive. For how could he imagine that we simpletons would go on using his jury plan after circumstances had stripped it of its usefulness, any more than he could imagine that we would go on using his candle-clock after we had invented chronometers? In his day news could not travel fast, and hence he could easily find a jury of honest, intelligent men who had not heard of the case they were called to try—but in our day of telegraphs and newspapers his plan compels us to swear in juries composed of fools and rascals, because the system rigidly excludes honest men and men of brains.

I remember one of those sorrowful farces, in Virginia, which we call a jury trial. A noted desperado killed Mr. B., a good citizen, in the most wanton and cold-blooded way. Of course the papers were full of it, and all men capable of reading, read about it. And of course all men not deaf and dumb and idiotic, talked about it. A jury-list was made out, and Mr. B. L., a prominent banker and a valued citizen, was questioned precisely as he would have been questioned in any court in America:

"Have you heard of this homicide?"

"Yes."

"Have you held conversations upon the subject?"

"Yes."

"Have you formed or expressed opinions about it?"

"Yes."

"Have you read the newspaper accounts of it?"

"Yes."

"We do not want you."

A minister, intelligent, esteemed, and greatly respected; a merchant of high character and known probity; a mining superintendent of intelligence and unblemished reputation; a quartz mill owner of excellent standing, were all questioned in the same way, and all set aside. Each said the public talk and the newspaper reports had not so biased his mind but that sworn testimony would overthrow his previously formed opinions and enable him to render a verdict without prejudice and in accordance with the facts. But of course such men could not be trusted with the case. Ignoramuses alone could mete out unsullied justice.

When the peremptory challenges were all exhausted, a jury of twelve men was empaneled—a jury who swore they had neither

THE UNPREJUDICED JURY.

heard, read, talked about nor expressed an opinion concerning a murder which the very cattle in the corrals, the Indians in the sagebrush and the stones in the streets were cognizant of! It was a jury composed of two desperadoes, two low beer-house politicians, three barkeepers, two ranchmen who could not read, and three dull, stupid, human donkeys! It actually came out afterward, that one of these latter thought that incest and arson were the same thing.

The verdict rendered by this jury was, Not Guilty. What else could one expect?

The jury system puts a ban upon intelligence and honesty, and a premium upon ignorance, stupidity and perjury. It is a shame that we must continue to use a worthless system because it *was* good a thousand years ago. In this age, when a gentleman of high social standing, intelligence and probity, swears that testimony given under solemn oath will outweigh, with him, street talk and newspaper reports based upon mere hearsay, he is worth a hundred jurymen who will swear to their own ignorance and stupidity, and justice would be far safer in his hands than in theirs. Why could not the jury law be so altered as to give men of brains and honesty an *equal chance* with fools and miscreants? Is it right to show the present favoritism to one class of men and inflict a disability on another, in a land whose boast is that all its citizens are free and equal? I am a candidate for the legislature. I desire to tamper with the jury law. I wish to so alter it as to put a premium on intelligence and character, and close the jury box against idiots, blacklegs, and people who do not read newspapers. But no doubt I shall be defeated—every effort I make to save the country "misses fire."

My idea, when I began this chapter, was to say something about desperadoism in the "flush times" of Nevada. To attempt a portrayal of that era and that land, and leave out the blood and carnage, would be like portraying Mormondom and leaving out polygamy. The desperado stalked the streets with a swagger graded according to the number of his homicides, and a nod of recognition from him was sufficient to make a humble admirer happy for the rest of the day. The deference that was paid to a desperado of wide reputation, and who "kept his private graveyard," as the phrase went, was marked, and cheerfully accorded. When he moved along the side-

A DESPERADO GIVING REFERENCE.

walk in his excessively long-tailed frock-coat, shiny stump-toed boots, and with dainty little slouch hat tipped over left eye, the small-fry roughs made room for his majesty; when he entered the restaurant, the waiters deserted bankers and merchants to overwhelm him with obsequious service; when he shouldered his way to a bar, the shouldered parties wheeled indignantly, recognized him, and—apologized. They got a look in return that froze their marrow, and by that time a curled and breast-pinned barkeeper was beaming over the counter, proud of the established acquaintanceship that permitted such a familiar form of speech as:

"How 're ye, Billy, old fel? Glad to see you. What'll you take—the old thing?"

The "old thing" meant his customary drink, of course.

The best known names in the Territory of Nevada were those belonging to these long-tailed heroes of the revolver. Orators, governors, capitalists and leaders of the legislature enjoyed a degree of fame, but it seemed local and meagre when contrasted with the fame of such men as Sam Brown, Jack Williams, Billy Mulligan, Farmer Pease, Sugarfoot Mike, Pock-Marked Jake, El Dorado Johnny, Jack McNabb, Joe McGee, Jack Harris, Six-fingered Pete, etc., etc. There was a long list of them. They were brave, reckless men, and traveled with their lives in their hands. To give them their due, they did their killing principally among themselves, and seldom molested peaceable citizens, for they considered it small credit to add to their trophies so cheap a bauble as the death of a man who was "not on the shoot," as they phrased it. They killed each other on slight provocation, and hoped and expected to be killed themselves—for they held it almost shame to die otherwise than "with their boots on," as they expressed it.

I remember an instance of a desperado's contempt for such small game as a private citizen's life. I was taking a late supper in a restaurant one night, with two reporters and a little printer named—Brown, for instance—any name will do. Presently a stranger with a long-tailed coat on came in, and not noticing Brown's hat, which was lying in a chair, sat down on it. Little Brown sprang up and became abusive in a moment. The stranger smiled, smoothed out the hat, and offered it to Brown with profuse apologies couched in caustic sarcasm, and begged Brown not to destroy him. Brown threw off his coat and challenged the man to fight—abused him, threatened him, impeached his courage, and urged and even implored him to fight; and in the meantime the smiling stranger placed himself under our protection in mock distress. But presently he assumed a serious tone, and said:

"Very well, gentlemen, if we must fight, we must, I suppose. But don't rush into danger and then say I gave you no warning. I am more than a match for all of you when I get started. I will give you proofs, and then if my friend here still insists, I will try to accommodate him."

The table we were sitting at was about five feet long, and unusually cumbersome and heavy. He asked us to put our hands on the dishes and hold them in their places a moment—one of them was a large oval dish with a portly roast on it. Then he sat down, tilted up one end of the table, set two of the legs on his knees, took the end of the table between his teeth, took his hands away, and pulled down with his teeth till the table came up to a level position, dishes and all! He said he could lift a keg of nails with his teeth. He

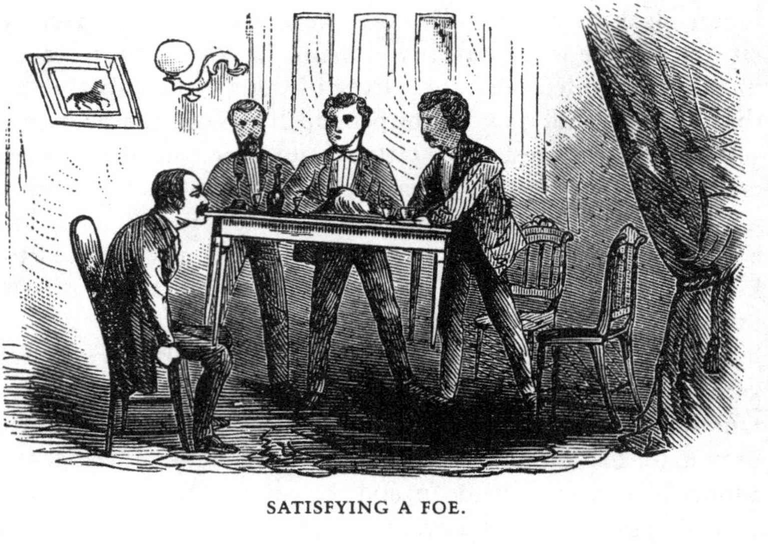

SATISFYING A FOE.

picked up a common glass tumbler and bit a semi-circle out of it. Then he opened his bosom and showed us a net-work of knife and bullet scars; showed us more on his arms and face, and said he believed he had bullets enough in his body to make a pig of lead. He was armed to the teeth. He closed with the remark that he was Mr.

—— of Cariboo—a celebrated name whereat we shook in our shoes. I would publish the name, but for the suspicion that he might come and carve me. He finally inquired if Brown still thirsted for blood. Brown turned the thing over in his mind a moment, and then—asked him to supper.

With the permission of the reader, I will group together, in the next chapter, some samples of life in our small mountain village in the old days of desperadoism. I was there at the time. The reader will observe peculiarities in our *official* society; and he will observe also, an instance of how, in new countries, murders breed murders.

CHAPTER 49

An extract or two from the newspapers of the day will furnish a photograph that can need no embellishment:

FATAL SHOOTING AFFRAY.—An affray occurred, last evening, in a billiard saloon on C street, between *Deputy Marshal Jack Williams* and Wm. Brown, which resulted in the immediate death of the latter. There had been some difficulty between the parties for several months.

An inquest was immediately held, and the following testimony adduced:

Officer GEO. BIRDSALL, sworn, says:—I was told Wm. Brown was drunk and was looking for Jack Williams; so soon as I heard that I started for the parties to prevent a collision; went into the billiard saloon; saw Billy Brown running around, saying if anybody had anything against him to show cause; he was talking in a boisterous manner, and officer Perry took him to the other end of the room to talk to him; Brown came back to me; remarked to me that he thought he was as good as anybody, and knew how to take care of himself; he passed by me and went to the bar; don't know whether he drank or not; Williams was at the end of the billiard-table, next to the stairway; Brown, after going to the bar, came back and said he was as good as any man in the world; he had then walked out to the end of the first billiard-table from the bar; I moved closer to them, supposing there would be a fight; as Brown drew his pistol I caught hold of it; he had fired one shot at Williams; don't know the effect of it; caught hold of him with one hand, and took hold of the pistol and turned it up; think he fired once after I caught hold of the pistol; I wrenched the pistol from him; walked to the end of the billiard-table and told a party that I had Brown's pistol, and to stop shooting; I think four shots were fired in all; after walking out, Mr. Foster remarked that Brown was shot dead.

Oh, there was no excitement about it—he merely "remarked" the small circumstance!

Four months later the following item appeared in the same paper (the *Enterprise*). In this item the name of one of the city officers above referred to (*Deputy Marshal Jack Williams*) occurs again:

Robbery and Desperate Affray.—On Tuesday night, a German named Charles Hurtzal, engineer in a mill at Silver City, came to this place, and visited the hurdy-gurdy house on B street. The music, dancing and Teutonic maidens awakened memories of Faderland until our German friend was carried away with rapture. He evidently had money, and was spending it freely. Late in the evening Jack Williams and Andy Blessington invited him down stairs to take a cup of coffee. Williams proposed a game of cards and went up stairs to procure a deck, but not finding any returned. On the stairway he met the German, and drawing his pistol knocked him down and rifled his pockets of some seventy dollars. Hurtzal dared give no alarm, as he was told, with a pistol at his head, if he made any noise or exposed them, they would blow his brains out. So effectually was he frightened that he made no complaint, until his friends forced him. Yesterday a warrant was issued, but the culprits had disappeared.

This efficient city officer, Jack Williams, had the common reputation of being a burglar, a highwayman and a desperado. It was said that he had several times drawn his revolver and levied money contributions on citizens at dead of night in the public streets of Virginia.

Five months after the above item appeared, Williams was assassinated while sitting at a card table one night; a gun was thrust through the crack of the door and Williams dropped from his chair riddled with balls. It was said, at the time, that Williams had been for some time aware that a party of his own sort (desperadoes) had sworn away his life; and it was generally believed among the people that Williams's friends and enemies would make the assassination memorable—and useful, too—by a wholesale destruction of each other.*

---

*However, one prophecy was verified, at any rate. It was asserted by the desperadoes that one of their brethren (Joe McGee, *a special policeman*) was known to be the conspirator chosen by lot to assassinate Williams; and they also asserted that doom had been pronounced against McGee, and that he would be assassinated in exactly the same manner that had been adopted for the destruction of Williams—a prophecy which came true a year later. After twelve months of distress (for McGee saw a fancied assassin in every man that approached him), he made the last of many efforts to get out of the country unwatched. He went to Carson and sat down in a saloon to wait for the stage—it would leave at four in the morning. But as the night waned and the crowd thinned, he grew uneasy, and told the barkeeper that assassins were on his track. The barkeeper told him to stay in the middle of the room, then, and not go near the door, or the window by the stove. But a fatal fascination seduced him to the neighborhood of the stove every now and then, and repeatedly the bar-

It did not so happen, but still, times were not dull during the next twenty-four hours, for within that time a woman was killed by a pistol shot, a man was brained with a slung shot, and a man named Reeder was also disposed of permanently. Some matters in the *Enterprise* account of the killing of Reeder are worth noting—especially the accommodating complaisance of a Virginia justice of the peace. The italics in the following narrative are mine:

MORE CUTTING AND SHOOTING.—The devil seems to have again broken loose in our town. Pistols and guns explode and knives gleam in our streets as in early times. When there has been a long season of quiet, people are slow to wet their hands in blood; but once blood is spilled, cutting and shooting come easy. Night before last Jack Williams was assassinated, and yesterday forenoon we had more bloody work, growing out of the killing of Williams, and on the same street in which he met his death. It appears that Tom Reeder, a friend of Williams, and George Gumbert were talking, at the meat market of the latter, about the killing of Williams the previous night, when Reeder said it was a most cowardly act to shoot a man in such a way, giving him "no show." Gumbert said that Williams had "as good a show as he gave Billy Brown," meaning the man killed by Williams last March. Reeder said it was a d—d lie, that Williams had no show at all. At this, Gumbert drew a knife and stabbed Reeder, cutting him in two places in the back. One stroke of the knife cut into the sleeve of Reeder's coat and passed downward in a slanting direction through his clothing, and entered his body at the small of the back; another blow struck more squarely, and made a much more dangerous wound. Gumbert gave himself up to the officers of justice, and was shortly after discharged by Justice Atwill, *on his own recognizance,* to appear for trial at six o'clock in the evening. In the meantime Reeder had been taken into the office of Dr. Owens, where his wounds were properly dressed. *One of his wounds was considered quite dangerous, and it was thought by many that it would prove fatal. But being considerably under the influence of liquor, Reeder did not feel his wounds as he otherwise would, and he got up and went into the street.* He went to the meat market and renewed his quarrel with Gumbert, threatening his life. Friends tried to

keeper brought him back to the middle of the room and warned him to remain there. But he could not. At three in the morning he again returned to the stove and sat down by a stranger. Before the barkeeper could get to him with another warning whisper, some one outside fired through the window and riddled McGee's breast with slugs, killing him almost instantly. By the same discharge the stranger at McGee's side also received attentions which proved fatal in the course of two or three days.

interfere to put a stop to the quarrel and get the parties away from each other. In the Fashion Saloon Reeder made threats against the life of Gumbert, saying he would kill him, and it is said that *he requested the officers not to arrest Gumbert, as he intended to kill him.* After these threats Gumbert went off and procured a double-barreled shot gun, loaded with buck-shot or revolver balls, and went after Reeder. Two or three persons were assisting him along the street, trying to get him home, and had him just in front of the store of Klopstock & Harris, when Gumbert came across toward him from the opposite side of the street with his gun. He came up within about ten or fifteen feet of Reeder, and called out to those with him to "look out! get out of the way!" and they had only time to heed the warning, when he fired. Reeder was at the time attempting to screen himself behind a large cask, which stood against the awning post of Klopstock & Harris's store, but some of the balls took effect in the lower part of his breast, and he reeled around forward and fell in front of the cask. Gumbert then raised his gun and fired the second barrel, which missed Reeder and entered the ground. At the time that this occurred, there were a great many persons on the street in the vicinity, and a number of them called out to Gumbert, when they saw him raise his gun, to "hold on," and "don't shoot!" The cutting took place about ten o'clock and the shooting about twelve. After the shooting the street was instantly crowded with the inhabitants of that part of the town, some appearing much excited and laughing—declaring that it looked like the "good old times of '60." Marshal Perry and officer Birdsall were near when the shooting occurred, and Gumbert was immediately arrested and his gun taken from him, when he was marched off to jail. Many persons who were attracted to the spot where this bloody work had just taken place, looked bewildered and seemed to be asking themselves what was to happen next, appearing in doubt as to whether the killing mania had reached its climax, or whether we were to turn in and have a grand killing spell, shooting whoever might have given us offence. It was whispered around that it was not all over yet—five or six more were to be killed before night. Reeder was taken to the Virginia City Hotel, and doctors called in to examine his wounds. They found that two or three balls had entered his right side; one of them appeared to have passed through the substance of the lungs, while another passed into the liver. Two balls were also found to have struck one of his legs. As some of the balls struck the cask, the wounds in Reeder's leg were probably from these, glancing downwards, though they might have been caused by the second shot fired. After being shot, Reeder said when he got on his feet—smiling as he spoke—"It will take better shooting than that to kill me." The doctors consider it almost impossible for him to recover, but as he has an excellent constitution he may survive, notwithstanding the number and dangerous character of the wounds he has received. The town appears to be perfectly quiet at present, as though the late stormy times had cleared our moral atmosphere; but who can tell in what quarter clouds are lowering or plots ripening?

Reeder—or at least what was left of him—survived his wounds two days! Nothing was ever done with Gumbert.

Trial by jury is the palladium of our liberties. I do not know what a palladium is, having never seen a palladium, but it is a good thing no doubt at any rate. Not less than a hundred men have been murdered in Nevada—perhaps I would be within bounds if I said three hundred—and as far as I can learn, only two persons have suffered the death penalty there. However, four or five who had no money and no political influence have been punished by imprisonment—one languished in prison as much as eight months, I think. However, I do not desire to be extravagant—it may have been less.

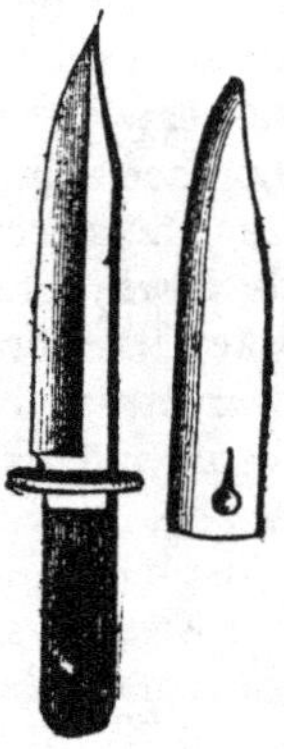

CHAPTER 50

THESE murder and jury statistics remind me of a certain very extraordinary trial and execution of twenty years ago; it is a scrap of history familiar to all old Californians, and worthy to be known by other peoples of the earth that love simple, straightforward justice unencumbered with nonsense. I would apologize for this digression but for the fact that the information I am about to offer is apology enough in itself. And since I digress constantly anyhow, perhaps it is as well to eschew apologies altogether and thus prevent their growing irksome.

Capt. Ned Blakely—that name will answer as well as any other fictitious one (for he was still with the living at last accounts, and may not desire to be famous)—sailed ships out of the harbor of San Francisco for many years. He was a stalwart, warm-hearted, eagle-eyed veteran, who had been a sailor nearly fifty years—a sailor from early boyhood. He was a rough, honest creature, full of pluck, and just as full of hard-headed simplicity, too. He hated trifling conventionalities—"business" was the word, with him. He had all a sailor's vindictiveness against the quips and quirks of the law, and steadfastly believed that the first and last aim and object of the law and lawyers was to defeat justice.

He sailed for the Chincha Islands in command of a guano ship. He had a fine crew, but his negro mate was his pet—on him he had for years lavished his admiration and esteem. It was Capt. Ned's first voyage to the Chinchas, but his fame had gone before him—the fame of being a man who would fight at the dropping of a handkerchief, when imposed upon, and would stand no nonsense. It was a fame well earned. Arrived in the islands, he found that the staple of conversation was the exploits of one Bill Noakes, a bully, the mate of a trading ship. This man had created a small reign of terror there. At nine o'clock at night, Capt. Ned, all alone, was pacing his deck in the starlight. A form ascended the side, and approached him. Capt. Ned said:

"Who goes there?"

"I'm Bill Noakes, the best man in the islands."

"What do you want aboard this ship?"

"I've heard of Capt. Ned Blakely, and one of us is a better man than t'other—I'll know which, before I go ashore."

"You've come to the right shop—I'm your man. I'll learn you to come aboard this ship without an *in*vite."

He seized Noakes, backed him against the mainmast, pounded his face to a pulp, and then threw him overboard.

IMPARTING INFORMATION.

Noakes was not convinced. He returned the next night, got the pulp renewed, and went overboard head first, as before. He was satisfied.

A week after this, while Noakes was carousing with a sailor crowd on shore, at noonday, Capt. Ned's colored mate came along, and Noakes tried to pick a quarrel with him. The negro evaded the trap, and tried to get away. Noakes followed him up; the negro began to run; Noakes fired on him with a revolver and killed him.

Half a dozen sea-captains witnessed the whole affair. Noakes retreated to the small after-cabin of his ship, with two other bullies, and gave out that death would be the portion of any man that intruded there. There was no attempt made to follow the villains; there was no disposition to do it, and indeed very little thought of such an enterprise. There were no courts and no officers; there was no government; the islands belonged to Peru, and Peru was far away; she had no official representative on the ground; and neither had any other nation.

However, Capt. Ned was not perplexing his head about such things. They concerned him not. He was boiling with rage and furious for justice. At nine o'clock at night he loaded a double-barreled gun with slugs, fished out a pair of handcuffs, got a ship's lantern, summoned his quartermaster, and went ashore. He said:

"Do you see that ship there at the dock?"

"Ay-ay, sir."

"It's the Venus."

"Ay-ay, sir."

"You—you know *me*."

"Ay-ay, sir."

"Very well, then. Take the lantern. Carry it just under your chin. I'll walk behind you and rest this gun-barrel on your shoulder, p'inting forward—so. Keep your lantern well up, so's I can see things ahead of you good. I'm going to march in on Noakes—and take him—and jug the other chaps. If you flinch—well, you know *me*."

"Ay-ay, sir."

In this order they filed aboard softly, arrived at Noakes's den, the quartermaster pushed the door open, and the lantern revealed the three desperadoes sitting on the floor. Capt. Ned said:

"I'm Ned Blakely. I've got you under fire. Don't you move without orders—any of you. You two kneel down in the corner; faces to the wall—now. Bill Noakes, put these handcuffs on; now come up close. Quartermaster, fasten 'em. All right. Don't stir, sir. Quartermaster, put the key in the outside of the door. Now, men, I'm going to lock you two in; and if you try to burst through this door—well, you've heard of *me*. Bill Noakes, fall in ahead, and march. All set. Quartermaster, lock the door."

Noakes spent the night on board Blakely's ship, a prisoner under strict guard. Early in the morning Capt. Ned called in all the sea-captains in the harbor and invited them, with nautical ceremony,

A WALKING BATTERY.

to be present on board his ship at nine o'clock to witness the hanging of Noakes at the yard-arm!

"What! The man has not been tried."

"Of course he hasn't. But didn't he kill the nigger?"

"Certainly he did; but you are not thinking of hanging him without a trial?"

"*Trial!* What do I want to try him for, if he killed the nigger?"

"Oh, Capt. Ned, this will *never* do. Think how it will sound."

"Sound be hanged! *Didn't he kill the nigger?*"

"Certainly, certainly, Capt. Ned,—nobody denies that,—but—"

"Then I'm going to *hang* him, that's all. Everybody I've talked to talks just the same way you do. Everybody says he killed the nigger, everybody knows he killed the nigger, and yet every lubber of you wants him *tried* for it. I don't understand such bloody foolishness as that. *Tried!* Mind you, I don't object to trying him, if it's got to be done to give satisfaction; and I'll be there, and chip in and help, too; but put it off till afternoon—put it off till afternoon, for I'll have my hands middling full till after the burying—"

"Why, what do you mean? Are you going to hang him *anyhow*—and try him afterward?"

"Didn't I *say* I was going to hang him? I never saw such people as you. What's the difference? You ask a favor, and then you ain't satisfied when you get it. Before or after's all one—*you* know how the trial will go. He killed the nigger. Say—I must be going. If your mate would like to come to the hanging, fetch him along. I like him."

There was a stir in the camp. The captains came in a body and pleaded with Capt. Ned not to do this rash thing. They promised that they would create a court composed of captains of the best character; they would empanel a jury; they would conduct everything in a way becoming the serious nature of the business in hand, and give the case an impartial hearing and the accused a fair trial. And they said it would be murder, and punishable by the American courts if he persisted and hung the accused on his ship. They pleaded hard. Capt. Ned said:

"Gentlemen, I'm not stubborn and I'm not unreasonable. I'm always willing to do just as near right as I can. How long will it take?"

"Probably only a little while."

"And can I take him up the shore and hang him as soon as you are done?"

"If he is proven guilty he shall be hanged without unnecessary delay."

"*If* he's proven guilty. Great Neptune, *ain't* he guilty? This beats my time. Why you all *know* he's guilty."

But at last they satisfied him that they were projecting nothing underhanded. Then he said:

"Well, all right. You go on and try him and I'll go down and overhaul his conscience and prepare him to go—like enough he needs it, and I don't want to send him off without a show for hereafter."

This was another obstacle. They finally convinced him that it was necessary to have the accused in court. Then they said they would send a guard to bring him.

"No, sir, I prefer to fetch him myself—he don't get out of *my* hands. Besides, I've got to go to the ship to get a rope, anyway."

The court assembled with due ceremony, empaneled a jury, and presently Capt. Ned entered, leading the prisoner with one hand and carrying a Bible and a rope in the other. He seated himself by the side of his captive and told the court to "up anchor and make sail." Then he turned a searching eye on the jury, and detected Noakes's friends, the two bullies. He strode over and said to them confidentially:

"You're here to interfere, you see. Now you vote right, do you hear?—or else there'll be a double-barreled inquest here when this trial's off, and your remainders will go home in a couple of baskets."

The caution was not without fruit. The jury was a unit—the verdict, "Guilty."

Capt. Ned sprung to his feet and said:

"Come along—you're my meat *now*, my lad, anyway. Gentlemen you've done yourselves proud. I invite you all to come and see that I do it all straight. Follow me to the cañon, a mile above here."

The court informed him that a sheriff had been appointed to do the hanging, and—

Capt. Ned's patience was at an end. His wrath was boundless. The subject of a sheriff was judiciously dropped.

When the crowd arrived at the cañon, Capt. Ned climbed a tree and arranged the halter, then came down and noosed his man. He opened his Bible, and laid aside his hat. Selecting a chapter at random, he read it through, in a deep bass voice and with sincere solemnity. Then he said:

"Lad, you are about to go aloft and give an account of yourself; and the lighter a man's manifest is, as far as sin's concerned, the better for him. Make a clean breast, man, and carry a log with you that'll bear inspection. You killed the nigger?"

No reply. A long pause.

The captain read another chapter, pausing, from time to time, to impress the effect. Then he talked an earnest, persuasive sermon to him, and ended by repeating the question:

"Did you kill the nigger?"

No reply—other than a malignant scowl. The captain now read the first and second chapters of Genesis, with deep feeling—paused a moment, closed the book reverently, and said with a perceptible savor of satisfaction:

"There. Four chapters. There's few that would have took the pains with you that I have."

OVERHAULING HIS MANIFEST.

Then he swung up the condemned, and made the rope fast; stood by and timed him half an hour with his watch, and then delivered the body to the court. A little after, as he stood contemplating the motionless figure, a doubt came into his face; evidently he felt a twinge of conscience—a misgiving—and he said with a sigh:

"Well, p'raps I ought to burnt him, maybe. But I was trying to do for the best."

When the history of this affair reached California (it was in the "early days") it made a deal of talk, but did not diminish the captain's popularity in any degree. It increased it, indeed. California had a population then that "inflicted" justice after a fashion that was simplicity and primitiveness itself, and could therefore admire appreciatively when the same fashion was followed elsewhere.

CHAPTER 51

VICE flourished luxuriantly during the hey-day of our "flush times." The saloons were overburdened with custom; so were the police courts, the gambling dens, the brothels and the jails—unfailing signs of high prosperity in a mining region—in any region for that matter. Is it not so? A crowded police court docket is the surest of all signs that trade is brisk and money plenty. Still, there is one other sign; it comes last, but when it does come it establishes beyond cavil that the "flush times" are at the flood. This is the birth of the "literary" paper. The *Weekly Occidental,* "devoted to literature," made its appearance in Virginia. All the literary people were engaged to write for it. Mr. F. was to edit it. He was a felicitous skirmisher with a pen, and a man who could say happy things in a crisp, neat way. Once, while editor of the *Union,* he had disposed of a labored, incoherent, two-column attack made upon him by a cotemporary, with a single line, which, at first glance, seemed to contain a solemn and tremendous compliment—viz.: "THE LOGIC OF OUR ADVERSARY RESEMBLES THE PEACE OF GOD,"—and left it to the reader's memory and after-thought to invest the remark with another and "more different" meaning by supplying for himself and at his own leisure the rest of the Scripture—"*in that it passeth understanding.*" He once said of a little, half-starved, wayside community that had no subsistence except what they could get by preying upon chance passengers who stopped over with them a day when traveling by the overland stage, that in their church service they had altered the Lord's Prayer to read: "Give us this day our daily stranger!"

We expected great things of the *Occidental.* Of course it could not get along without an original novel, and so we made arrangements to hurl into the work the full strength of the company. Mrs. F. was an able romancist of the ineffable school—I know no other name to apply to a school whose heroes are all dainty and all perfect. She wrote the opening chapter, and introduced a lovely blonde simpleton who talked nothing but pearls and poetry and who was virtuous to the verge of eccentricity. She also introduced a young French Duke of aggravated refinement, in love with the blonde. Mr. F. followed next week, with a brilliant lawyer who set about getting the Duke's estates into trouble, and a sparkling young lady of high society who fell to fascinating the Duke and impairing the appetite of the blonde. Mr. D., a dark and bloody editor of one of the dailies, followed Mr. F., the third week, introducing a mysterious Rosicrucian who transmuted metals, held consultations with the devil in a cave at dead of night, and cast the horoscope of the several heroes and heroines in such a way as to provide

THE HEROES AND HEROINES OF THE STORY.

plenty of trouble for their future careers and breed a solemn and awful public interest in the novel. He also introduced a cloaked and masked melodramatic miscreant, put him on a salary and set him on the midnight track of the Duke with a poisoned dagger. He also created an Irish coachman with a rich brogue and placed him in the service of the society-young-lady with an ulterior mission to carry billets-doux to the Duke.

About this time there arrived in Virginia a dissolute stranger with a literary turn of mind—rather seedy he was, but very quiet and unassuming; almost diffident, indeed. He was so gentle, and his manners were so pleasing and kindly, whether he was sober or intoxicated, that he made friends of all who came in contact with him. He applied for literary work, offered conclusive evidence that he wielded an easy and practiced pen, and so Mr. F. engaged him at once to help write the novel. His chapter was to follow Mr. D.'s, and mine was to come next. Now what does this fellow do but go off and get drunk and then proceed to his quarters and set to work with his imagination in a state of chaos, and that chaos in a condition of extravagant activity. The result may be guessed. He scanned the chapters of his predecessors, found plenty of heroes and heroines already created, and was satisfied with them; he decided to introduce no more; with all the confidence that whisky inspires and all the easy complacency it gives to its servant, he then launched himself lovingly into his work: he married the coachman to the society-young-lady for the sake of the scandal; married the Duke to the blonde's stepmother, for the sake of the sensation; stopped the desperado's salary; created a misunderstanding between the devil and the Rosicrucian; threw the Duke's property into the wicked lawyer's hands; made the lawyer's upbraiding conscience drive him to drink, thence to *delirium tremens,* thence to suicide; broke the coachman's neck; let his widow succumb to contumely, neglect, poverty and consumption; caused the blonde to drown herself, leaving her clothes on the bank with the customary note pinned to them forgiving the Duke and hoping he would be happy; revealed to the Duke, by means of the usual strawberry mark on left arm, that he had married his own long-lost mother and destroyed his long-lost sister; instituted the proper and necessary suicide of the Duke and the Duchess in order to compass poetical justice; opened the earth and let the Rosicrucian through,

DISSOLUTE AUTHOR.

accompanied with the accustomed smoke and thunder and smell of brimstone, and finished with the promise that in the next chapter, after holding a general inquest, he would take up the surviving character of the novel and tell what became of the devil!

It read with singular smoothness, and with a "dead" earnestness that was funny enough to suffocate a body. But there was war when it came in. The other novelists were furious. The mild stranger, not yet more than half sober, stood there, under a scathing fire of vituperation, meek and bewildered, looking from one to another of his assailants, and wondering what he could have done to invoke such a storm. When a lull came at last, he said his say gently and appealingly—said he did not rightly remember what he had written, but was sure he had tried to do the best he could, and knew his object had been to make the novel not only pleasant and plausible but instructive and—

The bombardment began again. The novelists assailed his ill-chosen adjectives and demolished them with a storm of denunciation and ridicule. And so the siege went on. Every time the stranger tried to appease the enemy he only made matters worse. Finally he offered to rewrite the chapter. This arrested hostilities. The indignation gradually quieted down, peace reigned again and the sufferer retired in safety and got him to his own citadel.

But on the way thither the evil angel tempted him and he got drunk again. And again his imagination went mad. He led the heroes and heroines a wilder dance than ever; and yet all through it ran that same convincing air of honesty and earnestness that had marked his first work. He got the characters into the most extraordinary situations, put them through the most surprising performances, and made them talk the strangest talk! But the chapter cannot be described. It was symmetrically crazy; it was artistically absurd; and it had explanatory foot-notes that were fully as curious as the text. I remember one of the "situations," and will offer it as an example of the whole. He altered the character of the brilliant lawyer, and made him a great-hearted, splendid fellow; gave him fame and riches, and set his age at thirty-three years. Then he made the blonde discover, through the help of the Rosicrucian and the melodramatic miscreant, that while the Duke loved her money ardently and wanted it, he secretly felt a sort of leaning toward the society-young-lady. Stung to the quick, she tore her affections from him and bestowed them with tenfold power upon the lawyer, who responded with consuming zeal. But the parents would none of it. What they wanted in the family was a Duke; and a Duke they were determined to have; though they confessed that next to the Duke the lawyer had their preference. Necessarily the blonde now went into a decline. The parents were alarmed. They pleaded with her to marry the Duke, but she steadfastly refused, and pined on. Then they laid a plan. They told her to wait a year and a day, and if at the end of that time she still felt that she could not marry the Duke, she might marry the lawyer with their full consent. The result was as they had foreseen: gladness came again, and the flush of returning health. Then the parents took the next step in their scheme. They had the family physician recommend a long sea voyage and much land travel for the thorough restoration of the blonde's strength; and they invited the Duke to be of the party. They judged that the Duke's constant presence and the lawyer's protracted absence would do the rest—for they did not invite the lawyer.

So they set sail in a steamer for America—and the third day out, when their sea-sickness called truce and permitted them to take their first meal at the public table, behold there sat the lawyer! The

UNLOOKED-FOR APPEARANCE OF THE LAWYER.

Duke and party made the best of an awkward situation; the voyage progressed, and the vessel neared America. But, by and by, two hundred miles off New Bedford, the ship took fire; she burned to the water's edge; of all her crew and passengers, only thirty were saved. They floated about the sea half an afternoon and all night long. Among them were our friends. The lawyer, by superhuman exertions, had saved the blonde and her parents, swimming back and forth two hundred yards and bringing one each time—(the girl first). The Duke had saved himself. In the morning two whaleships arrived on the scene and sent their boats. The weather was stormy and the embarkation was attended with much confusion and excitement. The lawyer did his duty like a man; helped his exhausted and insensible blonde, her parents and some others into a boat (the Duke helped himself in); then a child fell overboard at the other end of the raft and the lawyer rushed thither and helped half a dozen people fish it out, under the stimulus of its mother's screams. Then he ran back—a few seconds too late—the blonde's boat was under way. So he had to take the other boat, and go to the other ship. The storm increased and drove the vessels out of sight of each other—drove them whither it would. When it calmed, at the end of three days, the blonde's ship was seven hundred miles north of Boston and the other about seven hundred south of that port. The blonde's captain was bound on a whaling cruise in the North Atlantic and could not go back such a distance or make a port without orders; such being nautical law. The lawyer's captain was to cruise in the North Pacific, and *he* could not go back or make a port without orders. All the lawyer's money and baggage were in the blonde's boat and went to the blonde's ship—so his captain made him work his passage as a common sailor. When both ships had been cruising nearly a year, the one was off the coast of Greenland and the other in Behring's Strait. The blonde had long ago been well-nigh persuaded that her lawyer had been washed overboard and lost just before the whaleships reached the raft, and now, under the pleadings of her parents and the Duke she was at last beginning to nerve herself for the doom of the covenant, and prepare for the hated marriage. But she would not yield a day before the date set. The weeks dragged on, the time narrowed, orders were given to deck the ship for the wedding—a wedding at sea among icebergs and walruses. Five days more and all would be over. So the blonde reflected, with a sigh and a tear. Oh where was

THE STORM INCREASED.

her true love—and why, why did he not come and save her? At that moment he was lifting his harpoon to strike a whale in Behring's Strait, five thousand miles away, by the way of the Arctic Ocean, or twenty thousand by the way of the Horn—that was the reason. He struck, but not with perfect aim—his foot slipped and he fell in the whale's mouth and went down his throat. He was insensible five days. Then he came to himself and heard voices; daylight was streaming through a hole cut in the whale's roof. He climbed out and astonished the sailors who were hoisting blubber up a ship's side. He recognized the vessel, flew aboard, surprised the wedding party at the altar and exclaimed:

"Stop the proceedings—I'm here! Come to my arms, my own!"

There were foot-notes to this extravagant piece of literature wherein the author endeavored to show that the whole thing was within the possibilities; he said he got the incident of the whale traveling from Behring's Strait to the coast of Greenland, five thousand miles in five days, through the Arctic Ocean, from Charles Reade's "Love Me Little, Love Me Long," and considered that that established the fact that the thing could be done; and he instanced Jonah's adventure as proof that a man could live in a whale's belly, and added that if a preacher could stand it three days a lawyer could surely stand it five!

JONAH OUTDONE.

There was a fiercer storm than ever in the editorial sanctum now, and the stranger was peremptorily discharged, and his manuscript flung at his head. But he had already delayed things so much that there was not time for some one else to rewrite the chapter, and so the paper came out without any novel in it. It was but a feeble, struggling, stupid journal, and the absence of the novel probably shook public confidence; at any rate, before the first side of the next issue went to press, the *Weekly Occidental* died as peacefully as an infant.

An effort was made to resurrect it, with the proposed advantage of a telling new title, and Mr. F. said that *The Phenix* would be just the name for it, because it would give the idea of a resurrection from its dead ashes in a new and undreamed of condition of splendor; but some low-priced smarty on one of the dailies suggested that we call it the *Lazarus;* and inasmuch as the people were not profound in Scriptural matters but thought the resurrected Lazarus and the dilapidated mendicant that begged in the rich man's gateway were one and the same person, the name became the laughing stock of the town, and killed the paper for good and all.

I was sorry enough, for I was very proud of being connected with a literary paper—prouder than I have ever been of anything since, perhaps. I had written some rhymes for it—poetry I considered it—and it was a great grief to me that the production was on the "first side" of the issue that was not completed, and hence did not see the light. But time brings its revenges—I can put it in here; it will answer in place of a tear dropped to the memory of the lost *Occidental.* The idea (not the chief idea, but the vehicle that bears it) was probably suggested by the old song called "The Raging Canal," but I cannot remember now. I do remember, though, that at that time I thought my doggerel was one of the ablest poems of the age:

THE AGED PILOT MAN.

On the Erie Canal, it was,
All on a summer's day,
I sailed forth with my parents
Far away to Albany.

From out the clouds at noon that day
There came a dreadful storm,
That piled the billows high about,
And filled us with alarm.

A man came rushing from a house,
Saying, "Snub up* your boat I pray,
Snub up your boat, snub up, alas,
Snub up while yet you may."

Our captain cast one glance astern,
Then forward glancèd he,
And said, "My wife and little ones
I never more shall see."

*The customary canal technicality for "tie up."

Said Dollinger the pilot man,
In noble words, but few,—
"Fear not, but lean on Dollinger,
And he will fetch you through."

The boat drove on, the frightened mules
Tore through the rain and wind,
And bravely still, in danger's post,
The whip-boy strode behind.

"Come 'board, come 'board," the captain cried,
"Nor tempt so wild a storm;"
But still the raging mules advanced,
And still the boy strode on.

Then said the captain to us all,
"Alas, 'tis plain to me,
The greater danger is not there,
But here upon the sea.

So let us strive, while life remains,
To save all souls on board,
And then if die at last we must,
Let . . . . I *cannot* speak the word!"

DOLLINGER.

Said Dollinger the pilot man,
Tow'ring above the crew,
"Fear not, but trust in Dollinger,
And he will fetch you through."

"Low bridge! low bridge!" all heads went down,
The laboring bark sped on;
A mill we passed, we passed a church,
Hamlets, and fields of corn;
And all the world came out to see,
And chased along the shore
Crying, "Alas, alas, the sheeted rain,
The wind, the tempest's roar!
Alas, the gallant ship and crew,
Can *nothing* help them more?"

"LOW BRIDGE!"

And from our deck sad eyes looked out
Across the stormy scene:
The tossing wake of billows aft,
The bending forests green,
The chickens sheltered under carts
In lee of barn the cows,

The skurrying swine with straw in mouth,
   The wild spray from our bows!

      "She balances!
       She wavers!
Now let her go about!
   If she misses stays and broaches to,
We're all"—[then with a shout,]
      "Hurray! hurray!
       Avast! belay!
       Take in more sail!
       Lord, what a gale!
Ho, boy, haul taut on the hind mule's tail!"

SHORTENING SAIL.

"Ho! lighten ship! ho! man the pump!
   Ho, hostler, heave the lead!
And count ye all, both great and small,
   As numbered with the dead!
For mariner for forty year,
   On Erie, boy and man,
I never yet saw such a storm,
   Or one 't with it began!"

So overboard a keg of nails
And anvils three we threw,
Likewise four bales of gunny sacks,
Two hundred pounds of glue,
Two sacks of corn, four ditto wheat,
A box of books, a cow,
A violin, Lord Byron's works,
A rip-saw and a sow.

LIGHTENING SHIP.

A curve! a curve! the dangers grow!
"Labbord!—stabbord!—s-t-e-a-d-y!—so!—
Hard-a-port, Dol!—hellum-a-lee!
Haw the head mule!—the aft one gee!
Luff!—bring her to the wind!"

"A quarter-three!—'tis shoaling fast!
Three feet large!—t-h-r-e-e feet!—
Three feet scant!" I cried in fright
"Oh, is there *no* retreat?"

Said Dollinger, the pilot man,
As on the vessel flew,
"Fear not, but trust in Dollinger,
And he will fetch you through."

A panic struck the bravest hearts,
  The boldest cheek turned pale;
For plain to all, this shoaling said
A leak had burst the ditch's bed!
And, straight as bolt from crossbow sped,
Our ship swept on, with shoaling lead,
  Before the fearful gale!

"Sever the tow-line! Cripple the mules!"
  Too late! . . . . . There comes a shock!
* * * * * *
Another length, and the fated craft
  Would have swum in the saving lock!

Then gathered together the shipwrecked crew
  And took one last embrace,
While sorrowful tears from despairing eyes
  Ran down each hopeless face;
And some did think of their little ones
  Whom they never more might see,
And others of waiting wives at home,
  And mothers that grieved would be.

THE MARVELOUS RESCUE.

But of all the children of misery there
  On that poor sinking frame,

But one spake words of hope and faith,
  And I worshipped as they came:
Said Dollinger the pilot man,—
  (O brave heart, strong and true!)—
"Fear not, but trust in Dollinger,
  For he will fetch you through."

Lo! scarce the words have passed his lips
  The dauntless prophet say'th,
When every soul about him seeth
  A wonder crown his faith!

For straight a farmer brought a plank,—
  (Mysteriously inspired)—
And laying it unto the ship,
  In silent awe retired.

Then every sufferer stood amazed
  That pilot man before;
A moment stood. Then wondering turned,
  And speechless walked ashore.

CHAPTER 52

SINCE I desire, in this chapter, to say an instructive word or two about the silver mines, the reader may take this fair warning and skip, if he chooses. The year 1863 was perhaps the very top blossom and culmination of the "flush times." Virginia swarmed with men and vehicles to that degree that the place looked like a very hive—that is when one's vision could pierce through the thick fog of alkali dust that was generally blowing in summer. I will say, concerning this dust, that if you drove ten miles through it, you and your horses would be coated with it a sixteenth of an inch thick and present an outside appearance that was a uniform pale yellow color, and your buggy would have three inches of dust in it, thrown there by the wheels. The delicate scales used by the assayers were enclosed in glass cases intended to be air-tight, and yet some of this dust was so impalpable and so invisibly fine that it would get in, somehow, and impair the accuracy of those scales.

Speculation ran riot, and yet there was a world of substantial business going on, too. All freights were brought over the mountains from California (a hundred and fifty miles) by pack-train partly, and partly in huge wagons drawn by such long mule teams that each team amounted to a procession, and it did seem, sometimes, that the grand combined procession of animals stretched unbroken from Virginia to California. Its long route was traceable clear across the deserts of the Territory by the writhing serpent of dust it lifted up. By these wagons, freights over that hundred and fifty miles were two hundred dollars a ton for small lots (same price for all express matter brought by stage), and a hundred dollars a ton for full loads. One Virginia firm received one hundred tons of freight a month, and paid ten thousand dollars a month freightage. In the winter the freights were much higher. All the bullion was

SILVER BRICKS.

shipped in bars by stage to San Francisco (a bar was usually about twice the size of a pig of lead and contained from fifteen hundred to three thousand dollars according to the amount of gold mixed with the silver), and the freight on it (when the shipment was large) was one and a quarter per cent of its intrinsic value. So, the freight on these bars probably averaged something more than twenty-five dollars each. Small shippers paid two per cent. There were three stages a day, each way, and I have seen the out-going stages carry away a third of a ton of bullion each, and more than once I saw them divide a two-ton lot and take it off. However, these were extraordinary events.* Two tons of silver bullion would be in the

*Mr. Valentine, Wells Fargo's agent, has handled all the bullion shipped through the Virginia office for many a month. To his memory—which is excellent—we are indebted for the following exhibit of the company's business in the Virginia office since the first of January, 1862: From January 1st to April 1st, about $270,000 worth of bullion passed through that office; during the next quarter, $570,000; next quarter, $800,000; next quarter, $956,000; next quarter, $1,275,000; and for the quarter ending on the 30th of last June, about $1,600,000. Thus in a year and a half, the Virginia office only shipped $5,330,000 in bullion. During the year 1862 they shipped $2,615,000, so we perceive the average shipments have more than doubled in the last six months. This gives us room to promise for the Virginia office $500,000 a month for the year 1863 (though perhaps, judging by the steady increase in the business, we are underestimating, somewhat). This gives us $6,000,000 for the year. Gold Hill and Silver City together can beat us—we will give them $10,000,000. To Dayton, Empire City, Ophir and Carson City, we will allow an aggregate of $8,000,000, which is not over the mark, perhaps, and may possibly be a little under it. To Esmeralda we give $4,000,000. To Reese River and Humboldt $2,000,000, which is liberal now, but may not be before the year is out. So we prognosticate that the yield of bullion this year will be about $30,000,000. Placing the number of mills in the Territory at 100, this gives to each the labor of producing $300,000 in bullion during the twelve months. Allowing them to run 300 days in the year, (which none of them more than do) this makes their work average $1,000 a day. Say the mills average 20 tons of rock a day and this rock worth $50 as a general thing, and you

neighborhood of forty bars, and the freight on it over a thousand dollars. Each coach always carried a deal of ordinary express matter besides, and also from fifteen to twenty passengers at from twenty-five to thirty dollars a head. With six stages going all the time, Wells, Fargo and Co.'s Virginia City business was important and lucrative.

All along under the centre of Virginia and Gold Hill, for a couple of miles, ran the great Comstock silver lode—a vein of ore from fifty to eighty feet thick between its solid walls of rock—a vein as wide as some of New York's streets. I will remind the reader that in Pennsylvania a coal vein only eight feet wide is considered ample.

TIMBER SUPPORTS.

Virginia was a busy city of streets and houses above ground. Under it was another busy city, down in the bowels of the earth, where a great population of men thronged in and out among an intricate maze of tunnels and drifts, flitting hither and thither under a winking sparkle of lights, and over their heads towered a vast web of interlocking timbers that held the walls of the gutted Comstock apart. These timbers were as large as a man's body, and the framework stretched upward so far that no eye could pierce to its top through the closing gloom. It was like peering up through the clean-picked ribs and bones of some colossal skeleton. Imagine such a framework two miles long, sixty feet wide, and higher than any church spire in America.

have the actual work of our 100 mills figured down "to a spot"—$1,000 a day each, and $30,000,000 a year in the aggregate.—*Enterprise.*

[A considerable overestimate.—M. T.]

Imagine this stately lattice-work stretching down Broadway, from the St. Nicholas to Wall street, and a Fourth of July procession, reduced to pigmies, parading on top of it and flaunting their flags, high above the pinnacle of Trinity steeple. One can imagine that, but he cannot well imagine what that forest of timbers cost, from the time they were felled in the pineries beyond Washoe Lake, hauled up and around Mount Davidson at atrocious rates of freightage, then squared, let down into the deep maw of the mine and built up there. Twenty ample fortunes would not timber one of the greatest of those silver mines. The Spanish proverb says it requires a gold mine to "run" a silver one, and it is true. A beggar with a silver mine is a pitiable pauper indeed if he cannot sell.

I spoke of the underground Virginia as a city. The Gould & Curry is only one single mine under there, among a great many others; yet the Gould & Curry's streets of dismal drifts and tunnels were five miles in extent, altogether, and its population five hundred miners. Taken as a whole, the underground city had some thirty miles of streets and a population of five or six thousand. In this present day some of those populations are at work from twelve to sixteen hundred feet under Virginia and Gold Hill, and the signal-bells that tell them what the superintendent above ground desires them to do are struck by telegraph as we strike a fire alarm. Sometimes men fall down a shaft, there, a thousand feet deep. In such cases, the usual plan is to hold an inquest.

If you wish to visit one of those mines, you may walk through a tunnel about half a mile long if you prefer it, or you may take the quicker plan of shooting like a dart down a shaft, on a small platform. It is like tumbling down through an empty steeple, feet first. When you reach the bottom, you take a candle and tramp through drifts and tunnels where throngs of men are digging and blasting; you watch them send up tubs full of great lumps of stone—silver ore; you select choice specimens from the mass, as souvenirs; you admire the world of skeleton timbering; you reflect frequently that you are buried under a mountain, a thousand feet below daylight; being in the bottom of the mine you climb from "gallery" to "gallery," up endless ladders that stand straight up and down; when your legs fail you at last, you lie down in a small box-car in a

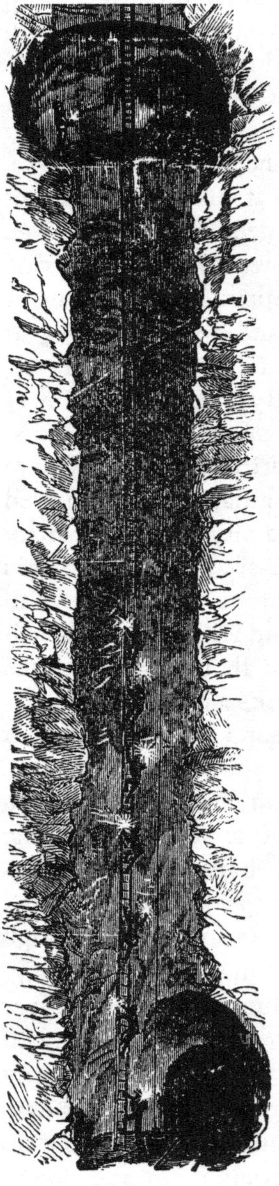

FROM GALLERY TO GALLERY.

cramped "incline" like a half-up-ended sewer and are dragged up to daylight feeling as if you are crawling through a coffin that has no end to it. Arrived at the top, you find a busy crowd of men receiving the ascending cars and tubs and dumping the ore from an elevation into long rows of bins capable of holding half a dozen tons each; under the bins are rows of wagons loading from chutes and trap-doors in the bins, and down the long street is a procession of these wagons wending toward the silver mills with their rich freight. It is all "done," now, and there you are. You need never go down again, for you have seen it all. If you have forgotten the process of reducing the ore in the mill and making the silver bars, you can go back and find it again in my Esmeralda chapters if so disposed.

Of course these mines cave in, in places, occasionally, and then it is worth one's while to take the risk of descending into them and observing the crushing power exerted by the pressing weight of a settling mountain. I published such an experience in the *Enterprise,* once, and from it I will take an extract:

AN HOUR IN THE CAVED MINES.—We journeyed down into the Ophir mine, yesterday, to see the earthquake. We could not go down the deep incline, because it still has a propensity to cave in places. Therefore we traveled through the long tunnel which enters the hill above the Ophir office, and then by means of a series of long ladders, climbed away down from the first to the fourth gallery. Traversing a drift, we came to the Spanish line, passed five sets of timbers still uninjured, and found the earthquake. Here was as complete a chaos as ever was seen—vast masses of earth and splintered and broken timbers piled confusedly together, with scarcely an aperture left large enough for a cat to creep through. Rubbish was still falling at intervals from above, and one timber which had braced others earlier in the day, was *now* crushed down out of its former position, showing that the caving and settling of the tremendous mass was still going on. We were in that portion of the Ophir known as the "north mines." Returning to the surface, we entered a tunnel leading into the Central, for the purpose of getting into the main Ophir. Descending a long incline in this tunnel, we traversed a drift or so, and then went down a deep shaft from whence we proceeded into the fifth gallery of the Ophir. From a side-drift we crawled through a small hole and got into the midst of the earthquake again—earth and broken timbers mingled together without regard to grace or symmetry. A large portion of the second, third and fourth galleries had caved in and gone to destruction—the two latter at seven o'clock on the previous evening.

At the turn-table, near the northern extremity of the fifth gallery, two big piles of rubbish had forced their way through from the fifth gallery, and from the looks of the timbers, more was about to come. These beams are solid—eighteen inches square; first, a great beam is laid on the floor, then upright ones, five feet high, stand on it, supporting another horizontal beam, and so on, square above square, like the framework of a window. The superincumbent weight was sufficient to mash the ends of those great upright beams fairly into the solid wood of the horizontal ones three inches, compressing and bending the upright beam till it curved like a bow. Before the Spanish caved in, some of their twelve-inch horizontal timbers were compressed in this way until they were only five inches thick! Imagine the power it must take to squeeze a solid log together in that way. Here, also, was a range of timbers, for a distance of twenty feet, tilted six inches out of the perpendicular by the weight resting upon them from the caved galleries above. You could hear things cracking and giving way, and it was not pleasant to know that the world overhead was slowly and silently sinking down upon you. The men down in the mine do not mind it, however.

Returning along the fifth gallery, we struck the safe part of the Ophir incline, and went down it to the sixth; but we found ten inches of water there, and had to come back. In repairing the damage done to the incline, the pump had to be stopped for two hours, and in the meantime the water gained about a foot. However, the pump was at work again, and the flood-water was decreasing. We climbed up to the fifth gallery again and sought a deep shaft, whereby we might descend to another part of the sixth, out of reach of the water, but suffered disappointment, as the men had gone to dinner, and there was no one to man the windlass. So, having seen the earthquake, we climbed out at the Union incline and tunnel, and adjourned, all dripping with candle grease and perspiration, to lunch at the Ophir office.

During the great flush year of 1863, Nevada [claims to have] produced $25,000,000 in bullion—almost, if not quite, a round million to each thousand inhabitants, which is very well, considering that she was without agriculture and manufactures.* Silver mining was her sole productive industry.

---

*Since the above was in type, I learn from an official source that the above figure is too high, and that the yield for 1863 did not exceed $20,000,000. However, the day for large figures is approaching; the Sutro Tunnel is to plow through the Comstock lode from end to end, at a depth of two thousand feet, and then mining will be easy and comparatively inexpensive; and the momentous matters of drainage, and hoisting and hauling of ore will cease to be burdensome. This vast work will absorb many years, and millions of dollars, in its completion; but it will early yield money, for that desirable epoch will begin as soon as it strikes the first end of the vein. The tunnel will be some eight miles long, and will develop astonishing riches. Cars will carry the ore through the tunnel and dump it in the mills and thus do away with the present costly system of double handling and transportation by mule teams. The water from the tunnel will furnish the motive power for the mills. Mr. Sutro, the originator of this prodigious enterprise, is one of the few men in the world who is gifted with the pluck and perseverance necessary to follow up and hound such an undertaking to its completion. He has converted several obstinate Congresses to a deserved friendliness toward his important work, and has gone up and down and to and fro in Europe until he has enlisted a great moneyed interest in it there.

CHAPTER 53

Every now and then, in these days, the boys used to tell me I ought to get one Jim Blaine to tell me the stirring story of his grandfather's old ram—but they always added that I must not mention the matter unless Jim was drunk at the time—just comfortably and sociably drunk. They kept this up until my curiosity was on the rack to hear the story. I got to haunting Blaine; but it was of no use, the boys always found fault with his condition; he was often moderately but never satisfactorily drunk. I never watched a man's condition with such absorbing interest, such anxious solicitude; I never so pined to see a man uncompromisingly drunk before. At last, one evening I hurried to his cabin, for I learned that this time his situation was such that even the most fastidious could find no fault with it—he was tranquilly, serenely, symmetrically drunk—not a hiccup to mar his voice, not a cloud upon his brain thick enough to obscure his memory. As I entered, he was sitting upon an empty powder-keg, with a clay pipe in one hand and the other raised to command silence. His face was round, red, and very serious; his throat was bare and his hair tumbled; in general appearance and costume he was a stalwart miner of the period. On the pine table stood a candle, and its dim light revealed "the boys" sitting here and there on bunks, candle-boxes, powder-kegs, etc. They said:

"Sh—! Don't speak—he's going to commence."

THE STORY OF THE OLD RAM.

I found a seat at once, and Blaine said:

"I don't reckon them times will ever come again. There never was a more bullier old ram than what he was. Grandfather fetched him from Illinois—got him of a man by the name of Yates—Bill Yates—maybe you might have heard of him; his father was a deacon—Baptist—and he was a rustler, too; a man had to get up ruther early to get the start of old Thankful Yates; it was him that put the Greens up to jining teams with my grandfather when he moved West. Seth Green was prob'ly the pick of

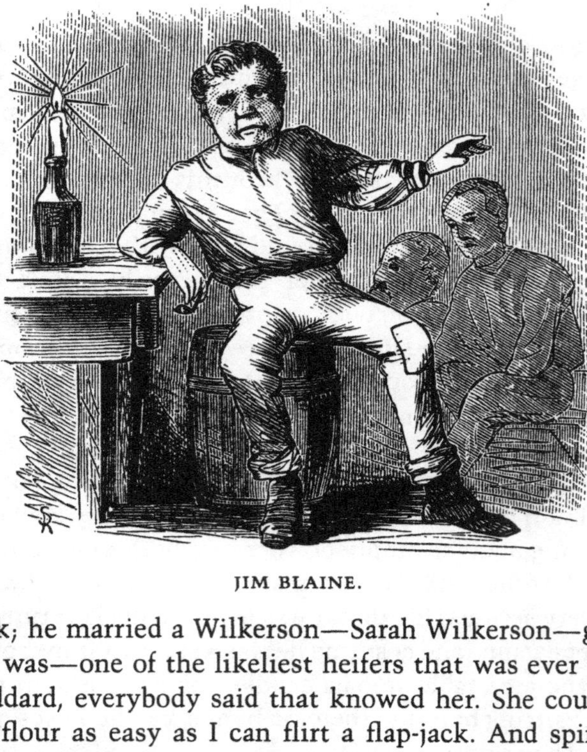

JIM BLAINE.

the flock; he married a Wilkerson—Sarah Wilkerson—good cretur, she was—one of the likeliest heifers that was ever raised in old Stoddard, everybody said that knowed her. She could heft a bar'l of flour as easy as I can flirt a flap-jack. And spin? Don't mention it! Independent? Humph! When Sile Hawkins come a browsing around her, she let him know that for all his tin he couldn't trot in harness alongside of *her.* You see, Sile Hawkins was—no, it warn't Sile Hawkins, after all—it was a galoot by the name of Filkins—I disremember his first name; but he *was* a stump—come into pra'r meeting drunk, one night, hooraying for Nixon, becuz he thought it was a primary; and old deacon Ferguson up and scooted him through the window and he lit on old Miss Jefferson's head, poor old filly. She was a good soul—had a glass eye and used to lend it to old Miss Wagner, that hadn't any, to receive company in; it warn't big enough, and when Miss Wagner warn't noticing, it would get twisted around in the socket, and look up, maybe, or out to one side, and every which way, while t'other one was looking as straight ahead as a spy-glass. Grown people didn't mind it, but it most always made the children cry, it was so sort of scary. She tried packing it in raw cotton, but it wouldn't work, somehow—the cotton would get loose

HURRAH FOR NIXON.

and stick out and look so kind of awful that the children couldn't stand it no way. She was always dropping it out, and turning up her old dead-light on the company empty, and making them oncomfortable, becuz *she* never could tell when it hopped out, being blind on that side, you see. So somebody would have to hunch her and say, 'Your game eye has fetched loose, Miss Wagner dear'—and then all of them would have to sit and wait till she jammed it in again—wrong side before, as a general thing, and green as a bird's egg, being a bashful cretur and easy sot back before company. But being wrong side before warn't much difference, anyway, becuz her own eye was sky-blue and the glass one was yaller on the front side, so whichever way she turned it it didn't match nohow. Old Miss Wagner was considerable on the borrow, she was. When she had a quilting, or Dorcas S'iety at her house she gen'ally borrowed Miss Higgins's wooden leg to stump around on; it was considerable shorter than her other pin, but much *she* minded that. She said she couldn't abide crutches when she had company, becuz they were so slow; said when she had company and things had to be done, she wanted to get up and hump herself. She was as bald as a jug, and so she used to borrow Miss Jacops's wig—Miss Jacops was the coffin-peddler's wife—a ratty old buzzard, he was, that used to go roosting around where people was sick, waiting for 'em; and there that old rip would sit all day, in the shade, on a coffin that he judged would fit the can'idate; and if it was a slow customer and kind of uncertain, he'd fetch his rations and a blanket along and sleep in the coffin nights. He was anchored out that way, in frosty weather, for about three weeks, once, before old Robbins's place, waiting for him; and after that, for as much as two years, Jacops was not on speaking terms with the old man, on account of his disapp'inting him. He got one of his feet froze, and lost money, too, becuz old Robbins took a favorable turn and got well. The next time Robbins got sick, Jacops tried to make up with him, and varnished up the same old coffin and fetched it along; but old Robbins was too many for him; he had him in, and 'peared

MISS WAGNER.

to be powerful weak; he bought the coffin for ten dollars and Jacops was to pay it back and twenty-five more besides if Robbins didn't like the coffin after he'd tried it. And then Robbins died, and at the funeral he bursted off the lid and riz up in his shroud and told the parson to let up on the performances, becuz he could *not* stand such a coffin as that. You see he had been in a trance once before, when he was young, and he took the chances on another, cal'lating that if he made the trip it was money in his pocket, and if he missed fire he couldn't lose a cent. And by George he sued Jacops for the rhino and got jedgment; and he set up the coffin in his back parlor and said he 'lowed to take his time, now. It was always an aggravation to Jacops, the way that miserable old thing acted. He moved back to Indiany pretty soon—went to Wellsville—Wellsville was the place the Hogadorns was from. Mighty fine family. Old Maryland stock. Old Squire Hogadorn could carry around more mixed licker, and cuss better than most any man I ever see. His second wife was the widder Billings—she that was Becky Martin; her dam was deacon Dunlap's first wife. Her oldest child, Maria, married a missionary and died in grace—et up by the savages. They et *him*, too, poor feller—biled him. It warn't the custom, so they say, but

WAITING FOR A CUSTOMER.

they explained to friends of his'n that went down there to bring away his things, that they'd tried missionaries every other way and never could get any good out of 'em—and so it annoyed all his relations to find out that that man's life was fooled away just out of a dern'd experiment, so to speak. But mind you, there ain't anything ever reely lost; everything that people can't understand and don't see the reason of does good if you only hold on and give it a fair shake; Prov'dence don't fire no blank ca'tridges, boys. That there missionary's substance, unbeknowns to himself, actu'ly converted every last one of them heathens that took a chance at the barbacue. Nothing ever fetched them but that. Don't tell *me* it was an accident that he was biled. There ain't no such a thing as an accident. When my uncle Lem was leaning up agin a scaffolding once, sick, or drunk, or suthin, an Irishman with a hod full of bricks fell on him out of the third story and broke the old man's back in two places. People said it was an accident. Much accident there was about that. He didn't know what he was there for, but he was there for a good object. If he hadn't been there the Irishman would have been killed. Nobody can ever make me believe anything different from that. Uncle Lem's dog was there. Why didn't the Irishman fall on the dog? Becuz the dog would a seen him a coming and stood from under. That's the reason the dog warn't appinted. A dog can't be depended on to carry out a special providence. Mark my words it was a put-up thing. Accidents don't happen, boys. Uncle Lem's dog—I wish you could a seen that dog. He was a reglar shepherd—or ruther he was part bull and part shepherd—

WAS TO BE THERE.

splendid animal; belonged to parson Hagar before uncle Lem got him. Parson Hagar belonged to the Western Reserve Hagars; prime family; his mother was a Watson; one of his sisters married a Wheeler; they settled in Morgan County, and he got nipped by the machinery in a carpet factory and went through in less than a quarter of a minute; his widder bought the piece of carpet that had his remains wove in, and people come a hundred mile to 'tend the funeral. There was fourteen yards in the piece. She wouldn't let them roll him up, but planted him just so—full length. The church was middling small where they preached the funeral, and they had to let one end of the coffin stick out of the window. They didn't bury him—they planted one end, and let him stand up, same as a monument. And they nailed a sign on it and put—put on—put on it—sacred to—the m-e-m-o-r-y—of fourteen y-a-r-d-s—of three-ply—car - - - pet—containing all that was—m-o-r-t-a-l—of—of—W-i-l-l-i-a-m—W-h-e—"

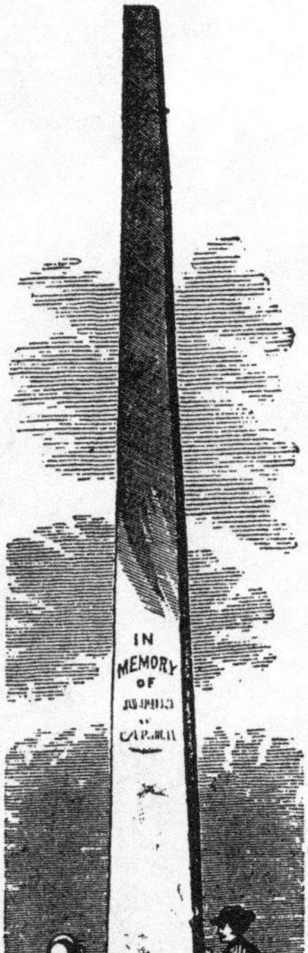

THE MONUMENT.

Jim Blaine had been growing gradually drowsy and drowsier—his head nodded, once, twice, three times—dropped peacefully upon his breast, and he fell tranquilly asleep. The tears were running down the boys' cheeks—they were suffocating with suppressed laughter—and had been from the start, though I had never noticed it. I perceived that I was "sold." I learned then that Jim Blaine's peculiarity was that whenever he reached a certain stage of intoxication, no human power could keep him from setting out, with impressive unction, to tell about a wonderful adventure which he had once had with his grandfather's old ram—and the mention of the ram in the first sentence was as far as any man had ever heard him get, concerning it. He always maundered off, interminably, from one thing to another, till his whisky got the best of him and he fell asleep. What the thing was that happened to him and his grandfather's old ram is a dark mystery to this day, for nobody has ever yet found out.

CHAPTER 54

Of course there was a large Chinese population in Virginia—it is the case with every town and city on the Pacific coast. They are a harmless race when white men either let them alone or treat them no worse than dogs; in fact they are almost entirely harmless anyhow, for they seldom think of resenting the vilest insults or the cruelest injuries. They are quiet, peaceable, tractable, free from drunkenness, and they are as industrious as the day is long. A disorderly Chinaman is rare, and a lazy one does not exist. So long as a Chinaman has strength to use his hands he needs no support from anybody; white men often complain of want of work, but a Chinaman offers no such complaint; he always manages to find something to do. He is a great convenience to everybody—even to the worst class of white men, for he bears the most of their sins, suffering fines for their petty thefts, imprisonment for their robberies, and death for their murders. Any white man can swear a Chinaman's life away in the courts, but no Chinaman can testify against a white man. Ours is the "land of the free"—nobody denies that—nobody challenges it. [Maybe it is because we won't let other people testify.] As I write, news comes that in broad daylight in San Francisco, some boys have stoned an inoffensive Chinaman to death, and that although a large crowd witnessed the shameful deed, no one interfered.

There are seventy thousand (and possibly one hundred thousand) Chinamen on the Pacific coast. There were about a thousand in Virginia. They were penned into a "Chinese quarter"—a thing which they do not particularly object to, as they are fond of herding together. Their buildings were of wood; usually only one story high, and set thickly together along streets scarcely wide enough for a wagon to pass through. Their quarter was a little removed from the rest of the town. The chief employment of Chinamen in towns is to wash clothing. They always send a bill, like this below, pinned to the clothes. It is mere ceremony, for it does not enlighten the customer much. Their price for washing was $2.50 per dozen—rather cheaper than white people could afford to wash for at that time. A very common sign on the Chinese houses was: "See Yup, Washer and Ironer;" "Hong Wo, Washer;" "Sam Sing & Ah Hop, Washing." The house servants, cooks, etc., in California and Nevada, were chiefly Chinamen. There were few white servants and no Chinawomen so employed. Chinamen make good house servants, being quick, obedient, patient, quick to learn and tirelessly industrious. They do not need to be taught a thing twice, as a general thing. They are imitative. If a Chinaman were to see his master break up a centre table, in a passion, and kindle a fire with it, that Chinaman would be likely to resort to the furniture for fuel forever afterward.

All Chinamen can read, write and cipher with easy facility—pity but all our petted *voters* could. In California they rent little patches of ground and do a deal of gardening. They will raise surprising crops of vegetables on a sand pile. They waste nothing. What is rubbish to a Christian, a Chinaman carefully preserves and makes useful in one way or another. He gathers up all the old oyster and sardine cans that white people throw away, and procures marketable tin and solder from them by melting. He gathers up old bones and turns them into manure. In California he gets a living out of old mining claims that white men have abandoned as exhausted and worthless—and then the officers come down on him once a month with an exorbitant swindle to which the legislature has given the broad, general name of "foreign" mining tax, but it is usually inflicted on no foreigners but Chinamen. This swindle has in some cases been repeated once or twice on the same victim in the course of the same month—but the public treasury was not additionally enriched by it, probably.

Chinamen hold their dead in great reverence—they worship their departed ancestors, in fact. Hence, in China, a man's front yard, back yard, or any other part of his premises, is made his family burying ground, in order that he may visit the graves at any and

IMITATION.

all times. Therefore that huge empire is one mighty cemetery; it is ridged and wrinkled from its centre to its circumference with graves—and inasmuch as every foot of ground must be made to do its utmost, in China, lest the swarming population suffer for food, the very graves are cultivated and yield a harvest, custom holding this to be no dishonor to the dead. Since the departed are held in such worshipful reverence, a Chinaman cannot bear that any indignity be offered the places where they sleep. Mr. Burlingame said that herein lay China's bitter opposition to railroads; a road could not be built anywhere in the empire without disturbing the graves of their ancestors or friends.

A Chinaman hardly believes he could enjoy the hereafter except his body lay in his beloved China; also, he desires to receive, himself, after death, that worship with which he has honored his dead that preceded him. Therefore, if he visits a foreign country, he makes arrangements to have his bones returned to China in case he dies; if he hires to go to a foreign country on a labor contract, there is always a stipulation that his body shall be taken back to China if he dies; if the government sells a gang of Coolies to a foreigner for the usual five-year term, it is specified in the contract that their bodies shall be restored to China in case of death. On the Pacific coast the Chinamen all belong to one or another of several great companies or organizations, and these companies keep track of their members, register their names, and ship their bodies home when they die. The See Yup Company is held to be the largest of these. The Ning Yeong Company is next, and numbers eighteen thousand members on the coast. Its headquarters are at San Francisco, where it has a costly temple, several great officers (one of whom keeps regal state in seclusion and cannot be approached by common humanity), and a numerous priesthood. In it I was shown a register of its members, with the dead and the date of their shipment to China duly marked. Every ship that sails from San Francisco carries away a heavy freight of Chinese corpses—or did, at least, until the legislature, with an ingenious refinement of Christian cruelty, forbade the shipments, as a neat underhanded way of deterring Chinese immigration. The bill was offered, whether it passed or not. It is my impression that it passed. There was another bill—it became a law—compelling every incoming Chinaman to be vaccinated on the wharf and pay a duly appointed quack (no decent doctor would defile himself with such legalized robbery) ten dollars for it. As few importers of Chinese would want to go to an expense like that, the law-makers thought this would be another heavy blow to Chinese immigration.

What the Chinese quarter of Virginia was like—or, indeed, what the Chinese quarter of any Pacific coast town was and is like—may be gathered from this item which I printed in the *Enterprise* while reporting for that paper:

CHINATOWN.—Accompanied by a fellow reporter, we made a trip through our Chinese quarter the other night. The Chinese have built their portion of the city to suit themselves; and as they keep neither carriages nor wagons, their streets are not wide enough, as a general thing, to admit of the passage of vehicles. At ten o'clock at night the Chinaman may be seen in all his glory. In every little cooped-up, dingy cavern of a hut, faint with the odor of burning Josh-lights and with nothing to see the gloom by save the sickly, guttering tallow candle, were two or three yellow, long-tailed vagabonds, coiled up on a sort of short truckle-bed, smoking opium, motionless and with their lustreless eyes turned inward from excess of satisfaction—or rather the recent smoker looks thus, immediately after having passed the pipe to his neighbor—for opium-smoking is a comfortless operation, and requires constant attention. A lamp sits on the bed, the length of the long pipe-stem from the smoker's mouth; he puts a pellet of opium on the end of a wire, sets it on fire, and plasters it into the pipe much as a Christian would fill a hole with putty; then he applies the bowl to the lamp and proceeds to smoke—and the stewing and frying of the drug and the gurgling of the juices in the stem would wellnigh turn the stomach of a statue. John likes it, though; it soothes him, he takes about two dozen whiffs, and then rolls over to dream, Heaven only knows what, for we could not imagine by looking at the soggy creature. Possibly in his visions he travels far away from the gross world and his regular washing, and feasts on succulent rats and birds'-nests in Paradise.

Mr. Ah Sing keeps a general grocery and provision store at No. 13 Wang street. He lavished his hospitality upon our party in the friendliest way. He had various kinds of colored and colorless wines and brandies, with unpronounceable names, imported from China in little crockery jugs, and which he offered to us in dainty little miniature wash-basins of porcelain. He offered us a mess of birds'-nests; also, small, neat sausages, of which we could have swallowed several yards if we had chosen to try, but we suspected that each link contained the corpse of a mouse, and therefore refrained. Mr. Sing had in his store a thousand articles of merchandise, curious to behold, impossible to imagine the uses of, and beyond our ability to describe.

His ducks, however, and his eggs, we could understand; the former were split open and flattened out like codfish, and came from China in that shape, and the latter were plastered over with some kind of paste which kept them fresh and palatable through the long voyage.

We found Mr. Hong Wo, No. 37 Chow-chow street, making up a lottery scheme—in fact we found a dozen others occupied in the same way in various parts of the quarter, for about every third Chinaman runs a lottery, and the balance of the tribe "buck" at it. "Tom," who speaks faultless English, and used to be chief and only cook to the *Territorial Enterprise,* when the establishment kept bachelor's hall two years ago, said that "Sometime Chinaman buy ticket one dollar hap, ketch um two tree hundred, sometime no ketch um anyting; lottery like one man fight um seventy—may-be he whip, may-be he get whip heself, welly good." However, the percentage being sixty-nine against him, the chances are, as a general thing, that "he get whip heself." We could not see that these lotteries differed in any respect from our own, save that the figures being Chinese, no ignorant white man might ever hope to succeed in telling "t'other from which;" the manner of drawing is similar to ours.

Mr. See Yup keeps a fancy store on Live Fox street. He sold us fans of white feathers, gorgeously ornamented; perfumery that smelled like Limburger cheese, Chinese pens, and watch-charms made of a stone unscratchable with steel instruments, yet polished and tinted like the inner

CHINESE LOTTERY.

coat of a sea-shell.* As tokens of his esteem, See Yup presented the party with gaudy plumes made of gold tinsel and trimmed with peacocks' feathers.

We ate chow-chow with chop-sticks in the celestial restaurants; our comrade chided the moon-eyed damsels in front of the houses for their want of feminine reserve; we received protecting Josh-lights from our hosts and "dickered" for a pagan God or two. Finally, we were impressed with the genius of a Chinese book-keeper; he figured up his accounts on a machine like a gridiron with buttons strung on its bars; the different rows represented units, tens, hundreds and thousands. He fingered them with incredible rapidity—in fact, he pushed them from place to place as fast as a musical professor's fingers travel over the keys of a piano.

They are a kindly disposed, well-meaning race, and are respected and well treated by the upper classes, all over the Pacific coast. No

*A peculiar species of the "jade-stone"—to a Chinaman peculiarly precious.

Californian *gentleman or lady* ever abuses or oppresses a Chinaman, under any circumstances, an explanation that seems to be much needed in the east. Only the scum of the population do it—they and their children; they, and, naturally and consistently, the policemen and politicians, likewise, for these are the dust-licking pimps and slaves of the scum, there as well as elsewhere in America.

CHAPTER 55

I BEGAN to get tired of staying in one place so long. There was no longer satisfying variety in going down to Carson to report the proceedings of the legislature once a year, and horse-races and pumpkin-shows once in three months; (they had got to raising pumpkins and potatoes in Washoe Valley, and of course one of the first achievements of the legislature was to institute a ten-thousand-dollar Agricultural Fair to show off forty dollars' worth of those pumpkins in—however, the Territorial legislature was usually spoken of as the "asylum"). I wanted to see San Francisco. I wanted to go somewhere. I wanted—I did not know *what* I wanted. I had the "spring fever" and wanted a change, principally, no doubt. Besides, a convention had framed a State Constitution; nine men out of every ten wanted an office; I believed that these gentlemen would "treat" the moneyless and the irresponsible among the population into adopting the Constitution and thus well-nigh killing the country (it could not well carry such a load as a State government, since it had nothing to tax that could stand a tax, for undeveloped mines could not, and there were not fifty developed ones in the land, there was but little realty to tax, and it did seem as if nobody was ever going to think of the simple salvation of inflicting a money penalty on murder). I believed that a State government would destroy the "flush times," and I wanted to get away. I believed that the mining stocks I had on hand would soon be worth a hundred thousand dollars, and thought if they reached that before the Constitution was adopted, I would sell out and make myself secure from the crash the change of government was going to bring. I considered a hundred thousand dollars sufficient to go home with decently, though it was but a small amount compared to what I had been expecting to return with. I felt rather down-hearted about it, but I tried to comfort myself with the reflection that with such a sum I could not fall into want. About this time a schoolmate of mine whom I had not seen since boyhood, came tramping in on foot from Reese river, a very allegory of Poverty. The son of wealthy parents, here he was, in a strange land, hungry, bootless, mantled in an ancient horse-blanket, roofed with a brimless hat, and so generally and so extravagantly dilapidated that he could have "taken the shine out of the Prodigal Son himself," as he pleasantly remarked. He wanted to borrow forty-six dollars—twenty-six to take him to San Francisco, and twenty for something else; to buy some soap with, maybe, for he needed it. I found I had but little more than the amount wanted, in my pocket; so I stepped in and borrowed forty-six dollars of a banker (on twenty days' time, without the formality of a note), and gave it him, rather than walk half a block to the office, where I had some specie laid up. If anybody had told me that it would take me two years to pay back that forty-six dollars to the banker (for I did not expect it of the Prodigal, and was not disappointed), I would have felt injured. And so would the banker.

AN OLD FRIEND.

I wanted a change. I wanted variety of some kind. It came. Mr. Goodman went away for a week and left me the post of chief editor. It destroyed me. The first day, I wrote my "leader" in the forenoon. The second day, I had no subject and put it off till the afternoon. The third day I put it off till evening, and then copied an elaborate editorial out of the "American Cyclopedia," that steadfast friend of the editor, all over this land. The fourth day I "fooled around" till midnight, and then fell back on the Cyclopedia again. The fifth day I cudgeled my brain till midnight, and then kept the press waiting while I penned some bitter personalities on six different people. The sixth day I labored in anguish till far into the night and brought forth—nothing. The paper went to press without an editorial. The seventh day I resigned. On the eighth, Mr. Goodman returned and found six duels on his hands—my personalities had borne fruit.

Nobody, except he has tried it, knows what it is to be an editor. It is easy to scribble local rubbish, with the facts all before you; it is easy to clip selections from other papers; it is easy to string out a correspondence from any locality; but it is unspeakable hardship to write editorials. *Subjects* are the trouble—the dreary lack of them, I mean. Every day, it is drag, drag, drag—think, and worry and suffer—all the world is a dull blank, and yet the editorial columns *must* be filled. Only give the editor a *subject,* and his work is done—it is no trouble to write it up; but fancy how you would feel if you had to pump your brains dry every day in the week, fifty-two weeks in the year. It makes one low spirited simply to think of it. The matter that each editor of a daily paper in America writes in the course of a year would fill from four to eight bulky volumes like this book! Fancy what a library an editor's work would make, after twenty or thirty years' service. Yet people often marvel that Dickens, Scott, Bulwer, Dumas, etc., have been able to produce so many books. If these authors had wrought as voluminously as newspaper editors do, the result would be something to marvel at, indeed. How editors can continue this tremendous labor, this exhausting consumption of brain fibre (for their work is creative, and not a mere mechanical laying-up of facts, like reporting), day after day and year after year, is incomprehensible. Preachers take two months' holiday in midsummer, for they find that to produce two sermons a week is wearing, in the long run. In truth it must be so, and is so; and therefore, how an editor can take from ten to twenty texts and build upon them from ten to twenty painstaking editorials a week and keep it up all the year round, is farther beyond comprehension than ever. Ever since I survived my week as editor, I have found at least one pleasure in any newspaper that comes to my hand; it is in admiring the long columns of editorial, and wondering to myself how in the mischief he did it!

Mr. Goodman's return relieved me of employment, unless I chose to become a reporter again. I could not do that; I could not serve in the ranks after being General of the army. So I thought I would depart and go abroad into the world somewhere. Just at this juncture, Dan, my associate in the reportorial department, told me, casually, that two citizens had been trying to persuade him to go with them to New York and aid in selling a rich silver mine which they had discovered and secured in a new mining district in our neighborhood. He said they offered to pay his expenses and give him one-third of the proceeds of the sale. He had refused to go. It was the very opportunity I wanted. I abused him for keeping so quiet about it, and not mentioning it sooner. He said it had not occurred to him that I would like to go, and so he had recommended them to apply to Marshall, the reporter of the other paper. I asked Dan if it was a good, honest mine, and no swindle. He said the men had shown him nine tons of the rock, which they had got out to take to New York, and he could cheerfully say that he had seen but little rock in Nevada that was richer; and moreover, he said that they had secured a tract of valuable timber and a mill-site, near the mine. My first idea was to kill Dan. But I changed my mind, notwithstanding I was so angry, for I thought maybe the chance was not yet lost. Dan said it was by no means lost; that the men were absent at the mine again, and would not be in Virginia to leave for the east for some ten days; that they had requested him to do the talking to Marshall, and he had promised that he would either secure Marshall or somebody else for them by the time they got back; he would now say nothing to anybody till they returned, and then fulfil his promise by furnishing me to them.

It was splendid. I went to bed all on fire with excitement; for nobody had yet gone east to sell a Nevada silver mine, and the field was white for the sickle. I felt that such a mine as the one described by Dan would bring a princely sum in New York, and sell without delay or difficulty. I could not sleep, my fancy so rioted through its castles in the air. It was the "blind lead" come again.

Next day I got away, on the coach, with the usual eclat attending departures of old citizens,—for if you have only half a dozen friends out there they will make noise for a hundred rather than let you seem to go away neglected and unregretted—and Dan promised to keep strict watch for the men that had the mine to sell.

The trip was signalized but by one little incident, and that occurred just as we were about to start. A very seedy looking vagabond passenger got out of the stage a moment to wait till the usual ballast of silver bricks was thrown in. He was standing on the pavement, when an awkward express employé, carrying a brick weighing a hundred pounds, stumbled and let it fall on the bummer's foot. He instantly dropped on the ground and began to howl in the most heart-breaking way. A sympathizing crowd gathered around and were going to pull his boot off; but he screamed louder than ever and they desisted; then he fell to gasping, and between the gasps ejaculated "Brandy! for Heaven's sake, brandy!" They poured half a pint down him, and it wonderfully restored and comforted him. Then he begged the people to assist him to the stage, which was done. The express people urged him to have a doctor at their expense, but he declined, and said that if he only had a little brandy to take along with him, to soothe his paroxysms of pain when they came on, he would be grateful and content. He was quickly supplied with two bottles, and we drove off. He was so smiling and happy after that, that I could not refrain from asking him how he could possibly be so comfortable with a crushed foot.

"Well," said he, "I hadn't had a drink for twelve hours, and hadn't a cent to my name. I was most perishing—and so, when that duffer dropped that hundred-pounder on my foot, I see my chance. Got a cork leg, you know!" and he pulled up his pantaloons and proved it.

He was as drunk as a lord all day long, and full of chucklings over his timely ingenuity.

One drunken man necessarily reminds one of another. I once heard a gentleman tell about an incident which he witnessed in a Californian bar-room. He entitled it "Ye Modest Man Taketh a Drink." It was nothing but a bit of acting, but it seemed to me a perfect rendering, and worthy of Toodles himself. The modest man, tolerably far gone with beer and other matters, enters a saloon (twenty-five cents is the price for anything and everything, and specie the only money used) and lays down a half dollar; calls for whisky and drinks it; the barkeeper makes change and lays the

FAREWELL AND ACCIDENT.

quarter in a wet place on the counter; the modest man fumbles at it with nerveless fingers, but it slips and the water holds it; he contemplates it, and tries again; same result; observes that people are interested in what he is at, blushes; fumbles at the quarter again—blushes—puts his forefinger carefully, slowly down, to make sure of his aim—pushes the coin toward the barkeeper, and says with a sigh:

"('ic!) Gimme a cigar!"

Naturally, another gentleman present told about another drunken man. He said he reeled toward home late at night; made a mistake and entered the wrong gate; thought he saw a dog on the stoop; and it was—an iron one. He stopped and considered; wondered if it was a dangerous dog; ventured to say "Be (hic) begone!" No effect. Then he approached warily, and adopted conciliation; pursed up his lips and tried to whistle, but failed; still approached, saying, "Poor dog!—doggy, doggy, doggy!—poor doggy-dog!" Got up on the stoop, still petting with fond names; till master of the advantages; then exclaimed, "Leave, you thief!"—planted a vindictive kick in his ribs, and went head-over-heels overboard, of course. A pause; a sigh or two of pain, and then a remark in a reflective voice:

"GIMME A CIGAR!"

"Awful solid dog. What could he ben eating? ('ic!) Rocks, p'raps. Such animals is dangerous. 'At's what *I* say—they're dangerous. If a man—('ic!)—if a man wants to feed a dog on rocks, let him *feed* him on rocks; 'at's all right; but let him keep him at *home*—not have him layin' round promiscuous, where ('ic!) where people's liable to stumble over him when they ain't noticin'!"

It was not without regret that I took a last look at the tiny flag (it was thirty-five feet long and ten feet wide) fluttering like a lady's handkerchief from the topmost peak of Mount Davidson, two thousand feet above Virginia's roofs, and felt that doubtless I was bidding a permanent farewell to a city which had afforded me the most vigorous enjoyment of life I had ever experienced. And this reminds me of an incident which the dullest memory Virginia could boast at the time it happened must vividly recall, at times, till its possessor dies. Late one summer afternoon we had a rain shower. That was astonishing enough, in itself, to set the whole town buzzing, for it only rains (during a week or two weeks) in the winter in Nevada, and even then not enough at a time to make it worth while for any merchant to keep umbrellas for sale. But the rain was not the chief wonder. It only lasted five or ten minutes; while the people were still talking about it all the heavens gathered to themselves a dense blackness as of midnight. All the vast eastern front of Mount Davidson, overlooking the city, put on such a funereal gloom that only the nearness and solidity of the mountain made its outlines even faintly distinguishable from the dead blackness of the heavens they rested against. This unaccustomed sight turned all eyes toward the mountain; and as they looked, a little tongue of rich golden flame was seen waving and quivering in the heart of the midnight, away up on the extreme summit! In a few minutes the streets were packed with people, gazing with hardly an uttered word, at the one brilliant mote in the brooding world of darkness. It flicked like a candle-flame, and looked no larger; but with such a background it was wonderfully bright, small as it was. It was the flag!—though no one suspected it at first, it seemed so like a supernatural visitor of some kind—a mysterious messenger of good tidings, some were fain to believe. It was the nation's emblem transfigured by the departing rays of a sun that was entirely palled from view; and on no other object did the glory fall, in all the broad panorama of mountain ranges and deserts. Not even upon the staff of the flag—for that, a needle in the distance at any time, was now untouched by the light and undistinguishable in the gloom. For a whole hour the weird visitor winked and burned in its lofty solitude, and still the thousands of uplifted eyes watched it with fascinated interest. How the people were wrought up! The superstition grew apace that this was a mystic courier come with great news from the war—the poetry of the idea excusing and commending it—and on it spread, from heart to heart, from lip to lip and from street to street, till there was a general impulse to have out the military and welcome the bright waif with a salvo of artillery!

And all that time one sorely tried man, the telegraph operator sworn to official secrecy, had to lock his lips and chain his tongue with a silence that was like to rend them; for he, and he only, of all the speculating multitude, knew the great things this sinking sun had seen that day in the east—Vicksburg fallen, and the Union arms victorious at Gettysburg!

THE HERALD OF GLAD NEWS.

But for the journalistic monopoly that forbade the slightest revealment of eastern news till a day after its publication in the California papers, the glorified flag on Mount Davidson would have been saluted and re-saluted, that memorable evening, as long as there was a charge of powder to thunder with; the city would have been illuminated, and every man that had any respect for himself would have got drunk,—as was the custom of the country on all occasions of public moment. Even at this distant day I cannot think of this needlessly marred supreme opportunity without regret. What a time we might have had!

CHAPTER 56

We rumbled over the plains and valleys, climbed the Sierras to the clouds, and looked down upon summer-clad California. And I will remark here, in passing, that all scenery in California requires *distance* to give it its highest charm. The mountains are imposing in their sublimity and their majesty of form and altitude, from any point of view—but one must have distance to soften their ruggedness and enrich their tintings; a Californian forest is best at a little distance, for there is a sad poverty of variety in species, the trees being chiefly of one monotonous family—redwood, pine, spruce, fir—and so, at a near view there is a wearisome sameness of attitude in their rigid arms, stretched downward and outward in one continued and reiterated appeal to all men to "Sh!—don't say a word!—you might disturb somebody!" Close at hand, too, there is a reliefless and relentless smell of pitch and turpentine; there is a ceaseless melancholy in their sighing and complaining foliage; one walks over a soundless carpet of beaten yellow bark and dead spines of the foliage till he feels like a wandering spirit bereft of a footfall; he tires of the endless tufts of needles and yearns for substantial, shapely leaves; he looks for moss and grass to loll upon, and finds none, for where there is no bark there is naked clay and dirt, enemies to pensive musing and clean apparel. Often a grassy plain in California, is what it should be, but often, too, it is best contemplated at a distance, because although its grass blades are tall, they stand up vindictively straight and self-sufficient, and are unsociably wide apart, with uncomely spots of barren sand between.

One of the queerest things I know of, is to hear tourists from "the States" go into ecstasies over the loveliness of "ever-blooming California." And they always do go into that sort of ecstasies. But perhaps they would modify them if they knew how old Californians, with the memory full upon them of the dust-covered and questionable summer greens of Californian "verdure," stand astonished, and filled with worshipping admiration, in the presence of the lavish richness, the brilliant green, the infinite freshness, the spendthrift variety of form and species and foliage that make an eastern landscape a vision of Paradise itself. The idea of a man

AN EASTERN LANDSCAPE.

falling into raptures over grave and sombre California, when that man has seen New England's meadow-expanses and her maples, oaks and cathedral-windowed elms decked in summer attire, or the opaline splendors of autumn descending upon her forests, comes very near being funny—would be, in fact, but that it is so pathetic. No land with an unvarying climate can be very beautiful. The tropics are not, for all the sentiment that is wasted on them. They seem beautiful at first, but sameness impairs the charm by and by. *Change* is the handmaiden Nature requires to do her miracles with. The land that has four well-defined seasons, cannot lack beauty, or pall with monotony. Each season brings a world of enjoyment and interest in the watching of its unfolding, its gradual, harmonious development, its culminating graces—and just as one

A VARIABLE CLIMATE.

begins to tire of it, it passes away and a radical change comes, with new witcheries and new glories in its train. And I think that to one in sympathy with nature, each season, in its turn, seems the loveliest.

San Francisco, a truly fascinating city to live in, is stately and handsome at a fair distance, but close at hand one notes that the architecture is mostly old-fashioned, many streets are made up of decaying, smoke-grimed, wooden houses, and the barren sand hills toward the outskirts obtrude themselves too prominently. Even the kindly climate is sometimes pleasanter when read about than personally experienced, for a lovely, cloudless sky wears out its welcome by and by, and then when the longed for rain does come it *stays.* Even the playful earthquake is better contemplated at a dis—

However there are varying opinions about that.

The climate of San Francisco is mild and singularly equable. The thermometer stands at about seventy degrees the year round. It hardly changes at all. You sleep under one or two light blankets summer and winter, and never use a mosquito bar. Nobody ever wears summer clothing. You wear black broadcloth—if you have it—in August and January, just the same. It is no colder, and no warmer, in the one month than the other. You do not use overcoats and you do not use fans. It is as pleasant a climate as could well be contrived, take it all around, and is doubtless the most unvarying in the whole world. The wind blows there a good deal in the summer months, but then you can go over to Oakland, if you choose—three or four miles away—it does not blow there. It has only snowed twice in San Francisco in nineteen years, and then it only remained on the ground long enough to astonish the children, and set them to wondering what the feathery stuff was.

During eight months of the year, straight along, the skies are bright and cloudless, and never a drop of rain falls. But when the other four months come along, you will need to go and steal an umbrella. Because you will require it. Not just one day, but one hundred and twenty days in hardly varying succession. When you want to go visiting, or attend church, or the theatre, you never look up at the clouds to see whether it is likely to rain or not—you look at the almanac. If it is winter, it will *rain*—and if it is summer, it *won't* rain, and you cannot help it. You never need a lightning-rod, because it never thunders and it never lightens. And after you have listened for six or eight weeks, every night, to the dismal monotony of those quiet rains, you will wish in your heart the thunder *would* leap and crash and roar along those drowsy skies once, and make everything alive—you will wish the prisoned lightnings *would* cleave the dull firmament asunder and light it with a blinding glare for *one* little instant. You would give *anything* to hear the old familiar thunder again and see the lightning strike somebody. And along in the summer, when you have suffered about four months of lustrous, pitiless sunshine, you are ready to go down on your knees and plead for rain—hail—snow—thunder and lightning—anything to break the monotony—you will take an earthquake, if you cannot do any better. And the chances are that you'll get it, too.

San Francisco is built on sand hills, but they are prolific sand hills. They yield a generous vegetation. All the rare flowers which people in "the States" rear with such patient care in parlor flower pots and greenhouses, flourish luxuriantly in the open air there all the year round. Calla lilies, all sorts of geraniums, passion flowers, moss roses—I do not know the names of a tenth part of them. I only know that while New Yorkers are burdened with banks and drifts of snow, Californians are burdened with banks and drifts of flowers, if they only keep their hands off and let them grow. And I have heard that they have also that rarest and most curious of all the flowers, the beautiful *Espiritu Santo,* as the Spaniards call it—or flower of the Holy Spirit—though I thought it grew only in Central America—down on the Isthmus. In its cup is the daintiest little fac-simile of a dove, as pure as snow. The Spaniards have a superstitious reverence for it. The blossom has been conveyed to the States, submerged in ether; and the bulb has been taken thither also, but every attempt to make it bloom after it arrived, has failed.

I have elsewhere spoken of the endless winter of Mono, California, and but this moment of the eternal spring of San Francisco. Now if we travel a hundred miles in a straight line, we come to the eternal summer of Sacramento. One never sees summer clothing or mosquitoes in San Francisco—but they can be found in Sacramento. Not always and unvaryingly, but about one hundred and forty-three months out of twelve years, perhaps. Flowers bloom there, always, the reader can easily believe—people suffer and sweat, and swear, morning, noon and night, and wear out their stanchest energies fanning themselves. It gets hot there, but if you go down to Fort Yuma you will find it hotter. Fort Yuma is probably the hottest place on earth. The thermometer stays at one hundred and twenty in the shade there all the time—except when it varies and goes higher. It is a U. S. military post, and its occupants get so used to the terrific heat that they suffer without it. There is a tradition (attributed to John Phoenix*) that a very, very wicked soldier died there, once, and of course, went straight to the hottest corner of perdition,—and the next day he *telegraphed back for his blankets.* There is no doubt about the truth of this statement—there can be no doubt about it. I have seen the place where that soldier used to board. In Sacramento it is fiery summer always, and you can gather roses, and eat strawberries and ice-cream, and wear white linen clothes, and pant and perspire at eight or nine o'clock

*It has been purloined by fifty different scribblers who were too poor to invent a fancy but not ashamed to steal one.—M. T.

in the morning, and then take the cars, and at noon put on your furs and your skates, and go skimming over frozen Donner Lake,

SACRAMENTO. THREE HOURS AWAY.

seven thousand feet above the valley, among snow banks fifteen feet deep, and in the shadow of grand mountain peaks that lift their frosty crags ten thousand feet above the level of the sea. There is a transition for you! Where will you find another like it in the Western hemisphere? And some of us have swept around snow-walled curves of the Pacific Railroad in that vicinity, six thousand feet above the sea, and looked down as the birds do, upon the deathless summer of the Sacramento Valley, with its fruitful fields, its feathery foliage, its silver streams, all slumbering in the mellow haze of its enchanted atmosphere, and all infinitely softened and spiritualized by distance—a dreamy, exquisite glimpse of fairy-land, made all the more charming and striking that it was caught through a forbidding gateway of ice and snow and savage crags and precipices.

CHAPTER 57

It was in this Sacramento Valley, just referred to, that a deal of the most lucrative of the early gold mining was done, and you may still see, in places, its grassy slopes and levels torn and guttered and disfigured by the avaricious spoilers of fifteen and twenty years ago. You may see such disfigurements far and wide over California—and in some such places, where only meadows and forests are visible—not a living creature, not a house, no stick or stone or remnant of a ruin, and not a sound, not even a whisper to disturb the Sabbath stillness—you will find it hard to believe that there stood at one time a fiercely-flourishing little city, of two thousand or three thousand souls, with its newspaper, fire company, brass band, volunteer militia, bank, hotels, noisy Fourth of July processions and speeches, gambling hells crammed with tobacco smoke, profanity, and rough-bearded men of all nations and colors, with tables heaped with gold dust sufficient for the revenues of a German principality—streets crowded and rife with business—town lots worth four hundred dollars a front foot—labor, laughter, music, dancing, swearing, fighting, shooting, stabbing—a bloody inquest and a man for breakfast every morning—*everything* that delights and adorns existence—all the appointments and appurtenances of a thriving and prosperous and promising young city,—and *now* nothing is left of it all but a lifeless, homeless solitude. The men are gone, the houses have vanished, even the *name* of the place is forgotten. In no other land, in modern times, have towns so absolutely died and disappeared, as in the old mining regions of California.

It was a driving, vigorous, restless population in those days. It was a *curious* population. It was the *only* population of the kind that the world has ever seen gathered together, and it is not likely that the world will ever see its like again. For, observe, it was an assemblage of two hundred thousand *young* men—not simpering, dainty, kid-gloved weaklings, but stalwart, muscular, dauntless young braves, brim full of push and energy, and royally endowed with every attribute that goes to make up a peerless and magnificent manhood—the very pick and choice of the world's glorious ones. No women, no children, no gray and stooping veterans,—none but erect, bright-eyed, quick-moving, strong-handed young giants—the strangest population, the finest population, the most gallant host that ever trooped down the startled solitudes of an unpeopled land. And where are they now? Scattered to the ends of the earth—or prematurely aged and decrepit—or shot or stabbed in street affrays—or dead of disappointed hopes and broken hearts—all gone, or nearly all—victims devoted upon the altar of the golden calf—the noblest holocaust that ever wafted its sacrificial incense heavenward. It is pitiful to think upon.

It was a splendid population—for all the slow, sleepy, sluggish-brained sloths staid at home—you never find that sort of people among pioneers—you cannot build pioneers out of that sort of material. It was that population that gave to California a name for getting up astounding enterprises and rushing them through with a magnificent dash and daring, and a recklessness of cost or consequences, which she bears unto this day—and when she projects a new surprise, the grave world smiles as usual, and says "well, that is California all over."

But they were rough in those times! They fairly reveled in gold, whisky, fights and fandangoes, and were unspeakably happy. The honest miner raked from a hundred to a thousand dollars out of his claim a day, and what with the gambling dens and the other entertainments, he hadn't a cent the next morning, if he had any sort of luck. They cooked their own bacon and beans, sewed on their own buttons, washed their own shirts—blue woolen ones—and if a man wanted a fight on his hands without any annoying delay, all he had to do was to appear in public in a white shirt or a stove-pipe hat, and he would be accommodated. For those people hated aristocrats. They had a particular and malignant animosity toward what they called a "biled shirt."

It was a wild, free, disorderly, grotesque society! *Men*—only swarming hosts of stalwart *men*—nothing juvenile, nothing feminine, visible anywhere!

In those days miners would flock in crowds to catch a glimpse of that rare and blessed spectacle, a woman! Old inhabitants tell how, in a certain camp, the news went abroad early in the morning that a woman was come! They had seen a calico dress hanging out of a wagon down at the camping ground—sign of emigrants from over the great plains. Everybody went down there, and a shout went up when an actual, bona-fide dress was discovered fluttering in the wind! The male emigrant was visible. The miners said:

"Fetch her out!"

He said: "It is my wife, gentlemen—she is sick—we have been robbed of money, provisions, everything, by the Indians—we want to rest."

"Fetch her out! We've got to see her!"

"But, gentlemen, the poor thing, she—"

"FETCH HER OUT!"

He "fetched her out," and they swung their hats and sent up three rousing cheers and a tiger; and they crowded around and

"FETCH HER OUT!"

gazed at her, and touched her dress, and listened to her voice with the look of men who listened to a *memory* rather than a present reality—and then they collected twenty-five hundred dollars in gold and gave it to the man, and swung their hats again and gave three more cheers, and went home satisfied.

Once I dined in San Francisco with the family of a pioneer, and talked with his daughter, a young lady whose first experience in San Francisco was an adventure, though she herself did not remember it, as she was only two or three years old at the time. Her father said that, after landing from the ship, they were walking up the street, a servant leading the party with the little girl in her arms. And presently a huge miner, bearded, belted, spurred, and bristling with deadly weapons—just down from a long campaign in the mountains, evidently—barred the way, stopped the servant, and stood gazing, with a face all alive with gratification and astonishment. Then he said, reverently:

"Well, if it ain't a child!" And then he snatched a little leather sack out of his pocket and said to the servant:

"WELL, IF IT AIN'T A CHILD!"

"There's a hundred and fifty dollars in dust, there, and I'll give it to you to let me kiss the child!"

That anecdote is *true.*

But see how things change. Sitting at that dinner table, listening to that anecdote, if I had offered double the money for the privilege of kissing the same child, I would have been refused. Seventeen added years have far more than doubled the price.

And while upon this subject I will remark that once in Star City, in the Humboldt Mountains, I took my place in a sort of long, post-office single file of miners, to patiently await my chance to peep through a crack in the cabin and get a sight of the splendid new sensation—a genuine, live Woman! And at the end of half an hour

A GENUINE LIVE WOMAN.

my turn came, and I put my eye to the crack, and there she was, with one arm akimbo, and tossing flap-jacks in a frying pan with the other. And she was one hundred and sixty-five* years old, and hadn't a tooth in her head.

*Being in calmer mood, now, I voluntarily knock off a hundred from that.—M. T.

CHAPTER 58

FOR a few months I enjoyed what to me was an entirely new phase of existence—a butterfly idleness; nothing to do, nobody to be responsible to, and untroubled with financial uneasiness. I fell in love with the most cordial and sociable city in the Union. After the sage-brush and alkali deserts of Washoe, San Francisco was Paradise to me. I lived at the best hotel, exhibited my clothes in the most conspicuous places, infested the opera, and learned to seem enraptured with music which oftener afflicted my ignorant ear than enchanted it, if I had had the vulgar honesty to confess it. However, I suppose I was not greatly worse than the most of my countrymen in that. I had longed to be a butterfly, and I was one at last. I attended private parties in sumptuous evening dress, simpered and aired my graces like a born beau, and polked and schottisched with a step peculiar to myself—and the kangaroo. In a word, I kept the due state of a man worth a hundred thousand dollars (prospectively,) and likely to reach absolute affluence when that silver-mine sale should be ultimately achieved in the east. I spent money with a free hand, and meantime watched the stock sales with an interested eye and looked to see what might happen in Nevada.

Something very important happened. The property holders of Nevada voted against the State Constitution; but the folks who had nothing to lose were in the majority, and carried the measure over their heads. But after all it did not immediately look like a disaster, though unquestionably it was one. I hesitated, calculated the chances, and then concluded not to sell. Stocks went on rising; speculation went mad; bankers, merchants, lawyers, doctors, mechanics, laborers, even the very washerwomen and servant girls, were putting up their earnings on silver stocks, and every sun that rose in the morning went down on paupers enriched and rich men beggared. What a gambling carnival it was! Gould & Curry soared to six thousand three hundred dollars a foot! And then—all of a sudden, out went the bottom and everything and everybody went

THE GRACE OF A KANGAROO.

to ruin and destruction! The wreck was complete. The bubble scarcely left a microscopic moisture behind it. I was an early beggar and a thorough one. My hoarded stocks were not worth the paper they were printed on. I threw them all away. I, the cheerful idiot that had been squandering money like water, and thought myself beyond the reach of misfortune, had not now as much as fifty dollars when I gathered together my various debts and paid them. I removed from the hotel to a very private boarding house. I took a reporter's berth and went to work. I was not entirely broken in spirit, for I was building confidently on the sale of the silver mine in the east. But I could not hear from Dan. My letters miscarried or were not answered.

One day I did not feel vigorous and remained away from the office. The next day I went down toward noon as usual, and found a note on my desk which had been there twenty-four hours. It was signed "Marshall"—the Virginia reporter—and contained a request that I should call at the hotel and see him and a friend or two that night, as they would sail for the east in the morning. A postscript added that their errand was a big mining speculation! I was hardly ever so sick in my life. I abused myself for leaving Virginia and entrusting to another man a matter I ought to have attended to myself; I abused myself for remaining away from the office on the one day of all the year that I should have been there. And thus berating myself I trotted a mile to the steamer wharf and arrived just in time to be too late. The ship was in the stream and under way.

DREAMS DISSIPATED.

I comforted myself with the thought that maybe the speculation would amount to nothing—poor comfort at best—and then went back to my slavery, resolved to put up with my thirty-five dollars a week and forget all about it.

A month afterward I enjoyed my first earthquake. It was one which was long called the "great" earthquake, and is doubtless so distinguished till this day. It was just after noon, on a bright October day. I was coming down Third street. The only objects in motion anywhere in sight in that thickly built and populous quarter, were a man in a buggy behind me, and a street car wending slowly up the cross street. Otherwise, all was solitude and a Sabbath stillness. As I turned the corner, around a frame house, there was a great rattle and jar, and it occurred to me that here was an item!—no doubt a fight in that house. Before I could turn and seek the door, there came a really terrific shock; the ground seemed to roll under me in waves, interrupted by a violent joggling up and down, and there was a heavy grinding noise as of brick houses rubbing together. I fell up against the frame house and hurt my elbow. I knew what it was, now, and from mere reportorial instinct, nothing else, took out my watch and noted the time of day; at that moment a third and still severer shock came, and as I reeled about on the pavement trying to keep my footing, I saw a sight! The entire front of a tall four-story brick building in Third street sprung outward like a door and fell sprawling across the street, raising a dust like a great volume of smoke! And here came the buggy—overboard

THE "ONE-HORSE SHAY" OUTDONE.

went the man, and in less time than I can tell it the vehicle was distributed in small fragments along three hundred yards of street. One could have fancied that somebody had fired a charge of chair-rounds and rags down the thoroughfare. The street car had stopped, the horses were rearing and plunging, the passengers were pouring out at both ends, and one fat man had crashed half way through a glass window on one side of the car, got wedged fast and was squirming and screaming like an impaled madman. Every door, of every house, as far as the eye could reach, was vomiting a stream of human beings; and almost before one could execute a wink and begin another, there was a massed multitude of people stretching in endless procession down every street my position commanded. Never was solemn solitude turned into teeming life quicker.

Of the wonders wrought by "the great earthquake," these were all that came under my eye; but the tricks it did, elsewhere, and far and wide over the town, made toothsome gossip for nine days. The destruction of property was trifling—the injury to it was widespread and somewhat serious.

The "curiosities" of the earthquake were simply endless. Gentlemen and ladies who were sick, or were taking a siesta, or had dissipated till a late hour and were making up lost sleep, thronged into the public streets in all sorts of queer apparel, and some without any at all. One woman who had been washing a naked child, ran down the street holding it by the ankles as if it were a dressed turkey. Prominent citizens who were supposed to keep the Sabbath strictly, rushed out of saloons in their shirt-sleeves, with billiard cues in their hands. Dozens of men with necks swathed in napkins, rushed from barber-shops, lathered to the eyes or with one cheek clean shaved and the other still bearing a hairy stubble. Horses broke from stables, and a frightened dog rushed up a short attic ladder and out on to a roof, and when his scare was over had not the nerve to go down again the same way he had gone up. A prominent editor flew down stairs, in the principal hotel, with nothing on but one brief undergarment—met a chambermaid, and exclaimed:

HARD ON THE INNOCENTS.

DRY BONES SHAKEN.

"Oh, what *shall* I do! Where shall I go!"

She responded with naive serenity:

"If you have no choice, you might try a clothing-store!"

"OH, WHAT *SHALL* I DO!"

A certain foreign consul's lady was the acknowledged leader of fashion, and every time she appeared in anything new or extraordinary, the ladies in the vicinity made a raid on their husbands' purses and arrayed themselves similarly. One man who had suffered considerably and growled accordingly, was standing at the window when the shocks came, and the next instant the consul's wife, just out of the bath, fled by with no other apology for clothing than—a bath-towel! The sufferer rose superior to the terrors of the earthquake, and said to his wife:

"GET OUT YOUR TOWEL MY DEAR!"

"Now *that* is something *like!* Get out your towel my dear!"

The plastering that fell from ceilings in San Francisco that day, would have covered several acres of ground. For some days afterward, groups of eyeing and pointing men stood about many a building, looking at long zig-zag cracks that extended from the eaves to the ground. Four feet of the tops of three chimneys on one house were broken square off and turned around in such a way as to completely stop the draft. A crack a hundred feet long gaped open six inches wide in the middle of one street and then shut together again with such force, as to ridge up the meeting earth like a slender grave. A lady sitting in her rocking and quaking parlor, saw the wall part at the ceiling, open and shut twice, like a mouth, and then—drop the end of a brick on the floor like a tooth. She was a woman easily disgusted with foolishness, and she arose and went out of there. One lady who was coming down stairs was astonished to see a bronze Hercules lean forward on its pedestal as if to strike her with its club. They both reached the bottom of the flight at the same time,—the woman insensible from the fright. Her child, born some little time afterward, was club-footed. However—on second thought,—if the reader sees any coincidence in this, he must do it at his own risk.

"WE WILL OMIT THE BENEDICTION!"

The first shock brought down two or three huge organ-pipes in one of the churches. The minister, with uplifted hands, was just closing the services. He glanced up, hesitated, and said:

"However, we will omit the benediction!"—and the next instant there was a vacancy in the atmosphere where he had stood.

After the first shock, an Oakland minister said:

"Keep your seats! There is no better place to die than this"—

And added, after the third:

"But outside is good enough!" He then skipped out at the back door.

Such another destruction of mantel ornaments and toilet bottles as the earthquake created, San Francisco never saw before. There was hardly a girl or a matron in the city but suffered losses of this kind. Suspended pictures were thrown down, but oftener still, by a curious freak of the earthquake's humor, they were whirled completely around with their faces to the wall! There was great difference of opinion, at first, as to the course or direction the earthquake traveled, but water that splashed out of various tanks and buckets settled that. Thousands of people were made so sea-sick by the rolling and pitching of floors and streets that they were weak and bedridden for hours, and some few for even days afterward. Hardly an individual escaped nausea entirely.

The queer earthquake-episodes that formed the staple of San Francisco gossip for the next week would fill a much larger book than this, and so I will diverge from the subject.

By and by, in the due course of things, I picked up a copy of the *Enterprise* one day, and fell under this cruel blow:

NEVADA MINES IN NEW YORK.—G. M. Marshall, Sheba Hurst and Amos H. Rose, who left San Francisco last July for New York City, with ores from mines in Pine Wood District, Humboldt County, and on the Reese River range, have disposed of a mine containing six thousand feet and called the Pine Mountains Consolidated, for the sum of $3,000,000. The stamps on the deed, which is now on its way to Humboldt County, from New York, for record, amounted to $3,000, which is said to be the largest amount of stamps ever placed on one document. A working capital of $1,000,000 has been paid into the treasury, and machinery has already been purchased for a large quartz mill, which will be put up as soon as possible. The stock in this company is all full paid and entirely unassessable. The ores of the mines in this district somewhat resemble those of the Sheba mine in Humboldt. Sheba Hurst, the discoverer of the mines, with his friends corralled all the best leads and all the land and timber they desired before making public their whereabouts. Ores from there, assayed in this city, showed them to be exceedingly rich in silver and gold—silver predominating. There is an abundance of wood and water in the District. We are glad to know that New York capital has been enlisted in the development of the mines of this region. Having seen the ores and assays, we are satisfied that the mines of the District are very valuable—anything but wild-cat.

Once more native imbecility had carried the day, and I had lost a million! It was the "blind lead" over again.

Let us not dwell on this miserable matter. If I were inventing these things, I could be wonderfully humorous over them; but they are too true to be talked of with hearty levity, even at this distant day.* Suffice it that I so lost heart, and so yielded myself up to repinings and sighings and foolish regrets, that I neglected my duties and became about worthless, as a reporter for a brisk newspaper. And at last one of the proprietors took me aside, with a charity I still remember with considerable respect, and gave me an opportunity to resign my berth and so save myself the disgrace of a dismissal.

---

*True, and yet not exactly as given in the above figures, possibly. I saw Marshall, months afterward, and although he had plenty of money he did not claim to have captured an entire *million.* In fact I gathered that he had not then received $50,000. Beyond that figure his fortune appeared to consist of uncertain vast expectations rather than prodigious certainties. However, when the above item appeared in print I put full faith in it, and incontinently wilted and went to seed under it.

CHAPTER 59

For a time I wrote literary screeds for the *Golden Era.* C. H. Webb had established a very excellent literary weekly called the *Californian,* but high merit was no guaranty of success; it languished, and he sold out to three printers, and Bret Harte became editor at twenty dollars a week, and I was employed to contribute an article a week at twelve dollars. But the journal still languished, and the printers sold out to Capt. Ogden, a rich man and a pleasant gentleman who chose to amuse himself with such an expensive luxury without much caring about the cost of it. When he grew tired of the novelty, he re-sold to the printers, the paper presently died a peaceful death, and I was out of work again. I would not mention these things but for the fact that they so aptly illustrate the ups and downs that characterize life on the Pacific coast. A man could hardly stumble into such a variety of queer vicissitudes in any other country.

SLINKING.

For two months my sole occupation was avoiding acquaintances; for during that time I did not earn a penny, or buy an article of any kind, or pay my board. I became a very adept at "slinking." I slunk from back street to back street, I slunk away from approaching faces that looked familiar, I slunk to my meals, ate them humbly and with a mute apology for every mouthful I robbed my generous landlady of, and at midnight, after wanderings that were but slinkings away from cheerfulness and light, I slunk to my bed. I felt meaner, and lowlier and more despicable than the worms. During all this time I had but one piece of money—a silver ten-cent piece—and I held to it and would not spend it on any account, lest the consciousness coming strong upon me that I was *entirely* penniless, might suggest suicide. I had pawned everything but the clothes I had on; so I clung to my dime desperately, till it was smooth with handling.

However, I am forgetting. I did have one other occupation besides that of "slinking." It was the entertaining of a collector (and being entertained by him,) who had in his hands the Virginia banker's bill for the forty-six dollars which I had loaned my schoolmate, the "Prodigal." This man used to call regularly once a week and dun me, and sometimes oftener. He did it from sheer force of habit, for he knew he could get nothing. He would get out his bill, calculate the interest for me, at five per cent a month, and show me clearly that there was no attempt at fraud in it and no mistakes; and then plead, and argue and dun with all his might for any sum—any little trifle—even a dollar—even half a dollar, on account. Then his duty was accomplished and his conscience free. He immediately dropped the subject there always; got out a couple of cigars and divided, put his feet in the window, and then we would have a long, luxurious talk about everything and everybody, and he would furnish me a world of curious dunning adventures out of the ample store in his memory. By and by he would clap his hat on his head, shake hands and say briskly:

"Well, business is business—can't stay with you always!"—and was off in a second.

The idea of pining for a dun! And yet I used to long for him to come, and would get as uneasy as any mother if the day went by without his visit, when I was expecting him. But he never collected that bill, at last, nor any part of it. I lived to pay it to the banker myself.

Misery loves company. Now and then at night, in out-of-the-way, dimly lighted places, I found myself happening on another child of misfortune. He looked so seedy and forlorn, so homeless and friendless and forsaken, that I yearned toward him as a brother. I wanted to claim kinship with him and go about and enjoy our wretchedness together. The drawing toward each other must have been mutual; at any rate we got to falling together oftener, though still seemingly by accident; and although we did not speak or evince any recognition, I think the dull anxiety passed out of both of us when we saw each other, and then for several hours we would idle along contentedly, wide apart, and glancing furtively in at home lights and fireside gatherings, out of the night shadows, and very much enjoying our dumb companionship.

Finally we spoke, and were inseparable after that. For our woes were identical, almost. He had been a reporter too, and lost his berth, and this was his experience, as nearly as I can recollect it. After losing his berth, he had gone down, down, down, with never a halt: from a boarding house on Russian Hill to a boarding house in Kearny street; from thence to Dupont; from thence to a low sailor den; and from thence to lodgings in goods boxes and empty hogsheads near the wharves. Then, for a while, he had gained a meagre living by sewing up bursted sacks of grain on the piers; when that failed he had found food here and there as chance threw it in his way. He had ceased to show his face in daylight, now, for a reporter knows everybody, rich and poor, high and low, and cannot well avoid familiar faces in the broad light of day.

This mendicant Blucher—I call him that for convenience—was a splendid creature. He was full of hope, pluck and philosophy; he was well read and a man of cultivated taste; he had a bright wit and was a master of satire; his kindliness and his generous spirit made him royal in my eyes and changed his curb-stone seat to a throne and his damaged hat to a crown.

He had an adventure, once, which sticks fast in my memory as the most pleasantly grotesque that ever touched my sympathies. He had been without a penny for two months. He had shirked about obscure streets, among friendly dim lights, till the thing had become second nature to him. But at last he was driven abroad in daylight. The cause was sufficient; *he had not tasted food for forty-eight hours,* and he could not endure the misery of his hunger in idle hiding. He came along a back street, glowering at the loaves in bake-shop windows, and feeling that he could trade his life away for a morsel to eat. The sight of the bread doubled his hunger; but it was good to look at it, anyhow, and imagine what one might do if one only had it. Presently, in the middle of the street he saw a shining spot—looked again—did not, and could not, believe his eyes—turned away, to try them, then looked again. It was a verity—no vain, hunger-inspired delusion—it was a silver dime! He snatched it—gloated over it; doubted it—bit it—found it genuine—choked his heart down, and smothered a halleluiah. Then he looked around—saw that nobody was looking at him—threw the dime down where it was before—walked away a few steps, and approached again, pretending he did not know it was there, so that he could re-enjoy the luxury of finding it. He walked around it, viewing it from different points; then sauntered about with his hands in his pockets, looking up at the signs and now and then glancing at

A PRIZE.

it and feeling the old thrill again. Finally he took it up, and went away, fondling it in his pocket. He idled through unfrequented streets, stopping in doorways and corners to take it out and look at it. By and by he went home to his lodgings—an empty queensware hogshead,—and employed himself till night trying to make up his mind what to buy with it. But it was hard to do. To get the most for it was the idea. He knew that at the Miners' Restaurant he could get a plate of beans and a piece of bread for ten cents; or a fish-ball and some few trifles, but they gave "no bread with one fish-ball" there. At French Pete's he could get a veal cutlet, plain, and some radishes and bread, for ten cents; or a cup of coffee—a pint at least—and a slice of bread; but the slice was not thick enough by the eighth of an inch, and sometimes they were still more criminal than that in the cutting of it. At seven o'clock his hunger was wolfish; and still his mind was not made up. He turned out and went up Merchant street, still ciphering; and chewing a bit of stick, as is the way of starving men. He passed before the lights of Martin's restaurant, the most aristocratic in the city, and stopped. It was a place where he had often dined, in better days, and Martin knew him well. Standing aside, just out of the range of the light, he worshipped the quails and steaks in the show window, and imagined that maybe the fairy times were not gone yet and some prince in disguise would come along presently and tell him to go in there and take whatever he wanted. He chewed his stick with a hungry interest as he warmed to his subject. Just at this juncture he was conscious of some one at his side, sure enough; and then a finger touched his arm. He looked up, over his shoulder, and saw an apparition—a very allegory of Hunger! It was a man six feet high, gaunt, unshaven, hung with rags; with a haggard face and sunken cheeks, and eyes that pleaded piteously. This phantom said:

A LOOK IN AT THE WINDOW.

"Come with me—please."

He locked his arm in Blucher's and walked up the street to where the passengers were few and the light not strong, and then facing about, put out his hands in a beseeching way, and said:

"Friend—stranger—look at me! Life is easy to you—you go about, placid and content, as I did once, in my day—you have been in there, and eaten your sumptuous supper, and picked your teeth, and hummed your tune, and thought your pleasant thoughts, and said to yourself it is a good world—but you've never *suffered!* You don't know what trouble is—you don't know what misery is—nor hunger! Look at me! Stranger have pity on a poor friendless, homeless dog! As God is my judge, I have not tasted food for eight and forty hours!—look in my eyes and see if I lie! Give me the least trifle in the world to keep me from starving—anything—twenty-five cents! Do it, stranger—do it, *please.* It will be nothing to you, but

"DO IT, STRANGER."

life to me. Do it, and I will go down on my knees and lick the dust before you! I will kiss your footprints—I will worship the very ground you walk on! Only twenty-five cents! I am famishing—perishing—starving by inches! For God's sake don't desert me!"

Blucher was bewildered—and touched, too—stirred to the depths. He reflected. Thought again. Then an idea struck him, and he said:

"Come with me."

He took the outcast's arm, walked him down to Martin's restaurant, seated him at a marble table, placed the bill of fare before him, and said:

"Order what you want, friend. Charge it to me, Mr. Martin."

"All right, Mr. Blucher," said Martin.

Then Blucher stepped back and leaned against the counter and watched the man stow away cargo after cargo of buckwheat cakes at seventy-five cents a plate; cup after cup of coffee, and porter house steaks worth two dollars apiece; and when six dollars and a half's worth of destruction had been accomplished, and the stranger's hunger appeased, Blucher went down to French Pete's, bought a veal cutlet plain, a slice of bread, and three radishes, with his dime, and set to and feasted like a king!

Take the episode all around, it was as odd as any that can be culled from the myriad curiosities of Californian life, perhaps.

CHAPTER 60

By and by, an old friend of mine, a miner, came down from one of the decayed mining camps of Tuolumne, California, and I went back with him. We lived in a small cabin on a verdant hillside, and there were not five other cabins in view over the wide expanse of hill and forest. Yet a flourishing city of two or three thousand population had occupied this grassy dead solitude during the flush times of twelve or fifteen years before, and where our cabin stood had once been the heart of the teeming hive, the centre of the city. When the mines gave out the town fell into decay, and in a few years wholly disappeared—streets, dwellings, shops, everything—and left no sign. The grassy slopes were as green and smooth and desolate of life as if they had never been disturbed. The mere handful of miners still remaining, had seen the town spring up, spread, grow and flourish in its pride; and they had seen it sicken and die, and pass away like a dream. With it their hopes had died, and their zest of life. They had long ago resigned themselves to their exile, and ceased to correspond with their distant friends or turn longing eyes toward their early homes. They had accepted banishment, forgotten the world and been forgotten of the world. They were far from telegraphs and railroads, and they stood, as it were, in a living grave, dead to the events that stirred the globe's great populations, dead to the common interests of men, isolated and outcast from brotherhood with their kind. It was the most singular, and almost the most touching and melancholy exile that fancy can imagine. One of my associates in this locality, for two or three months, was a man who had had a university education; but now for eighteen years he had decayed there by inches, a bearded, rough-clad, clay-stained miner, and at times, among his sighings and soliloquizings, he unconsciously interjected vaguely remembered Latin and Greek sentences—dead and musty tongues, meet vehicles for the thoughts of one whose dreams were all of the past, whose life was a failure; a tired man, burdened with the present, and indifferent to the future; a man without ties, hopes, interests, waiting for rest and the end.

THE OLD COLLEGIATE.

In that one little corner of California is found a species of mining which is seldom or never mentioned in print. It is called "pocket-mining" and I am not aware that any of it is done outside of that little corner. The gold is not evenly distributed through the surface dirt, as in ordinary placer mines, but is collected in little spots, and they are very wide apart and exceedingly hard to find, but when you do find one you reap a rich and sudden harvest. There are not now more than twenty pocket-miners in that entire little region. I think I know every one of them personally. I have known one of them to hunt patiently about the hillsides every day for eight months without finding gold enough to make a snuff-box—his grocery bill running up relentlessly all the time—and then find a pocket and take out of it two thousand dollars in two dips of his shovel. I have known him to take out three thousand dollars in two hours, and go and pay up every cent of his indebtedness, then enter on a dazzling spree that finished the last of his treasure before the night was gone. And the next day he bought his groceries on credit as usual, and shouldered his pan and shovel and went off to the hills hunting pockets again happy and content. This is the most fascinating of all the different kinds of mining, and furnishes a very handsome percentage of victims to the lunatic asylum.

Pocket hunting is an ingenious process. You take a spadeful of earth from the hillside and put it in a large tin pan and dissolve and wash it gradually away till nothing is left but a teaspoonful of fine sediment. Whatever gold was in that earth has remained, because, being the heaviest, it has sought the bottom. Among the sediment you will find half a dozen yellow particles no larger than pinheads. You are delighted. You move off to one side and wash another pan. If you find gold again, you move to one side further, and wash a third pan. If you find *no* gold this time, you are delighted again, because you know you are on the right scent. You lay an imaginary plan, shaped like a fan, with its handle up the hill—for just where the end of the handle is, you argue that the rich deposit lies hidden, whose vagrant grains of gold have escaped and been washed down the hill, spreading farther and farther apart as they wandered. And so you proceed up the hill, washing the earth and narrowing your lines every time the absence of gold in the pan shows that you are outside the spread of the fan; and at last, twenty yards up the hill your lines have converged to a point—a single foot from that point you cannot find any gold. Your breath comes short and quick, you are feverish with excitement; the dinner-bell may ring its clapper off, you pay no attention; friends may die, weddings transpire, houses burn down, they are nothing to you; you sweat and dig and delve with a frantic interest—and all at once you strike it! Up comes a spadeful of earth and quartz that is all lovely with soiled lumps and leaves and sprays of gold. Sometimes that one spadeful is all—five hundred dollars. Sometimes the nest contains ten thousand dollars, and it takes you three or four days to get it all out. The pocket-miners tell of one nest that yielded sixty thousand dollars and two men exhausted it in two weeks, and then sold the ground for ten thousand dollars to a party who never got three hundred dollars out of it afterward.

STRIKING A POCKET.

The hogs are good pocket hunters. All the summer they root around the bushes, and turn up a thousand little piles of dirt, and then the miners long for the rains; for the rains beat upon these little piles and wash them down and expose the gold, possibly right over a pocket. Two pockets were found in this way by the same man in one day. One had five thousand dollars in it and the other eight thousand dollars. That man could appreciate it, for he hadn't had a cent for about a year.

In Tuolumne lived two miners who used to go to the neighboring village in the afternoon and return every night with household supplies. Part of the distance they traversed a trail, and nearly always sat down to rest on a great boulder that lay beside the path. In the course of thirteen years they had worn that boulder tolerably smooth, sitting on it. By and by two vagrant Mexicans came along and occupied the seat. They began to amuse themselves by chipping off flakes from the boulder with a sledge-hammer. They examined one of these flakes and found it rich with gold. That boulder paid them eight hundred dollars afterward. But the aggravating circumstance was that these "Greasers" knew that there must be more gold where that boulder came from, and so they went panning up the hill and found what was probably the richest pocket that region has yet produced. It took three months to exhaust it, and it yielded a hundred and twenty thousand dollars. The two American miners who used to sit on the boulder are poor yet, and they take turn about in getting up early in the morning to curse those Mexicans—and when it comes down to pure ornamental cursing, the native American is gifted above the sons of men.

I have dwelt at some length upon this matter of pocket-mining because it is a subject that is seldom referred to in print, and therefore I judged that it would have for the reader that interest which naturally attaches to novelty.

CHAPTER 61

One of my comrades there—another of those victims of eighteen years of unrequited toil and blighted hopes—was one of the gentlest spirits that ever bore its patient cross in a weary exile: grave and simple Dick Baker, pocket-miner of Dead-Horse Gulch. He was forty-six, gray as a rat, earnest, thoughtful, slenderly educated, slouchily dressed and clay-soiled, but his heart was finer metal than any gold his shovel ever brought to light—than any, indeed, that ever was mined or minted.

Whenever he was out of luck and a little down-hearted, he would fall to mourning over the loss of a wonderful cat he used to own (for where women and children are not, men of kindly impulses take up with pets, for they must love something.) And he always spoke of the strange sagacity of that cat with the air of a man who believed in his secret heart that there was something human about it—maybe even supernatural.

TOM QUARTZ.

I heard him talking about this animal once. He said, "Gentlemen, I used to have a cat here, by the name of Tom Quartz, which you'd a took an interest in I reckon—most anybody would. I had him here eight year—and he was the remarkablest cat *I* ever see. He was a large gray one of the Tom specie, an' he had more hard, natchral sense than any man in this camp—'n' a *power* of dignity—he wouldn't a let the Gov'ner of Californy be familiar with him. He never ketched a rat in his life—'peared to be above it. He never cared for nothing but mining. He knowed more about mining, that cat did, than any man *I* ever

ever see. You couldn't tell *him* noth'n' 'bout placer diggin's—'n' as for pocket-mining, why he was just born for it. He would dig out after me an' Jim when we went over the hills prospect'n', and he would trot along behind us for as much as five mile, if we went so fur. An' he had the best judgment about mining ground—why you never see anything like it. When we went to work, he'd scatter a glance around, 'n' if he didn't think much of the indications, he would give a look as much as to say, 'Well, I'll have to get you to excuse *me*,' 'n' without another word he'd hyste his nose into the air 'n' shove for home. But if the ground suited him, he would lay low 'n' keep dark till the first pan was washed, 'n' then he would sidle up 'n' take a look, an' if there was about six or seven grains of gold *he* was satisfied—he didn't want no better prospect 'n that—'n' then he would lay down on our coats and snore like a steamboat till we'd struck the pocket, an' then get up 'n' superintend. He was nearly lightnin' on superintending.

"Well, by an' by, up comes this yer quartz excitement. Everybody was into it—everybody was pick'n' 'n' blast'n' instead of shovelin' dirt on the hillside—everybody was put'n' down a shaft instead of scrapin' the surface. Noth'n' would do Jim, but *we* must tackle the ledges, too, 'n' so we did. We commenced put'n' down a shaft, 'n' Tom Quartz he begin to wonder what in the Dickens it was all about. *He* hadn't ever seen any mining like that before, 'n' he was all upset, as you may say—he couldn't come to a right understanding of it no way—it was too many for *him*. He was down on it, too, you bet you—he was down on it powerful—'n' always appeared to consider it the cussedest foolishness out. But that cat, you know, was *always* agin new fangled arrangements—somehow he never could abide 'em. *You* know how it is with old habits. But by an' by Tom Quartz begin to git sort of reconciled a little, though he never *could* altogether understand that eternal sinkin' of a shaft an' never pannin' out anything. At last he got to comin' down in the shaft, hisself, to try to cipher it out. An' when he'd git the blues, 'n' feel kind o' scruffy, 'n' aggravated 'n' disgusted—knowin' as he did, that the bills was runnin' up all the time an' we warn't makin' a cent—he would curl up on a gunny sack in the corner an' go to sleep. Well, one day when the shaft was down about eight foot, the rock got so hard that we had to put in a blast—the first blast'n' we'd ever done since Tom Quartz was born. An' then we lit the fuse 'n' clumb out 'n' got off 'bout fifty yards—'n' forgot 'n' left Tom Quartz sound asleep on the gunny sack. In 'bout a minute we seen a puff of smoke bust up out of the hole, 'n' then everything let go with an awful crash, 'n' about four million ton of rocks 'n' dirt 'n' smoke 'n' splinters shot up 'bout a mile an' a half into the air, an' by George, right in the dead centre of it was old Tom Quartz a goin' end over end, an' a snortin' an' a sneez'n', an' a clawin' an' a reachin' for things like all possessed. But it warn't no use, you know, it warn't no use. An' that was the last we see of *him* for about two minutes 'n' a half, an' then all of a sudden it begin to rain rocks and rubbage, an' directly he come down ker-whop about ten foot off f'm where we stood. Well, I reckon he was p'raps the orneriest lookin' beast you ever see. One ear was sot back on his neck, 'n' his tail was stove up, 'n' his eye-winkers was swinged off, 'n' he was all blacked up with powder an' smoke, an' all sloppy with mud 'n' slush f'm one end to the other. Well sir, it

AN ADVANTAGE TAKEN.

warn't no use to try to apologize—we couldn't say a word. He took a sort of a disgusted look at hisself, 'n' then he looked at us—an' it was just exactly the same as if he had said—'Gents, maybe *you* think it's smart to take advantage of a cat that ain't had no experience of quartz minin', but *I* think *different*'—an' then he turned on his heel 'n' marched off home without ever saying another word.

AFTER AN EXCURSION.

"That was jest his style. An' maybe you won't believe it, but after that you never see a cat so prejudiced agin quartz mining as what he was. An' by an' by when he *did* get to goin' down in the shaft agin, you'd a been astonished at his sagacity. The minute we'd tetch off a blast 'n' the fuse'd begin to sizzle, he'd give a look as much as to say: 'Well, I'll have to git you to excuse *me*,' an' it was surpris'n', the way he'd shin out of that hole 'n' go f'r a tree. Sagacity? It ain't no name for it. 'Twas *inspiration!*"

I said, "Well, Mr. Baker, his prejudice against quartz mining *was* remarkable, considering how he came by it. Couldn't you ever cure him of it?"

"*Cure him!* No! When Tom Quartz was sot once, he was *always* sot—and you might a blowed him up as much as three million times 'n' you'd never a broken him of his cussed prejudice agin quartz mining."

The affection and the pride that lit up Baker's face when he delivered this tribute to the firmness of his humble friend of other days, will always be a vivid memory with me.

At the end of two months we had never "struck" a pocket. We had panned up and down the hillsides till they looked plowed like a field; we could have put in a crop of grain, then, but there would have been no way to get it to market. We got many good "prospects," but when the gold gave out in the pan and we dug down, hoping and longing, we found only emptiness—the pocket that should have been there was as barren as our own. At last we shouldered our pans and shovels and struck out over the hills to try new localities. We prospected around Angel's Camp, in Calaveras County, during three weeks, but had no success. Then we wandered on foot among the mountains, sleeping under the trees at night, for the weather was mild, but still we remained as centless as the last rose of summer. That is a poor joke, but it is in pathetic harmony with the circumstances, since we were so poor ourselves. In accordance with the custom of the country, our door had always stood open and our board welcome to tramping miners—they drifted along nearly every day, dumped their post shovels by the threshold and took "pot luck" with us—and now on our own tramp we never found cold hospitality.

Our wanderings were wide and in many directions; and now I could give the reader a vivid description of the Big Trees and the marvels of the Yo Semite—but what has this reader done to me that I should persecute him? I will deliver him into the hands of less conscientious tourists and take his blessing. Let me be charitable, though I fail in all virtues else.

Some of the phrases in the above are mining technicalities, purely, and may be a little obscure to the general reader. In "*placer diggings*" the gold is scattered all through the surface dirt; in "*pocket*" diggings it is concentrated in one little spot; in "*quartz*" the gold is in a solid, continuous vein of rock, enclosed between distinct walls of some other kind of stone—and this is the most laborious and expensive of all the different kinds of mining. "*Prospecting*" is hunting for a "*placer;*" "*indications*" are signs of its presence; "*panning out*" refers to the washing process by which the grains of gold are separated from the dirt; a "*prospect*" is what one finds in the first panful of dirt—and its value determines whether it is a good or a bad prospect, and whether it is worth while to tarry there or seek further.

CHAPTER 62

AFTER a three months' absence, I found myself in San Francisco again, without a cent. When my credit was about exhausted, (for I had become too mean and lazy, now, to work on a morning paper, and there were no vacancies on the evening journals,) I was created San Francisco correspondent of the *Enterprise*, and at the end of five months I was out of debt, but my interest in my work was gone; for my correspondence being a daily one, without rest or respite, I got unspeakably tired of it. I wanted another change. The vagabond instinct was strong upon me. Fortune favored and I got a new berth and a delightful one. It was to go down to the Sandwich Islands and write some letters for the Sacramento *Union*, an excellent journal and liberal with employés.

We sailed in the propeller Ajax, in the middle of winter. The almanac called it winter, distinctly enough, but the weather was a compromise between spring and summer. Six days out of port, it became summer altogether. We had some thirty passengers; among them a cheerful soul by the name of Williams, and three sea-worn old whaleship captains going down to join their vessels. These latter played euchre in the smoking room day and night, drank astonishing quantities of raw whisky without being in the least affected by it, and were the happiest people I think I ever saw. And then there was "the old Admiral"—a retired whaleman. He was a roaring, terrific combination of wind and lightning and thunder, and earnest, whole-souled profanity. But nevertheless he was tender-hearted as a girl. He was a raving, deafening, devastating typhoon, laying waste the cowering seas but with an unvexed refuge in the centre where all comers were safe and at rest. Nobody could know the "Admiral" without liking him; and in a sudden and dire emergency I think no friend of his would know which to

THE THREE CAPTAINS.

choose—to be cursed by him or prayed for by a less efficient person.

His title of "Admiral" was more strictly "official" than any ever worn by a naval officer before or since, perhaps—for it was the voluntary offering of a whole nation, and came direct from the *people* themselves without any intermediate red tape—the people of the Sandwich Islands. It was a title that came to him freighted with affection, and honor, and appreciation of his unpretending merit. And in testimony of the genuineness of the title it was publicly ordained that an exclusive flag should be devised for him and used solely to welcome his coming and wave him God-speed in his going. From that time forth, whenever his ship was signaled in the offing, or he catted his anchor and stood out to sea, that ensign streamed from the royal halliards on the parliament house and the nation lifted their hats to it with spontaneous accord.

Yet he had never fired a gun or fought a battle in his life. When I knew him on board the Ajax, he was seventy-two years old and had

THE OLD ADMIRAL.

plowed the salt water sixty-one of them. For sixteen years he had gone in and out of the harbor of Honolulu in command of a whaleship, and for sixteen more had been captain of a San Francisco and Sandwich Island passenger packet and had never had an accident or lost a vessel. The simple natives knew him for a friend who never failed them, and regarded him as children regard a father. It was a dangerous thing to oppress them when the roaring Admiral was around.

Two years before I knew the Admiral, he had retired from the sea on a competence, and had sworn a colossal nine-jointed oath that he would "never go within *smelling* distance of the salt water again as long as he lived." And he had conscientiously kept it. That is to say, *he* considered he had kept it, and it would have been more than dangerous to suggest to him, even in the gentlest way, that making eleven long sea voyages, as a passenger, during the two years that had transpired since he "retired," was only keeping the general spirit of it and not the strict letter.

The Admiral knew only one narrow line of conduct to pursue in any and all cases where there was a fight, and that was to shoulder his way straight in without an inquiry as to the rights or the merits of it, and take the part of the weaker side. And this was the reason why he was always sure to be present at the trial of any universally execrated criminal to oppress and intimidate the jury with a vindictive pantomime of what he would do to them if he ever caught them out of the box. And this was why harried cats and outlawed dogs that knew him confidently took sanctuary under his chair in time of trouble. In the beginning he was the most frantic and bloodthirsty Union man that drew breath in the shadow of the Flag; but the instant the Southerners began to go down before the sweep of the Northern armies, he ran up the Confederate colors and from that time till the end was a rampant and inexorable secessionist.

He hated intemperance with a more uncompromising animosity than any individual I have ever met, of either sex; and he was never tired of storming against it and beseeching friends and strangers alike to be wary and drink with moderation. And yet if any creature had been guileless enough to intimate that his absorbing nine gallons of "straight" whisky during our voyage was any fraction short of rigid or inflexible abstemiousness, in that self-same moment the old man would have spun him to the uttermost parts of the earth in the whirlwind of his wrath. Mind, I am not saying his whisky ever affected his head or his legs, for it did not, in even the slightest degree. He was a capacious container, but he did not hold enough for that. He took a level tumblerful of whisky every morning before he put his clothes on—"to sweeten his bilgewater," he said. He took another after he got the most of his clothes on, "to settle his mind and give him his bearings." He then shaved, and put on a clean shirt; after which he recited the Lord's Prayer in a fervent, thundering bass that shook the ship to her kelson and suspended all conversation in the main cabin. Then, at this stage, being invariably "by the head," or "by the stern," or "listed to port or starboard," he took one more to "put him on an even keel so that he would mind his hellum and not miss stays and go about, every time he came up in the wind." And now, his state-room door swung open and the sun of his benignant face beamed redly out upon men and women and children, and he roared his "Shipmets a'hoy!" in a way that was calculated to wake the dead and precipitate the final resurrection; and forth he strode, a picture to look at and a presence to enforce attention. Stalwart and portly; not a gray hair; broad-brimmed slouch hat; semi-sailor toggery of blue navy flannel—roomy and ample; a stately expanse of shirt-front and a liberal amount of black silk neck-cloth tied with a sailor knot; large chain and imposing seals impending from his fob; awe-inspiring feet, and "a hand like the hand of Providence," as his whaling brethren expressed it; wrist-bands and sleeves pushed back half way to the elbow, out of respect for the warm weather, and exposing hairy arms, gaudy with red and blue anchors, ships, and goddesses of liberty tattooed in India ink. But these details were only secondary matters—his face was the lodestone that chained the eye. It was a sultry disk, glowing determinedly out through a weather beaten mask of mahogany, and studded with warts, seamed with scars, "blazed" all over with unfailing fresh slips of the razor; and with cheery eyes, under shaggy brows, contemplating the world from over the back of a gnarled crag of a nose that loomed vast and lonely out of the undulating immensity that spread away from its foundations. At his heels frisked the darling of his bachelor estate, his terrier "Fan," a creature no larger than a squirrel. The main part of his daily life was occupied in looking after "Fan," in a motherly way, and doctoring her for a hundred ailments which existed only in his imagination.

The Admiral seldom read newspapers; and when he did he never believed anything they said. He read nothing, and believed in nothing, but "The Old Guard," a secession periodical published in New York. He carried a dozen copies of it with him, always, and referred to them for all required information. If it was not there, he supplied it himself, out of a bountiful fancy, inventing history, names, dates, and everything else necessary to make his point good in an argument. Consequently he was a formidable antagonist in a dispute. Whenever he swung clear of the record and began to create history, the enemy was helpless and had to surrender. Indeed, the enemy could not keep from betraying some little spark of indignation at his manufactured history—and when it came to indignation, that was the Admiral's very "best hold." He was always ready for a political argument, and if nobody started one he would do it himself. With his third retort his temper would begin to rise, and within five minutes he would be blowing a gale, and within fifteen his smoking-room audience would be utterly stormed away and the old man left solitary and alone, banging the table with his fist, kicking the chairs, and roaring a hurricane of profanity. It got so, after a while, that whenever the Admiral approached, with politics in his eye, the passengers would drop out with quiet accord, afraid to meet him; and he would camp on a deserted field.

DESERTED FIELD.

But he found his match at last, and before a full company. At one time or another, everybody had entered the lists against him and been routed, except the quiet passenger Williams. He had never been able to get an expression of opinion out of him on politics. But now, just as the Admiral drew near the door and the company were about to slip out, Williams said:

"Admiral, are you *certain* about that circumstance concerning the clergymen you mentioned the other day?"—referring to a piece of the Admiral's manufactured history.

Every one was amazed at the man's rashness. The idea of deliberately inviting annihilation was a thing incomprehensible. The retreat came to a halt; then everybody sat down again wondering, to await the upshot of it. The Admiral himself was as surprised as any one. He paused in the door, with his red handkerchief half raised to his sweating face, and contemplated the daring reptile in the corner.

"*Certain* of it? Am I *certain* of it? Do you think I've been lying about it? What do you take me for? Anybody that don't know that

WILLIAMS.

circumstance, don't know anything; a child ought to know it. Read up your history! Read it up —— —— —— ——, and don't come asking a man if he's *certain* about a bit of A B C stuff that the very southern niggers know all about."

Here the Admiral's fires began to wax hot, the atmosphere thickened, the coming earthquake rumbled, he began to thunder and lighten. Within three minutes his volcano was in full eruption and he was discharging flames and ashes of indignation, belching black volumes of foul history aloft, and vomiting red-hot torrents of profanity from his crater. Meantime Williams sat silent, and apparently deeply and earnestly interested in what the old man was saying. By and by, when the lull came, he said in the most deferential way, and with the gratified air of a man who has had a mystery cleared up which had been puzzling him uncomfortably:

"*Now* I understand it. I always thought I knew that piece of history well enough, but was still afraid to trust it, because there was not that convincing particularity about it that one likes to have in history; but when you mentioned every name, the other day, and every date, and every little circumstance, in their just order and sequence, I said to myself, *this* sounds something like—*this* is history—*this* is putting it in a shape that gives a man confidence; and I said to myself afterward, I will just ask the Admiral if he is perfectly certain about the details, and if he is I will come out and thank him for clearing this matter up for me. And that is what I want to do now—for until you set that matter right it was nothing but just a confusion in my mind, without head or tail to it."

Nobody ever saw the Admiral look so mollified before, and so pleased. Nobody had ever received his bogus history as gospel before; its genuineness had always been called in question either by words or looks; but here was a man that not only swallowed it all down, but was grateful for the dose. He was taken aback; he hardly knew what to say; even his profanity failed him. Now, Williams continued, modestly and earnestly:

"But Admiral, in saying that this was the first stone thrown, and that this precipitated the war, you have overlooked a circumstance which you are perfectly familiar with, but which has escaped your memory. Now I grant you that what you have stated is correct in every detail—to wit: that on the 16th of October, 1860, two Massachusetts clergymen, named Waite and Granger, went in disguise to the house of John Moody, in Rockport, at dead of night, and dragged forth two Southern women and their two little children, and after tarring and feathering them conveyed them to Boston and burned them alive in the State House square; and I also grant your proposition that this deed is what led to the secession of South Carolina on the 20th of December following. Very well." [Here the company were pleasantly surprised to hear Williams proceed to come back at the Admiral with his own invincible weapon—clean, pure, *manufactured history,* without a word of truth in it.] "Very well, I say. But Admiral, why overlook the Willis and Morgan case in South Carolina? You are too well informed a man not to know all about that circumstance. Your arguments and your conversations have shown you to be intimately conversant with every detail of this national quarrel. You develop matters of history every day that show plainly that you are no smatterer in it, content to nibble about the surface, but a man who has searched the depths and possessed yourself of everything that has a bearing upon the great question. Therefore, let me just recall to your mind that Willis and Morgan case—though I see by your face that the whole thing is already passing through your memory at this moment. On the 12th of August, 1860, *two months* before the Waite and Granger affair, two South Carolina clergymen, named John H. Morgan and Winthrop L. Willis, one a Methodist and the other an Old School Baptist, disguised themselves, and went at midnight to the house of a planter named Thompson—Archibald F. Thompson, Vice President under Thomas Jefferson,—and took thence, at midnight, his widowed aunt, (a Northern woman,) and her adopted child, an orphan named Mortimer Highie, afflicted with epilepsy and suffering at the time from white swelling on one of his legs, and compelled to walk on crutches in consequence; and the two ministers, in spite of the pleadings of the victims, dragged them to the bush, tarred and feathered them, and afterward burned them at the stake in the city of Charleston. You remember perfectly well what a stir it made; you remember perfectly well that even the Charleston *Courier* stigmatized the act as being unpleasant, of questionable propriety, and scarcely justifiable, and likewise that it would not be matter of surprise if retaliation ensued. And you remember also, that this thing was the *cause* of the Massachusetts outrage. Who, indeed, were the two Massachusetts ministers? and who were the two Southern women they burned? I do not need to remind *you*, Admiral, with your intimate knowledge of history, that Waite was the nephew of the woman burned in Charleston; that Granger was her cousin in the second degree, and that the women they burned in Boston were the wife of John H. Morgan, and the still loved but divorced wife of Winthrop L. Willis. Now, Admiral, it is only fair that you should acknowledge that the first provocation came from the Southern preachers and that the Northern ones were justified in retaliating. In your arguments you never yet have shown the least disposition to withhold a just verdict or be in anywise unfair, when authoritative history condemned your position, and therefore I have no hesitation in asking you to take the original blame from the Massachusetts ministers, in this matter, and transfer it to the South Carolina clergymen where it justly belongs."

The Admiral was conquered. This sweet spoken creature who swallowed his fraudulent history as if it were the bread of life; basked in his furious blasphemy as if it were generous sunshine; found only calm, even-handed justice in his rampant partisanship; and flooded him with invented history so sugar-coated with flattery and deference that there was no rejecting it, was "too many" for him. He stammered some awkward, profane sentences about the —— —— —— —— Willis and Morgan business having escaped his memory, but that he "remembered it now," and then, under pretense of giving Fan some medicine for an imaginary cough, drew out of the battle and went away, a vanquished man. Then cheers and laughter went up, and Williams, the ship's benefactor, was a hero. The news went about the vessel, champagne was ordered, an enthusiastic reception instituted in the smoking room, and everybody flocked thither to shake hands with the conqueror. The wheelsman said afterward, that the Admiral stood up behind the pilot house and "ripped and cursed all to himself" till he loosened the smoke-stack guys and becalmed the mainsail.

The Admiral's power was broken. After that, if he began an argument, somebody would bring Williams, and the old man would grow weak and begin to quiet down at once. And as soon as he was done, Williams in his dulcet, insinuating way, would invent some history (referring for proof, to the old man's own excellent memory and to copies of "The Old Guard" known not to be in his possession) that would turn the tables completely and leave the Admiral all abroad and helpless. By and by he came to so dread Williams and his gilded tongue that he would stop talking when he saw him approach, and finally ceased to mention politics altogether, and from that time forward there was entire peace and serenity in the ship.

CHAPTER 63

On a certain bright morning the Islands hove in sight, lying low on the lonely sea, and everybody climbed to the upper deck to look. After two thousand miles of watery solitude the vision was a welcome one. As we approached, the imposing promontory of Diamond Head rose up out of the ocean, its rugged front softened by the hazy distance, and presently the details of the land began to make themselves manifest: first the line of beach; then the plumed cocoanut trees of the tropics; then cabins of the natives; then the white town of Honolulu, said to contain between twelve and fifteen thousand inhabitants, spread over a dead level; with streets from twenty to thirty feet wide, solid and level as a floor, most of them straight as a line and a few as crooked as a corkscrew.

The further I traveled through the town the better I liked it. Every step revealed a new contrast—disclosed something I was unaccustomed to. In place of the grand mud-colored brown stone fronts of San Francisco, I saw dwellings built of straw, *adobes* and cream-colored pebble-and-shell-conglomerated coral cut into oblong blocks and laid in cement; also a great number of neat white cottages, with green window-shutters; in place of front yards like billiard-tables with iron fences around them, I saw these homes surrounded by ample yards, thickly clad with green grass, and shaded by tall trees, through whose dense foliage the sun could scarcely penetrate; in place of the customary geranium, calla lily, etc., languishing in dust and general debility, I saw luxurious banks and thickets of flowers, fresh as a meadow after a rain, and glowing with the richest dyes; in place of the dingy horrors of San Francisco's pleasure grove, the "Willows," I saw huge-bodied, wide-spreading forest trees, with strange names and stranger appearance—trees that cast a shadow like a thunder-cloud, and were able to stand alone without being tied to green poles; in place of gold-fish, wiggling around in glass globes, assuming countless shades and degrees of distortion through the magnifying and diminishing qualities of their transparent prison houses, I saw cats—Tom-cats, Mary Ann cats, long-tailed cats, bob-tail cats,

SCENE ON THE ISLANDS.

blind cats, one-eyed cats, wall-eyed cats, cross-eyed cats, gray cats, black cats, white cats, yellow cats, striped cats, spotted cats, tame cats, wild cats, singed cats, individual cats, groups of cats, platoons of cats, companies of cats, regiments of cats, armies of cats, multitudes of cats, millions of cats, and all of them sleek, fat, lazy and sound asleep.

I looked on a multitude of people, some white, in white coats, vests, pantaloons, even white cloth shoes, made snowy with chalk duly laid on every morning; but the majority of the people were almost as dark as negroes—women with comely features, fine black eyes, rounded forms, inclining to the voluptuous, clad in a single bright red or white garment that fell free and unconfined from shoulder to heel, long black hair falling loose, gypsy hats, encircled with wreaths of natural flowers of a brilliant carmine tint; plenty of dark men in various costumes, and some with nothing on but a battered stove-pipe hat tilted on the nose, and a very scant breech-clout;—certain smoke-dried children were clothed in nothing but sunshine—a very neat fitting and picturesque apparel indeed.

FASHIONABLE ATTIRE.

In place of roughs and rowdies staring and blackguarding on the corners, I saw long-haired, saddle-colored Sandwich Island maidens sitting on the ground in the shade of corner houses, gazing indolently at whatever or whoever happened along; instead of wretched cobble-stone pavements, I walked on a firm foundation of coral, built up from the bottom of the sea by the absurd but persevering insect of that name, with a light layer of lava and cinders overlying the coral, belched up out of fathomless perdition long ago through the seared and blackened crater that stands dead and harmless in the distance now; instead of cramped and crowded street cars, I met dusky native women sweeping by, free as the wind, on fleet horses and astride, with gaudy riding-sashes streaming like banners behind them; instead of the combined stenches of Chinadom and Brannan street slaughter-houses, I breathed the balmy fragrance of jessamine, oleander, and the Pride of India; in place of the hurry and bustle and noisy confusion of San Francisco, I moved in the midst of a summer calm as tranquil as dawn in the Garden of Eden; in place of the Golden City's skirting sand hills and the placid bay, I saw on the one side a framework of tall, precipitous mountains close at hand, clad in refreshing green, and cleft by deep, cool, chasm-like valleys—and in front the grand sweep of the ocean: a brilliant, transparent green near the shore, bound and bordered by a long white line of foamy spray dashing against the reef, and further out the dead blue water of the deep sea, flecked with "white caps," and in the far horizon a single, lonely sail—a mere accent-mark to emphasize a slumberous calm and a solitude that were without sound or limit. When the sun sunk down—the one intruder from other realms and persistent in suggestions of them—it was tranced luxury to sit in the perfumed air and forget that there was any world but these enchanted islands.

It was such ecstasy to dream, and dream—till you got a bite. A scorpion bite. Then the first duty was to get up out of the grass and

A BITE.

kill the scorpion; and the next to bathe the bitten place with alcohol or brandy; and the next to resolve to keep out of the grass in future. Then came an adjournment to the bed-chamber and the pastime of writing up the day's journal with one hand and the destruction of mosquitoes with the other—a whole community of them at a slap. Then, observing an enemy approaching,—a hairy tarantula on stilts—why not set the spittoon on him? It is done, and the projecting ends of his paws give a luminous idea of the magnitude of his reach. Then to bed and become a promenade for a centipede with forty-two legs on a side and every foot hot enough to burn a hole through a raw-hide. More soaking with alcohol, and a resolution to examine the bed before entering it, in future. Then wait, and suffer, till all the mosquitoes in the neighborhood have crawled in under the bar, then slip out quickly, shut them in and sleep peacefully on the floor till morning. Meantime it is comforting to curse the tropics in occasional wakeful intervals.

We had an abundance of fruit in Honolulu, of course. Oranges, pine-apples, bananas, strawberries, lemons, limes, mangoes, gua-

RECONNOITERING.

vas, melons, and a rare and curious luxury called the chirimoya, which is deliciousness itself. Then there is the tamarind. I thought tamarinds were made to eat, but that was probably not the idea. I ate several, and it seemed to me that they were rather sour that year. They pursed up my lips, till they resembled the stem-end of a tomato, and I had to take my sustenance through a quill for twenty-four hours. They sharpened my teeth till I could have shaved with them, and gave them a "wire edge" that I was afraid would stay; but a citizen said "no, it will come off when the enamel does"—which was comforting, at any rate. I found, afterward, that only strangers eat tamarinds—but they only eat them once.

EATING TAMARINDS.

CHAPTER 64

In my diary of our third day in Honolulu, I find this:

I am probably the most sensitive man in Hawaii to-night—especially about sitting down in the presence of my betters. I have ridden fifteen or twenty miles on horseback since 5 P.M., and to tell the honest truth, I have a delicacy about sitting down at all.

An excursion to Diamond Head and the King's Cocoanut Grove was planned to-day—time, 4:30 P.M.—the party to consist of half a dozen gentlemen and three ladies. They all started at the appointed hour except myself. I was at the Government Prison, (with Capt. Fish and another whaleship-skipper, Capt. Phillips,) and got so interested in its examination that I did not notice how quickly the time was passing. Somebody remarked that it was twenty minutes past five o'clock, and that woke me up. It was a fortunate circumstance that Capt. Phillips was along with his "turn-out," as he calls a top-buggy that Capt. Cook brought here in 1778, and a horse that was here when Capt. Cook came. Capt. Phillips takes a just pride in his driving and in the speed of his horse, and to his passion for displaying them I owe it that we were only sixteen minutes coming from the prison to the American Hotel—a distance which has been estimated to be over half a mile. But it took some fearful driving. The captain's whip came down fast, and the blows started so much dust out of the horse's hide that during the last half of the journey we rode through an impenetrable fog, and ran by a pocket compass in the hands of Capt. Fish, a whaler of twenty-six years' experience, who sat there through the perilous voyage as self-possessed as if he had been on the euchre-deck of his own ship, and calmly said, "Port your helm—port," from time to time, and "Hold her a little free—steady—so-o," and "Luff—hard down to starboard!" and never once lost his presence of mind or betrayed the least anxiety by voice or manner. When we came to anchor at last, and Capt. Phillips looked at his watch and said, "Sixteen minutes—I told you it was in her! that's over three miles an hour!" I could see he felt entitled to a compliment, and so I said I had never seen lightning go like that horse. And I never had.

The landlord of the American said the party had been gone nearly an hour, but that he could give me my choice of several horses that could overtake them. I said, never mind—I preferred a safe horse to a fast one—I would like to have an excessively gentle horse—a horse with no spirit whatever—a lame one, if he had such a thing. Inside of five minutes I was mounted, and perfectly satisfied with my outfit. I had no time to label him "This is a horse," and so if the public took him for a sheep I cannot help it. I was satisfied, and that was the main thing. I could see that he had as many fine points as any man's horse, and so I hung my hat on one of them, behind the saddle, and swabbed the perspiration from my face and started. I named him after this island, "Oahu" (pronounced O-waw-hoo). The first gate he came to he started in; I had neither whip nor spur, and so I simply argued the case with him. He resisted argument, but ultimately yielded to insult and abuse. He backed out of that gate and steered for another one on the other side of the street. I triumphed by my former process. Within the next six hundred yards he crossed the street fourteen times and attempted thirteen gates, and in the meantime the tropical sun was beating down and threatening to cave the top of my head in, and I was literally dripping with perspiration. He abandoned the gate business after that and went along peaceably enough, but absorbed in meditation. I noticed this latter circumstance, and it soon began to fill me with apprehension. I said to myself, this creature is planning some new outrage, some fresh deviltry or other—no horse ever thought over a subject so profoundly as this one is doing just for nothing. The more this thing preyed upon my mind the more uneasy I became, until the suspense became almost unbearable and I dismounted to see if there was anything wild in his eye—for I had heard that the eye of this noblest of our domestic animals is very expressive. I cannot describe what a load of anxiety was lifted from my mind when I found that he was only asleep. I woke him up and started him into a faster walk, and then the villainy of his nature came out again. He tried to climb over a stone wall, five or

LOOKING FOR MISCHIEF.

six feet high. I saw that I must apply force to this horse, and that I might as well begin first as last. I plucked a stout switch from a tamarind tree, and the moment he saw it, he surrendered. He broke into a convulsive sort of a canter, which had three short steps in it and one long one, and reminded me alternately of the clattering shake of the great earthquake, and the sweeping plunging of the Ajax in a storm.

And now there can be no fitter occasion than the present to pronounce a left-handed blessing upon the man who invented the American saddle. There is no seat to speak of about it—one might as well sit in a shovel—and the stirrups are nothing but an ornamental nuisance. If I were to write down here all the abuse I expended on those stirrups, it would make a large book, even without pictures. Sometimes I got one foot so far through, that the stirrup partook of the nature of an anklet; sometimes both feet were through, and I was handcuffed by the legs; and sometimes my feet got clear out and left the stirrups wildly dangling about my shins. Even when I was in proper position and carefully balanced upon the balls of my feet, there was no comfort in it, on account of my nervous dread that they were going to slip one way or the other in a moment. But the subject is too exasperating to write about.

A mile and a half from town, I came to a grove of tall cocoanut trees, with clean, branchless stems reaching straight up sixty or seventy feet and topped with a spray of green foliage sheltering clusters of cocoanuts—not more picturesque than a forest of colossal ragged parasols, with bunches of magnified grapes under

A FAMILY LIKENESS.

them, would be. I once heard a grouty northern invalid say that a cocoanut tree might be poetical, possibly it was; but it looked like a feather-duster struck by lightning. I think that describes it better than a picture—and yet, without any question, there is something fascinating about a cocoanut tree—and graceful, too.

About a dozen cottages, some frame and the others of native grass, nestled sleepily in the shade here and there. The grass cabins are of a grayish color, are shaped much like our own cottages, only with higher and steeper roofs usually, and are made of some kind of weed strongly bound together in bundles. The roofs are very thick, and so are the walls; the latter have square holes in them for windows. At a little distance these cabins have a furry appearance, as if they might be made of bear skins. They are very cool and pleasant inside. The King's flag was flying from the roof of one of the cottages, and his Majesty was probably within. He owns the whole concern thereabouts, and passes his time there frequently, on sultry days "laying off." The spot is called "The King's Grove."

Near by is an interesting ruin—the meagre remains of an ancient heathen temple—a place where human sacrifices were offered up in those old bygone days when the simple child of nature, yielding momentarily to sin when sorely tempted, acknowledged his error when calm reflection had shown it to him, and came forward with noble frankness and offered up his grandmother as an atoning sacrifice—in those old days when the luckless sinner could keep on cleansing his conscience and achieving periodical happiness as long as his relations held out; long, long before the missionaries braved a thousand privations to come and make them permanently miserable by telling them how beautiful and how blissful a place heaven is, and how nearly impossible it is to get there; and showed the poor native how dreary a place perdition is and what unnecessarily liberal facilities there are for going to it; showed him how, in his ignorance, he had gone and fooled away all his kin-folks to no purpose; showed him what rapture it is to work all day long for fifty cents to buy food for next day with, as compared with fishing for pastime and lolling in the shade through eternal summer, and eating of the bounty that nobody labored to provide but Nature. How sad it is to think of the multitudes who have gone to their graves in this beautiful island and never knew there was a hell!

This ancient temple was built of rough blocks of lava, and was simply a roofless enclosure a hundred and thirty feet long and seventy wide—nothing but naked walls, very thick, but not much higher than a man's head. They will last for ages, no doubt, if left unmolested. Its three altars and other sacred appurtenances have crumbled and passed away years ago. It is said that in the old times thousands of human beings were slaughtered here, in the presence of naked and howling savages. If these mute stones could speak, what tales they could tell, what pictures they could describe, of fettered victims writhing under the knife; of massed forms straining forward out of the gloom, with ferocious faces lit up by the sacrificial fires; of the background of ghostly trees; of the dark pyramid of Diamond Head standing sentinel over the uncanny scene, and the peaceful moon looking down upon it through rifts in the cloud-rack!

When Kamehameha (pronounced Ka-may-ha-may-ah) the Great—who was a sort of a Napoleon in military genius and uniform success—invaded this island of Oahu three-quarters of a century ago, and exterminated the army sent to oppose him, and took full and final possession of the country, he searched out the dead body of the King of Oahu, and those of the principal chiefs, and impaled their heads on the walls of this temple.

Those were savage times when this old slaughter-house was in its prime. The King and the chiefs ruled the common herd with a rod of iron; made them gather all the provisions the masters needed; build all the houses and temples; stand all the expenses, of whatever kind; take kicks and cuffs for thanks; drag out lives well flavored with misery, and then suffer death for trifling offenses or yield up their lives on the sacrificial altars to purchase favors from the gods for their hard rulers. The missionaries have clothed them, educated them, broken up the tyrannous authority of their chiefs, and given them freedom and the right to enjoy whatever their hands and brains produce, with equal laws for all and punishment for all alike who transgress them. The contrast is so strong—the benefit conferred upon this people by the missionaries is so prominent, so palpable and so unquestionable, that the frankest compliment I can pay them, and the best, is simply to point to the condition of the Sandwich Islanders of Capt. Cook's time, and their condition to-day. Their work speaks for itself.

CHAPTER 65

By and by, after a rugged climb, we halted on the summit of a hill which commanded a far-reaching view. The moon rose and flooded mountain and valley and ocean with a mellow radiance, and out of the shadows of the foliage the distant lights of Honolulu glinted like an encampment of fire-flies. The air was heavy with the fragrance of flowers. The halt was brief. Gayly laughing and talking, the party galloped on, and I clung to the pommel and cantered after. Presently we came to a place where no grass grew—a wide expanse of deep sand. They said it was an old battle-ground. All around everywhere, not three feet apart, the bleached bones of men gleamed white in the moonlight. We picked up a lot of them for mementoes. I got quite a number of arm bones and leg bones—of great chiefs, maybe, who had fought savagely in that fearful battle in the old days, when blood flowed like wine where we now stood—and wore the choicest of them out on Oahu afterward, trying to make him go. All sorts of bones could be found except skulls; but a citizen said, irreverently, that there had been an unusual number of "skull-hunters" there lately—a species of sportsmen I had never heard of before.

Nothing whatever is known about this place—its story is a secret that will never be revealed. The oldest natives make no pretense of being possessed of its history. They say these bones were here when they were children. They were here when their grandfathers were children—but how they came here, they can only conjecture. Many people believe this spot to be an ancient battleground, and it is usual to call it so; and they believe that these skeletons have lain for ages just where their proprietors fell in the great fight. Other people believe that Kamehameha I fought his first battle here. On this point, I have heard a story, which may have been taken from one of the numerous books which have been written concerning these islands—I do not know where the narrator got it. He said that when Kamehameha (who was at first merely a subordinate chief on the island of Hawaii), landed here, he brought a large army with him, and encamped at Waikiki. The Oahuans marched against him, and so confident were they of success that they readily acceded to a demand of their priests that they should draw a line where these bones now lie, and take an oath that, if forced to retreat at all, they would never retreat beyond this boundary. The priests told them that death and everlasting punishment would overtake any who violated the oath, and the march was resumed. Kamehameha drove them back step by step; the priests fought in the front rank and exhorted them both by voice and inspiriting example to remember their oath—to die, if need be, but never cross the fatal line. The struggle was manfully maintained, but at last the chief priest fell, pierced to the heart with a spear, and the unlucky omen fell like a blight upon the brave souls at his back; with a triumphant shout the invaders pressed forward—the line was crossed—the offended gods deserted the despairing army, and, accepting the doom their perjury had brought upon them, they broke and fled over the plain where Honolulu stands now—up the beautiful Nuuanu Valley—paused a moment, hemmed in by precipitous mountains on either hand and the frightful precipice of the Pari in front, and then were driven over—a sheer plunge of six hundred feet!

The story is pretty enough, but Mr. Jarves's excellent history says the Oahuans were intrenched in Nuuanu Valley; that Kamehameha ousted them, routed them, pursued them up the valley and drove them over the precipice. He makes no mention of our bone-yard at all in his book.

Impressed by the profound silence and repose that rested over the beautiful landscape, and being, as usual, in the rear, I gave voice to my thoughts. I said:

"What a picture is here slumbering in the solemn glory of the moon! How strong the rugged outlines of the dead volcano stand out against the clear sky! What a snowy fringe marks the bursting of the surf over the long, curved reef! How calmly the dim city sleeps yonder in the plain! How soft the shadows lie upon the stately mountains that border the dream-haunted Manoa Valley! What a grand pyramid of billowy clouds towers above the storied Pari! How the grim warriors of the past seem flocking in ghostly squadrons to their ancient battlefield again—how the wails of the dying well up from the—"

At this point the horse called Oahu sat down in the sand. Sat down to listen, I suppose. Never mind what he heard. I stopped

SAT DOWN TO LISTEN.

apostrophising and convinced him that I was not a man to allow contempt of court on the part of a horse. I broke the back-bone of a chief over his rump and set out to join the cavalcade again.

Very considerably fagged out we arrived in town at nine o'clock at night, myself in the lead—for when my horse finally came to understand that he was homeward bound and hadn't far to go, he turned his attention strictly to business.

This is a good time to drop in a paragraph of information. There is no regular livery stable in Honolulu, or, indeed, in any part of the kingdom of Hawaii; therefore, unless you are acquainted with wealthy residents (who all have good horses), you must hire animals of the wretchedest description from the Kanakas (*i. e.* natives.) Any horse you hire, even though it be from a white man, is not often of much account, because it will be brought in for you from some ranch, and has necessarily been leading a hard life. If the Kanakas who have been caring for him (inveterate riders they are) have not ridden him half to death every day themselves, you can depend upon it they have been doing the same thing by proxy, by clandestinely hiring him out. At least, so I am informed. The result is, that no horse has a chance to eat, drink, rest, recuperate, or look well or feel well, and so strangers go about the Islands mounted as I was to-day.

In hiring a horse from a Kanaka, you must have all your eyes about you, because you can rest satisfied that you are dealing with a shrewd unprincipled rascal. You may leave your door open and your trunk unlocked as long as you please, and he will not meddle with your property; he has no important vices and no inclination to commit robbery on a large scale; but if he can get ahead of you in the horse business, he will take a genuine delight in doing it. This trait is characteristic of horse-jockeys, the world over, is it not? He will overcharge you if he can; he will hire you a fine-looking horse at night (anybody's—maybe the King's, if the royal steed be in convenient view), and bring you the mate to my Oahu in the morning, and contend that it is the same animal. If you make trouble, he will get out by saying it was not himself who made the bargain with you, but his brother, "who went out in the country this morning." They have always got a "brother" to shift the responsibility upon. A victim said to one of these fellows one day:

"But I know I hired the horse of you, because I noticed that scar on your cheek."

The reply was not bad: "Oh, yes—yes—my brother all same—we twins!"

A friend of mine, J. Smith, hired a horse yesterday, the Kanaka warranting him to be in excellent condition. Smith had a saddle and blanket of his own, and he ordered the Kanaka to put these on the horse. The Kanaka protested that he was perfectly willing to trust the gentleman with the saddle that was already on the ani-

"MY BROTHER ALL SAME—WE TWINS!"

mal, but Smith refused to use it. The change was made; then Smith noticed that the Kanaka had only changed the saddles, and had left the original blanket on the horse; he said he forgot to change the blankets, and so, to cut the bother short, Smith mounted and rode away. The horse went lame a mile from town, and afterward got to cutting up some extraordinary capers. Smith got down and took off the saddle, but the blanket stuck fast to the horse—glued to a procession of raw places. The Kanaka's mysterious conduct stood explained.

Another friend of mine bought a pretty good horse from a native, a day or two ago, after a tolerably thorough examination of the animal. He discovered to-day that the horse was as blind as a bat, in one eye. He meant to have examined that eye, and came home with a general notion that he had done it; but he remembers now that every time he made the attempt his attention was called to something else by his victimizer.

One more instance, and then I will pass to something else. I am informed that when a certain Mr. L., a visiting stranger, was here he bought a pair of very respectable-looking match horses from a native. They were in a little stable with a partition through the middle of it—one horse in each apartment. Mr. L. examined one of them critically through a window (the Kanaka's "brother" having gone to the country with the key), and then went around the house and examined the other through a window on the other side. He said it was the neatest match he had ever seen, and paid for the horses on the spot. Whereupon the Kanaka departed to join his brother in the country. The fellow had shamefully swindled L. There was only one "match" horse, and he had examined his starboard side through one window and his port side through another! I decline to believe this story, but I give it because it is worth something as a fanciful illustration of a fixed fact—namely, that the Kanaka horse-jockey is fertile in invention and elastic in conscience.

EXTRAORDINARY CAPERS.

You can buy a pretty good horse for forty or fifty dollars, and a good enough horse for all practical purposes for two dollars and a half. I estimate Oahu to be worth somewhere in the neighborhood of thirty-five cents. A good deal better animal than he is was sold here day before yesterday for a dollar and seventy-five cents, and sold again to-day for two dollars and twenty-five cents; Williams bought a handsome and lively little pony yesterday for ten dollars; and about the best common horse on the island (and he is a really good one) sold yesterday, with Mexican saddle and bridle, for seventy dollars—a horse which is well and widely known, and greatly respected for his speed, good disposition and everlasting bottom. You give your horse a little grain once a day; it comes from San

Francisco, and is worth about two cents a pound; and you give him as much hay as he wants; it is cut and brought to the market by natives, and is not very good; it is baled into long, round bundles, about the size of a large man; one of them is stuck by the middle on each end of a six-foot pole, and the Kanaka shoulders the pole

A LOAD OF HAY.

and walks about the streets between the upright bales in search of customers. These hay bales, thus carried, have a general resemblance to a colossal capital H.

The hay-bundles cost twenty-five cents apiece, and one will last a horse about a day. You can get a horse for a song, a week's hay for another song, and you can turn your animal loose among the luxuriant grass in your neighbor's broad front yard without a song at all—you do it at midnight, and stable the beast again before morning. You have been at no expense thus far, but when you come to buy a saddle and bridle they will cost you from twenty to thirty-five dollars. You can hire a horse, saddle and bridle at from seven to ten dollars a week, and the owner will take care of them at his own expense.

It is time to close this day's record—bed time. As I prepare for sleep, a rich voice rises out of the still night, and, far as this ocean rock is toward the ends of the earth, I recognize a familiar home air. But the words seem somewhat out of joint:

Waikiki lantani oe Kaa hooly hooly wawhoo.

Translated, that means "When we were marching through Georgia."

CHAPTER 66

PASSING through the market place we saw that feature of Honolulu under its most favorable auspices—that is, in the full glory of Saturday afternoon, which is a festive day with the natives. The native girls by twos and threes and parties of a dozen, and sometimes in whole platoons and companies, went cantering up and down the neighboring streets astride of fleet but homely horses,

SANDWICH ISLAND GIRLS.

and with their gaudy riding habits streaming like banners behind them. Such a troop of free and easy riders, in their natural home, the saddle, makes a gay and graceful spectacle. The riding habit I speak of is simply a long, broad scarf, like a tavern table-cloth brilliantly colored, wrapped around the loins once, then apparently passed between the limbs and each end thrown backwards over the same, and floating and flapping behind on both sides beyond the horse's tail like a couple of fancy flags; then, slipping the stirrup-irons between her toes, the girl throws her chest forward, sits up like a Major General and goes sweeping by like the wind.

The girls put on all the finery they can on Saturday afternoon—fine black silk robes; flowing red ones that nearly put your eyes out; others as white as snow; still others that discount the rainbow; and they wear their hair in nets, and trim their jaunty hats with fresh flowers, and encircle their dusky throats with home-made necklaces of the brilliant vermillion-tinted blossom of the *ohia;* and they fill the markets and the adjacent streets with their bright presences, and smell like a rag factory on fire with their offensive cocoanut oil.

Occasionally you see a heathen from the sunny isles away down in the South Seas, with his face and neck tattooed till he looks like the customary mendicant from Washoe who has been blown up in a mine. Some are tattooed a dead blue color down to the upper lip—masked, as it were—leaving the natural light yellow skin of Micronesia unstained from thence down; some with broad marks drawn down from hair to neck, on both sides of the face, and a strip of the original yellow skin, two inches wide, down the centre—a gridiron with a spoke broken out; and some with the entire face discolored with the popular mortification tint, relieved only by one or two thin, wavy threads of natural yellow running across the face from ear to ear, and eyes twinkling out of this darkness, from under shadowing hat-brims, like stars in the dark of the moon.

Moving among the stirring crowds, you come to the poi merchants, squatting in the shade on their hams, in true native fashion, and surrounded by purchasers. (The Sandwich Islanders always squat on their hams, and who knows but they may be the old original "ham sandwiches?" The thought is pregnant with interest.) The poi looks like common flour paste, and is kept in large bowls formed of a species of gourd, and capable of holding from one to three or four gallons. Poi is the chief article of food among the natives, and is prepared from the *taro* plant. The *taro* root looks like a thick, or, if you please, a corpulent sweet potato, in shape, but is of a light purple color when boiled. When boiled it answers as a passable substitute for bread. The buck Kanakas bake it under ground, then mash it up well with a heavy lava pestle, mix water with it until it becomes a paste, set it aside and let it ferment, and then it is poi—and an unseductive mixture it is, almost tasteless before it ferments and too sour for a luxury afterward. But nothing is more nutritious. When solely used, however, it produces acrid humors, a fact which sufficiently accounts for the humorous character of the Kanakas. I think there must be as much of a knack in handling poi as there is in eating with chopsticks. The forefinger is thrust into the mess and stirred quickly round several times and drawn as quickly out, thickly coated, just as if it were poulticed; the head is thrown back, the finger inserted in the mouth and the delicacy stripped off and swallowed—the eye closing gently, meanwhile, in a languid sort of ecstasy. Many a different finger goes into the same bowl and many a different kind of dirt and shade and quality of flavor is added to the virtues of its contents.

ORIGINAL HAM SANDWICH.

Around a small shanty was collected a crowd of natives buying the *awa* root. It is said that but for the use of this root the destruction of the people in former times by certain imported diseases would have been far greater than it was, and by others it is said that this is merely a fancy. All agree that poi will rejuvenate a man who is used up and his vitality almost annihilated by hard drinking, and that in some kinds of diseases it will restore health after all medicines have failed; but all are not willing to allow to the *awa* the virtues claimed for it. The natives manufacture an intoxicating drink from it which is fearful in its effects when persistently indulged in. It covers the body with dry, white scales, inflames the eyes, and causes premature decrepitude. Although the man before whose establishment we stopped has to pay a Government license of eight hundred dollars a year for the exclusive right to sell *awa* root, it is said that he makes a small fortune every twelve-month; while saloon-keepers, who pay a thousand dollars a year for the privilege of retailing whisky, etc., only make a bare living.

We found the fish market crowded; for the native is very fond of fish, and *eats the article raw and alive!* Let us change the subject.

In old times here Saturday was a grand gala day indeed. All the native population of the town forsook their labors, and those of the surrounding country journeyed to the city. Then the white folks had to stay indoors, for every street was so packed with charging cavaliers and cavalieresses that it was next to impossible to thread one's way through the cavalcades without getting crippled.

At night they feasted and the girls danced the lascivious *hula-hula*—a dance that is said to exhibit the very perfection of educated motion of limb and arm, hand, head and body, and the exactest uniformity of movement and accuracy of "time." It was performed by a circle of girls with no raiment on them to speak of, who went through an infinite variety of motions and figures without prompting, and yet so true was their "time," and in such perfect concert did they move that when they were placed in a straight line, hands, arms, bodies, limbs and heads waved, swayed, gesticulated, bowed, stooped, whirled, squirmed, twisted and undulated as if they were part and parcel of a single individual; and it was difficult to believe they were not moved in a body by some exquisite piece of mechanism.

Of late years, however, Saturday has lost most of its quondam gala features. This weekly stampede of the natives interfered too much with labor and the interests of the white folks, and by sticking in a law here, and preaching a sermon there, and by various other means, they gradually broke it up. The demoralizing *hula-hula* was forbidden to be performed, save at night, with closed doors, in presence of few spectators, and only by permission duly procured from the authorities and the payment of ten dollars for the same. There are few girls now-a-days able to dance this ancient national dance in the highest perfection of the art.

The missionaries have christianized and educated all the natives. They all belong to the Church, and there is not one of them, above the age of eight years, but can read and write with facility in the native tongue. It is the most universally educated race of people outside of China. They have any quantity of books, printed in the Kanaka language, and all the natives are fond of reading. They are inveterate church-goers—nothing can keep them away. All this ameliorating cultivation has at last built up in the native women a profound respect for chastity—in other people. Perhaps that is enough to say on that head. The national sin will die out when the race does, but perhaps not earlier. But doubtless this purifying is not far off, when we reflect that contact with civilization and the whites has reduced the native population from *four hundred thousand* (Capt. Cook's estimate,) to *fifty-five thousand* in something over eighty years!

Society is a queer medley in this notable missionary, whaling and governmental centre. If you get into conversation with a stranger, and experience that natural desire to know what sort of ground you are treading on by finding out what manner of man your stranger is, strike out boldly and address him as "Captain." Watch him narrowly, and if you see by his countenance that you are on the wrong tack, ask him where he preaches. It is a safe bet that he is either a missionary or captain of a whaler. I am now personally acquainted with seventy-two captains and ninety-six missionaries. The captains and ministers form one-half of the population; the third fourth is composed of common Kanakas and mercantile foreigners and their families, and the final fourth is made up of high officers of the Hawaiian Government. And there are just about cats enough for three apiece all around.

A solemn stranger met me in the suburbs the other day, and said:

"Good morning, your reverence. Preach in the stone church yonder, no doubt?"

"No, I don't. I'm not a preacher."

"Really, I beg your pardon, Captain. I trust you had a good season. How much oil—"

"Oil? What do you take me for? I'm not a whaler."

"Oh, I beg a thousand pardons, your Excellency. Major General in the household troops, no doubt? Minister of the Interior, likely?

Secretary of War? First Gentleman of the Bed-chamber? Commissioner of the Royal—"

"Stuff! I'm no official. I'm not connected in any way with the Government."

"Bless my life! Then, who the mischief are you? what the mischief are you? and how the mischief did you get here, and where in thunder did you come from?"

"I'm only a private personage—an unassuming stranger—lately arrived from America."

"No? Not a missionary! not a whaler! not a member of his Majesty's Government! not even Secretary of the Navy! Ah, Heaven! it is too blissful to be true; alas, I do but dream. And yet that noble,

I KISSED HIM FOR HIS MOTHER.

honest countenance—those oblique, ingenuous eyes—that massive head, incapable of—of—anything; your hand; give me your hand, bright waif. Excuse these tears. For sixteen weary years I have yearned for a moment like this, and—"

Here his feelings were too much for him, and he swooned away. I pitied this poor creature from the bottom of my heart. I was deeply moved. I shed a few tears on him and kissed him for his mother. I then took what small change he had and "shoved."

CHAPTER 67

I STILL quote from my journal:

I found the national Legislature to consist of half a dozen white men and some thirty or forty natives. It was a dark assemblage. The nobles and Ministers (about a dozen of them altogether) occupied the extreme left of the hall, with David Kalakaua (the King's Chamberlain) and Prince William at the head. The President of the Assembly, his Royal Highness M. Kekuanaoa,* and the Vice President (the latter a white man,) sat in the pulpit, if I may so term it.

The President is the King's father. He is an erect, strongly built, massive featured, white-haired, tawny old gentleman of eighty years of age or thereabouts. He was simply but well dressed, in a blue cloth coat and white vest, and white pantaloons, without spot, dust or blemish upon them. He bears himself with a calm, stately dignity, and is a man of noble presence. He was a young man and a distinguished warrior under that terrific fighter, Kamehameha I, more than half a century ago. A knowledge of his career suggested some such thought as this: "This man, naked as the day he was born, and war-club and spear in hand, has charged at the head of a horde of savages against other hordes of savages more than a generation and a half ago, and reveled in slaughter and carnage; has worshipped wooden images on his devout knees; has seen hundreds of his race offered up in heathen temples as sacrifices to wooden idols, at a time when no missionary's foot had ever pressed this soil, and he had never heard of the white man's God; has believed his enemy could secretly pray him to death; has seen the day, in his childhood, when it was a crime punishable by death for a man to eat with his wife, or for a plebeian to let his shadow fall upon the King—and now look at him: an educated Christian;

*Since dead.

neatly and handsomely dressed; a high-minded, elegant gentleman; a traveler, in some degree, and one who has been the honored guest of royalty in Europe; a man practiced in holding the reins of an enlightened government, and well versed in the politics of his country and in general, practical information. Look at him, sitting there presiding over the deliberations of a legislative body, among whom are white men—a grave, dignified, statesmanlike personage, and as seemingly natural and fitted to the place as if he had been born in it and had never been out of it in his lifetime. How the experiences of this old man's eventful life shame the cheap inventions of romance!"

Kekuanaoa is not of the blood royal. He derives his princely rank from his wife, who was a daughter of Kamehameha the Great. Under other monarchies the male line takes precedence of the female in tracing genealogies, but here the opposite is the case—the female line takes precedence. Their reason for this is exceedingly sensible, and I recommend it to the aristocracy of Europe: They say it is easy to know who a man's mother was, but, etc., etc.

The christianizing of the natives has hardly even weakened some of their barbarian superstitions, much less destroyed them. I have just referred to one of these. It is still a popular belief that if your enemy can get hold of any article belonging to you he can get down on his knees over it and *pray you to death.* Therefore many a native gives up and dies merely because he *imagines* that some enemy is putting him through a course of damaging prayer. This praying an individual to death seems absurd enough at a first glance, but then when we call to mind some of the pulpit efforts of certain of our own ministers the thing looks plausible.

AN ENEMY'S PRAYER.

In former times, among the Islanders, not only a plurality of wives was customary, but a *plurality of husbands* likewise. Some native women of noble rank had as many as six husbands. A woman thus supplied did not reside with all her husbands at once, but lived several months with each in turn. An understood sign hung at her door during these months. When the sign was taken down, it meant "NEXT."

In those days woman was rigidly taught to "know her place." Her place was to do all the work, take all the cuffs, provide all the food, and content herself with what was left after her lord had finished his dinner. She was not only forbidden, by ancient law, and under penalty of death, to eat with her husband or enter a canoe, but was debarred, under the same penalty, from eating bananas, pine-apples, oranges and other choice fruits at any time or in any place. She had to confine herself pretty strictly to "poi" and hard work. These poor ignorant heathen seem to have had a sort of groping idea of what came of woman eating fruit in the Garden of Eden, and they did not choose to take any more chances. But the missionaries broke up this satisfactory arrangement of things. They liberated woman and made her the equal of man.

The natives had a romantic fashion of burying some of their children alive when the family became larger than necessary. The missionaries interfered in this matter too, and stopped it.

To this day the natives are able to *lie down and die whenever they want to,* whether there is anything the matter with them or not. If a Kanaka takes a notion to die, that is the end of him; nobody can persuade him to hold on; all the doctors in the world could not save him.

A luxury which they enjoy more than anything else, is a large funeral. If a person wants to get rid of a troublesome native, it is only necessary to promise him a fine funeral and name the hour and he will be on hand to the minute—at least his remains will.

All the natives are Christians, now, but many of them still desert to the Great Shark God for temporary succor in time of trouble. An eruption of the great volcano of Kilauea, or an earthquake, always brings a deal of latent loyalty to the Great Shark God to the surface. It is common report that the King, educated, cultivated and refined Christian gentleman as he undoubtedly is, still turns to the idols of his fathers for help when disaster threatens. A planter caught a shark, and one of his christianized natives testified his emancipation from the thrall of ancient superstition by assisting to dissect the shark after a fashion forbidden by his abandoned creed. But remorse shortly began to torture him. He grew moody and sought solitude; brooded over his sin, refused food, and finally said he must die and ought to die, for he had sinned against the Great Shark God and could never know peace any more. He was proof against persuasion and ridicule, and in the course of a day or two took to his bed and died, although he showed no symptom of disease. His young daughter followed his lead and suffered a like fate within the week. Superstition is ingrained in the native blood and bone and it is only natural that it should crop out in time of distress. Wherever one goes in the Islands, he will find small piles of stones by the wayside, covered with leafy offerings, placed there by the natives to appease evil spirits or honor local deities belonging to the mythology of former days.

In the rural districts of any of the Islands, the traveler hourly comes upon parties of dusky maidens bathing in the streams or in the sea without any clothing on and exhibiting no very intemperate zeal in the matter of hiding their nakedness. When the mis-

VISITING THE MISSIONARIES.

sionaries first took up their residence in Honolulu, the native women would pay their families frequent friendly visits, day by day, not even clothed with a blush. It was found a hard matter to convince them that this was rather indelicate. Finally the missionaries provided them with long, loose calico robes, and that ended the difficulty—for the women would troop through the town, stark naked, with their robes folded under their arms, march to the missionary houses and then proceed to dress! The natives soon manifested a strong proclivity for clothing, but it was shortly apparent that they only wanted it for grandeur. The missionaries imported a quantity of hats, bonnets, and other male and female wearing apparel, instituted a general distribution, and begged the people not to come to church naked, next Sunday, as usual. And they did not; but the national spirit of unselfishness led them to divide up with neighbors who were not at the distribution, and next Sabbath the poor preachers could hardly keep countenance before their vast congregations. In the midst of the reading of a hymn a brown, stately dame would sweep up the aisle with a world of airs, with nothing in the world on but a "stove-pipe" hat and a pair of cheap gloves; another dame would follow, tricked out in a man's shirt, and nothing else; another one would enter with a flourish, with simply the sleeves of a bright calico dress tied around her waist and the rest of the garment dragging behind like a peacock's tail off duty; a stately "buck" Kanaka would stalk in with a woman's bonnet on, wrong side before—only this, and nothing more; after him would stride his fellow, with the legs of a pair of pantaloons tied around his neck, the rest of his person untrammeled; in his rear would come another gentleman simply gotten up in a fiery neck-tie and a striped vest. The poor creatures were beaming with complacency and wholly unconscious of any absurdity in their appearance. They gazed at each other with happy admiration, and it was plain to see that the young girls were taking note of what each other had on, as naturally as if they had always lived in a land of Bibles and knew what churches were made for; here was the evidence of a dawning civilization. The spectacle which the congregation presented was so extraordinary and withal so moving, that the missionaries found it difficult to keep to the text and go on with the services; and by and by when the simple children of the sun began a general swapping of garments in open meeting and produced some irresistibly grotesque effects in the course of re-dressing, there was nothing for it but to cut the thing short with the benediction and dismiss the fantastic assemblage.

In our country, children play "keep house;" and in the same high-sounding but miniature way the grown folk here, with the

FULL CHURCH DRESS.

poor little material of slender territory and meagre population, play "empire." There is his royal Majesty the King, with a New York detective's income of thirty or thirty-five thousand dollars a year from the "royal civil list" and the "royal domain." He lives in a two-story frame "palace."

PLAYING EMPIRE.

And there is the "royal family"—the customary hive of royal brothers, sisters, cousins and other noble drones and vagrants usual to monarchy,—all with a spoon in the national pap-dish, and all bearing such titles as his or her Royal Highness the Prince or Princess So-and-so. Few of them can carry their royal splendors far enough to ride in carriages, however; they sport the economical Kanaka horse or "hoof it"* with the plebeians.

Then there is his Excellency the "royal Chamberlain"—a sinecure, for his Majesty dresses himself with his own hands, except

ROYALTY AND ITS SATELLITES.

when he is ruralizing at Waikiki and then he requires no dressing.

Next we have his Excellency the Commander-in-chief of the Household Troops, whose forces consist of about the number of soldiers usually placed under a corporal in other lands.

Next comes the royal Steward and the Grand Equerry in Waiting—high dignitaries with modest salaries and little to do.

Then we have his Excellency the First Gentleman of the Bedchamber—an office as easy as it is magnificent.

Next we come to his Excellency the Prime Minister, a renegade American from New Hampshire, all jaw, vanity, bombast and ignorance, a lawyer of "shyster" calibre, a fraud by nature, a humble worshipper of the sceptre above him, a reptile never tired of sneer-

*Missionary phrase.

ing at the land of his birth or glorifying the ten-acre kingdom that has adopted him—salary, four thousand dollars a year, vast consequence, and no perquisites.

Then we have his Excellency the Imperial Minister of Finance, who handles a million dollars of public money a year, sends in his annual "budget" with great ceremony, talks prodigiously of "finance," suggests imposing schemes for paying off the "national debt" (of a hundred and fifty thousand dollars,) and does it all for four thousand dollars a year and unimaginable glory.

Next we have his Excellency the Minister of War, who holds sway over the royal armies—they consist of two hundred and thirty uniformed Kanakas, mostly Brigadier Generals, and if the country ever gets into trouble with a foreign power we shall probably hear from them. I knew an American whose copper-plate visiting card bore this impressive legend: "Lieutenant-Colonel in the Royal Infantry." To say that he was proud of this distinction is stating it but tamely. The Minister of War has also in his charge some venerable swivels on Punch-Bowl Hill wherewith royal salutes are fired when foreign vessels of war enter the port.

Next comes his Excellency the Minister of the Navy—a nabob who rules the "royal fleet," (a steam-tug and a sixty-ton schooner.)

And next comes his Grace the Lord Bishop of Honolulu, the chief dignitary of the "Established Church"—for when the American Presbyterian missionaries had completed the reduction of the nation to a compact condition of Christianity, native royalty stepped in and erected the grand dignity of an "Established (Episcopal) Church" over it, and imported a cheap ready-made Bishop from England to take charge. The chagrin of the missionaries has never been comprehensively expressed, to this day, profanity not being admissible.

Next comes his Excellency the Minister of Public Instruction.

Next, their Excellencies the Governors of Oahu, Hawaii, etc., and after them a string of High Sheriffs and other small fry too numerous for computation.

Then there are their Excellencies the Envoy Extraordinary and Minister Plenipotentiary of his Imperial Majesty the Emperor of the French; her British Majesty's Minister; the Minister Resident, of the United States; and some six or eight representatives of other foreign nations, all with sounding titles, imposing dignity and prodigious but economical state.

Imagine all this grandeur in a play-house "kingdom" whose population falls absolutely short of sixty thousand souls!

The people are so accustomed to nine-jointed titles and colossal magnates that a foreign prince makes very little more stir in Honolulu than a western Congressman does in New York.

And let it be borne in mind that there is a strictly defined "court costume" of so "stunning" a nature that it would make the clown in a circus look tame and commonplace by comparison; and each Hawaiian official dignitary has a gorgeous vari-colored, gold-laced uniform peculiar to his office—no two of them are alike, and it is hard to tell which one is the "loudest." The King has a "drawing-room" at stated intervals, like other monarchs, and when these varied uniforms congregate there weak-eyed people have to contemplate the spectacle through smoked glass. Is there not a gratifying contrast between this latter-day exhibition and the one the ancestors of some of these magnates afforded the missionaries the Sunday after the old-time distribution of clothing? Behold what religion and civilization have wrought!

CHAPTER 68

While I was in Honolulu I witnessed the ceremonious funeral of the King's sister, her Royal Highness the Princess Victoria. According to the royal custom, the remains had lain in state at the palace *thirty days*, watched day and night by a guard of honor. And during all that time a great multitude of natives from the several islands had kept the palace grounds well crowded and had made the place a pandemonium every night with their howlings and wailings, beating of tom-toms and dancing of the (at other times) forbidden *hula-hula* by half-clad maidens to the music of songs of questionable decency chanted in honor of the deceased. The printed programme of the funeral procession interested me at the time; and after what I have just said of Hawaiian grandiloquence in the matter of "playing empire," I am persuaded that a perusal of it may interest the reader:

After reading the long list of dignitaries, etc., and remembering the sparseness of the population, one is almost inclined to wonder where the material for that portion of the procession devoted to "Hawaiian Population Generally" is going to be procured:

Undertaker.

Royal School. Kawaiahao School. Roman Catholic School.

Maemae School.

Honolulu Fire Department.

Mechanics' Benefit Union.

Attending Physicians.

Konohikis (Superintendents) of Crown Lands, Konohikis of Private Lands of His Majesty, Konohikis of Private Lands of Her late Royal Highness.

Governor of Oahu and Staff.

Hulumanu (Military Company).

The Prince of Hawaii's Own (Military Company).

Household Troops.

The King's Household Servants.
Servants of Her late Royal Highness.
Protestant Clergy. The Clergy of the Roman Catholic Church.
His Lordship Louis Maigret, the Rt. Rev. Bishop of Arathea,
Vicar-Apostolic of the Hawaiian Islands.
The Clergy of the Hawaiian Reformed Catholic Church.
His Lordship the Right Reverend Bishop of Honolulu.

Escort Haw. Cavalry.
Large Kahilis.
Small Kahilis.
PALL BEARERS.

[HEARSE.]

PALL BEARERS.
Small Kahilis.
Large Kahilis.*
Escort Haw. Cavalry.

Her Majesty Queen Emma's Carriage.
His Majesty's Staff.
Carriage of Her late Royal Highness.
Carriage of Her Majesty the Queen Dowager.
The King's Chancellor.
Cabinet Ministers.
His Excellency the Minister Resident of the United States.
H. I. M.'s Commissioner.
H. B. M.'s Acting Commissioner.
Judges of Supreme Court.
Privy Councillors.
Members of the Legislative Assembly.
Consular Corps.
Circuit Judges.
Clerks of Government Departments.
Members of the Bar.
Collector General, Custom House Officers and Officers of the Customs.
Marshal and Sheriffs of the different Islands.
King's Yeomanry.
Foreign Residents.
Ahahui Kaahumanu.

*Ranks of long-handled mops made of gaudy feathers—sacred to royalty. They are stuck in the ground around the tomb and left there.

Hawaiian Population Generally.
Hawaiian Cavalry.
Police Force.

I resume my journal at the point where the procession arrived at the royal mausoleum:

As the procession filed through the gate, the military deployed handsomely to the right and left and formed an avenue through which the long

A MODERN FUNERAL.

column of mourners passed to the tomb. The coffin was borne through the door of the mausoleum, followed by the King and his chiefs, the great officers of the kingdom, foreign Consuls, Embassadors and distinguished guests (Burlingame and Gen. Van Valkenburgh). Several of the *kahilis* were then fastened to a framework in front of the tomb, there to remain until they decay and fall to pieces, or, forestalling this, until another scion of royalty dies. At this point of the proceedings the multitude set up such a heart-broken wailing as I hope never to hear again. The soldiers fired three volleys of musketry—the wailing being previously silenced to permit of the guns being heard. His Highness Prince William, in a showy military uniform (the "true prince," this—scion of the house over-thrown by the present dynasty—he was formerly betrothed to the Princess but was not allowed to marry her), stood guard and paced back and forth within the door. The privileged few who followed the coffin into the mausoleum remained some time, but the King soon came out and stood in the door and near one side of it. A stranger could have guessed his rank (although he was so simply and unpretentiously dressed) by the profound deference paid him by all persons in his vicinity; by seeing his high officers receive his quiet orders and suggestions with bowed and uncovered heads; and by observing how careful those persons who came out of the mausoleum were to avoid "crowding" him (although there was room enough in the doorway for a wagon to pass, for that matter); how respectfully they edged out sideways, scraping their backs against the wall and always presenting a front view of their persons to his Majesty, and never putting their hats on until they were well out of the royal presence.

He was dressed entirely in black—dress-coat and silk hat—and looked rather democratic in the midst of the showy uniforms about him. On his breast he wore a large gold star, which was half hidden by the lappel of his coat. He remained at the door a half hour, and occasionally gave an order to the men who were erecting the *kahilis* before the tomb. He had the good taste to make one of them substitute black crape for the ordinary hempen rope he was about to tie one of them to the framework with. Finally he entered his carriage and drove away, and the populace shortly began to drop into his wake. While he was in view there was but one man who attracted more attention than himself, and that was Harris (the Yankee Prime Minister). This feeble personage had crape enough around his hat to express the grief of an entire nation, and as usual he neglected no opportunity of making himself conspicuous and exciting the admiration of the simple Kanakas. Oh! noble ambition of this modern Richelieu!

It is interesting to contrast the funeral ceremonies of the Princess Victoria with those of her noted ancestor Kamehameha the Conqueror, who died fifty years ago—in 1819, the year before the first missionaries came:

On the 8th of May, 1819, at the age of sixty-six, he died as he had lived, in the faith of his country. It was his misfortune not to have come in contact with men who could have rightly influenced his religious aspirations. Judged by his advantages, and compared with the most eminent of his countrymen, he may be justly styled, not only great, but good. To this day his memory warms the heart and elevates the national feelings of Hawaiians. They are proud of their old warrior-king; they love his name; his deeds form their historical age; and an enthusiasm everywhere prevails, shared even by foreigners who knew his worth, that constitutes the firmest pillar of the throne of his dynasty.

In lieu of human victims (the custom of that age), a sacrifice of three hundred dogs attended his obsequies; no mean holocaust, when their national value and the estimation in which they were held are considered. The bones of Kamehameha after being kept for a while, were so carefully concealed that all knowledge of their final resting place is now lost. There was a proverb current among the common people that the bones of a cruel king could not be hid; they made fish-hooks and arrows of them, upon which in using them they vented their abhorrence of his memory in bitter execrations.

The account of the circumstances of his death, as written by the native historians, is full of minute detail, but there is scarcely a line of it which does not mention or illustrate some bygone custom of the country. In this respect it is the most comprehensive document I have yet met with. I will quote it entire:

When Kamehameha was dangerously sick and the priests were unable to cure him, they said, "Be of good courage, and build a house for the god" (his own private god or idol), "that thou mayest recover." The chiefs corroborated this advice of the priests, and a place of worship was prepared for Kukailimoku, and consecrated in the evening. They proposed also to the king, with a view to prolong his life, that human victims should be sacrificed to his deity; upon which the greater part of the people absconded through fear of death, and concealed themselves in hiding-places till the tabu,* in which destruction impended, was past. It is doubtful whether Kamehameha approved of the plan of the chiefs and priests to sacrifice men, as he was known to say, "The men are sacred for the king;" meaning that they were for the service of his successor. This information was derived from his son, Liholiho.

After this, his sickness increased to such a degree that he had not strength to turn himself in his bed. When another season, consecrated for worship at the new temple—heiau—arrived, he said to his son Liholiho, "Go thou and make supplication to thy god; I am not able to go and will offer my prayers at home." When his devotions to his feathered god, Kukailimoku, were concluded, a certain religiously disposed individual, who had a bird-god, suggested to the king that through its influence his sickness might be removed. The name of this god was Pua; its body was made of a bird, now eaten by the Hawaiians, and called in their language *alae.* Kamehameha was willing that a trial should be made, and two houses were constructed to facilitate the experiment; but while dwelling in them, he became so very weak as not to receive food. After lying there three days, his wives, children, and chiefs, perceiving that he was very low, returned him to his own house. In the evening he was carried to the

***Tabu* (pronounced tah-boo,) means prohibition (we have borrowed it,) or sacred. The *tabu* was sometimes permanent, sometimes temporary; and the person or thing placed under *tabu* was for the time being sacred to the purpose for which it was set apart. In the above case the victims selected under the *tabu* would be sacred to the sacrifice.

eating-house,* where he took a little food in his mouth, which he did not swallow; also a cup of water. The chiefs requested him to give them his counsel. But he made no reply, and was carried back to the dwelling-house; but when near midnight, ten o'clock, perhaps, he was carried again to the place to eat; but, as before, he merely tasted of what was presented to him. Then Kaikioewa addressed him thus: "Here we all are, your younger brethren, your son, Liholiho, and your foreigner; impart to us your dying charge, that Liholiho and Kaahumanu may hear." Then Kamehameha inquired, "What do you say?" Kaikioewa repeated, "Your counsels for us." He then said, "Move on in my good way, and ——." He could proceed no further. The foreigner—Mr. Young—embraced and kissed him. Hoapili also embraced him, whispering something in his ear, after which he was taken back to the house. About twelve, he was carried once more to the house for eating, into which his head entered, while his body was in the dwelling-house immediately adjoining. It should be remarked, that this frequent carrying of a sick chief to and fro from one house to another, resulted from the tabu system then in force. There were at that time six houses (huts) connected with an establishment; one was for worship, one for the men to eat in, an eating-house for the women, a house to sleep in, a house in which to manufacture kapa (native cloth), and one where at certain intervals the women might dwell in seclusion.

The sick king was once more taken to his house, when he expired; this was at two o'clock—a circumstance from which Leleiohoku derived his name. As he breathed his last Kalaimoku came to the eating-house to order those in it to go out. There were two aged persons thus directed to depart; one went, the other remained on account of love to the king, by whom he had formerly been kindly sustained. The children also were sent away. Then Kalaimoku came to the house, and the chiefs had a consultation. One of them spoke thus: "This is my thought, we will eat him raw."† Kaahumanu (one of the dead king's widows) replied, "Perhaps his body is not at our disposal; that is more properly with his successor. Our part in him—the breath—has departed; his remains will be disposed of by Liholiho."

After this conversation, the body was taken into the consecrated house for the performance of the proper rites by the priest and the new king. The name of this ceremony is *uko;* and when the sacred hog was baked, the priest offered it to the dead body and it became a god, the king at the same time repeating the customary prayers.

*It was deemed pollution to eat in the same hut a person slept in—the fact that the patient was dying could not modify the rigid etiquette.

†This sounds suspicious, in view of the fact that all Sandwich Island historians, white and black, protest that cannibalism never existed in the Islands. However, since they only proposed to "eat him raw" we "won't count that." But it would certainly have been cannibalism if they had cooked him.—M. T.

Then the priest, addressing himself to the king and chiefs, said, "I will now make known to you the rules to be observed respecting persons to be sacrificed on the burial of this body. If you obtain one man before the corpse is removed, one will be sufficient; but after it leaves this house four will be required. If delayed until we carry the corpse to the grave, there must be ten; but after it is deposited in the grave, there must be fifteen. To-morrow morning there will be a tabu, and if the sacrifice be delayed until that time, forty men must die."

Then the high priest Hewahewa, inquired of the chiefs, where shall be the residence of King Liholiho? They replied, "Where, indeed? you of all men ought to know." Then the priest observed, "There are two suitable places; one is Kau, the other is Kohala." The chiefs preferred the latter, as it was more thickly inhabited. The priest added, "These are proper places for the king's residence, but he must not remain in Kona, for it is polluted." This was agreed to. It was now break of day. As he was being carried to the place of burial, the people perceived that their king was dead, and they wailed. When the corpse was removed from the house to the tomb, a distance of one chain, the procession was met by a certain man who was ardently attached to the deceased. He leaped upon the chiefs who were carrying the king's body; he desired to die with him, on account of his love. The chiefs drove him away. He persisted in making numerous attempts, which were unavailing. Kalaimoku also had it in his heart to die with him, but was prevented by Hookio.

The morning following Kamehameha's death, Liholiho and his train departed for Kohala according to the suggestions of the priest, to avoid the defilement occasioned by the dead. At this time, if a chief died the land was polluted, and the heirs sought a residence in another part of the country, until the corpse was dissected and the bones tied in a bundle, which being done, the season of defilement terminated. If the deceased were not a chief, the house only was defiled, which became pure again on the burial of the body. Such were the laws on this subject.

On the morning in which Liholiho sailed in his canoe for Kohala, the chiefs and people mourned after their manner on occasion of a chief's death, conducting themselves like madmen, and like beasts. Their conduct was such as to forbid description. The priests, also, put into action the sorcery apparatus, that the person who had prayed the king to death might die; for it was not believed that Kamehameha's departure was the effect either of sickness or old age. When the sorcerers set up by their fire-places sticks with a strip of kapa flying at the top, the chief Keeaumoku, Kaahumanu's brother, came, in a state of intoxication, and broke the flag-staff of the sorcerers, from which it was inferred that Kaahumanu and her friends had been instrumental in the king's death. On this account they were subjected to abuse.

You have the contrast, now, and a strange one it is. This great Queen, Kaahumanu, who was "subjected to abuse" during the frightful orgies that followed the King's death, in accordance with ancient custom, afterward became a devout Christian and a steadfast and powerful friend of the missionaries.

Dogs were, and still are, reared and fattened for food, by the natives—hence the reference to their value in one of the above paragraphs.

Forty years ago it was the custom in the Islands to suspend all law for a certain number of days after the death of a royal personage; and then a saturnalia ensued which one may picture to himself after a fashion, but not in the full horror of the reality. The people shaved their heads, knocked out a tooth or two, plucked out an eye sometimes, cut, bruised, mutilated or burned their flesh, got drunk, burned each other's huts, maimed or murdered one another according to the caprice of the moment, and both sexes gave themselves up to brutal and unbridled licentiousness. And after it all,

FORMER FUNERAL ORGIES.

came a torpor from which the nation slowly emerged bewildered and dazed, as if from a hideous half-remembered nightmare. They were not the salt of the earth, those "gentle children of the sun."

The natives still keep up an old custom of theirs which cannot be comforting to an invalid. When they think a sick friend is going to die, a couple of dozen neighbors surround his hut and keep up a deafening wailing night and day till he either dies or gets well. No doubt this arrangement has helped many a subject to a shroud before his appointed time.

They surround a hut and wail in the same heart-broken way when its occupant returns from a journey. This is their dismal idea of a welcome. A very little of it would go a great way with most of us.

CHAPTER 69

BOUND for Hawaii, (a hundred and fifty miles distant,) to visit the great volcano and behold the other notable things which distinguish that island above the remainder of the group, we sailed from Honolulu on a certain Saturday afternoon, in the good schooner Boomerang.

The Boomerang was about as long as two street cars, and about as wide as one. She was so small (though she was larger than the majority of the inter-island coasters) that when I stood on her deck I felt but little smaller than the Colossus of Rhodes must have felt when he had a man-of-war under him. I could reach the water when she lay over under a strong breeze. When the captain and my comrade (a Mr. Billings), myself and four other persons were all assembled on the little after portion of the deck which is sacred to the cabin passengers, it was full—there was not room for any more quality folks. Another section of the deck, twice as large as ours, was full of natives of both sexes, with their customary dogs, mats, blankets, pipes, calabashes of poi, fleas, and other luxuries and baggage of minor importance. As soon as we set sail the natives all lay down on the deck as thick as negroes in a slave-pen, and smoked, conversed, and spit on each other, and were truly sociable.

The little low-ceiled cabin below was rather larger than a hearse, and as dark as a vault. It had two coffins on each side—I mean two bunks. A small table, capable of accommodating three persons at dinner, stood against the forward bulkhead, and over it hung the dingiest whale-oil lantern that ever peopled the obscurity of a dungeon with ghostly shapes. The floor room unoccupied was not extensive. One might swing a cat in it, perhaps, but not a long cat. The hold forward of the bulkhead had but little freight in it, and from morning till night a portly old rooster, with a voice like Balaam's ass, and the same disposition to use it, strutted up and down in that part of the vessel and crowed. He usually took dinner at six o'clock, and then, after an hour devoted to meditation, he mounted a barrel and crowed a good part of the night. He got hoarser and hoarser all the time, but he scorned to allow any personal consideration to interfere with his duty, and kept up his labors in defiance of threatened diphtheria.

A PASSENGER.

Sleeping was out of the question when he was on watch. He was a source of genuine aggravation and annoyance. It was worse than useless to shout at him or apply offensive epithets to him—he only took these things for applause, and strained himself to make more noise. Occasionally, during the day, I threw potatoes at him through an aperture in the bulkhead, but he only dodged and went on crowing.

The first night, as I lay in my coffin, idly watching the dim lamp swinging to the rolling of the ship, and snuffing the nauseous odors of bilge water, I felt something gallop over me. I turned out promptly. However, I turned in again when I found it was only a rat. Presently something galloped over me once more. I knew it was not a rat this time, and I thought it might be a centipede, because the captain had killed one on deck in the afternoon. I turned out. The first glance at the pillow showed me a repulsive sentinel perched upon each end of it—cockroaches as large as peach leaves—fellows with long, quivering antennæ and fiery, malignant eyes. They were grating their teeth like tobacco worms, and appeared to be dissatisfied about something. I had often heard that these reptiles were in the habit of eating off sleeping sailors' toe nails down to the quick, and I would not get in the bunk any more. I lay down on the floor. But a rat came and bothered me, and shortly afterward a procession of cockroaches arrived and camped in my hair. In a few moments the rooster was crowing with uncommon spirit and a party of fleas were throwing double summersets about my person in the wildest disorder, and taking a bite every time they struck. I was beginning to feel really annoyed. I got up and put my clothes on and went on deck.

The above is not overdrawn; it is a truthful sketch of inter-island schooner life. There is no such thing as keeping a vessel in elegant condition, when she carries molasses and Kanakas.

It was compensation for my sufferings to come unexpectedly upon so beautiful a scene as met my eye—to step suddenly out of the sepulchral gloom of the cabin and stand under the strong light of the moon—in the centre, as it were, of a glittering sea of liquid

MOONLIGHT ON THE WATER.

silver—to see the broad sails straining in the gale, the ship heeled over on her side, the angry foam hissing past her lee bulwarks, and sparkling sheets of spray dashing high over her bows and raining upon her decks; to brace myself and hang fast to the first object that presented itself, with hat jammed down and coat tails whipping in the breeze, and feel that exhilaration that thrills in one's hair and quivers down his back-bone when he knows that every inch of canvas is drawing and the vessel cleaving through the waves at her utmost speed. There was no darkness, no dimness, no obscurity there. All was brightness, every object was vividly defined. Every prostrate Kanaka; every coil of rope; every calabash of poi; every puppy; every seam in the flooring; every bolthead; every object, however minute, showed sharp and distinct in its every outline; and the shadow of the broad mainsail lay black as a pall upon the deck, leaving Billings's white upturned face glorified and his body in a total eclipse.

Monday morning we were close to the island of Hawaii. Two of its high mountains were in view—Mauna Loa and Hualalai. The latter is an imposing peak, but being only ten thousand feet high is seldom mentioned or heard of. Mauna Loa is said to be sixteen thousand feet high. The rays of glittering snow and ice, that clasped its summit like a claw, looked refreshing when viewed from the blistering climate we were in. One could stand on that mountain (wrapped up in blankets and furs to keep warm), and while he nibbled a snow-ball or an icicle to quench his thirst he could look down the long sweep of its sides and see spots where plants are growing that grow only where the bitter cold of winter prevails; lower down he could see sections devoted to productions that thrive in the temperate zone alone; and at the bottom of the mountain he could see the home of the tufted cocoa palms and other species of vegetation that grow only in the sultry atmosphere of eternal summer. He could see all the climes of the world at a single glance of the eye, and that glance would only pass over a distance of four or five miles as the bird flies!

By and by we took boat and went ashore at Kailua, designing to ride horseback through the pleasant orange and coffee region of Kona, and rejoin the vessel at a point some leagues distant. This journey is well worth taking. The trail passes along on high ground—say a thousand feet above sea level—and usually about a mile distant from the ocean, which is always in sight, save that occasionally you find yourself buried in the forest in the midst of a rank, tropical vegetation and a dense growth of trees, whose great boughs overarch the road and shut out sun and sea and everything, and leave you in a dim, shady tunnel, haunted with invisible singing birds and fragrant with the odor of flowers. It was pleasant to ride occasionally in the warm sun, and feast the eye upon the ever-changing panorama of the forest (beyond and below us), with its many tints, its softened lights and shadows, its billowy undulations sweeping gently down from the mountain to the sea. It was pleasant also, at intervals, to leave the sultry sun and pass into the cool, green depths of this forest and indulge in sentimental reflections under the inspiration of its brooding twilight and its whispering foliage.

GOING INTO THE MOUNTAINS.

We rode through one orange grove that had ten thousand trees in it! They were all laden with fruit.

At one farmhouse we got some large peaches of excellent flavor. This fruit, as a general thing, does not do well in the Sandwich Islands. It takes a sort of almond shape, and is small and bitter. It needs frost, they say, and perhaps it does; if this be so, it will have a good opportunity to go on needing it, as it will not be likely to get it. The trees from which the fine fruit I have spoken of came had been planted and replanted *sixteen times*, and to this treatment the proprietor of the orchard attributed his success.

We passed several sugar plantations—new ones and not very extensive. The crops were, in most cases, third rattoons. [NOTE.—The first crop is called "plant cane;" subsequent crops which spring from the original roots, without replanting, are called "rattoons."] Almost everywhere on the island of Hawaii sugar-cane matures in twelve months, both rattoons and plant, and although it ought to be taken off as soon as it tassels, no doubt, it is not absolutely necessary to do it until about four months afterward. In Kona, the average yield of an acre of ground is *two tons* of sugar, they say. This is only a moderate yield for these islands, but would be astounding for Louisiana and most other sugar growing countries. The plantations in Kona being on pretty high ground—up among the light and frequent rains—no irrigation whatever is required.

CHAPTER 70

We stopped some time at one of the plantations, to rest ourselves and refresh the horses. We had a chatty conversation with several gentlemen present; but there was one person, a middle aged man, with an absent look in his face, who simply glanced up, gave us good-day and lapsed again into the meditations which our coming had interrupted. The planters whispered us not to mind him—crazy. They said he was in the Islands for his health; was a preacher; his home, Michigan. They said that if he woke up presently and fell to talking about a correspondence which he had some time held with Mr. Greeley about a trifle of some kind, we must humor him and listen with interest; and we must humor his fancy that this correspondence was the talk of the world.

It was easy to see that he was a gentle creature and that his madness had nothing vicious in it. He looked pale, and a little worn, as if with perplexing thought and anxiety of mind. He sat a long time,

THE DEMENTED.

looking at the floor, and at intervals muttering to himself and nodding his head acquiescingly or shaking it in mild protest. He was lost in his thought, or in his memories. We continued our talk with the planters, branching from subject to subject. But at last the word "circumstance," casually dropped, in the course of conversation, attracted his attention and brought an eager look into his countenance. He faced about in his chair and said:

"Circumstance? What circumstance? Ah, I know—I know too well. So you have heard of it too." [With a sigh.] "Well, no matter—all the world has heard of it. All the world. The whole world. It is a large world, too, for a thing to travel so far in—now isn't it? Yes, yes—the Greeley correspondence with Erickson has created the saddest and bitterest controversy on both sides of the ocean—and still they keep it up! It makes us famous, but at what a sorrowful sacrifice! I was so sorry when I heard that it had caused that bloody and distressful war over there in Italy. It was little comfort to me, after so much bloodshed, to know that the victors sided with me, and the vanquished with Greeley. It is little comfort to know that Horace Greeley is responsible for the battle of Sadowa, and not me. Queen Victoria wrote me that she felt just as I did about it—she said that as much as she was opposed to Greeley and the spirit he showed in the correspondence with me, she would not have had Sadowa happen for hundreds of dollars. I can show you her letter, if you would like to see it. But gentlemen, much as you may think you know about that unhappy correspondence, you cannot know the *straight* of it till you hear it from my lips. It has always been garbled in the journals, and even in history. Yes, even in history—think of it! Let me—*please* let me, give you the matter, exactly as it occurred. I truly will not abuse your confidence."

Then he leaned forward, all interest, all earnestness, and told his story—and told it appealingly, too, and yet in the simplest and most unpretentious way; indeed, in such a way as to suggest to one, all the time, that this was a faithful, honorable witness, giving evidence in the sacred interest of justice, and under oath. He said:

"Mrs. Beazeley—Mrs. Jackson Beazeley, widow, of the village of Campbellton, Kansas,—wrote me about a matter which was near her heart—a matter which many might think trivial, but to her it was a thing of deep concern. I was living in Michigan, then—serving in the ministry. She was, and is, an estimable woman—a woman to whom poverty and hardship have proven incentives to industry, in place of discouragements. Her only treasure was her son William, a youth just verging upon manhood; religious, amiable, and sincerely attached to agriculture. He was the widow's comfort and her pride. And so, moved by her love for him, she wrote me about a matter, as I have said before, which lay near her heart—because it lay near her boy's. She desired me to confer with Mr. Greeley about turnips. Turnips were the dream of her child's young ambition. While other youths were frittering away in frivolous amusements the precious years of budding vigor which God had given them for useful preparation, this boy was patiently enriching his mind with information concerning turnips. The sentiment which he felt toward the turnip was akin to adoration. He could not think of the turnip without emotion; he could not speak of it calmly; he could not contemplate it without exaltation. He could not eat it without shedding tears. All the poetry in his sensitive nature was in sympathy with the gracious vegetable. With the earliest pipe of dawn he sought his patch, and when the curtaining night drove him from it he shut himself up with his books and garnered statistics till sleep overcame him. On rainy days he sat and talked hours together with his mother about turnips. When company came, he made it his loving duty to put aside everything

DISCUSSING TURNIPS.

else and converse with them all the day long of his great joy in the turnip. And yet, was this joy rounded and complete? Was there no secret alloy of unhappiness in it? Alas, there was. There was a canker gnawing at his heart; the noblest inspiration of his soul eluded his endeavor—viz.: he could not make of the turnip a climbing vine. Months went by; the bloom forsook his cheek, the fire faded out of his eye; sighings and abstraction usurped the place of smiles and cheerful converse. But a watchful eye noted these things and in time a motherly sympathy unsealed the secret. Hence the letter to me. She pleaded for attention—she said her boy was dying by inches.

"I was a stranger to Mr. Greeley, but what of that? The matter was urgent. I wrote and begged him to solve the difficult problem if possible and save the student's life. My interest grew, until it partook of the anxiety of the mother. I waited in much suspense. At last the answer came.

"I found that I could not read it readily, the handwriting being unfamiliar and my emotions somewhat wrought up. It seemed to refer in part to the boy's case, but chiefly to other and irrelevant matters—such as paving-stones, electricity, oysters, and something which I took to be 'absolution' or 'agrarianism,' I could not be certain which; still, these appeared to be simply casual mentions, nothing more; friendly in spirit, without doubt, but lacking the connection or coherence necessary to make them useful. I judged that my understanding was affected by my feelings, and so laid the letter away till morning.

"In the morning I read it again, but with difficulty and uncertainty still, for I had lost some little rest and my mental vision seemed clouded. The note was more connected, now, but did not meet the emergency it was expected to meet. It was too discursive. It appeared to read as follows, though I was not certain of some of the words:

> Polygamy dissembles majesty; extracts redeem polarity; causes hitherto exist. Ovations pursue wisdom, or warts inherit and condemn. Boston, botany, cakes, folony undertakes, but who shall allay? We fear not.
>
> Yrxwly, HEVACE EVEELOJ.

"But there did not seem to be a word about turnips. There seemed to be no suggestion as to how they might be made to grow

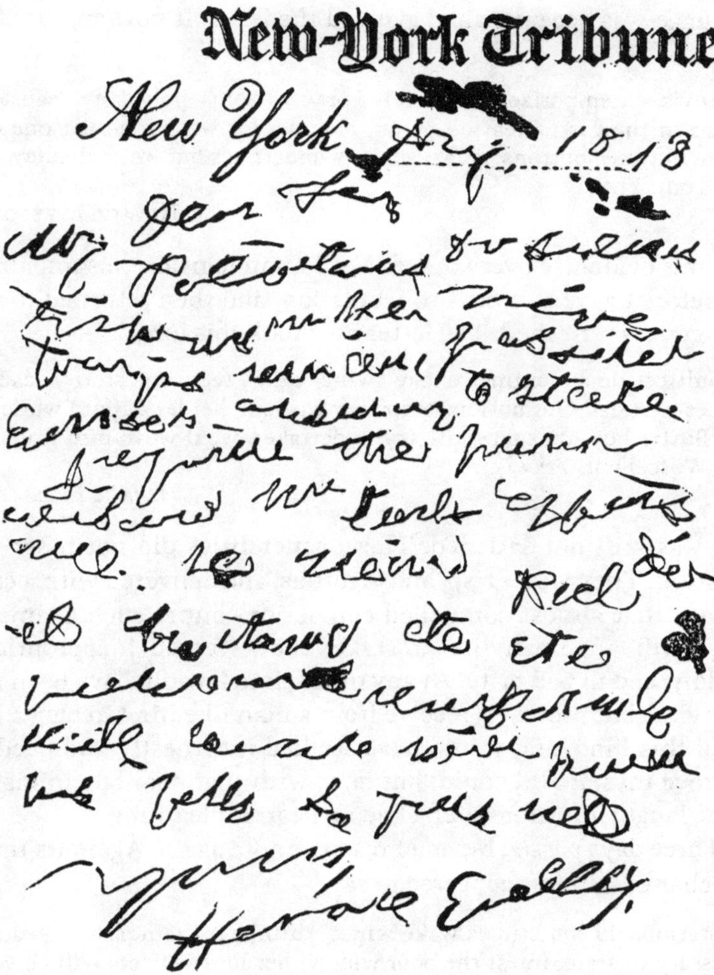

New-York Tribune.

New York Aug. 18

Dear Sir

Yours,
Horace Greeley.

like vines. There was not even a reference to the Beazeleys. I slept upon the matter; I ate no supper, neither any breakfast next morning. So I resumed my work with a brain refreshed, and was very hopeful. *Now* the letter took a different aspect—all save the signature, which latter I judged to be only a harmless affectation of Hebrew. The epistle was necessarily from Mr. Greeley, for it bore the printed heading of *The Tribune,* and I had written to no one else there. The letter, I say, had taken a different aspect, but still its language was eccentric and avoided the issue. It now appeared to say:

> Bolivia extemporizes mackerel; borax esteems polygamy; sausages wither in the east. Creation perdu, is done; for woes inherent one can damn. Buttons, buttons, corks, geology underrates but we shall allay. My beer's out. Yrxwly,
>
> HEVACE EVEELOJ.

"I was evidently overworked. My comprehension was impaired. Therefore I gave two days to recreation, and then returned to my task greatly refreshed. The letter now took this form:

> Poultices do sometimes choke swine; tulips reduce posterity; causes leather to resist. Our notions empower wisdom, her let's afford while we can. Butter but any cakes, fill any undertaker, we'll wean him from his filly. We feel hot. Yrxwly,
>
> HEVACE EVEELOJ.

"I was still not satisfied. These generalities did not meet the question. They were crisp, and vigorous, and delivered with a confidence that almost compelled conviction; but at such a time as this, with a human life at stake, they seemed inappropriate, worldly, and in bad taste. At any other time I would have been not only glad, but proud, to receive from a man like Mr. Greeley a letter of this kind, and would have studied it earnestly and tried to improve myself all I could; but now, with that poor boy in his far home languishing for relief, I had no heart for learning.

"Three days passed by, and I read the note again. Again its tenor had changed. It now appeared to say:

> Potations do sometimes wake wines; turnips restrain passion; causes necessary to state. Infest the poor widow; her lord's effects will be void. But dirt, bathing, etc., etc., followed unfairly, will worm him from his folly—so swear not. Yrxwly,
>
> HEVACE EVEELOJ.

"This was more like it. But I was unable to proceed. I was too much worn. The word 'turnips' brought temporary joy and encouragement, but my strength was so much impaired, and the delay might be so perilous for the boy, that I relinquished the idea of pursuing the translation further, and resolved to do what I ought to have done at first. I sat down and wrote Mr. Greeley as follows:

Dear Sir: I fear I do not entirely comprehend your kind note. It cannot be possible, sir, that 'turnips restrain passion'—at least the study or contemplation of turnips cannot—for it is this very employment that has scorched our poor friend's mind and sapped his bodily strength. But if they *do* restrain it, will you bear with us a little further and explain how they should be prepared? I observe that you say 'causes necessary to state,' but you have omitted to state them.

Under a misapprehension, you seem to attribute to me interested motives in this matter—to call it by no harsher term. But I assure you, dear sir, that if I seem to be 'infesting the widow,' it is all *seeming,* and void of reality. It is from no seeking of mine that I am in this position. She asked me, herself, to write you. I never have infested her—indeed I scarcely know her. I do not infest anybody. I try to go along, in my humble way, doing as near right as I can, never harming anybody, and never *throwing out insinuations.* As for 'her lord and his effects,' they are of no interest to me. I trust I have effects enough of my own—shall endeavor to get along with them, at any rate, and not go mousing around to get hold of somebody's that are 'void.' But do you not see?—this woman is a *widow*—she has no 'lord.' He is dead—or pretended to be, when they buried him. Therefore, no amount of 'dirt, bathing,' etc., etc., howsoever 'unfairly followed' will be likely to 'worm him from his folly'—if being dead and a ghost is 'folly.' Your closing remark is as unkind as it was uncalled for; and if report says true you might have applied it to yourself, sir, with more point and less impropriety. Very Truly Yours,

Simon Erickson.

"In the course of a few days, Mr. Greeley did what would have saved a world of trouble, and much mental and bodily suffering and misunderstanding, if he had done it sooner. To wit, he sent an intelligible rescript or translation of his original note, made in a plain hand by his clerk. Then the mystery cleared, and I saw that his heart had been right, all the time. I will recite the note in its clarified form:

[Translation.]

Potatoes do sometimes make vines; turnips remain passive: cause unnecessary to state. Inform the poor widow her lad's efforts will be vain. But diet, bathing, etc. etc., followed uniformly, will wean him from his folly—so fear not. Yours,

Horace Greeley.

"But alas, it was too late, gentlemen—too late. The criminal delay had done its work—young Beazeley was no more. His spirit had taken its flight to a land where all anxieties shall be charmed away, all desires gratified, all ambitions realized. Poor lad, they laid him to his rest with a turnip in each hand."

So ended Erickson, and lapsed again into nodding, mumbling, and abstraction. The company broke up, and left him so. . . . But they did not say what drove him crazy. In the momentary confusion, I forgot to ask.

CHAPTER 71

At four o'clock in the afternoon we were winding down a mountain of dreary and desolate lava to the sea, and closing our pleasant land journey. This lava is the accumulation of ages; one torrent of fire after another has rolled down here in old times, and built up the island structure higher and higher. Underneath, it is honey-combed with caves; it would be of no use to dig wells in such a place; they would not hold water—you would not find any for them to hold, for that matter. Consequently, the planters depend upon cisterns.

The last lava flow occurred here so long ago that there are none now living who witnessed it. In one place it enclosed and burned down a grove of cocoanut trees, and the holes in the lava where the trunks stood are still visible; their sides retain the impression of the bark; the trees fell upon the burning river, and becoming partly submerged, left in it the perfect counterpart of every knot and branch and leaf, and even nut, for curiosity seekers of a long distant day to gaze upon and wonder at.

There were doubtless plenty of Kanaka sentinels on guard hereabouts at that time, but they did not leave casts of their figures in the lava as the Roman sentinels at Herculaneum and Pompeii did. It is a pity it is so, because such things are so interesting, but so it is. They probably went away. They went away early, perhaps. However, they had their merits; the Romans exhibited the higher pluck, but the Kanakas showed the sounder judgment.

Shortly we came in sight of that spot whose history is so familiar to every school-boy in the wide world—Kealakekua Bay—the place where Capt. Cook, the great circumnavigator, was killed by the natives nearly a hundred years ago. The setting sun was flaming upon it, a summer shower was falling, and it was spanned by two magnificent rainbows. Two men who were in advance of us rode through one of these, and for a moment their garments shone with a more than regal splendor. Why did not Capt. Cook have taste enough to call his great discovery the Rainbow Islands? These charming spectacles are present to you at every turn; they are common in all the islands; they are visible every day, and frequently at night also—not the silvery bow we see once in an age in the States, by moonlight, but barred with all bright and beautiful colors, like the children of the sun and rain. I saw one of them a few nights ago. What the sailors call "rain-dogs"—little patches of rainbow—are often seen drifting about the heavens in these latitudes, like stained cathedral windows.

Kealakekua Bay is a little curve like the last kink of a snail shell, winding deep into the land, seemingly not more than a mile wide from shore to shore. It is bounded on one side—where the murder was done—by a little flat plain, on which stands a cocoanut grove and some ruined houses; a steep wall of lava, a thousand feet high at the upper end and three or four hundred at the lower, comes down from the mountain and bounds the inner extremity of it. From this wall the place takes its name, *Kealakekua*, which in the native tongue signifies "The Pathway of the Gods." They say (and still believe, in spite of their liberal education in Christianity), that the great god Lono, who used to live upon the hillside, always traveled that causeway when urgent business connected with heavenly affairs called him down to the seashore in a hurry.

As the red sun looked across the placid ocean through the tall, clean stems of the cocoanut trees, like a blooming whisky bloat through the bars of a city prison, I went and stood in the edge of the water on the flat rock pressed by Capt. Cook's feet when the blow was dealt which took away his life, and tried to picture in my mind the doomed man struggling in the midst of the multitude of exasperated savages—the men in the ship crowding to the vessel's side and gazing in anxious dismay toward the shore—the—but I discovered that I could not do it.

It was growing dark, the rain began to fall, we could see that the distant Boomerang was helplessly becalmed at sea, and so I adjourned to the cheerless little box of a warehouse and sat down to smoke and think, and wish the ship would make the land—for we had not eaten much for ten hours and were viciously hungry.

Plain unvarnished history takes the romance out of Capt. Cook's assassination, and renders a deliberate verdict of justifiable homicide. Wherever he went among the islands he was cordially received and welcomed by the inhabitants, and his ships lavishly supplied with all manner of food. He returned these kindnesses with insult and ill-treatment. Perceiving that the people took him for the long vanished and lamented god Lono, he encouraged them in the delusion for the sake of the limitless power it gave him; but during the famous disturbance at this spot, and while he and his comrades were surrounded by fifteen thousand maddened savages, he received a hurt and betrayed his earthly origin with a groan. It was his death-warrant. Instantly a shout went up: "He groans!—he is not a god!" So they closed in upon him and dispatched him.

His flesh was stripped from the bones and burned (except nine pounds of it which were sent on board the ships). The heart was hung up in a native hut, where it was found and eaten by three children, who mistook it for the heart of a dog. One of these children grew to be a very old man, and died in Honolulu a few years ago. Some of Cook's bones were recovered and consigned to the deep by the officers of the ships.

Small blame should attach to the natives for the killing of Cook. They treated him well. In return, he abused them. He and his men inflicted bodily injury upon many of them at different times, and killed at least three of them before they offered any proportionate retaliation.

Near the shore we found "Cook's Monument"—only a cocoanut stump, four feet high, and about a foot in diameter at the butt. It had lava boulders piled around its base to hold it up and keep it in its place, and it was entirely sheathed over, from top to bottom, with rough, discolored sheets of copper, such as ships' bottoms are coppered with. Each sheet had a rude inscription scratched upon it—with a nail, apparently—and in every case the execution was wretched. Most of these merely recorded the visits of British naval commanders to the spot, but one of them bore this legend:

"Near this spot fell
CAPTAIN JAMES COOK,
The Distinguished Circumnavigator, who Discovered these
Islands A. D. 1778."

After Cook's murder, his second in command, on board the ship, opened fire upon the swarms of natives on the beach, and one of

KEALAKEKUA BAY AND COOK'S MONUMENT.

his cannon balls cut this cocoanut tree short off and left this monumental stump standing. It looked sad and lonely enough to us, out there in the rainy twilight. But there is no other monument to Capt. Cook. True, up on the mountain side we had passed by a large enclosure like an ample hog-pen, built of lava blocks, which marks the spot where Cook's flesh was stripped from his bones and burned; but this is not properly a monument, since it was erected by the natives themselves, and less to do honor to the circumnavigator than for the sake of convenience in roasting him. A thing like a guide-board was elevated above this pen on a tall pole, and formerly there was an inscription upon it describing the memorable occurrence that had there taken place; but the sun and the wind have long ago so defaced it as to render it illegible.

Toward midnight a fine breeze sprang up and the schooner soon worked herself into the bay and cast anchor. The boat came ashore for us, and in a little while the clouds and the rain were all gone. The moon was beaming tranquilly down on land and sea, and we two were stretched upon the deck sleeping the refreshing sleep and dreaming the happy dreams that are only vouchsafed to the weary and the innocent.

CHAPTER 72

In the breezy morning we went ashore and visited the ruined temple of the lost god Lono. The high chief cook of this temple—the priest who presided over it and roasted the human sacrifices—was uncle to Obookiah, and at one time that youth was an apprentice-priest under him. Obookiah was a young native of fine mind, who, together with three other native boys, was taken to New England by the captain of a whaleship during the reign of Kamehameha I, and they were the means of attracting the attention of the religious world to their country. This resulted in the sending of missionaries there. And this Obookiah was the very same sensitive savage who sat down on the church steps and wept because his people did not have the Bible. That incident has been very elaborately painted in many a charming Sunday school book—aye, and told so plaintively and so tenderly that I have cried over it in Sunday school myself, on general principles, although at a time when I did not know much and could not understand why the people of the Sandwich Islands needed to worry so much about it as long as they did not know there was a Bible at all.

Obookiah was converted and educated, and was to have returned to his native land with the first missionaries, had he lived. The other native youths made the voyage, and two of them did good service, but the third, William Kanui, fell from grace afterward, for a time, and when the gold excitement broke out in California he journeyed thither and went to mining, although he was fifty years old. He succeeded pretty well, but the failure of Page, Bacon & Co. relieved him of six thousand dollars, and then, to all intents and purposes, he was a bankrupt in his old age and he resumed service in the pulpit again. He died in Honolulu in 1864.

Quite a broad tract of land near the temple, extending from the sea to the mountain top, was sacred to the god Lono in olden times—so sacred that if a common native set his sacrilegious foot upon it it was judicious for him to make his will, because his time had come. He might go around it by water, but he could not cross it. It was well sprinkled with pagan temples and stocked with awkward, homely idols carved out of logs of wood. There was a temple devoted to prayers for rain—and with fine sagacity it was placed at a point so well up on the mountain side that if you prayed there twenty-four times a day for rain you would be likely to get it every time. You would seldom get to your Amen before you would have to hoist your umbrella.

And there was a large temple near at hand which was built in a single night, in the midst of storm and thunder and rain, by the ghastly hands of dead men! Tradition says that by the weird glare

THE GHOSTLY BUILDERS.

of the lightning a noiseless multitude of phantoms were seen at their strange labor far up the mountain side at dead of night—flitting hither and thither and bearing great lava blocks clasped in their nerveless fingers—appearing and disappearing as the pallid lustre fell upon their forms and faded away again. Even to this day, it is said, the natives hold this dread structure in awe and reverence, and will not pass by it in the night.

At noon I observed a bevy of nude native young ladies bathing in the sea, and went and sat down on their clothes to keep them from being stolen. I begged them to come out, for the sea was rising and I was satisfied that they were running some risk. But they were not

ON GUARD.

afraid, and presently went on with their sport. They were finished swimmers and divers, and enjoyed themselves to the last degree. They swam races, splashed and ducked and tumbled each other about, and filled the air with their laughter. It is said that the first thing an Islander learns is how to swim; learning to walk being a matter of smaller consequence, comes afterward. One hears tales of native men and women swimming ashore from vessels many miles at sea—more miles, indeed, than I dare vouch for or even mention. And they tell of a native diver who went down in thirty or forty-foot waters and brought up an anvil! I think he swallowed the anvil afterward, if my memory serves me. However I will not urge this point.

I have spoken, several times, of the god Lono—I may as well furnish two or three sentences concerning him.

The idol the natives worshipped for him was a slender, unornamented staff twelve feet long. Tradition says he was a favorite god on the island of Hawaii—a great king who had been deified for meritorious services—just our own fashion of rewarding heroes, with the difference that we would have made him a Postmaster instead of a god, no doubt. In an angry moment he slew his wife, a goddess named Kaikilani Alii. Remorse of conscience drove him mad, and tradition presents us the singular spectacle of a god traveling "on the shoulder;" for in his gnawing grief he wandered about from place to place boxing and wrestling with all whom he met. Of course this pastime soon lost its novelty, inasmuch as it must necessarily have been the case that when so powerful a deity sent a frail human opponent "to grass" he never came back any more. Therefore, he instituted games called makahiki, and ordered that they should be held in his honor, and then sailed for foreign lands on a three-cornered raft, stating that he would return some day—and that was the last of Lono. He was never seen any more; his raft got swamped, perhaps. But the people always expected his return, and thus they were easily led to accept Capt. Cook as the restored god.

Some of the old natives believed Cook was Lono to the day of their death; but many did not, for they could not understand how he could die if he was a god.

Only a mile or so from Kealakekua Bay is a spot of historic interest—the place where the last battle was fought for idolatry. Of course we visited it, and came away as wise as most people do who go and gaze upon such mementoes of the past when in an unreflective mood.

While the first missionaries were on their way around the Horn, the idolatrous customs which had obtained in the Islands as far back as tradition reached were suddenly broken up. Old Kamehameha I was dead, and his son, Liholiho, the new King, was a free liver, a roystering, dissolute fellow, and hated the restraints of the ancient *tabu*. His assistant in the Government, Kaahumanu, the Queen dowager, was proud and high-spirited, and hated the *tabu* because it restricted the privileges of her sex and degraded all women very nearly to the level of brutes. So the case stood. Liholiho had half a mind to put his foot down, Kaahumanu had a whole mind to badger him into doing it, and whisky did the rest. It was probably the first time whisky ever prominently figured as an aid to civilization. Liholiho came up to Kailua as drunk as a piper, and attended a great feast; the determined Queen spurred his drunken courage up to a reckless pitch, and then, while all the multitude stared in blank dismay, he moved deliberately forward and sat down with the women! They saw him eat from the same vessel with them, and were appalled! Terrible moments drifted slowly by, and still the King ate, still he lived, still the lightnings of the insulted gods were withheld! Then conviction came like a revelation—the superstitions of a hundred generations passed from before the people like a cloud, and a shout went up, "The *tabu* is broken! the *tabu* is broken!"

THE *TABU* BROKEN.

Thus did King Liholiho and his dreadful whisky preach the first sermon and prepare the way for the new gospel that was speeding southward over the waves of the Atlantic.

The *tabu* broken and destruction failing to follow the awful sacrilege, the people, with that childlike precipitancy which has always characterized them, jumped to the conclusion that their gods were a weak and wretched swindle, just as they formerly jumped to the conclusion that Capt. Cook was no god, merely because he groaned, and promptly killed him without stopping to inquire whether a god might not groan as well as a man if it suited his convenience to do it; and satisfied that the idols were powerless to protect themselves they went to work at once and pulled them down—hacked them to pieces—applied the torch—annihilated them!

The pagan priests were furious. And well they might be; they had held the fattest offices in the land, and now they were beggared; they had been great—they had stood above the chiefs—and now they were vagabonds. They raised a revolt; they scared a number of people into joining their standard, and Kekuokalani, an ambitious offshoot of royalty, was easily persuaded to become their leader.

In the first skirmish the idolaters triumphed over the royal army sent against them, and full of confidence they resolved to march upon Kailua. The King sent an envoy to try and conciliate them, and came very near being an envoy short by the operation; the savages not only refused to listen to him, but wanted to kill him. So the King sent his men forth under Major General Kalaimoku and the two hosts met at Kuamoo. The battle was long and fierce—men and women fighting side by side, as was the custom—and when the day was done the rebels were flying in every direction in hopeless panic, and idolatry and the *tabu* were dead in the land!

The royalists marched gayly home to Kailua glorifying the new dispensation. "There is no power in the gods," said they; "they are a vanity and a lie. The army with idols was weak; the army without idols was strong and victorious!"

The nation was without a religion.

The missionary ship arrived in safety shortly afterward, timed by providential exactness to meet the emergency, and the gospel was planted as in a virgin soil.

CHAPTER 73

AT noon, we hired a Kanaka to take us down to the ancient ruins at Honaunau in his canoe—price two dollars—reasonable enough, for a sea voyage of eight miles, counting both ways.

The native canoe is an irresponsible looking contrivance. I cannot think of anything to liken it to but a boy's sled runner hollowed out, and that does not quite convey the correct idea. It is about fifteen feet long, high and pointed at both ends, is a foot and a half or two feet deep, and so narrow that if you wedged a fat man into it you might not get him out again. It sits on top of the water like a duck, but it has an outrigger and does not upset easily if you keep still. This outrigger is formed of two long bent sticks, like plow handles, which project from one side, and to their outer ends is bound a curved beam composed of an extremely light wood, which skims along the surface of the water and thus saves you from an upset on that side, while the outrigger's weight is not so easily lifted as to make an upset on the other side a thing to be greatly feared. Still, until one gets used to sitting perched upon this knife-blade, he is apt to reason within himself that it would be more comfortable if there were just an outrigger or so on the other side also.

I had the bow seat, and Billings sat amidships and faced the Kanaka, who occupied the stern of the craft and did the paddling. With the first stroke the trim shell of a thing shot out from the shore like an arrow. There was not much to see. While we were on the shallow water of the reef, it was pastime to look down into the limpid depths at the large bunches of branching coral—the unique shrubbery of the sea. We lost that, though, when we got out into the dead blue water of the deep. But we had the picture of the surf, then, dashing angrily against the crag-bound shore and sending a foaming spray high into the air. There was interest in this beetling border, too, for it was honey-combed with quaint caves and arches and tunnels, and had a rude semblance of the dilapidated architecture of ruined keeps and castles rising out of the restless sea. When this novelty ceased to be a novelty, we turned our eyes shoreward and gazed at the long mountain with its rich green forests stretching up into the curtaining clouds, and at the specks of houses in the rearward distance and the diminished schooner riding sleepily at anchor. And when these grew tiresome we dashed boldly into the midst of a school of huge, beastly porpoises engaged at their eternal game of arching over a wave and disappearing, and then doing it over again and keeping it up—always circling over, in that way, like so many well-submerged wheels. But the porpoises wheeled themselves away, and then we were thrown upon our own

SURF-BATHING—SUCCESS.

resources. It did not take many minutes to discover that the sun was blazing like a bonfire, and that the weather was of a melting temperature. It had a drowsing effect, too.

In one place we came upon a large company of naked natives, of both sexes and all ages, amusing themselves with the national pastime of surf-bathing. Each heathen would paddle three or four hundred yards out to sea, (taking a short board with him), then face the shore and wait for a particularly prodigious billow to come along; at the right moment he would fling his board upon its foamy crest and himself upon the board, and here he would come whizzing by like a bombshell! It did not seem that a lightning express train could shoot along at a more hair-lifting speed. I tried surf-bathing once, subsequently, but made a failure of it. I got the board placed right, and at the right moment, too; but missed the connection myself. The board struck the shore in three-quarters of a second, without any cargo, and I struck the bottom about the same time, with a couple of barrels of water in me. None but natives ever master the art of surf-bathing thoroughly.

SURF-BATHING—FAILURE.

At the end of an hour we had made the four miles, and landed on a level point of land, upon which was a wide extent of old ruins, with many a tall cocoanut tree growing among them. Here was the ancient City of Refuge—a vast enclosure, whose stone walls were twenty feet thick at the base, and fifteen feet high; an oblong square, a thousand and forty feet one way, and a fraction under seven hundred the other. Within this enclosure, in early times, had been three rude temples; each was two hundred and ten feet long by one hundred wide, and thirteen high.

In those days, if a man killed another anywhere on the island the relatives were privileged to take the murderer's life; and then a chase for life and liberty began—the outlawed criminal flying through pathless forests and over mountain and plain, with his hopes fixed upon the protecting walls of the City of Refuge, and the avenger of blood following hotly after him! Sometimes the race was kept up to the very gates of the temple, and the panting pair sped through long files of excited natives, who watched the contest with flashing eye and dilated nostril, encouraging the hunted refugee with sharp, inspiriting ejaculations, and sending up a ringing shout of exultation when the saving gates closed upon him and the cheated pursuer sank exhausted at the threshold. But sometimes the flying criminal fell under the hand of the avenger

THE CITY OF REFUGE.

at the very door, when one more brave stride, one more brief second of time would have brought his feet upon the sacred ground and barred him against all harm. Where did these isolated pagans get this idea of a City of Refuge—this ancient Oriental custom?

This old sanctuary was sacred to all—even to rebels in arms and invading armies. Once within its walls, and confession made to the priest and absolution obtained, the wretch with a price upon his head could go forth without fear and without danger—he was *tabu,* and to harm him was death. The routed rebels in the lost battle for idolatry fled to this place to claim sanctuary, and many were thus saved.

Close to a corner of the great enclosure is a round structure of stone, some six or eight feet high, with a level top about ten or twelve feet in diameter. This was the place of execution. A high palisade of cocoanut piles shut out its cruel scenes from the vulgar multitude. Here criminals were killed, the flesh stripped from the bones and burned, and the bones secreted in holes in the body of the structure. If the man had been guilty of a high crime, the entire corpse was burned.

The walls of the temple are a study. The same food for speculation that is offered the visitor to the Pyramids of Egypt he will find here—the mystery of how they were constructed by a people unacquainted with science and mechanics. The natives have no invention of their own for hoisting heavy weights, they had no beasts of burden, and they have never even shown any knowledge of the properties of the lever. Yet some of the lava blocks quarried out, brought over rough, broken ground, and built into this wall, six or seven feet from the ground, are of prodigious size and would weigh tons. How did they transport and how raise them?

Both the inner and outer surfaces of the walls present a smooth front and are very creditable specimens of masonry. The blocks are of all manner of shapes and sizes, but yet are fitted together with the neatest exactness. The gradual narrowing of the wall from the base upward is accurately preserved. No cement was used, but the edifice is firm and compact and is capable of resisting storm and decay for centuries. Who built this temple, and how it was built, and when, are mysteries that may never be unraveled.

Outside of these ancient walls lies a sort of coffin-shaped stone eleven feet four inches long and three feet square at the small end (it would weigh a few thousand pounds), which the high chief who held sway over this district many centuries ago brought thither on his shoulder one day to use as a lounge! This circumstance is established by the most reliable traditions. He used to lie down on it, in his indolent way, and keep an eye on his subjects at work for him and see that there was no "soldiering" done. And no doubt there was not any done to speak of, because he was a man of that sort of build that incites to attention to business on the part of an employé. He was fourteen or fifteen feet high. When he stretched himself at full length on his lounge, his legs hung down over the end, and when he snored he woke the dead. These facts are all attested by irrefragable tradition.

On the other side of the temple is a monstrous seven-ton rock, eleven feet long, seven feet wide and three feet thick. It is raised a foot or a foot and a half above the ground, and rests upon half a dozen little stony pedestals. The same old fourteen-footer brought it down from the mountain, merely for fun (he had his own notions about fun), and propped it up as we find it now and as others may find it a century hence, for it would take a score of horses to budge it from its position. They say that fifty or sixty years ago the proud Queen Kaahumanu used to fly to this rock for safety, whenever she had been making trouble with her fierce husband, and hide under it until his wrath was

THE QUEEN'S ROCK.

appeased. But these Kanakas will lie, and this statement is one of their ablest efforts—for Kaahumanu was six feet high—she was bulky—she was built like an ox—and she could no more have squeezed herself under that rock than she could have passed between the cylinders of a sugar mill. What could she gain by it, even if she succeeded? To be chased and abused by a savage husband could not be otherwise than humiliating to her high spirit, yet it could never make her feel so flat as an hour's repose under that rock would.

We walked a mile over a raised macadamized road of uniform width; a road paved with flat stones and exhibiting in its every detail a considerable degree of engineering skill. Some say that that wise old pagan Kamehameha I planned and built it, but others say it was built so long before his time that the knowledge of who constructed it has passed out of the traditions. In either case, however, as the handiwork of an untaught and degraded race it is a thing of pleasing interest. The stones are worn and smooth, and pushed apart in places, so that the road has the exact appearance of those ancient paved highways leading out of Rome which one sees in pictures.

The object of our tramp was to visit a great natural curiosity at the base of the foothills—a congealed cascade of lava. Some old forgotten volcanic eruption sent its broad river of fire down the mountain side here, and it poured down in a great torrent from an overhanging bluff some fifty feet high to the ground below. The flaming torrent cooled in the winds from the sea, and remains there to-day, all seamed, and frothed and rippled—a petrified Niagara. It is very picturesque, and withal so natural that one might almost imagine it still flowed. A smaller stream trickled over the cliff and built up an isolated pyramid about thirty feet high, which has the semblance of a mass of large gnarled and knotted vines and roots and stems intricately twisted and woven together.

We passed in behind the cascade and the pyramid, and found the bluff pierced by several cavernous tunnels, whose crooked courses we followed a long distance.

Two of these winding tunnels stand as proof of Nature's mining abilities. Their floors are level, they are seven feet wide, and their roofs are gently arched. Their height is not uniform, however. We passed through one a hundred feet long, which leads through a spur of the hill and opens out well up in the sheer wall of a precipice whose foot rests in the waves of the sea. It is a commodious tunnel, except that there are occasional places in it where one must stoop to pass under. The roof is lava, of course, and is thickly studded with little lava-pointed icicles an inch long, which hardened as they dripped. They project as closely together as the iron teeth of a corn-sheller, and if one will stand up straight and walk any distance there, he can get his hair combed free of charge.

CHAPTER 74

We got back to the schooner in good time, and then sailed down to Kau, where we disembarked and took final leave of the vessel. Next day we bought horses and bent our way over the summer-clad mountain-terraces, toward the great volcano of Kilauea (Ke-low-way-ah). We made nearly a two days' journey of it, but that was on account of laziness. Toward sunset on the second day, we reached an elevation of some four thousand feet above sea level, and as we picked our careful way through billowy wastes of lava long generations ago stricken dead and cold in the climax of its tossing fury, we began to come upon signs of the near presence of the volcano—signs in the nature of ragged fissures that discharged jets of sulphurous vapor into the air, hot from the molten ocean down in the bowels of the mountain.

Shortly the crater came into view. I have seen Vesuvius since, but it was a mere toy, a child's volcano, a soup-kettle, compared to this. Mount Vesuvius is a shapely cone thirty-six hundred feet high; its crater an inverted cone only three hundred feet deep, and not more than a thousand feet in diameter, if as much as that; its fires meagre, modest, and docile. But here was a vast, perpendicular, walled cellar, nine hundred feet deep in some places, thirteen hundred in others, level-floored, and *ten miles in circumference!* Here was a yawning pit upon whose floor the armies of Russia could camp, and have room to spare.

Perched upon the edge of the crater, at the opposite end from where we stood, was a small lookout house—say three miles away. It assisted us, by comparison, to comprehend and appreciate the great depth of the basin—it looked like a tiny martin-box clinging at the eaves of a cathedral. After some little time spent in resting and looking and ciphering, we hurried on to the hotel.

By the path it is half a mile from the Volcano House to the lookout house. After a hearty supper we waited until it was thoroughly dark and then started to the crater. The first glance in that direction revealed a scene of wild beauty. There was a heavy fog over the crater and it was splendidly illuminated by the glare from the fires below. The illumination was two miles wide and a mile high, perhaps; and if you ever, on a dark night and at a distance beheld the light from thirty or forty blocks of distant buildings all on fire at once, reflected strongly against overhanging clouds, you can form a fair idea of what this looked like.

A colossal column of cloud towered to a great height in the air immediately above the crater, and the outer swell of every one of its vast folds was dyed with a rich crimson lustre, which was subdued to a pale rose tint in the depressions between. It glowed like a muffled torch and stretched upward to a dizzy height toward the zenith. I thought it just possible that its like had not been seen since the children of Israel wandered on their long march through the desert so many centuries ago over a path illuminated by the mysterious "pillar of fire." And I was sure that I now had a vivid conception of what the majestic "pillar of fire" was like, which almost amounted to a revelation.

THE PILLAR OF FIRE.

Arrived at the little thatched lookout house, we rested our elbows on the railing in front and looked abroad over the wide crater and down over the sheer precipice at the seething fires beneath us. The view was a startling improvement on my daylight experience. I turned to see the effect on the balance of the company and found the reddest-faced set of men I almost ever saw. In the strong light every countenance glowed like red-hot iron, every shoulder was suffused with crimson and shaded rearward into dingy, shapeless obscurity! The place below looked like the infernal regions and these men like half-cooled devils just come up on a furlough.

I turned my eyes upon the volcano again. The "cellar" was tolerably well lighted up. For a mile and a half in front of us and half a mile on either side, the floor of the abyss was magnificently illuminated; beyond these limits the mists hung down their gauzy curtains and cast a deceptive gloom over all that made the twinkling fires in the remote corners of the crater seem countless leagues removed—made them seem like the camp-fires of a great army far away. Here was room for the imagination to work! You could imagine those lights the width of a continent away—and that hidden under the intervening darkness were hills, and winding rivers, and weary wastes of plain and desert—and even then the tremendous vista stretched on, and on, and on!—to the fires and far beyond! You could not compass it—it was the idea of eternity made tangible—and the longest end of it made visible to the naked eye!

The greater part of the vast floor of the desert under us was as black as ink, and apparently smooth and level; but over a mile square of it was ringed and streaked and striped with a thousand branching streams of liquid and gorgeously brilliant fire! It looked like a colossal railroad map of the State of Massachusetts done in chain lightning on a midnight sky. Imagine it—imagine a coal-black sky shivered into a tangled net-work of angry fire!

Here and there were gleaming holes a hundred feet in diameter, broken in the dark crust, and in them the melted lava—the color a dazzling white just tinged with yellow—was boiling and surging furiously; and from these holes branched numberless bright torrents in many directions, like the spokes of a wheel, and kept a tolerably straight course for a while and then swept round in huge rainbow curves, or made a long succession of sharp worm-fence angles, which looked precisely like the fiercest jagged lightning. These streams met other streams, and they mingled with and crossed and recrossed each other in every conceivable direction, like skate tracks on a popular skating ground. Sometimes streams twenty or thirty feet wide flowed from the holes to some distance without dividing—and through the opera glasses we could see that they ran down small, steep hills and were genuine cataracts of fire, white at their source, but soon cooling and turning to the richest red, grained with alternate lines of black and gold. Every now and then masses of the dark crust broke away and floated slowly down

THE CRATER.

these streams like rafts down a river. Occasionally the molten lava flowing under the superincumbent crust broke through—split a dazzling streak, from five hundred to a thousand feet long, like a sudden flash of lightning, and then acre after acre of the cold lava parted into fragments, turned up edgewise like cakes of ice when a great river breaks up, plunged downward and were swallowed in the crimson cauldron. Then the wide expanse of the "thaw" maintained a ruddy glow for a while, but shortly cooled and became black and level again. During a "thaw," every dismembered cake was marked by a glittering white border which was superbly shaded inwards by aurora borealis rays, which were a flaming yellow where they joined the white border, and from thence toward their points tapered into glowing crimson, then into a rich, pale carmine, and finally into a faint blush that held its own a moment and then dimmed and turned black. Some of the streams preferred to mingle together in a tangle of fantastic circles, and then they looked something like the confusion of ropes one sees on a ship's deck when she has just taken in sail and dropped anchor—provided one can imagine those ropes on fire.

Through the glasses, the little fountains scattered about looked very beautiful. They boiled, and coughed, and spluttered, and discharged sprays of stringy red fire—of about the consistency of mush, for instance—from ten to fifteen feet into the air, along with a shower of brilliant white sparks—a quaint and unnatural mingling of gouts of blood and snow-flakes!

We had circles and serpents and streaks of lightning all twined and wreathed and tied together, without a break throughout an area more than a mile square (that amount of ground was covered, though it was not strictly "square"), and it was with a feeling of placid exultation that we reflected that many years had elapsed since any visitor had seen such a splendid display—since any visitor had seen anything more than the now snubbed and insignificant "North" and "South" lakes in action. We had been reading old files of Hawaiian newspapers and the "Record Book" at the Volcano House, and were posted.

I could see the North Lake lying out on the black floor away off in the outer edge of our panorama, and knitted to it by a webwork of lava streams. In its individual capacity it looked very little more respectable than a schoolhouse on fire. True, it was about nine hundred feet long and two or three hundred wide, but then, under the present circumstances, it necessarily appeared rather insignificant, and besides it was so distant from us.

I forgot to say that the noise made by the bubbling lava is not great, heard as we heard it from our lofty perch. It makes three distinct sounds—a rushing, a hissing, and a coughing or puffing sound; and if you stand on the brink and close your eyes it is no trick at all to imagine that you are sweeping down a river on a large low-pressure steamer, and that you hear the hissing of the steam about her boilers, the puffing from her escape-pipes and the churning rush of the water abaft her wheels. The smell of sulphur is strong, but not unpleasant to a sinner.

We left the lookout house at ten o'clock in a half cooked condition, because of the heat from Pele's furnaces, and wrapping up in blankets, for the night was cold, we returned to our hotel.

CHAPTER 75

THE next night was appointed for a visit to the bottom of the crater, for we desired to traverse its floor and see the "North Lake" (of fire) which lay two miles away, toward the further wall. After dark half a dozen of us set out, with lanterns and native guides, and climbed down a crazy, thousand-foot pathway in a crevice fractured in the crater wall, and reached the bottom in safety.

The eruption of the previous evening had spent its force and the floor looked black and cold; but when we ran out upon it we found it hot yet, to the feet, and it was likewise riven with crevices which revealed the underlying fires gleaming vindictively. A neighboring cauldron was threatening to overflow, and this added to the dubiousness of the situation. So the native guides refused to continue the venture, and then everybody deserted except a stranger named Marlette. He said he had been in the crater a dozen times in daylight and believed he could find his way through it at night. He thought that a run of three hundred yards would carry us over the hottest part of the floor and leave us our shoe-soles. His pluck gave me back-bone. We took one lantern and instructed the guides to hang the other to the roof of the lookout house to serve as a beacon for us in case we got lost, and then the party started back up the precipice and Marlette and I made our run. We skipped over the hot floor and over the red crevices with brisk dispatch and reached the cold lava safe but with pretty warm feet. Then we took things leisurely and comfortably, jumping tolerably wide and probably bottomless chasms, and threading our way through picturesque lava upheavals with considerable confidence. When we got fairly away from the cauldrons of boiling fire, we seemed to be in a gloomy desert, and a suffocatingly dark one, surrounded by dim walls that seemed to tower to the sky. The only cheerful objects were the glinting stars high overhead.

By and by Marlette shouted "Stop!" I never stopped quicker in my life. I asked what the matter was. He said we were out of the path. He said we must not try to go on till we found it again, for we were surrounded with beds of rotten lava through which we could easily break and plunge down a thousand feet. I thought eight hundred would answer for me, and was about to say so when Marlette partly proved his statement by accidentally crushing through and

BREAKING THROUGH.

disappearing to his arm-pits. He got out and we hunted for the path with the lantern. He said there was only one path and that it was but vaguely defined. We could not find it. The lava surface was all alike in the lantern light. But he was an ingenious man. He said it was not the lantern that had informed him that we were out of the path, but his *feet*. He had noticed a crisp grinding of fine lava-needles under his feet, and some instinct reminded him that in the path these were all worn away. So he put the lantern behind him, and began to search with his boots instead of his eyes. It was good sagacity. The first time his foot touched a surface that did not grind under it he announced that the trail was found again; and after that we kept up a sharp listening for the rasping sound and it always warned us in time.

It was a long tramp, but an exciting one. We reached the North Lake between ten and eleven o'clock, and sat down on a huge overhanging lava-shelf, tired but satisfied. The spectacle presented was worth coming double the distance to see. Under us, and stretching away before us, was a heaving sea of molten fire of seemingly limitless extent. The glare from it was so blinding that it was some time before we could bear to look upon it steadily. It was like gazing at the sun at noonday, except that the glare was not quite so white. At unequal distances all around the shores of the lake were nearly white-hot chimneys or hollow drums of lava, four or five feet high, and up through them were bursting gorgeous sprays of lava-gouts and gem spangles, some white, some red and some

FIRE FOUNTAINS.

golden—a ceaseless bombardment, and one that fascinated the eye with its unapproachable splendor. The more distant jets, sparkling up through an intervening gossamer veil of vapor, seemed miles away; and the further the curving ranks of fiery fountains receded, the more fairy-like and beautiful they appeared.

Now and then the surging bosom of the lake under our noses would calm down ominously and seem to be gathering strength for an enterprise; and then all of a sudden a red dome of lava of the bulk of an ordinary dwelling would heave itself aloft like an escaping balloon, then burst asunder, and out of its heart would flit a pale-green film of vapor, and float upward and vanish in the darkness—a released soul soaring homeward from captivity with the damned, no doubt. The crashing plunge of the ruined dome into the lake again would send a world of seething billows lashing against the shores and shaking the foundations of our perch. By and by, a loosened mass of the hanging shelf we sat on tumbled into the lake, jarring the surroundings like an earthquake and delivering a suggestion that may have been intended for a hint, and may not. We did not wait to see.

We got lost again on our way back, and were more than an hour hunting for the path. We were where we could see the beacon lantern at the lookout house at the time, but thought it was a star and paid no attention to it. We reached the hotel at two o'clock in the morning pretty well fagged out.

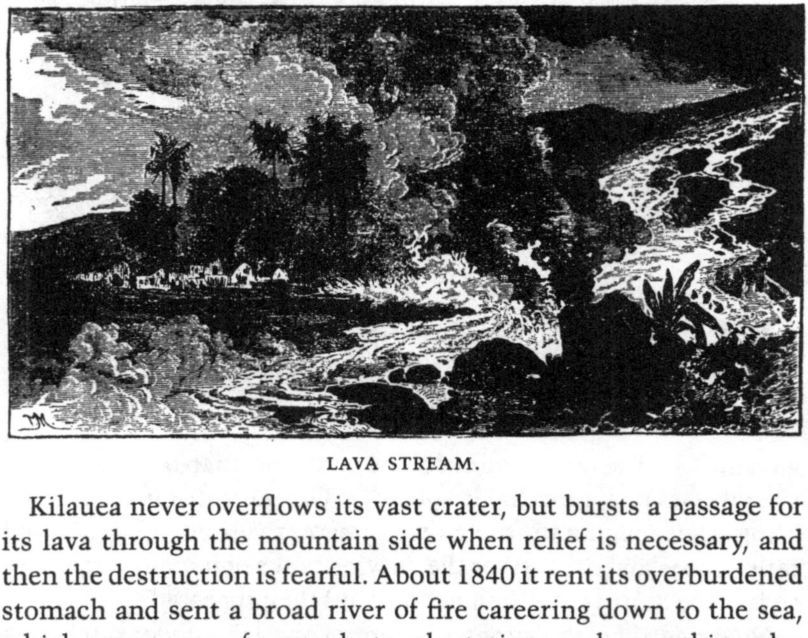

LAVA STREAM.

Kilauea never overflows its vast crater, but bursts a passage for its lava through the mountain side when relief is necessary, and then the destruction is fearful. About 1840 it rent its overburdened stomach and sent a broad river of fire careering down to the sea, which swept away forests, huts, plantations and everything else that lay in its path. The stream was *five miles broad,* in places, and *two hundred feet deep,* and the distance it traveled was forty miles. It tore up and bore away acre-patches of land on its bosom like rafts—rocks, trees and all intact. At night the red glare was visible a hundred miles at sea; and at a distance of forty miles fine print could be read at midnight. The atmosphere was poisoned with sulphurous vapors and choked with falling ashes, pumice stones and cinders; countless columns of smoke rose up and blended together in a tumbled canopy that hid the heavens and glowed with a ruddy flush reflected from the fires below; here and there jets of lava sprung hundreds of feet into the air and burst into rocket-sprays that returned to earth in a crimson rain; and all the while the laboring mountain shook with Nature's great palsy, and voiced its distress in moanings and the muffled booming of subterranean thunders.

Fishes were killed for twenty miles along the shore, where the lava entered the sea. The earthquakes caused some loss of human life, and a prodigious tidal wave swept inland, carrying everything

A TIDAL WAVE.

before it and drowning a number of natives. The devastation consummated along the route traversed by the river of lava was complete and incalculable. Only a Pompeii and a Herculaneum were needed at the foot of Kilauea to make the story of the eruption immortal.

CHAPTER 76

We rode horseback all around the island of Hawaii (the crooked road making the distance two hundred miles), and enjoyed the journey very much. We were more than a week making the trip, because our Kanaka horses would not go by a house or a hut without stopping—whip and spur could not alter their minds about it, and so we finally found that it economized time to let them have their way. Upon inquiry the mystery was explained: the natives are such thorough-going gossips that they never pass a house without stopping to swap news, and consequently their horses learn to regard that sort of thing as an essential part of the whole duty of man, and his salvation not to be compassed without it. However, at a former crisis of my life I had once taken an aristocratic young lady out driving, behind a horse that had just retired from a long and honorable career as the moving impulse of a milk wagon, and so this present experience awoke a reminiscent sadness in me in place of the exasperation more natural to the occasion. I remembered how helpless I was that day, and how humiliated; how ashamed I was of having intimated to the girl that I had always owned the horse and was accustomed to grandeur; how hard I tried to appear easy, and even vivacious, under suffering that was consuming my vitals; how placidly and maliciously the girl smiled, and kept on smiling, while my hot blushes baked themselves into a permanent blood-pudding in my face; how the horse ambled from one side of the street to the other and waited complacently before every third house two minutes and a quarter while I belabored his back and reviled him in my heart; how I tried to keep him from turning corners, and failed; how I moved heaven and earth to get him out of town, and did not succeed; how he traversed the entire settlement and delivered imaginary milk at a hundred and sixty-two different domiciles, and how he finally brought up at

TRIP ON THE MILKY WAY.

a dairy depot and refused to budge further, thus rounding and completing the revealment of what the plebeian service of his life had been; how, in eloquent silence, I walked the girl home, and how, when I took leave of her, her parting remark scorched my soul and appeared to blister me all over: she said that my horse was a fine, capable animal, and I must have taken great comfort in him in my time—but that if I would take along some milk-tickets next time, and appear to deliver them at the various halting places, it might expedite his movements a little. There was a coolness between us after that.

In one place in the island of Hawaii, we saw a laced and ruffled cataract of limpid water leaping from a sheer precipice fifteen hundred feet high; but that sort of scenery finds its stanchest ally in the arithmetic rather than in spectacular effect. If one desires to be so stirred by a poem of Nature wrought in the happily commingled graces of picturesque rocks, glimpsed distances, foliage, color, shifting lights and shadows, and falling water, that the tears almost come into his eyes so potent is the charm exerted, he need not go away from America to enjoy such an experience. The Rainbow Fall, in Watkins Glen (N. Y.), on the Erie railway, is an example. It would recede into pitiable insignificance if the callous tourist drew an arithmetic on it; but left to compete for the honors simply on scenic grace and beauty—the grand, the august and the sublime being barred the contest—it could challenge the old world and the new to produce its peer.

In one locality, on our journey, we saw some horses that had been born and reared on top of the mountains, above the range of running water, and consequently they had never drank that fluid in their lives, but had been always accustomed to quenching their thirst by eating dew-laden or shower-wetted leaves. And now it was destructively funny to see them sniff suspiciously at a pail of water, and then put in their noses and try to take a *bite* out of the fluid, as if it were a solid. Finding it liquid, they would snatch away their heads and fall to trembling, snorting and showing other evidences of fright. When they became convinced at last that the water was friendly and harmless, they thrust in their noses up to their eyes, brought out a mouthful of the water, and proceeded to *chew* it complacently. We saw a man coax, kick and spur one of them five or ten minutes before he could make it cross a running stream. It spread its nostrils, distended its eyes and trembled all over, just as horses customarily do in the presence of a serpent—and for aught I know it thought the crawling stream *was* a serpent.

In due course of time our journey came to an end at Kawaihae (usually pronounced To-a-*hi*—and before we find fault with this elaborate orthographical method of arriving at such an unostentatious result, let us lop off the *ugh* from our word "though"). I made this horseback trip on a mule. I paid ten dollars for him at Kau (Kah-oo), added four to get him shod, rode him two hundred miles, and then sold him for fifteen dollars. I mark the circumstance with a white stone (in the absence of chalk—for I never saw a white stone that a body could mark anything with, though out of respect for the ancients I have tried it often enough); for up to that day and date it was the first strictly commercial transaction I had ever entered into, and come out winner. We returned to Honolulu, and from thence sailed to the island of Maui, and spent several weeks there very pleasantly. I still remember, with a sense of indolent luxury, a pic-nicking excursion up a romantic gorge there, called

A VIEW IN THE IAO VALLEY.

the Iao Valley. The trail lay along the edge of a brawling stream in the bottom of the gorge—a shady route, for it was well roofed with the verdant domes of forest trees. Through openings in the foliage we glimpsed picturesque scenery that revealed ceaseless changes and new charms with every step of our progress. Perpendicular walls from one to three thousand feet high guarded the way, and were sumptuously plumed with varied foliage, in places, and in places swathed in waving ferns. Passing shreds of cloud trailed their shadows across these shining fronts, mottling them with blots; billowy masses of white vapor hid the turreted summits, and far above the vapor swelled a background of gleaming green crags and cones that came and went, through the veiling mists, like islands drifting in a fog; sometimes the cloudy curtain descended till half the cañon wall was hidden, then shredded gradually away till only airy glimpses of the ferny front appeared through it—then swept aloft and left it glorified in the sun again. Now and then, as our position changed, rocky bastions swung out from the wall, a mimic ruin of castellated ramparts and crumbling towers clothed with mosses and hung with garlands of swaying vines, and as we moved on they swung back again and hid themselves once more in the foliage. Presently a verdure-clad needle of stone, a thousand feet high, stepped out from behind a corner, and mounted guard over the mysteries of the valley. It seemed to me that if Capt. Cook needed a monument, here was one ready made—therefore, why not put up his sign here, and sell out the venerable cocoanut stump?

But the chief pride of Maui is her dead volcano of Haleakala—which means, translated, "the house of the sun." We climbed a thousand feet up the side of this isolated colossus one afternoon; then camped, and next day climbed the remaining nine thousand feet, and anchored on the summit, where we built a fire and froze and roasted by turns, all night. With the first pallor of dawn we got up and saw things that were new to us. Mounted on a commanding pinnacle, we watched Nature work her silent wonders. The sea was spread abroad on every hand, its tumbled surface seeming only wrinkled and dimpled in the distance. A broad valley below appeared like an ample checker-board, its velvety green sugar plantations alternating with dun squares of barrenness and groves of trees diminished to mossy tufts. Beyond the valley were mountains picturesquely grouped together; but bear in mind, we fancied that we were looking *up* at these things—not down. We seemed to sit in the bottom of a symmetrical bowl ten thousand feet deep, with the valley and the skirting sea lifted away into the sky above us! It was curious; and not only curious, but aggravating; for it was having our trouble all for nothing, to climb ten thousand feet toward heaven and then have to look *up* at our scenery. However, we had to be content with it and make the best of it; for all we could do we could not coax our landscape down out of the clouds. Formerly, when I had read an article in which Poe treated of this singular fraud perpetrated upon the eye by isolated great altitudes, I had looked upon the matter as an invention of his own fancy.

I have spoken of the outside view—but we had an inside one, too. That was the yawning dead crater, into which we now and then tumbled rocks, half as large as a barrel, from our perch, and saw them go careering down the almost perpendicular sides, bounding three hundred feet at a jump; kicking up dust-clouds wherever they struck; diminishing to our view as they sped farther into distance; growing invisible, finally, and only betraying their course by faint little puffs of dust; and coming to a halt at last in the bottom of the abyss, two thousand five hundred feet down from where they started! It was magnificent sport. We wore ourselves out at it.

The crater of Vesuvius, as I have before remarked, is a modest pit about a thousand feet deep and three thousand in circumference; that of Kilauea is somewhat deeper, and *ten miles* in circumference. But what are either of them compared to the vacant stomach of Haleakala? I will not offer any figures of my own, but give official ones—those of Commander Wilkes, U. S. N., who surveyed it and testifies that it is *twenty-seven miles in circumference!* If it had a level bottom it would make a fine site for a city like London. It must have afforded a spectacle worth contemplating in the old days when its furnaces gave full rein to their anger.

Presently vagrant white clouds came drifting along, high over the sea and the valley; then they came in couples and groups; then in imposing squadrons; gradually joining their forces, they banked themselves solidly together, a thousand feet under us, and *totally shut out land and ocean*—not a vestige of *anything* was left in view but just a little of the rim of the crater, circling away from the

MAGNIFICENT SPORT.

pinnacle whereon we sat (for a ghostly procession of wanderers from the filmy hosts without had drifted through a chasm in the crater wall and filed round and round, and gathered and sunk and blended together till the abyss was stored to the brim with a fleecy fog). Thus banked, motion ceased, and silence reigned. Clear to the horizon, league on league, the snowy floor stretched without a break—not level, but in rounded folds, with shallow creases between, and with here and there stately piles of vapory architecture lifting themselves aloft out of the common plain—some near at hand, some in the middle distances, and others relieving the monotony of the remote solitudes. There was little conversation, for the impressive scene overawed speech. I felt like the Last Man, neglected of the judgment, and left pinnacled in mid-heaven, a forgotten relic of a vanished world.

While the hush yet brooded, the messengers of the coming resurrection appeared in the east. A growing warmth suffused the horizon, and soon the sun emerged and looked out over the cloud-waste, flinging bars of ruddy light across it, staining its folds and billow-caps with blushes, purpling the shaded troughs between, and glorifying the massy vapor-palaces and cathedrals with a wasteful splendor of all blendings and combinations of rich coloring.

It was the sublimest spectacle I ever witnessed, and I think the memory of it will remain with me always.

CHAPTER 77

I STUMBLED upon one curious character in the island of Maui. He became a sore annoyance to me in the course of time. My first glimpse of him was in a sort of public room in the town of Lahaina. He occupied a chair at the opposite side of the apartment, and sat eyeing our party with interest for some minutes, and listening as critically to what we were saying as if he fancied we were talking to him and expecting him to reply. I thought it very sociable in a stranger. Presently, in the course of conversation, I made a statement bearing upon the subject under discussion—and I made it with due modesty, for there was nothing extraordinary about it, and it was only put forth in illustration of a point at issue. I had barely finished when this person spoke out with rapid utterance and feverish anxiety:

"Oh, that was certainly remarkable, after a fashion, but you ought to have seen *my* chimney—you ought to have seen *my* chimney, sir! Smoke! I wish I may hang if—Mr. Jones, *you* remember that chimney—you *must* remember that chimney! No, no—I recollect, now, you warn't living on this side of the island then. But I am telling you nothing but the truth, and I wish I may never draw another breath if that chimney didn't smoke so that the smoke actually got *caked* in it and I had to dig it out with a pickaxe! You may smile, gentlemen, but the High Sheriff's got a hunk of it which I dug out before his eyes, and so it's perfectly easy for you to go and examine for yourselves."

The interruption broke up the conversation, which had already begun to lag, and we presently hired some natives and an outrigger canoe or two, and went out to overlook a grand surf-bathing contest.

Two weeks after this, while talking in a company, I looked up and detected this same man boring through and through me with his intense eye, and noted again his twitching muscles and his feverish anxiety to speak. The moment I paused, he said:

"*Beg* your pardon, sir, beg your pardon, but it can only be considered remarkable when brought into strong outline by isolation. Sir, contrasted with a circumstance which occurred in my own experience, it instantly becomes commonplace. No, not that—for I will not speak so discourteously of any experience in the career of a stranger and a gentleman—but I am *obliged* to say that you could not, and you *would* not ever again refer to this tree as a *large* one, if you could behold, as I have, the great Yakmatack tree, in the island of Ounaska, sea of Kamtchatka—a tree, sir, not one inch less than four hundred and fifteen feet in solid diameter!—and I wish I may die in a minute if it isn't so! Oh, you needn't look so questioning, gentlemen; here's old Cap Saltmarsh can say whether I know what I'm talking about or not. I showed him the tree."

Capt. Saltmarsh.—"Come, now, cat your anchor, lad—you're heaving too taut. You *promised* to show me that stunner, and I

ELEVEN MILES TO SEE.

walked more than eleven mile with you through the cussedest jungle *I* ever see, a hunting for it; but the tree you showed me finally warn't as big around as a beer cask, and *you* know that your own self, Markiss."

"Hear the man talk! Of *course* the tree was reduced that way, but didn't I *explain* it? Answer me, didn't I? Didn't I say I wished you could have seen it when *I* first saw it? When you got up on your ear and called me names, and said I had brought you eleven miles to look at a sapling, didn't I *explain* to you that all the whaleships in the North Seas had been wooding off of it for more than twenty-seven years? And did you s'pose the tree could last for-*ever,* con-*found* it? I don't see why you want to keep back things that way, and try to injure a person that's never done *you* any harm."

Somehow this man's presence made me uncomfortable, and I was glad when a native arrived at that moment to say that Mucka-wow, the most companionable and luxurious among the rude war-chiefs of the Islands, desired us to come over and help him enjoy a missionary whom he had found trespassing on his grounds.

I think it was about ten days afterward that, as I finished a statement I was making for the instruction of a group of friends and acquaintances, and which made no pretense of being extraordinary, a familiar voice chimed instantly in on the heels of my last word, and said:

"But, my dear sir, there was *nothing* remarkable about that horse, or the circumstance either—nothing in the world! I mean no sort of offense when I say it, sir, but you really do not know anything whatever about speed. Bless your heart, if you could only have seen my mare Margaretta; *there* was a beast!—*there* was lightning for you! Trot! Trot is no name for it—she flew! How she *could* whirl a buggy along! I started her out once, sir—Col. Bilgewater, *you* recollect that animal perfectly well—I started her out about thirty or thirty-five yards ahead of the awfullest storm I ever saw in my life, and it chased us upwards of eighteen miles! It did, by the everlasting hills! And I'm telling you nothing but the unvarnished truth when I say that not one single drop of rain fell on me—not a single *drop,* sir! And I swear to it! But my dog was a swimming behind the wagon all the way!"

For a week or two I stayed mostly within doors, for I seemed to meet this person everywhere, and he had become utterly hateful to me. But one evening I dropped in on Capt. Perkins and his friends, and we had a sociable time. About ten o'clock I chanced to be talking about a merchant friend of mine, and without really intending it, the remark slipped out that he was a little mean and parsimonious about paying his workmen. Instantly, through the steam of a hot whisky punch on the opposite side of the room, a

CHASED BY A STORM.

remembered voice shot—and for a moment I trembled on the imminent verge of profanity:

"Oh, my dear sir, really you expose yourself when you parade *that* as a surprising circumstance. Bless your heart and hide, you are ignorant of the very A B C of meanness! ignorant as the unborn babe! ignorant as unborn *twins!* You don't know *anything* about it! It is pitiable to see you, sir, a well-spoken and prepossessing stranger, making such an enormous pow-wow here about a subject concerning which your ignorance is perfectly humiliating! Look me in the eye, if you please; look me in the eye. John James Godfrey was the son of poor but honest parents in the State of Mississippi—boyhood friend of mine—bosom comrade in later years. Heaven rest his noble spirit, he is gone from us now. John James Godfrey was hired by the Hayblossom Mining Company in California to do some blasting for them—the 'Incorporated Company of Mean Men,' the boys used to call it. Well, one day he drilled a hole about four feet deep and put in an awful blast of powder, and was standing over it ramming it down with an iron crowbar about nine foot long, when the cussed thing struck a spark and fired the powder, and scat! away John Godfrey whizzed like a sky-rocket, him and his crowbar! Well, sir, he kept on going up in the air higher and higher, till he didn't look any bigger than a boy—and he kept going on up higher and higher, till he didn't look any bigger than a doll—and he kept on going up higher and higher, till he didn't look any bigger than a little small bee—and then he went out of sight! Presently he came in sight again, looking like a little small bee—and he came along down further and further, till he looked as big as a doll again—and down further and further, till he was as big as a boy again—and further and further, till he was a full-sized man once more; and then him and his crowbar came a wh-izzing down and lit right exactly in the same old tracks and went to r-ramming down, and r-ramming down, and r-ramming down again, just the same as if nothing had happened! Now do you know, that poor cuss warn't gone only sixteen minutes, and yet that Incorporated Company of Mean Men DOCKED HIM FOR THE LOST TIME!"

LEAVING WORK.

I said I had the headache, and so excused myself and went home. And on my diary I entered "another night spoiled" by this offensive loafer. And a fervent curse was set down with it to keep the item company. And the very next day I packed up, out of all patience, and left the island.

Almost from the very beginning, I regarded that man as a liar.

. . . . .

The line of points represents an interval of years. At the end of which time the opinion hazarded in that last sentence came to be gratifyingly and remarkably endorsed, and by wholly disinterested persons. The man Markiss was found one morning hanging to a beam of his own bedroom (the doors and windows securely fastened on the inside), dead, and on his breast was pinned a paper in his own handwriting begging his friends to suspect no innocent person of having anything to do with his death, for that it was the work of his own hands entirely. Yet the jury brought in the astounding verdict that deceased came to his death "by the hands of some person or persons unknown!" They explained that the perfectly undeviating consistency of Markiss's character for thirty years towered aloft as colossal and indestructible testimony, that whatever statement he chose to make was entitled to instant and unquestioning acceptance as a *lie.* And they furthermore stated their belief that he was not dead, and instanced the strong circumstantial evidence of his own word that he *was* dead—and beseeched the coroner to delay the funeral as long as possible, which was done. And so in the tropical climate of Lahaina the coffin stood open for seven days, and then even the loyal jury gave him up. But they sat on him again, and changed their verdict to "suicide induced by mental aberration"—because, said they, with penetration, "he said he was dead, and he *was* dead; and would he have told the truth if he had been in his right mind? *No,* sir."

CHAPTER 78

AFTER half a year's luxurious vagrancy in the Islands, I took shipping in a sailing vessel, and regretfully returned to San Francisco—a voyage in every way delightful, but without an incident: unless lying two long weeks in a dead calm, eighteen hundred miles from the nearest land, may rank as an incident. Schools of whales grew so tame that day after day they played about the ship among the porpoises and the sharks without the least apparent fear of us, and we pelted them with empty bottles for lack of better sport. Twenty-four hours afterward these bottles would be still lying on the glassy water under our noses, showing that the ship had not moved out of her place in all that time. The calm was absolutely breathless, and the surface of the sea absolutely without a wrinkle. For a whole day and part of a night we lay so close to another ship that had drifted to our vicinity, that we carried on conversations with her passengers, introduced each other by name, and became pretty intimately acquainted with people we had never heard of before, and have never heard of since. This was the only vessel we saw during the whole lonely voyage. We had fifteen passengers, and to show how hard pressed they were at last for occupation and amusement, I will mention that the gentlemen gave a good part of their time every day, during the calm, to trying to sit on an empty champagne bottle (lying on its side), and thread a needle without touching their

OUR AMUSEMENTS.

heels to the deck, or falling over; and the ladies sat in the shade of the mainsail, and watched the enterprise with absorbing interest. We were at sea five Sundays; and yet, but for the almanac, we never would have known but that all the other days were Sundays too.

I was home again, in San Francisco, without means and without employment. I tortured my brain for a saving scheme of some kind, and at last a public lecture occurred to me! I sat down and wrote one, in a fever of hopeful anticipation. I showed it to several friends, but they all shook their heads. They said nobody would come to hear me, and I would make a humiliating failure of it. They said that as I had never spoken in public, I would break down in the delivery, anyhow. I was disconsolate now. But at last an editor slapped me on the back and told me to "go ahead." He said, "Take the largest house in town, and charge a dollar a ticket." The audacity of the proposition was charming; it seemed fraught with practical worldly wisdom, however. The proprietor of the several theatres endorsed the advice, and said I might have his handsome new opera-house at half price—fifty dollars. In sheer desperation I took it—on credit, for sufficient reasons. In three days I did a hundred and fifty dollars' worth of printing and advertising, and was the most distressed and frightened creature on the Pacific coast. I could not sleep—who could, under such circumstances? For other people there was facetiousness in the last line of my posters, but to me it was plaintive with a pang when I wrote it:

Doors open at 7½. The trouble will begin at 8.

That line has done good service since. Showmen have borrowed it frequently. I have even seen it appended to a newspaper advertisement reminding school pupils in vacation what time next term would begin. As those three days of suspense dragged by, I grew more and more unhappy. I had sold two hundred tickets among my personal friends, but I feared they might not come. My lecture, which had seemed "humorous" to me, at first, grew steadily more and more dreary, till not a vestige of fun seemed left, and I grieved that I could not bring a coffin on the stage and turn the thing into a funeral. I was so panic-stricken, at last, that I went to three old friends, giants in stature, cordial by nature, and stormy-voiced, and said:

"This thing is going to be a failure; the jokes in it are so dim that nobody will ever see them; I would like to have you sit in the parquette, and help me through."

They said they would. Then I went to the wife of a popular citizen, and said that if she was willing to do me a very great kindness, I would be glad if she and her husband would sit prominently in the left-hand stage-box, where the whole house could see them. I explained that I should need help, and would turn toward her and smile, as a signal, when I had been delivered of an obscure joke—"and then," I added, "don't wait to investigate, but *respond!*"

She promised. Down the street I met a man I never had seen before. He had been drinking, and was beaming with smiles and good nature. He said:

"My name's Sawyer. You don't know me, but that don't matter. I haven't got a cent, but if you knew how bad I wanted to laugh, you'd give me a ticket. Come, now, what do you say?"

"Is your laugh hung on a hair-trigger?—that is, is it critical, or can you get it off *easy?*"

My drawling infirmity of speech so affected him that he laughed a specimen or two that struck me as being about the article I wanted, and I gave him a ticket, and appointed him to sit in the second circle, in the centre, and be responsible for that division of the house. I gave him minute instructions about how to detect indistinct jokes, and then went away, and left him chuckling placidly over the novelty of the idea.

I ate nothing on the last of the three eventful days—I only suffered. I had advertised that on this third day the box-office would be opened for the sale of reserved seats. I crept down to the theatre at four in the afternoon to see if any sales had been made. The ticket seller was gone, the box-office was locked up. I had to swallow suddenly, or my heart would have got out. "No sales," I said to myself; "I might have known it." I thought of suicide, pretended illness, flight. I thought of these things in earnest, for I was very miserable and scared. But of course I had to drive them away, and prepare to meet my fate. I could not wait for half past seven—I wanted to face the horror, and end it—the feeling of many a man doomed to hang, no doubt. I went down back streets at six o'clock, and entered the theatre by the back door. I stumbled my way in the dark among the ranks of canvas scenery, and stood on the stage.

The house was gloomy and silent, and its emptiness depressing. I went into the dark among the scenes again, and for an hour and a half gave myself up to the horrors, wholly unconscious of everything else. Then I heard a murmur; it rose higher and higher, and ended in a crash, mingled with cheers. It made my hair rise, it was so close to me, and so loud. There was a pause, and then another; presently came a third, and before I well knew what I was about, I was in the middle of the stage, staring at a sea of faces, bewildered by the fierce glare of the lights, and quaking in every limb with a terror that seemed like to take my life away. The house was full, aisles and all!

SEVERE CASE OF STAGE-FRIGHT.

The tumult in my heart and brain and legs continued a full minute before I could gain any command over myself. Then I recognized the charity and the friendliness in the faces before me, and little by little my fright melted away, and I began to talk. Within three or four minutes I was comfortable, and even content. My three chief allies, with three auxiliaries, were on hand, in the parquette, all sitting to-

MY THREE PARQUETTE ALLIES.

gether, all armed with bludgeons, and all ready to make an onslaught upon the feeblest joke that might show its head. And whenever a joke did fall, their bludgeons came down and their faces seemed to split from ear to ear; Sawyer, whose hearty countenance was seen looming redly in the centre of the second circle, took it up, and the house was carried handsomely. Inferior jokes never fared so royally before. Presently I delivered a bit of serious matter with impressive unction (it was my pet), and the audience listened with an absorbed hush that gratified me more than any applause; and as I dropped the last word of the clause, I happened to turn and catch Mrs. ——'s intent and waiting eye; my conversation with her flashed upon me, and in spite of all I could do I smiled. She took it for the signal, and promptly delivered a mellow laugh that touched off the whole audience; and the explosion that followed was the triumph of the evening. I thought that that honest man Sawyer would choke himself; and as for the bludgeons, they performed like pile-drivers. But my poor little morsel of pathos was ruined. It was taken in good faith as an intentional joke, and the prize one of the entertainment, and I wisely let it go at that.

SAWYER IN THE CIRCLE.

All the papers were kind in the morning; my appetite returned; I had abundance of money. All's well that ends well.

CHAPTER 79

I LAUNCHED out as a lecturer, now, with great boldness. I had the field all to myself, for public lectures were almost an unknown commodity in the Pacific market. They are not so rare, now, I suppose. I took an old personal friend along to play agent for me, and for two or three weeks we roamed through Nevada and California and had a very cheerful time of it. Two days before I lectured in Virginia City, two stage-coaches were robbed within two miles of the town. The daring act was committed just at dawn, by six masked men, who sprang up alongside the coaches, presented revolvers at the heads of the drivers and passengers, and commanded a general dismount. Everybody climbed down, and the robbers took their watches and every cent they had. Then they took gunpowder and blew up the express specie boxes and got their contents. The leader of the robbers was a small, quick-spoken man, and the fame of his vigorous manner and his intrepidity was in everybody's mouth when we arrived.

The night after instructing Virginia, I walked over the desolate "divide" and down to Gold Hill, and lectured there. The lecture done, I stopped to talk with a friend, and did not start back till eleven. The "divide" was high, unoccupied ground, between the towns, the scene of twenty midnight murders and a hundred robberies. As we climbed up and stepped out on this eminence, the Gold Hill lights dropped out of sight at our backs, and the night closed down gloomy and dismal. A sharp wind swept the place, too, and chilled our perspiring bodies through.

"I tell you I don't like this place at night," said Mike the agent.

"Well, don't speak so loud," I said. "You needn't remind anybody that we are here."

Just then a dim figure approached me from the direction of Virginia—a man, evidently. He came straight at me, and I stepped aside to let him pass; he stepped in the way and confronted me again. Then I saw that he had a mask on and was holding something in my face—I heard a click-click and recognized a revolver in dim outline. I pushed the barrel aside with my hand and said:

"Don't!"

He ejaculated sharply:

"Your watch! Your money!"

I said:

"You can have them with pleasure—but take the pistol away from my face, please. It makes me shiver."

"No remarks! Hand out your money!"

"Certainly—I—"

"Put up your hands! Don't you go for a weapon! Put 'em up! Higher!"

I held them above my head.

A pause. Then:

"Are you going to hand out your money or not?"

I dropped my hands to my pockets and said:

"Certainly! I—"

"Put up your *hands!* Do you want your head blown off? Higher!"

I put them above my head again.

Another pause.

"*Are* you going to hand out your money or *not?* Ah-ah—again? Put up your hands! By George, you want the head shot off you awful bad!"

"Well, friend, I'm trying my best to please you. You tell me to give up my money, and when I reach for it you tell me to put up my hands. If you would only—. Oh, now—don't! All six of you at me! That other man will get away while—. Now please take some of those revolvers out of my face—*do,* if you *please!* Every time one of them clicks, my liver comes up into my throat! If you have a mother—any of you—or if any of you have ever *had* a mother—or a—grandmother—or a—"

"Cheese it! *Will* you give up your money, or have we got to—. There-there—none of that! Put up your *hands!*"

"Gentlemen—I know you are gentlemen by your—"

"Silence! If you want to be facetious, young man, there are times and places more fitting. *This* is a serious business."

"You prick the marrow of my opinion. The funerals I have attended in my time were comedies compared to it. Now *I* think—"

"Curse your palaver! Your money!—your money!—your money! Hold!—put up your hands!"

"Gentlemen, listen to reason. You *see* how I am situated—now *don't* put those pistols so close—I smell the powder. You see how I am situated. If I had four hands—so that I could hold up two and—"

A PREDICAMENT.

"Throttle him! Gag him! Kill him!"

"Gentlemen, *don't!* Nobody's watching the other fellow. Why don't some of you—. Ouch! Take it away, please! Gentlemen, you see that I've got to hold up my hands; and so I can't take out my money—but if you'll be so kind as to take it out for me, I will do as much for you some—"

"Search him Beauregard—and stop his jaw with a bullet, quick, if he wags it again. Help Beauregard, Stonewall."

Then three of them, with the small, spry leader, adjourned to Mike and fell to searching him. I was so excited that my lawless fancy tortured me to ask my two men all manner of facetious questions about their rebel brother-generals of the South, but, considering the order they had received, it was but common prudence to keep still. When everything had been taken from me,—watch, money, and a multitude of trifles of small value,—I supposed I was free, and forthwith put my cold hands into my empty pockets and began an inoffensive jig to warm my feet and stir up some latent courage—but instantly all pistols were at my head, and the order came again:

"Be still! Put up your hands! And *keep* them up!"

They stood Mike up alongside of me, with strict orders to keep his hands above his head, too, and then the chief highwayman said:

"Beauregard, hide behind that boulder; Phil Sheridan, you hide behind that other one; Stonewall Jackson, put yourself behind that sage-bush there. Keep your pistols bearing on these fellows, and if they take down their hands within ten minutes, or move a single peg, let them have it!"

Then three disappeared in the gloom toward the several ambushes, and the other three disappeared down the road toward Virginia.

It was depressingly still, and miserably cold. Now this whole thing was a practical joke, and the robbers were personal friends of ours in disguise, and twenty more lay hidden within ten feet of us during the whole operation, listening. Mike knew all this, and was in the joke, but I suspected nothing of it. To me it was most uncomfortably genuine.

When we had stood there in the middle of the road five minutes, like a couple of idiots, with our hands aloft, freezing to death by inches, Mike's interest in the joke began to wane. He said:

"The time's up, now, ain't it?"

"No, you keep still. Do you want to take any chances with those bloody savages?"

Presently Mike said:

"*Now* the time's up, anyway. I'm freezing."

"Well freeze. Better freeze than carry your brains home in a basket. Maybe the time *is* up, but how do *we* know?—got no watch to tell by. I mean to give them good measure. I calculate to stand here fifteen minutes or die. Don't you move."

So, without knowing it, I was making one joker very sick of his contract. When we took our arms down at last, they were aching with cold and fatigue, and when we went sneaking off, the dread I was in that the time might not yet be up and that we would feel bullets in a moment, was not sufficient to draw all my attention from the misery that racked my stiffened body.

The joke of these highwayman friends of ours was mainly a joke upon themselves; for they had waited for me on the cold hill-top two full hours before I came, and there was very little fun in that; they were so chilled that it took them a couple of weeks to get warm again. Moreover, I never had a thought that they would kill me to get money which it was so perfectly easy to get without any such folly, and so they did not really frighten me bad enough to make their enjoyment worth the trouble they had taken. I was only afraid that their weapons would go off accidentally. Their very numbers inspired me with confidence that no blood would be intentionally spilled. They were not smart; they ought to have sent only *one* highwayman, with a double-barreled shotgun, if they desired to see the author of this volume climb a tree.

However, I suppose that in the long run I got the largest share of the joke at last; and in a shape not foreseen by the highwaymen; for

BEST PART OF THE JOKE.

the chilly exposure on the "divide" while I was in a perspiration gave me a cold which developed itself into a troublesome disease and kept my hands idle some three months, besides costing me quite a sum in doctor's bills. Since then I play no practical jokes on people and generally lose my temper when one is played upon me.

When I returned to San Francisco I projected a pleasure journey to Japan and thence westward around the world; but a desire to see home again changed my mind, and I took a berth in the steamship, bade good-bye to the friendliest land and livest, heartiest community on our continent, and came by the way of the Isthmus to New York—a trip that was not much of a pic-nic excursion, for the cholera broke out among us on the passage and we buried two or three bodies at sea every day. I found home a dreary place after my long absence; for half the children I had known were now wearing whiskers or waterfalls, and few of the grown people I had been acquainted with remained at their hearthstones prosperous and happy—some of them had wandered to other scenes, some were in jail, and the rest had been hanged. These changes touched me deeply, and I went away and joined the famous Quaker City European Excursion and carried my tears to foreign lands.

Thus, after seven years of vicissitudes, ended a "pleasure trip" to the silver mines of Nevada which had originally been intended to occupy only three months. However, I usually miss my calculations further than that.

MORAL.

If the reader thinks he is done, now, and that this book has no moral to it, he is in error. The moral of it is this: If you are of any account, stay at home and make your way by faithful diligence; but if you are "no account," go away from home, and then you will *have* to work, whether you want to or not. Thus you become a blessing to your friends by ceasing to be a nuisance to them—if the people you go among suffer by the operation.

The End.

APPENDIX A

BRIEF SKETCH OF MORMON HISTORY

MORMONISM is only about forty years old, but its career has been full of stir and adventure from the beginning, and is likely to remain so to the end. Its adherents have been hunted and hounded from one end of the country to the other, and the result is that for years they have hated all "Gentiles" indiscriminately and with all their might. Joseph Smith, the finder of the Book of Mormon and founder of the religion, was driven from State to State with his mysterious copperplates and the miraculous stones he read their inscriptions with. Finally he instituted his "church" in Ohio and Brigham Young joined it. The neighbors began to persecute, and apostasy commenced. Brigham held to the faith and worked hard. He arrested desertion. He did more—he added converts in the midst of the trouble. He rose in favor and importance with the brethren. He was made one of the Twelve Apostles of the church. He shortly fought his way to a higher post and a more powerful—President of the Twelve. The neighbors rose up and drove the Mormons out of Ohio, and they settled in Missouri. Brigham went with them. The Missourians drove them out and they retreated to Nauvoo, Illinois. They prospered there, and built a temple which made some pretensions to architectural grace and achieved some celebrity in a section of country where a brick court-house with a tin dome and a cupola on it was contemplated with reverential awe. But the Mormons were badgered and harried again by their neighbors. All the proclamations Joseph Smith could issue denouncing polygamy and repudiating it as utterly anti-Mormon were of no avail; the people of the neighborhood, on both sides of the Mississippi, claimed that polygamy was practiced by the Mormons, and not only polygamy but a little of everything that was bad. Brigham returned from a mission to England, where he had established a Mormon newspaper, and he brought back with him several hundred converts to his preaching. His influence among the brethren augmented with every move he made. Finally Nauvoo was invaded by the Missouri and Illinois Gentiles, and Joseph Smith killed. A Mormon named Rigdon assumed the Presidency of the Mormon church and government, in Smith's place, and even tried his hand at a prophecy or two. But a greater than he was at hand. Brigham seized the advantage of the hour and without other authority than superior brain and nerve and will, hurled Rigdon from his high place and occupied it himself. He did more. He launched an elaborate curse at Rigdon and his disciples; and he pronounced Rigdon's "prophecies" emanations from the devil, and ended by "handing the false prophet over to the buffetings of Satan for a thousand years"—probably the longest term ever inflicted in Illinois. The people recognized their master. They straightway elected Brigham Young President, by a prodigious majority, and have never faltered in their devotion to him from that day to this. Brigham had forecast—a quality which no other prominent Mormon has probably ever possessed. He recognized that it was better to move to the wilderness than *be* moved. By his command the people gathered together their meagre effects, turned their backs upon their homes, and their faces toward the wilderness, and on a bitter night in February filed in sorrowful procession across the frozen Mississippi, lighted on their way by the glare from their burning temple, whose sacred furniture their own hands had fired! They camped, several days afterward, on the western verge of Iowa, and poverty, want, hunger, cold, sickness, grief and persecution did their work, and many succumbed and died—martyrs, fair and true, whatever else they might have been. Two years the remnant remained there, while Brigham and a small party crossed the country and founded Great Salt Lake City, purposely choosing a land which was *outside the ownership and jurisdiction of the hated American nation.* Note that. This was in 1847. Brigham moved his people there and got them settled just in time to see disaster fall again. For the war closed and Mexico ceded Brigham's refuge to the enemy—the United States! In 1849 the Mormons organized a "free and independent" government and erected the

"State of Deseret," with Brigham Young as its head. But the very next year Congress deliberately snubbed it and created the "Territory of Utah" out of the same accumulation of mountains, sagebrush, alkali and general desolation,—but made Brigham Governor of it. Then for years the enormous migration across the plains to California poured through the land of the Mormons and yet the church remained staunch and true to its lord and master. Neither hunger, thirst, poverty, grief, hatred, contempt, nor persecution could drive the Mormons from their faith or their allegiance; and even the thirst for gold, which gleaned the flower of the youth and strength of many nations, was not able to entice them! That was the final test. An experiment that could survive that was an experiment with some substance to it somewhere.

Great Salt Lake City throve finely, and so did Utah. One of the last things which Brigham Young had done before leaving Iowa, was to appear in the pulpit dressed to personate the worshipped and lamented prophet Smith, and confer the prophetic succession, with all its dignities, emoluments and authorities, upon "President Brigham Young!" The people accepted the pious fraud with the maddest enthusiasm, and Brigham's power was sealed and secured for all time. Within five years afterward he openly added polygamy to the tenets of the church by authority of a "revelation" which he pretended had been received nine years before by Joseph Smith, albeit Joseph is amply on record as denouncing polygamy to the day of his death.

Now was Brigham become a second Andrew Johnson in the small beginning and steady progress of his official grandeur. He had served successively as a disciple in the ranks; home missionary; foreign missionary; editor and publisher; Apostle; President of the Board of Apostles; President of all Mormondom, civil and ecclesiastical; successor to the great Joseph by the will of heaven; "prophet," "seer," "revelator." There was but one dignity higher which he *could* aspire to, and he reached out modestly and took that—he proclaimed himself a God!

He claims that he is to have a heaven of his own hereafter, and that he will be its God, and his wives and children its goddesses, princes and princesses. Into it all faithful Mormons will be admitted, with their families, and will take rank and consequence according to the number of their wives and children. If a disciple dies before he has had time to accumulate enough wives and children to enable him to be respectable in the next world any friend can marry a few wives and raise a few children for him *after he is dead,* and they are duly credited to his account and his heavenly status advanced accordingly.

Let it be borne in mind that the majority of the Mormons have always been ignorant, simple, of an inferior order of intellect, unacquainted with the world and its ways; and let it be borne in mind that the wives of these Mormons are necessarily after the same pattern and their children likely to be fit representatives of such a conjunction; and then let it be remembered that *for forty years* these creatures have been driven, driven, driven, relentlessly! and mobbed, beaten, and shot down; cursed, despised, expatriated; banished to a remote desert, whither they journeyed gaunt with famine and disease, disturbing the ancient solitudes with their lamentations and marking the long way with graves of their dead—and all because they were simply trying to live and worship God in the way which *they* believed with all their hearts and souls to be the true one. Let all these things be borne in mind, and then it will not be hard to account for the deathless hatred which the Mormons bear our people and our government.

That hatred has "fed fat its ancient grudge" ever since Mormon Utah developed into a self-supporting realm and the church waxed rich and strong. Brigham as Territorial Governor made it plain that Mormondom was for the Mormons. The United States tried to rectify all that by appointing Territorial officers from New England and other anti-Mormon localities, but Brigham prepared to make their entrance into his dominions difficult. Three thousand U. S. troops had to go across the plains and put these gentlemen in office. And after they were in office they were as helpless as so many stone images. They made laws which nobody minded and which could not be executed. The Federal judges opened court in a land filled with crime and violence and sat as holiday spectacles for insolent crowds to gape at—for there was nothing to try, nothing to do, nothing on the dockets! And if a Gentile brought a suit, the Mormon jury would do just as it pleased about bringing in a verdict, and when the judgment of the court was rendered no Mormon cared for it and no officer could execute it. Our Presidents shipped one cargo of officials after another to Utah, but the result was always the same—they sat in a blight for a while, they fairly feasted on scowls and insults day by day, they saw every attempt to do their official duties find its reward in darker and darker looks, and in secret threats and warnings of a more and more dismal nature—and at last they either succumbed and became despised tools and toys of the Mormons, or got scared and discomforted beyond all endurance and left the Territory. If a brave officer kept on courageously till his pluck was proven, some pliant Buchanan or Pierce would remove him and appoint a stick in his place. In 1857 Gen. Harney came very near being appointed Governor of Utah. And so it came very near being Harney Governor and Cradlebaugh Judge!—two men who never had any idea of fear further than the sort of murky comprehension of it which they were enabled to gather from the dictionary. Simply (if for nothing else) for the variety they would have made in a rather monotonous history of Federal servility and helplessness, it is a pity they were not fated to hold office together in Utah.

Up to the date of our visit to Utah, such had been the Territorial record. The Territorial government established there had been a hopeless failure, and Brigham Young was the only real power in the land. He was an absolute monarch—a monarch who defied our President—a monarch who laughed at our armies when they camped about his capital—a monarch who received without emotion the news that the august Congress of the United States had enacted a solemn law against polygamy, and then went forth calmly and married twenty-five or thirty more wives.

APPENDIX B

THE MOUNTAIN MEADOWS MASSACRE

THE persecutions which the Mormons suffered so long—and which they consider they still suffer in not being allowed to govern themselves—they have endeavored and are still endeavoring to repay. The now almost forgotten "Mountain Meadows massacre" was their work. It was very famous in its day. The whole United States rang with its horrors. A few items will refresh the reader's memory. A great emigrant train from Missouri and Arkansas passed through Salt Lake City and a few disaffected Mormons joined it for the sake of the strong protection it afforded for their escape. In that matter lay sufficient cause for hot retaliation by the Mormon chiefs. Besides, these one hundred and forty-five or one hundred and fifty unsuspecting emigrants being in part from Arkansas, where a noted Mormon missionary had lately been killed, and in part from Missouri, a State remembered with execrations as a bitter persecutor of the saints when they were few and poor and friendless, here were substantial additional grounds for lack of love for these wayfarers. And finally, this train was rich, very rich in cattle, horses, mules and other property—and how could the Mormons consistently keep up their coveted resemblance to the Israelitish tribes and not seize the "spoil" of an enemy when the Lord had so manifestly "delivered it into their hand?"

Wherefore, according to Mrs. C. V. Waite's entertaining book, "The Mormon Prophet," it transpired that—

A "revelation" from Brigham Young, as Great Grand Archee, or God, was despatched to President J. C. Haight, Bishop Higbee, and J. D. Lee (adopted son of Brigham), commanding them to raise all the forces they could muster and trust, follow those cursed gentiles (so read the revelation), attack them, disguised as Indians, and with the arrows of the Almighty make a clean sweep of them, and leave none to tell the tale; and if they needed any assistance, they were commanded to hire the Indians as their allies, promising them a share of the booty. They were to be neither slothful nor negligent in their duty, and to be punctual in sending the teams back to him before winter set in, for this was the mandate of Almighty God.

The command of the "revelation" was faithfully obeyed. A large party of Mormons, painted and tricked out as Indians, overtook the train of emigrant wagons some three hundred miles south of Salt Lake City, and made an attack. But the emigrants threw up earthworks, made fortresses of their wagons and defended themselves gallantly and successfully for five days! Your Missouri or Arkansas gentleman is not much afraid of the sort of scurvy apologies for "Indians" which the southern part of Utah affords. He would stand up and fight five hundred of them.

At the end of the five days the Mormons tried military strategy. They retired to the upper end of the "Meadows," resumed civilized apparel, washed off their paint, and then, heavily armed, drove down in wagons to the beleaguered emigrants, bearing a flag of truce! When the emigrants saw white men coming they threw down their guns and welcomed them with cheer after cheer! And, all unconscious of the poetry of it, no doubt, they lifted a little child aloft, dressed in white, in answer to the flag of truce!

The leaders of the timely white "deliverers" were President Haight and Bishop John D. Lee, of the Mormon church. Mr. Cradlebaugh, who served a term as a Federal Judge in Utah and afterward was sent to Congress from Nevada, tells in a speech delivered in Congress how these leaders next proceeded:

> They professed to be on good terms with the Indians, and represented them as being very mad. They also proposed to intercede, and settle the matter with the Indians. After several hours of parley, they, having (apparently) visited the Indians, gave the *ultimatum* of the savages; which was, that the emigrants should march out of their camp, leaving everything behind them, even their guns. It was promised by the Mormon bishops that they would bring a force, and guard the emigrants back to the settlements.
>
> The terms were agreed to,—the emigrants being desirous of saving the lives of their families. The Mormons retired, and subsequently appeared with thirty or forty armed men. The emigrants were marched out, the women and children in front, and the men behind, the Mormon guard

being in the rear. When they had marched in this way about a mile, at a given signal, the slaughter commenced. The men were almost all shot down at the first fire from the guard. Two only escaped, who fled to the desert, and were followed 150 miles before they were overtaken and slaughtered.

The women and children ran on, two or three hundred yards further, when they were overtaken, and with the aid of the Indians they were slaughtered. Seventeen individuals only, of all the emigrant party, were spared, and they were little children, the eldest of them being only seven years old. Thus, on the 10th day of September, 1857, was consummated one of the most cruel, cowardly, and bloody murders known in our history.

The number of persons butchered by the Mormons on this occasion was *one hundred and twenty.*

With unheard-of temerity Judge Cradlebaugh opened his court and proceeded to make Mormondom answer for the massacre. And what a spectacle it must have been to see this grim veteran, solitary and alone in his pride and his pluck, glowering down on his Mormon jury and Mormon auditory, deriding them by turns, and by turns "breathing threatenings and slaughter!"

An editorial in the *Territorial Enterprise* of that day says of him and of the occasion:

He spoke and acted with the fearlessness and resolution of a Jackson; but the jury failed to indict, or even report on the charges, while threats of violence were heard in every quarter, and an attack on the U. S. troops intimated, if he persisted in his course.

Finding that nothing could be done with the juries, they were discharged, with a scathing rebuke from the Judge. And then, sitting as a committing magistrate, *he commenced his task alone.* He examined witnesses, made arrests in every quarter, and created a consternation in the camps of the saints, greater than any they had ever witnessed before, since Mormondom was born. At last accounts, terrified elders and bishops were decamping to save their necks; and developments of the most startling character were being made, implicating the highest church dignitaries in the many murders and robberies committed upon the gentiles during the past eight years.

Had Harney been Governor, Cradlebaugh would have been supported in his work, and the absolute proofs adduced by him of Mormon guilt in this massacre and in a number of previous murders, would have conferred gratuitous coffins upon certain citizens, together with occasion to use them. But Cumming was the Federal

Governor, and he, under a curious pretense of impartiality, sought to screen the Mormons from the demands of justice. On one occasion he even went so far as to publish his protest against the use of the U. S. troops in aid of Cradlebaugh's proceedings.

Mrs. C. V. Waite closes her interesting detail of the great massacre with the following remark and accompanying summary of the testimony—and the summary is concise, accurate and reliable:

> For the benefit of those who may still be disposed to doubt the guilt of Young and his Mormons in this transaction, the testimony is here collated, and circumstances given, which go, not merely to implicate, but to fasten conviction upon them, by "confirmations strong as proofs of Holy Writ."
>
> 1. The evidence of Mormons themselves, engaged in the affair, as shown by the statements of Judge Cradlebaugh and Deputy U. S. Marshal Rogers.
>
> 2. The failure of Brigham Young to embody any account of it in his Report as Superintendent of Indian Affairs. Also his failure to make any allusion to it whatever from the pulpit, until several years after the occurrence.
>
> 3. The flight to the mountains of men high in authority in the Mormon Church and State, when this affair was brought to the ordeal of a judicial investigation.
>
> 4. The failure of the "Deseret News," the Church organ, and the only paper then published in the Territory, to notice the massacre, until several months afterward, and then only to deny that Mormons were engaged in it.
>
> 5. The testimony of the children saved from the massacre.
>
> 6. The children and the property of the emigrants found in possession of the Mormons, and that possession traced back to the very day after the massacre.
>
> 7. The statements of Indians in the neighborhood of the scene of the massacre: these statements are shown, not only by Cradlebaugh and Rogers, but by a number of military officers, and by J. Forney, who was, in 1859, Superintendent of Indian Affairs for the Territory. To all these were such statements freely and frequently made by the Indians.
>
> 8. The testimony of R. P. Campbell, Capt. 2d Dragoons, who was sent in the spring of 1859 to Santa Clara, to protect travellers on the road to California, and to inquire into Indian depredations.

APPENDIX C

CONCERNING A FRIGHTFUL ASSASSINATION THAT WAS NEVER CONSUMMATED

[If ever there was a harmless man, it is Conrad Wiegand, of Gold Hill, Nevada. If ever there was a gentle spirit that thought itself unfired gunpowder and latent ruin, it is Conrad Wiegand. If ever there was an oyster that fancied itself a whale; or a jack-o'lantern, confined to a swamp, that fancied itself a planet with a billion-mile orbit; or a summer zephyr that deemed itself a hurricane, it is Conrad Wiegand. Therefore, what wonder is it that when he says a thing, he thinks the world listens; that when he does a thing the world stands still to look; and that when he suffers, there is a convulsion of nature? When I met Conrad, he was "Superintendent of the Gold Hill Assay Office"—and he was not only its Superintendent, but its entire force. And he was a street preacher, too, with a mongrel religion of his own invention, whereby he expected to regenerate the universe. This was years ago. Here latterly he has entered journalism; and his journalism is what it might be expected to be: colossal to ear, but pigmy to the eye. It is extravagant grandiloquence confined to a newspaper about the size of a double letter sheet. He doubtless edits, sets the type, and prints his paper, all alone; but he delights to speak of the concern as if it occupies a block and employs a thousand men.

[Something less than two years ago, Conrad assailed several people mercilessly in his little "People's Tribune," and got himself into trouble. Straightway he airs the affair in the *Territorial Enterprise,* in a communication over his own signature, and I propose to reproduce it here, in all its native simplicity and more than human candor. Long as it is, it is well worth reading, for it is the richest specimen of journalistic literature the history of America can furnish, perhaps:]

From the Territorial Enterprise, Jan. 20, 1870.

A SEEMING PLOT FOR ASSASSINATION MISCARRIED.

TO THE EDITOR OF THE ENTERPRISE,

Months ago, when Mr. Sutro incidentally exposed mining mismanagement on the Comstock, and among others roused me to protest against its continuance, in great kindness you warned me that any attempt by publications, by public meetings and by legislative action, aimed at the correction of chronic mining evils in Storey County, must entail upon me (a) business ruin, (b) the burden of all its costs, (c) personal violence, and if my purpose were persisted in, then (d) assassination; and after all nothing would be effected.

YOUR PROPHECY FULFILLING.

In large part at least your prophecies have been fulfilled, for (a) assaying, which was well attended to in the Gold Hill Assay Office (of which I am superintendent), in consequence of my publications has been taken elsewhere, so the President of one of the companies assures me. With no reason *assigned,* other work has been taken away. With but one or two important exceptions, our assay business now consists simply of the *gleanings* of the vicinity. (b) Though my own personal donations to the People's Tribune Association have already exceeded $1,500, outside of our own numbers we have received (in money) less than $300 as contributions and subscriptions for the journal. (c) On Thursday last, on the main street in Gold Hill, near noon, with neither warning nor cause assigned, by a powerful blow I was felled to the ground, and while down I was kicked by a man who it would seem had been led to *believe* that I had spoken derogatorily of him. By whom he was so induced to believe I am as yet unable to say. On Saturday last I was again assailed and beaten by a man who first informed me why he did so, and who persisted in making his assault even after the erroneous impression under which he *also* was at first laboring had been clearly and repeatedly pointed out. This same man, after failing through intimidation to elicit from me the names of our editorial contributors, against giving which he knew me to be pledged, beat himself weary upon me with a rawhide, I not resisting, and then pantingly threatened me with permanent disfiguring mayhem, if ever again I should introduce his name into print, and who but a few minutes before his attack upon me assured me that the only reason I was "permitted" to reach home alive on Wednesday evening last (at which time the *People's Tribune* was issued) was, that he deems me only half-witted, and be it remembered the very next morning I *was* knocked down and kicked by a man who seemed to be *prepared* for flight.

[*He sees doom impending:*]

WHEN WILL THE CIRCLE JOIN?

How long before the *whole* of your prophecy will be fulfilled I cannot say, but under the shadow of so much fulfillment in so short a time, and with such direct threats from a man who is one of the most prominent exponents of the San Francisco mining Ring staring me and this whole community boldly and defiantly in the face and *pointing* to a completion of your augury, do you blame me for feeling that this communication is the last I shall ever write for the Press, especially when a sense alike of personal self-respect, of duty to this money-oppressed and fear-ridden community, and of American fealty to the spirit of true Liberty all command me, and each more loudly than love of life itself, to declare the name of that prominent man to be JOHN B. WINTERS, President of the Yellow Jacket Company, a political aspirant and a military General. The name of his partially duped accomplice and abettor in this last marvelous assault, is no other than PHILIP LYNCH, Editor and proprietor of the Gold Hill *News*.

Despite of the insult and wrong heaped upon me by John B. Winters, on Saturday afternoon, only a glimpse of which I shall be able to afford your readers, so much do I deplore clinching (by publicity) a serious mistake of any one, man or woman, committed under natural and not self-wrought passion, in view of his great apparent excitement at the time and in view of the almost perfect privacy of the assault, I am far from sure that I should not have given him space for repentance before exposing him, were it not that he himself has so far exposed the matter as to make it the common talk of the town that he has horsewhipped me. That fact having been made public, all the facts in connection need to be also, or silence on my part would seem *more* than singular, and with many would be proof either that I was conscious of some unworthy aim in publishing the article, or else that my "non-combatant" principles are but a convenient cloak alike of physical and moral cowardice. I therefore shall try to present a graphic but truthful picture of this whole affair, but shall forbear all comments, presuming that the editors of our own journal, if others do not, will speak freely and fittingly upon this subject in our next number, whether I shall then be dead or living, for my death will not stop, though it may suspend, the publication of the *People's Tribune.*

[*The "non-combatant" sticks to principle, but takes along a friend or two of a conveniently different stripe:*]

THE TRAP SET.

On Saturday morning John B. Winters sent verbal word to the Gold Hill Assay Office that he desired to see me at the Yellow Jacket office. Though such a request struck me as decidedly cool in view of his own recent discourtesies to me there alike as a publisher and as a stockholder in the Yellow Jacket mine, and though it seemed to me more like a summons than the courteous request by one gentleman to another for a favor, hoping that some conference with Sharon looking to the betterment of mining matters in Nevada might arise from it, I felt strongly inclined to overlook what *possibly* was simply an oversight in courtesy. But as then it had only been two days since I had been bruised and beaten under a hasty and false apprehension of facts, my caution was somewhat aroused. Moreover I remembered sensitively his contemptuousness of manner to me at my last interview in his office. I therefore felt it needful, if I went at all, to go accompanied by a friend whom he would not dare to treat with incivility, and whose presence with me might secure me exemption from insult. Accordingly I asked a neighbor to accompany me.

THE TRAP ALMOST DETECTED.

Although I was not then aware of this fact, it would seem that previous to my request this same neighbor had heard Dr. Zabriskie state publicly in a saloon, that Mr. Winters had told him he had decided either to kill or to horsewhip me, but had not finally decided on which. My neighbor, therefore, felt unwilling to go down with me until he had *first* called on Mr. Winters alone. He therefore paid him a visit. From that interview he assured me that he gathered the impression that he did not believe I would have any difficulty with Mr. Winters, and that he (Winters) would call on me at 4 o'clock in my own office.

MY OWN PRECAUTIONS.

As Sheriff Cummings was in Gold Hill that afternoon, and as I desired to converse with him about the previous assault, I invited him to my office, and he came. Although a half-hour had passed beyond 4 o'clock, Mr. Winters had not called, and we both of us began preparing to go home. Just then, Philip Lynch, Publisher of the Gold Hill *News,* came in and said, blandly and cheerily, as if bringing good news:

"Hello, John B. Winters wants to see you."

I replied, "Indeed! Why he sent me word that he would call on me *here* this afternoon at 4 o'clock!"

"O, well, it don't do to be too ceremonious just now, he's in my office, and that will do as well—come on in, Winters wants to consult with you alone. He's got something to say to you."

Though slightly uneasy at this change of programme, yet believing that in an *editor's* house I ought to be safe, and anyhow that I would be within hail of the street, I hurriedly, and but partially whispered my dim apprehensions to Mr. Cummings, and asked him if he would not keep near enough to hear my voice in case I should call. He consented to do so while waiting for some other parties, and to come in if he heard my voice or thought I had need of protection.

On reaching the editorial part of the *News* office, which viewed from the street is dark, I did not see Mr. Winters, and again my misgivings arose. Had I paused long enough to consider the case, I should have invited Sheriff Cummings in, but as Lynch went down stairs, he said: "*This* way, Wiegand—it's best to be private," or some such remark.

[*I do not desire to strain the reader's fancy, hurtfully, and yet it would be a favor to me if he would try to fancy this lamb in battle, or the duelling ground or at the head of a vigilance committee—M. T.:*]

I followed, and *without* Mr. Cummings, and without arms, which I never do or will carry, unless as a soldier in war, or unless I should yet come to feel I must fight a duel, or to join and aid in the ranks of a *necessary* Vigilance Committee. But by following I made a fatal mistake. Following was entering a trap, and whatever animal suffers itself to be *caught* should expect the common fate of a caged rat, as I fear events to come will prove.

Traps commonly are not set for *benevolence.*

[*His body-guard is shut out:*]

THE TRAP INSIDE.

I followed Lynch down stairs. At their foot a door to the left opened into a small room. From *that* room another door opened into yet *another* room, and once entered I found myself inveigled into what many will ever henceforth regard as a private subterranean Gold Hill den, admirably adapted in proper hands to the purposes of murder, raw or disguised, for from it with both or even one door closed, when too late, I saw that I *could* not be heard by Sheriff Cummings, and from it, BY VIOLENCE AND BY FORCE, I was prevented from making a peaceable exit, when I thought I saw the studious object of this "consultation" was no other than to compass my killing, *in the presence of Philip Lynch as a witness,* as soon as by insult a proverbially excitable man should be exasperated to the point of assailing Mr. Winters, so that Mr. Lynch, by his conscience and by his well known tenderness of heart toward the rich and potent would be *compelled* to testify that he saw Gen. John B. Winters kill Conrad Wiegand in "self-defense." But I am going too fast.

OUR HOST.

Mr. Lynch was present during most of the time (say a little short of an hour,) but three times he left the room. His testimony, therefore, would be available only as to the bulk of what transpired. On entering this carpeted den I was invited to a seat near one corner of the room. Mr. Lynch took a seat near the window. J. B. Winters sat (at first) near the door, and began his remarks essentially as follows:

"I have come here to exact of you a retraction, in black and white, of those damnably false charges which you have preferred against me in that —— —— infamous lying sheet of yours, and you must declare yourself their author; that you published them knowing them to be false, and that your motives were malicious."

"Hold, Mr. Winters. Your language is insulting and your demand an enormity. I trust I was not invited here either to be insulted or coerced. I supposed myself here by invitation of Mr. Lynch, at your request."

"Nor did I come here to insult you. I have already told you that I am here for a very different purpose."

"Yet your language *has* been offensive, and even now shows strong excitement. If insult is repeated I shall either leave the room or call in Sheriff Cummings, whom I just left standing and waiting for me outside the door."

"No, you won't, sir. You may just as well understand it at once as not. *Here* you are my man, and I'll tell you why! Months ago you put your property out of your hands, boasting that you did so to escape losing it on prosecution for libel."

"It is true that I did convert all my immovable property into personal property, such as I could trust safely to others, and chiefly to escape ruin through possible libel suits."

"Very good, sir. Having placed yourself beyond the pale of the law, *may God help your soul* if you DON'T make precisely such a retraction as I have demanded. I've got you now, and by ——, before you can get out of this room you've *got* to both write and sign precisely the retraction I have demanded, and before you go, anyhow—you —— —— low-lived —— lying —— ——, I'll teach you what *personal* responsibility is *outside* of the law; and, by ——, Sheriff Cummings and all the friends you've got in the world, besides, can't save you, you —— ——, etc.! *No,* sir. I'm *alone* now, and I'm *prepared* to be shot down just here and now rather than be vilified by you as I have been, and suffer you to escape me after publishing those charges, not only here where I am known and universally respected, but where I am *not* personally known and may be injured."

I confess this speech, with its terrible and but too plainly *implied* threat of killing me if I did not sign the paper he demanded, terrified me, especially as I saw he was working himself up to the highest possible pitch of passion, and instinct told me that *any* reply other than one of seeming concession to his demands would only be fuel to a raging fire, so I replied:

"Well, if I've *got* to sign ——," and then I paused some time. Resuming, I said, "But, Mr. Winters, you are greatly excited. Besides, I see you are laboring under a total misapprehension. It is your duty not to inflame but to calm yourself. I am prepared to show you, if you will only point out the article that you allude to, that *you* regard as 'charges' what no calm and logical mind has any *right* to regard as such. *Show* me the charges, and I will try, at all events; and if it becomes plain that no charges *have* been preferred, then plainly there can be nothing to retract, and no one could rightly *urge* you to demand a retraction. You should beware of making so serious a mistake, for however *honest* a man may be, every one is liable to misapprehend.

"Besides you *assume* that *I* am the author of some certain article which you have not pointed out. It is *hasty* to do so."

He then pointed to some numbered paragraphs in a *Tribune* article, headed "What's the Matter with Yellow Jacket?" saying "*That's* what I refer to."

To gain time for general reflection and resolution, I took up the paper and looked it over for a while, he remaining silent, and as I hoped, cooling. I then resumed, saying, "As I supposed. I do not *admit* having written that article, nor have you any right to *assume* so important a point, and then base important action upon your assumption. You might deeply regret it afterwards. In my published Address to the People, I notified the world that no information as to the authorship of any article would be given without the consent of the writer. I therefore cannot honorably tell you *who* wrote that article, nor can you exact it."

"If you are *not* the author, then I *do* demand to know who is?"

"I must decline to say."

"Then by ——, I brand *you* as its author, and shall treat you accordingly."

"Passing that point, the most important misapprehension which I notice is, that you regard them as 'charges' at all, when their context, both at their beginning and end, show they are not. These words introduce them: *'Such an investigation* [just before indicated,] *we think MIGHT result in showing some of the following points.'* Then follow eleven specifications, and the succeeding paragraph shows that the suggested investigation 'might EXONERATE those who are generally believed guilty.' You see, therefore, the context *proves* they are not preferred *as* charges, and this you seem to have overlooked."

While making those comments, Mr. Winters frequently interrupted me in such a way as to convince me that he was *resolved* not to consider candidly the thoughts contained in my words. He insisted upon it that they *were* charges, and "By ——," he would make me take them back *as* charges, and he referred the question to Philip Lynch, to whom I then appealed as a literary man, as a logician, and as an editor, calling his attention especially to the introductory paragraph just before quoted.

He replied, "If they are *not* charges, they certainly are *insinuations,*" whereupon Mr. Winters renewed his demands for retraction precisely such as he had before named, except that he would allow me to state who *did* write the article if I did not myself, and this time shaking his fist in my face with more cursings and epithets.

When he threatened me with his clenched fist, instinctively I tried to rise from my chair, but Winters then forcibly thrust me down, as he did every other time (at least seven or eight,) when under similar imminent danger of bruising by his fist, (or for aught I could know worse than that after the first stunning blow,) which he could easily and safely to himself have dealt me so long as he kept me down and stood over me.

This fact it was, which more than anything else, convinced me that by plan and plot I was purposely made powerless in Mr. Winters' hands, and that he did not mean to allow me that advantage of being afoot which he possessed. Moreover, I then became convinced that Philip Lynch (and for what *reason* I wondered,) would do absolutely nothing to protect me in his own house. I realized then the situation thoroughly. I had found it equally vain to protest or argue, and I would make no unmanly appeal for pity, still less apologize. Yet my life had been by the plainest possible implication threatened. I was a weak man. I was unarmed. I was helplessly down, and Winters was afoot and probably armed. Lynch was the only "witness." The statements demanded, if given and not explained, would utterly sink me in my own self-respect, in my family's eyes, and in the eyes of the community. On the other hand, should I give the author's name how could I ever expect that confidence of the People which I should no longer deserve, and how much dearer to me and to my family was *my* life than the life of the real author to *his* friends. Yet life seemed dear and each minute that remained seemed precious if not solemn. I sincerely trust that neither you nor any of your readers, and especially none with families, may ever be placed in such seeming *direct* proximity to death while obliged to decide the one question I was compelled to, viz: What should I do—I, a man of family, and *not* as Mr. Winters is, "alone."

[*The reader is requested not to skip the following.—M. T.:*]

STRATEGY AND MESMERISM.

To gain time for further reflection, and hoping that by a *seeming* acquiescence I might regain my personal liberty, at least till I could give an alarm, or take advantage of some momentary inadvertence of Winters, and then without a *cowardly* flight escape, I resolved to write a certain kind of retraction, but previously had inwardly decided

First. That I would studiously avoid every action which might be *construed* into the drawing of a weapon, even by a self-infuriated man, no matter what amount of insult might be heaped upon me, for it seemed to me that this great excess of compound profanity, foulness and epithet must be more than a mere indulgence, and therefore must have some object. "Surely in vain the net is spread in the sight of any bird." Therefore, as before without thought, I thereafter by intent kept my hands away from my pockets, and generally in sight and spread upon my knees.

Second. I resolved to make no motion with my arms or hands which could possibly be construed into aggression.

Third. I resolved completely to govern my outward manner and suppress indignation. To do this, I must govern my spirit. To do that, by force of imagination I was obliged like actors on the boards to resolve myself into an unnatural mental state and see all things through the eyes of an assumed *character*.

Fourth. I resolved to try on Winters, silently, and unconsciously to himself a mesmeric power which I possess over certain kinds of people, and which at times I have found to work even in the dark over even the lower animals.

Does any one smile at these last counts? God save you from ever being *obliged* to beat in a game of chess, whose stake is your life, you having but four poor pawns and pieces and your adversary with his full force unshorn. But if you do, provided you have any strength with breadth of will, do not despair. Though mesmeric power may not *save* you it may help you; *try* it at all events. In this instance I was conscious of power coming into me, and by a law of nature, I know Winters was correspondingly weakened. If I could have gained more time I am sure he would not even have struck me.

It takes time both to form such resolutions and to recite them. That time, however, I gained while thinking of my retraction, which I first wrote in pencil, altering it from time to time till I got it to suit me, my aim being to make it look like a concession to demands, while in fact it should tersely speak the truth into Mr. Winters' mind. When it was finished, I copied it in ink, and if correctly copied from my first draft it should read as follows. In copying I do not think I made any material change:

COPY.

TO PHILIP LYNCH, EDITOR OF THE GOLD HILL NEWS:

I learn that Gen. John B. Winters believes the following (pasted on) clipping from the *People's Tribune* of January to contain distinct charges of mine against him personally, and that as such he desires me to retract them unqualifiedly.

In compliance with his request, permit me to say that, although Mr. Winters and I see this matter differently, in view of his strong feelings in the premises, I hereby declare that I do not know those "charges" (if such they are) to be true, and I hope that a critical examination would altogether disprove them.

CONRAD WIEGAND.

Gold Hill, January 15, 1870.

I then read what I had written and handed it to Mr. Lynch, whereupon Mr. Winters said:

"That's not satisfactory, and it won't do;" and then addressing himself to Mr. Lynch, he further said: "How does it strike *you?*"

"Well, I confess I don't see that it *retracts* anything."

"Nor do I," said Winters; "In fact, I regard it as adding insult to injury. Mr. Wiegand, you've got to do better than that. *You* are not the man who can pull wool over *my* eyes."

"That, sir, is the only retraction I can write."

"No it isn't, sir, and if you so much as *say* so again you do it at your peril, for I'll thrash you to within an inch of your life, and by ——, sir, I don't pledge myself to spare you even that inch either. I want you to understand I have asked you for a very different paper, and that paper you've got to sign."

"Mr. Winters, I assure you that I *do* not wish to irritate you, but, at the same time, it is utterly *impossible* for me to write any other paper than that which I have written. If you are resolved to *compel* me to *sign* something, Philip Lynch's hand must write it at your dictation, and if, when written, I *can* sign it I will do so, but such a document as you say you *must* have from me I never can sign. I mean what I say."

"Well, sir, what's to be done must be done quickly, for I've been here long enough already. I'll put the thing in another shape (and then pointing to the paper;) Don't you know those charges are false?"

"I do not."

"Do you know them to be true?"

"Of my own personal knowledge I do not."

"Why then print them?"

"Because rightly considered in their connection they are *not* charges, but pertinent and useful *suggestions* in answer to the queries of a correspondent who stated facts which are inexplicable."

"Don't you know that *I* know they are false?"

"If you *do,* the proper course is simply to deny them and court an investigation."

"And do YOU claim the right to make ME come out and deny anything you may choose to write and print?"

To that question I think I made no reply, and he then further said: "Come, now, we've talked about this matter long enough. I want your final answer—Did you write that article or not?"

"I cannot in honor tell you *who* wrote it."

"Did you not see it before it was printed?"

"Most certainly, sir."

"And did you deem it a fit thing to publish?"

"Most assuredly, sir, or I would never have consented to its appearance. Of its *authorship* I can say nothing whatever, but for its *publication* I assume full, sole and personal responsibility."

"And do you then retract it or not?"

"Mr. Winters, if my refusal to sign such a paper as you have demanded *must* entail upon me all that your language in this room fairly implies, then I ask a few minutes for prayer."

"Prayer! —— —— you, this is not your *hour* for prayer—your time to pray was when you were writing those —— lying charges. Will you sign or not?"

"You already have my answer."

"What! do you still refuse?"

"I do sir."

"Take *that*, then," and to my amazement and inexpressible relief he drew only a raw-hide instead of what I expected—a bludgeon or pistol. With it, as he spoke, he struck at my left ear downwards, as if to tear it off, and afterwards on the side of the head. As he moved away to get a better chance for a more effective shot, for the first time I gained a chance under peril to rise, and I did so pitying him from the very bottom of my soul, to think that one so naturally capable of true dignity, power and nobility could, by the temptations of this State, and by unfortunate associations and aspirations, be so deeply debased as to find in such brutality anything which he could call satisfaction—but the great hope for us all is in progress and growth, and John B. Winters, I trust, will yet be able to comprehend my feelings.

He continued to beat me with all his great force, until absolutely weary, exhausted and panting for breath. I still adhered to my purpose of non-aggressive defense, and made no other use of my arms than to defend my head and face from further disfigurement. The mere pain arising from the blows he inflicted upon my person was of course transient, and my clothing to some extent deadened its severity, as it now hides all remaining traces.

When I supposed he was through, taking the butt end of his weapon and shaking it in my face, he warned me, if I correctly understood him, of more yet to come, and furthermore said, if ever I again dared introduce his name to print, in either my own or any other public journal, he would cut off my left ear (and I do not *think* he was jesting) and send me home to my family a visibly mutilated man, to be a standing warning to all low-lived puppies who seek to blackmail gentlemen and to injure their good names. And when he *did* so operate, he informed me that his implement would not be a whip but a knife.

When he had said this, unaccompanied by Mr. Lynch, as I remember it, he left the room, for I sat down by Mr. Lynch exclaiming: "The man is mad—he is *utterly* mad—this step is his ruin—it is a mistake—it would be ungenerous in me, despite of all the ill usage I have here received, to expose him, at least till he has had an opportunity to reflect upon the matter. I shall be in no haste."

"Winters *is* very mad just now," replied Mr. Lynch, "but when he is himself he is one of the finest men I ever met. In fact, he told me the reason he did not meet you up stairs was to spare you the humiliation of a beating in the sight of others."

I submit that that unguarded remark of Philip Lynch convicts him of having been privy in advance to Mr. Winters' intentions whatever they may have been, or at least to his meaning to make an assault upon me, but I leave to others to determine how much censure an *editor* deserves for inveigling a weak, non-combatant man, also a publisher, to a pen of his own to be horsewhipped, if no worse, for the simple printing of what is verbally in the mouth of nine out of ten men, and women too, upon the street.

While writing this account two theories have occurred to me as *possibly* true respecting this most remarkable assault:

First. The aim *may* have been simply to extort from me such admissions as in the hands of money and influence would have sent me to the Penitentiary for libel. This however seems unlikely, because any statements elicited by fear or force could not be evidence in law or could be so explained as to have no force. The statements wanted so badly must have been desired for some other purpose.

Second. The other theory has so dark and wilfully murderous a look that I shrink from writing it, yet as in all probability my death at the earliest practicable moment has already been decreed, I feel I should do all I can before my hour arrives, at least to show others how to break up that aristocratic rule and combination which has robbed all Nevada of true freedom, if not of manhood itself. Although I do not prefer this hypothesis as a *"charge,"* I feel that as an American citizen I still have a right both to think and to speak my thoughts even in the land of Sharon and Winters, and as much so respecting the theory of a brutal assault (especially when I have been its subject) as respecting any other apparent enormity. I give the matter simply as a suggestion which may explain to the proper authorities and to the people whom they should represent, a well ascertained but notwithstanding a darkly mysterious fact. The scheme of this assault *may* have been

First. To terrify me by making me conscious of my utter helplessness after making actual though not legal threats against my life.

Second. To imply that I could *save* my life only by writing or signing certain specific statements which if not subsequently explained would eternally have branded me as infamous, and would have consigned my family to shame and want, or to the dreadful compassion and patronage of the rich.

Third. To blow my brains out *the moment I had signed,* thereby preventing me from making any such subsequent explanation as *could* remove the infamy.

Fourth. Philip Lynch to be compelled to testify that I was killed by John B. Winters in self-defense, for the conviction of Winters would bring *him* in as an accomplice. If that *was* the programme in John B. Winters' mind nothing saved my life but my persistent *refusal* to sign, when that refusal seemed clearly to me to be the choice of death.

The remarkable assertion made to me by Mr. Winters, that pity only spared my life on Wednesday evening last, almost compels me to believe that at first he *could* not have intended me to leave that room alive; and why I was allowed to, unless through mesmeric or some other invisible influence, I cannot divine. The more I reflect upon this matter, the more probable as true does this horrible interpretation become.

The narration of these things I might have spared both to Mr. Winters and to the public had he himself observed silence, but as he has both verbally spoken and suffered a thoroughly garbled statement of facts to appear in the Gold Hill *News*, I feel it due to myself no less than to this community, and to the entire independent press of America and Great Britain, to give a true account of what even the Gold Hill *News* has pronounced a disgraceful affair, and which it deeply regrets because of some telegraphic mistake in the account of it.

Though he may not deem it prudent to take my life just now, the publication of this article I feel sure must compel Gen. Winters (with his peculiar views about *his* right to exemption from criticism by *me*) to resolve on my violent death, though it may take years to compass it. Notwithstanding *I* bear *him* no ill will; and if W. C. Ralston and William Sharon, and other members of the San Francisco mining and milling Ring feel that he above all other men in this State and California is the most fitting man to supervise and control Yellow Jacket matters, until I am able to vote more than half their stock I presume he will be retained to grace his present post.

Meantime, I cordially invite all who know of any sort of important villainy which only *can* be cured by exposure (and who would expose it if they felt sure they would not be betrayed under bullying threats,) to communicate with the *People's Tribune*; for until I *am* murdered, so long as I can raise the means to publish, I propose to continue my *efforts* at least to revive the liberties of the State, to curb oppression, and to benefit this part of man's world and God's earth.

CONRAD WIEGAND.

[It does seem a pity that the Sheriff was shut out, since the good sense of a general of militia and of a prominent editor failed to teach them that the merited castigation of this weak, half-witted child was a thing that ought to have been done in the street, where the poor thing could have a chance to run. When a journalist maligns a citizen, or attacks his good name on hearsay evidence, he deserves to be thrashed for it, even if he *is* a "non-combatant" weakling; but a generous adversary would at least allow such a lamb the use of his legs at such a time.—M. T.]

REFERENCE MATERIAL

EXPLANATORY NOTES

In his Prefatory to *Roughing It* Mark Twain confessed, "Yes, take it all around, there is quite a good deal of information in the book." These notes are intended to clarify and supplement this information by identifying people, places, and incidents, and by explaining literary allusions and topical references. In addition, they attempt to demonstrate the factuality of the narrative, so that the reader may more fully appreciate the artistry that Mark Twain used to shape his experiences into a work of literature.

The notes also identify portions of the text based on earlier printings—both of his own works that Mark Twain revised for inclusion in the book, and of works he quoted from other authors. Thus whenever mention is made that he incorporated into the text one of his pieces from, for example, the Buffalo *Express* or the Sacramento *Union*, the reader may find in Emendations of the Copy-Text and Rejected Substantives, found in the Works of Mark Twain edition (1993), a record of the revisions he carried out while composing *Roughing It*. Likewise, when a note identifies the source of a quotation from the work of another author, the reader may find a record of any alterations Mark Twain is presumed to have made in the borrowed material. All references to the Introduction are to the Works of Mark Twain edition (1993).

All references in the text are keyed to this volume by page and line: for example, 1.1 means page 1, line 1. Chapter titles and picture captions are *not* included in the line count. Frequently cited works have been assigned an abbreviation, which in citations is followed by a page (or volume and page) number: "*L2*, 298" or "*MTB*, 1:337." But most works are cited by the author's last name ("Hunter, 254" or "Root and Connelley, 44") or by a short title ("*Tribute*, 23"). When two or more works by the same author are cited in this way, the date of publication is used to distinguish them: "Fatout 1964, 80" and "Fatout 1976, 10." Works by members of the Clemens family may be found under their initials: SLC, OC, and MEC. All abbreviations, authors, and short titles used in citations are fully defined in References. For the reader's convenience, citations to works available in numerous editions may supply a chapter number (or its equivalent, such as a book or act number) rather than a page number. All quotations from holograph documents are transcribed verbatim from the originals (or photocopies thereof), even when a published form is also cited for the reader's convenience. The location of every unique document or manuscript is identified by the standard Library of Congress abbreviation, or the last name of the owner, always defined in References. Previously unpublished words by Mark Twain are identified by a dagger (†) in the citation and are ©1993 by Manufacturers Hanover Trust Company as Trustee of the Mark Twain Foundation, which reserves all reproduction rights or dramatization rights in every medium.

1.1–2 My brother had just been appointed Secretary of Nevada Territory] Orion Clemens (1825–97) learned of his appointment as secretary of Nevada Territory by President Lincoln on 27 March 1861, obtained his commission on 20 April, and received his final instructions on 2 July. The position had been secured for him by Edward Bates (1793–1869), Lincoln's newly appointed attorney general, who wrote to Secretary of State William Seward on 12 March 1861:

> I have just received a letter from *Orion Clemens* of M° begging me to help him to an office suitable to his degree & qualifications—& he indicates the post of Secretary of a Territory—any Territory except *Utah*—
>
> Mr C was bred a printer—I knew him in his apprenticeship—a good boy, anxious to learn, using all means in his power to do so. He edited a newspaper in a country town of M°, with fair success. Studied law, & practiced for several years, in N.E. M°. His success as a lawyer was not great, chiefly, I am told, because his politics did not suit his locality—He *was* a Whig, but joined the Republicans, & that, while it was honest & manly, subjected him to an opposition amounting almost to persecution.
>
> I consider him an honest man of fair mediocrity of talents & learning—more indeed of both, than I have seen in several Territorial secretaries.
>
> Without being very urgent with you, I commend Mr Clemens to you, as a worthy & competent man, who will be grateful for a favor. (Bates to Seward, 12 Mar 61, *Letters of Application*)

In 1860 Orion had campaigned vigorously on behalf of Lincoln and the Republican Party (MEC, 10; Miller, 1–2; Mack 1961b, 69).

1.7–11 I envied my brother . . . I never had been away from home] To create a fictional persona for the narrator, Clemens departed in several ways from the facts. In reality, he had left home in June 1853 at the age of seventeen. After working for four years as a journeyman typesetter in various midwestern and eastern cities, he began his training in April 1857 as a cub pilot on the Mississippi. As a licensed pilot he earned as much as $250 a month. For a period in 1860–61 he even provided financial support for Orion, who was ten years his senior and had been married since 1854. Still, Clemens had left the river by May 1861 (see the note at 2.18–20), and may well have felt some envy toward his brother (*L1*, 1–3, 44–46, 58–59, 69–71, 102, 103–4, 112; AD, 29 Mar 1906, CU-MARK, in *MTA*, 2:290–91).

2.14–15 he offered me . . . the sublime position of private secretary under him] Orion's official instructions stipulated that "as a general thing, the Secretary can, *in person*, perform *all* the duties pertaining to his office" (Miller, 2). He therefore had no authority to offer his brother a secretarial position. But that did not deter Clemens, who had saved enough money from his pilot's wages to pay for both stage fares to Carson City (see the note at 4.2–3) and provide approximately $800 more for expenses. During the sixty-day session of the first Territorial Legislature, from 1 October through 29 November 1861, Orion did hire his brother as a clerk, at $8 a day, for a total of $480 (Miller, 1–3; AD, 29 Mar 1906, CU-MARK, in *MTA*, 2:291).

2.16–17 the heavens and the earth passed away, and the firmament was rolled together as a scroll] Revelation 6:14 and 21:1: "And the heaven departed as a scroll when it is rolled together; and every mountain and island were moved out of their places. . . . And I saw a new heaven and a new earth: for the first heaven and the first earth were passed away; and there was no more sea."

2.18–20 At the end of an hour or two I was ready . . . because we were going in the overland stage] Clemens did not in fact decide to go with Orion until early July 1861. For several weeks after Orion was told of his appointment on 27 March, Clemens continued to work as a pilot, completing his final run in New Orleans on 8 May and returning to St. Louis as a passenger on 21 May, by which date the Civil War had virtually halted commercial river traffic. From mid-June until early July he belonged to a small band of Confederate volunteers, an episode he later fictionalized in "The Private History of a Campaign That Failed" (SLC 1885). On 4 July he met in St. Louis with Orion, who had left behind his wife and daughter in Keokuk, Iowa; on 18 July the brothers embarked from St. Louis on the *Sioux City,* bound up the Missouri River for the overland stagecoach at St. Joseph (*L1*, 121–22; MEC, 10–11).

2.24–28 I only proposed to stay in Nevada three months . . . seven uncommonly long years] In August 1866 Clemens recalled that when he left for Nevada he expected "to be gone 3 months . . . thinking the war would be closed & the river open again by that time" (*L1*, 357). But the War lasted until April 1865, and he remained in the West until December 1866, returning to St. Louis in March 1867, after an absence of nearly six years (*L2*, 1, 18 n. 1).

3.1–3 sand-bars which we roosted on . . . and then got out our crutches and sparred over] To spar a vessel over a sand-bar, long stout poles were lashed to either side of it,

> by means of which the bow was lifted as on crutches. The wheels were then put in forward motion and the boat driven ahead for a short distance, perhaps no more than a few feet. . . . This operation was repeated as often as necessary to enable the boat partly to hobble over, partly to dig its way through the bar into the deeper water of the pool beyond. (Hunter, 254–55)

3.4 she was walking most of the time] This passage resembles a description in Albert D. Richardson's *Beyond the Mississippi,* a book Clemens probably read while working on *Roughing It* (SLC to Bliss, 29 Oct 70,

Daley). Richardson had taken a steamboat in 1857 at Jefferson City, Missouri, to connect with the overland stage at Kansas City. "Navigating the Missouri, at low water," he wrote, "is like putting a steamer upon dry land, and sending a boy ahead with a sprinkling pot. Our boat rubbed and scraped upon sand-bars, and they stopped us abruptly a dozen times a day" (Richardson, 21–22, 25, 33).

3.7 "shear"] More commonly "sheer," the curvature from bow to stern of a ship's deck as shown in side elevation.

4.2–3 a hundred and fifty dollars apiece for tickets] Mark Twain evidently misremembered the actual cost. The receipt for the two fares, issued by the Central Overland California and Pike's Peak Express Company on 25 July 1861 for the trip from St. Joseph to Carson City, indicates that after an initial payment of $300, another $100 was due within thirty days, bringing the total to $200 per passenger. Three months later, in October 1861, the fare was reduced to $150, after the start of the line was moved from St. Joseph to nearby Atchison, Kansas (receipt in CU-MARK, facsimile in *L1,* 122; "The Overland Mail Route," San Francisco *Evening Bulletin,* 24 June 61, 3; "Overland Mail" and "Greatly Reduced Rates," Atchison *Freedom's Champion,* 12 Oct 61, 2, 3; Root and Connelley, 44).

5.3–9 a pitiful little Smith & Wesson's seven-shooter . . . you could not hit anything with it] Smith and Wesson's first production, introduced in 1857, was a twenty-two-caliber "Patent Breech-Loading 7 Shot Revolver," which weighed eight ounces and had a barrel less than four inches long. It was not accurate beyond ten or fifteen yards: "In a day when large-calibered guns were the rule, it must have been regarded as little more than a toy" (McHenry and Roper, 27, 139–40, 182).

5.16 Mr. George Bemis] Presumably Mark Twain invented Bemis. "Capt G. T. Hicher" and one other man accompanied the Clemens brothers when they called on Brigham Young in Salt Lake City (see the note at 92.22–93.3), but nothing has been found to suggest that either man accompanied them from St. Joseph.

5.18–19 an old original "Allen" revolver . . . a "pepper-box."] Bemis's weapon was not properly speaking a revolver (which has a single barrel), but a small-caliber pistol with six barrels (see the illustration on page 5), first manufactured by Ethan Allen in 1837. Its hammer cocked automatically with each pull of the trigger until all of its barrels, which revolved around a common axis, were fired. The name "pepper-box" derived from its resemblance (when viewed from the front) to the "perforations in the top of an old-fashioned pepper shaker." Such pistols were very popular, in spite of their inaccuracy at a range of more than a few feet (Chapel, 84–88, 92).

6.5–6 We jumped into the stage . . . and we bowled away] Orion kept a journal of the trip, which Clemens borrowed to help him write the opening chapters (SLC to OC, 15 July 70, CU-MARK, in *MTL*, 1:174–75). The journal itself is no longer extant, but some—or possibly all—of its contents survive, transcribed by Orion in a letter of 8 and 9 September 1861 to his wife, Mollie. This journal transcript provides a cursory account of the brothers' journey, from their 26 July departure from St. Joseph to their 14 August arrival in Carson City, with a brief description of the stopover at Salt Lake City on 6–7 August. It is printed in supplement A, together with a schematic comparison of Orion's account with the account in *Roughing It.* Maps 1A–1D in supplement B show the overland route and locate all of the stagecoach stations and other significant landmarks mentioned in the text and notes.

6.6 and left "the States" behind us] After the travelers ferried across the river at St. Joseph they disembarked in Kansas, which had become a state in January 1861; they would not leave "the States" proper until they entered Nebraska Territory (see the note at 12.18–19).

7.4 an imposing cradle on wheels] The Concord coach, manufactured by the Abbot-Downing Company of Concord, New Hampshire, was the standard vehicle used on all the major western stage lines at the time. Its body "rested on stout leather straps, called thorough braces, which rocked the stage body back and forth in a motion more pleasant to passengers than the ordinary jars of a wagon" and also diminished "the violence of jolts transmitted from the coach to the animals" (Hafen, 306; Greever, 44).

7.11–13 we had three days' delayed mails with us] On 1 July 1861 daily mail service was begun over a central overland route from St. Joseph to Sacramento. The Central Overland California and Pike's Peak Express Company (which until July had transported mail only semimonthly) was assigned responsibility for the line from St. Joseph to Salt Lake City, and from there the route was managed by the Butterfield Overland Mail Company, which until March 1861 had been carrying the daily mail over a southern route. The Butterfield Company had abandoned this southern route because of Confederate depredations, and, under an agreement with the Central Overland Company, moved its stock and equipment to the central route. The closure of the southern route, plus the inability of steamers to depart New York City after 20 June, led by early July to the accumulation of over twelve tons of mail at the St. Joseph office, some of which no doubt accompanied the Clemens brothers (Hafen, 92–94, 161, 211–14, 217–18; Conkling and Conkling, 2:325–26, 337–38; "Progress of the Continental Telegraph—The Overland Mail Company—Complaints as to the Newspaper Carriage Answered," San Francisco *Evening Bulletin*, 6 Sept 61, 2).

7.27–28 we would unload the most of our mail . . . on the Plains] Contemporary accounts, including the postmaster general's, confirm that in order to lighten their loads overland drivers sometimes stashed mail (especially printed material) along the route for a later stage to pick up, or even abandoned it altogether. The San Francisco *Evening Bulletin* commented in September 1861:

> Our literary folks subscribe for Harper and the Atlantic, and the people of the Great Basin and eastward get them; our "girls" subscribe for Bonner's Ledger, and the girls over the mountains get them; our babies' mothers "take Godey for the patterns," and the Brigham Young and eastward babies have the benefit of the patterns for their Sunday dresses. ("Literary Overlanders," 21 Sept 61, 3)

By June 1862 the problem had become so acute that overburdened drivers were even accused of wantonly destroying mail, sometimes while disguised as Indians (Blair, 561; Burton, 214; "The Overland Mail Troubles," San Francisco *Alta California,* 23 June 62, 1, reprinting the Carson City *Silver Age* of 19 June; Chapman, 264–67).

9.8–10 The fountains of her great deep . . . forty nights] Genesis 7:11–12: "In the six hundredth year of Noah's life . . . were all the fountains of the great deep broken up. . . . And the rain was upon the earth forty days and forty nights."

12.18–19 Little Sandy . . . Big Sandy] Actually, the trail crossed Little Sandy Creek about twenty-five miles beyond the Nebraska border, and then, another three miles or so further on, Big Sandy Creek. Clemens's memory of this section of the route was not helped by Orion's journal, which made no mention of the river crossings (see supplement A, item 1, and supplement B, map 1A).

13.26–15.7 "sage-brush," . . . "greasewood,"] This description of sagebrush and greasewood faintly echoes a similar passage in a letter Clemens wrote to his mother and then edited for publication in the Keokuk *Gate City* on 20 November 1861, in which he likened sage-brush to "a liliputian cedar tree" and characterized greasewood as "a perfect imitation, in miniature, of the live-oak tree, 'barring' the color of it" (SLC 1861). A clipping of this letter may well have been available in one of Clemens's scrapbooks.

14.8–10 lilliputian . . . Brobdingnag] Terms derived from imaginary countries in Swift's *Gulliver's Travels* (1726).

15.30–31 In Syria . . . a camel took charge of my overcoat] Clemens was in the vicinity of the headwaters of the Jordan on 17 and 18 September 1867, during the Holy Land excursion described in *The Innocents Abroad* (*N&J1*, 417, 420–22; SLC 1869a, chapter 42). No previous written version of this obviously fictional episode has been found, either in his letters to the *Alta California,* in *Innocents*, or in his extant notebook for the period, but Clemens did tell of "a ferocious and voracious camel" in at least one of his 1868 lectures about the excursion ("Opera

House—Mark Twain's Lecture," Virginia City *Territorial Enterprise*, 28 Apr 68, 3).

23.6–7 a great long "navy" revolver] A large-caliber revolver with a barrel measuring seven and one-half inches, first manufactured in 1851 by Samuel Colt (1814–62) and shortly thereafter adopted as a sidearm by the United States Navy. The revolver (with its imitators) predominated in the West in the latter half of the nineteenth century, becoming "Colt's passport to undying fame" (Edwards, 277–79, 283–84; Mathews, 1115).

24.7 Nicolson pavement] A type of street pavement, patented in 1854 by Samuel Nicolson (1791–1868), which was used in numerous American cities during the 1860s. Consisting of thick blocks of wood embedded in asphalt, it was less expensive than stone, rapidly laid, smooth, and relatively durable (*Mining and Scientific Press:* "The Chicago, or 'Nicholson' Pavement," 7 [21 Dec 63]: 4; "Patent Department," 8 [16 Jan 64]: 39).

25.1–2 We could not eat the bread or the meat, nor drink the "slumgullion."] The brothers' meal was evidently typical. Richard Burton, who traveled west by stagecoach in August 1860, described a breakfast "prepared in the usual prairie style": the stale coffee of "burnt beans" was simmered "till every noxious principle was duly extracted from it," the bacon was "rusty," the antelope steak was "cut off a corpse suspended for the benefit of flies outside," and the bread was prepared with "sour milk, . . . saleratus or prepared carbonate of soda or alkali, and other vile stuff, which communicates to the food the green-yellow tinge, and suggests many of the properties of poison" (Burton, 104).

25.3 the anecdote (a very, very old one, even at that day)] At least two writers known to Mark Twain published versions of this joke: John Phoenix (George H. Derby) in 1855, and Albert D. Richardson in 1867 (Bellamy, 39–40; Fried, 42–43; Derby, 211; Richardson, 493).

26.20–21 At 4 P.M. we crossed a branch of the river, and at 5 P.M. we crossed the Platte itself] The route reached the south bank of the Platte River at this point, but did not cross it. Orion's journal makes no mention of river crossings near Fort Kearny, and places the fort itself only seven miles beyond the sighting of the "Timber of Platte" (supplement A, item 1).

26.34–28.5 At . . . *out.*] This paragraph was reprinted, with a few minor changes, from the New York *Times* of 28 June 1869 (1–2). The article from which it was taken was the last of a series published by Clemens's friend William Swinton (1833–92), who had been a *Times* staff member since 1858. As the newspaper's special correspondent, he traveled to California in the spring of 1869 on the first run of the Pacific Railroad to employ "Pullman palace cars." His train departed Omaha on Sunday,

13 June, and arrived at Sacramento four days later. On 8 July Swinton accepted a professorship at the University of California in Berkeley, where he remained until 1874 (New York *Times:* "We had a dispatch . . . ," 9 July 69, 5; "The New West," 11 June 69, 5, and 14 June 69, 8; Ohles, 3:1262–63; Swinton to A. J. Moulder, 8 July 69, Regents' Records, Box 2:16, University Archives, CU-BANC).

27.5 Delmonico] New York restaurateur Lorenzo Delmonico (1813–81), whose principal establishment, at Broadway and Chambers Street, was internationally renowned for the quality and variety of its menu.

30.5–7 the first prairie-dog villages . . . the regular *cayote*] With few exceptions, the chronology of the overland trip described in *Roughing It* accords exactly with Orion's journal of the actual journey (see supplement A, item 1). In this instance, however, the first sight of prairie dogs and coyotes is assigned to the fourth day, one day later than Orion's reference to them.

31.22 you need a minie rifle] This muzzle-loading rifle fired a bullet invented in 1849 by Claude Étienne Minié (1804–79), which expanded to fit tightly into the grooves of the rifling, thereby improving its accuracy. The rifle had greater range and accuracy than earlier types, and made a significant impact on military tactics when it came into wide use in the 1850s. It became obsolete soon after 1865, when it was superseded by breech-loading firearms.

35.4–7 the trip was often made in fifteen days . . . eighteen or nineteen days, if I remember rightly] The scheduled passenger trip from Atchison to Placerville (about sixty miles shorter than the trip from St. Joseph to Sacramento) actually took seventeen days. Clemens's trip to Carson City (a day short of Placerville) took twenty days, including a stop of two nights and two days at Salt Lake City. The government contract with the stage company provided for "the transportation of the entire letter mail six times a week on the central route, to be carried through in twenty days eight months in the year, and in twenty-three days four months in the year, from St. Joseph, Missouri, (or Atchison, Kansas,) to Placerville" (Blair, 560; "Greatly Reduced Rates," Atchison *Freedom's Champion,* 12 Oct 61, 3; Root and Connelley, 43, 63; Kelly 1862, 12).

37.36–38.1 this vast machinery . . . was in the hands of Mr. Ben Holladay. All the western half . . . was in his hands] In mid-1861 Benjamin Holladay (1819–87) held an unrecorded deed of trust giving him effective control of the stage line, but he did not become its official owner until March 1862. His interest was not in "the western half of the business," but in the line between the Missouri River and Salt Lake City. Popular with his employees, punctilious as an administrator, and sometimes unscrupulous in his business methods, Holladay was exceedingly prosperous and had achieved near-legendary status by the time he sold his stage operations to Wells, Fargo and Company in November 1866, anticipating the completion of the transcontinental railroad. Thereafter he concentrated his business interests in the West, where he operated railroads, steamship lines, a hotel, and a sawmill (Ralph Moody, 202–5, 211–13; Frederick, 63–64, 71–75, 80–81, 260, 272; Hafen, 227–28).

38.1–3 an incident of Palestine travel . . . set down in my Holy Land note-book] The incident is not mentioned in Clemens's extant notebooks or in *The Innocents Abroad.* Mark Twain did, however, tell the story in several of his 1868 and 1869 lecture appearances, and included it in "I Rise to a Question of Privilege," written in May 1868 for the San Francisco *News Letter and California Advertiser* but never published (SLC 1868d). Clemens's remarks in a letter of 2 December 1868 to Jervis Langdon confirm that it was based on fact (*L2*, 298, 299 n. 2).

38.8–19 a young New York boy by the name of Jack . . . an elderly pilgrim . . . learned in the Scriptures] Mark Twain refers to John A. (Jack) Van Nostrand (1847?–79) of New York City and Greenville, New Jersey, and to (Confederate) Colonel William Ritenour Denny (1823–1904), a Sunday-school superintendent from Winchester, Virginia, who were members of the *Quaker City* excursion and of Clemens's party during a three-week trip on horseback through the Holy Land. While at Jericho, Denny noted in his journal, "We tried to select what might be the spot (Pisgah) where Moses viewed the promised land and died on the mountains of Moab beyond Jordan but we could not" (Denny, entries for 11 and 25 Sept 67; *L2*, 64, 93, 395–96; *MTB*, 3:1290).

39.17–18 Ben Holladay would have fetched them through in thirty-six hours] Holladay was fond of performing dramatic feats of travel. In 1862 he made the trip from San Francisco to New York City in sixteen days (a clipping describing this event may be found in Clemens's December 1866 notebook); the following year he traveled from Folsom, California (near Sacramento), to Atchison, Kansas, in twelve days. On both occasions he used specially selected teams of horses. Albert D. Richardson, correspondent for the Boston *Journal* in 1863, estimated that the latter trip "cost him 20,000 dollars in wear and tear of stock and vehicles"—evidently a small price to pay for the publicity it received (Ralph Moody, 255; "Telegraphic," Sacramento *Bee,* 16 Sept 62, 3; *N&J1*, 265 n. 30).

40.5 "Julesburg," *alias* "Overland City,"] Named for Jules Bene (also known as Jules Beni or Reni, and as René Jules), a French-Canadian trader who settled on the site in 1859, this town consisted of no more than a dozen buildings by the time it was destroyed by Indians in February 1865. It marked a major junction—the point at which the stage line to Denver diverged toward the southwest, while the main overland route crossed the South Platte River and headed northwest. By the time of the Clemenses' visit, the town had a reputation for lawlessness, which had prompted the stage company to rename it Overland City in official documents. Present-day Julesburg, Colorado, was established in 1884 by the Union Pacific Railroad, across the river and several miles north of the original site (Root and Connelley, 65, 213–15, 360–61; Thrapp, 1:92; Mattes, 279; Work, 24; see also the notes at 60.26–63.3 and 66.24–67.7).

41.8–9 a less sumptuous affair, called a "mud-wagon"] On the rougher sections of the route the Concord coaches were replaced by "mud-wagons," which carried the same number of inside passengers but were faster on mountain roads and less likely to capsize because they were both lighter and lower to the ground (Rusling, 143; Hafen, 96; George R. Stewart 1968, 6, 7, 11).

41.28–30 we took horses . . . on a buffalo hunt] Orion's journal makes no mention of such a hunt, although the entry for 29 July describes the area beyond Fort Kearny as "the Buffalo region" (supplement A, item 1). This side trip, which falls two days later in the *Roughing It* chronology, is undoubtedly imaginary.

48.6–7 talking about the king, and the sacred white elephant, the Sleeping Idol] The Buddhists of Thailand (formerly Siam) believe that an albino elephant is the incarnation of the soul of a king or a great hero and is therefore sacred. The Sleeping Idol, an enormous statue of a reclining Buddha in the Wat Poh temple in Bangkok, is one hundred and fifty feet long and forty feet high, covered in gold leaf. Clemens probably read about both in *The English Governess at the Siamese Court,* Anna Leonowens's personal reminiscence of her employment by King Mongkut, ruler of Thailand from 1851 until his death in 1868. Clemens owned an American edition of Leonowens's work (Boston: Osgood and Co.), which he inscribed "Saml L. Clemens / 1871," indicating that he may have added the Eckert incident long after first drafting chapter 6 in the fall of 1870 (Gribben, 1:406; Leonowens, 49–50, 140–41; O'Donnell, 72–73).

50.3–4 carrying letters nineteen hundred miles in eight days] The pony express provided mail service—at first weekly, and then semiweekly—for nearly nineteen months, starting on 3 April 1860; it was officially discontinued on 26 October 1861, two days after the completion of the overland telegraph line. The service had been established by the freighting firm of Russell, Majors and Waddell (which also owned the Central Overland California and Pike's Peak Express Company) to demonstrate the practicality of the central route, in an attempt to win the overland-mail contract away from the Butterfield Overland Mail. The full nineteen-hundred-mile route, from St. Joseph to Sacramento, required about ten days of nonstop travel, in relays, with each rider covering at least fifty miles (and sometimes as much as a hundred). By late July 1861, when the Clemenses started overland, telegraph stations had been established some fifty miles west of Fort Kearny, Nebraska, and the same distance east of Fort Churchill, Nevada; the transmission of messages therefore required pony-express travel only between these two stations, which took as little as eight days (Chapman, 301; Hafen, 169–74, 179, 185–87; Blair, 560).

50.15 the blackness of darkness] Jude 13.

50.27 *two dollars an ounce*] The cost of operating the pony express turned out to be much greater than the income generated, contributing to the eventual bankruptcy of Russell, Majors and Waddell. The initial fee for a letter was five dollars per half ounce, in addition to the basic ten-cent United States postage. Over the life of the service, the charge was gradually reduced: at the time of the Clemens brothers' trip it had recently been cut to the rate named here (Hafen, 180; "Pony Express," St. Louis *Missouri Democrat,* 1 July 61, 4; *DAH,* 4:306–7; see the textual note at 50.27).

53.14–54.10 the Indian mail robbery and massacre of 1856 . . . Babbitt, survived the massacre, . . . desperately wounded] Undoubtedly based on a story which the brothers heard and which Orion recorded in his journal, Mark Twain's account conflates several related incidents involving Cheyenne Indians, mislocates them by a hundred miles or more, and supplies a fictional embellishment—the "desperately wounded" survivor. On 24 August 1856, near Fort Kearny (about two hundred and fifty miles east of the scene of Mark Twain's account), a frightened mail conductor fired on two young Indians who approached to ask for tobacco. One of the Indians responded by wounding him with an arrow, but was restrained and punished by his fellow tribesmen. The following day soldiers from Fort Kearny retaliated by attacking the offending group of Indians, killing at least six, wounding many others, and taking their horses and other possessions. The surviving Indians then attacked a small wagon train carrying official supplies to the Utah government on behalf of Almon Whiting Babbitt (1813–56), secretary of Utah Territory since 1853. Two members of the company, which did not include Babbitt, survived the attack. Babbitt himself and two companions were killed thirteen days later, on 7 September, about a hundred miles east of the spot identified by Mark Twain. The Cheyenne plundered Babbitt's light carriage, taking his mules, jewelry, and gold coin (supplement A, item 1; McClelland, 1:650–54; Jefferson Davis, 106–12; Schindler, 230–36; Joseph Smith, 76; Jenson, 1:284–86; Van Wagoner and Walker, 5–9).

55.1–2 Fort Laramie . . . the Black Hills, with Laramie Peak] Fort Laramie "marked the transition from the Great Plains to the Rocky Mountains" (Mattes, 6). The Black Hills (now known as the Laramie Mountains), forested with dark conifers, are dominated by Laramie Peak, rising more than a mile above the surrounding land forty miles west of Fort Laramie (Mattes, 501; Urbanek 1974, 125; Lavender 1983, 10–11; Burton, 174).

58.10 We never did get much satisfaction about that dark occurrence] The altercation may have been less serious than the brothers thought. An unpublished account in the Library of Congress, said to be by someone "well acquainted with the stage route in the early sixties," mentions

> "Play Killings" which caused the green travelers to tremble with fear, often pulled off by stage drivers and wranglers, for the traveler's benefit. . . . these "Play Killings" were often written up afterwards as real, which caused eastern people to suppose that eight men out of ten were shot in the west each year. (Dick Clayton, 1, 3)

This account is clearly apocryphal in its other details, however, since it places Clemens—supposedly already calling himself "Mark Twain"—at Weber Station, Utah, in 1862, socializing with (among others) Jack Slade (see the next note), Lotta Crabtree (1847–1924), and the famous Indian scout Sacagawea (1784?–?1884).

58.36–38 Even before we got to Overland City, we had begun to hear about Slade and his "division"] From here through chapter 11, Mark Twain describes the career of the notorious Joseph A. (Jack) Slade (1829?–64). When returning to this section of his narrative in March 1871, Clemens asked Orion to set down his own recollections of what they had learned about Slade on the trip (SLC to OC, 10 Mar 71, NN-B). Orion's response, a letter written on 11 March, is reproduced in supplement A, item 3. Orion expressed confusion about where the brothers first heard Slade's name. In any case, Mark Twain's claim here that they had heard of Slade even before arriving in Overland City, some four hundred miles east of Rocky Ridge Station, was clearly intended to heighten the dramatic effect of their eventual encounter with him, described at the end of chapter 10. Slade had been an overland agent at least since 1859, first overseeing the route west from Fort Kearny, and then the entire division from Julesburg to Rocky Ridge Station. Spending much of his time inspecting the stations along the route, he was an efficient superintendent and a ruthless exterminator of thieves and other outlaws (Callaway, 101–8; Root and Connelley, 216–18; McClernan, 22 n. 10).

60.5–6 I will reduce all this mass of overland gossip to one straightforward narrative] Slade's biographers, from Mark Twain's time to the present, have found it impossible to distinguish fact from fiction. Mark Twain first described his meeting with Slade in an "Around the World" letter published in the Buffalo *Express* on 22 January 1870 (SLC 1870b). In this much fuller account in chapters 10 and 11, he combined popular lore with accurate history, relying on his own recollection of "overland gossip" and early 1860s newspaper reports, on Orion's letter of 11 March 1871, and on chapter 23 of Thomas J. Dimsdale's *Vigilantes of Montana* (166–77), a book that he later explicitly identifies as a source (see 64.1). Mark Twain probably received a copy of Dimsdale's book from Hezekiah Hosmer of Virginia City, Montana Territory, to whom he had written on 15 September 1870, requesting newspaper documentation about Slade (MtHI). See the Introduction, page 811.

60.8 Slade was born in Illinois, of good parentage] Dimsdale states merely that Slade "was raised in Clinton County, Ill., and was a member of a highly respectable family" (166). In fact he was born in 1829 or 1830 in Carlyle, Illinois, a town founded by his father, Charles Slade—a mill owner, merchant, and legislator who served in Congress briefly before his death in 1834. His mother, born Mary D. Kane, came from a wealthy and influential family (McClernan, 13, 22 n. 8, 37–42; Callaway, 97–98).

60.8–9 At about twenty-six years of age he killed a man in a quarrel and fled the country] Dimsdale asserts that "Slade was, at the time of his coming West, a fugitive from justice in Illinois, where he killed a man with whom he had been quarreling," by throwing a stone at his head. No source giving Slade's age as twenty-six at the time has been found (Dimsdale, 175–76).

60.12–18 he had an angry dispute with one of his wagon-drivers . . . and shot him dead] Dimsdale does not report this story, but Orion set down a version of it in his 11 March 1871 letter (supplement A, item 3). Slade's career in the late 1850s, before his employment as a division agent, has not been documented. There is some evidence that he worked with a freighting company on the overland trail, or possibly for John M. Hockaday and Company, which transported mail over the route in 1858–59. The incident Mark Twain describes may or may not have occurred, but the story was widely repeated, in several different versions. The brothers could have heard it on their overland trip, or read it during their stay in Nevada: it appeared in the Carson City *Silver Age* in June 1862 (Chapman, 184–85; Bloss, 86–87; Hafen, 109–110; Callaway, 113; McClernan, 26–27; "A Disreputable Agent," Sacramento *Union*, 24 June 62, 2, reprinting the Carson City *Silver Age* of 21 June).

60.22–24 he killed three savages . . . and afterward cut their ears off and sent them . . . to the chief of the tribe] No source for this episode has been discovered, although its atrocities are like those commonly attributed to Slade (McClernan, 42–43).

60.26–63.3 the important post of overland division-agent at Julesburg, in place of Mr. Jules . . . dead or alive] Jules Bene (see the note at 40.5), a dishonest station keeper, was dismissed when Slade took charge of the division; Slade, under orders to recover stolen company property, seized some horses from him. Mark Twain's version of the ensuing feud follows Dimsdale for the most part, but incorporates from Orion's report the detail that the two men fired at each other through a doorway, while Dimsdale and others assert that Jules attacked Slade when he was unarmed (Dimsdale, 173–75; Thrapp, 1:92; supplement A, item 3; McClernan, 13; Callaway, 102, 106–7; Langford, 2:293–95).

63.35–39 On one occasion . . . killing three, and wounding the fourth] Mark Twain copied these two sentences almost verbatim from Dimsdale (175).

64n.1 Prof. Thos. J. Dimsdale] Thomas J. Dimsdale (1831–66), an educated Englishman suffering from tuberculosis, went to Virginia City, Idaho Territory, in the summer of 1863, seeking improved health. (On 26 May 1864 this area became part of the newly formed territory of Montana.) He taught school, served as the territory's first superintendent of public instruction, and edited the *Montana Post,* its first newspaper of consequence. *The Vigilantes of Montana,* based on a series of articles which appeared in the *Post* in 1865–66, was published shortly before his death (DeGolyer, ix).

64.16–65.15 he saw a man approaching who had offended him . . . one of the deadest men that ever lived] No source for these two alleged murders has been identified. The account here became itself part of the tradition in which "every sort of homicidal exploit was attributed to Slade," most or even all of which are probably "unworthy of belief" (Callaway, 112–13).

66.5–23 a Frenchman who had offended Slade . . . they mounted double and galloped away unharmed] Dimsdale does not recount these incidents. Orion set down a version of them, and they were also reported in the Carson City *Silver Age* in June 1862. Both accounts link the two incidents, identifying one of the would-be lynchers and his family as the victims of the burning (supplement A, item 3; "A Disreputable Agent," Sacramento *Union,* 24 June 62, 2, reprinting the Carson City *Silver Age* of 21 June).

66.24–67.7 Slade's myrmidons captured his ancient enemy Jules . . . correct in all essential particulars] This incident probably took place in 1860. Mark Twain first made passing reference to it in his January 1870 "Around the World" letter (SLC 1870b). His account here is greatly expanded, but does not seem to draw on either Orion's or Dimsdale's versions, from which it varies considerably. He may well have seen a report published in western newspapers in June 1862, which claimed that Jules begged Slade to spare his life in return for "his entire stock, which was valued at $3,000," and which also noted that Slade put

Jules's ears in his pocket, remarking that he planned to "make soup of them" ("The Overland Mail Troubles," San Francisco *Alta California,* 23 June 62, 1, reprinting the Carson City *Silver Age* of 19 June). Nathaniel P. Langford, in his authoritative 1890 account, establishes that there is little doubt that Slade acted in self-defense, that Jules was the vengeful aggressor, that Slade's contemporaries felt his killing of Jules was justified under the circumstances, and that the reports of Jules's torture were greatly exaggerated, if not utterly false (supplement A, item 3; Dimsdale, 174–75; Thrapp, 1:92, 3:1318; Langford, 2:295–301).

67.8 we rattled up to a stage station] Before writing *Roughing It* Clemens mentioned breakfasting with Slade at Rocky Ridge Station (which they reached on the morning of 3 August, the ninth day of their trip) on three different occasions: in his January 1870 "Around the World" letter, in his September 1870 letter to Hosmer, and in his March 1871 letter to Orion (see the notes at 58.36–38, 60.5–6, and 66.24–67.7). In the *Roughing It* chronology, he moved the encounter with Slade to the morning of the eighth day, leaving the location—the name of the station and its distance from St. Joseph—deliberately vague.

67.21 He was so friendly and so gentle-spoken] Dimsdale noted that Slade was "a kind hearted and intelligent gentleman" when alcohol had not transformed him into "a reckless demon," and reported that "no man in the Territory had a greater faculty of attracting the favorable notice of even strangers" (Dimsdale, 167). William F. ("Buffalo Bill") Cody, who worked under Slade for two years as a pony-express rider and stage driver, described him as kind, generous, and concerned for the welfare of his employees. A year before the Clemenses' trip, Slade had been so solicitous of a baby girl in Richard Burton's party of travelers that he drove them part of the way in his own buckboard with "an outriding escort" of "sixteen of the most villa[i]nous cut throats on the Plains" (Hale, 7–8; Cody, 104–5).

67.26–28 his face was rather broad . . . lips peculiarly thin and straight] Mark Twain chose not to use all of the description that Orion provided (supplement A, item 3). An 1862 newspaper story reported that Slade was "of small stature, very wiry, with sharp cheek bones, an aquiline nose and brown hair" ("A Disreputable Agent," Sacramento *Union,* 24 June 62, 2, reprinting the Carson City *Silver Age* of 21 June).

69.2–4 the Vigilance Committee in Montana . . . had hanged him] In June 1863 Slade moved to Virginia City, Idaho Territory, where he operated a freighting business and began ranching. He had been fired the previous November from the overland stage line at the insistence of the authorities at Fort Halleck, where he had wrecked the sutler's store on a drunken spree. Slade's execution on 10 March 1864 no doubt came to Clemens's attention in Nevada, when he was reporting for the Virginia City *Territorial Enterprise.* The files of the *Enterprise* for that period are lost, but the town's other major newspaper published two accounts of "the shocking event" (Virginia City *Union:* "Execution at Bannock City," 3 Apr 64, 2; "The Slade Scene in the Doings of the Idaho Vigilance Committee," 5 May 64, 1; Callaway, 118–19, 121–23; McClernan, 14, 25 n. 22, 27–28 n. 24; Chapman, 193–96; Root and Connelley, 466).

69.6–7 being a Reliable Account . . . Band:] This subtitle is evidently Mark Twain's own composite of the subtitles on the paper cover and on the title page of Dimsdale's book. The subtitle on the cover reads, "TRIAL, CAPTURE AND EXECUTION OF HENRY PLUMMER'S NOTORIOUS ROAD AGENT BAND! FORMING THE ONLY RELIABLE WORK EVER OFFERED TO THE PUBLIC." The subtitle on the title page reads, "OR POPULAR JUSTICE IN THE ROCKY MOUNTAINS. BEING A CORRECT AND IMPARTIAL NARRATIVE OF THE CHASE, TRIAL, CAPTURE AND EXECUTION OF HENRY PLUMMER'S ROAD AGENT BAND, . . . Forming the only reliable work on the subject ever offered the public."

69.13–17 "Those who saw him . . . would pronounce him a fiend incarnate."] An essentially accurate quotation from Dimsdale (167).

69.17–20 From Fort Kearny . . . anything in literature] Mark Twain was responsible for some of the "compactness, simplicity and vigor of expression" in this sentence; Dimsdale actually wrote, "He was feared a great deal more, generally, than the Almighty, from Kearney, West" (Dimsdale, 175).

69.22 After the execution of the five men, on the 14th of January] In an earlier chapter, Dimsdale described the hanging of five desperadoes on 14 January 1864: Boone Helm, Jack Gallagher, Frank Parish, Haze Lyons, and "Club-Foot George" Lane (Dimsdale, 136–46).

70.10–11 On returning from Milk River] Earlier in the chapter Dimsdale reported that Slade, shortly after arriving in Virginia City in 1863, undertook to fetch a load of merchandise from the Milk River in northwestern Idaho Territory; he and his teamsters successfully completed the seven-hundred-mile round trip through hostile Indian country. One writer described him as "the only man to be found in the mines willing to encounter the risk" of such an enterprise, through an area "full half of which was unmarked by a road" (Dimsdale, 167; Langford, 2:302–4).

72.26–31 Nevada . . . Virginia] Nevada City and Virginia City, two miles apart, were the largest mining camps in Alder Gulch, Idaho Territory (Langford, 1:377).

76.1–7 a Mormon emigrant train . . . the distance our stage had come in *eight days and three hours*] Orion's account indicates that the travelers actually encountered the emigrants on their seventh day of travel, probably between Horseshoe and La Prele stations (supplement A, item 1). Some four or five thousand emigrants, as estimated in October 1861 by the Salt Lake City *Deseret News,* made the trip to Utah in the summer of 1861 ("Last Immigrant Company," Salt Lake City *Deseret News,* 2 Oct 61, 180).

76.10 Horse Creek] This is the only place name in Mark Twain's account of the overland trip which is not mentioned in Orion's journal. Having followed the valley of the North Platte River for about two hundred miles, the trail left the river valley upstream from present-day Casper, Wyoming, and continued in a more westerly direction toward the Sweetwater River and Independence Rock, crossing on the way Horse Creek, the site of a stage station (Urbanek 1974, 104; Urbanek 1978, 43–44).

76.19–20 Independence Rock, Devil's Gate and the Devil's Gap] Independence Rock is a granite monolith covering over twenty acres and rising one hundred and ninety feet above the valley floor. Four miles upstream, the Sweetwater River flows through Devil's Gate, a deep, narrow gorge. To pass this obstacle, the trail traversed the ridge to the south through a "natural opening," which was very likely known as Devil's Gap, although the name has not been independently documented (Urbanek 1978, 49–51).

77.15 South Pass City] This settlement was situated near the place where the overland route left the Sweetwater River; it was less than a year old, being "one of the many mushroom growths which the presence of gold in the Rocky Mountains . . . caused to spring up" (Burton, 199–200). (Another town of the same name, still in existence today as a historic site, was founded several miles north in 1867: see WPA, 319–20.)

78.14–80.4 SOUTH PASS . . . Mount Washington] South Pass (elevation 7,550 feet) is a long, treeless valley, twenty-five miles wide, from which several mountains rising over twelve thousand feet are visible in the distance (WPA, 321). Mount Washington in New Hampshire (elevation 6,288 feet) is the highest point in the northeastern United States.

81.3–4 a spring which spent its water through two outlets and sent it in opposite directions] Mark Twain apparently alludes to Pacific Springs, situated in South Pass about four miles west of the Continental Divide. The notion of a single spring with "two outlets" sending the waters in "opposite directions" is evidently his alone; Orion claimed, in his letter of 11 March 1871, that at this spot one "spring with waters destined for the Atlantic stood within a man's length (or within sight) of another spring whose waters were about to commence a voyage to the Pacific," and in his journal he made only passing mention of the spring (supplement A, items 1 and 3; WPA, 323).

81.38–82.1 I freighted a leaf . . . But I put no stamp on it] Mark Twain's manuscript draft of this passage was longer; he later reduced it to this brief remark: see the manuscript page reproduced on page 798.

82.9–17 a boyish prank of mine . . . to drop the melon on his head] In his Autobiographical Dictation of 29 March 1906, Clemens told a greatly expanded version of the watermelon incident, identifying his brother Henry as the victim (CU-MARK, in *MTA*, 2:282–84). No evidence has been found that he actually encountered an old friend on the summit.

85.7 sixty U. S. soldiers from Camp Floyd] Located some forty miles southwest of Salt Lake City, Camp Floyd was built in 1858 to house federal troops during the Mormon conflict of 1857–58. The soldiers met by the Clemens brothers must have been among the last to leave the camp, which the army had fully abandoned by the end of July 1861 (Alexander and Arrington, 3–7, 18). The Clemenses reached "the remnant and ruin" of this "important military station" on 8 August, shortly after leaving Salt Lake City (122.1–2).

85.33–34 took supper with a Mormon "Destroying Angel."] The brothers' last stop before Salt Lake City was Mountain Dell Station, operated by Ephraim Knowlton Hanks (1826–96). Born and raised in Ohio, Hanks ran away from home and joined the navy for three years before converting to Mormonism in about 1846. He served the church as a mail carrier, negotiator with the Indians, and in 1857–58 as guerrilla and scout. The Sons of Dan, or Danites—also known among non-Mormons as the Avenging or Destroying Angels—was a secret, paramilitary society formed in 1838 by the Missouri Mormons to defend themselves and punish apostates. Members swore to obey the head of the church "the same as the Supreme God," pledging secrecy upon pain of death. The society's name derived from Genesis 49:17: "Dan shall be a serpent by the way, an adder in the path, that biteth the horse heels, so that his rider shall fall backward." Richard Burton, who had stopped at Mountain Dell Station one year earlier, reported that Hanks made "a facetious allusion to all our new dangers under the roof of a Danite." In fact, the Sons of Dan may well have been officially dissolved in Missouri, but because Mormon vigilantism continued in Utah, the popular view (clearly known to Hanks) routinely blamed the Danites, with their reputation for vengeance. Burton (and others) described Hanks as "a middle-sized, light haired, good looking man, with regular features, a pleasant and humorous countenance, and the manly manner of his early sailor life, touched with the rough cordiality of the mountaineer." Mark Twain, whose description contrasts markedly with Burton's, may have confused Hanks with Heber C. Kimball's son (see the next note) (Burton, 237–38; Fike and Headley, 28; Hanks and Hanks, 15, 40, 57–58, 62, 191–94, 296; Schindler, 26–39, 200 n. 18, 258, 354; Hyde, 104–5; Hilton, 12–13; Nels Anderson, 27 n. 27, 149, 167).

86.10–11 one person that looked like a gentleman—Heber C. Kimball's son] Almost certainly William Henry Kimball (1826–1907), eldest son of Heber C. Kimball (see the note at 92.9–10) and an officer in the territorial militia. In a letter dated 19 August 1861 to the St. Louis *Missouri Democrat,* Orion quoted Kimball's identification of himself as Heber Kimball's "hell-roaring son" (OC, 1). The description seems apt: in 1857 he had been implicated in two murders (for one of which he was later indicted but never tried), and in 1860 he had been disfellowshiped temporarily for drunkenness. It has been suggested that Mark Twain had access to Orion's newspaper letter while writing *Roughing It,* and that he deliberately reversed the two characters (making Hanks the rowdy, and Kimball the gentleman) in order to "temper the heated passions and violent controversies visible just below the surface of his brother's letter" (Rogers 1961, 46). But it seems at least as likely that, ten years after the fact, Mark Twain merely confused the two men (Kimball 1981, 223, 232, 311; Kimball 1988, 9, 106; Schindler, 193 n. 1, 251, 280 n. 42, 357, 359–60; Bancroft 1882–90, 21:509; Hickman, 125, 128–29; Hilton, 69–70, 77–78).

86.14–15 said to be the wives of the Angel—or some of them, at least] Like many prominent Mormons, Hanks was a polygamist, but a modest one at this time: he had only two wives in 1861 (Hanks and Hanks, 131, 251–52).

86.19–87.1 "peculiar institution,"] Polygamy. The term was also commonly used to refer to black slavery in the United States (Arrington 1985, 247, 323; Waite, 30; O'Dea, 105).

87.5 Salt Lake House] According to Burton, this "grand," two-story hotel was "the principal, if not the only establishment of the kind" in the city. It had "a long verandah, supported by trimmed and painted posts," and a large central courtyard "for cor[r]alling cattle" (Burton, 247).

88.14 the Acting Governor of the Territory] In 1906 Clemens mistakenly recalled that Frank Fuller "was acting Governor, and he gave us a very good time during those two or three days that we rested in Great Salt Lake City" (AD, 11 Apr 1906, CU-MARK, in *MTA,* 2:350). The acting governor (as Orion noted at this time in his newspaper letter) was actually the territorial secretary, Francis H. Wootton, standing in for Governor Alfred Cumming, a secessionist who had departed for his native Georgia in May (see the note at 552.40–553.2). Wootton, also a secessionist, had already tendered his resignation, preferring not to serve under Lincoln, but he could not leave until his replacement, Frank Fuller, arrived, which he did on 10 September, a month after the

Clemens brothers had gone on to Carson City. Clemens and Fuller did not meet until 1862, after which they became lifelong friends (OC, 1; "Departure of the Governor," Salt Lake City *Deseret News*, 22 May 61, 96; "Affairs in Utah," New York *Times*, 8 July 61, 2; *L2*, 5; Bancroft 1882–90, 21:604–5).

88.15–16 "Gentiles" are people who are not Mormons] Because they identified themselves with the Hebrews of the Old Testament, Mormons early applied this biblical term to all non-Mormons (Arrington and Bitton, 128).

88.30 the exclusively Mormon refresher, "valley tan."] Burton claimed that this local whiskey made from wheat, "being generally pure," was better than what "sold under the name of cognac" (Burton, 388). Edward P. Hingston, who visited Salt Lake City with Artemus Ward in 1864, pronounced it "the vilest whisky I remember tasting" (Hingston, 457). The term originally referred to leather tanned in the Salt Lake Valley, but came to apply to anything manufactured in Utah, including crockery, medicines, furniture, and gold coin (Bancroft 1882–90, 21:540 n. 44).

89.4–7 no public drinking saloons were allowed . . . and no private drinking . . . except . . . "valley tan."] Beer was also produced and privately consumed. At this time the Mormons emphasized temperance rather than abstinence, although by the end of the century alcohol use was virtually prohibited. Hingston noted that Brigham Young himself owned a distillery and sold valley tan at a "properly appointed office, where it is only to be bought wholesale by those who are permitted to purchase, and who must take it to their own homes for private consumption" (Hingston, 457–58; Bush, 64 n. 48; McCue, 70–71; Burton, 388).

89.5 Brigham Young] Young (1801–77) was born in Vermont, raised in New York, and, as a young man, trained as a carpenter and painter. In 1831 he converted to Mormonism, whose founder, Joseph Smith, he met the following year. He rose quickly in the church ranks, becoming, after Smith's murder in 1844, the second prophet of the church and later its president. He was largely responsible for organizing and leading the Mormon exodus to Utah, begun in 1846. After serving as the first governor of Utah Territory from 1851 to 1858, he was obliged to give up all civil office, but still exercised nearly unquestioned authority among Mormons, warranting Mark Twain's description of him as an "absolute monarch" (87.3–4) (Arrington 1985, 413–17; Jenson, 1:8–14; Kimball 1981, 206).

90.10–16 The armorial crest of my own State . . . was always too figurative . . . a GOLDEN BEEHIVE . . . all at work] The Missouri state and Utah territorial seals are pictured below. The Missouri motto acknowledged the importance of preserving the Union, despite the long-standing conflict between slave and free states. (The Missouri Compromise of 1820 admitted Missouri to the Union as a slave state.) The beehive was a favorite Mormon emblem, signifying both the virtue of industry and the overall social order they sought to create, after a passage in the Book of Mormon: "And they did also carry with them Deseret, which, by interpretation, is a honey bee" (*Book of Mormon* 1866, Ether 1:3 [Ether 2:3]; Carter, 4:67–70; Houck, 3:269–71).

90.17–19 The city lies in the edge of a level plain as broad as the State of Connecticut . . . under a curving wall of mighty mountains] At the time, Salt Lake City occupied the northern edge of the valley, which extends roughly twenty-four miles north to south, and eighteen miles east to west. Connecticut is roughly sixty by ninety miles. The valley is surrounded by mountains, the tallest rising more than seven thousand feet above the valley floor.

91.7 Salt Lake City was healthy—an extremely healthy city] A commonplace: Burton, for example, claimed that its "climate of arid heat and dry cold is eminently suited to most healthy and to many sickly constitutions: children and adults have come from England, apparently in a dying state, and have lived to be strong and robust men" (Burton, 337).

92.8–9 the foundation of the prodigious temple] The Mormons began the temple at Salt Lake City in 1853, but suspended work in 1858 in anticipation of hostilities with federal troops (see the note at 548.26–31). Construction resumed in October 1861, shortly after the Clemenses left, and was completed in 1893. The foundation measured 186½ by 99 feet and consisted of footings 16 by 8 feet, designed to support walls at least 6 feet thick and 167½ feet high, with towers rising 15 to 43 feet higher. The building material was syenite (rock composed primarily of feldspar), quarried in the mountains and transported twenty miles by teams of horses and oxen (Rich, 307–8; *House of the Lord,* 12–13; "The Temple," Salt Lake City *Deseret News,* 18 Dec 61, 196).

92.9–10 that shrewd Connecticut Yankee, Heber C. Kimball] Heber Chase Kimball (1801–68) was born in Vermont and grew up there and in New York, where he became a Mormon in 1832. Rising rapidly in the church ranks, he led the first two Mormon missions to England. He was among the first Mormon settlers of Utah in 1847, and from then until his death was second only to Young in the church hierarchy. He served as chief justice, lieutenant governor, and ex-officio president of the senate of the provisional state of Deseret (1849–50), and as a member of the legislative council under the territorial government of Utah (1851–59). His widespread business interests included farming, ranching (cattle, sheep, and horses), milling, freighting, real-estate investment, and the vigorous promotion of domestic manufacture (Jenson, 1:34–37; Kimball 1981, 197–98, 206, 219–25; Esshom, 986–87).

92.11–12 the "Tithing-House,"] Devout Mormons began tithing (giving a tithe, or one-tenth, of their income to the church) in the late 1830s. The Salt Lake City Tithing Office and Deseret Store was a long narrow building with "cellars, store-rooms, receiving-rooms, pay-rooms, and writing offices" on Main Street, across from the building site of the temple (Burton, 302–3). There Mormons brought their tithes, either in coin or in produce and materials, which were then displayed for sale or distributed to the poor (Arrington and Bitton, 210; Cameron, 205, 227).

92.12 the "Lion House,"] So called after a sculpted lion over its entrance, it was one of a complex of buildings owned by Young, and it served as home for many of his wives and children. It contained a separate room for each wife, as well as a communal kitchen, dining room (large enough to seat fifty), nursery, schoolroom, and prayer room. Built in 1856 for sixty-five thousand dollars, it was located near the Tithing Office (Arrington 1985, 170; Burton, 301–2; Cameron, 227).

92.17–18 Mr. Street (since deceased)] James Street (d. 1867), whose experiences as an agent of the Overland Telegraph Company Mark Twain discusses in chapter 14, went to California in the early 1850s. He engaged in business in the southern part of the state, and later worked on the construction of a telegraph line between Los Angeles and San Francisco ("Death of James Street," San Francisco *Alta California,* 7 Jan 67, 2). Street may have accompanied the Clemens brothers on their visit to Young, although he is not named in Young's office journal for that day (see the next note). It has been suggested that the Clemenses did not meet Street in Salt Lake City, but only at Camp Floyd after leaving the city (Rogers 1961, 47). In 1874, however, Clemens wrote Street's daughter, "I remember your father very well indeed. His courtesies to us in Salt Lake City were of so pleasant a nature that even the fourteen years that have rolled by since have not sufficed to obliterate the memory of them" (SLC to Miss Street, 1 Dec 74, ViU†).

92.22–93.3 He talked about Utah . . . with our Secretary and certain government officials who came with us] Young's office journal for 7 August 1861 reads as follows:

> Br William Clayton, read the pony dispatch to some of the members of the club; Pres^{t} Young ‸Heber‸ & Wells were present.
>
> Br. W^{m}. Clayton, introduced: Mr Clements Sec^{y} of the Territory of Nevada who was on his way to Carson, ~~also~~ accompanied by ‸his Brother & Capt G. T. Hicher &‸ Sec^{y} Wootten of this Ter. and ~~three~~ ‸one‸ other gentlemen. ~~Capt G. T. Hincher~~
>
> They conversed with Pres. Young & Wells principally about this Territory, situation of Big Cotton wood Lake, the health of the Country. Opinion of Mr Bridger who said he would be willing to give \$50^{00} for the first bushel of wheat raised in this barren Country. The improvements in the Valley far exceeded their expectations, after the conversation they politely took their leave. (Young, entry for 7 Aug 61, used by permission)

William Clayton (1814–79), originally from Lancashire, England, went to Utah with Young in 1847 and became his clerk. Heber C. Kimball (see the note at 92.9–10) and Daniel Hanmer Wells (1814–91) were Young's first and second counselors, respectively; the three together were known as the First Presidency. Captain G. T. Hicher has not been identified; Secretary Wootton was the acting governor of Utah Territory (see the note at 88.14) (Kimball 1981, 45; Jenson, 1:36, 62, 717–18; Arrington and Bitton, 339). The "Opinion of Mr Bridger" refers to frontiersman and scout James Bridger (1804–81), who, according to an eyewitness in 1847, "considered it important not to bring a large population into the Great Basin until it was ascertained that grain could be raised; he said he would give one thousand dollars for a bushel of corn raised in the Basin" (Arrington 1985, 141, 458 n. 58).

93.4–5 I made several attempts to "draw him out" on Federal politics and his high-handed attitude toward Congress] Orion may have had explicit orders from the State Department to inquire into Mormon intentions following the secession of the Southern states. His letter to the *Democrat* indicated that he, rather than his brother, attempted to "draw out" the Mormon officials. Orion did not report Young's comments, but quoted the following speech of Kimball's:

> It's my opinion you won't see peace any more; the United States will go all to pieces, and the Mormons will take charge of and rule all the country; republicanism will be overthrown, but I won't say what will take its place, nor when, nor at what time the Mormons will commence their rule. You are going to have trouble in Nevada. But mind, I am a Union man, we are Union men, we are going to stand by the country. Now, tell it just as I say it. (OC, 1)

At the time of Clemens's visit, Young had done nothing that showed a particularly "high-handed attitude toward Congress." The phrase is probably a vestigial reference to material Mark Twain removed from the chapter, in proof, but ultimately included as appendix A when the book manuscript proved too short to fill the six hundred pages his publisher expected. Originally, the material in appendix A probably fell just after the previous paragraph (ending with "satisfied." at 92.16), and therefore before this reference to Young's "high-handed attitude." The final paragraph in appendix A makes clear that the "attitude" referred to was Young's response to events that occurred *after* "the date of our visit to Utah" (549.20), principally the federal law against polygamy passed in 1862 (see the note at 549.26–28). Appendix A and much else in these chapters on the Mormons derived from Mark Twain's reading of Catharine V. Waite's *Mormon Prophet and His Harem* (1868; first edition, 1866). He mentions her book in chapter 17 (117.2–3) and cites it as the source of his account of the Mountain Meadows massacre, which was evidently drafted as a chapter following chapter 14, but was likewise removed in proof, and ultimately restored as appendix B. Waite's view of Young was decidedly hostile (Waite, 20, 23, 25, 48, 89–90, 92–93, 295).

94.1–4 Mr. Street . . . had eight or nine hundred miles . . . to traverse with his wire] In June 1860 Congress passed the Pacific Telegraph Act, which authorized the construction, within two years, of a telegraph line from the Missouri River to San Francisco. In April 1861, several California telegraph companies merged to form the Overland Telegraph Company, which won the contract to build the line between Salt Lake City and Carson City, the eastern terminus of the existing line from San Francisco. Street, formerly the manager of the Pacific and Atlantic Telegraph Company in San Francisco, was placed in charge of the crew building west from Salt Lake City, while another crew worked east from Carson. Street's section covered about three hundred miles, half the distance to Carson (Thompson, 349, 354–55, 360–67; Gamble, 556–58; Reid, 501).

96.14–15 I believe his story. I knew him well . . . afterward in San Francisco] Street's story is confirmed, in its essentials, by his immediate superior, James Gamble, general superintendent of the Overland Telegraph Company. Gamble explained that "the first contract made with the Mormons was also a failure. Young denounced the contractors who agreed to furnish the poles from the pulpit, and said the work of furnishing the poles should and must be carried out" (Gamble, 559). After the line between Carson and Salt Lake was completed on 24 October 1861, Street returned to San Francisco, where he continued to work for several years for the California State Telegraph Company, which had absorbed the Overland Company. Clemens's surviving letters of the period, however, do not mention him (Gamble, 562; Langley 1861, 321, 493; Langley 1862, 369, 580; Langley 1865, 418).

97.9 these poor, ungainly and pathetically "homely" creatures] The supposedly dreary appearance of Mormon women was a popular myth. Clemens was undoubtedly familiar with Richardson's description in *Beyond the Mississippi:* "Few of the women are comely. . . . Nearly all are plain—many extremely so. . . . they bear the indelible impress of poverty, hard labor and stinted living. In those faces is little breadth, thought or self-reliant reasoning, but much narrowness, grave sincerity and unreflecting earnestness" (Richardson, 357). He is not known to have read Fitz Hugh Ludlow's similar assertion in *The Heart of the Continent,* that he "had not met a single woman who looked high-toned, first-class, capable of poetic enthusiasm or heroic self-devotion; . . . not one to whom a finely organized intellectual man could come for companionship" (Ludlow, 375).

98n.2 Appendices A and B] As first drafted, appendix A was almost certainly part of chapter 13 (see the note at 93.4–5), and appendix B a separate chapter following chapter 14. Mark Twain cut out both, probably in proof during August 1871, and only later agreed to make them into appendixes to help lengthen his book, possibly as late as December 1871. See the Introduction, pages 844, 846, 865, 873.

98 *illus*] Strictly speaking, this drawing does not illustrate anything in the text. Elisha Bliss, Mark Twain's publisher, probably inserted it here to help fill up the white space on the last page of chapter 14. The engraving was not made for *Roughing It,* but borrowed from a book Bliss had published in 1870: Nelson Winch Green's *Mormonism,* an anti-Mormon polemic based on an autobiographical account by Mary Ettie V. Smith, a former Mormon. No evidence has been found that Clemens himself was familiar with Green's book. Although the illustration appears here without a caption, it is called "The Endowment" in the List of Illustrations (xxvi.6). That title was derived from Green's caption, "The Oath of the Endowment": in Green's text the picture illustrates a secret Mormon initiation ceremony in which, according to Mary Smith, the temptation scene in the Garden of Eden was re-enacted in a fashion "*too monstrous for human belief.*" Her description of these "infernal rites" makes clear that the apron pictured was decorated with "green silk, to represent fig leaves," but it does not explain the significance of the dagger (Green, 41–53, illustration facing 343).

99.4–6 how Burton galloped in among the . . . defenceless "Morrisites" and shot them down . . . like so many dogs] Joseph Morris (1824–62) was an English convert to Mormonism who emigrated to Utah in 1853. In 1857 he claimed the first of a series of revelations which led him to believe that he, rather than Brigham Young, was the true prophet. In April 1861, shortly after being excommunicated, Morris organized his own church, whose tenets included the imminence of a Second Coming and the rejection of polygamy. Within a year he had attracted several hundred followers, who established a stronghold some thirty miles north of Salt Lake City. In the spring of 1862 (several months after the Clemens brothers had passed through Salt Lake City) the Morrisites captured several would-be defectors, and then refused a judge's order to release them. To enforce the order, Acting Governor Frank Fuller sent a force of five hundred men, primarily Mormons, under the command of Deputy Territorial Marshal Robert T. Burton (1821–1907), also a Mormon. After a three-day battle, the Morrisites surrendered and stacked their guns. Burton then rode into the stronghold and, according to an eyewitness account reproduced in Waite's *Mormon Prophet*, murdered the unarmed Morris and three of his followers, including two women. Burton claimed that he had fired only at Morris, and only when Morris urged his followers to retrieve their weapons. In 1863, several Morrisites were tried, and seven were convicted of second-degree murder for the deaths of two militiamen, while others were fined. All were pardoned three days later by Governor Stephen S. Harding, who believed that Burton had acted out of vengeance and religious zeal. (Burton himself was tried and acquitted much later, in 1879.) Mark Twain could have learned of these events from Frank Fuller, or contemporary news reports, or both. His characterization of Burton may, however, indicate the influence of a source hostile to Mormons, such as Waite's *Mormon Prophet* (Howard, 112–32; Bancroft 1882–90, 21:615–21; Rich, 299–301; Neff, 650–52; Waite, 39, 136–41; Esshom, 784; Hickman, 211–17).

99.6–8 Bill Hickman, a Destroying Angel, shot Drown and Arnold dead for bringing suit against him for a debt] William Adams Hickman (1815–83) joined the Mormon church in 1838 and was active in Mormon affairs until 1863, five years before being excommunicated. He served both Smith and Young as a bodyguard, and was known as an Indian fighter, cattle rustler, and vigilante. He also sat in the Utah territorial legislature and served as a mail carrier, county sheriff, assessor, tax collector, and prosecuting attorney. Beginning in 1863, he worked as a spy and guide for the federal forces in Utah. C. M. Drown and Josiah Arnold, a former Mormon, were murdered together in Salt Lake City in July 1859. Mark Twain found a brief account of the murder in Waite's *Mormon Prophet:*

> A man by the name of Drown, brought suit upon a promissory note for $480, against the Danite captain, Bill Hickman. The case being submitted to the court, Drown obtained a judgment. A few days afterwards, Drown and a companion named Arnold were stopping at the house of a friend in Salt Lake City, when Hickman, with some seven or eight of his band, rode up to the house, and called for Drown to come out. Drown, suspecting foul play, refused to do so, and locked the doors. The Danites thereupon dismounted from their horses, broke down the doors, and shot down both Drown and Arnold. Drown died of his wounds next morning, and Arnold a few days afterwards. Hickman and his band rode off unmolested. (Waite, 84)

Although Hickman was indicted for murdering Drown, he was never brought to trial. In 1872, too late to affect *Roughing It*, J. H. Beadle edited and published Hickman's sensational autobiography, *Brigham's Destroying Angel*. There Hickman confessed to a number of grisly killings committed at the behest of Young, but he denied killing Drown and Arnold, pointing the finger instead at "a man by the name of Matthews," who had acted upon Young's remark that Drown was a "bad man, and should be used up" (Hickman, 110–11, 133–35; Hilton, ix–xi, 7–13, 43, 84, 85–86, 87, 108–9, 114, 119, 125–31; Schindler, 280 n. 42, 357; Van Wagoner and Walker, 119–24).

99.8–9 how Porter Rockwell did this and that dreadful thing] As a boy, Orrin Porter Rockwell (1813–78) knew and idolized Joseph Smith. In 1830, he became one of the earliest converts to Mormonism, serving as Smith's bodyguard in Illinois. Rockwell was notorious even before the Mormons left Illinois: he was arrested in 1843 for the attempted murder of Lilburn W. Boggs, a former governor of Missouri, and again in 1845 for killing a man implicated in Smith's murder the year before. Neither charge resulted in conviction. Rockwell was in the first party of Mormon immigrants to Utah in 1847. Known for his skills as a rider and marksman, he served as a scout, hunter, deputy marshal, express rider and, in 1857–58, guerrilla leader. Among the crimes ascribed to him was the 1857 killing of four wealthy travelers in Utah whom the Mormons suspected of being federal spies. No one was ever convicted of their murders. Rockwell was alleged to have killed as many as a hundred men, and was routinely identified as a "Destroying Angel" (Schindler, 3–6, 61–62, 70–73, 82, 94, 99, 148–49, 181, 192, 193, 223, 251, 268–78; Van Wagoner and Walker, 249–53).

99.27–29 their religion teaches them that the more wives a man has . . . the higher the place they will all have in the world to come] Beginning in 1835, Mormon doctrine held that the marriage bonds continued in an afterlife, an idea essential to the theological rationale for plural marriage, according to which a man's progression toward "exalted godhood" in heaven depended on the number of wives and children "sealed to him for eternity" (Van Wagoner, 56). Founder Joseph Smith was the first to practice plural marriage, albeit surreptitiously, as early as the 1830s. He did not develop the theological justification for it until 1843, when he claimed that a revelation from God called for the restoration of biblical polygamy. That revelation was known only to his closest associates, however, and he never publicly acknowledged it. In 1852, when the church under the leadership of Brigham Young announced plural marriage as a tenet, Mormons were exhorted, even commanded, to practice it, but only a small minority ever did so (Van Wagoner, 4–6, 85–86, 90–92, 97–98).

100.1–6 Brigham Young's harem contains twenty or thirty wives . . . children—fifty altogether] At the time of the Clemenses' visit, Young had seventeen wives (two of them sisters), ranging in age from about thirty-one to fifty-nine, and at least forty-one children (Arrington 1985, 420–21).

100.10–11 Johnson professed to have enjoyed a sociable breakfast in the Lion House] No evidence has been found that Johnson was modeled on a real person. Mark Twain's description of Young's family closely resembles the farcical treatment that Artemus Ward had used to poke fun at Mormon polygamy. Clemens was probably familiar with Ward's "A Visit to Brigham Young," first published in *Vanity Fair* on 10 November 1860 as "Artemus Ward Visits Brigham Young" and collected two years later in *Artemus Ward: His Book:*

> He don't pretend to know his children, thare is so many of um, tho they all know him. He sez about every child he meats call him Par, & he takes it for grantid it is so. His wives air very expensiv. Thay allers want suthin & ef he don't buy it for um thay set the house in a uproar. He sez he don't have a minit's peace. . . . "I find that the keers of a marrid life way hevy onto me," sed the Profit, "& sumtimes I wish I'd remaned singel." (Charles Farrar Browne 1862, 99–100)

Clemens met Ward in Virginia City in late 1863, and the two men quickly developed a mutual affection and professional respect (*L1*, 267–68, 269–70 n. 5). For further discussion of Ward's influence on Mark Twain, see Branch 1967, Branch 1978, Rowlette, and Cracroft.

103.13 Joseph Smith] See the note at 107.5–10.

103.13–14 By the slaughtered body of St. Parley Pratt] Parley Parker Pratt (1807–57) from New York joined the church in 1830 and five years later became one of Joseph Smith's original twelve apostles. He served as a missionary in the United States, Canada, Great Britain, the Pacific islands, and South America, and published several theological defenses of Mormon doctrine. He helped organize the first government in Utah and served in the territorial senate. He was murdered in Arkansas in May 1857 by the undivorced husband of his tenth plural wife, and was thereafter regarded by Mormons as a martyr (Van Wagoner and Walker, 217–23; Jenson, 1:83–85).

103.24–25 I will hang him higher than Haman] Haman, the chief minister of King Ahasuerus (Xerxes), persuaded the king to massacre all the Jews, and prepared a gallows to hang his own enemy, Mordecai. Queen Esther, a Jew, intervened, and Haman was hanged on his own gallows (Esther 3–7).

103.26 Shade of Nephi] See the note at 107.12.

103.34–36 I had married her . . . and of course I could not remember her name] Mark Twain may have known a similar anecdote in Richardson's *Beyond the Mississippi* in which Young, startled by a woman's claim to be his wife, consults his records and remarks, "Well, I believe you are right. I *knew* your face was familiar!" (Richardson, 355).

104.1–2 by the ghost of Orson Hyde] Originally from Connecticut, Orson Hyde (1805–78) was no ghost when *Roughing It* was published. He joined the Mormon church in 1831, became an apostle in 1835, and in the next few years led important missions to England and Jerusalem. For most of 1855 and 1856 he served as ecclesiastical leader and probate judge for newly formed Carson County, Utah (later Nevada) Territory. In 1858 he was appointed by Young to preside over a district of south-central Utah, where he lived until his death in 1878. Hyde was also elected to several terms in the Utah legislature, serving a total of more than fifteen years (Jenson, 1:80–82).

107.2–3 I brought away a copy from Salt Lake] The edition Mark Twain almost certainly used when writing this chapter was the "sixth European," published in 1866 and therefore not the copy he may have "brought away" with him in 1861.

107.5–10 If Joseph Smith . . . merely translated it from certain . . . plates of copper . . . in an out-of-the-way locality] Smith (1805–44), the founder and first prophet of the Mormon church (officially, the Church of Jesus Christ of Latter-day Saints), was born in Vermont and moved with his family to western New York in 1816. He claimed that a series of visions in the 1820s led him to discover certain metal plates buried under a stone near Manchester, New York. Smith's own statements and the Book of Mormon itself indicate variously that the plates were gold, or brass, or simply "ore." Smith's brother William, however, identified the metal as copper sometime after *Roughing It* was published, which suggests that Mark Twain had a contemporary source for this information, as yet unidentified (Hyde, 212–13; Donna Hill, 71). Engraved on these plates were ostensibly ancient characters which Smith called "Reformed Egyptian," and which he claimed to be able to translate by gazing into special "seer" stones. After dictating his translation over a period of months in 1828–29, he published it in March 1830 as the Book of Mormon. Eleven days later he founded his church, and over the next decade led a growing membership westward to various locations in Ohio, Missouri, and Illinois. In 1844, conflict both within the church and with non-Mormon neighbors at Nauvoo, Illinois, precipitated his arrest and, on 27 June, his murder in the Carthage, Illinois, jail (Brodie, 6–9, 37–43, 57, 60–62, 82, 87, 98–99, 208–9; Van Wagoner and Walker, 288–94; Donna Hill, 71–73; Arrington and Bitton, 13). See the first paragraph of appendix A for Mark Twain's summary of the history of the Mormon church under Smith.

107.12 The book seems to be merely a prosy detail of imaginary history] According to a modern (1981) introduction, the Book of Mormon is a "record of God's dealings with the ancient inhabitants of the Americas," principally the descendants and followers of Nephi and Laman, two sons of Lehi, who leave Jerusalem for the New World in 600 B.C.;

and the Jaredites, descendants and followers of Jared, who leave Babel after the destruction of the tower in 2500 B.C. The narrative culminates with the reappearance of Christ in America, heralding a period of harmony between the chronically warring Nephites and Lamanites. Ultimately the iniquitous Lamanites (the supposed forebears of the American Indians) destroy the Nephites. The chronicle is supposed to have been recorded on metal plates by several historians—first Nephi himself, and later Mormon and his son Moroni, the last surviving Nephite, who buried the plates around 421 A.D. Smith claimed that Moroni appeared to him as an angel in 1823 and revealed the location of the plates, but did not allow him to take possession of them until 1827 (Donna Hill, 98–100; Arrington and Bitton, 9, 14, 31–33; Hyde, 212–13; Brodie, 39–40, 43–44, 70–71).

108.14–39 THE TESTIMONY OF THREE WITNESSES . . . OLIVER COWDERY, DAVID WHITMER, MARTIN HARRIS] Responding to demands that someone besides himself be allowed to see the plates, in March 1829 Smith announced a revelation instructing him to show them to three persons, unnamed. In June, when he had nearly completed his work on the Book of Mormon, he claimed a further revelation naming his three associates: Oliver Cowdery (1806–50), David Whitmer (1805–88), and Martin Harris (1783–1875). Harris and Cowdery had both assisted him by transcribing his dictations; Harris had also agreed to pay for publication; and Smith was living in Whitmer's home when he completed his work. The three witnesses subsequently gave varying accounts of the plates, and all became alienated from Smith and his church. Their testimony has appeared in every edition of the Book of Mormon (Brodie, 53, 60–62, 76–78; Donna Hill, 84–85, 89–97; Arrington and Bitton, 12–14; *Doctrine and Covenants,* sections 5 and 17; Jenson, 1:246–51, 263–76).

109.8–29 AND ALSO THE TESTIMONY OF EIGHT WITNESSES . . . if the entire Whitmer family had testified] Familial connections among all eleven witnesses were even closer than their names might suggest. The five Whitmers—David, Christian (1798–1835), Jacob (1800–56), John (1802–78), and Peter, Jr. (1809–36)—were brothers; Oliver Cowdery and Hiram Page (1800–52) were married to the Whitmers' sisters; and Joseph Smith, Sr. (1771–1840), Hyrum Smith (1800–44), and Samuel Harrison Smith (1808–44) were Joseph's father and brothers (Jenson, 1: 52–53, 181–82, 251–52, 276–82; Brodie, 78–79).

109.31 Zeniff] Although the table of contents in the sixth European edition of the Book of Mormon (probably used by Mark Twain) lists the Record of Zeniff as a separate book, this record is actually a subsection of the Book of Mosiah; in addition, the text includes a fourth book of Nephi not listed in the contents (*Book of Mormon* 1866, viii, xi, Mosiah 6–13, 4 Nephi [492–96]).

109.33–111.21 first book of Nephi . . . reached it in safety] Mark Twain paraphrases and quotes from *Book of Mormon* 1866, 1 Nephi 1:11–5:43 (1 Nephi 2:1–18:23), with the exception of the phrase "children of Lehi" (109.34–35), which is found in Mormon 2:2 (Mormon 4:12).

110.5–6 He finished the ship *in a single day,* while his brethren stood by and made fun of it] Mark Twain simplified and summarized several pages of exceptionally turgid narrative. Nephi's brothers opposed his plan to construct a ship "even for the space of many days," but through divine intervention, he eventually enlisted their help, with construction taking longer than a single day (*Book of Mormon* 1866, 1 Nephi 5:22, 28–34 [1 Nephi 17:17, 49–18:4]).

111.22–24 Polygamy . . . was added by Brigham Young . . . it was regarded as an "abomination."] Following Waite's *Mormon Prophet,* Mark Twain assumed that Young's 1852 public endorsement of polygamy was also its introduction. In fact, polygamy had been practiced in secret by Joseph Smith and others during his lifetime, possibly as early as the 1830s (see the note at 99.27–29). Waite presented the same evidence of doctrinal inconsistency, quoting both of the passages from the Book of Mormon which Mark Twain quoted here (111.26–35, 112.1–5). The conflict between Mormon scripture and practice, as well as Smith's lifelong denial of polygamy (despite strong evidence to the contrary), caused confusion among Mormons and led to many defections (see *Book of Mormon* 1866, Jacob 2:6,9 [Jacob 2:23–26, 3:5]; Waite, 176–79; Van Wagoner, 3–4, 12–13, 54–55, 72–74, 79; Foster, 130–39, 146–51).

112.1–2 the Lamanites . . . because of their filthiness and the cursings which hath come upon their skins] The Lamanites, the supposed ancestors of the American Indians, were cursed by God with a dark skin because of their iniquities, and became "a filthy people, full of idleness and all manner of abominations" (Brodie, 43–49; *Book of Mormon* 1866, 1 Nephi 3:31 [1 Nephi 12:23], 2 Nephi 4:4 [2 Nephi 5:21], 3 Nephi 1:9 [3 Nephi 2:14–15]).

112.16 now these were the names of the disciples whom Jesus had chosen] According to the third Book of Nephi, Jesus, after appearing in the New World, chose twelve disciples before returning to heaven. One of these disciples, named Nephi, was a descendant of the original Nephi, who had emigrated from Jerusalem six hundred years earlier (*Book of Mormon* 1866, 3 Nephi 1:1, 8:10–11, 9:1–2 [3 Nephi 1:1–2, 18:36–39, 19:1, 4]).

112.17–20 how much more grandeur and picturesqueness . . . accompanied one of the tenderest episodes in the life of our Savior . . . I quote the following] Mark Twain alludes to Christ's blessing of the children in the New Testament:

And they brought young children to him, that he should touch them; and his disciples rebuked those that brought them. But when Jesus saw it, he was much displeased, and said unto them, Suffer the little children to come unto me, and forbid them not; for of such is the kingdom of God. Verily I say unto you, Whosoever shall not receive the kingdom of God as a little child, he shall not enter therein. And he took them up in his arms, put his hands upon them, and blessed them. (Mark 10:13–16)

The passage quoted from the *Book of Mormon* 1866 is 3 Nephi 8:5 (3 Nephi 17:19–25).

112.38–114.44 The book of Ether is an incomprehensible medley . . . I have not written] The Book of Ether recounts the history of the Jaredites (see the note at 107.12). The names and events mentioned here occur in *Book of Mormon* 1866, Ether 5–6 (Ether 12–15); the quoted extract is from Ether 6:7–9 (Ether 15:12–33).

113.21–22 that of the Kilkenny cats, which it resembles] Proverbial: two cats from Kilkenny County, Ireland, fought until they killed each other, leaving nothing behind but their tails. The story probably derived from the long-standing enmity between two "municipalities of Kilkenny . . . who contendeth so severely about boundaries and dues to the end of the 17th century that they mutually ruined each other" (Lean, 1:276). About 1700, their enmity gave rise to a nursery rhyme: "There were two cats at Kilkenny; Each thought there was one too many" (Stevenson, 799). A rather less plausible theory traces the expression to Hessian soldiers, garrisoned at Kilkenny during the Irish rebellion of 1798, who, for sport, forced cats to fight to the death (Harvey, 448).

116.3 the "Mormon question,"] Public policy toward the Mormons remained unsettled for much of the century. Concern over their political intransigence, religious eccentricity and dogmatism, and especially polygamy constituted the "Mormon question" or "Mormon problem," which Fitz Hugh Ludlow identified as "the engrossing question, 'What shall we do with the Mormons?'" (Ludlow, iii; Allen and Leonard, 296–97; Arrington and Bitton, 173–74, 176, 179; Bancroft 1882–90, 21:495–96 n. 30; Lingenfelter, Dwyer, and Cohen, 226).

116.8–117.6 "Mountain Meadows massacre" . . . the Mormons *were* the assassins] Mark Twain's account of this episode, based on Waite's *Mormon Prophet,* is in appendix B (see the note at 93.4–5).

122.11–13 there was no well or spring . . . a stage station there] There was in fact a spring at Fish Springs Station (or Fish Creek Station, as Orion called it in his journal), but it consisted merely of pot-holes full of warm, sulfurous water (supplement A, item 1; Root and Connelley, 103; Burton, 558). In the fall of 1871, after he had long since completed the printer's copy of his book, Mark Twain was obliged to rewrite part of this chapter when the printers lost the manuscript for it. He evidently rewrote it in October, while on lecture tour, and therefore without access to Orion's journal. See the Introduction, pages 869–70.

124.23–24 the station on the farther verge of the desert] The travelers arrived at Willow Springs Station at 2 P.M. on 9 August, having taken twenty-two hours to traverse some sixty-eight miles along the southern edge of the vast Great Salt Lake Desert (supplement A, item 1; Root and Connelley, 103).

124.31 "gild refined gold or paint the lily."] *King John*, act 4, scene 2.

126.2–3 Rocky Cañon, two hundred and fifty miles from Salt Lake] Mark Twain's source for this identification was undoubtedly Orion's journal entry of 10 August, but the forbidding canyon located at this point of the overland route was actually named Egan Canyon. Situated between "steep high rugged mountains," Egan Canyon had been the site of more than one attack by Goshute Indians (Mason, 51–53, 60–62; supplement A, item 1; Burton, 617; see supplement B, map 1C).

126.5–6 the wretchedest type of mankind I have ever seen, . . . the Goshoot Indians] This small tribe—whose name is now more commonly spelled "Goshute" (from the Indian word for "parched or dry earth" plus the suffix "ute")—were members of the Shoshoni family. They inhabited northwestern Utah and eastern Nevada, numbering fewer than five hundred by the 1870s (Hodge, 1:496–97; see also the note at 128.19–129.12).

126.8 the despised Digger Indians of California] The name "Digger" was originally applied to one Paiute tribe, which alone among the Paiutes practiced agriculture. In time it came to refer instead to numerous root-eating Paiute tribes inhabiting several western states, including California, Nevada, and Utah; "as the root-eaters were supposed to represent a low type of Indian, the term speedily became one of opprob[r]ium" (Hodge, 1:390).

126.12–127.3 Wood's "Uncivilized Races of Men" . . . Bosjesmans (Bushmen) of South Africa] In the fall of 1870, when beginning work on *Roughing It*, Mark Twain asked Elisha Bliss to send him a copy of John George Wood's two-volume work, *The Uncivilized Races, or Natural History of Man*, first published in London in 1868–70 and reissued by the American Publishing Company in 1870 (SLC to Bliss, 29 Oct 70, Daley). Mark Twain's own copy of the book, presumably the one Bliss sent him, survives with his marginalia sprinkled throughout (NvU); it contains no holograph comments, however, about the tribes he lists here. Wood, an "armchair" naturalist who compiled his book without leaving England, included articles—often contemptuously critical—on the Fuegians, Hottentots, Kytch, and Bushmen (as well as many others), but did not mention the Goshutes or Diggers in his brief article on the Indians of North America. Wood's conclusions were somewhat at variance with Mark Twain's: he seems to have found the Fuegians and the Kytch even more "degraded" than the Bushmen (John George Wood, 1:269, 485, 2:514, 515).

127.9–21 like all the other "Noble Red Men" . . . thinking whisky is referred to] The concept of the "Noble Red Man" has been traced at least as far back as the work of John Dryden, who wrote of "the noble savage" uncorrupted by "the base laws of servitude" (*The Conquest of Granada* [1670], act 1, scene 1); Mark Twain was most familiar with its embodiment in James Fenimore Cooper's Indian heroes (see the note at 128.19–129.12). In describing the Goshutes he may have recalled a passage in *Beyond the Mississippi* in which Richardson expressed similar sentiments:

> Near a little road-side grocery, supported by a post and flanked by an empty cask, stood a Noble Red Man. Indifferent to his tattered clothing, which afforded no protection from the sharp, wintry nights—with his long black locks flying in the wind—his whole soul was wrapped in a whisky bottle. He regarded it with a fixed stare, in which satisfaction at the quality of its contents and pensive regret at their diminishing quantity were ludicrously blended. Mr. Cooper died too early. I think one glimpse of *this* Aboriginal would have saved his pen much labor, and early American literature many Indian heroes. (Richardson, 512)

127.29–30 whichever animal-Adam the Darwinians trace them to] Mark Twain was no doubt referring to Charles Darwin's most recent work, *The Descent of Man,* volume 1 of which was published in the United States in mid-February 1871, and volume 2 in late March (D. Appleton and Co.). Clemens purchased and read at least the first volume (his copy is in CU-MARK)—probably by early April, when he evidently revised this chapter, and certainly no later than 2 July, when he wrote to Jim Gillis (see the note at 412.1–3), "Say, old philosopher, would you like to read Darwin? If you would, let me know, & I will get the books & forward them to you" (SLC to Gillis, PH in CU-MARK, courtesy of CCamarSJ†; New York *Tribune:* "New Publications," 10 Feb 71, 6, and "Books of the Week," 25 Mar 71, 6).

127.35–128.17 they attacked the stage-coach . . . the soldierly driver was dead] This is an essentially accurate account of the start of the Goshute War of 1863, which began on 22 March of that year and concluded in October when the Indians sued for peace. (Mark Twain's version differs from contemporary newspaper reports only in its failure to mention three other passengers—an old man, who was wounded and recovered, and his two little sons.) The attack occurred near Eight Mile Station, which in 1863 was in western Utah but is now in eastern Nevada (Angel, 180–83; "More Indian Difficulties," Salt Lake City *Deseret News,* 25 Mar 63, 312; "The Attack on the Overland Stage," Sacramento *Union,* 31 Mar 63, 3, reprinting the Virginia City *Union* of 28 March).

128.2 Judge Mott] Gordon Newell Mott (1812–87) was born in Ohio and practiced law in California before moving to Nevada Territory in 1861. From 1861 to 1863 he served as judge of the district comprising Lake, Storey, and Washoe counties, and as associate justice of the territorial supreme court. In 1863–64 he was a territorial representative to the United States Congress (*BDUSC*, 1544; Kelly 1862, 10; Kelly 1863, 9).

128.19–129.12 a disciple of Cooper . . . over-estimating the Red Man while viewing him through the mellow moonshine of romance] Mark Twain's disdain for the idealized image of the American Indian—especially as found in James Fenimore Cooper's Leather-Stocking Tales (of which *The Last of the Mohicans* [1826] was the second)—is evident as early as 25 June 1862 in a letter published in the Keokuk *Gate City* (SLC 1862b) and as late as 1884 in the unfinished tale "Huck Finn and Tom Sawyer among the Indians" (SLC 1884b). See, for example, his remarks in an 1867 letter to the San Francisco *Alta California* (SLC 1867j); in "A Day at Niagara," an August 1869 Buffalo *Express* contribution (SLC 1869e); and in "The Noble Red Man," a piece in the September 1870 *Galaxy* (SLC 1870j). For analyses of Mark Twain's treatment of this subject see Denton, Harris, Lorch 1945, and McNutt.

129.7 Emerson Bennett's works] Bennett (1822–1905) wrote melodramatic adventure fiction, much of it set on the frontier. Two such novels of his, both published in 1849, sold a hundred thousand copies each: *The Prairie Flower* and its sequel, *Leni-Leoti.*

129.7–8 studying frontier life at the Bowery Theatre] Since its construction in 1826 on the west side of the Bowery just below Canal Street, this theater had been quite popular for productions of all types; it specialized, however, in melodramas and thrillers, some of which were dramatized versions of dime novels by authors like Bennett (King, 578; Odell, 7:224–27).

129.20–21 the Baltimore and Washington Railroad Company . . . are Goshoots] The specific reason for Mark Twain's grievance against this railroad, the Washington branch line of the Baltimore and Ohio Railroad, is not now known.

130.1–24 the highest mountain peaks we had yet seen . . . the "Sink" of the Carson] Mark Twain's geographical description is not entirely accurate. His remark about the mountain peaks is clearly derived from Orion's record, which reads "Passed points declared by the driver to be the highest we had crossed." In fact, when the travelers crossed the Ruby Mountains through the Overland Pass they were several hundred feet lower than they had been at both South Pass and Big Mountain, and the highest mountains in view were more than a thousand feet lower than those of the Wind River and Uinta mountains visible from South

Pass and beyond. The "Great American Desert" was more commonly known as the Forty Mile Desert, a fact he alludes to in his description of it as "forty memorable miles of bottomless sand." It was so named by early emigrants, whose route took them across the desert from north to south, a distance of some forty miles. The overland-mail route, however, traversed the desert from east to west, a considerably shorter distance. Finally, Carson Lake and Carson Sink are separate features, although they are connected by sloughs (Angel, 359, 360, 365; Townley, 46–47; supplement A, item 1; see supplement B, maps 1D and 2).

130.5–6 the eastward-bound telegraph-constructors] See the note at 94.1–4.

130.7 his Excellency Gov. Nye] James Warren Nye (1815–76), an outspoken Republican politician from New York, served in the late 1850s as police commissioner and first president of the New York City Metropolitan Board of Police. In 1860 he campaigned vigorously for Lincoln, who rewarded him the following year with an appointment as governor of the newly formed Nevada Territory. Nye arrived at Carson City early in July 1861. After Nevada became a state, he was elected United States senator from 1864 to 1873. During his frequent absences from the territory, Orion, as territorial secretary, served as acting governor. Both the Clemenses enjoyed consistently friendly relations with Nye during their stay in Nevada, although he later reportedly dismissed Clemens as "nothing but a damned Secessionist" (Frank Fuller to A. B. Paine, 7 Dec 1910, Chester L. Davis 1956d, 1; Mack 1961a, 9–11; *BDUSC*, 1579; *L1*, 145–46 n. 2). Clemens later recalled,

> Governor Nye was an old and seasoned politician from New York—politician, not statesman. He had white hair. He was in fine physical condition. He had a winningly friendly face and deep lustrous brown eyes that could talk as a native language the tongue of every feeling, every passion, every emotion. His eyes could outtalk his tongue, and this is saying a good deal, for he was a very remarkable talker, both in private and on the stump. He was a shrewd man. He generally saw through surfaces and perceived what might be going on inside without being suspected of having an eye on the matter. (AD, 2 Apr 1906, CU-MARK, in *MTA*, 2:305)

131.7–8 Ragtown] This settlement on the Carson River, which marked the end of the arduous desert passage for early emigrants on the trail to the California gold fields, probably derived its name from the worn-out clothes they washed and draped over bushes to dry (Townley, 31; Carlson, 197).

131.12 Horace Greeley] Greeley (1811–72) had been the influential editor of the New York *Tribune* since 1841, and was a prolific author and a political leader as well. Two years before the Clemens brothers went west, Greeley had taken the overland stagecoach to San Francisco as a correspondent for the *Tribune;* his travel letters were later published in *An Overland Journey, from New York to San Francisco, in the Summer of 1859* (Greeley 1860). He was one of Mark Twain's favorite targets for good-humored satire: see chapter 70.

131.13–132.6 Hank Monk . . . what was left of him] Henry James Monk (1826–83), the "king of stage drivers" (as Mark Twain referred to him in 1863), was born in New York; in 1852 he went to California, and for over thirty years drove stages there and in Nevada, working first for the California Stage Company and then, after 1857, for the Pioneer Stage Line (SLC 1863m). Monk was immortalized in western legend by virtue of a single accomplishment: a sixty-mile stagecoach trip over the Sierra Nevada on 30 July 1859, transporting Greeley from an inn fifteen miles west of Genoa, Nevada Territory, to Sportsman's Hall, California (a reception committee took Greeley in a carriage the remaining twelve miles to Placerville). Over the roughest and most dangerous forty miles of the trip Monk drove his horses at a "break-neck rate," as Greeley himself reported it (Greeley 1860, 281–82). Monk enjoyed recounting the adventure; the most reliable surviving version of the story appeared in the San Francisco *Golden Era* in April 1860, in a letter signed "Cornish." In December 1863 Mark Twain attended (and reported) a ceremony at which Monk's admirers presented him with a "superb gold watch . . . gorgeously embellished with coaches and horses" and engraved with "Hank's famous remark to Horace Greeley" (SLC 1863y; Cornish, 5; Lillard and Hood, 7–11, 41 n. 1, 44 nn. 13, 15; see Lillard and Hood for an exhaustive treatment of the incident).

132.8–9 Gregory Diggings] John H. Gregory of Georgia made a rich gold strike in May 1859 on the north fork of Clear Creek in Colorado, attracting thousands of prospectors. The diggings ultimately proved to be the richest in the state, producing $85 million in gold. The site is now near Central City, about thirty miles west of Denver (Bancroft 1882–90, 20:377–78; State Historical Society of Colorado, 41–42).

135.10–12 I . . . listened to that deathless incident four hundred and eighty-one or eighty-two times] Lillard and Hood make clear that the Greeley-Monk anecdote was indeed an exceedingly familiar story on the West Coast for many years. Mark Twain evidently first experimented with repeating the story for the sake of humorous satire sometime after delivering his first Sandwich Islands lecture in San Francisco on 2 October 1866, trying it out during his October–November lecture tour in California and Nevada ("Robbery of Mark Twain," Virginia City *Union,* 12 Nov 66, 3; *L1,* 361–62, 366–67 n. 4; Lorch 1966, 45–46). He then included the anecdote in his second San Francisco lecture, on 16 November, an occasion he described in detail many years later:

> For repetition is a mighty power in the domain of humor. If frequently used, nearly any precisely worded and unchanging formula will eventually compel laughter if it be gravely & earnestly repeated, at intervals, five or six times. I undertook to prove the truth of this, forty years ago, in San Francisco, on the occa-

> sion of my second attempt at lecturing. My first lecture had succeeded to my satisfaction. Then I prepared another one, but was afraid of it because the first fifteen minutes of it was not humorous. I felt the necessity of preceding it with something which would break up the house with a laugh and get me on pleasant and friendly terms with it at the start, instead of allowing it leisure to congeal into a critical mood, since that could be disastrous. With this idea in mind, I prepared a scheme of so daring a nature that I wonder now that I ever had the courage to carry it through. San Francisco had been persecuted for five or six years with a silly and pointless and unkillable anecdote which everybody had long ago grown weary of—weary unto death. It was as much as a man's life was worth to tell that moldy anecdote to a citizen. I resolved to begin my lecture with it, and keep on repeating it until the mere repetition should conquer the house and make it laugh. That anecdote is in one of my books. . . .
>
> I told it in a level voice, in a colorless and monotonous way, without emphasizing any word in it, and succeeded in making it dreary and stupid to the limit. Then I paused and looked very much pleased with myself, and as if I expected a burst of laughter. Of course there was no laughter, nor anything resembling it.

Mark Twain told the story three times in all; after the third telling, the audience finally broke into a "tempest" of laughter:

> It was a heavenly sound to me, for I was nearly exhausted with weakness and apprehension, and was becoming almost convinced that I should have to stand there and keep on telling that anecdote all night, before I could make those people understand that I was working a delicate piece of satire. I am sure I should have stood my ground and gone on favoring them with that tale until I broke them down, under the unconquerable conviction that the monotonous repetition of it would infallibly fetch them some time or other. (AD, 31 Aug 1906, CU-MARK, in *AMT,* 143–46)

The following spring, Mark Twain again included the anecdote in his New York lecture, delivered in Cooper Union on 6 May 1867,

> remarking when he did so that it had not the slightest connection with the subject of his lecture; but that every one who had been to California held it to be a solemn duty to inflict this story on any innocent Eastern man whom fate might place in his power. (Review of Richardson's *Beyond the Mississippi* in the New York *Citizen,* 24 Aug 67, 3)

135.18 sozodont] Sozodont—a red liquid containing 37 percent alcohol—was a popular dentifrice manufactured since early 1859 by Hall and Ruckel of Brooklyn; the advertisements for it, which appeared in newspapers and magazines throughout the country for several decades, contained the claim that it "purifies and perfumes the BREATH" (Wharton, 139; Presbrey, 339, 340, 382, 402).

135.26–28 Bayard Taylor has written about this hoary anecdote . . . and every other correspondence-inditing being] No version of the anecdote has been found in the western writings of Bayard Taylor (1825–78) or J. Ross Browne (1821–75). Taylor, a renowned travel writer, poet, novelist, translator, and New York *Tribune* correspondent, was in California at the same time as Greeley, arriving in August 1859 for a three-month lecture tour. His account of the tour—"New Pictures from California," included in *At Home and Abroad* (second series, 1862)—makes no mention of the Greeley-Monk anecdote. Browne, also an indefatigable traveler and prolific writer, served for a time in the West as special inspector of Indian affairs and commissioner of mines for the federal government. He and Clemens had known each other since at least 1866 (*L1*, 368). Albert D. Richardson (1833–69), a journalist and western traveler, corresponded for the *Tribune* for many years. His western writings from 1857–67 were incorporated into *Beyond the Mississippi*, which included a version of what he termed the "apocryphal" Greeley-Monk anecdote (Richardson, 382–84). Mark Twain almost certainly read Olive Logan's version of the yarn in her article "Does It Pay to Visit Yo Semite?" in the October 1870 *Galaxy*, which also included his own "Memoranda"; Logan explained that although "everybody has heard" the anecdote, "no matter, everybody must hear it again" (Logan, 503). And, finally, the joke was alluded to, if not actually recounted, in the following works, any of which Mark Twain could have read: *Artemus Ward: His Travels* (Charles Farrar Browne 1865, 156–62); Samuel Bowles's *Across the Continent* (137–38); Charles Wentworth Dilke's *Greater Britain* (1:188); and Harvey Rice's *Letters from the Pacific Slope* (50–51).

136n.1–2 the adventure it celebrates *never occurred*] It was Joseph Goodman (see the note at 274.25–26) who initially informed Clemens that Greeley had denied the truth of the anecdote. Shortly after the publication of *Roughing It*, when Greeley was running for president, Goodman wrote an anti-Greeley editorial for the *Enterprise*, which read in part:

> In the Fall of 1869, we met Hank Monk at Reno, as we were about leaving for the East. With the recollection of that ride fresh in his memory, and a sentiment of fellowship toward his illustrious passsenger, with whom he had passed hand in hand into literature and fame, Hank requested us to call upon Mr. Greeley and tell him that in memory of their celebrated mountain ride he wished him to procure a pass that would enable him to visit his friends in the East. . . . We met the philosopher at the Astor House, and briefly delivered our message. The reply was concise and emphatic. "Damn him! that fellow has done me more harm than any man in America!" We protested our ignorance of any injury. "But there was not a damned word of truth in the whole story!" rejoined Mr. Greeley. . . .
>
> In telling the story of the Placerville ride, will Democratic orators append this sequel, illustrative of the overbearing and illiberal nature of Mr. Greeley? . . . Hank Monk still handles the whip and reins, but we fancy he has more friends on this coast than Horace Greeley—though he is running for President. (Goodman 1872, 2; see also *MTB*, 1:303 n. 1)

On 24 March 1871—not long after the present chapter was written—Goodman began a visit with Clemens in Elmira, where he read part of the *Roughing It* manuscript. Presumably he then reported his 1869 encounter with Greeley. In August, when Clemens probably read this chapter in proof, he decided to ask Greeley himself whether the disclaimer was accurate, explaining that "a newspaper editor, who said he got it from you," had told him that it had "*never occurred*" (SLC to Greeley, 17 Aug 71, NN†; "City and Neighborhood," Elmira *Adver-*

tiser, 25 Mar 71, 4). Greeley's reply, if any, is not known to survive, but it is clear that he had ample reason to resent the story, which had been used by his political enemies to ridicule him. In March 1866 a congressman from New York who disagreed with a *Tribune* editorial had caused Artemus Ward's version to be read aloud to the entire House of Representatives (Lillard and Hood, 17).

136n.5–6 but what does the thirteenth chapter of Daniel say? Aha!] Although the book of Daniel in the King James Bible has only twelve chapters, the Catholic Bible includes two additional chapters that Protestants regard as apocryphal. Chapter thirteen—the story of Susanna, in which two elders who falsely accuse her of adultery are exposed by Daniel and put to death—was undoubtedly familiar to Mark Twain, since the Clemens family's 1817 King James Bible included the Apocrypha (CU-MARK). Mark Twain's intent here, admittedly somewhat obscure, seems to be to endorse the death penalty for "a man who would wantonly contrive so flat a [story] as this." The possibility remains, however, that he teasingly referred to a nonexistent book of the Bible so as to reinforce his allegation that the Greeley-Monk anecdote was utterly "apocryphal."

138.20–31 Mr. Harris . . . rode by . . . with a bullet through one of his lungs, and several in his hips] John (Jack) Harris was a notorious stagecoach bandit who nevertheless enjoyed the "general esteem" of the Nevada community, which considered the stage company to be among "the biggest robbers in all the world." No jury would convict him, even when a member of his gang turned state's evidence against him (Considine 1923b; Angel, 568). The gunfight that Mark Twain describes here, which occurred on 14 August 1861, was reported in the *Enterprise:* Harris, who "had some grudge against" a man named Julien, fired on him and missed; he himself was wounded in the chest and thigh ("Shooting Scrape," San Francisco *Evening Bulletin,* 21 Aug 61, 3, reprinting the Virginia City *Territorial Enterprise* of 17 August). Harris later went to Pioche, in eastern Nevada, where Wells, Fargo and Company hired him to prevent his depredations; Harris still managed to hold up the stagecoaches, taking a shortcut back to the station in time to meet them upon their arrival. Shortly before his death in 1875, allegedly caused by "a general breaking up of the system" (the result of his having been shot "several times" over the years), he confessed that his real name was Amos Huxford, and that he had been raised in Maine by a relative named Harris (Ashbaugh, 31; "Death of a Noted Character," San Francisco *Alta California,* 3 May 75, 1, reprinting the Pioche [Nev.] *Record* of 27 April).

138.36–139.11 the daily "Washoe Zephyr" set in . . . a skurrying storm of emigrating roofs and vacant lots] Exaggerated claims and comic tales about the Washoe winds were a staple of 1860s Nevada journalism.

Dan De Quille (William Wright), a colleague of Mark Twain's on the *Enterprise,* wrote his share of such items, as did J. Ross Browne and Mark Twain: see Lillard, 257–60, which presents a full discussion of the subject and reprints items by Wright in the Cedar Falls (Iowa) *Gazette,* as well as a passage from "A Peep at Washoe" (J. Ross Browne 1860–61, 289–90). Two items that appeared in the *Enterprise* local column in late 1862 have been attributed to Mark Twain: "A Gale" and "Blown Down" (SLC 1862d, 1862j). In the latter piece he remarked, "At sunset yesterday, the wind commenced blowing after a fashion to which a typhoon is mere nonsense, and in a short time the face of heaven was obscured by vast clouds of dust all spangled over with lumber, and shingles, and dogs and things."

140.4 Washoe is a pet nickname for Nevada] "Washoe" comes from the word "washiu," which means "person" in the language of the Washo Indians. The Washo, traditional enemies of the Paiute, were a small tribe inhabiting the region around Carson City and Lake Tahoe; in 1859 they numbered only about nine hundred (Hodge, 2:920).

140.5–6 Scriptural wind . . . "whence it cometh."] John 3:8.

140.21 newly arrived Chief and Associate Justices of the Territory] Upon the creation of Nevada Territory in March 1861, President Lincoln appointed George Turner (d. 1885) as chief justice, and Gordon N. Mott (see the note at 128.2) and Horatio M. Jones as associate justices. Mott was already in Carson City when the Clemenses arrived; but Turner, a lawyer and jurist from Ohio, and Jones, who was born in Pennsylvania but had become a resident of Missouri, did not arrive until the second week in September (*L1,* 126 n. 2, 128–29 n. 2, 243 n. 4; James W. Nye to William Seward, 19 July 61, *Territorial Papers;* Marsh, 691 n. 255).

141.4 Bridget O'Flannigan] A fictional name for Mrs. Margret Murphy, whose boarding house was on the north side of the plaza (*L1,* 134 n. 2; Kelly 1862, 85).

141.18–142.6 made of old flour sacks . . . pictures from *Harper's Weekly* on them] This description is similar to a passage in the letter Clemens published in the Keokuk *Gate City* on 20 November 1861. He may have referred to a clipping of the letter to refresh his memory:

> The houses are mostly frame, and unplastered; but "papered" inside with flour-sacks sewn together—with the addition, in favor of the parlor, of a second papering composed of engravings cut from "Harper's Weekly;" so you will easily perceive that the handsomer the "brand" upon the flour-sacks is, and the more spirited the pictures are, the finer the house looks. (SLC 1861)

143.1–2 voluntary camp followers of the Governor] Only three of these "camp followers" are known by name: Will H. Wagner, James Neary, and Clement T. Rice (see the notes at 147.17–19 and 278.11–12).

145.6–8 Bob H—— sprung up . . . the tarantulas is loose] This anecdote was evidently based on an actual incident, which Clemens recorded in his notebook in February 1865: "Time Bob Howland came into Mrs. Murphy's corral in Carson, drunk, knocked down Wagners bottles of tarantulas & scorpions & spilled them on the floor" (*N&J1,* 80). Clemens first met Robert Muir Howland (1838–90) in late August 1861 when Howland, who lived in Aurora (in the Esmeralda mining district), stayed at Mrs. Murphy's while serving as a delegate to the Union Convention in Carson City. A native of New York, he emigrated to California and then, in the summer of 1861, to Nevada Territory. He was the co-owner and superintendent of several mines in Aurora, marshal of that town, and, in 1864, was appointed warden of the territorial prison in Carson City by Governor Nye. In later life he continued his mining activities and acted as a mining consultant. For many years Howland and his wife, Louise (whom he married in 1867), maintained a friendship with Clemens and his wife, chiefly through correspondence (*L1,* 142 n. 2; "Married," Virginia City *Territorial Enterprise,* 12 Nov 67, 3).

147.7–8 as the historian Josephus phrases it, in his fine chapter upon the destruction of the Temple] Flavius Josephus (A.D. 37–?100), historian of the Jews, described the destruction of the temple of Solomon in Jerusalem by the Babylonians in Book 10, chapter 8, of *Antiquities of the Jews.* Clemens owned *The Genuine Works of Josephus* (Philadelphia: 1829), which included *Antiquities,* although it is not known when he acquired it (Gribben, 1:361).

147.11–12 I had nothing to do and no salary] See the note at 2.14–15.

147.13–15 Johnny K—— . . . the young son of an Ohio nabob] John D. Kinney (1840–78), whom Clemens described to his mother in September 1861 as a "first-rate fellow," had worked as a teller in his father's Cincinnati bank until his trip west (*L1,* 124). He arrived in Carson City during the second week in September 1861, on the same stagecoach as justices Turner and Jones. During his brief stay in Nevada Territory he worked as a realtor and speculated heavily in mining claims. In March 1862 he returned to Cincinnati, and by 1870 had become a partner in his father's bank (*L1,* 126 n. 2; SLC to Robert and Louise Howland, 6 Mar 70, Gunn).

147.16–17 the marvelous beauty of Lake Tahoe . . . drove us thither to see it] This lake west of Carson City (see supplement B, map 3) spans the California-Nevada border and is about twenty-two miles long by twelve miles wide. It was officially named Lake Bigler, after John Bigler, California's third governor (1852–56); the Washo name "Tahoe" (meaning "water" or "lake") came into use during the Civil War because of Bigler's unpopular secessionist views, but was not officially adopted until 1945. Clemens's trip to the lake probably took place on 14–17

September, shortly after Kinney's arrival in Carson City, not at the "end of August," as Mark Twain claims (Hart, 48, 268; *L1*, 126 n. 3).

147.17–19 Three or four members of the Brigade . . . located some timber lands] In a "Memorandum of Agreement and Copartnership" dated 24 August 1861, eleven men laid claim to a "certain parcel of Timber Land" on the northeast shore of Lake Tahoe, in the name of "John Nye & Co" (PH in CU-MARK, courtesy of Michael H. Marleau). In addition to John Nye, the governor's brother (see the note at 228.2–4), the signers included: John Ives, the governor's physician, who had accompanied him from New York; Will H. Wagner, presumably the boarder at Mrs. Murphy's who collected tarantulas (see the note at 145.6–8); and James Neary, another of Mrs. Murphy's boarders (*L1*, 143 n. 9, 200 n. 2; Kelly 1862, 85).

147.29–30 We . . . hired a couple of Chinamen to curse those people who had beguiled us] In writing to his mother in September 1861 about this trip, Clemens described Kinney's indulgence in restorative profanity while slyly affirming his own restraint. Kinney supposedly asked him, "Why don't you *curse* the infernal place? You know you *want* to. *I* do, and *will* curse the ——— thieving country as long as I live" (*L1*, 125).

152.2 the next two or three weeks] In a letter to his mother written immediately upon his return from Lake Tahoe (conjecturally dated 18–21 September 1861), Clemens stated that he had stayed there only four days (*L1*, 124; see the next note).

157.11 We made many trips to the lake after that] The "fence" and "house" that Clemens and Kinney built to secure their three-hundred-acre timber claim were destroyed by the forest fire. Nevertheless, on 25 October 1861 Clemens wrote his sister and mother, "I have already laid a timber claim on the borders of a Lake (Bigler) which throws Como in the shade. . . . In that claim I took up about two miles in length by one in width" (*L1*, 129). It is possible that Clemens made this claim of two square miles (slightly less than thirteen hundred acres), as Albert Bigelow Paine has suggested, during a later trip to Lake Tahoe, possibly on 22–28 September 1861. A second visit to the lake so soon after his first may explain why Mark Twain mistakenly remembered spending two or three weeks there. Only one additional trip of Clemens's to the lake has been documented, in August 1863 (*MTB*, 1:180; *L1*, 127 n. 7, 264).

158.24 *tapaderas*] Stirrup covers, which protected the rider's feet.

158.24–25 the ungainly sole-leather covering with the unspellable name] Mark Twain refers to a *mochila*, a removable piece of heavy leather—usually rectangular—which covered the frame of a Spanish (i.e., western) saddle, with openings for the horn and cantle. Pony-express riders used *mochilas* fitted with mail pouches at each corner, which could be rapidly switched from one saddle to another (Ahlborn, 39–40, 50, 54–55, 142).

159 *illus*] In July 1871 Orion described the artist's sketch of this illustration in a letter to Clemens: "I told Frank [Bliss, i.e., Elisha's son] to take the tree out of Carson and put the auctioneer on the horse. He said he would take the tree out, but people here wouldn't understand the idea of an auctioneer on a horse" (4 July 71, CU-MARK). Orion's view clearly prevailed.

162.5 Old *Abe* Curry] Abraham V. Z. Curry (1815–73) came from New York, where he had worked first as a baker and then in the shipping trade on Lake Erie. He emigrated to California in about 1852, and then to Eagle Valley, in what was then Utah Territory, in 1858. There he laid out Carson City and built many of its buildings, establishing himself as a leading merchant, zealous champion of his town, and a public-spirited citizen. In 1859 he and Alva Gould located a claim on the Comstock lode, which later became the immensely profitable Gould and Curry mine (see the note at 301.3–13). Curry later served in the second and third territorial legislatures (1862 and 1864). Mark Twain mentioned him frequently—always with admiration and affection—in his 1863–64 letters to the Virginia City *Territorial Enterprise* ("Abraham Curry," Carson City *Appeal*, 21 Oct 73, 2; Mack 1936, 178; Marsh, 669–70 n. 37; *MTEnt*, passim).

162.21–22 the Speaker of the House] The Speaker for the first Territorial Legislature (1861) was Miles N. Mitchell (b. 1819) of New York, who went to California in 1851 and then to Utah Territory in 1860. He served in the legislature again in 1862, was a member of the first constitutional convention (1863), and in January 1864 was elected governor. The election was invalidated, however, when the voters rejected the constitution. On 4 January 1864 Mark Twain correctly anticipated this outcome and posted a slate of candidates as "For Sale or Rent" to "any small State, lying around anywhere"; his advertisement for Mitchell read: "One Governor, entirely new. Attended Sunday-school in his youth, and still remembers it. Never drinks. In other respects, however, his habits are good. As Commander-in-Chief of the Militia, he would be an ornament. Most Governors are" (SLC 1864a; Marsh, 668 n. 24; Angel, 85).

163.8 the Clerk of the House] The clerk in both the first and second territorial legislatures was William M. Gillespie (1838–85), a New York journalist who traveled to Nevada with Governor Nye in July 1861 and worked briefly on the Carson City *Silver Age*. He served as a delegate to the third Territorial Legislature, as well as the constitutional conventions of 1863 and 1864, earning from Clemens the nickname "Jefferson's Manual" for his knowledge of parliamentary rules (SLC 1864b). Later in the decade Gillespie was the clerk and official reporter for the Nevada State Assembly. He practiced law and journalism in Salt Lake City, Honolulu, and San Francisco, returning eventually to Virginia City (Marsh, 3, 668–69 n. 29).

163.8–9 the Dana silver mine] Possibly a reference to the rich Daney mine, located in November 1861 on the Comstock lode in the Devil's Gate district (*ET&S1*, 492; see the textual note).

164.33–165.4 the regular price of hay . . . carpeted with their carcases] The prices given here may be somewhat exaggerated, but the description of the winter of 1859–60, "one of unusual length and severity," is essentially true: "Hay, for example, sold at the rate of four and five and barley at six and eight hundred dollars per ton, provisions of all kinds being also excessively scarce and dear. Many of the horses and two-thirds of the cattle in the country died from starvation" (DeGroot 1876b).

165.5–6 I gave the Genuine Mexican Plug to a passing Arkansas emigrant] This "emigrant" is almost certainly fictional; on 1 December 1861 Clemens sold a horse—presumably the model for the Mexican plug—to his friend William Clagett (see the note at 180.9–10) for forty-five dollars (PH of receipt in CU-MARK, courtesy of Fred Clagett, reproduced in *L1*, 169 n. 18).

166.22 In 1858 silver lodes were discovered in "Carson County,"] Actually, the first vein of silver—a low-grade extension of what was later called the Comstock lode—was discovered in 1856 near present-day Silver City by Ethan Allen Grosh and Hosea Ballou Grosh, sons of a Pennsylvania clergyman and veterans of the California gold fields. The Groshes were prospecting in Gold Canyon, where they and other miners had been recovering modest amounts of gold from placer diggings for several years. Both brothers died in late 1857, however, before they could record their silver claim. In the spring of 1859, two placer miners working farther north, at Gold Hill, uncovered a gold-bearing quartz vein which, although poor in silver, was actually a section of the Comstock lode. Then in June, near what was later the site of Virginia City, Peter O'Riley and Patrick McLaughlin accidentally uncovered a deposit of rich black sand, but failed to recognize that it contained large amounts of silver. Henry T. P. Comstock (who had taken over the Groshes' cabin and was searching for their claim) deceived O'Riley and McLaughlin into sharing their claim—which still appeared to be merely another placer—with himself and his partner, Emanuel Penrod. It was not until 27 June that rock from the vein was assayed and found to yield $3,876 per ton, of which three-fourths were silver and one-fourth gold. This news set off the great mining boom of the early 1860s. The lode was unofficially named after Comstock, in spite of the fact that he deserved little credit for its discovery (Grant H. Smith, 1–11, 17–18; Lord, 22-55; Angel, 51–59).

166.24–29 Allegiance to Brigham Young and Utah was renounced . . . "Nevada Territory,"] In July 1859 delegates from Carson County (western Utah Territory) and the Honey Lake Valley region of northern California (east of the summit of the Sierra Nevada), impatient with Congress's failure to set up a territorial government, drafted a "Declaration" of "entire and unconditional separation" from Mormon government, citing "a long train of abuses and usurpations on the part of the Mormons of Eastern Utah towards the people of Western Utah" (Carson Valley *Territorial Enterprise,* 30 July 59, facsimile in Angel, 70). At an election held in September 1859, a large majority of voters approved the constitution and elected Isaac Roop governor (see the next note). The provisional territory, however, failed to obtain the recognition of Congress, and its government, in the absence of a mandate, never functioned effectively. The Territory of Nevada was not officially established until 2 March 1861, when the Organic Act was signed into law by President Buchanan, two days before the inauguration of President Lincoln (Angel, 61–66, 69–72; Kelly 1862, 25–36).

166.27 Gov. Roop] Isaac N. Roop (1822–69), a native of Maryland, emigrated to northern California in 1850 and three years later settled in the Honey Lake Valley region, where he founded Susanville, named after his daughter. Roop had been active in two earlier attempts (in 1856 and 1857) to form a territory from parts of eastern California and western Utah. He later served in the first Territorial Legislature (1861) and as a boundary commissioner for Nevada (1862), and was twice elected district attorney of Lassen County, California (1865 and 1867) (Shuck, 405–10; *ET&S1,* 482; see also chapter 34 and the note at 223.19).

167.1–2 the population of the Territory was about twelve or fifteen thousand] According to the official census taken in August 1861, the population of the territory was 16,374 (Angel, 78).

168.7–8 Congress had appropriated only twenty thousand dollars a year] Orion Clemens reported to the Territorial Council (or Senate, as Mark Twain calls it in this chapter) on 11 November 1861:

> The expense of the present session of the Legislature will probably amount to $35,000, being $15,000 more than the appropriation made by Congress. The current expenses of the two Houses have amounted already to $13,000, and will probably reach $15,000 before the end of the session; and the printing is estimated at $20,000. (Marsh, 245)

He later informed William H. Jones, acting first comptroller of the Treasury Department after the death of Elisha Whittlesey (see the next note), "When I first arrived here people were surprised and incredulous when I talked of making the appropriation answer the purposes it was intended for in this Territory—they said it ought to be three times as much" (OC to William H. Jones, 29 Apr 63, "Territorial Letters Received").

168.16–17 Ours had a trying time of it] The claims that Mark Twain makes about the difficulties of the new territorial government are true in a general sense—as evidenced by the voluminous correspondence between Orion and the Treasury Department in Washington—although not every example in this chapter has been independently documented. Mark Twain's intention to be factual is clear, however, from the letter he sent Orion from Elmira, shortly before writing this chapter in April 1871:

> In moving from Buffalo here I have lost certain notes & documents—among them what you wrote for me about the difficulties of opening up the Territorial government in Nevada & getting the machinery to running. And now, just at the moment that I want it, it is gone. I don't even know what it was you wrote, for I did not intend to read it until I was ready to use it. Have you time to scribble something again, to aid my memory. Little characteristic items like Whittlesey's refusing to allow for the knife, &c are the most illuminating things—the difficulty of getting credit for the Gov't—& all that sort of thing. Incidents are better, any time, than dry history. Don't tax yourself—I can make a little go a great way. (SLC to OC, 4 Apr 71, CU-MARK, in *MTLP*, 62)

Elisha Whittlesey (1783–1863) was first comptroller of the Treasury Department from 1849 to 1857 and again from 1861 until his death.

168.17–20 The Organic Act and the "instructions" from the State Department . . . at such-and-such a date] The Organic Act stipulated that the election of delegates be "held at such time and places, and be conducted in such manner, as the governor shall appoint and direct," and that the delegates "thus elected . . . shall meet at such place and on such day as the governor shall appoint" (Kelly 1862, 38–39). Prior to the Clemenses' arrival, Governor Nye had established 31 August as the election date, and 1 October as the date for the convening of the legislature (OC to Elisha Whittlesey, 21 Aug 61 [1st of 2], "Territorial Letters Received"). The Organic Act also granted a *per diem* to legislators of three dollars, and another three dollars for every twenty miles traveled to attend the legislative session (Kelly 1862, 43). No copy of Orion's fourteen pages of handwritten "instructions" can now be located (they were originally enclosed in a letter of 26 June 1861 to him from Elisha Whittlesey); William C. Miller indicated in a 1973 article that he had seen the instructions, but quoted only a few words from them (Miller, 2).

169.3–4 He offered his large stone building . . . rent-free] Curry provided, free of charge, the entire unpartitioned second story of his hotel (which was also his residence) at Warm Springs, about two miles outside Carson City: in the voucher of expenses for the first legislative session submitted to the Treasury Department by Orion, the cost of rent was listed as "0000.00." The building had "a penitential look," having been built "on speculation, ostensibly as a hotel for sick people, but really with a view to its ultimate conversion into a prison" (Marsh, 2).

Curry was also landlord to the legislature at its second session, beginning in November 1862—but he required a rent of $1,500 at that time for the new premises, more conveniently located within Carson City at the Great Basin Hotel (OC to Elisha Whittlesey, 21 Aug 61 [1st of 2], "Territorial Letters Received"; "Abstract of Disbursements" 1861; Kelly 1862, 65, 70; Marsh, 408, 411).

169.4–5 a horse-railroad from town to the Capitol] Andrew J. Marsh described this railroad for the Sacramento *Union:*

> It runs—or rather trots—from Carson City across the Eagle Valley. . . . The rolling stock consists of a platform car, which carries freight from Curry's stone quarry to Carson, and a windowless passenger car of primitive construction. Two mules . . . act in the capacity of locomotives. Into this car the assembled wisdom climb in the morning to be carted over the rough scantling track to the Capitol, and at night to be carted home again. The car has no springs, and the members think their daily rides afford excellent exercise for the dyspeptic. (Marsh, 47)

169.6–8 pine benches and . . . clean saw-dust by way of carpet and spittoon combined] When Orion defended the legislative expenses to the Treasury Department comptroller, he explained that the "members of the House of Representatives of the first session sat on borrowed pine benches," and that he "bought no carpets for the first session . . . but covered the floor with saw dust" (OC to William H. Jones, 29 Apr 63, "Territorial Letters Received").

169.9–17 canvas partition . . . three dollars and forty cents would be subtracted . . . and it *was*] According to the Carson City *Silver Age:*

> This large Hall is to be divided into four apartments, by partitions. The eastern end of the building is to be assigned to the Council, and the western end to the House of Representatives, while the central part is to contain two middling sized rooms for the use of the Committees and the Sergeant-at-Arms, of each House. ("Items from Washoe," San Francisco *Alta California*, 11 Sept 61, 4, reprinting the Carson City *Silver Age* of 6 September)

In a letter of 13 March 1862, the Treasury Department comptroller questioned Orion about a voucher he had submitted for cotton fabric and thread, totaling $103.07. Orion explained:

> This was for the walls and ceiling of the Legislative Halls, partition and Committee rooms, in lieu of plastering. In this part of the country, few houses are plastered. The custom is to take cotton cloth, stitch it together, cover the walls and ceiling with it, and cover the cloth on the walls with wall paper. (OC to Elisha Whittlesey, 2 May 62, "Official Correspondence")

Orion's explanation was apparently accepted, and the $103.07 was not "subtracted" from his salary.

169.23–25 one dollar and fifty cents . . . for press-work, in greenbacks] That is, $1.50 for setting 1,000 ems of type, and $1.50 for printing 250 sheets (Ringwalt, 156, 464–65). The comptroller's office set the prices to be allowed for territorial printing after submitting a detailed questionnaire to local printers to determine current market rates. Mark

Twain takes some liberty with historical chronology here, since the prices he quotes were established in March 1863 for the printing of the laws and journals of the second Territorial Legislature, which had met in late 1862 (William H. Jones to OC, 5 Mar 63, "Territorial Letters Sent"). Moreover, the problems associated with the deflated value of greenbacks (legal tender notes unsecured by gold, made necessary by the tremendous cost of the Civil War) had not yet arisen in the fall of 1861, since the first greenbacks were not issued until April 1862. Although Congress stipulated that these notes be accepted "in payment of all debts, public and private, within the United States," businessmen on the Pacific Coast continued to deal in specie and were unwilling to accept payment in greenbacks except "at their gold, not at their nominal, value," which fluctuated widely in response to military and political developments (Mitchell, 142–44, 185, 210–38; *DAH*, 3:261; Barrett, 30–31). This custom prevailed in Nevada, as Orion patiently explained to the comptroller in 1863:

> Legal tender notes . . . are here merchandise (we have no bank notes in circulation) and gold and silver coin is the currency, while in the States the reverse is the case. . . . Any man in this Territory having a legal tender note must sell it for its market price in coin, or submit to an equivalent advance in price, before he can buy . . . any article of food or clothing or merchandise, or pay for freight or printing material or hire of hands. (OC to William H. Jones, 29 Apr 63, "Territorial Letters Received")

169.27–34 When greenbacks had gone down to forty cents on the dollar . . . the printing of the journals was discontinued] Although Orion did have difficulty arranging for the printing of the laws and journals of the first (1861) legislative session, his problems did not become insurmountable until 1863, when he attempted to contract for the printing of the laws and journals of the second (1862) session. By that time, the gold value of greenbacks had fallen precipitously for ten months, dropping from $.98 to $.57 between April 1862 and February 1863 (it did not reach $.40 until June 1864) (*L1*, 223–24 n. 2; Mitchell, 211, 425–27). When Joseph T. Goodman of the Virginia City *Territorial Enterprise* responded in February 1863 to the government questionnaire about prevailing rates for printing, he indicated his willingness to take on the job of publishing the laws and journals in book form for $.75 "per 1,000 ems" and the same "per token." Although these rates were only one-half the government allowance in greenbacks, Goodman still insisted on payment in gold. But the comptroller informed Orion on 5 March that greenbacks were the "only basis upon which you can contract for the execution of the Territorial printing" (Goodman to OC, 28 Jan and 16 Feb 63, enclosed with OC to Elisha Whittlesey, 5 Feb and 23 Feb 63, "Territorial Letters Received"; William H. Jones to OC, 5 Mar 63, "Territorial Letters Sent"). In July, Orion wrote to Robert W. Taylor, who had succeeded Whittlesey as first comptroller of the Treasury Department, giving a full account of his "trouble" over the public printing and explaining the reluctance of territorial printers to accept payment in greenbacks:

> Finally, about a month ago, I prevailed on [the *Territorial Enterprise*] (after they had held the copy several months) to undertake the printing of the laws, by promising to advance on delivery the whole amount allowed by the Government, on bills made out by them in such amounts as they might think they ought to have, giving them a chance to get more if they could. I expect the laws to be delivered to me soon. Shall I make the same offer to induce them to undertake the printing of the Journals? . . . Nobody seems to care much about the printing of the Journals, and it is so late now that I think it is hardly worth while to have them printed. (OC to Robert W. Taylor, 9 July 63, "Territorial Letters Received")

The journals for the second legislative session were never printed; the manuscript copy for them is preserved in the Archives Division of the Office of the Secretary of State in Carson City (Marsh, ix, 662; *RI 1972*, 576, mistakenly states that the 1862 journals were printed "without interruption").

169.37–170.2 with full exhibits of the high prices . . . a printed market report] In his explanatory letter of 29 April 1863, Orion wrote:

> [The printers] express the opinion that they will do "pretty well" if they realize expenses from what the Department allows them. To show more clearly the difficulty the printer has to contend with in this respect, I enclose some advertisements clipped from a daily (loyal) paper published in the town of Virginia in this Territory. I do not see that there is any practicable remedy, but it will serve to throw further light on the probable cause of the high prices asked by the printers. (OC to William H. Jones, 29 Apr 63, "Territorial Letters Received")

The enclosed "advertisements"—Mark Twain's "full exhibits" and "printed market report"—do not survive.

170.3–5 The United States responded by subtracting the printing-bill from the Secretary's suffering salary] Although Orion's salary was paid quarterly, in full, his ongoing correspondence with the Treasury Department clearly indicates that he was expected to reimburse the government for all "disallowed" expenses. The dispute over the printing bill for the 1862 laws continued for several years. Mark Twain clearly had in mind two letters that the Treasury Department sent Orion in 1869 requesting him to reimburse, from his own pocket, $1330.08 of "disallowed" payments he had made to printers (including Goodman) between July 1863 and October 1864. In October 1869 Orion unsuccessfully appealed the request. Later that year, or early in 1870, Clemens asked his old Virginia City acquaintance Thomas Fitch (see the note at 339.11–13), then a Nevada Congressman, to intercede for Orion in the dispute, and indicated his own willingness to guarantee payment of the debt if necessary. The official resolution of the case is unknown (Robert W. Taylor to OC, 9 June 69 [two letters] and 30 Oct 69, CU-MARK; OC to Robert W. Taylor, 4 Oct 69, CU-MARK; *L3*, 386; SLC to PAM, 14 Jan 70, NPV).

170.16–20 kept his office in his bedroom . . . if I had been Secretary myself] When he first arrived in Nevada, Orion used his bedroom at Mrs. Murphy's Carson City boarding house as his office, paying for it himself. At the end of 1862, after Clemens's repeated urgings that he find a more suitable office and fit it up "superbly," he rented a three-room suite and furnished it at government expense (*L1*, 213). To this the comptroller (or some unidentified auditor) objected, but then relented and noted on the verso of Orion's letter of explanation, "In consideration of the fact that he paid his own office rent for the first three or four months of his incumbency—perhaps the rent should be allowed him for the past" (OC to William H. Jones, 29 Apr 63, with notes on the verso in an unidentified hand, "Territorial Letters Received"). Orion voluntarily reimbursed the government $339.25 for his bed, table, chairs, washstand, and window coverings (*L1*, 183–84 n. 5, 186, 196, 208–9, 212 n. 12).

170.31–35 The knives cost three dollars apiece . . . out of the Secretary's salary] Orion's purchase of pocket knives for the second Territorial Legislature was challenged in Washington, prompting him to submit the following explanation:

> The 16 pocket knives were disposed of as follows: I and my clerk had one each. There were six extra clerks employed by the Legislature, and I gave knives to five of them. The Legislature employed two pages. I gave one to each. Some of the members lost their knives and I replaced them; and several members who were not present when the session opened came afterwards, and I gave them knives.

On the verso of Orion's letter an unidentified auditor noted:

> Allow the expense for knives, except to extra clerks as a *specialty*, & instruct the Sec. not to furnish duplicates to those who may lose them. . . . The Legislature had no right to employ those 4 extra clerks—the Sec. could not pay them & should not have furnished them either with knives or Blank books. (OC to William H. Jones, 29 Apr 63, with notes on the verso in an unidentified hand, "Territorial Letters Received")

171.2–19 he got an Indian to saw . . . it went through all right] In March 1862 the comptroller informed Orion that a payment of $1.50 " 'To an Indian' For cutting 1⅓ cords wood" was disallowed for lack of a receipt bearing "signature or mark" (Elisha Whittlesey to OC, 13 Mar 62, "Territorial Letters Sent"). In the 1861–62 "Abstract of Disbursements," three similar payments—this time presumably accompanied by a voucher signed with a "mark"—passed without challenge.

172.2–6 member proposed to save three dollars a day . . . during the morning prayer] Mark Twain's description of this legislator appears to conflate facts about two different Nevada characters, Jacob L. Van Bokkelen and Colonel Jonathan Williams. Van Bokkelen (d. 1873) had been a member of the 1851 San Francisco Vigilance Committee; in Nevada he served in both the first and second territorial legislatures and during the Civil War was Lincoln's appointee as provost marshal for the territory (Marsh, 666 n. 11). On 17 October 1861, while president of the Council in the first Territorial Legislature, Van Bokkelen objected to the appointment of a chaplain, remarking that "he did not think it was necessary to go to an expense of a dollar and a half a day for a short and concise prayer in the morning. . . . He had sat under prayers costing ten thousand dollars a year and did not know that they did him much good" (Marsh, 90). The member who "sat with his feet on his desk, eating raw turnips," however, was clearly Colonel Williams, whose unusual habit Mark Twain first mentioned in a dispatch from Carson City to the Virginia City *Territorial Enterprise:*

> Col. Williams, of the House, who says I mutilate his eloquence, addressed a note to me this morning, to the effect that I had given his constituents wrong impressions concerning him, and nothing but blood would satisfy him. I sent him that turnip on a hand-barrow, requesting him to extract from it a sufficient quantity of blood to restore his equilibrium—(which I regarded as a very excellent joke.) Col. Williams ate it (raw) during the usual prayer by the chaplain. . . . Col. Williams had his feet on his desk at the time. (SLC 1862h)

In 1866 Mark Twain again mentioned that Williams "used to always" engage in this irreverent activity "during prayer by the Chaplain" (SLC 1866w). Clemens had a more personal reason for lampooning Williams: in July 1863 Orion, in his capacity as acting governor, discharged him as a notary public for Lander County for being "a loud mouthed Copperhead"; Williams responded by calling Orion a specimen of "political vermin" ("Caustic Letter," Placerville [Calif.] *Mountain Democrat,* 8 Aug 63, 3). Williams was a proprietor of the *Enterprise* from 1859 until early 1862; Rollin Daggett described him as "an erratic old gentleman who wrote strong, but in villainous English, and was given a great deal to his cups" (Daggett, 15). Williams later "drifted about Nevada for many years, ultimately committing suicide at Pioche in January of 1876" (Lingenfelter and Gash, 253–54).

172.7–8 The legislature sat sixty days, and passed private toll-road franchises] The first legislature, which met from 1 October to 29 November 1861, approved six franchises to construct toll roads. Twenty-two roads were franchised at the second session (1862), and twenty-seven at the third (1864). Such franchises were an effective way to provide for the transportation of passengers and freight to and from the various mining regions springing up in previously undeveloped areas of the territory (*Laws* 1862, 602; *Laws* 1863, 16–17, 213; *Laws* 1864, 178–79; Maule, 17).

174.4–7 "Gould & Curry" . . . "Ophir"] These mines were among the first, and richest, on the Comstock lode. The Gould and Curry claim, located in 1859 by Alva Gould and Abraham Curry but soon sold to others, was incorporated in June 1860 (see the note at 301.3–13). The company operated "in a small way" until the end of 1861, when its tunnel under D Street in Virginia City "penetrated 40 feet of rich solid ore" and the mine began to overtake the Ophir in productivity. At the time of the Clemenses' arrival in August, Gould and Curry stock was worth $225 per foot; between mid-February and May 1862 it rose from $375 to $850 per foot (Kelly 1862, 14; Grant H. Smith, 26, 84; *Mining and Scientific Press:* "Sales Mining Stocks," 3 [17 Aug 61]: 6; "Mining Stock," 4 [15 Feb 62]: 5; "Stock Quotations," 5 [8 May 62]: 5). The Ophir mine, the first and most famous claim on the Comstock, was incorporated in April 1860. Throughout 1861 and early 1862 Ophir stock sold in the range of $800 to $1,250 per foot. The stock price peaked at $3,800 in October 1862, not in late 1861, as Mark Twain implies here (Grant H. Smith, 80 n. 1; *Mining and Scientific Press:* mining-stock quotations in issues between January 1861 and April 1862; "Stock Quotations," 6 [7 Oct 62]: 2).

174.20–21 had found a "clay casing" and knew they were "right on the ledge"] Since sheets of clay often encased the quartz veins on the Comstock lode, they were regarded as good evidence of an ore deposit (Angel, 118).

175.1 And so on] Although some of the mines mentioned in this paragraph were real, the anecdotes are fictional ("List of Incorporated Mining Companies," *Mining and Scientific Press* 6 [10 Aug 63]: 1–7).

175.13 "Esmeralda" had just had a run] The principal town in the Esmeralda mining district was Aurora (claimed by both California and Nevada, until the resolution of the boundary dispute in the fall of 1863), which was located in the Sierra Nevada foothills about a hundred miles southeast of Carson City (see supplement B, map 3). Following the organization of the district in August 1860, Aurora experienced a boom, reaching a population of nearly two thousand by August 1861. Typical of the glowing reports from the area is this one from the Carson City *Silver Age* for early September: "Now is the time for capitalists to invest. Ground that can be bought at the present time for ten and fifteen dollars, in six months cannot be bought for five times that amount" ("Summary of Mining News," *Mining and Scientific Press* 4 [5 Oct 61]: 5, reprinting the Carson City *Silver Age;* Kelly 1862, 14, 238–42; Paher, 466). Spurred by such reports, Clemens visited Aurora briefly in September 1861, returning in April 1862 for a five-month stay. Aurora's prosperity reached its peak in early 1864; by the spring of 1865 half the population had left (*L1,* 122, 184–241; Angel, 418).

175.13–14 "Humboldt" was beginning to shriek for attention] This mining region was situated about a hundred seventy-five miles northeast of Carson City in the West Humboldt Mountains (see supplement B, map 2). Silver and gold were discovered in the area in 1860, and over the next year, Unionville, Humboldt City, and Star City—each in a separate mining district—emerged as the principal centers of mining activity. News of a rich strike in June 1861, before Clemens arrived in Nevada, caused a rush to the Humboldt region from the Comstock; but it was not until the fall that Humboldt mining fever heated up in earnest. In November a correspondent from the Santa Clara district reported:

> The great extent and richness of the Humboldt mines have long since ceased to be questions of doubt. . . . New leads are being located almost daily beyond the limits of the mining districts now formed. The irresistible conviction is forced upon all who have prospected here during the past Summer that this is not only the richest but most extensive quartz region extant. (Simmons, 1)

The Humboldt region continued to attract miners, mill operators, and investors for a time, except for a decline in 1864–65 which temporarily emptied the mining camps (Kelly 1862, 13, 235–38; *Mining and Scientific Press:* "Interesting Correspondence from Nevada Territory," 3 [15 June 61]: 2; "Nevada Territory," 4 [2 Nov 61]: 5); Angel, 449–54).

176.6–28 But . . . incalculable.] Neither this extract, nor the one at 177.3–178.19, can be dated precisely, since the *Enterprise* for this period is not extant, and no reprintings of these items have been found. Certain details (the discovery of coal, the length of the Sheba tunnel) suggest, however, that they appeared in late 1862 or early 1863, a year later than Mark Twain implies. He probably pasted the actual clippings of these extracts into his printer's copy, after removing them from the "coffin of 'Enterprise' files" he received from his family in the spring of 1870 (SLC to JLC and family, 26 Mar 70, NPV, in *MTBus,* 112).

176.19 Col. Whitman] In October 1861 George W. Whitman (1811?–1891), the former state controller of California (1856–58), announced his recent discovery of extensive coal beds fifteen miles southeast of Virginia City: "I am greatly mistaken if the supply of coal at this point is not more than sufficient to meet every demand for a period much longer than you or I will need fire in an earthly habitation." This discovery of a potential source of fuel in timber-scarce Nevada was as significant as a major ore strike (*Mining and Scientific Press:* "Nevada Territory," 4 [12 Oct 61]: 5; "Regular Correspondence," 4 [1 Feb 62]: 5; Curry, 644; *Hutchings' California Magazine* 2 [Mar 58]: 390).

176.23 Captain Burch] The Indian agent "for the several bands of Indians" in the Humboldt area in 1863–64, and presumably earlier as well (Sage Brush, 208–9).

177.17 The Sheba mine] The Sheba mine, located by William M. Hurst in May 1861, was very near Star City. Following its first shipment of ore to San Francisco in August 1861, it proved to be one of the richest Humboldt mines ("Humbol[d]t District," *Mining and Scientific Press* 4 [14 Dec 61]: 5; Ransome, 41–43). Upon his return from the Humboldt area, Clemens sent a sample of Sheba casing rock to his brother-in-law, William A. Moffett, in St. Louis (*L1,* 154).

178.6 the Mexican] See the note at 301.14–21.

179.4–6 We . . . drove out of Carson on a chilly December afternoon] Clemens left Carson City with three companions (identified below) during the first or second week of December 1861 and was away approximately seven weeks, returning by the end of January 1862. For his other accounts of this trip to Humboldt see his letter of 30 January 1862 to his mother (published in the Keokuk *Gate City*), his letter of 12 February 1866 to the Virginia City *Territorial Enterprise*, and chapter 27 of *The Innocents Abroad* (SLC 1862a, 1866d, 1869a).

180.9–10 Young Clagett (now member of Congress from Montana)] William Horace Clagett (1838–1901) was an old friend of Clemens's from Keokuk, Iowa, who arrived in Nevada Territory in September 1861. Having recently been appointed notary public for Unionville, he was now on his way there to assume his duties. In 1866, after serving as a representative in the Nevada territorial and state legislatures, Clagett left his Virginia City law practice and relocated to Montana. Elected Republican congressman from Montana in August 1871 (at which time Clemens inserted the parenthetical identification), he served in Washington, D.C., from December 1871 to March 1873 (*L1*, 123 n. 1, 150–51 n. 4; Clagett, 9, 16; *BDUSC*, 777).

180.11 Oliphant] A fictional name for Augustus W. (Gus) Oliver (1835–?1918), a lawyer who in 1860 emigrated from Maine to California and afterward to Carson City, where he worked briefly as a journalist. Recently appointed probate judge for Humboldt County, he, like Clagett, was traveling there to take up his post. His later career took him to California, where he was employed as a schoolteacher and a judge (*L1*, 150–51 n. 4; biographical information courtesy of H. LeRoy Oliver).

180.12–13 old Mr. Ballou the blacksmith] Cornbury S. Tillou, a Carson City blacksmith and jack-of-all-trades. Oliver later noted that Tillou was "a Frenchman, an elderly man," but according to the 1860 census he was born about 1820, and was therefore not "sixty years of age," as Mark Twain describes him (Oliver to A. B. Paine, 24 Apr 1910, in Delaney, 3; *Carson County Census*, 133; *L1*, 150–51, n. 4).

180.17–18 We were fifteen days making the trip—two hundred miles; thirteen, rather] Clemens wrote his mother on 30 January 1862 that he had arrived in Unionville after "pushing that wagon nearly 200 miles, and taking eleven days to do it in" (*L1*, 149).

180.37–181.1 his Partingtonian fashion] Benjamin P. Shillaber (1814–90), an American journalist and humorist, was the creator of Mrs. Ruth Partington, a New England widow given to malapropisms whose sayings were widely reprinted in American newspapers during Clemens's apprentice years. In May 1852 Shillaber had published Clemens's sketch "The Dandy Frightening the Squatter" in his magazine, the Boston *Carpet-Bag;* he and Clemens met sometime before *Roughing It* was written (*ET&S1*, 63–65; Shillaber to SLC, 1 Jan 70, CU-MARK).

183.2 the Great American Desert] Sam and Orion Clemens had crossed this desert from east to west in the overland-mail stagecoach in August 1861 (see the note at 130.1–24). Traveling to Unionville, Clemens and his party left the overland route at Ragtown Station and struck out across the desert through miles of "sand to the fetlock," alkali flats, and the slough of the Humboldt River (Doctor 1862a; see supplement B, map 2).

183.8–9 the "Sink of the Humboldt."] This inhospitable marsh containing Humboldt Lake is about eighty-five miles northeast of Carson City. A traveler crossing the Sink in October 1863 described it as "a large, dry, depressed plain, white with alkali, and glittering in the fierce rays of the sun like some polished crust of snow" ("Washoe as It Is," Sacramento *Union*, 2 Feb 64, 1).

184.14–19 Unionville consisted of eleven cabins . . . in the bottom of a crevice] Unionville, in the Buena Vista mining district, was laid out in July 1861 in a canyon in the Humboldt range, and in November became the Humboldt County seat. Although it apparently had only a handful of inhabitants when Clemens arrived in December 1861, by the following September the population was estimated at three hundred, and the town's buildings—constructed of adobe, slate, brush, and canvas—lined the canyon for almost a mile. The area was reportedly "well stocked with liquor, lice and loafers; and [at] the same time is greatly in want of water power, wood and women" ("Nevada Territory," *Mining and Scientific Press* 5 [14 June 62]: 5; *L1*, 151–52 n. 9; *Laws* 1862, 291; "Letter from the Humboldt Mines," Sacramento *Union*, 6 May 62, 1; "The Humboldt Mining District," San Francisco *Alta California*, 24 June 62, 1; Nomad, 1).

184.24 through which the cattle used to tumble occasionally] Clemens described Oliver's experiences with such intrusive cattle in chapter 27 of *The Innocents Abroad*—an account that Oliver himself claimed was apocryphal (Delaney, 3).

184.26 Indians brought brush and bushes] Indians from Captain John's band of Paiutes at Humboldt Lake supplied labor at Unionville for one dollar per day and board (Nomad, 1; Doctor 1862b).

188.11 "all that glitters is not gold."] An expression already proverbial in Shakespeare's time: "All that glisters is not gold— / Often have you heard that told" (*The Merchant of Venice*, act 2, scene 7).

190.7 "Monarch of the Mountains"] There is no evidence that Clemens participated in locating such a claim; he evidently was involved, however, in the location of one near Unionville named the "Annie Moffett" (or "Anne Moffatt"), after his niece. Nothing is known about this claim beyond his mentions of it in letters to Clagett in February and March 1862 (*L1*, 164, 168 n. 6, 170).

193.19–24 we owned largely in the "Gray Eagle," . . . the "Grand Mogul,"] In January 1862 Clemens purchased ten feet in the Alba Nueva ledge near Unionville from Hugo Pfersdorff (see the note at 197.15–16); no additional holdings of his in the Humboldt region at this time—aside from his shares in the Annie Moffett—have been documented (*L1*, 167 n. 2). Most of the mines listed here are presumably fictional.

193.34 no milling] John C. Fall's Pioneer Mill, the first in Unionville, did not begin operation until November 1862 (*L1*, 152 n. 11).

197.8–9 the Secretary and I had purchased "feet" from various Esmeralda stragglers] Before Clemens left Carson City for the Humboldt region he had acquired feet in at least two Esmeralda mines, the Black Warrior and the Farnum, the latter with his brother Orion. These shares were purchased from Horatio G. Phillips—who was associated with the Clemens brothers in several mining ventures in 1861 and 1862—and Noah T. Carpenter (*L1*, 140, 141 n. 1, 189 n. 11).

197.15–16 with Mr. Ballou and a gentleman named Ollendorff] Clemens spent New Year's Day in Unionville before beginning his return trip to Carson City, having stayed "two or three weeks" in Humboldt (SLC 1866d). His companions on the return trip were Colonel John B. Onstine and Captain Hugo Pfersdorff. Tillou ("Mr. Ballou") was almost certainly not with them: references in Clemens's correspondence with Clagett between February and September 1862 suggest that he remained in Humboldt during that time. Onstine was a lawyer from Ohio who established a practice in Carson City, and then in Unionville, in the early 1860s. Pfersdorff, one of the pioneers of the Unionville area, served as district recorder there from 1861 to about 1865 (*L1*, 150, 152 n. 13, 164, 166, 170, 171, 193, 239; "From the Humboldt Mines," Stockton *Independent*, 8 Feb 62, 2, reprinting the Carson City *Silver Age* of 21 January; Knight 1863, 359–60; Knight 1864, 285).

197.16–18 not the party . . . foreign grammars, with their interminable repetitions of questions] Heinrich Gottfried Ollendorff (1802–65) was a grammarian and teacher of languages resident in Paris for most of his career. Beginning in the late 1830s, he published a series of textbooks—each issued in numerous editions—on how to become proficient within six months in reading, writing, and speaking the major modern languages. His method, "based on the principle that a foreign language should be taught in the same way in which a child learns to speak its mother tongue," relied upon conversational question-and-answer exercises rather than upon memorizing and applying rules of grammar and syntax (Singer, 9:395).

197.21 "Honey Lake Smith's,"] A trading post and stage station about thirty-six miles northeast of Carson City, named for its proprietor, formerly of Honey Lake, California. The site is now submerged by the waters of the Lahontan Reservoir (Carlson, 135–36; Gianella, 5–7; Kelly 1862, 13; see supplement B, map 2).

200.18–22 We remained cooped up eight days . . . their profusion is simply inconceivable] In his letter to the Virginia City *Territorial Enterprise* dated 12 February 1866, Clemens recalled his stay at Honey Lake Smith's:

> I was 15 days on the road back to Carson on horseback, with Colonel Onstein and Captain Pfersdorff, nine of which were spent at Honey Lake Smith's, when there was but two hundred feet of dry ground around the house, and the whole desert for miles around was under water. The whole place was crowded with teamsters, and we wore out every deck of cards on the place, and then had no amusement left but to scrape up a handful of vermin off the floor or the beds, and "shuffle" them, and bet on odd or even. Even this poor excuse for a game broke up in a row at last when it was discovered that Colonel Onstein kept a "cold deck" down the back of his neck! He would persist in cheating, and so we played no more. Take it altogether, that was the funniest trip I ever made. (SLC 1866d)

201.6 "old sledge"] This card game, also known as "seven-up," was the subject of Mark Twain's sketch "Science vs. Luck," published in the *Galaxy* for October 1870 (SLC 1870*l*).

201.13–14 a stalwart ruffian called "Arkansas,"] Arkansas also figures in an unpublished play fragment by Clemens which Albert Bigelow Paine labeled, "Original form of 'Arkansaw' incident in 'Roughing It'—Probably written in Buffalo. 1870" (SLC 1873a). The manuscript, however, is written on paper which Clemens seems not to have used before early 1873, and therefore must date from after the publication of *Roughing It*. In the play, Arkansas is bullying two inoffensive customers in a Virginia City saloon when Scotty Briggs and Buck Fanshaw (featured in chapter 47) intervene and rout him and his gang. Briggs and Fanshaw then rebuke the barkeeper for not taking charge of the situation, as required by his exalted status in Virginia City society, a theme developed in chapter 48.

217.12 a stage station] Clemens and his companions had probably arrived at Desert Well Station, about twelve miles southwest of Honey Lake Smith's (Carlson, 97; Townley, 30–31; see supplement B, map 2).

219.36–220.1 We reached Carson . . . kept us there a week] Because of the heavy flooding on the road to Carson City, Clemens found his journey broken again at Virginia City, where he and his party (which reportedly included a "Capt. Cathburt," possibly a mistake for Pfersdorff) arrived on 19 January 1862. Their arrival was notable enough to be mentioned in several newspapers: "They were sixteen days on the route, being water-bound for eight days at Honey Lake Smith's and finally had to swim out. The desert road this side of Smith's was covered with snow and water, and traveling was, of course, slow and tiresome" ("From the Humboldt Mines," Stockton *Independent,* 8 Feb 62, 2, and "Humboldt," Marysville *Appeal,* 2 Feb 62, 3, both reprinting the Carson City *Silver Age* of 21 January). Clemens remained in Virginia City at least a week, but was back in Carson City by 28 January. His departure for the Esmeralda district did not take place until early April 1862 (*L1,* 150 n. 3, 184–85 n. 1).

220.2 the trial of the great land-slide case of Hyde *vs.* Morgan] Mark Twain had already published two versions of the story he is about to tell in the next chapter. The first, entitled "A Rich Decision," appeared in an August 1863 letter to the San Francisco *Morning Call.* The second, which appeared in the Buffalo *Express* in April 1870, was revised for inclusion in *Roughing It* (SLC 1863p, 1870e). Both earlier versions are reprinted in *The Great Landslide Case,* together with a discussion of the historical background and the evolution of the text (Anderson and Branch). James C. Merrell, who claimed to have shared a cabin with Clemens in Aurora, asserted that Clemens wrote an even earlier version of the story there during his 1862 sojourn. Merrell's account, which incorrectly implies that the landslide itself occurred in Aurora, may well be apocryphal (see the note at 221.20–29):

> I believe that I heard read the first letter which ever gave him encouragement to become a writer. There had been an avalanche, which carried down a miner's cabin and deposited it on top of another miner's cabin. This appealed to Clemens as a most amusing mix-up, and he wrote a long letter to the *Virginia Enterprise,* describing the incident and making a long argument as to which miner could claim the entire property.
>
> He chuckled over it a good deal while he was writing it and when he had finished he brought it to us and said, "Listen, boys, to what I told 'em about the late catastrophe." Then he read it all through to us.
>
> Not long after, he got a letter from the *Enterprise.* I do not know the contents of it, but at supper table Clemens said, "I guess those fellows liked my stuff pretty well." Soon afterwards he had money to pay his bills, and I always supposed the paper gave him something for the letter. (Cyril Clemens, 19–21)

221.11–15 Gen. Buncombe . . . his salary was Territorially meagre] "Buncombe" is a facetious name for Benjamin B. Bunker (b. 1815), a New Hampshire lawyer appointed United States attorney for Nevada Territory in March 1861. Because Bunker was expected to earn substantial fees in private legal practice, his annual salary as United States attorney was merely $250, as compared with the top salary of $3,000 for a territorial official. By July he had established a law practice in Carson City, but his residence in the territory was short-lived: in January 1862 he requested a leave of absence, and on 1 May he left the West, never to return. In June 1863 President Lincoln removed the absentee attorney from office. Clemens's letters of the period reveal that he was well acquainted with Bunker, toward whom he developed a decidedly irreverent attitude, adopting his name for the plodding, ruminative horse he rode on the trip to Humboldt (Anderson and Branch, 9–13; *L1*, 131, 135 n. 6, 147–48, 234, 235 n. 4).

221.20–29 Dick Hyde . . . his ranch was situated just in the edge of the valley] In his two earlier versions of the landslide case, Mark Twain used the real name of the plaintiff, Richard D. Sides (1825–1901). (Mark Twain may have been influenced by a historical connection between Sides and the Mormon leader Orson Hyde when he made this revision for *Roughing It:* see Anderson and Branch, 14–16, 24–27, 50). Sides, who was well known throughout the region, began ranching in Washoe Valley in the early 1850s, held offices in Carson County during the period of Mormon colonization, and staked an early claim on the Comstock lode. His ranch was outside Franktown, near the lower slopes of the Sierra Nevada (*Carson County Census*, 123; Doten, 3:2106; see supplement B, map 3).

222.1 Tom Morgan] Clemens's 1863 *Call* letter and an entry in his 1865 notebook identify the defendant as Tom Rust, about whom nothing further is known (SLC 1863p; *N&J1*, 79; Anderson and Branch, 54 n. 25).

223.17 Hal Brayton, a very smart lawyer] Clemens's friend Patrick Henry (Hal) Clayton (d. 1874), an early settler of Carson City. Clayton, who was appointed prosecuting attorney for the county in 1860, was a noted secessionist and a central figure in the boisterous proceedings of the Third House, Nevada's burlesque territorial legislature. He appeared as counsel for the defense in at least one other mock trial, in Virginia City in 1865 (Anderson and Branch, 13–14, 19; Marsh, 677 n. 108).

223.18–19 the courts being in vacation, it was to be tried before a referee] Nevada tradition and internal evidence suggest that the mock trial, intended as an elaborate practical joke on Bunker, actually took place in Carson City sometime during the first two weeks of February 1862, before the courts began their regular session on 17 February (Anderson and Branch, 19, 23–24).

223.19 ex-Governor Roop] Isaac N. Roop's title dated from his brief tenure in 1859 as governor of the unauthorized provisional territory of Nevada. He also served as a recorder of land deeds for a number of years in this period and was known as an expert on property rights (Anderson and Branch, 16–18; see also the notes at 166.24–29 and 166.27). Mark Twain called Roop "that remorseless old joker" in his 1870 Buffalo *Express* version of the tale (SLC 1870e).

227.4 Hoosac Tunnel] When *Roughing It* was published, this five-mile railroad tunnel through the Hoosac Mountains in western Massachusetts—the second longest in the world at that time—had been under construction for nearly fifteen years. In November 1873 its excavation was finally complete; the tunnel was opened in 1876 (*Annual Cyclopaedia 1873*, 355–58; *DAH*, 3:45).

228.1–2 WHEN we finally left for Esmeralda . . . we had an addition to the company] This second trip of Clemens's to Aurora, in the Esmeralda district (he had visited the area previously in September 1861: see the note at 175.13–14), came early in April 1862 after several weeks spent in Carson City. As noted earlier, the *Roughing It* narrative telescopes the actual chronology; it also implies that Mark Twain's traveling party still included his Humboldt friends Ballou (Tillou) and Ollendorff (Pfersdorff). Clemens's actual traveling companions have not been identified; Ballou, however, was probably not one of them (see the note at 197.15–16).

228.2–4 Capt. John Nye, the Governor's brother . . . a tongue hung in the middle] John Nye emigrated to California in 1848 after living for some years in Alabama, where he left a wife; unlike his brother, Governor James Nye, he was evidently a Southern sympathizer during the Civil War. He was "an enthusiastic entrepreneur in mining and timber projects and an incorporator of the Aurora and Walker River Railroad," and a principal in John Nye and Company, which located timber claims at Lake Tahoe in August 1861 (*L1*, 134 n. 2; see also the note at 147.17–18). Listed as a resident of Aurora in 1863, he moved to San Francisco soon thereafter: his name appears in San Francisco directories from 1864 through 1901, primarily as a real-estate agent. In 1867–68 Nye was also the steward of the United States Marine Hospital in San Francisco. In March 1868 the Washington, D.C., correspondent of the San Francisco *Evening Bulletin* noted the presence of "Capt. Nye of San Francisco" in the capital and characterized him as an effective and influential lobbyist for federal appointments on the Pacific Coast, "one of the fiercest and most vehement talkers that is to be found anywhere" (Jorkins, 5; Nye-Starr, 95, 96, 100–101; Kelly 1863, 432; Langley 1867, 373).

229.21–26 The Board were living on the "assessments." . . . the ledge . . . was as barren of silver as a curb-stone] Eastern capitalists, like other investors in mining property, were subject to frequent, onerous, and sometimes fraudulent assessments. In January 1863 easterners, principally New Yorkers, were reported to be investing heavily in Washoe mines. By the spring of 1864 this practice had "become all the rage in New York City," where "the people take as lively an interest in 'feet' . . . as we do here" (*Mining and Scientific Press:* "Lively Times" and "Eastern Capital," 8 [14 May 64]: 329; "Stock Remarks," 6 [12 Jan 63]: 5). Mark Twain's remarks recall his bitter indictment of mining-company assessment policies—in particular, those of the Hale and Norcross company, in which he owned stock—in the San Francisco *Morning Call* of 19 August 1864 (SLC 1864*l*; *L1*, 309 n. 5, 319 n. 5).

229.26–230.17 Jim Townsend's tunnel . . . two hundred and twenty-five feet of your tunnel on trestle-work] Mark Twain included a version of this tale in a letter to the San Francisco *Alta California* published on 26 May 1867 (SLC 1867e). James William Emery ("Lying Jim") Townsend (1838–1900) learned the printing trade in his home state of New Hampshire and began his journalism career on the San Francisco *Golden Era* in 1859, working alongside Joseph Goodman, Bret Harte, and Denis McCarthy (see the notes at 274.25–26, 405.4, and 537.4). He worked as a printer on the *Territorial Enterprise* from the fall of 1862 until the winter of 1863–64, when he joined the staff of the Virginia City *Union*. For the next forty years he was connected with a variety of California and Nevada newspapers as a printer, reporter, editor, and proprietor. Townsend, perhaps the original of Harte's "Truthful James," became widely known on the Pacific Coast as a wit and a raconteur of Münchausen-like adventures. Examples of his humorous journalism may be found in *Lying on the Eastern Slope* (Dwyer and Lingenfelter, 7–16). "Daley" is evidently a fictional name.

230.20–231.9 We took up various claims . . . we never ceased to expect fortune . . . to burst upon us some day] This paragraph sums up Clemens's unrewarding efforts, made with such friends as Robert Howland, Horatio Phillips, and Calvin Higbie, to locate and work numerous mines in Aurora from April to September 1862 (*L1*, 184–241 passim).

231.13–14 I went to work as a common laborer in a quartz mill, at ten dollars a week and board] Clemens worked in Joshua E. Clayton's mill on Martinez Hill just east of Aurora for about a week during the latter part of June 1862. Clayton proposed to teach Clemens his process for reducing gold and silver ore. Clemens wrote to Orion on 2 June, "When I have learned it, he wants Raish [Horatio Phillips] and me to go out to Humboldt, get it used by Humboldt Mills, and stay there and work it." One week later he claimed in another letter to his brother, "I know all the chemicals, and the manner of using them, shall begin practice in a week or so" (*L1*, 188 n. 9, 194 n. 3, 216, 219). Many years afterward, in 1906, Clemens again described his pay as "ten dollars a week and board," claiming that "the board was worth while, because it consisted not only of bacon, beans, coffee, bread, and molasses, but we had stewed dried apples every day in the week" (AD, 27 Mar 1906, CU-MARK, in *MTA*, 2:258).

232.6 This mill was a six-stamp affair] Clayton's mill, which was in operation by February 1862, actually had twelve stamps for crushing ore. The "Clayton & Veatch process" employed there, which Mark Twain describes in this chapter, was a variation of John A. Veatch's steam-tub method of amalgamation (Kelly 1862, 244; *L1*, 188 n. 9, 194 n. 3).

232–34 *illus*] These engravings were reused from two earlier works—Browne's "Reese River Country" and Richardson's *Beyond the Mississippi*—and do not illustrate the process in use at Clayton's mill. The first one, which accompanied Browne's description of mining in the Reese River area of central Nevada, apparently depicts the "Freiberg or barrel process, which is conducted by means of revolving barrels" (J. Ross Browne 1866, 42–43). The second one depicts the Washoe wet process, employing shallow pans, which became the most widely used in the Nevada silver mills (Richardson, 502; Küstel, 117–18, 122–24; Hodges, 2–3, 8–9).

233.30 "earn his bread by the sweat of his brow."] Compare Genesis 3:19: "In the sweat of thy face shalt thou eat bread."

234.10–11 screening tailings . . . with a long-handled shovel, is the most undesirable] In 1906 Clemens recalled: "I hate a long-handled shovel. I never could learn to swing it properly. As often as any other way the sand didn't reach the screen at all, but went over my head and down my back, inside of my clothes. It was the most detestable work I have ever engaged in" (AD, 27 Mar 1906, CU-MARK, in *MTA*, 2:258).

235.14–15 The first one in Nevada was built at Egan Cañon and was a small insignificant affair] Most sources agree that the first mill in Nevada was Almarin B. Paul's Pioneer Mill, which began crushing ore on 11 August 1860 in Gold Canyon. (Angel's *History of Nevada* awards the distinction to Logan and Holmes's mill, also in Gold Canyon, but this rudimentary operation—established in October 1859—"could only be called a mill by courtesy," according to Lord [86 n. 2].) The mistaken reference here to Egan Canyon may derive from Mark Twain's misreading of a remark in Richardson's *Beyond the Mississippi.* Describing his travels from Utah to Nevada in 1865, Richardson noted the first evidence of mining activity he had seen on his route: "Two hundred and fifty miles west of Salt Lake we encountered the first quartz mining of Nevada, at Egan Canyon, a picturesque valley. Only one mill was running. It had but five stamps" (369). Nearby appeared an illustration—later appropriated for use in *Roughing It* (reproduced on page 235)—deceptively captioned "Egan Canyon and First Quartz Mill" (368). Clemens passed through Egan Canyon, the site of a pony-express and overland-mail station, on his trip to Carson City. A small mill was built there in 1864 (Hodges, 2–3; Lord, 84–86; Angel, 60; Paher, 242).

235.18–236.22 the "fire-assay" . . . Nothing now remains but to weigh it] Clemens had the opportunity to observe this fire-assay process in February 1863 in the assaying rooms of Theall and Company in Virginia City; he described the technique at humorous length in his sketch "Silver Bars—How Assayed," probably published between 17 and 22 February in the *Territorial Enterprise* (SLC 1863b).

236.36–237.14 One assayer got such rich results . . . left town "between two days."] This anecdote was apparently a folktale. William F. Rae recounted it, for example, in his *Westward by Rail* (215), and it has been included in an anthology of Mormon folklore (Fife and Fife, 286; L. L. Lee, 47).

237.16–32 I only remained in the milling business one week . . . I was ordered off the premises] Clemens explained to his brother Orion in a letter of 9 July: "I caught a violent cold at Clayton's, which lasted two weeks, and I came near getting salivated, working in the quicksilver and chemicals. I hardly think I shall try the experiment again. It is a confining business, and [I] will not be confined, for love nor money" (*L1*, 225). In 1906 he described his departure: "On my side, I could not endure the heavy labor; and on the company's side, they did not feel justified in paying me to shovel sand down my back; so I was discharged just at the moment that I was going to resign" (AD, 27 Mar 1906, CU-MARK, in *MTA*, 2:258).

238.1–240.5 It . . . desires.] Mark Twain first published this passage in a Buffalo *Express* "Around the World" letter on 11 December 1869; he revised the earlier printing for inclusion in *Roughing It* (SLC 1869n).

238.1–2 It was somewhere in the neighborhood of Mono Lake that the marvelous Whiteman cement mine was supposed to lie] Mark Twain recounts his own version of a persistent legend about a rich gold-bearing cement mine allegedly located south of Mono Lake on the Owens River. (The term "cement" was commonly applied by miners in the area to lava or—more specifically—to "any firmly compacted mass of detrital auriferous material . . . of volcanic origin" [*Century Dictionary*, s.v. "cement"].) The mine was named after Gideon F. Whiteman, "who played a prominent part in the intense searches for it that began in 1861" (*L1*, 226–27 n. 2). Whiteman purportedly continued his search for the mine "until August of 1880, when paralysis forced him to permanently retire to San Francisco. There he allegedly died in 1883" (James W. A. Wright, 13, 51 n. 7).

238.4–20 we would have a wild excitement . . . the whole population gone chasing after W.] On 3 July 1862 an Aurora correspondent of the Sacramento *Bee* (possibly Daniel Twing, one of Clemens's cabinmates; see *L1*, 237 n. 2) wrote:

> Our town is all excitement to-day, from the reported discovery of rich and extensive gold diggings over in the vicinity of Owens river. . . . Directly parties of horsemen were noticed to leave town during the still hours of night, stealthily moving away to the west. . . . Well, the next day succeeding the night of mystification, another and another party quietly took themselves out of town. . . . The cause of this epidemic is reports now industriously circulated through the

camp, that . . . digging of surpassing richness had been discovered along the sides of the hills—gold lying in seams of cement, in the most prolific abundance. (Veni, Vidi, 1862a)

238.21–239.36 The tradition was . . . for twelve or thirteen years] This version of the legend differs significantly from a reputedly authoritative one written in 1879 by James W. A. Wright, a mining correspondent for the San Francisco *Evening Post*, who attempted to piece together a factual history of the mine from interviews with Whiteman and others. According to Wright, the "reddish, rusty looking cement . . . thickly spangled with flakes of purest gold" was discovered in 1857 by two emigrants crossing the Sierra who stopped to rest along the Owens River. In 1860 one of the two men, on his deathbed, gave a specimen of the cement to a San Francisco doctor, who in turn continued the search in 1861 and 1862, employing Whiteman on the latter occasion. Wright acknowledged Mark Twain's precedence in relating the cement-mine story, but claimed that his version of events—such as the statement that by 1862 Whiteman had been searching for the mine for "twelve or thirteen years"—was "humor rather than history" (James W. A. Wright, 11–14, 49).

239.36–37 Some people believed . . . he had not] On 28 July 1862 the Aurora correspondent of the Sacramento *Bee* commented:

One of the adventurers to the Cement diggings has just returned, and he tells me he thinks the diggings are a humbug, or else the first discoverers are humbugging everybody else by putting them on the wrong scent, and keeping them there till they get tired of prospecting and return home disgusted, when the pioneers will quietly take possession of their rich discoveries again and work them when and as they please, with no one to molest or make them afraid—except Indians. From what I accidentally heard one of the original proprietors say a day or two since, I am constrained to believe the latter conclusion is the correct one. (Veni, Vidi 1862b)

240.6 A new partner of ours, a Mr. Higbie] On 9 July 1862 Clemens reported to Orion that his cabinmate Calvin H. Higbie (1831?–1914)—the "Honest Man . . . Genial Comrade, and . . . Steadfast Friend" to whom *Roughing It* is dedicated—was among the cement-mine searchers: "I had a whispered message from him last night, in which he said he had arrived safely on the ground, and was in with the discoverers, turning the river out of its bed"; Clemens was relying on Higbie to determine whether the cement-mine rumors were a "steamboat": "Higbie is a large, strong man, and has the perseverance of the devil. If there is anything there, he will find it" (*L1*, 225). Higbie, a civil engineer who had lived for a time in Tuolumne County, California, arrived in Aurora in the spring of 1861. In the mid-1870s, after many years of traveling and engaging in mining ventures, he settled in Greenville, in northern California, where he lived until his death. In 1906 Clemens described him as "a most kindly, engaging, frank, unpretentious, unlettered, and utterly honest, truthful, and honorable giant; practical, unimaginative, destitute of humor, well endowed with good plain common sense, and as simple-hearted as a child" (AD, 10 Aug 1906, CU-MARK†; Higbie to SLC, 4 Dec 86, CU-MARK). Late in life Higbie wrote memoirs about his friendship with Clemens, who found them riddled with "extravagant distortions" and advised against their publication; portions of them were ultimately printed, however, after Higbie's death (AD, 10 Aug 1906, CU-MARK†; *L1*, 227 n. 3; Phillips, 22–23, 69–70, 73–74).

240.7–10 a friend of ours, a Mr. Van Dorn . . . join the next cement expedition] This friend was actually William Van Horn (b. 1820?), who came originally from Tennessee but had lived for a time in Keokuk, Iowa. Clemens described him in a 6 September 1862 letter to Clagett as "a comical old cuss, [who] can keep a camp alive with fun when he chooses" (*L1*, 239). According to Wright's history, Van Horn—a member of Whiteman's search party—actually located the cement mine with another prospector in the summer of 1862. Van Horn and his friend allegedly carried off thirty thousand dollars worth of gold at that time, but, on a subsequent visit, were forced to withdraw by hostile Indians. Van Horn reportedly died about 1865 without ever having returned to the site (*L1*, 240 n. 2; James W. A. Wright, 22–27).

240.16–18 We were to leave town . . . and meet at dawn on the "divide" overlooking Mono Lake] The prospectors apparently followed a wagon road leading south out of Aurora which traversed a ridge and descended into the Mono Lake basin (see supplement B, map 3). It is not known whether Clemens actually embarked on such an expedition to the Owens River cement mine, or when he visited Mono Lake. In a letter of 9 September 1862 he referred to a recent two-week trip "slashing around in the White Mountain District, partly for pleasure and partly for other reasons." Some have assumed that this late August–early September trip was the one described in chapters 37–39 of *Roughing It* (see *L1*, 239, 240 n. 2). But since the White Mountain district is considerably east of the Owens River and Mono Lake, this identification seems unlikely. Although Albert Bigelow Paine states that Clemens and Higbie made several long walking trips out of Aurora—including one to Yosemite, across the Sierra to the west of Mono Lake—none has been independently documented (*MTB*, 1:200).

243.7–8 Mono, it is sometimes called, and sometimes the "Dead Sea of California."] Mono Lake was named after the Monache Indians (members of the Shoshoni family), who inhabited the surrounding region. Their name meant "fly people" in the language of their Yokuts neighbors, who applied the term because "their chief food staple and trading article was the pupae of a fly . . . found in great quantities on the shores of the Great Basin lakes" (Gudde, 196; see also the note at 247.16–34). The comparison of Mono Lake to the Dead Sea seems to have originated with Henry DeGroot, an early visitor to the area, who stated: "It is literally a Dead Sea: not even a fish or frog can endure its acrid properties" (DeGroot 1860, 6–7). Browne popularized the name in his 1865 series for *Harper's* magazine, "A Trip to Bodie Bluff and the Dead Sea of the West," which Clemens had almost certainly read (J. Ross Browne 1865b, 416).

243.13–16 we traveled around . . . and then we went regularly into camp] Clemens's party probably went west along the north shore of the lake, possibly camping slightly beyond Black Point, at the spot where Mill Creek enters the lake (Frank J. Thomas, 2–3; see supplement B, map 3).

245.1–249.15 MONO LAKE . . . true.] Mark Twain first published this chapter in a Buffalo *Express* "Around the World" letter on 16 October 1869; he revised the earlier printing for inclusion in *Roughing It* (SLC 1869k).

245.1–7 MONO LAKE lies in a lifeless, treeless, hideous desert . . . a hundred miles in circumference, with two islands in its centre] Mono Lake is situated in an independent drainage basin, "a shallow, bathtub-shaped depression cupped by the lofty Sierra Nevada on its west and rolling volcanic uplands on its north, east and south" (Gaines, 16–17). The area around the northern shore is a "level-floored desert, scantily clothed in sage-brush and bunch-grass" (Russell, 272). At the time of Clemens's visit, the surface of the lake was slightly more than sixty-four hundred feet above sea level. The adjacent Sierra rises above thirteen thousand feet, while the White Mountains, visible to the southeast, tower to over fourteen thousand feet. In 1862 the lake was approximately fourteen miles east to west, and nine miles north to south; its circumference was probably about sixty miles. (Since 1941, water diversion has made it smaller, shallower, and saltier.) Its two volcanic islands are of contrasting appearance: the larger one, Paoha Island, is covered with light-colored lake sediment; Negit Island (now actually a peninsula) is formed of black lava (Gaines, 2, 8, 17, 25–26, 40–41, 66, 83; DeGroot 1863; Russell, 269, 278–79).

245.12–20 The lake is two hundred feet deep . . . so strong with alkali . . . the white lather would pile up three inches high] In the early 1860s the lake's maximum depth was about one hundred and ninety feet, and its average depth about seventy-five feet (it is now less than fifty feet). "Because of Mono's high carbonate concentrations, the lake is alkaline as well as salty. . . . Alkalinity imparts a slippery feel and bitter taste to the water, as well as those cleansing qualities praised by Twain" (Gaines, 17, 20–21). Browne remarked, in his 1865 article, "For washing purposes [the water] is admirable. I washed my head in it, and was astonished at the result" (J. Ross Browne 1865b, 417).

247.16–34 a white feathery sort of worm . . . a fly . . . the Indians eat all three] The lake waters contain vast numbers of brine shrimp (Mark

Twain's "feathery sort of worm") as well as immature (larval) brine flies, both of which feed on algae. Female brine flies lay their eggs by enveloping themselves in a "globule of air" to descend underwater, where they cling to the rocks; when they have finished laying, they simply "pop up to the surface." After the larvae are sufficiently developed, they attach themselves to rocks on the lakeshore and pupate, emerging in several weeks as adult flies, which "darken the shore for mile after mile; four thousand have been tallied in a square foot" (Gaines, 42–48). Browne explained that the fly pupae were a "fruitful source of subsistence" for the Mono Indians: "By drying them in the sun and mixing them with acorns, berries, grass-seeds, and other articles of food gathered up in the mountains, they make a conglomerate called *cuchaba,* which they use as a kind of bread" (J. Ross Browne 1865b, 417). In 1863 a member of the California geological survey described this delicacy in his journal:

> The Indians come far and near to gather them. The worms are dried in the sun, the shell rubbed off, when a yellowish kernel remains, like a small yellow grain of rice. This is oily, very nutritious, and not unpleasant to the taste, and under the name of *koo-chah-bee* forms a very important article of food. The Indians gave me some; it does not taste bad, and if one were ignorant of its origin, it would make fine soup. (Brewer, 417)

248.7–11 an unfailing spring of boiling water . . . a spring of pure cold water, sweet and wholesome] Browne also described these springs:

> The larger island [Paoha] has a singular volcano in the interior, from which issues hot water and steam. Within a few yards of the boiling spring, the water of which is bitter, a spring of pure fresh water gushes out of the rocks. This is justly regarded as the greatest natural wonder of the lake. (J. Ross Browne 1865b, 418)

248.19–20 what it does with its surplus water is a dark and bloody mystery] The lake's water level is maintained by evaporation (Gaines, 25).

249.3 the little town of Mono] The now-vanished mining camp of Monoville was situated a few miles north of Mono Lake and twenty-five miles southwest of Aurora. Prospectors rushed to the area following the discovery of rich gold deposits in July 1859, and within a few months the population reached seven hundred. Deep snows during the winter of 1859–60, and the discovery of gold and silver at Aurora the following summer, just as quickly depopulated the town. By January 1864, according to the Aurora *Times,* Monoville was "almost wholly deserted" ("A Deserted City," Virginia City *Union,* 5 Jan 64, 1, reprinting the Aurora *Times;* Chalfant, 40–42).

250.9–10 twelve miles, straight out to the islands] An exaggeration: the islands were no farther than seven miles from any point on the lake shore. From the northwest shore, where Clemens and his party probably camped, the distance was even less—perhaps four miles at most.

253.4–5 It was only a long swim that could be fatal] Browne also warned of the caustic qualities of the lake waters: "It shrinks up the flesh when steeped in it for any great length of time, like a strong decoction of lye. . . . One might almost as well sink as float in a case of wreck; for in either event his chance of life would be slender" (J. Ross Browne 1865b, 417–18). Modern assessment of the lake differs considerably: "Swimming in Mono Lake is a delightfully buoyant experience, for you cannot sink in the dense water. Old-timers claim a soak cures almost anything. But keep the water out of eyes and cuts—it stings! After a float, rinse the salts off your skin with fresh water" (Gaines, 4).

254.1–2 around its shores stand picturesque turret-looking masses] These mineral formations, or tufa towers, were created by underwater springs that bubbled up through the lake in past millennia; when the lake receded, they were exposed. Calcium in the spring water combined with carbonates in the lake water to form the precipitate calcite, which piled up on the lake bottom (Gaines, 21–22).

254.10–12 Castle Peak, and . . . a bright, miniature lake . . . between ten and eleven thousand feet] This twelve-thousand-foot peak (renamed Dunderberg Peak in 1878) is ten miles northwest of Mono Lake. The "miniature lake" is probably Trumbull Lake, "at the southern base of Castle Peak," some twenty-five hundred feet lower in elevation (Williams, 68; Browning, 59–60; see supplement B, map 3).

254.18–19 Mr. Ballou] See the notes at 180.12–13, 197.15–16, and 228.1–2.

256.17–28 the Wide West had "struck it rich!" . . . black, decomposed stuff . . . gold and particles of "native" silver] The Wide West claim was located in 1860 on Last Chance Hill, Aurora; its mining company was incorporated the following January with a capital stock of 2,400 shares valued at $600,000 (*L1*, 217 n. 2). The rich strike mentioned here occurred toward the end of May 1862; Clemens was among those who obtained a sample of the ore, "a *pinch* of decom, . . . pinched with thumb and finger, from Wide West ledge," as he wrote to Orion on 2 June (*L1*, 217). The Esmeralda *Star* reported on 31 May: "We have been in California since the spring of '49, visited many of the mines, but never saw anything to compare in richness with the ledge of the 'Wide West,' we have only spoken of the gold which could be seen and we were told that it was equally as rich in silver" (quoted in Mack 1947, 165–66).

257.12–16 a sixteen-hundred-pound parcel . . . to San Francisco] The details of this anecdote suggest that Mark Twain used as a source a clipping of a report in the Virginia City *Territorial Enterprise* for 20 July 1862, presumably preserved in a scrapbook. This report—from "a correspondent, writing from Esmeralda, July 13th"—had almost certainly been written by Clemens himself: "Sol. Carter purchased sixteen hundred pounds of decomposed Pride of Utah rock from the company, in the beginning of the week, for which he paid one dollar a pound in cash, and shipped said rock to San Francisco by his pack train" (SLC 1862c). When Mark Twain adapted this anecdote for use in *Roughing It,* he altered only the name of the mine, from the "Pride of Utah" to the "Wide West." The history of the Wide West was closely tied to that of the Pride of Utah, situated slightly above and parallel to it on Last Chance Hill. A rich strike was made in the Pride of Utah in mid-June, two or three weeks after the one in the Wide West. By early July it was known that the two ledges were intersected by the same rich cross vein, which was the source of both strikes. By the end of 1862 the two claims were owned by one company, and this consolidated Wide West mine was ultimately among the most productive in Esmeralda. In chapters 40–41 Mark Twain conflated the facts about the Wide West and the Pride of Utah, evidently in order to simplify his story of the blind lead as well as make it more dramatic, while still drawing on certain essential facts. The note at 269.25–26 discusses the question of whether the tale is fact or fiction.

257.27–258.11 he meant to have a look into the Wide West shaft . . . IT'S A BLIND LEAD] According to Higbie's recollection, the superintendent of the Wide West invited him to inspect the excavation:

> While walking about and trying to get at the shape and formation of the deposit I discovered a cross vein running diagonally across this chimney and entering the walls at both sides. I called the attention of the superintendent to it. He thought it only a short spur and worthy of no attention, but as I had seen it entering both walls I was confident it was a permanent and distinct vein from the Wide West. Accordingly I made a mining location on this cross vein, as the mining laws permitted me to do, and put Sam L. Clemens' name on the location notice. (Phillips, 70)

259.5–6 even the Wide West people themselves did not suspect it] In reality, the owners of the Wide West quickly realized that the source of their rich strike was not their own claim but a cross ledge, apparently already located by someone else, called the "Dimes." In a letter of 22 June Clemens told Orion, "You see the grand rock comes from the 'Dimes,' in reality, and not from the W. W., although the latter said nothing about it until they had bought into the former" (*L1,* 220; Esmeralda district mining deeds, Book B:299–300, Mono County Archives).

259.14 the foreman of the Wide West] In the next chapter (268.29–30) Mark Twain identifies the foreman as A. D. Allen, an identification confirmed by the Esmeralda *Star* report of 31 May 1862 (quoted in Mack 1947, 165–66). Allen was an early locator of mining property on the Comstock lode, in Aurora, and in the Bodie mining district southwest of Esmeralda. In 1862 he was also president of Aurora's Live Yankee Mining Company. In September of that year he was elected a representative from Esmeralda County to the second Territorial Legislature, but failed to serve his term (*L1,* 191 n. 1; Angel, 402).

260.1–2 take possession of this blind lead, record it and establish ownership] Since the 1862 mining locations for the Esmeralda district (as opposed to mining deeds, which were entered in separate books) are not known to survive, it has not been possible to confirm whether Clemens and Higbie recorded a claim to the blind lead, or cross ledge, where it intersected the Pride of Utah tunnel. It is clear, however, that it turned out to be a continuation of the Dimes cross ledge. While the Wide West worked along the Dimes, the Pride of Utah followed its own rich strike, and the excavations soon met, which resulted in several months of legal "warfare" between the two companies ("The Wealth of Esmeralda," San Francisco *Alta California*, 3 Aug 62, 2).

260.2–3 and then forbid the Wide West company to take out any more of the rock] On 13 July, an Aurora correspondent—probably Clemens—reported that the excavations of the two companies had "run together." The Wide West served an injunction on the Pride of Utah (not the other way around) and, in addition, seized over one hundred pounds of its bullion from Clayton's mill. In retaliation, the Pride of Utah men "built a fire of such aromatic fuel as old boots, rags, etc., in the bottom of their shaft, and closed up the top, thus converting the Wide West shaft into a chimney"—which necessarily led to a suspension of work, at least temporarily (SLC 1862c).

262.38–263.2 By the laws of the district . . . obliged to do a fair and reasonable amount of work . . . within ten days] The first laws of the Esmeralda mining district were passed in August 1860, amended in June 1861, and amended again in June 1862. Although it is difficult to determine which laws were current and which were superseded by later ones, it appears that no provision such as the one that Mark Twain describes was in effect in June 1862. Mark Twain's reference to a ten-day period suggests that he was recalling Section 11 of the original code, which applied only to *surface* claims: "All surface claims shall be worked within ten days after there is sufficient water to successfully work said claims." It may be significant, in spite of Mark Twain's (and Higbie's) unequivocal assertion that they officially recorded their claim, that Section 5 read, "All quartz claims shall be duly recorded within ten days from the time of location." The law regarding labor that actually governed Clemens's claim was a recent amendment, passed on 1 June, which applied to both surface and underground (blind) leads: "There shall be ($20) twenty dollars' worth of work, or four days of useful labor, . . . done on each claim of two hundred feet . . . on or before the first day of December, 1862; said work to hold the claim good until the first day of June, 1863" (*Mining Laws*, 4, 6; Phillips, 70). Clemens and his partners would thus have had to perform twelve days of labor—at any time prior to 1 December—to secure their six-hundred-foot claim for a year. To obtain a perpetual title, they needed to do fifteen days of work on each two-hundred-foot claim, a total of forty-five days of labor. In a letter of 22 June 1862 Clemens indicated that he was familiar with this provision: "By the new law I can get a perpetual title to our ground very easily," he wrote Orion (in reference to another claim) (*L1,* 221). In retelling the blind-lead story many years later, in 1906, he described a different version of the labor requirement, claiming that he and his partners could have made their "ownership of that exceedingly rich property permanent by doing ten days' work on it, as required by the mining laws" (AD, 26 Mar 1906, CU-MARK, in *MTA,* 2:253).

263.6–7 a Mr. Gardiner . . . "Nine-Mile Ranch"] The owner of this ranch, located about nine miles northwest of Aurora, has not been conclusively identified. Two Gardiners are listed as Aurora residents: E. L. H. Gardiner, deputy recorder for the Esmeralda district, and T. W. Gardiner (Kelly 1863, 425, 427; *Mining Laws,* 2). Another early settler in the area, George Albert Green, has also been named as an owner of the ranch, probably at a later date (see supplement B, map 3; Fox, foldout map; Wedertz, 43).

264.1 CAPT. NYE was very ill indeed, with spasmodic rheumatism] On 12 July 1862 the Esmeralda *Star* reported that John Nye was bedridden at Nine Mile Ranch, "an invalid, lying upon his back, all stiffened and swollen up by that excruciating disease—inflammatory rheumatism" ("Captain John Nye," Forest Hill [Calif.] *Placer Courier,* 26 July 62, 3, reprinting the Esmeralda *Star* of 12 July). Clemens described the illness many years later as "a violent case of spasmodic rheumatism or blind staggers, or some malady of the kind" (AD, 26 Mar 1906, CU-MARK, in *MTA,* 2:254). Clemens's 1862 correspondence confirms that he was absent from Aurora nursing Nye sometime between 25 June and 9 July (*L1,* 223, 224).

264.12–13 I had seen him nurse a sick man himself and put up patiently with the inconveniences] See the note at 265.22–24.

264.28–29 my late grandfather had had a coachman and such things] Although Clemens's paternal grandfather, Samuel B. Clemens of Virginia (d. 1805), and his maternal grandfather, Benjamin Lampton of Kentucky (d. 1837), were both moderately prosperous slave owners, this claim is clearly facetious (Wecter 1952, 6–9, 22–24, 46–47).

265.9 my share of the Tennessee land] Around 1830, in an effort to insure the family's future prosperity, John Marshall Clemens had purchased a tract of some seventy-five thousand acres near Jamestown, Fentress County, Tennessee. "Although after the father's death in 1847 responsibility for realizing income from the land fell chiefly to Orion, every member of the Clemens family, at one time or another, cherished schemes for exploiting it" (*L1,* 79 n. 11). Clemens's own efforts to sell the land in 1865–66 to grape-growing interests were frustrated by Orion's inconvenient temperance beliefs. In about 1887 Orion traded away what the family believed to be the last of the Tennessee land—a ten-thousand-acre parcel—but in 1906, Clemens was surprised by a proposal that he sell a remaining thousand acres (*L1*, 326, 327 n. 2, 341–42; AD, 5 Apr 1906, CU-MARK, in *MTA*, 2:320–21; SLC 1897–98, 30).

265.10–12 the typographical union of which I had long been a member in good standing] Clemens joined a printers' union in the summer of 1853 when he began work as a typesetter in St. Louis, probably the St. Louis Typographical Union No. 8—a charter member of the National Typographical Union, established in May 1852 (*L1*, 11 n. 2).

265.22–24 He raved like a maniac . . . and swore a world of oaths that he would kill me] Clemens wrote Orion on 9 July, upon his return from nursing Nye:

> Capt. Nye, as his disease grew worse, grew so peevish and abusive, that I quarrelled with him and left. He required almost constant attention, day and night, but he made no effort to hire anyone to assist me. He said he nursed the Governor three weeks, day and night—which is a d—d lie, I suspect. He told Mrs. Gardiner he would take up the quarrel with me again when he gets well. (*L1*, 224)

266.28–29 Higbie had depended on me, as I had on him] Higbie claimed in his reminiscences that he was in no way responsible for the loss of the claim. Having been called away to help some friends, he had exacted a promise from Clemens to "take care of things" by performing the "assessment work" (Phillips, 70).

268.11 as he came into Esmeralda by one road, I entered it by another] The dramatic coincidence of Higbie's and Clemens's entering Aurora by different roads minutes before the relocation, which presumably occurred at midnight on 30 June (see the next note), was certainly Clemens's invention. Clemens's letter of 9 July 1862 to Orion indicates that he did not return to Aurora until about 8 July, and that Higbie had left Aurora for the cement diggings during the first week in July and had not yet returned (*L1*, 224–25, 229–30 n. 1).

268.27–32 fourteen men, duly armed . . . proclaimed their ownership of the blind lead, under the new name of the "Johnson." . . . A. D. Allen . . . said his name must be added] On 1 July 1862 Peter Johnson—an owner of the Pride of Utah mine and of the Union Mill near Aurora—recorded the relocation of a ledge he named the "Johnson," in partnership with A. D. Allen and several others,

> said location being a re-location of the ledges or claims known as the Harlem and Zenobia ledges and being a claim of One thousand (1000) feet, described as commencing at the Notice in the Pride of Utah Tunnel, and thence running on the Lode Eight hundred (800) feet east and Two hundred (200) feet West. (Esmeralda district mining deeds, Book E:44–45, Mono County Archives)

(See the note at 269.10–12; "From the Esmeralda Mining District," San Francisco *Alta California*, 23 June 62, 1; Esmeralda district mining deeds, Book B:488–90, Mono County Archives.) It may have been this relocation that an Aurora correspondent of the Sacramento *Bee* reported on 3 July:

[The Wide West and the Pride of Utah] companies struck the cross lead about the same time, and worked towards each other. . . . The men who work for the two companies located claims immediately after the discovery of the cross vein covering nearly the whole of it, as it was not the lead claimed by the original companies. (Veni, Vidi 1862a)

Johnson's relocation did not go unchallenged. In December 1862 the Zenobia Lode Company published a notice that asserted

a superior title to the Johnson Co., claiming the same ground so far as said localities conflict. This ground is a portion of that now held by the Company known as the Wide West Company. The notice is signed by A. Waddell, J. C. Dorsey, S. P. Dorsey and James Elder. ("Esmeralda Mining Notices," *Mining and Scientific Press* 6 [20 Dec 62]: 2, repeated weekly through 2 Mar 63)

269.1–9 Higbie and I cleared out . . . and after a month or two . . . returned to Esmeralda] Clemens's letters of July and August 1862 disprove this statement: he did not absent himself from Aurora for any long period until late August, when he went to the White Mountains for about two weeks. In fact on 21 July Clemens, apparently still hoping that he could profit from the Johnson strike, purchased twenty-five feet in the "First East Extension of the 'Johnson' Lode, situated on Last Chance Hill" for $500; the deed for this purchase was "Filed for Record Octr 3^{d} a.d. 1862 . . . at the request of C. H. Higbie" (deed, item B12, NPV).

269.10–12 the Wide West and the Johnson companies had consolidated . . . five thousand feet, or shares] The Pride of Utah and the Johnson companies consolidated on 27 September 1862. The new corporation was capitalized for $1,400,000 with 5,600 shares; among the first trustees of the new company was A. D. Allen. On 3 December, the Wide West purchased the combined Johnson and Pride of Utah Mining Company for $200,000. By early 1863 the newly consolidated Wide West owned a controlling interest in the Dimes ledge as well (San Francisco *Evening Bulletin:* "More Mining Companies," 30 Sept 62, 3; "San Francisco Mining Companies," 6 Jan 63, 3; Esmeralda district mining deeds, Book C:743–44, Book E:44–45, Mono County Archives; "The Esmeralda Mines," letter dated 12 Feb 63, undated clipping, San Francisco *Alta California,* Bancroft Scraps, Set W [Nevada Mining], 94:1:50, CU-BANC; Sahab, 1).

269.12–15 the foreman . . . had sold his hundred feet . . . and gone home to the States to enjoy it] In January 1863 an Aurora correspondent for the San Francisco *Evening Bulletin* commented: "The Gambles and the Johnsons and the Allens are sure to sell stock in claims which have long since been given up by poor miners, while many rich ledges lie neglected because confidence is only reposed in the wealthy" (Sahab, 1). In an "Around the World" letter published in the Buffalo *Express* in January 1870 Clemens wrote of his two partners, Allen and Higbie: "The sensible one is still worth a hundred thousand dollars or so—he never lost his wits—but the other one (and by far the best and worthiest of our trio), can't pay his board" (SLC 1870a).

269.19–20 We would have been millionaires] The richness of the Johnson ledge is indisputable. The reputation of the consolidated Wide West mine (which included the rich Johnson lead) blossomed in late 1862, gaining "world-wide notoriety" in 1863 (Kelly 1863, 410). William H. Bunker, who explored the abandoned Johnson excavation in 1879, found that "occasionally a pillar of rich ore was left to sustain the walls. . . . The ore in the existing pillars assays as high as $10,000 per ton" (Bunker, 13). Nevertheless, the claim proved to be a "chamber mine"—that is, the rich ore was not dispersed throughout but was found in a single large chamber, reportedly large enough to "turn a wagon and horses in" (Wasson, 45; Joshua E. Clayton, 145)—and this chamber was soon exhausted. Confidence in the Wide West—and in the Esmeralda mining region as a whole—was short-lived. The value of Wide West stock began a precipitous decline in mid-1863, in spite of attempts to suppress the information that the original rich strike was depleted. By early the following year the mine's yield was negligible (*Mining and Scientific Press:* "Esmeralda," 6 [20 July 63]: 1; "Wide West Mining Company" and "Romance of the Wide West Continued," 8 [5 Mar 64]: 147, 148; "Esmeralda Stock List," 6 [25 May 63]: 5; "Report of Bids," 7 [21 Dec 63]: 5; Grant H. Smith, 48; Paher, 466).

269.22–24 the evidence of . . . the official records of Esmeralda District, is . . . proof that it is a true history] See the note at 260.1–2.

269.25–26 I was absolutely and unquestionably worth a million dollars, once] Independent documentary evidence proves that the story of the Wide West mine and its associated rich blind lead took place essentially as Mark Twain recounts it. It has not been demonstrated, however, that Clemens and Higbie were directly involved, in spite of their virtually identical recollections that they made a claim and lost it by default. Furthermore, Mark Twain's explanation of the applicable mining law does not seem to correspond to recoverable fact. That the story was at best an exaggeration is suggested by the content of Clemens's letters of the period, which make little mention of the Johnson lead, focusing instead on the nearby Annapolitan—a claim located in September 1861 which he, Higbie, and several other partners owned. On 22 June 1862, for example—two days after he is conjectured to have located the blind lead—he wrote to Orion:

> We are most damnably "mixed" as to whether the "Annipolitan" will prove to be the "Dimes" or the "Pride of Utah." We want it to be the former—for in that case we can hold all our ground—but if it be the "Pride of Utah," we shall lose all of

> it except fifty feet, as the "P. of U." was located first. There is an extension on the "P. of U.," and in order to be on the safe side, we have given them notice not to work on it. (*L1*, 220)

Three days later, on 25 June, he informed Orion, "No—haven't struck anything in the 'Annipolitan.' No—down 12 feet—am not afraid of it. It will come out well I think" (*L1*, 223). In his next extant letter—written on 9 July, after his return from nursing Captain Nye and nine days after the relocation of the Johnson ledge—he told Orion, "From what I can learn, the Pride of Utah and the Dimes have run together, at a depth of less than 100 feet, and now form one immense ledge, of fabulous richness. I suppose the Annipolitan will share the same fate" (*L1*, 225). A week or so later Orion, who had evidently learned something of the Johnson excitement from Tom Nye (Captain Nye's son), wrote to ask Clemens about his involvement, prompting his only known mention of the Johnson claim: "No, I don't own a foot in the 'Johnson' ledge—I will tell the story some day in a more intelligible manner than Tom [Nye] has told it" (*L1*, 228). These letters suggest that it may have been the Annapolitan's proximity to the rich strikes which stimulated Clemens's dreams of wealth, and that the true story of the blind lead has not yet been told. For a full anaylsis see Edgar M. Branch's article "Fact and Fiction in the Blind Lead Episode of *Roughing It*" (Esmeralda district mining deeds, Book B:501–3, Book G:383–84, Mono County Archives; *L1*, 134 n. 2, 216–224, 230 n. 6).

269.27–270.1 A year ago . . . Higbie, wrote me] The earliest surviving letter from Higbie dates from 1886, when he wrote to Clemens from Greenville requesting a $20,000 loan to buy out two mining partners. Clemens responded with a good-natured refusal (Higbie to SLC, 4 Dec 86, CU-MARK; SLC to Higbie, 16 Dec 86, *Saturday Evening Post* 193 [11 Sept 1920]: 74).

271.2–4 I had gone out into the world . . . my father had endorsed for friends] Clemens's father, Virginia-born John Marshall Clemens, died on 24 March 1847 virtually bankrupt. His financial collapse—the inevitable result of years of unremunerative mercantile enterprises and real-estate investments—was apparently hastened by his dealings with Hannibal land speculator Ira Stout. Clemens later asserted that Stout got his father "to go security for a large sum, 'took the benefit of the bankrupt law' and ruined him—in fact made a pauper of him," condemning the Clemens family to years of "grinding poverty and privation" (SLC 1897, 31; AD, 28 Mar 1906, CU-MARK, in *MTA*, 2:274). When his father died, Clemens, aged eleven, became an apprentice (probably part time) at Henry La Cossitt's Hannibal *Gazette*, but he may be dating his entry "into the world" from his employment as a printer's devil, for board but no wages, at Joseph P. Ament's Hannibal *Missouri Courier* in the spring of 1848 (Wecter 1952, 122–23, 202; *Inds*, 314).

271.11–272.1 grocery clerk . . . studied law . . . blacksmithing . . . printer . . . pilot] Although it is possible that in his early years Clemens tried his hand as a clerk, law student, and blacksmith, these experiences have not been documented. His work as a printer and pilot is discussed in the note at 1.7–11.

271.26–27 Esmeralda *Union*] In 1862 Aurora's only newspaper was the Esmeralda *Star.* The Esmeralda *Union* did not begin publication until March 1864 (Angel, 295–97).

272.3–4 I did long to stand behind a wheel again] The frustration of his mining hopes may have caused Clemens privately to regret his piloting days, but in August 1862 he dashed off an emphatic disclaimer to his family: "What in thunder are pilot's wages to me? . . . I never have *once* thought of returning home to go on the river again, and I never expect to do any more piloting at any price. . . . Do not tell any one that I had any idea of piloting again at present—for it is all a mistake" (*L1*, 235–36). In early 1866, however, twenty months after leaving Nevada for San Francisco, he wrote his mother and sister, "I wish I was back there piloting up & down the river again. Verily, all is vanity and little worth—except piloting" (*L1*, 327).

272.5–6 grandiloquent letters home about my blind lead and my European excursion] On the whole Clemens seems to have kept his expectations to himself: "You must do all the writing home," he advised Orion in a letter of 9 June 1862 from Aurora, "I haven't written a word home since I left Carson. I am afraid the folks will not hear from me again while I remain in this part of Cal[i]fornia" (*L1*, 219). In fact, there are no letters extant from Clemens to his St. Louis family between early April 1862, when he left Carson City for Aurora, and mid-August, well after the blind-lead excitement of late June and early July.

273.10–28 I had amused myself with writing letters . . . city editor of the *Enterprise*] In the spring of 1862 Clemens began sending correspondence from Aurora to the Virginia City *Territorial Enterprise* under the pen name "Josh." These letters—now lost—were apparently humorous or satirical in tone, and met with the enthusiastic approval of the *Enterprise* staff. Joseph Goodman, the newspaper's proprietor and editor-in-chief, later recalled these "voluntary contributions": "They struck us as so funny that we sent him word to come to Virginia City and take a job on the paper" ("Jos. Goodman's Memories of Humorist's Early Days," San Francisco *Examiner*, 22 Apr 1910, 3; see also the note at 220.2). Goodman was particularly struck by one item, a burlesque Fourth of July oration that commenced "Fellow Citizens:—I was sired by the great American eagle, and borne by a continental dam!" (This item has been identified as a lampoon of the platform style of Nevada Chief Justice George Turner, whom the *Enterprise* was then attacking for official corruption. It has also sometimes been conflated with another Clemens piece apparently entitled "Lecture of Mr. Personal Pronoun." Clemens himself later recalled that his place on the *Enterprise* was secured by a burlesque of a Turner speech.) At the end of July Clemens received a letter from William H. Barstow, who worked in the business office of the *Enterprise,* offering him the "post of local reporter . . . at $25 a week," which he accepted in early August (*L1,* 201 n. 8, 231, 233; Putnam, 3; Daggett, 15; Sam P. Davis, 1:393–94; Johnson, 266; AD, 2 Oct 1906, CU-MARK, in *MTE,* 390–91; *ET&S1,* 13–17).

274.8–9 I went up to Virginia . . . rusty looking city editor] Clemens postponed his journey to Virginia City for several weeks, taking up his new position in late September. According to Dennis Driscoll, one of the *Enterprise* proprietors, Clemens walked "all the way from Aurora, packing his blankets on his back," and announced his arrival with the remark, "Dang my buttons, if I don't believe I'm lousy"; among "all the compositors turning at the uncouth figure presented to them, . . . there was not a man to dispute Mark's assertion" ("The Pioneer Journal Dead," Virginia City *Evening Chronicle,* 16 Jan 93, 2; *L1,* 241 n. 5).

274.25–26 the chief editor and proprietor (Mr. Goodman] At this time the *Enterprise* had three proprietors: Joseph Thompson Goodman (1838–1917), editor-in-chief; Denis E. McCarthy, print-shop supervisor (see the note at 537.4); and Dennis Driscoll (1823–76), business manager. Goodman went to California from New York in 1854 and learned the printer's trade in San Francisco, working along with McCarthy at the San Francisco *Mirror* and the *Golden Era.* In March 1861 he and McCarthy purchased the *Enterprise,* transforming it from a weekly to a daily and greatly enlarging its circulation. From early 1862 until October 1863 Driscoll joined Goodman and McCarthy in ownership of the paper. After McCarthy sold out in September 1865, Goodman stayed on as sole proprietor until 1874, when he sold his interest (reportedly for half a million dollars) and became a San Francisco stockbroker and speculator, first gaining and then losing a fortune. From 1880 to 1891 he operated a raisin vineyard in Fresno County, California. During his retirement he devoted most of his time to deciphering the Maya inscriptions of Central America and Yucatan, about which he published a monograph, entitled *The Archaic Maya Inscriptions,* in London in 1897 (William Wright 1893a; "Death of D. E. McCarthy," Virginia City *Evening Chronicle,* 17 Dec 85, 2; *L1,* 242 n. 2; Lingenfelter and Gash, 253–54; Rawls, 8; Goodman to Alfred B. Nye, 6 Nov 1905 and 17 Nov 1905, Alfred B. Nye Papers, CU-BANC; "Joseph T. Goodman Comes into His Own," San Francisco *Chronicle,* 21 Sept 1930, F5; for a fuller history of the *Enterprise,* see the note at 292.1–7).

275.9 Dan] William Wright (1829–98), who wrote under the pseudonym "Dan De Quille," was widely known throughout the West as a mining reporter and humorist. Born in Ohio, he moved with his family to West

Liberty, Iowa, in 1847, and in 1857 emigrated to California. For five years he prospected and mined in California and Nevada, publishing occasional pieces of humorous journalism, notably in the San Francisco *Golden Era.* Since May 1862 he had been the local editor of the *Enterprise,* continuing his connection with the newspaper until it suspended publication in 1893. In 1897, in failing health and reduced circumstances, he retired to the home of his daughter in Iowa. His major work was *The History of the Big Bonanza* (1876), completed at Clemens's Hartford home and issued by Clemens's own publisher, the American Publishing Company (William Wright 1876, vii–ix, xv–xxv; Berkove 1988b; *L1,* 265–66; *ET&S1,* 171–72). Despite the impression given here that Clemens immediately assumed full duties as the *Enterprise*'s city editor, he actually shared the post with Wright for several weeks, until Wright departed on 27 December 1862 to visit his family in Iowa. When Wright returned in September 1863 he resumed his place on the *Enterprise,* sharing reportorial duties, as well as lodgings, with Clemens.

275.21 Two nonpareil columns] Nonpareil was one of the smallest type sizes, equivalent to modern six-point type; it was "extensively used, though mostly on newspapers" (A. A. Stewart, 163; MacKellar, 56). In later years Clemens recalled that his obligation to the *Enterprise* was "to furnish one column of leaded nonpareil every day, and as much more as I could get on paper before the paper should go to press at two o'clock in the morning" (AD, 9 Jan 1906, CU-MARK, in *MTA,* 1:271).

276.17–35 I discovered some emigrant wagons . . . no parallel in history] Clemens's sensational accounts of the beleaguered wagon trains have been identified as two *Enterprise* items of 1 October 1862, extant only as reprinted in the Marysville (Calif.) *Appeal* of 5 October (SLC 1862e–f).

277.2–3 Mr. Goodman said that I was as good a reporter as Dan] Goodman, in later years, reportedly had this to say about the relative abilities of his two local reporters:

> Isn't it so singular that Mark Twain should live and Dan De Quille fade out? If anyone had asked me in 1863 which was to be an immortal name, I should unhesitatingly have said Dan De Quille. They had about equal talent and sense of humor, but the difference was the way in which they used their gifts. One shrank from the world; the other braved it, and it recognized his audacity. (Drury, 216)

278.11–12 My great competitor . . . was Boggs of the *Union*] The character Boggs was based upon Clement T. Rice. Rice went to Nevada from New York in 1861, "having received an appointment under Gov. Nye" (Rice to A. W. Clark, 8 July 61, quoted in Marsh, 680 n. 144). He prospected for a time, and like Clemens owned shares in many mining claims. Clemens had met him in Carson City in 1861 when Rice was a reporter on the *Silver Age.* Rice remained with the newspaper when it moved to Virginia City on 4 November 1862—under the proprietorship of Sam A. Glessner, James L. Laird, and John Church—and changed its name to the *Union,* soon becoming the major competitor of the *Enterprise.* Despite their elaborate journalistic sparring (with Rice figuring as "the Unreliable" in Clemens's columns), the two were good friends, visiting San Francisco together in May and June 1863 and collaborating in reporting the third Territorial Legislature in 1864 for their respective newspapers. By 1867, reputedly a wealthy man, Rice had entered the insurance business in New York City (*L1,* 131, 135 n. 6; Lingenfelter and Gash, 32, 255; *ET&S1,* 22, 193; *MTEnt,* 11–12).

278.17–18 because the principal hated the *Enterprise*] William E. Mellvile had been the principal of—and a teacher at—Virginia City's single public school since its establishment in 1862. During 1863 he was mentioned in the press as a possible candidate for political office and described as a superior teacher and a man of excellent character and fluent speech. He resigned in February 1864, perhaps as the result of unspecified charges brought against him by school trustee William H. Barstow. Clemens explained Mellvile's animosity toward the *Enterprise* in an earlier account of the school-report incident in an 1867 letter to the *Enterprise:* "The scrub who had charge of the public school would not let me have the report for the ENTERPRISE, because it had said he was an ass, which was true, and if he had been half a man he would have been flattered by it" (SLC 1868a; Angel, 571; Kelly 1863, 167; "Our Public School," Virginia City *Evening Bulletin,* 8 July 63, 3; Argentoro, 1; "Board of Education," Virginia City *Union,* 4, 7, and 25 Feb 64, 3; "Certificate of Incorporation of the Virginia Literary & Scientific Association," dated 22 Jan 62, Book A: 3637–38, Storey County Archives, PH in CU-MARK, courtesy of Michael H. Marleau).

279.17 the proprietor of the *Union*] In his 1867 *Enterprise* account Clemens identified this proprietor as John Church (SLC 1868a).

280.7–8 there was no school report in the *Union,* and Boggs held me accountable] In an 1881 letter Rice teased Clemens about the school-report incident, alluding to "the 'influence' you dosed me with in the Territorial Enterprise office, to get my 'school report' that I obtained for the Union" (Rice to SLC, 4 Dec 81, CU-MARK).

280.12 the proprietor of the "Genesee" mine] The Genesee, located in the Devil's Gate district five or six miles southeast of Virginia City, aroused interest among speculators in late 1862 and early 1863. The mine "proprietor" who requested the inspection may have been one of two owners mentioned by Mark Twain in an 1868 letter to the Chicago *Republican:* "Where is the famous Genessee, which United State[s] Senator Stewar[t] and 'uncle' Johnny Atchison bought for so fabulous a sum?" (SLC 1868e). John H. Atchison invested widely in Comstock mines, including the Ophir and the Mexican; in 1862 he and William M. Stewart (see the note at 288.16–17) lived at the same Carson City address ("Mining Matters in Nevada Territory," San Francisco *Alta California*, 28 Nov 62, 1, reprinting the Virginia City *Union* of 22 November; Quartz, 1; Marsh, 686 n. 198; Grant H. Smith, 80–81 n. 1; Kelly 1862, 67, 89).

281.4–6 the grand "flush times" . . . continued with unabated splendor for three years] The population boom, lavish spending habits, and jubilant spirits characterizing the Comstock in 1863 did not continue with "unabated splendor" for three years. The Washoe economy entered a major depression as early as May 1864 (right before Clemens's departure for San Francisco), which "culminated in the panic of December 1865" (Grant H. Smith, 48–50). In his *Enterprise* letter of 29 December 1865 Mark Twain spoke of the "list of rich stock operators of two years ago" who were "busted": "All the nabobs of '63 are pretty much ruined. . . . These are sad, sad times" (SLC 1866a).

282.36–37 It claimed a population of fifteen thousand to eighteen thousand] Although no official figures are available, it is estimated that between the fall of 1862 and midsummer 1863 the population of Virginia City increased from four thousand to fifteen thousand or more (Grant H. Smith, 28).

285.1 My salary was increased to forty dollars a week] This salary, Clemens later confessed, was "all of forty dollars more than I was worth, and I had always wanted a position which paid in the opposite proportion of value to amount of work" (AD, 9 Jan 1906, CU-MARK, in *MTA*, 1:271).

286.16–287.1 give the reporters forty or fifty "feet," and get them to . . . publish a notice of it] Clemens, for example, made favorable mention of the Echo mine, in which he was a shareholder, in three letters to the San Francisco *Morning Call* in July and August 1863. In the first of them he went so far as to claim that the Echo was "probably the richest mine in Gold Hill District" (SLC 1863f, 1863i, 1863*l*; *L1*, 258–59 n. 1).

287.25 We received presents of "feet" every day] Fully realizing the extent to which his reports affected the value of mining stock, Clemens learned, as he wrote home, "how to levy black-mail on the mining companies" in exchange for shares of stock (*L1*, 253). When his mother later inquired how he supported his extravagant living in San Francisco during May and June 1863, he answered, "Why I sold 'wildcat' mining ground that was given me, & my credit was always good at the bank for two or three thousand dollars, & is yet" (*L1*, 259–60).

288.16–17 Mr. Stewart (Senator, now, from Nevada)] William M. Stewart (1827?–1909), originally from New York, had emigrated to California in 1850; he practiced law and served as state attorney general before relocating to Nevada in 1860. There he invested in mining properties and maintained a highly lucrative law practice, earning immense fees for representing several of the largest mining companies. He was a member of the Territorial Council in 1861 and a delegate to the constitutional convention of 1863. When Nevada achieved statehood, Stewart was elected one of its first senators, serving from 1864 to 1875 and again from 1887 to 1905 (*L1*, 243 n. 4; Elliott, 4–5, 11, 17–26, 277 n. 1).

288.17–26 he would give me twenty feet of "Justis" stock . . . nothing could make that man yield] The Justis (sometimes spelled "Justice") mine, located in 1859, was in the Gold Hill district on the west side of Gold Canyon, conveniently situated near the main road and several mills. In mid-November 1863 Justis stock was hovering in the range of $10 a foot; on 11 December it had reached $70. By mid-February 1864, following a rich strike earlier that month, the price had risen to over $150 a foot (Lamb, 2; Virginia City *Union:* "Rich Strike," 10 Feb 64, 3; "Justice Company," 27 Mar 64, 3; "Washoe Stock and Exchange Board," Virginia City *Evening Bulletin,* various dates in Nov 63–Feb 64). Mark Twain gave a similar account of Stewart's offer in his letter to the *Enterprise* of 12 December 1863, taking the opportunity to launch an attack on the "disreputable old cottonhead":

> [Stewart] as good as promised me ten feet in the "Justis," and then backed down again when the stock went up to $80 a foot. . . . Bill Stewart is always construing something—eternally distorting facts and principles. He would climb out of his coffin and construe the burial service. He is a long-legged, bull-headed, whopper-jawed, constructionary monomaniac. . . . I have my own opinion of Bill Stewart, and if it would not appear as if I were a little put out about that Justis (that was an almighty mean thing), I would as soon express it as not. (SLC 1863y)

288.27–28 My revenge will be found in the accompanying portrait] See the illustration on page 289. According to Stewart, Clemens exacted this "revenge" for quite another offense, dating from the winter of 1867–68. Stewart employed Clemens then as his private secretary and shared lodgings with him in Washington, D.C., an arrangement that allowed Clemens to begin work on his manuscript for *The Innocents Abroad.* Reportedly Clemens's irregular and obtrusive living habits so bedeviled their elderly landlady that Stewart was forced to call him to account. "I called Sam in and repeated to him what the landlady had said," Stewart recalled in 1891,

> I told him I would thrash him if I ever heard another complaint. I said that I did not want to turn him out because I wanted him to finish his book. He made one of his smart replies at the expense of the landlady and I told him that I would thrash him then and there. He begged in a most pitiful way for me not to do so and I could not help laughing.
>
> Seeing that he had gotten me into a good humor again he said that he would not annoy the old woman again, but that he would certainly get even with me for having threatened to thrash him if it took him 10 years to do so. ("Mark Twain's Revenge," New York *Recorder,* 5 Apr 91, clipping enclosed in Robert W. Carl to SLC, 5 Apr 91, CU-MARK)

In his autobiography, published in 1908, Stewart told substantially the same story, adding, "I was confident that he would come to no good end, but I have heard of him from time to time since then, and I understand that he has settled down and become respectable" (William M. Stewart, 224). Albert Bigelow Paine maintained that this mildly provocative portrait (which does not particularly resemble Stewart, who had a distinctive flowing beard) was an "unforgivable offense to [Stewart's] dignity," which rankled long after and influenced Stewart's unflattering—and at times untruthful—recollections of Clemens (*MTB*, 1:347 n. 1). But Clemens's friend Steve Gillis believed that Stewart's "malicious stories" were not the result of any real offense. In a letter to Paine, Gillis transmitted Joseph Goodman's remarks "about that Stewart fling":

> "If Mark didn't see fit to come back at the Senator, why should Paine take up the cudgel now? I have always thought that Stewart considered that attack a masterpiece of humor, and that his object was to draw Mark into a controversy and thereby attract attention to his (Stewart's) book." . . .
>
> There you have Stewart's animus in a nutshell. (Gillis to Paine, 26 Feb 1911, Daley)

288.29–37 they had been buying "Overman" stock . . . These are actual facts] Between March and August 1863, the value of stock in the Overman mine, in the Gold Hill district, increased from $12 to over $600 a foot (*Mining and Scientific Press:* "Washoe Stock Remarks," 6 [23 Mar 63]: 5; "The Mining Share Market," 6 [31 Aug 63]: 4). In a letter written to his family on 18 July 1863, shortly after returning to Virginia City from a visit to San Francisco, Clemens gave a slightly different account of this failed opportunity:

> A gentleman in San Francisco told me to call at his office, & he would give me five feet of "Overman." Well, do you know I never went after it? The stock is worth $400^{00} a foot, now—$2,000 thrown away. I don't care a straw, for myself, but I ought to have had more thought for you. (*L1*, 260)

The value of the stock on 16 July was in fact $400 a foot (*L1*, 261 n. 2).

289.20–22 the government holds the primary right to mines . . . or at least did then] In the early 1860s there were no national laws regulating mining claims, nor any way to acquire legal title to claims located on public lands. By long-established custom, however, the rights of "squatter sovereignty" prevailed, and miners observed the laws set forth by each mining district. The National Mining Law of 1866, sponsored by Senator Stewart, gave legal status to local regulations and provided for the patenting of mining claims at a fee of five dollars per acre (Elliott, 49–55).

289.23–24 Imagine a stranger staking out a mining claim . . . in your front yard] The conflicting rights of "owners of gold and silver ledges lying under the earth, and the owners of lots lying on the top of the earth" were a topic of lively discussion in Nevada and California newspapers in 1863 and 1864 ("The Conflict in Washoe between Mining Claims and Surface Lots," San Francisco *Evening Bulletin,* 30 Apr 63, 3). The principle that "*no surface location of ground on mineral land can be made to the exclusion of mining interests*" prevailed in the courts, although owners of condemned houses, crops, or other improvements were entitled to compensation (San Francisco *Evening Bulletin:* "Further of the Conflict of Surface and Ledge Interests at Washoe," 5 May 63, 2; "Mining Companies vs. Lot Owners in Washoe," 7 Sept 63, 2). Mark Twain took note of this conflict of interests in "A Big Thing," published in the Buffalo *Express* in March 1870: "When you have 'taken up' a mine you have a legal right to dig for it,—and if another man owns the farm that is on top of it, it is a very grave misfortune for him, because the only way he has of protecting that farm from destruction, is to move it" (SLC 1870d).

289.30–35 I owned in another claim . . . "East India" stock . . . did not cut a quartz ledge or anything that remotely resembled one] Clemens wrote to his family in April 1863:

> Some of the boys made me a present of fifty feet in the East India G & S. M. Company, ten days ago. I was offered ninety-five dollars a foot for it, yesterday, in gold. *I refused it*—not because I think the claim is worth a cent, for I *don't,* but because I had a curiosity to see how high it *would* go, before people find out how worthless it is. (*L1,* 247)

The East India "humbug," Clemens later noted, was located "right in the middle of C. street" (SLC 1868e).

290.7–291.10 "North Ophir." . . . the mine had been "salted" with melted half dollars] The North Ophir was southwest of Virginia City in the Argentine district. It first attracted attention in March 1863, but its shares were not actively traded until a sudden "excitement" in the stock in early July sent prices soaring from below $10 up to $60 a foot. On 6 July, however, the Virginia City *Evening Bulletin* reported that "one individual who had some rock assayed and found silver alloyed with copper, swears that somebody melted a lot of half dollars and poured them into the ledge" ("Fluctuations of North Ophir," 6 July 63, 2). In spite of this accusation, Clemens puffed the mine in mid-July in exchange for five feet, claiming that expert testimony had "removed the stain from the North Ophir's character" (SLC 1863i). Years later he admitted that he had "bought that mine," and then "adjourned to the poor-house again" when a "painful case of 'salting' was apparent" (SLC 1869j). In an ironic conclusion to the hoax, the Virginia City correspondent of the San Francisco *Evening Bulletin* maintained in October 1863 that the "salting" conspirators had taken care to "preserve small portions of the milling of the coin, which on being detected would at once disclose the artifice," thereby depressing the value of the stock and permitting them to purchase it at cheap prices ("Review of Things in Washoe," San Francisco *Evening Bulletin,* 14 Oct 63, 1; "Struck It

Rich," Sacramento *Union*, 9 Mar 63, 1, reprinting an item possibly by Clemens in the Virginia City *Territorial Enterprise* of 6 March; *L1*, 260, 260–61 n. 1).

291.3–15 the world-renowned tragedian, McKean Buchanan . . . we might have lost . . . from the stage] According to the Virginia City *Evening Bulletin* of 6 July 1863, a "prominent theatrical man" (presumably Buchanan) purchased a block of North Ophir stock for less than $10 a foot, sold out for $30, and then the next day bought it back for $60, believing it would rise still further ("Fluctuations of North Ophir," 2). Instead, he lost everything when the stock collapsed. McKean Buchanan (1823–72) abandoned a lucrative mercantile career to pursue his theatrical ambitions after making a decided hit as an amateur in New Orleans. He made his New York debut in 1849 and toured extensively over the succeeding years, appearing in California, Great Britain, and Australia. He and his company toured Nevada in 1862—meeting with little success—and returned in May 1863 for an extended engagement in Virginia City. Buchanan had an established reputation as a tragedian, although his overblown, bombastic style did not endear him to the critics. Mark Twain himself remarked in 1869 in the Buffalo *Express:*

> The great McKean Buchanan having been driven from all the world's great cities many years ago, still keeps up a pitiless persecution of the provinces, ranting with undiminished fury before audiences composed of one sad manager, one malignant reporter, and a Sheriff waiting to collect the license, and still pushes his crusade from village to village, strewing his disastrous wake with the corpses of country theatres. (SLC 1869f)

And upon Buchanan's death, the New York *Times* commented that many of his "warm personal friends . . . regretted his persistence in continuing on the dramatic stage" ("Obituary. McKean Buchanan," 18 Apr 72, 2; Odell, 5:444–45, 7:3; "McKean Buchanan's Death—Biographical Sketch of the Noted Actor," Denver *Rocky Mountain News*, 17 Apr 72, 1; Rambler, 1; Watson, 91–94, 125–26, 145).

292.1–7 over two years before, Mr. Goodman and another journeyman printer . . . bought it . . . for a thousand dollars] The weekly *Territorial Enterprise* had been established in December 1858 by William L. Jernegan and Alfred James in Genoa, Utah Territory. The struggling paper moved to Carson City in November 1859. By November 1860, Colonel Jonathan Williams, who had purchased James's interest in August 1859, was the sole proprietor and had relocated the paper to fast-growing Virginia City. Williams soon acquired a new partner, I. B. Wollard, whose interest was in turn bought in March 1861 by Goodman and McCarthy, who had recently arrived from San Francisco. Goodman later recalled that since he and McCarthy were penniless, the paper was "to be paid for out of its earnings." (The actual price is not known; in 1906 Clemens contradicted his statement here, claiming that it was only $214.) Goodman and McCarthy "turned the old weekly into a daily, and made enough in a single month to pay the whole purchase price" (Goodman to Alfred B. Nye, 17 Nov 1905, Alfred B. Nye Papers, CU-BANC). "Virginia City legend has it that Goodman and McCarthy every Saturday night divided the take in equal halves and each one carried his share home in a fire bucket filled with golden eagles" (Beebe, 32; Lingenfelter and Gash, 253–54; AD, 9 Jan 1906, CU-MARK, in *MTA*, 1:274).

292.7–11 The editorial sanctum . . . compressed into one apartment . . . general dinner table] The first Virginia City office of the *Enterprise* was on A Street near Sutton Avenue. Dan De Quille described the premises as

> a one-story frame with a shed addition on the north side. In the main structure were the cases of the compositors, the table at which all the writing, local and editorial, was done, and the old Washington hand-press on which the papers were worked off.
>
> The shed addition was used as a kitchen (an old Chinaman called "Joe" doing the cooking) and eating-room, and ranged on the sides were sleeping bunks, one above another in ship-shape. Here all hands ate at a long table, and here nearly all slept. (William Wright 1893a)

When Clemens joined the newspaper in September 1862, the office had been relocated to North C Street over a clothing store ("The Pioneer Journal Dead," Virginia City *Evening Chronicle*, 16 Jan 93, 2).

292.12–13 The paper was . . . printed by steam] The *Enterprise*'s new steam press—the first in Nevada—was brought in sections by ox-drawn wagon from San Francisco. The press began production the night of 31 July 1863 with editors and compositors alike taking part in a riotous celebration. The next morning's edition was several hours late and typographically chaotic, but sported "an entirely new and improved shape" of "increased and ponderous dimensions . . . nearly double" in size ("The Enterprise," Virginia City *Evening Bulletin*, 1 Aug 63, 3; Beebe, 87; Angel, 292).

292.13 there were five editors and twenty-three compositors] According to a correspondent for the Sacramento *Bee*, in January 1864 the *Enterprise* employed "nine compositors on the paper with a foreman, two or three in the job room, and one pressman," in addition to "four editors, viz: J. T. Goodman, Mr. [Charles A. V.] Putnam, 'Dan de Quille,' and 'Mark Twain'" (Curtis, 1). Putnam had joined the staff in May 1863. Clemens's fifth editor may have been George F. Dawson, an Englishman, who worked as an assistant editor in 1864 (Putnam, 3; *L1*, 304 n. 2).

292.16–18 the "Enterprise Building" was . . . fire-proof brick] The *Enterprise* moved to its third and final Virginia City location, a three-story brick building on South C Street, in August 1863 (*L1*, 243; William Wright 1893a).

292.21–23 The "Gould & Curry" company were erecting a monster hundred-stamp mill at a cost . . . of a million dollars] The imposing Gould and Curry mill was located about two miles northeast of Virginia City. As first constructed it had forty stamps for crushing ore; these were later increased to eighty. Its main structure, built in the form of a Greek cross, featured an ornamental pool graced by an elaborate fountain. While the mill was under construction, it was regarded as "the model mill of the country, and . . . the greatest piece of work of the sort in the world" ("Notes of Nevada Travel," Marysville [Calif.] *Appeal*, 28 June 62, 3). According to Eliot Lord, however, the mill—which had cost nearly $900,000 by the end of 1863—proved to be "the most conspicuous monument of inexperience and extravagance ever erected in a mining district," for it "was not yet fairly completed when its entire machinery for ore reduction was discarded" as unsatisfactory. In 1864 the mill was rebuilt, "almost from the foundation," at a cost of over $560,000 (Lord, 124–25; Grant H. Smith, 85; "Mill Reduction and Works of the Gould & Curry Company," Sacramento *Union*, 14 Nov 62, 4, reprinting the Virginia City *Union*).

292.23 Gould & Curry stock paid heavy dividends] The Gould and Curry Silver Mining Company paid its first monthly dividend, $24 a foot, in December 1862; in January 1863 the dividend rose to $100 per foot, and by June it had increased to $150. The first full year of dividends totaled $1,464,400 ($1,220 per foot), a sum representing about 40 percent of the company's gross receipts. For an investor who purchased stock in December 1862, at $2,600 per foot, this represented an annual return of nearly 47 percent (*Mining and Scientific Press:* "Mining Stock Report," 6 [20 Dec 62]: 5, and 6 [29 Dec 62]: 5; "Stock Remarks," 6 [2 Feb 63]: 5; "The Mining Share Market," 6 [29 June 63: 4]; "Cost and Result of Silver Mining," Virginia City *Union*, 14 Jan 64, 1).

292.25 The Superintendent of the Gould & Curry] The superintendent of the mine from its incorporation in 1860 was Charles Lyman Strong (1826–83), a self-educated mining engineer. He had arrived in California about 1850 as an agent for Wells and Company, and spent the next ten years in a variety of commercial pursuits. Encouraged by the Gould and Curry's owners to give free rein to his ideas, Strong was largely responsible for the construction of the company's extravagant mill. In 1864 the strain of his responsibilities caused him to resign his position in order to travel.

292.29–293.2 The Superintendent . . . was to have had one per cent . . . of the bullion likewise] Mark Twain refers to Walter W. Palmer, superintendent of the Ophir Silver Mining Company, who was employed during 1863 for a monthly salary of $2,500. On 1 January 1864 his salary was changed to $1,000, plus 2 percent "on the dividends to be thereafter declared by the Company, in lieu of the old contract salary" (SLC

1864n). Apparently some misunderstanding about the exact terms of this agreement led to a dispute. In May 1864 the company asked Palmer to resign (for unstated reasons), and he complied. On 19 August the company filed suit for the recovery of $8,456, which Palmer claimed was rightfully his. It was almost certainly Clemens who reported this case for the San Francisco *Morning Call* (SLC 1864n, 1864s).

293.6–33 U. S. Sanitary Commission . . . the wildest mob . . . came there "flush" and went away "busted."] The United States Sanitary Commission was officially established in June 1861 by an order of the secretary of war, but it owed its existence to a coalition of relief associations formed by women in the Northern states. During its first year its revenues were very limited, but in the fall of 1862—under the energetic leadership of its president, the Reverend Henry W. Bellows (1814–82)—it began to receive substantial contributions from across the nation and around the world. The clamorous mob described here gathered in front of the International Hotel on C Street during Clemens's first month on the *Enterprise*—on 26 October 1862—at a meeting organized by the Central Committee of the Storey County Patriotic Fund Association. This meeting represented Virginia City's effort to contribute its share to the $20,000 total that Storey County had pledged to raise. Nearly $3,000 was collected on the spot, which was added to $16,000 in silver bullion already donated. (The meeting was reported in the *Enterprise,* possibly by Clemens, on 28 October.) The president, or chairman, of the Central Committee was Almarin B. Paul (1823–1909) of Gold Hill (formerly of St. Louis), a prominent banker and mill operator reputed to be one of the wealthiest men in Nevada. Paul had pioneered the Washoe wet process for crushing ore, and established the Pioneer Mill, probably the first mill on the Comstock (see the note at 235.14–15; Stillé, 63–69, 197–204, 539–42; Sacramento *Union:* "Relief in Nevada Territory," 30 Oct 62, 2, reprinting the Virginia City *Territorial Enterprise* of 28 October; "Those Silver Brick," 4 Nov 62, 3; *L1,* 278 n. 6).

294.1–8 the famous "Sanitary Flour Sack" came our way . . . Reuel Gridley . . . was defeated] A year and a half passed before the Sanitary Flour Sack excitement began in April 1864. Clemens had last seen Reuel Colt Gridley (1829–70) in 1846 or 1847, when Gridley left their Hannibal, Missouri, school to join a company of infantry bound for the Mexican War. Barton S. Bowen, a steamboat captain with whom Clemens had served as a pilot, claimed in 1865 that he had once tried to "teach young Gridley" to be a pilot, "but found him so much given to larking, that he couldn't learn" ("River News," Cincinnati *Commercial,* 13 Feb 65, 4). In 1852 Gridley emigrated to California, and about ten years later relocated to Nevada, where, late in 1863, he started the grocery firm of Gridley, Hobart, and Jacobs at Austin, in the Reese

River area of central Nevada. (Reese River was the center of a mining "excitement" in 1862–63.) Gridley was not himself a mayoral candidate in the 19 April 1864 election that resulted in the Sanitary Flour Sack auction; he placed a bet on the Democratic candidate, David E. Buel, against the Republican candidate, Charles Holbrook. Gridley—who, as Clemens wrote his family on 17 May 1864, was "Union to the backbone, but a Copperhead in sympathies"—lost his bet to a Republican supporter, Dr. H. S. Herrick, the Lander County assessor and superintendent of schools. Mark Twain intentionally simplified the story of Gridley's bet: he described it correctly not only in his 1864 letter, but also in a December 1870 letter to the New York *Tribune* announcing Gridley's death (*L1*, 282; AD, 16 Mar 1906, CU-MARK, in *MTA*, 2:216–17; Elizabeth H. Smith, 11–13; Angel, 268–70, 461, 464; SLC 1870o).

295.10–12 he . . . had taken in eight thousand dollars in gold] The amount realized by the auction of Gridley's flour sack in Austin, together with additional donations and subscriptions, totaled $5,300 ("Sanitary Fund Meetings Yesterday!" Virginia City *Union*, 17 May 64, 3; "The Austin Flour Sack," Gold Hill *News*, 17 May 64, 2; *L1*, 282).

295.14–20 The news came to Virginia . . . Gridley arrived . . . only five thousand dollars had been secured] Three weeks elapsed before Gridley arrived in Virginia City with the flour sack. On Sunday, 15 May, he auctioned it during a fund-raising meeting in Maguire's Opera House for the disappointing sum of $570; by the end of the afternoon, however, the combined proceeds from the meeting totaled more than $3,700 in cash, mining stock, and silver bullion ("The Sanitary Meeting Sunday Afternoon," Virginia City *Union*, 17 May 64, 3; *L1*, 285 n. 9).

295.25–26 the next morning a procession of open carriages] The Sanitary Flour Sack procession of Monday, 16 May, was the subject of two reports, probably written by Clemens, in the *Enterprise* of 17 and 18 May (extant as reprinted in the San Francisco *Evening Bulletin* of 19 and 20 May). In the first of these, the procession was dubbed the "Army of the Lord," by which name it became known; Almarin Paul credited Mark Twain with this expression in a newspaper letter dated 21 May (Paul, 1; SLC 1864d–e). On 17 May Clemens also wrote an enthusiastic account of the event to his mother and sister, which was printed in an unidentified St. Louis newspaper. It was probably Pamela, his sister, who was involved in organizing a St. Louis fair to be held in May and June, who arranged for the letter's publication (*L1*, 281–87, 528–29).

297.8–10 Gen. W. said . . . The Yellow Jacket . . . offers a thousand dollars, coin] The bidder—at $500—for the Yellow Jacket mine was its newly elected president and superintendent, John B. Winters, known as "General Winters" because he was an officer in the Nevada militia. The Yellow Jacket, one of the first and richest of the Comstock mines, was located near Gold Hill on a southern extension of the lode (see the notes at 556.26–28 and 556.27; SLC 1864d; Grant H. Smith, 90–91, 93, 292–93; *RI 1972,* 587, misidentifies "Gen. W." as Charles H. S. Williams).

297.19–21 Gold Hill's . . . grand total was displayed] The contributions from Gold Hill totaled $6,588. Since this total was the first to exceed Austin's, Gridley "mounted the rostrum and threw up a sponge according to promise" (SLC 1864d–e).

297.22 refreshed with new lager beer and plenty of it] The first *Enterprise* report noted that "the boys" twice stopped to "moisten themselves" along the way. The reporter for the Gold Hill *News* remarked: "'Tone' was given to the procession by the presence of Gov. Twain and his staff of bibulous reporters, who came down in a free carriage, ostensibly for the purpose of taking notes, but in reality in pursuit of free whiskey" ("The Austin Flour Sack," 17 May 64, 2). (Clemens earned the title of "Gov. Twain" when he delivered a burlesque "Governor's Message" to Nevada's Third House, a mock legislative body, in December 1863: see *MTEnt,* 100–110, 144; *L1,* 272–73 n. 1.)

297.24–34 the expedition had carried Silver City and Dayton . . . forty thousand dollars in greenbacks] Silver City donated $1,800, and Dayton $1,865. Virginia City pledged $12,945 in gold, or $22,300 in greenbacks, not "forty thousand." The combined total earned for the Sanitary Commission on 16 May, however, *was* about $23,200 in gold, or $40,000 in greenbacks (SLC 1864d–e; Mitchell, 427). Contemporary newspaper stories, as well as later secondary accounts, frequently disagree about the totals for the flour-sack auctions. Since Mark Twain's source for his *Roughing It* account—if any—has not been determined, it is impossible to ascertain whether he intentionally inflated his figures.

298.3 Gridley sold the sack in Carson City] No auction was held in Carson City, as Clemens explained to his family in May 1864:

> Carson is considerably larger than either of these three towns [Gold Hill, Dayton, Silver City], but it has a lousy, lazy, worthless, poverty-stricken population, and the universal opinion was that we couldn't raise $500 dollars there. So we started home again. (*L1,* 283)

In the *Enterprise* Clemens provided another—even more offensive—reason for the procession's failure to go to Carson:

> The money raised at the Sanitary Fancy Dress Ball, recently held in Carson for the St. Louis Fair, had been diverted from its legitimate course, and was to be sent to aid a Miscegenation Society somewhere in the East; and it was feared the proceeds of the sack might be similarly disposed of. (Citizen, 2)

He explained to his sister-in-law that he was "not sober" when he wrote the item, and that he had not expected it to appear in print. For the resulting controversy, see *L1*, 287–89, 296–99.

298.3–4 and several California towns; also in San Francisco] Gridley left Virginia City on 17 May for Sacramento, where the sack was first sold at a picnic outside the city, and then auctioned again in the evening at a lecture given by Dr. Bellows (see the note at 293.6–33), earning $2,150 for the Sanitary Commission. The next day Gridley proceeded to San Francisco; journalist J. Ross Browne described his arrival: "It was the memorable event of the times. Never did Montgomery Street present a more imposing appearance. The beauty and the fashion of the city were there; and so was Gridley, decked out in glorious array, the observed of all observers" (J. Ross Browne 1866, 35). Ten days later the sack of flour was sold for the last time in the West, after the presentation of a comedy at the Metropolitan Theatre, bringing in $2,800. Gridley's celebrity was augmented by the sale of photographs taken by a San Francisco photographer; an engraving of one of these appeared in *Harper's Weekly* in January 1865 with the remark, "No lady's album in Nevada or California is considered complete without a photograph of GRIDLEY and his sack of flour" ("Mr. Gridley and His Sack of Flour," 21 Jan 65, 45; the engraving is reproduced in *L1*, 286). The flour sack reportedly earned in California and Nevada "the sum of $63,000 in coin, and it owned three blocks of lots in Austin worth $7,000, and a house and lot in Dayton" (*Tribute*, 23). Gridley's efforts were warmly praised by Dr. Bellows in a letter of 24 May: "The history of your Sanitary Sack of Flour is undoubtedly more interesting and peculiar than that of any sack recorded, short of the sack of Troy—and it would take another Homer to write it" ("Great Excitement about the Gridley-Sanitary Sack of Flour," Austin *Reese River Reveille*, 7 June 64, 1; "Departures Yesterday," Virginia City *Union*, 18 May 64, 3; "The Sanitary Gala Day," Sacramento *Union*, 19 May 64, 3; San Francisco *Evening Bulletin*: "Travels and Fortunes of the Great Austin Sack of Flour," 20 May 64, 1; "The Austin Sanitary Sack in Town," 21 May 64, 5; "Sale of the Gridley-Sanitary Sack of Flour at the Metropolitan Theatre," 30 May 64, 5).

298.4–5 he took it east and sold it in one or two Atlantic cities] Before sailing for the East, Gridley returned home to Austin for six months because of family illness. After leaving San Francisco for New York on 13 December 1864, he evidently visited several eastern cities in the spring of 1865; his exact itinerary, however, has not been determined. Of Gridley's tour "on the Atlantic side," Browne recalled reading "wonderful newspaper accounts. He was fêted, and gazed at, and admired, and hurrahed, and printed in weekly pictorials, and puffed, and joked—was the irrepressible Gridley" (J. Ross Browne 1866, 36; "Return of Mr.

Gridley," Austin *Reese River Reveille,* 5 June 64, 2; "The Famous Sanitary Flour Sack," San Francisco *Alta California,* 14 Dec 64, 1).

298.6–10 he finally carried it to St. Louis . . . small cakes and retailed them at high prices] Gridley took his flour sack to St. Louis in the summer of 1865. Since it was illegal in Missouri to auction the same item repeatedly, "it was suggested that the flour be baked into cakes which could be sold. Gridley refused, for he felt that the flour came from the West and that was where it belonged. Thus the tour ended on a sour note" (Elizabeth W. Smith, 16). Curiously, the idea of selling the flour as small cakes may have originated with Clemens a year earlier. In May 1864 an *Enterprise* reporter, probably Clemens, listed the amounts already realized by the flour-sack auctions in Nevada and estimated how much could be raised in California and the East, computing a total of over $500,000. He continued,

> Now supposing that the managers of the St. Louis Fair are smart enough to have this historical sack of flour ultimately made into thin wafer cakes—500 to the pound—it strikes us that 25,000 people would willingly give $5 a cake for it, if only for the sake of telling their children and friends that they had eaten a cake made out of flour that had sold for over $500,000 per sack! (SLC 1864g)

298.11–13 when the flour sack's mission was ended . . . a hundred and fifty thousand dollars in greenbacks] The final total of Gridley's proceeds cannot be determined with any certainty. Since the estimates of others range from $40,000 to $275,000, in gold, Mark Twain's figure is quite plausible (*Tribute,* 24; Webb 1865b; Stillé, 238).

298.16–22 the expenses of his Sanitary flour sack expedition . . . He died at Stockton, California, in December, 1870] Gridley returned home in mid-July 1865, "completely broken down in health" and "almost bankrupt" (Tinkham, 66). He died on 24 November 1870 in Paradise City, California (a small town in Stanislaus County, not far from Stockton). In his December 1870 letter to the New York *Tribune* Mark Twain praised Gridley's "integrity, benevolence, and enterprise" (SLC 1870o). A commemorative statue, depicting Gridley and the flour sack, was erected in 1887 at his gravesite in the Stockton Rural Cemetery. The original buckskin-covered flour sack is now in the State Historical Museum in Reno ("Arrival of the 'Golden City,'" San Francisco *Alta California,* 10 July 65, 1; Tinkham, 64–66, 241–42; Elizabeth W. Smith, 16–18).

299.7–301.31 Two . . . him.] Mark Twain first published this passage in a Buffalo *Express* "Around the World" letter on 8 January 1870; he revised the earlier printing for inclusion in *Roughing It* (SLC 1870a).

299.7–14 Two cousins . . . a hundred thousand dollars a year] In the earlier version of this passage in the *Express,* the two teamsters are called brothers, rather than cousins. Mark Twain may therefore have originally had in mind Theodore and Joseph Winters—both of whom he knew—who hauled logs on the Truckee River ditch before the snows drove them into Carson Valley at the right time in 1859 to establish early and profitable claims on the Comstock ("Returns from Washoe," Marysville [Calif.] *Appeal*, 10 Nov 63, 2; *ET&S1*, 339–42, 461; *L1*, 275, 279–80 n. 11).

300.5–301.2 John Smith . . . I'll take that money, if you please] Mark Twain is alluding to Lemuel Sanford (Sandy) Bowers (1830–68), an unlettered nabob famous for his conspicuous display of wealth. According to the reminiscences of Almarin B. Paul and C. C. Stevenson, both pioneer settlers of Gold Hill, Bowers located his ten-foot claim in Gold Hill gulch in the fall of 1858, before the discovery of the Comstock lode. His claim, later combined with the adjoining ten feet held by his wife, Eilley Orrum (1826–1903), proved to be on the richest section of the lode. Bowers built a ten-stamp mill in Crown Point Ravine in 1861 and enlarged it to twenty stamps in 1862. The Bowerses traveled in Europe in 1862–63, during which time their mansion in Washoe Valley was constructed and furnished in lavish style. An 1864 *Enterprise* item, possibly by Clemens, described the costly fittings of the house and put Bowers's monthly income at $70,000. Bowers died in April 1868, leaving a surprisingly depleted estate of $638,000. Mrs. Bowers, prey to poor management and a variety of swindlers, lost everything—including her house—over a period of years, and was forced to eke out a living as the "Washoe seeress." This anecdote about the ship's pool was published in California newspapers in May 1865; the incident allegedly occurred a few months earlier on board the steamer *Champion* (Angel, 39, 58, 68; Hermann, 12–17; "Pioneer Reminiscences in Washoe," Sacramento *Union*, 9 Oct 63, 4, reprinting the Virginia City *Territorial Enterprise* of 7 October; "A Washoe Palace," Stockton *Independent*, 30 Sept 63, 3, reprinting the Carson City *Independent*; "The Bowers Mill," Virginia City *Union*, 28 Apr 64, 3; Addenbrooke, 36; "A Washoe Nabob," *Mining and Scientific Press* 8 [13 Feb 64]: 102, reprinting the Virginia City *Territorial Enterprise*; "Death of a Good Citizen," Gold Hill *Evening News*, 21 Apr 68, 3; "Out of His Reckoning," Sacramento *Bee*, 2 May 65, 2).

301.3–13 The Gould & Curry claim . . . was worth . . . seven million six hundred thousand dollars in gold coin] In January 1867, during his voyage from San Francisco to New York, Mark Twain made the following notebook entry—one of several entries recording anecdotes later included in *Roughing It:* "Curry sold 600 feet of Gould & Curry for $2,600. Gould sold 600 feet for $250, an old plug horse, a jug of whisky & a pair of blankets" (*N&J1*, 293; see the notes at 301.14–21, 301.22–28, 318.1–2, 322.14–15, and 331.10). Alva Gould (1815–?93) emigrated from Michigan to California in 1849–50. He was a placer miner there until 1858, when he went to Carson County, Utah Territory. His later accounts—dictated in 1877 and 1891—of locating a claim, with Abraham Curry (see the note at 162.5), on the Comstock in early 1859 are contradictory. He consistently asserted, however, that Curry sold his share in their claim to Henry Meredith for $2,400, while he was defrauded of his own interest. In 1863, Gould unsuccessfully sued the Gould and Curry Silver Mining Company "for the recovery of 70 feet of their ground," claiming that since he had never sold his share, it remained his "by right of location" ("Suit against the Gould & Curry Co.," Eureka [Calif.] *Humboldt Times*, 17 Oct 63, 3). Gould also figured in a well-known Comstock anecdote, involving his sale of what may have been a different claim, in which he accepted $450 from a California speculator and then rode drunkenly down Gold Canyon shouting, "Oh, I've fooled the Californian!" (Lord, 60). Gould spent his last years as a fruit peddler at the Reno train depot. At its peak price of $6,300 a foot in June 1863, the 1,200-foot Gould and Curry mine was worth, as Mark Twain states, about $7.6 million (Gould, 1–20; "Chapter about Closed," Sacramento *Record-Union*, 2 Sept 93, 1; "Alva Gould," San Francisco *Morning Call*, 10 Mar 91, 7; "General Mining Stock Report," *Mining and Scientific Press* 6 [29 June 63]: 5).

301.14–21 a poverty-stricken Mexican . . . one million five hundred thousand dollars] Compare this January 1867 entry in Clemens's notebook: "100 feet of Ophir (the present Mexican) was segregated for a stream of water as large as your wrist to some Spaniards. Afterwards worth $18,000 a foot" (*N&J1*, 294). While giving slightly different figures for its later value, this entry and *Roughing It* both give condensed versions of the early history of the Mexican, or Spanish, mine, a 100-foot claim reportedly traded in mid-1859 by the original owners of the Ophir claim to Henry Comstock and Emanuel Penrod in return for water rights. Later that year Gabriel Maldonado, a Mexican, and Francis J. Hughes bought the claim for $9,500 and organized the Mexican Company. In 1864 the value of the dividend-paying Mexican mine was judged to be $1 million; the value of the company's mill at Empire City (east of Carson) is not known. Mark Twain published accounts of his two descents into the mine in October 1862 and February 1863 ("Silver in Nevada," Sacramento *Union*, 2 May 64, 4; SLC 1862g, 1863a).

301.22–28 An individual who owned . . . a sixty-thousand-dollar horse] Another January 1867 notebook entry reads, "A man sold 26 feet of Ophir or Yellow Jacket for an old plug horse—called him the $26,000 horse" (*N&J1*, 293). The allusion may be to James Finney, who sold to Henry Comstock his interest in the Ophir claim for "a certain Indian pony, bob-tailed, lean and aged. . . . According to some authorities, divers bottles of exhilarating fluids formed part of the consideration by Finney received on that occasion" (DeGroot 1876a).

301.32–37 A youth of nineteen . . . made himself rich by watching the mining telegrams] John William (Johnny) Skae (1841?–85) was a native of Canada who emigrated in the late 1850s to California, and shortly thereafter to Nevada. In the early 1860s he used his position with the Virginia City telegraph office to gain inside information: "He soon acquired such profits from his speculations that he abandoned his profession and launched out as a capitalist" (*ET&S2*, 72–73, 77–78, 123, 254–60; "Death of 'Johnny' Skae," San Francisco *Morning Call*, 17 July 85, 1). Skae's abuse of his position may have prompted the California State Telegraph Company (which had jurisdiction over the Virginia City office) in April 1863 to prohibit "persons employed by them from owning feet in mining ground" ("Taking the Feet from Telegraph Employees," San Francisco *Evening Bulletin*, 22 Apr 63, 1, reprinting the Virginia City *Union* of 17 April). Skae, whom Mark Twain portrayed in three 1864–65 sketches as a convivial companion and "inimitable punster," also served as a trustee and vice-president of the Virginia and Gold Hill Water Company, and in 1863 became superintendent of the Hale and Norcross mine, in which Clemens invested (Angel, 588; "Death of John Skae, the Mining Operator," San Francisco *Evening Bulletin*, 17 July 85, 2; "Death of John Skae," Virginia City *Evening Chronicle*, 17 July 85, 3; *L1*, 300–301 n. 4).

302.9–303.15 Another telegraph operator . . . a fortune was the result] Mark Twain may be recalling David C. Williams, a San Francisco stockbroker and former telegraph operator who was implicated in more than one incident involving the use of the wires to make a profit on Nevada mining stocks. In July 1864 Williams, posing as a teamster, spent more than a week at a stage and telegraph station near Placerville. He made note of the messages being transmitted, and even tried to bribe the operator to let him handle the wires, hoping to overhear the decision in the Savage and North Potosi lawsuit and wire it to his confederates in San Francisco so that they could buy shares in the victorious company before the news became public. Unlike the character in the *Roughing It* account, however, Williams was unsuccessful: the operator summoned a detective, who arrested him ("Williams, the Wire-Worker," San Francisco *Morning Call*, 12 Aug 64, 1; "Monopolizing the Line," Virginia City *Union*, 19 Apr 64, 3).

303.25–27 a friend . . . sought him out, bought his "feet" . . . and sold the property for seventy-five thousand dollars] A similar story is told of John W. Mackay (1831–1902), who became famous in the 1870s as a "Big Bonanza" millionaire. In 1863 the owners of the Kentuck mine were prevented from incorporating by the disappearance of one of the original locators, who still owned several shares in the mine. Learning that he was with the Confederate army in Tennessee, Mackay traced him and returned

> with the missing block of feet and a bill of sale to show his ownership. Mackay never revealed how he secured them but the legend insists he dogged his man into the front lines before Chattanooga and wrangled over the price while Parrott rifles boomed and Minié balls ripped overhead. (Beebe and Clegg, 66)

303.35–304.2 I was . . . again.] This paragraph, like the first part of the chapter, was based on an earlier printing in the Buffalo *Express* for 8 January 1870 (SLC 1870a). When Mark Twain was composing *Roughing It,* he discarded a sheet of manuscript on which he had pasted and revised a clipping of this passage from the *Express;* it is reproduced on page 800.

308.10–16 grand time over Buck Fanshaw when he died . . . high position in the fire department] The prototype of Buck Fanshaw was Thomas Peasley, a well-known Virginia City figure. Born in New York, Peasley went to Virginia City from Calaveras County, California, in 1860 and became the owner of the city's most elegant and popular saloon, the Sazerac. He helped to organize the city's volunteer fire department, and in 1862 became its first chief engineer. The charismatic and athletic Peasley was also the "proprietor," as Mark Twain puts it, of Julia Bulette, Virginia City's first and most famous courtesan, and made her the "queen," in full fire regalia, of Engine Company No. 1. An aggressive Unionist, he was widely acknowledged as a leader both in local and national political campaigns in Virginia City. He had "killed his man," a young tough named "Sugarfoot Jack" Jenkins, although not in defense of a stranger (see the note at 323.17). By 1866 Peasley had given up his saloon business and become manager and coproprietor of Maguire's Opera House and sergeant-at-arms of the Nevada State Senate. On 2 February 1866 Peasley, aged about thirty-eight, engaged in a gunfight with Martin V. Barnhart in the bar of the Ormsby House in Carson City, which resulted in the death of both men. Obituary notices called Peasley the "acknowledged political head of the Fire and Police Departments of Virginia, and . . . a man of great influence with the sports and roughs," and asserted that the vote of the "Peasley crowd" was essential to a politician's success. Peasley's body was removed to Virginia City, where a resplendent and well-attended funeral was held. Clemens remained in San Francisco at the time ("Two Men Killed, in Carson," San Francisco *Morning Call,* 3 Feb 66, 3; "A Terrible Tragedy," Carson City *Appeal,* 3 Feb 66, 2; "Funeral Yesterday," Virginia City *Union,* 5 Feb 66, 3; *ET&S1,* 473–74; Angel, 599; Lyman, 119–22; Mack 1947, 195–98; Beebe and Clegg, 16–18).

308.16 a very Warwick in politics] Richard Neville (1428–71), earl of Warwick and Salisbury, was known as "the Kingmaker" during the early years of the Wars of the Roses. He helped Edward, duke of York, to secure the English throne in 1461 as Edward IV, and served as his powerful great chamberlain. Falling out with Edward, he drove him from the throne, and in 1470 restored Henry VI of the house of Lancaster.

308.23–24 a verdict of death "by the visitation of God."] Clemens included a similar anecdote in his "People and Things" column in the Buffalo *Express* for 18 August 1869:

> In Nevada, a man with the consumption took the small-pox from a negro, the cholera from a Chinaman, and the yellow fever and the erysipelas from other parties, and swallowed fifteen grains of strychnine and fell out of the third-story window and broke his neck. Verdict of the jury, "Died by the visitation of God." (SLC 1869d)

309.13–14 the short-haired brotherhood] The term "short hairs" was apparently used for "roughs" in general, because they wore their hair in a short "fighting cut." From the mid-1860s the expression was sometimes used in politics to designate the party or faction of the "common man or 'toughs'" (Winfield J. Davis, 213–14; Morton, 111; Mathews, 2:1530).

309.17–20 minister . . . as yet unacquainted with the ways of the mines] Mark Twain's portrait of the young minister—here and in his earlier *Enterprise* piece (see the next note)—was based on his friend the Reverend Franklin S. Rising (1833?–68), the rector of St. Paul's Episcopal Church in Virginia City. (Rising did not, however, conduct the religious service at Peasley's funeral: the Reverend William M. Martin of Virginia City's Presbyterian Church officiated.) Rising arrived in Virginia City from New York in April 1862, formally opened his new church the following February, and helped establish Episcopal parishes in neighboring cities. He resigned his position in 1866 because of poor health and traveled to the Sandwich Islands, where he met Clemens again. The two men returned to the States together in July 1866 on the clipper *Smyrniote.* Hearing of Rising's death in an Ohio River steamboat collision in December 1868, Clemens described his association with this "noble young fellow" in a letter to Olivia Langdon: "I used to try to teach him how he ought to preach in order to get at the better natures of the rough population about him, & he used to try hard to learn—for I *knew* them & he did not, for he was refined & sensitive & not intended for such a people as that" (*L2,* 333, 337 n. 2; *L1,* 352, 354 n. 3; Doten, 2:877; Angel, 199–202, 215).

309.20 The committeeman, "Scotty" Briggs, made his visit] Mark Twain apparently returned to one of his early *Enterprise* pieces for the germ of his description of Scotty Briggs's interview with the minister. This recently discovered *Enterprise* article survives only in part, as a paraphrase quoted in the San Francisco *Call and Post* of 1 April 1921, and is reprinted here for the first time. The author of the article explained that Clemens had been dispatched by Goodman to interview the clergymen of the area; he "began with the Baptist Church, at Gold Hill," and reported as follows:

> The high price charged for water by the water company renders it impossible to immerse any but wealthy converts. For this and other reasons the pastor of the church informs me that he will be compelled to resign. His salary is small, only $24 a month. But the irregularity with which it is paid, or, to speak more accurately, the regularity with which it is not paid, is very distressing to him. He

keeps bachelor's quarters and is in debt to his butcher, and when the preacher calls for a beefsteak the butcher, in a sort of absent-minded way cuts him off a piece of liver. His congregation has dwindled to nine regular attendants, eight of whom are women, and his collection last Sabbath amounted to only twenty cents. On the whole it may be said that the condition of the cause of Christ in Gold Hill leaves very much to be desired.

The Methodist Church, in Virginia City, presents different conditions. The congregation is large and contributions are liberal. The pastor is a broad man—as broad as he is long. He measures 62 inches around the waist and 62 inches from keel to main yard.

The Episcopal clergyman is a charming little gentleman just out from the effete East. He is as unlearned in sporting nomenclature as sporting men are unlearned in the technicalities of orthodoxy.

Last week, on the day before Andy Brown died, his brother Steve went to the Episcopal clergyman and said: "My brother is about to pass in his checks and he wants you to come down to the joint and start him off square before he becomes a stiff."

"I am not a banker," said the clergyman, "and I can not aid your brother in passing checks."

"You don't tumble," said Andy. "My brother is going to die, and he wants you to do some praying over him before he goes. He doesn't feel sure as to where he will land, and he thinks that your prayers might keep him out of a hot climate."

"I see," said the divine. "Is your brother a professor?"

"He was," said Andy, "but since Baldy Thompson licked him in their last fight he has given up the profession of pugilism."

"Do you think," said the clergyman, "that your brother would like the Eucharist administered?"

"Well, partner," said Andy, dubiously, "it looks to me like a queer time for that sort of thing. But you know best, and you can take your deck along or I'll get you a pack of cards at the saloon." (Wells 1921a)

Mark Twain's portrait of Scotty Briggs, like his Buck Fanshaw, undoubtedly owed some of its features to actual Nevada figures. Briggs may have been drawn from John Van Buren (Jack) Perry, Virginia City's popular marshal and, like his friend Thomas Peasley, an ardent Unionist and a mainstay of the Virginia Volunteer Fire Department. Just as Scotty Briggs brawled alongside of Buck Fanshaw, so Perry joined Peasley and other Unionists in defending a Union recruiter attacked by a Secessionist in a Virginia City street. Mark Twain at least twice made reference to Perry's mastery of "vulgar phraseology" and recorded examples of his vivid slang quite similar to those of his fictional counterpart (SLC 1863c, 1863m). George Wharton James, an intimate friend of Perry's, claimed that Clemens became "very fond" of the marshal and spent many hours listening to his stories: "It was Jack who told several of the stories that appear in 'Roughing It'" (James, 530). Steve Gillis (see the note at 323.30–325.2), in later years, claimed that Scotty Briggs was drawn from one Ruef Williams, a neighbor at Jackass Hill in Tuolumne County—and possibly the "Riff Williams" whom Goodman mentioned as one of Peasley and Perry's cronies in the Virginia Fire Department. Nothing further is known about Williams, except that he was probably the "M. R. Williams" who was chief of the department at the time of Peasley's death ("A Card," Virginia City *Union,* 5 Feb 66, 2; Angel, 266, 600; AD, 26 May 1907, CU-MARK, in *MTE,* 361; Fulton, 55; Goodman 1892a).

313.18–314.1 some roughs jumped the Catholic bone-yard and started in to stake out town lots] The *Enterprise* local (possibly Clemens) reported on 25 December 1862:

> On Saturday last, parties in this city took possession of the Catholic cemetery, located in the southeast part of the town, and commenced the work of fencing it in and building thereon a house. When this became known throughout the city, there came near being a most bloody row over the matter. Many armed themselves and were for proceeding instantly to the burying ground to drive the jumpers away by force of arms.

But peaceful counsel prevailed, while a decision regarding ownership of the ground was awaited ("Jumping a Graveyard at Washoe," San Francisco *Evening Bulletin,* 29 Dec 62, 1, reprinting the Virginia City *Territorial Enterprise* of 25 December).

314.24–28 It was him that put down the riot last election . . . in less than three minutes] Paul Fatout has suggested that the model for this free-for-all was not an election riot, but a brawl that broke out between two rival fire companies after a major fire in Virginia City on 28 August 1863. The Virginia City *Union* reported:

> Fire Companies Nos. 1 and 2 met at the intersection of Taylor and C streets, and by some means became involved in a general row. . . . Trumpets, sticks and faucets were freely used, and blood streamed from numerous heads. The efforts of the police to stop it were at first futile, the Marshal himself [i.e., Perry] receiving a severe blow on the head with a club. ("The Fire at Virginia, N. T.," Sacramento *Union,* 31 Aug 63, 4, reprinting the Virginia City *Union* of 29 August)

Clemens reported on the fire and the riot in a dispatch to the San Francisco *Morning Call* (SLC 1863o). In composing this chapter, he may have conflated the riot with an incident in which Peasley made a lone stand before an anti-Union election rally in Virginia City on 22 October 1864:

> Fiery speeches and a street parade were features of the demonstration. As the parade neared the International Hotel, . . . Tom Peasley advanced to the middle of the street, faced the leaders of the line, which numbered thousands, and leveled two six-shooters at their heads. They came to an abrupt halt. Peasley pointed to a picture of President Lincoln that had been suspended from a window of the hotel, head downward, to indicate the derision of the anti-Unionists for the president.

He demanded that the picture be righted, and the parade leaders, "knowing the deadly earnestness of the man, and not caring to trifle with one of his reputation," complied; "only then did Peasley step aside and give the word for the parade to move on" (Levison, 7; "An Insult," Virginia City *Union,* 23 Oct 64, 3; Fatout 1964, 81–82).

318.1–2 THE first twenty-six graves in the Virginia cemetery were occupied by *murdered* men] In December 1866 Clemens wrote in his notebook, "First 26 buried in Va killed. First 6 buried in Carson" (*N&J1*, 251). He made the same claim about Virginia City in a May 1868 letter to the Chicago *Republican*, and again in a Buffalo *Express* "Around the World" letter published on 22 January 1870 (SLC 1868e, 1870b), which also contains remarks about two of the desperadoes mentioned later in this chapter—Sam Brown and Jack Williams—as well as Joseph Slade (see chapters 10 and 11; see also the note at 330.7–10).

319.10–11 Alfred the Great, when he invented trial by jury] Although Alfred (or Aelfred, 849–901), king of the West Saxons, may have introduced legal reforms "out of which sprang our present judicial system," the notion that he invented trial by jury is merely persistent legend. Trial by jury has ancient Teutonic roots, but "the first glimmerings of its actual existing shape cannot be seen till ages after Aelfred's day" (*DNB*, s.v. "Aelfred").

320.8 his candle-clock] King Alfred reportedly devised a clock consisting of candles, each of which burned for four hours, enclosed within a wood and horn lantern for protection from drafts (Asser, 86–87).

320.16–20 noted desperado . . . Mr. B. . . . Mr. B. L.] Unidentified.

322.14–15 a desperado of wide reputation, and who "kept his private graveyard,"] In a notebook entry of December 1866 Clemens made reference to the popular legend that the notorious Sam Brown (see the next note) kept his own cemetery: "Brown's Ranch—11 men he killed buried together & self at head" (*N&J1*, 251; Lyman, 146).

323.16 Sam Brown] Sam Brown, the most heartless bully of all Nevada "bad men," specialized in killing inoffensive, helpless people—the "peaceable citizens" whom most of the desperadoes, as Mark Twain wrote, left alone. According to Dan De Quille, "He was a big chief, and when he walked into a saloon, a side at a time, with his big Spanish spurs clanking along the floor, and his six-shooter flapping under his coat-tails, the little 'chiefs' hunted their holes and talked small on back seats" (William Wright 1876, 87). Brown allegedly killed at least sixteen persons in Texas, California, and Nevada. His three Nevada murders—the first in Carson City and two others in Virginia City—were committed over a two-year period beginning in February 1859. After the last of these, he reportedly wiped his bloody knife, lay down on a billiard table, and went to sleep. On 6 July 1861, his thirtieth birthday, he attacked hotel-keeper Henry Van Sickle near the town of Genoa, totally without provocation. Van Sickle escaped into the hotel, armed himself, and pursued Brown down the road, killing him in an exchange of gunfire (Angel, 343–44, 356–57; Van Sickle, 9–13). Van Sickle was fully exonerated when the jury found that Brown had died "from a just dispensation of an all-wise Providence" (Thrapp, 1:179).

323.16 Jack Williams] A gunman and robber responsible for the deaths of several men in California and Nevada, Williams was also a Virginia City deputy marshal in 1862. He was murdered on 9 December of that year by an assailant (probably Joseph McGee) who "fired through a door and escaped" ("A Desperado Killed—A Shooting Affair," Sacramento *Union,* 11 Dec 62, 3; see the note on McGee at 323.18). Clemens included a brief ironic description of Williams as "a kind-hearted man" who "gave all his custom to a poor undertaker who was trying to get along," in a January 1870 "Around the World" letter (SLC 1870b; "Shooting Affray at Virginia City," Sacramento *Union,* 8 Feb 62, 2; *CofC,* 8). He also probably wrote "Particulars of the Assassination of Jack Williams," reprinted from the *Territorial Enterprise* in the San Francisco *Morning Call* of 14 December 1862 (SLC 1862i). For more on Williams see chapter 49.

323.16 Billy Mulligan] "Mulligan was a natty little sport and gambler, who had been very active in San Francisco's ward politics at the time of the formation of the second vigilance committee in 1856, and had been ordered by that body to leave California" (Considine 1923c). After several years in New York, Mulligan turned up in Nevada, where he fought a much-publicized duel near Austin in April 1864. He died in a very public and bloody shoot-out on 7 July 1865 in San Francisco. The incident began when Mulligan, crazed from delirium tremens, fired a shot into the street from his room at the St. Francis Hotel. Over the next several hours he killed two people—one of them his friend Jack McNabb (see the note at 323.18), who had courageously tried to subdue him. Mulligan was finally killed by a police officer. Charles Henry Webb commemorated Mulligan's "Bad End" in verse in the San Francisco *Evening Bulletin* the following day (Webb 1865a; Richard Coke Wood, 75–80; "The Record of Blood," Virginia City *Territorial Enterprise,* 9 Apr 71, 3; "The Austin Duel," Virginia City *Union,* 23 Apr 64, 2).

323.17 Farmer Pease] Actually Langford ("Farmer") Peel, known as Virginia City's coolest, most gentlemanly gunman. Born in Liverpool, Peel had lived in Kansas and Salt Lake City before he fled to California in 1858 after killing a man in a duel. In 1863 he arrived in Virginia City, where on 30 September he seriously wounded the prize fighter Richard Paddock in a shoot-out following a saloon argument. About a month later, on 24 October, he shot and killed John ("El Dorado Johnny") Dennis, who had challenged him to a gunfight; Peel was acquitted on the grounds of self-defense. On another occasion he severely beat a judge who had sentenced him, and then walked calmly out of the courtroom when none of the officers present dared to apprehend him. According to Goodman, the next morning William Wright (Dan De Quille)

> took occasion to review the whole career of Peel in the local columns of the *Enterprise*. . . . He did not mince matters. He pictured the character of the desperado in its true light, spoke of his misdeeds in the plain and forcible terms they deserved, and called upon the authorities to overcome this terror and bring him to summary punishment.

When Wright's friends, as a joke, led him to believe that Peel was seeking vengeance for this column, Wright went looking for the desperado and found him in a saloon. He grabbed Peel, held a knife to his throat, and said, "I understand you are hunting for me. If there is any grudge we will settle it right here." Peel responded, "There's no hard feeling on my part, I assure you. . . . You wrote nothing about me but what was true and deserved, and I admire a man who is brave enough to say publicly what he thinks about a character like me" (Goodman 1891). Peel left Virginia City in 1867; in July of that year, at the age of thirty-six, he was killed in Montana by a former partner (Langford, 2:270–87; Angel, 345, 357; Gillis, 42–46; "Shooting at Virginia City," San Francisco *Alta California,* 1 Oct 63, 1; "Fatal Shooting Affray," Gold Hill *News,* 26 Oct 63, 3; Considine 1923a).

323.17 Sugarfoot Mike] Undoubtedly "Sugarfoot Jack" Jenkins, a young Virginia City gunman who died shortly after being shot on 20 September 1863 by Thomas Peasley (see the note at 308.10–16). Peasley was later acquitted by a jury, but the incident reportedly caused him to leave the saloon business, reform his combative nature, and adopt a "restrained and gentle manner" (Goodman 1892b; Lyman, 344–45; Wells 1921b; "Bloodshed at Washoe—Life of No Account," San Francisco *Evening Bulletin,* 25 Sept 63, 2, reprinting the Virginia City *Territorial Enterprise* of 22 September).

323.17 Pock-Marked Jake] Unidentified.

323.17–18 El Dorado Johnny] See the note on "Farmer Pease" at 323.17.

323.18 Jack McNabb] John H. McNabb, a Virginia City "rough," was often in the news in 1863–64. According to one possibly apocryphal account, he disrupted the opening night of Maguire's Opera House on 2 July 1863 by emptying his revolver at an enemy seated in a box across the auditorium (Beebe and Clegg, 52–54; Lyman, 240; see also J. B. Graham, 159–60, and Watson, 134). Two months later Mark Twain reported in a dispatch to the San Francisco *Morning Call* that the "notorious desperado" McNabb had shot two Virginia City policemen, wounding one of them—officer George W. Birdsall—gravely (SLC 1863q). Early in March 1864 McNabb was involved in another shooting incident at the Clipper Saloon. On 19 March he was sentenced to six months in jail for shooting officer Birdsall, but was pardoned two months later by Governor Nye. McNabb was shot and killed in San Francisco in 1865 by Billy Mulligan (see the note at 323.16; Virginia City *Union:* "Shooting Affray," 8 Mar 64, 3; "Sentenced," 20 Mar 64, 3; "Jack McNabb Pardoned," 13 May 64, 3).

323.18 Joe McGee] Joseph McGee, a butcher by trade, took part in a number of violent incidents—some involving members of the notorious John Daly gang—between 1859 and 1862 in Marysville and Sacramento, California. McGee, who became a special policeman on the Virginia City force, is believed to have been the murderer of Jack Williams in December 1862 (see the note on Williams at 323.16). Late on the night of 4 July 1863 McGee, having been ejected from a saloon while attempting an arrest, riddled the closed door with bullets, killing one patron and seriously wounding another. Mark Twain mentioned this incident in his letter to the San Francisco *Morning Call* dated 5 July. As he explains in chapter 49 (327n.1–328n.7), McGee was killed in a Carson City saloon on 10 December 1863 by John Daly, who was avenging the murder of his friend Williams a year earlier. Daly reportedly used the same gun with which McGee had shot Williams (SLC 1863e; "The Fourth at Virginia [N. T.]," Sacramento *Union,* 7 July 63, 2; San Francisco *Alta California:* "Imposing Funeral Procession," 23 July 63, 1; "Another Man Shot," 11 Dec 63, 1; "Blood Demanding Blood," San Francisco *Evening Bulletin,* 14 Dec 63, 1; McGrath, 88–90).

323.18 Jack Harris] See the note at 138.20–31.

323.18 Six-fingered Pete] Possibly John ("Three-fingered Jack") McDowell, an Irish emigrant who had fought in the Mexican War before joining the 1849 gold rush and prospecting in Tuolumne County, California. There and later in Virginia City he gained notoriety as a gunman. Early in 1864 he was in Aurora, earning a living as a gambler and—along with other members of the John Daly gang—working as a hired gun for the Pond mining company. McDowell, Daly, and two other gang members were hanged on 9 February 1864 by the Citizens' Safety Committee of Aurora, a vigilante group, for the murder of William R. Johnson, operator of a nearby stage station (McGrath, 82, 86–87, 90–96; "The Execution at Aurora," Virginia City *Union,* 14 Feb 64, 2, reprinting the Aurora *Times* of 10 February).

323.26–27 they held it almost shame to die otherwise than "with their boots on,"] Only those gunfighters who made no claim to respectability preferred such a violent end—El Dorado Johnny, for example, went to have his boots polished before challenging Peel (Gillis, 43). Thomas Peasley, however, expressed a last wish to have his boots removed as he lay dying in a Carson City saloon: "And thus Tom Peasley went out of the world fearlessly and barefooted, which implied to him a more honorable ending than it is likely most of us will make" (Goodman 1892b; see the note at 308.10–16, and the note on "Farmer Pease" at 323.17).

323.30–325.2 a little printer . . . celebrated name whereat we shook in our shoes] The bellicose printer was Clemens's good friend Stephen Edward (Steve) Gillis (1838–1918), known as a scrappy fighter. Gillis grew up in Mississippi and Tennessee, where he was trained as a typesetter.

He went to San Francisco in 1853 with his mother (his father had been there since 1849). By 1862, when Clemens joined the *Enterprise* staff, he was the paper's foreman. Over the next thirty-two years he worked as a foreman, typesetter, and writer, first on the *Enterprise* and later on the Virginia City *Chronicle.* In 1894 he retired to live with his brothers James (see the note at 412.1–3) and William at Jackass Hill, California (*L1,* 291–92 n. 3; see also Goodman 1892a). The table-lifting, glass-biting stranger has been identified as Tom McNabb, brother of the desperado Jack McNabb (see the note at 323.18):

> Of the three McNabb brothers, Tom was the only one that didn't die with his boots on. In a row with another San Francisco sport he received a bullet in his brain. It didn't kill him, but it seemed to change his nature. From that time on he was as docile a man as could be found in the city. (Considine 1923c)

By the time of his death in June 1872 at age forty-nine, McNabb had been "shot, stabbed and otherwise wounded over and over again" (Sacramento *Union,* 28 June 72: "Died," 2; "By State Telegraph," 3).

325.1 Cariboo] Cariboo, a remote district in British Columbia between the Fraser River and the Cariboo Mountains, was the scene of a frenzied rush after gold was discovered in the fall of 1860.

326.3–27 FATAL SHOOTING AFFRAY . . . dead.] The original newspaper printings of this extract and of the extracts at 327.1–14 and 328.8–330.2 have not been found. Mark Twain may have incorporated into his manuscript three clippings from the "coffin of 'Enterprise' files" he received from his family in the spring of 1870 (SLC to JLC and family, 26 Mar 70, NPV, in *MTBus,* 112). Williams (identified in the note at 323.16) killed Brown (not further identified) in the Bank Exchange Billiard Saloon in Virginia City on the night of 6 February 1862. George W. Birdsall was a brave, highly respected policeman well known to Clemens (see the note on McNabb at 323.18); Marshal John Van Buren Perry is identified in the note at 309.20 ("Shooting Affray at Virginia City," Sacramento *Union,* 8 Feb 62, 2).

327.1–14 ROBBERY AND DESPERATE AFFRAY . . . disappeared.] No other record of this robbery, which evidently occurred in June or July 1862, has been located. The victim, Charles Hurtzal, was probably the "Charles Hutzel" listed in the Nevada directory as a mill employee boarding at the Golden Age Hotel in Silver City. Andy Blessington, residing at the Eastern Slope Lodging House in Virginia City, has been identified as "one of the slickest short-card players that ever struck 'the land of Washoe.' . . . He was a bundle of nervous energy, full of fun, and when on the street usually the center of a crowd of idlers who appreciated good jokes" (J. B. Graham, 156; Kelly 1862, 207; Kelly 1863, 175).

327.20–25 Williams was assassinated . . . had sworn away his life] See the notes on Williams and McGee at 323.16 and 323.18.

328.8–330.2 MORE CUTTING AND SHOOTING . . . ripening?] Gumbert (or Gumpert) attacked Reeder on 10 December 1862; the *Enterprise* account quoted here must have appeared on 11 December. Clemens could not have written the item, since he was in Carson City at the time reporting the second Territorial Legislature; its author was probably Wright (suggestion courtesy of Lawrence Berkove, who also ascribes the other two extracts in this chapter to Wright: see Berkove 1993). Justice Joseph F. Atwill was a real-estate and mining agent who had been justice of the peace for Virginia City since 1861. The doctor attending Reeder was Joseph R. N. Owen (Kelly 1862, 116; Kelly 1863, 20, 269; "A Desperado Killed—A Shooting Affair," Sacramento *Union*, 11 Dec 62, 3).

330.7–10 Not less than a hundred men have been murdered . . . death penalty there] There were in fact about two hundred and sixty murders between 1846 and 1871, but only two executions (aside from lynchings carried out by vigilantes). Clemens witnessed the first of these while visiting Virginia City on a lecture tour in April–May 1868—the hanging of John Milleain, a Frenchman, for the murder of the courtesan Julia Bulette. He included a detailed, dramatic description of the event in a letter to the Chicago *Republican*, explaining that this "heartless assassin" was "the first man ever hanged in this city (or country either), where the first twenty-six graves in the cemetery were those of men who died by shots and stabs" (SLC 1868e; Angel, 343–50; Doten, 2:994–95; Beebe and Clegg, 18–22).

331.10 Capt. Ned Blakely] In actuality Captain Edgar (Ned) Wakeman (1818–75), a well-known skipper for many years in the Pacific Ocean trade. Among Wakeman's commands was the steamer *America*, which carried Clemens from San Francisco to San Juan del Sur, Nicaragua, in December 1866, on the first leg of his journey to New York. "I had rather travel with that old portly, hearty, jolly, boisterous, good-natured old sailor, Capt Ned Wakeman than with any other man I ever came across," Clemens confided in his notebook at the time, also noting nearby, "Hanging the negro in the Chinchas," which indicates that the yarn as recounted in this chapter may in fact reverse the roles of the negro and the white bully, Bill Noakes (*N&J1*, 238–43, 253, 336). Clemens encountered Wakeman again in Panama while returning from San Francisco to New York in July 1868. The two men spent a convivial evening together, and Clemens reported that "the old gentleman," who was "as tempestuous of exterior, as hearty of manner and as stormy of voice as ever," regaled him with yarns, including the one "about hanging the negro in the Chincha Islands" (SLC 1868h). Wakeman's hold on Clemens's imagination is apparent in notebook entries and literary works spanning the author's career. He is Captain Waxman in three San Francisco *Alta California* letters, Captain Hurricane Jones in

"Some Rambling Notes of an Idle Excursion," Admiral Stormfield in "The Refuge of the Derelicts," and the title character in "Captain Stormfield's Visit to Heaven" (SLC 1867b–d, 1878, 1905–6, 1909). After Wakeman's death his reminiscences were edited by his daughter and published as *The Log of an Ancient Mariner, Being the Life and Adventures of Captain Edgar Wakeman* (San Francisco: A. L. Bancroft and Co., 1878).

339.9–10 The *Weekly Occidental* . . . made its appearance in Virginia] The first number of the *Occidental,* edited by Thomas Fitch with the assistance of his wife, Anna M. Fitch (see the notes at 339.11–13 and 339.29–30), appeared on Sunday, 6 March 1864. No issues of the magazine survive, but its prospectus described it as a "Literary and Miscellaneous Newspaper, containing Tales, Poems, Literary Reviews, Editorials, Humorous Sketches, Brevities and Localisms, from the pens of the best writers of Nevada and California, together with Stories, Sketches and Essays from the latest Foreign and Domestic periodicals"; in addition, it was to chronicle important local events and contain a "Ladies' and Home Department" ("Prospectus of the 'Occidental,'" Virginia City *Union,* 9 Feb 64, 2). Contributors included Dan De Quille (William Wright), Joseph Goodman, and Rollin Daggett (see the note at 340.8–9), as well as the Fitches. Although Fitch recalled that three issues of the *Occidental* appeared, and Mark Twain here implies that there were four, apparently at least five numbers—from 6 March to 3 April 1864—were published: on 9 April, the day before the sixth was due to appear, the Virginia City *Evening Bulletin* noted that the "Occidental, a very excellent literary paper, has ceased to exist" ("Dead," 3). The possibility remains that two additional issues appeared: an advertisement attributed to the *Occidental* of 17 April survives in the Virginia City *Union* of the same date ("Sheriff's Sale," 1; Lingenfelter and Gash, 257; Rogers 1957, 365–70; William Wright 1893c; Fitch, 54–55; Eric N. Moody 1977, 11–13).

339.11–13 Mr. F. was to edit it . . . editor of the *Union,*] Thomas Fitch (1838–1923), a journalist, lawyer, speculator, politician, and orator with literary ambitions, was born in New York City and emigrated from Wisconsin to California in 1860. He worked as a journalist in San Francisco and Placerville, earned admittance to the bar, and in 1862–63 was a member of the California legislature. He went to Virginia City in June 1863 and was engaged as an editor on the *Union.* He later served as a delegate from Storey County to the constitutional convention of 1864, as the district attorney of Washoe County in 1865–66, and as a Republican congressman from Nevada in 1869–71. In addition to his failed literary journal, Fitch started a short-lived Virginia City daily newspaper, the *Washoe Evening Herald,* in July 1864, and in 1868 briefly published the weekly Belmont (Nev.) *Mountain Champion.* His literary endeavors included a novel, *Better Days; or, A Millionaire of To-morrow* (1891), written in collaboration with his wife, and an unpublished play, *Old Titles* (1876). Clemens and Fitch were well acquainted: Fitch and his family lodged across the hall from the rooms that Clemens and Dan De Quille shared in the Daggett and Myers building, and Clemens was a guest at Fitch's home in Washoe City during his western lecture tour of 1866. Although Clemens expressed his admiration of Fitch's writing and oratorical abilities (which earned him the title of "Silver Tongued Orator of the Pacific"), he also characterized Fitch in November 1864 as a political opportunist, a "two-faced" dog (*L1*, 310–11 n. 3, 318, 319 n. 4, 366 n. 3; SLC 1863e; Angel, 86; *BDUSC*, 1000; William Wright 1893b; Lingenfelter and Gash, 19, 258; Eric N. Moody 1978, vii–viii).

339.17–21 THE PEACE OF GOD . . . *passeth understanding*] Philippians 4:7.

339.28–29 an original novel . . . the full strength of the company] According to Fitch, this serialized composite "original novel" was entitled *The Silver Fiend, a Tale of Washoe.* Whereas Mark Twain designated the order of the collaborating authors as Anna Fitch, Thomas Fitch, Rollin Daggett, and the "dissolute stranger," Fitch maintained that he opened the story and was followed by Daggett and Mrs. Fitch, with Mark Twain scheduled to be the fourth contributor. Fitch claimed that the novel began as a western adventure with a later admixture—supplied by Mrs. Fitch—of domestic manners and love interest, centering on "a beautiful Vermont girl, who was compelled by her father's loss of fortune and death to come to the Pacific Coast and seek employment as a teacher" (Fitch, 54–55). A contemporary article in the Virginia City *Union* supports Fitch's recollection: "We were favored, last evening, with a copy of the first number of 'The Occidental,' the new literary weekly. . . . This copy of the Occidental contains . . . an original tale of the early days of Washoe, fertile in fact and fancy, and skilfully told—name of author not given" ("Literary Paper," 6 Mar 64, 2). Yet another version of the *Silver Fiend* project was recorded in 1893 by Dan De Quille, who recalled that only the first chapter—written by Daggett—ever appeared, and that it featured standard Gothic trappings such as a demonic Rosicrucian and a "partially subterranean castle" (William Wright 1893c, 173–74).

339.29–30 Mrs. F. was an able romancist of the ineffable school] Anna Mariska Fitch was the "talented lady editress" in charge of the "Ladies' and Home Department" in the *Occidental.* In addition to the novel that she and her husband co-authored (see note at 339.11–13), she published a novel, *Bound Down; or, Life and Its Possibilities* (1870); a play, *Items: A Washington Society Play* (1874); and a volume of verse, *The Loves of Paul Fenly* (1893).

340.8–9 Mr. D., a dark and bloody editor of one of the dailies] Mark Twain is referring to Rollin Mallory Daggett (1831–1901), whom Charles C. Goodwin, a colleague, described as "swarthy, a remote strain of Iroquois in his veins, I think; heavy set . . . a face full of merriment generally, but savage as a trapped bear when he was angry" (Goodwin, 185). Daggett was born in New York and raised in Ohio. In 1849–50 he went overland to California, where he prospected for gold and worked as a printer. In 1852 he and J. Macdonough Foard founded and began co-editing the San Francisco *Golden Era*, a prestigious literary weekly (undoubtedly the model for Fitch's *Occidental*; see the note at 405.1). Eight years later he established the San Francisco *Evening Mirror*. Upon moving to Virginia City in 1862 he became a prominent stockbroker and notary public, as well as a part-time staff member on the *Territorial Enterprise*—the beginning of a seventeen-year connection with the newspaper. In 1874, when William Sharon acquired the paper, Daggett succeeded Joseph Goodman as editor-in-chief. He was an outspoken Republican in politics, serving on the Territorial Council in 1863 and as Nevada's representative in Congress from 1879 to 1881. The following year he was appointed United States minister to Hawaii (1882–85). Daggett's literary talent found expression in numerous poems published in the *Enterprise*, and in a novel, *Braxton's Bar: A Tale of Pioneer Years in California* (1882). In 1888 Mark Twain's publishing firm, Charles L. Webster and Company, issued a collaborative work by Daggett and King Kalakaua of Hawaii, *The Legends and Myths of Hawaii* (*BDUSC*, 864; *L1*, 310–11 n. 3; Kelly 1863, 203; Weisenburger, 20–27, 47, 52–54, 94–95, 162–64).

340.20–21 there arrived in Virginia a dissolute stranger with a literary turn of mind] The model for this literary collaborator may have been—as Franklin Rogers has suggested—Charles Henry Webb (1834–1905), a journalist well known in New York Bohemian circles. (Rogers was incorrect, however, in asserting that Webb was not yet in the West during the lifetime of the *Occidental*.) Webb, who ran away to sea as a boy and spent four years on whaling vessels, later worked as a columnist and correspondent for the New York *Times*. After relocating to San Francisco in April 1863 he served as a city editor for the *Evening Bulletin*, a correspondent (as "John Paul") for the Sacramento *Union*, and a regular contributor (as "Inigo") to the *Golden Era*. On 21 March 1864, one day after the publication of the third number of the *Occidental*, "J. Paul" arrived in Virginia City from San Francisco by the Pioneer Stage ("Arrivals," Virginia City *Union*, 22 Mar 64, 3). Mark Twain's claim (at 346.1–4) that the dissolute stranger's chapter of the *Silver Fiend* was borrowed from Charles Reade's *Love Me Little, Love Me Long* (1859) may well be a covert allusion to Webb, a punster and facile parodist. By the time *Roughing It* was written Webb had published *Liffith Lank; or,*

Lunacy (1867), a burlesque of Reade's *Griffith Gaunt; or, Jealousy* (1866). The two men improved their acquaintance after Clemens moved to San Francisco at the end of May 1864. On the twenty-eighth of that month Webb issued the first number of his new literary weekly, the *Californian*, to which Mark Twain soon became a contributor. In April 1866 Webb returned to New York, where in 1867 he edited and published Mark Twain's first book, *The Celebrated Jumping Frog of Calaveras County, And other Sketches* (Rogers 1960, 77; Walker 1969, 133–34, 179–80; *ET&S1*, 504–6, 536 n. 26; *ET&S2*, 380–82).

341.35–36 by means of the usual strawberry mark on left arm] In romantic literature the discovery of a strawberry birthmark, often located on the left arm, commonly disclosed a character's unsuspected aristocratic lineage. Variations of the device figure in Henry Fielding's *Joseph Andrews* (1742), Horace Walpole's *The Castle of Otranto* (1764), and Ann Radcliffe's *The Castles of Athlin and Dunbayne* (1789), among others. John Maddison Morton's *Box and Cox: A Romance of Real Life* (1847), a universally popular one-act farce that was performed in Virginia City while Clemens was there, ridiculed the device by establishing Cox's identity as the brother of Box through the *lack* of a strawberry mark on his left arm. Clemens made a brief use of this convention in two newspaper pieces of early 1866, "Romance in Real Life" and "Neodamode" (part of a "San Francisco Letter"), and burlesqued it in greater detail in an "Around the World" letter (SLC 1866b–c, 1870c).

346.4 "Love Me Little, Love Me Long,"] The hero of Reade's novel, David Dodd, relates the following incident: Jem Green, a harpooner on the English whaler *Connemara*, harpooned a right whale on 5 March 1820 in the Pacific Ocean, but "she broke the harpoon shaft just below the line, and away she swam." Four years later in Nantucket, as a result of a drinking session with sailors from an American whaler, Green was presented with a harpoon steel bearing the *Connemara* stamp and his own name scratched on it. The log of the American vessel revealed that the right whale, with an English harpoon in her, was taken on 25 March 1820 off Greenland—at least "five thousand miles of water" away from the place of Green's strike (Charles Reade, 51–52).

346.6–7 Jonah's adventure as proof that a man could live in a whale's belly . . . three days] Jonah 1:17.

347.5–6 the resurrected Lazarus and the dilapidated mendicant] John 11:1–44 and Luke 16:19–31.

347.14 time brings its revenges] *Twelfth Night*, act 5, scene 1.

347.17 "The Raging Canal,"] This humorous song was written and performed by the celebrated comic singer Pete Morris (b. 1821); a version of the text may be found in *The American Songbag* (Levy, 256–57, 259;

Sandburg, 178–79). While "The Aged Pilot Man" and "The Raging Canal" share a similar narrative idea, Mark Twain was also inspired by traditional sentimental sea ballads—and specifically by Samuel Taylor Coleridge's "Rime of the Ancient Mariner," published in 1798 (Liljegren, 24). Roger L. Brooks has also pointed out similarities in rhyme and phrasing between Coleridge's poem and Mark Twain's (Roger L. Brooks, 451–53), while Howard Baetzhold has further observed:

> Despite the reference to "The Raging Canal," the author almost surely expected his readers to see through his (or his narrator's) dodge. Recognition of the kinship with Coleridge's famous poem would, in turn, enhance the ridiculousness of Mark Twain's tempest on a canal. (Baetzhold, 277)

Dollinger's repeated assurance, "Fear not, but lean on Dollinger, / And he will fetch you through," echoes Jack's remark in chapter 6, "Ben Holladay would have fetched them through in thirty-six hours!" (39.17–18).

354.3–4 The year 1863 was perhaps the . . . culmination of the "flush times."] See the note at 281.4–6.

354.21–22 the grand combined procession . . . stretched unbroken from Virginia to California] Eliot Lord notes that the mule teams crossing the Sierra at this time "stretched along the highway for miles in an unbroken procession, and if a teamster by chance fell out of line he would often be compelled to wait for hours before he could regain a place in the column" (Lord, 192–93).

354.26–356.4 a hundred dollars a ton for full loads . . . passengers at from twenty-five to thirty dollars a head] Eliot Lord claims that a "computed average" of five cents per pound was paid to "teamsters and shippers in 1862" (confirming Mark Twain's "hundred dollars a ton") and cites an advertised price in 1863 of twenty-seven dollars per stagecoach passenger (Lord, 194). The rest of the figures in this paragraph, although plausible, have not been confirmed.

355n.1–356n.2 *Mr. Valentine . . . *Enterprise.*] This is an excerpt, edited by Mark Twain, from a much longer item he had written for the *Enterprise* of 27 August 1863, entitled "Ye Bulletin Cyphereth"—a response to gross overestimates of bullion yields which had appeared a few days earlier in the Virginia City *Evening Bulletin* (SLC 1863n; *ET&S1*, 414). Note that Mark Twain's sums are incorrect: according to his figures, in 1862 the Virginia City office of Wells, Fargo shipped $2,596,000 (not $2,615,000), and between January 1862 and June 1863 it shipped $5,471,000 (not $5,330,000).

355n.1 Mr. Valentine, Wells Fargo's agent] Wells, Fargo and Company was organized in May 1852 by Henry Wells (1805–78) and William G. Fargo (1818–81), both of whom had more than a decade of experience in the express business. Within six months of its organization the company was well established in California mining camps as a major carrier of mail, gold dust and bullion, and passengers. Soon it was the dominant express line in the West, connecting with affiliated companies for delivery throughout the United States, Canada, and Europe. In 1863 the company was so successful that it paid its stockholders 122 percent in dividends. John J. Valentine (1840–1901) learned the express business in Kentucky. He emigrated to California in the spring of 1862, where he went to work for Wells, Fargo and Company, but was soon transferred to Virginia City, where he became a joint agent for that company, the Overland Mail Company, and the Pioneer Stage Company. In 1866 he became Wells, Fargo's superintendent of express, and by 1884 he was vice-president and general manager. He was president of the company from 1892 until his death (Loomis, 15–18, 34, 167, 188, 255, 280).

356.17–19 Under it was another busy city, down in the bowels of the earth] Here Mark Twain touches on a theme often developed in the columns of the *Enterprise,* even before he joined the staff. For example, in August 1862 the *Enterprise* local wrote, "Who ever thinks, in walking the streets, that perhaps hundreds of feet beneath him—beneath the city, in the bowels of the earth, a fellow mortal may also be walking in the same direction, in one of the streets of the city below?" ("Underground Life in the Silver Mines," San Francisco *Alta California,* 5 Aug 62, 1, reprinting the Virginia City *Territorial Enterprise;* see also "Subterranean Washoe," San Francisco *Herald and Mirror,* 14 May 62, 1, and "Washoe Underneath," Stockton *Independent,* 21 June 62, 1, both reprinting the *Enterprise*).

356.25–26 a vast web of interlocking timbers] The method of timbering a mine in square sets—somewhat like a honeycomb—was invented in 1860 by Philipp Deidesheimer (b. 1832) for use in the Ophir mine, and was soon adopted throughout the Comstock. The Deidesheimer method made possible the extraction of large ore bodies and provided a degree of safety to miners not possible under the old method of support by posts and caps. In late October 1862, about a month after going to work for the *Enterprise,* Clemens described the Deidesheimer square sets in his account of his descent into the Spanish mine (Angel, 573–74; SLC 1862g).

357.1–4 from the St. Nicholas to Wall street . . . high above the pinnacle of Trinity steeple] The vast and splendid St. Nicholas Hotel was opened in 1853 on Broadway at Spring Street, over a mile north of Wall Street. It was one of Clemens's favorite stopping places in New York. Trinity Protestant Episcopal Church, on Broadway opposite the head of Wall Street, was completed in 1846; its steeple was 284 feet high (Kouwenhoven, 277; King, 341–42).

357.10–11 The Spanish proverb says it requires a gold mine to "run" a silver one] Richardson also referred to this proverb in *Beyond the Mis-*

sissippi (370), although he did not identify it as Spanish. George Lyman, in *The Saga of the Comstock Lode,* renders the original proverb as "Para trabajar una mina de plata se necesita una mina de oro" (Lyman, 361 n. 4).

358.29–360.2 AN HOUR IN THE CAVED MINES . . . office.] The *Territorial Enterprise* printing of this article is not known to survive. In addition to this account, which probably appeared on 17 July 1863, Mark Twain's descriptions of his descents into the Ophir mine immediately before and after the 15 July cave-in are preserved in his San Francisco *Morning Call* letters published on 15, 18, and 23 July; in excerpts of *Enterprise* items reprinted in the *Mining and Scientific Press* of 27 July; and in the San Francisco *Evening Bulletin* of 21 July (SLC 1863f–j).

359.8–9 the Central] The Central Mining Company owned 150 feet on the Comstock lode immediately south of the Ophir claim (Lord, 61).

359.44 the Union incline and tunnel] The Mexican, California, Central, and Ophir companies cooperated to construct this eleven-hundred-foot tunnel in 1860 in order to "drain the ledge to the depth of 200 feet" (Lord, 88–89).

360n.1–2 I learn from an official source . . . that the yield for 1863 did not exceed $20,000,000] In this chapter Mark Twain presents three estimates of 1863 Nevada bullion production: $30 million (355n.18), $25 million (360.4), and $20 million. It is possible that his unidentified "official source" for this last figure was one of the numerous reports prepared in conjunction with the Sutro tunnel project, or even Adolph Sutro himself (see the next two notes). The best estimates now available indicate that the Nevada bullion yield for 1863 was only about $13.1 million: $12.4 million for the Comstock, $.5 million for Esmeralda, and $.2 million for Reese River and Humboldt (Lord, 416; Wasson, 47; Angel, 464; J. Ross Browne 1868, 332, 387, 431).

360n.3–9 the Sutro Tunnel is to plow through the Comstock lode . . . and will develop astonishing riches] The Sutro Tunnel, planned and built by Adolph Sutro at a cost of about $5 million, was begun on 19 October 1869—after several years of heroic effort by Sutro to obtain the required political and financial backing. The main tunnel, which was bored from a spot near the Carson River, east of Virginia City, into the flank of Mount Davidson, was completed on 8 July 1878. According to the 1867 "Report of the Committee on Federal Relations, of the Nevada Legislature," it was designed to intersect the

> mines at a depth of 2,000 feet, draining off the water to that depth by its natural flow, securing the best ventilation, cooling the atmosphere in the mine, furnishing facilities for transportation, and making it possible to dispense with all pumping and hoisting machinery: for the miner can enter the mines from below, work upwards, and the ore will fall by its own gravity; whilst a railroad in

the tunnel will transport the same at small cost to the adjacent valley. (Adolph Sutro, 81)

In August 1871 Clemens queried Sutro (who was about to embark from New York for Europe) about the tunnel project, writing from Hartford, where he was hard at work revising the printer's copy of *Roughing It:* "Can't you run up here for one day? I'm awful busy on my new book on Nevada & California. And by the way you might tell me something about the tunnel that would make an interesting page, perhaps"; ten days later, apparently after a meeting with Sutro in New York, he sent a follow-up telegram requesting the length of the tunnel "when finished" (SLC to Sutro, 19 Aug 71, Koundakjian†, and 29 Aug 71, NvHi†). Sutro evidently supplied the information for this appended annotation: according to his own 1868 published defense of the project, the main tunnel was to run 4.0 miles, and the lateral branches to it another 3.4 miles, for a total of 7.4 miles. (As built, the branches were about a mile shorter than originally planned.) Although the tunnel was a benefit to the mines, especially as a means of drainage, it was built too late to be very profitable. No sizable bonanzas were discovered after its completion, and about fifty years later it was abandoned (Adolph Sutro, 23; Theodore Sutro, 37–38; Shinn, 194–208; Stewart and Stewart, 168).

360n.12 Mr. Sutro] Adolph Heinrich Joseph Sutro (1830–98), a native of Prussia, emigrated to America in 1850 and soon proceeded to the West Coast, where he became a successful merchant. Drawn to Nevada in 1860 by the silver discoveries, he built a quartz mill at Dayton, employing a process for extracting metals which he had helped to develop. Within a short time he conceived his tunnel project and devoted his energies to it for over fifteen years. In 1880, after the tunnel was completed, he sold his shares in the Sutro Tunnel Company and returned to San Francisco. Real-estate investments increased his fortune, much of which he devoted to construction projects beneficial to the city. He served as San Francisco's mayor from 1894 to 1896 (Stewart and Stewart, 9, 19, 26–27, 33, 36–38, 166–68, 181–90, 202–9). Mark Twain described a stagecoach trip with Sutro from Virginia City to Dayton in a letter to the *Enterprise* written in late 1863 or early 1864. There he briefly portrayed Sutro as a hardheaded, humorless businessman and an outspoken advocate of entrusting all public projects to individual enterprise (SLC 1863x).

361.2–3 get one Jim Blaine to tell me the stirring story of his grandfather's old ram] The ram story became one of Clemens's favorite platform pieces in later years. In 1907 he explained that the tale was intended "to exhibit certain bad effects of a good memory . . . which has no sense of proportion, and can't tell an important event from an unimportant one, but preserves them all, states them all, and thus retards the progress of a narrative, at the same time making a tangled, inextricable confusion of it" (AD, 13 Oct 1907, CU-MARK, in *MTE,* 217–18). It is unclear who the prototype was for Jim Blaine. In January 1865 Clemens commented in his notebook, "Mountaineers in habit [of] telling same old experiences over & over again in these little back settlements. Like Dan's old Ram, whi[c]h he always drivels about when drunk"; in an 1866 notebook entry he again alluded to "Dan's old Ram" (*N&J1,* 74–75, 172). The reference could be either to Dan De Quille (William Wright), whose fondness for liquor was well known on the Comstock, or Dan Twing, one of Clemens's Aurora cabinmates. It is also possible that Clemens heard the tale during his stay at Jackass Hill and Angel's Camp in the winter of 1864–65. On 10 August 1871, when Clemens was in Hartford revising the printer's copy for *Roughing It,* he told his wife, "I wrote a splendid chapter today, for the middle of the book"; this has been conjecturally identified as the present chapter (CU-MARK†; see the Introduction, pages 814–15, 863–64).

364.14 Dorcas S'iety] A common name for church sewing circles. The Biblical Dorcas was a Joppa woman "full of good works and almsdeeds," especially known for the "coats and garments" she made for the poor (Acts 9:36–42).

366.33–34 A dog can't be depended on to carry out a special providence] In 1907 Clemens described the most effective way to deliver this joke:

> A pause *after* the remark was absolutely necessary with any and all audiences, because no man, howsoever intelligent he may be, can instantly adjust his mind to a new and unfamiliar, and yet for a moment or two apparently plausible, logic which recognizes in a dog an instrument too indifferent to pious restraints and too alert in looking out for his own personal interest to be safely depended upon in an emergency requiring self-sacrifice for the benefit of another, even when the command comes from on high. The absurdity of the situation always worked its way into the audience's mind, but it had to have time. (AD, 14 Oct 1907, CU-MARK, in *MTE,* 227–28)

It has been suggested that this "caricature of the doctrine of special providences links the monologue with Roop's speech at the Buncombe trial" (Henry Nash Smith 1962, 67–68; see chapter 34).

367.4–21 he got nipped by the machinery in a carpet factory . . . W-i-l-l-i-a-m—W-h-e—"] This story is an embroidered version of the card stripper's tale in "A Yankee in a Cotton Factory," by "Gamboge" (not otherwise identified), which was reprinted for many years in the American press after its first appearance in the Boston *Yankee Blade* on 2 October 1847 (Dorson, 14–15, 70–72).

369.1 there was a large Chinese population] Mark Twain derived some of his remarks about the Chinese in this chapter from an "Around the World" letter published in the Buffalo *Express* on 22 January 1870 (SLC 1870b). The material also echoes some of Samuel Bowles's comments about the Chinese in *Our New West* (396–416), a book Mark Twain may have been familiar with. Before writing *Roughing It* he had expressed his interest in the Chinese in numerous writings: see *CofC,* 23–27, 69–84; *ET&S2,* 38–48, 62–65; SLC 1868g, 1870f–g, 1870i, 1870k–*l,* 1871a.

369.16–17 no Chinaman can testify against a white man] An 1850 California law provided that "No Black, or Mulatto person, or Indian shall be allowed to give evidence in favor of, or against a White man"; in 1854 the California Supreme Court ruled that "Chinese and all other people not white, are included in the prohibition" (*Reports,* 4:399). The Civil Rights Act of 1866 and the Fourteenth Amendment (1868) effectively nullified this law, but "it was not until the revised [California Code of Civil Procedure] took effect on January first, 1873, that witnesses were admitted to the courts of California regardless of color and nationality" (Coolidge, 76; Sandmeyer, 45).

369.19–22 As I write . . . some boys have stoned an inoffensive Chinaman to death . . . no one interfered] Clemens probably read the following item in the New York *Tribune* for 3 June 1871 (1):

> San Francisco, June 2.—The police are endeavoring to arrest a gang of boys who stoned to death an inoffensive Chinaman on Fourth-st. yesterday afternoon. Dozens of people witnessed the assault, but did not interfere until the murder was complete. No attempt was then made to arrest the murderers.

In May 1870 (and again in 1906), Clemens recalled having written a similar report himself in 1864, only to have it suppressed by his employer, the San Francisco *Morning Call,* because of the paper's anti-Chinese bias. The 1870 article, published in the *Galaxy,* included an ironic defense of a San Francisco youth arrested for stoning a Chinese, concluding that everything in the boy's training "conspired to teach him that it was a high and holy thing to stone a Chinaman, and yet he no sooner attempts to do his duty than he is punished for it" (SLC 1870f, 723; AD, 13 June 1906, CU-MARK, in *MTE,* 256–57; *CofC,* 24–27).

370.1 a bill, like this below] The Chinese characters in the accompanying illustration are not, in fact, a laundry bill. They were borrowed from an engraving in Richardson's *Beyond the Mississippi* entitled "Invitation to Chinese Dinner." The top character, turned sideways in *Roughing It,* is taken out of context from the last line of the invitation and means " 'light' (used by Chinese custom instead of the pronoun 'you,')"; the other characters are a formal salutation (Richardson, 436–37).

370.31–34 an exorbitant swindle . . . "foreign" mining tax . . . usually inflicted on no foreigners but Chinamen] In April 1850 California enacted a tax, in the form of an obligatory license, on all foreigners working mining claims; from 1856 to 1870 the fee for this license was four dollars a month. In practice the tax began within a few years to be "exacted exclusively from Chinese miners":

> The income from the Foreign Miners' licenses in the decade from 1854 to 1865, amounted to one-eighth, and for the whole period from 1850 to 1870, to one-half, of the total income of the State from all sources. From 1855 onward, it is conceded by all authorities that the Chinese paid practically the whole of these taxes—a sum amounting altogether to nearly five million dollars. (Coolidge, 36)

On 31 May 1870 the tax was invalidated by federal law (Wheat, 353–55 n. 4; Sanger, 140, 144).

371.10–13 Mr. Burlingame said that herein lay China's bitter opposition to railroads . . . graves of their ancestors or friends] Anson Burlingame (1820–70) was educated at the University of Michigan and Harvard Law School. He practiced law in Boston before turning to politics, serving first in the Massachusetts state legislature, and then as a United States congressman from 1855 to 1861, when he was appointed minister to China. Clemens first met Burlingame in Honolulu in June 1866, when he was en route to China after a leave of absence; he helped Clemens secure an exclusive interview with the survivors of the *Hornet* shipwreck (see *L1*, 343–48). In November 1867 Burlingame resigned his ministry and shortly thereafter accepted an appointment from the Chinese government as a special envoy to the West. In February 1868 he left China on a goodwill tour of Western capitals, traveling first across the United States. In Washington, D.C., he helped to draft a treaty with the United States, the first by a Western power to recognize China's sovereignty and allow unrestricted immigration (*L2*, 187 n. 2, 238–39 n. 1). Shortly after the ratification of the treaty in July, Clemens, with Burlingame's collaboration, wrote a lengthy and laudatory analysis of it for the New York *Tribune*, in which he cautioned,

> Let us remember that China is one colossal graveyard—a mighty empire so knobbed all over with graves that the level spaces left are hardly more than alleys and avenues among the clustering death-mounds. . . . The first railroad that plows its pitiless way through these myriads of sacred hillocks will carry dismay and distress into countless households. (SLC 1868g)

372.2–3 if the government sells a gang of Coolies to a foreigner for the usual five-year term] Mark Twain is repeating a common misconception. Although many Chinese emigrated in the 1840s and 1850s to Cuba and South America (and other tropical areas) under labor contracts requiring a lengthy term of service, such arrangements did not involve the Chinese Imperial government, which technically forbade expatriation. Moreover, virtually no contract laborers came to the United States: "Only a few contract coolies were ever brought here and those before 1853. . . . Chinese laborers came as voluntary immigrants, either paying their own passage or borrowing the money to pay it" (Coolidge, 16–18, 43–48).

372.5–15 the Chinamen all belong to one or another of several great companies . . . a costly temple . . . duly marked] These associations of Chinese male immigrants exerted a close control over every aspect of their lives, functioning as social, benevolent, political, and quasi-judicial agencies. The members of each association came primarily from the same district or districts in Kwangtung Province, whence virtually all the Chinese in California had emigrated. The associations—of which there were six from 1862 until 1892—were united into an umbrella organization, known as the Chinese Six Companies. The Sze Yap (Mark Twain's "See Yup") company, although one of the oldest of these, was not in fact the largest in the early 1860s, since by then many of its members had left to form two new companies, one of them the Ning Yeong. (This latter association soon became the largest, numbering seventy-five thousand members by 1876.) The lavishly appointed Ning Yeong temple, located on Broadway between Dupont and Kearny streets, was officially opened on 20 August 1864. Mark Twain visited the temple on this occasion and reported the event in several sketches for the San Francisco *Morning Call.* Clippings of these sketches may have served to refresh his memory when he wrote this chapter—providing, for example, the "eighteen thousand" membership figure for the Ning Yeong company (SLC 1864m, 1864o–q; Hoy, 1–16; Barth, 96–108, 123).

372.17–20 until the legislature . . . forbade the shipments . . . The bill was offered, whether it passed or not] No such proposed law has been identified, at least not before the mid-1870s. A quarantine law for San Francisco passed by the California state legislature in April 1870, however, stipulated that no exhumation could take place without a permit from the city health officer, and such permits were allegedly refused to Chinese applicants (Benjamin S. Brooks, 6; *Statutes* 1870, 720; Coolidge, 264; Sandmeyer, 54–55).

372.20–24 There was another bill . . . compelling every incoming Chinaman to be vaccinated . . . ten dollars for it] The quarantine law passed in April 1870 also required the city health officer to board any vessel arriving from an Asiatic port and "in his discretion, vaccinate each and every one" of the passengers for a fee of one dollar each (*Statutes* 1870, 716–21). It is possible that Mark Twain was confusing the vaccination regulation with an 1852 state law "requiring the masters of vessels to give a per capita bond of five hundred dollars as indemnity against the costs of medical and other relief of alien passengers; or to commute such bond by the payment of not less than five and not more than ten dollars per passenger"; these fees were to be distributed among the three principal state hospitals (Coolidge, 70; *Statutes* 1852, 78–82). The law remained in effect until 1870, when—like the foreign miners' tax—it was invalidated by federal statute. Between 1852 and 1870, Chinese immigrants paid from 45 to 85 percent of the nearly one-half million dollars thus collected (Coolidge, 70).

372.31–374.16 CHINATOWN . . . a piano.] The publication date of this *Enterprise* item is not known, but the reference to "gaudy plumes" (374.6) suggests that it might have appeared in the summer of 1863.

The local reporter for the Virginia City *Evening Bulletin,* addressing Mark Twain in print on 25 July of that year, recalled the "night we saw you coming in from Chinadom, with a 'feather in your cap'" ("Mark Twain," 3).

372.37 Josh-lights] Joss lights were votive candles, also used in Chinese temples; the term "joss" was not Chinese, but a pidgin English word for "deus," meaning "god."

373.34–36 "Tom," . . . used to be chief and only cook to the *Territorial Enterprise* . . . two years ago] Dan De Quille remembered the cook's name as "Joe" in his description of the *Enterprise*'s first Virginia City quarters (see the note at 292.7–11). According to him, Joe was considered the "boss cook of the town" because of his ability to mold table butter in the form of lions and dragons, until it was discovered that he did not bother to keep mouse hairs and bugs out of his cooking ("Newspaper of Early Days on Comstock Dead," San Francisco *Chronicle,* 4 June 1916, 19).

376.2–7 going down to Carson to report the proceedings of the legislature . . . Agricultural Fair] Clemens reported the second and third territorial legislatures (11 November–20 December 1862, 12 January–20 February 1864) for the *Enterprise.* On 19 December 1862 he was made recording secretary of the newly created Washoe Agricultural, Mining and Mechanical Society, and in that capacity attended its first fair, held in Carson City on 12–17 October 1863. Only his report of the fair's final day, which appeared in the *Enterprise* on 20 October, is extant (*L1,* 266; SLC 1863w).

376.12–18 a convention had framed a State Constitution . . . nothing to tax that could stand a tax, for undeveloped mines could not] The first Nevada constitutional convention (which Clemens also reported for the *Enterprise:* see Marsh, Clemens, and Bowman) met in Carson City between 2 November and 11 December 1863. The document its members drafted contained a provision "which asked the people to vote for ratification of the constitution and at the same time choose officers to serve under it"; the candidates for office—who naturally favored the adoption of the constitution, since its rejection would nullify their election—were nominated at a second convention, held from 31 December 1863 through 2 January 1864 (Elliott, 27; *L1,* 269 n. 4). Although the *Enterprise* initially supported passage of the constitution, by 4 January 1864 Mark Twain had serious doubts about certain "unfortunate defects" of the document. The chief of these was a clause authorizing the taxing of all mining property—as distinct from net mining proceeds. The bulk of Nevada's mining property, he wrote, was not yet "in a developed and paying condition, and will require an enormous outlay of capital to accomplish such a result. And until it does begin to pay dividends, the people will not consent that it shall be burdened and hindered by taxation"; he correctly predicted that the voters would not ratify the constitution at the election of 19 January (SLC 1864a). For a discussion of the constitution that was ultimately ratified in September 1864, see the note at 396.21–25.

377.3–12 a schoolmate of mine . . . could have "taken the shine out of the Prodigal Son himself,"] Mark Twain is referring to Cornelius (Neil) Moss (b. 1836) of Hannibal, a classmate of his in Sunday school at the Old Ship of Zion Methodist Church and later at the school kept by John D. Dawson. Moss, whose father owned a large meat-packing business, attended Yale. Clemens later described him as "an envied rich boy. . . . Spoiled and of small account. . . . At 30 he was a graceless tramp in Nevada, living by mendicancy and borrowed money. Disappeared" (SLC 1897, 4–5; *Inds*, 336). Clemens actually encountered Moss in San Francisco in May 1863; there is no evidence of a second meeting in Virginia City in 1864 (*L1*, 252).

377.21–23 so I stepped in and borrowed forty-six dollars of a banker] In September 1864 Clemens alluded to a debt of fifty-five dollars which he owed to "Paxton & Thornburgh, Bankers" of Virginia City, possibly resulting from this loan to Moss (*L1*, 309, 310 n. 2).

377.31–32 Mr. Goodman went away for a week and left me the post of chief editor] On 18 March 1864 Clemens remarked to his sister about his new assignment: "I stipulated, when I took his place, that I should never be expected to write editorials about politics or eastern news. I take no sort of interest in those matters" (*L1*, 275). Goodman was away from Virginia City more than once in the spring of 1864, but the exact dates of his departures and returns have not been determined. His first absence (dating from sometime after 20 February, when Clemens returned to Virginia City from Carson after reporting the third Territorial Legislature) must have lasted more than a week, if—as Clemens informed his sister on 18 March—he went to the Sandwich Islands; no confirmation of such a trip, however, has been located in Virginia City, San Francisco, or Honolulu newspapers. By 8 April Goodman had returned to Virginia City, remaining for an unknown period of time; Clemens's later recollections suggest that he may have departed again by 22 April (see the next note). In any event, on 26 May the Virginia City *Union* again included Goodman on its list of arriving stage passengers ("Arrivals Yesterday," 9 Apr 64, 3, and 26 May 64, 3). The anecdotes in this paragraph seem to telescope events actually occurring over two to three months into a period of only one week.

377.35–36 I . . . copied an elaborate editorial out of the "American Cyclopedia,"] *The New American Cyclopedia: A Popular Dictionary of General Knowledge* was published by D. Appleton and Company in sixteen volumes between 1858 and 1863. Edited by George Ripley and

Charles A. Dana, the work was immensely popular, eventually selling more than three million copies in two editions. In 1906 Clemens recalled that the *Cyclopedia* furnished him with his first editorial, written on 22 April on the occasion of the

> three-hundredth anniversary of Shakespeare's birthday. . . . There wasn't enough of what Shakespeare had done to make an editorial of the necessary length, but I filled it out with what he hadn't done—which in many respects was more important and striking and readable than the handsomest things he had really accomplished. (AD, 19 Jan 1906, CU-MARK, in *MTA*, 1:354–55)

Another instance of such "borrowing" from the *Cyclopedia*, possibly by Clemens, was noted by the editor of the Virginia City *Union*. On 12 March he observed that the *Enterprise*, in its review of Adah Isaacs Menken in *Mazeppa* (then playing in Virginia City), was "beginning to devote its leading editorial space" to discussing "The Rationale of Obscene Exhibitions." He further observed that "the historical allusion to 'Mazeppa' in the *Enterprise* of yesterday, is in the main correct. It was copied from the *American Cyclopedia*" ("A Few Words to the 'Modest' Women of San Francisco Who Ventured to See Menken," San Francisco *Evening Bulletin*, 15 Mar 64, 5, reprinting the Virginia City *Union* of 12 March; see *L1*, 276 n. 2).

378.6–8 Mr. Goodman returned and found six duels on his hands—my personalities had borne fruit] One of Clemens's provocative editorials may have been an item that appeared in the *Enterprise* on 30 March, entitled "An Item for Our Cotemporaries" and extant as reprinted in the Virginia City *Union* the next day. It charged collusion between the *Union* and several "careless or corrupt" legislators in "log rolling" a bill that appropriated $400 to the *Union* for printing a pamphlet version of the proposed constitution (see the note at 376.12–18), whereas the *Enterprise* and other newspapers had printed it "as a matter of news." The *Union* responded by accusing the *Enterprise* of "twaddling unscrupulousness" and characterizing the editorial as "boobyish snivel combined with flat sneakishness" ("Several Items for the People," Virginia City *Union*, 31 Mar 64, 2). Another humorous item by Mark Twain, in which he facetiously claimed that Thomas Fitch (see the note at 339.11–13) had lodged a complaint against Virginia City broker Warren F. Myers for voicing racial slurs, appeared in the *Enterprise* on 1 April and elicited a disgusted comment from the Virginia City *Evening Bulletin* to the effect that "he who is a fool all the rest of the year, has no special rights on this particular day" ("Another 'Goak,'" 1 Apr 64, 3). The *Bulletin* continued its attack the following day, alluding to the "bitterness of [Mark Twain's] remarks" in the morning's *Enterprise:* "Merciless himself in perpetrating jokes on others, he winces like a cur with a flea in his ear when others retort; showing conclusively that he has quite misconcieved the nature of the character he has assumed—that of being Washoe's wit!" ("A Misconception," 2 Apr 64, 3). Clemens's items and editorials in the *Enterprise* for 18–19 May nearly resulted in his fighting two duels (with Steve Gillis as his second), one of them with James L. Laird of the Virginia City *Union*. In 1906 Clemens recalled that Laird's

> editor had gone off to San Francisco too, and Laird was trying his hand at editing. I woke up Mr. Laird with some courtesies of the kind that were fashionable among newspaper editors in that region, and he came back at me the next day in a most vitriolic way. He was hurt by something I had said about him—some little thing—I don't remember what it was now—probably called him a horse-thief, or one of those little phrases customarily used to describe another editor. (AD, 19 Jan 1906, CU-MARK, partially published in *MTA*, 1:355)

Goodman, who may well have been absent during any or all of these controversies (see the note at 377.31–32), was evidently not himself called to account for Clemens's indiscretions (for a full discussion see *L1*, 287–301).

379.7–10 Dan . . . told me, casually, that two citizens . . . aid in selling a rich silver mine . . . in a new mining district] The two citizens were William M. Hurst and one of his partners, Amos H. Rose (see the next note). Hurst had prospected in the Humboldt mountains since at least 1861 and was known as the owner of the Sheba and Ben Franklin mines there. He and five others set out from Virginia City in early April 1864 on a prospecting expedition. They returned about a month later and announced their formation of a new mining district, called Pine Wood, about a hundred and eighty miles northeast of Virginia City, between Reese River and Humboldt. This new district was a ten-by-twelve-mile area rich in pine forests, streams, and promising silver ledges. A long report of the new district, based on an interview with Hurst and probably written by Dan De Quille, appeared in the *Enterprise* on 7 May ("Humboldt Mines," Sacramento *Union*, 15 Aug 62, 2; Virginia City *Union:* "Prospecting Expedition," 3 Apr 64, 3; "A New Mining District," 7 May 64, 3; William Wright 1864).

379.15–30 he had recommended them to apply to Marshall, the reporter of the other paper . . . furnishing me to them] Although Mark Twain's claim about his understanding with Dan De Quille may be a fiction (see also the note at 403.18–38), the account of the plan to sell the mine in New York is essentially true. George M. Marshall, the local reporter for the Virginia City *Union*, entered into a business arrangement with Hurst and Rose, who, although not a member of the April–May prospecting party, was evidently an early investor in Hurst's Pine Wood claim. On 29 June 1864 Marshall took the stage to San Francisco, where he met his two partners and shortly thereafter, on 4 July, sailed with them for the East ("Going to the States," Virginia City *Union*, 29 June 64, 3; Collins, 165; Marshall, 1). While in San Francisco he wrote to Dan De Quille, who also owned feet in the Pine Wood claim:

> An arrangement has been entered into & papers drawn up with a N.Y. firm by which they give us $10 per foot on our stock as a basis, and half what it is sold for afterward. So as you have 1800 feet . . . multiply it by ten and see how many

dollars you can count on. Don't get excited Dan, but I believe this is the biggest thing in existence, and for Gods sake dont breathe a word of it to anyone. (Marshall to Wright, 30 June 64, IaHi)

379.37 Next day I got away, on the coach, with the usual eclat] Clemens left Virginia City on 29 May 1864 on the California stage, accompanied by Steve Gillis and—unexpectedly—by Goodman, who had planned to accompany the travelers "a little way" and instead "kept clear on to San Francisco" (Goodman to A. B. Paine, 7 Apr 1911, Chester L. Davis 1956c, 4). Clemens's cronies may have attended his departure with the "usual eclat," but he was not universally regretted. The Gold Hill *Evening News* expressed no surprise at his disappearance in view of the "indignation aroused by his enormities" and remarked: "Mark Twain's beard is full of dirt, and his face is black before the people of Washoe" ("An Exile," Gold Hill *Evening News*, 30 May 64, 2). *Roughing It* makes no mention of a major reason for Clemens and Gillis's departure: the desire to avoid arrest for violating the law against dueling (see the note at 378.6–8).

380.36 Toodles] The comical drunkard Timothy Toodles was the chief character of a popular stage extravaganza, *The Toodles*. The role was made famous by William E. Burton on the New York stage in 1848. Clemens saw R. G. Marsh's Juvenile Comedians perform the play in Carson City on 12 January 1864 (*MTEnt*, 131–32; Watson, 46).

383.12–384.3 a little tongue of rich golden flame . . . Vicksburg fallen, and the Union arms victorious at Gettysburg] The Union victories at Vicksburg and Gettysburg took place on 4 July 1863. The Virginia City *Evening Bulletin* described the dazzling effect of early sunlight on the recently installed flag atop Mount Davidson on the morning of the Fourth. The event Clemens recalls here, however—the remarkable flamelike appearance of the flag in a storm-darkened sky—occurred a few weeks later, on 30 July (Virginia City *Evening Bulletin:* "Celebration of the 4th of July," 6 July 63, 3; "A Beautiful Sight," 31 July 63, 3). Anna Fitch commemorated the event in her poem "The Flag on Fire," explaining that

on the evening of July 30th, 1863, upon the breaking away of a storm, this banner was suddenly illuminated by some curious refraction of the rays of the setting sun. Thousands of awe struck persons witnessed the spectacle, which continued until the streets of Virginia, 1500 feet below, were in utter darkness. (Newman, 322)

387.18–392.24 The climate . . . over."] Mark Twain first published this passage in a Buffalo *Express* "Around the World" letter on 13 November 1869; he revised the earlier printing for inclusion in *Roughing It* (SLC 1869m).

389.22 Fort Yuma] Fort Yuma was established in November 1850 on the western bank of the lower Colorado River at its confluence with the

Gila, to guard the main mail, freight, and emigrant route as it entered California from New Mexico Territory (1854–63), or Arizona Territory (after 1863).

389.26–30 a tradition (attributed to John Phoenix*) that a very, very wicked soldier . . . *telegraphed back for his blankets*] Captain George Horatio Derby (1823–61) of the United States Army Corps of Topographical Engineers was best known for his humorous sketches, widely reprinted in newspapers during the 1850s under the pseudonyms "Squibob" and "John Phoenix," and collected in two volumes—*Phoenixiana; or, Sketches and Burlesques* (1856) and *The Squibob Papers* (1865). From 1849 to 1856 Derby was stationed on the Pacific Coast, leading an expedition up the Colorado River in the winter of 1850–51 to explore a route for the provisioning of Fort Yuma. Clemens was thoroughly familiar with Derby's writing (see Gribben, 1:185), but his attribution of the soldier-in-hell anecdote remains unsubstantiated: the story has not been found in Derby's works (George R. Stewart, 7, 59–72, 180, 196, 210–11). Richardson, however, possibly Mark Twain's source, printed a version of it—attributing it to an "unknown genius"—immediately after quoting the following remark about Fort Yuma from Derby's "Lectures on Astronomy": "Mercury . . . receives six and a half times as much heat from the Sun as we do; from which we conclude that the climate must be very similar to that of Fort Yuma, on the Colorado River" (Derby 1856, 59; quoted in Richardson, 581). J. Ross Browne also repeated the story in his description of Fort Yuma in *Adventures in the Apache Country* (J. Ross Browne 1869, 56).

390.7–8 some of us have swept around snow-walled curves of the Pacific Railroad in that vicinity] Clemens made the round trip from Sacramento to Virginia City and back on the Central Pacific Railroad in late April and early May 1868, traversing Donner Pass—where the track was not yet completed—by horse-drawn sleigh (*L2*, 211–14).

392.25–395.11 But . . . head.] Mark Twain first published this passage in a Buffalo *Express* "Around the World" letter on 11 December 1869; he revised the earlier printing for inclusion in *Roughing It* (SLC 1869n).

395.3 Star City] Clemens visited Star City, a few miles northeast of Unionville, during his prospecting trip to the Humboldt district in the winter of 1861–62 (see chapters 27–30 and supplement B, map 2). At its peak in 1864–65 Star City had a population of about twelve hundred, but by 1871 it was nearly abandoned (Angel, 458; Ransome, 10).

396.1–16 For a few months I enjoyed . . . a butterfly idleness . . . the due state of a man . . . likely to reach absolute affluence] Clemens's period of idleness actually lasted for only a week (see the note at 397.10–11). After the dust and wind of Washoe, however, his hotel, the Occidental, seemed like "Heaven on the half shell," and life in San Francisco was exhilarating: "The birds, and the flowers, and the Chinamen, and the winds, and the sunshine, and all things that go to make life happy, are present in San Francisco" (SLC 1864h). The amusements Mark Twain describes in this paragraph reflect to some extent his first visit to San Francisco a year earlier, in May and June 1863. At that time he enjoyed the luxuries of the Occidental Hotel and the Lick House, attended the opera, "lived like a lord," speculated feverishly, and moved, he claimed, in "the very best society to be found in San Francisco" (*L1,* 252–61, 302–3).

396.21–25 The property holders of Nevada voted against the State Constitution . . . unquestionably it was one] Presumably to intensify the dramatic impact of his 1864 financial reverses, Clemens misrepresented the facts surrounding the ratification of the constitution and inaccurately blamed it for the 1864 depression. As mentioned earlier (see the note at 376.12–18), the first proposed state constitution was rejected in January 1864, largely because of its provision for a mining-property tax—a provision that Clemens, among others, feared would be an economic burden on mining interests. Nevertheless, in spite of this rejection a significant depression set in (caused at least in part by the effects of chronic litigation over mining laws), which worsened throughout 1864. A revised constitution, which many believed would benefit the economy, was drafted during the summer; it provided for the taxation of net mining proceeds, while exempting unproductive mining property. With the united support of both large and small mining interests, this constitution was ratified by an overwhelming majority of the voters on 7 September 1864 (Elliott, 36, 41, 283 n. 11).

396.26–397.6 Stocks went on rising . . . My hoarded stocks were not worth the paper they were printed on] When Clemens arrived in San Francisco, a downward slide in mining-stock values had already begun, which continued (although mitigated by occasional rallies) through 1865. Nevertheless, there is some truth to his description of a frenzied "gambling carnival," a condition that evidently persisted in spite of falling prices. On 22 May a reporter for the San Francisco *Morning Call* deplored current uncontrolled mining speculation, the "insane traffic in all sorts of mining stocks" by "demented creatures" with "feet on the brain." Recent failures and suicides, he continued, were "slight tremblings" betokening "the financial earthquake approaching" ("The Mining Mania," 22 May 64, 2; Grant H. Smith, 48–50, 99). The *Call*'s prediction proved correct: the decline in stock prices became precipitous in June and July, wiping out many wildcat-mine investors like Clemens (whose losses, however, have not been documented). In the week ending 30 July, for example, Gould and Curry stock fell from about $1,600 to $1,000 per foot. (The price of $6,300 for Gould and Curry stock mentioned at 397.1 was a year out of date: the stock had peaked at that level in June 1863.) An item in the *Call* for 28 July, almost certainly written by Clemens, described the Gould and Curry's "mighty descent," which "mashed and flattened out all the little wild-cats like mice under a deadfall" (SLC 1864k; *Mining and Scientific Press:* "San Francisco Stock and Exchange Board and Pacific Board of Brokers," 9 [30 July 64]: 69; "San Francisco Stock and Exchange Board," 6 [29 June 63]: 5).

397.10–11 I removed from the hotel to a very private boarding house. I took a reporter's berth and went to work] Clemens started working as the local reporter for the San Francisco *Morning Call* around 6 June, much earlier than he implies here. It has not been established when he and Steve Gillis moved together from the Occidental to a boarding house, but by 15 July they had already relocated once again, leaving behind an irate landlady who reportedly described the two of them to Gillis's father as "a couple of desperate characters from Washoe—gamblers and murd[er]ers of the very worst description!" (*L1*, 303).

397.17–398.3 It was signed "Marshall" . . . as they would sail for the east in the morning] Marshall, Hurst, and Rose embarked from San Francisco on 4 July 1864 aboard the *Golden City:* see the notes at 379.7–10 and 379.15–30.

398.19–20 thirty-five dollars a week] When Clemens first went to work for the *Morning Call* his salary was forty dollars a week; by 25 September, however, he had given up night work and accepted a lower wage: "I told the 'Call' folks to pay me $25 a week, & let me work only in daylight" (*L1*, 302, 312).

398.21–24 A month afterward I enjoyed my first earthquake . . . on a bright October day] Clemens freely reordered the chronology of the events of 1864 and 1865 in chapters 58 through 61 of *Roughing It.* The severe earthquake of 8 October 1865 occurred not one month, but fifteen months after Marshall and his companions sailed for New York, and more than seven months after Clemens's return to San Francisco from the mining camps of Tuolumne and Calaveras counties (see chapters 60 and 61). Clemens published four sketches about the quake that have survived wholly or in part, and possibly others no longer extant. His *Roughing It* account draws on details recorded in three of the surviving sketches—"The Cruel Earthquake," "Popper Defieth Ye Earthquake," and "The Great Earthquake in San Francisco"—and, no doubt, upon his recollection of the anecdotes and "toothsome gossip" that circulated in the city for days following the quake (SLC 1865s–u, 1865aa).

403.18–38 NEVADA MINES IN NEW YORK . . . wild-cat.] The *Territorial Enterprise* printing of this article is not known to survive. It probably appeared on 8 November 1864, the day on which a virtually identical report was published in the Virginia City *Union* ("Sale of a Nevada Mine in New York City," 2). In a later article the *Union* explained the eastern system of organizing mining companies, which it deemed superior to the western system:

A number of capitalists bargain with the owners of the mine to give them a certain sum of money and a certain portion of the stock for it. They then form a joint stock incorporation; issue, say one-half of the stock and sell it in the market for cash, which constitutes the "working fund." The stock, it must be borne in mind, is made unassessable. . . . As work is done and machinery erected the mine becomes valuable and the stock saleable, enabling the originators who hold the balance of the stock to sell, and thus realize more money. ("How Our Mines are Sold in the Eastern Market," Virginia City *Union,* 16 Nov 64, 2)

Hurst (nicknamed "Sheba" from his most famous mine), Rose, and Marshall thus received a large lump-sum payment and a sizeable block of unassessable shares. Clemens may only have learned of their lucrative deal during his stay at Angel's Camp, when he made the following entry in his notebook (probably on 24 January 1865), which suggests little or no personal knowledge of the transaction: "Geo N. Marshall, Geo. Hurst & another have sold a new mine in Humboldt for $3,000,000 in N. York" (*N&J1,* 73). In discussing "abortive mining enterprises" in his *Story of the Mine,* Charles Howard Shinn may have been alluding to the sale of "Pine Mountains Consolidated": "Over in the lava of Pine Woods district in 1863 some Virginia City men sold a group of mythical mines and received a very large payment down. The New York buyers spent another fortune and departed, leaving the holes in the desert" (Shinn, 143).

404.4–9 I neglected my duties . . . one of the proprietors . . . save myself the disgrace of a dismissal] On or about 10 October 1864 George E. Barnes, one of the proprietors of the San Francisco *Morning Call,* gave Clemens the opportunity—which he took—to resign his position as local reporter. As Barnes later recalled, Clemens left the *Call* "on the most friendly terms, when it was found necessary to make the local department more efficient, admitting his reportorial shortcomings and expressing surprise they were not sooner discovered" (Barnes, 1; *CofC,* 23–24). One of the *Call*'s other proprietors, James J. Ayers, admitted that Clemens's resignation was a relief:

However valuable his services had proven to a Nevada paper, where he might give full play to his fertile imagination and dally with facts to suit his fancy, that kind of reporting on a newspaper in a settled community, where the plain, unvarnished truth was an essential element in the duties of a reporter, could hardly be deemed satisfactory. It was true that we had long desired to dispense with Mark's services, but had a delicacy about bluntly telling him so. (Ayers, 223–24)

404n.1–2 I saw Marshall, months afterward] Clemens encountered Marshall in San Francisco in December 1865, and satirized his tiresome and profane travel reminiscences in a letter to the Virginia City *Territorial Enterprise* written on 23 December (SLC 1865ff).

405.1 I wrote literary screeds for the *Golden Era*] The San Francisco *Golden Era* was founded on 19 December 1852 by Rollin M. Daggett (see the note at 340.8–9) and J. Macdonough Foard, and purchased in 1860 by Joseph E. Lawrence and James Brooks. It quickly became the leading literary paper on the West Coast. Its luxurious office was the gathering place for local literary figures as well as distinguished visitors. The *Era* had already published (or reprinted) seven contributions by Mark Twain in 1863 and early 1864, and now—after his return to San Francisco in late May 1864—published three more (see SLC 1863d, 1863r–v, 1864f, 1864h–j). The *Golden Era* declined after the 1860s, finally ceasing publication in 1893.

405.1–18 C. H. Webb had established . . . the *Californian* . . . the paper presently died a peaceful death, and I was out of work again . . . queer vicissitudes] The first issue of the *Californian,* founded by Charles Henry Webb (see the note at 340.20–21), appeared on 28 May 1864 and soon earned favorable reviews from both the California and the eastern press. Nevertheless, in September 1864 Webb sold out to Richard L. Ogden (see the note at 405.7–8), who in turn relinquished his interest two months later to "three printers"—P. J. Thomas, A. M. Kenaday, and A. A. Stickney—together constituting the Californian Printing and Publishing Company. In January 1866 Webb again became a coproprietor along with Stickney, J. P. Bogardus, and William J. Bingham. During its first two years, the *Californian* was edited alternately by Webb and Bret Harte: Harte replaced Webb from 10 September to 19 November 1864, from 15 or 22 April to 30 December 1865, and from Webb's departure for New York on 18 April 1866 to 1 August 1866. In August 1866 Stickney and Bingham sold their interest to Bogardus, and James F. Bowman replaced Harte as editor; in October Bowman purchased Webb's remaining interest in the paper. Bowman and Bogardus continued together until January 1868, when the latter became sole proprietor, with Tremenheere L. Johns listed as his co-editor. The *Californian* survived—under different owners and editors—for several months longer: contrary to the statement in *Roughing It,* its "peaceful death" came with the issue of 21 November 1868, almost two years after Clemens had left the West (*Californian:* 1 [6 Aug 64]: 9; 1 [3 Sept 64]: 8; 1 [26 Nov 64]: 8; 2 [15 Apr 65]: 8; 4 [6 Jan 66]: 8; 4 [13 Jan 66]: 8; 4 [21 Apr 66]: 8; 5 [18 Aug 66]: 8; 5 [20 Oct 66]: 8; 7 [11 Jan 68]: 8; 7 [18 Jan 68]: 8; "Opening Chorus," 8 [21 Nov 68]: 2; *L1,* 314 n. 5, 330 n. 4; *ET&S2,* 144–45 n. 2; Harte to Webb, 18 Oct 66, CU-BANC).

405.4 Bret Harte] Harte (born Francis Brett Harte, 1836–1902), a native of New York, went to California in 1854 and worked in a variety of occupations before settling in San Francisco in 1860. After setting type for the *Golden Era* he began publishing pieces of his own in that journal. In the fall of 1864, during his first stint as editor of the *Californian,* he presumably accepted the first nine of Mark Twain's contributions (see the next note). In January 1866 he invited Clemens to collaborate on a collection of sketches, which, however, they never produced (see *L1*, 328). From July 1868 he served as the first editor of the *Overland Monthly,* for which he wrote some of his best work. After his departure for the East in February 1871, he contributed pieces to the *Atlantic Monthly,* but their quality was disappointing. From 1878 until his death he lived abroad, serving for a time as a consul in Prussia and then in Scotland. The work of his later years lacked the "vigor, color, and wit" of his early material, and "for the rest of his life he was little better than a hack writer" (*DAB*, 4:362–65).

405.5–6 I was employed to contribute an article a week at twelve dollars] On 25 September 1864, almost three months after his final contribution to the *Golden Era* and six days before his first sketch appeared in the *Californian,* Clemens wrote to his family:

> I have engaged to write for the new literary paper—the "Californian"—same pay I used to receive on the "Golden Era"—one article a week, fifty dollars a month. I quit the "Era," long ago. It wasn't high-toned enough. I thought that whether I was a literary "jackleg" or not, I wouldn't class myself with that style of people, anyhow. The "Californian" circulates among the highest class of the community, & is the best weekly literary paper in the United States—& I suppose I ought to know. (*L1*, 312)

Mark Twain's debut sketch, "A Notable Conundrum," was the first of twenty-seven original contributions to the *Californian* between 1 October 1864 and 29 September 1866 (SLC 1864t–bb, 1865a, 1865c–f, 1865h–j, 1865m, 1865o, 1865q–r, 1865v, 1865z, 1865dd–ee, 1866dd, 1866jj).

405.7–8 Capt. Ogden, a rich man and a pleasant gentleman] Richard Livingston Ogden (1825–1900), a native of New York, joined the army early in his life and served in the Mexican War, after which he settled in California and tried his hand at mining. He attained the rank of captain in the United States Army Quartermaster Corps, serving in San Francisco in 1863–64. After leaving military service, he successfully pursued careers both in journalism and in business. As "Podgers," he corresponded for the New York *Times* and the San Francisco *Alta California* (an 1865 letter to the *Alta* described the favorable reception in New York of Mark Twain's "Jumping Frog" tale: see Ogden, 1). His business interests included the management of George P. Kimball and Company of San Francisco, manufacturer of carriages and cars (Shuck et al., 1015–20). An item in the San Francisco *Morning Call* of 4 September 1864, probably by Clemens, reported Ogden's purchase of the *Californian:* "Mr. Webb has sold the paper to Captain Ogden, a gentleman of fine literary attainments, an able writer, and the possessor of a happy bank account" (SLC 1864r). Writing to Clemens in 1883, Ogden explained why he sold the *Californian* after only two months. He recalled

> settling every Saturday with the literary talent—at a considerable loss over receipts—all because the public was not as appreciative as at the present day, i e

the enterprise was a little too early. Webb found that out, and after having borrowed all the money I had, to keep it up, generously walked off and left me to run it for fun. When I had got about $5000 worth of fun out of it—I sold out for what I could get and never got that.—Some of the things you wrote in those days were as good if not better than you ever wrote since. I can safely say it in Hartes case. (Ogden to SLC, 19 June 83, CU-MARK)

405.20–25 For two months . . . I did not earn a penny . . . I became a very adept at "slinking."] Mark Twain may be drawing upon memories of two periods of financial distress during his residence in San Francisco—the first in 1864, and the second in 1865—but he was not wholly unemployed at either time. The *Roughing It* chronology places the two-month "slinking" period in late 1864—from about 10 October, when he lost his position with the *Morning Call,* until he departed in early December for Jackass Hill in Tuolumne County. During this period he apparently earned only $84 ($12 for each of seven sketches he published in the *Californian*); his departure from the *Call* cost him $200 in lost wages ($25 per week for eight weeks). In addition, on 21 October he was obliged to pay an assessment of $100 on four shares of Hale and Norcross stock, even though, when he left for Jackass Hill, he was able to take $300 with him, perhaps from the sale of one of these shares (SLC 1864v–bb; *L1,* 312, 315, 316 n. 5, 318, 319 n. 5, 320). Clemens continued in straitened circumstances throughout the first half of 1865, but his situation seems to have become acute in the late summer and fall, even occasioning comment in the press. An item entitled "A Sheik on the Move," presumably written by William K. McGrew, the *Call*'s local editor (see *ET&S2,* 546), appeared in the *Call* on 29 October 1865:

There is now, and has been for a long time past, camping about through town, a melancholy-looking Arab, known as Marque Twein. . . . His favorite measure is a pint measure. He is said to be a person of prodigious capacity, and addicted to a great flow of spirits. He moves often. Like all Arabs, Marque Twein is instinctively itinerant. He moves periodically. These periods occur at the end of his credit. . . . This Arab . . . wants to claim kin with respectable folks, but he labors under a difficulty in finding persons who are "on it." He may feel all right, but he don't *look* affectionate. His hat is an old one, and comes too far down over his eyes, and his clothes don't fit as if they were made for him. . . . Beware of him. (McGrew, 3)

Nine days earlier, Clemens had written a letter to Orion and Mollie Clemens which tends to confirm McGrew's description:

I have a religion—but you will call it blasphemy. It is that there is a God for the rich man but none for the poor.

You are in trouble, & in debt—so am I. I am utterly miserable—so are you. Perhaps your religion will sustain you, will feed you—I place no dependence in mine. Our religions are alike, though, in one respect—neither can make a man happy when he is out of luck. If I do not get out of debt in 3 months,—pistols or poison for one—exit *me.* (*L1,* 324)

406.10–11 the entertaining of a collector (and being entertained by him,)] This collector may have been Clemens's friend John Henry Riley, the same man who figures later in this chapter as the mendicant

Blucher (see the note at 406.35–407.22). The identification is suggested by the fact that Riley evidently pursued a variety of unusual occupations during his years in San Francisco, several of which Clemens described for humorous effect in a November 1870 *Galaxy* sketch entitled "Riley—Newspaper Correspondent." (The San Francisco city directory provides some corroboration of Riley's employment history, listing him in 1862 as a "collector" for a grain brokerage.) Riley's ability as a raconteur—as well as his love of smoking—endeared him to Clemens, who recalled the "unfailing vein of irony which makes his conversation to the last degree entertaining" (SLC 1870m; Langley 1862, 330, 381).

406.13 the "Prodigal."] See the note at 377.3–12.

406.35–407.22 another child of misfortune . . . This mendicant Blucher] Clemens explicitly identified this Blucher (not to be confused with the callow "Blucher" of *The Innocents Abroad*) as John Henry Riley in a letter of 29 June 1871 to Mary Mason Fairbanks. Riley (1830?–72) was a Philadelphian who emigrated to California in 1849 and held a variety of jobs, including that of a newspaper reporter in San Francisco, before he sailed for Washington, D.C., in November 1865. There he worked for congressional committees, corresponded for the San Francisco *Alta California,* and attained prominence among the corps of journalists. For a time in the winter of 1867–68 he and Clemens shared lodgings in Washington. Late in 1870, Clemens persuaded him to collaborate on a book about the South African diamond mines. He spent several months of 1871 in South Africa at Clemens's expense, gathering material for the project, and at the same time managed to secure an appointment as consul-general in the United States for the Orange Free State. He died of cancer in September 1872—about a year after his return from Africa—and the diamond-mine book was never written (SLC to Fairbanks, 29 June 71, CSmH, in *MTMF,* 155–56; *MTMF,* 115; SLC 1870m; biographical information in CU-MARK, courtesy of Gerald Thompson; Langley 1863, 306; "For the East," San Francisco *Alta California,* 10 Nov 65, 1; obituary notice dated 4 Dec 72, Bloemfontein [Orange Free State] *Gouvernements Courant,* PH in CU-MARK; SLC to Riley, 2 Dec 70, CU-MARK; Riley to SLC, 23 Mar 71 and 3 Dec 71, CU-MARK).

408.27–409.1 the Miners' Restaurant . . . French Pete's . . . Martin's restaurant] The Miners' Restaurant was a chophouse on Commercial Street—near the offices of the San Francisco *Morning Call*—known for its "square meals," evidently paying "more regard . . . to . . . quantity than quality" ("An Old Land-Mark Gone," Virginia City *Evening Bulletin,* 24 Oct 63, 4). Although "French Pete's" is not listed in the San Francisco directories, it may have been a nickname for a second Miners' Restaurant (run by the same proprietors as the original one—Pierre and Francis Cordier), located at the corner of Sansome and Merchant streets (see also the next note). Martin's (proprietor, Francisco Martin) was a high-toned establishment, also on Commercial Street, said to rival the better restaurants of New York; it was "much patronized by the Old Comstock crowd" (Edwords, 15; Langley 1860, 101, 210, 369; Langley 1859, 188; Neville, 136; Fletcher, 40).

411.7 Take the episode all around] A fragment of manuscript in Clemens's hand mentions an anecdote known to involve Riley, and then outlines the story related here, presumably also linked to him: "Found a dime—went up Kearney street—met poor man hungry—took him to Martin's and fed him—then we went to the miner's restaurant" (Anderson Auction Company, item 11: "we" may be a mistranscription of "he"). Clemens's inscription of "miner's restaurant" in this context supports the conjecture that "French Pete's" was the Cordiers' second Miners' Restaurant.

412.1–3 an old friend of mine, a miner, came down . . . and I went back with him] The old friend was James Norman (Jim) Gillis (1830–1907), the brother of Steve Gillis (see the note at 323.30–325.2). He was born in Georgia, and in 1848 obtained a medical degree in Memphis, Tennessee. The following year he went to San Francisco with his father, Angus Gillis. After an early period of ranching in Sacramento County, he spent most of the remainder of his life mining in Tuolumne County, living on Jackass Hill near Tuttletown. Periodically he visited San Francisco, where his parents lived; following such a visit late in 1864, he took Clemens back with him to his cabin on Jackass Hill. Clemens was spurred to leave San Francisco not only by his straitened financial circumstances, but by his fear that he would be called to honor a $500 bail bond he had posted for Steve Gillis, who had injured someone in a bar fight and fled to Nevada to escape prosecution. (In November 1866 the receipts from Clemens's second San Francisco lecture were confiscated to satisfy this bond: see "A Missionary's Troubles," San Francisco *Morning Call,* 18 Nov 66, 3.) Clemens arrived at Jackass Hill on 4 December 1864 and remained until 23 February 1865. Jim Gillis's wide-ranging intelligence and humor, his hospitality, and his love of nature were well known: Dan De Quille dubbed him the "Thoreau of the Sierras" and noted that his cabin was the "headquarters of all Bohemians visiting the mountains" (William Wright 1891). Clemens considered Gillis a "born humorist," a facile and imaginative spinner of "impromptu tales" (AD, 26 May 1907, CU-MARK, in *MTE,* 358–62). Among his creations were Dick Baker's tale of Tom Quartz, in the next chapter; the blue-jay yarn, in chapter 3 of *A Tramp Abroad;* and "The Tragedy of the Burning Shame," the basis for the Royal Nonesuch episode in chapter 23 of *Huckleberry Finn* ("James N. Gillis—His Life and Death," Sonora [Calif.] *Sierra Times,* 14 Apr 1907, clipping in CU-

MARK; Gillis, 17, 57–59; *L1*, 320–21; Fulton, 54–55; Goodwin, 90–94).

412.5–10 a flourishing city . . . fell into decay, and in a few years wholly disappeared] The first recorded discovery of gold on Jackass Hill was made in 1848 by the Means brothers, who earned an estimated ten thousand dollars from their claim. By 1849 well over three thousand miners were working in the immediate area, which was considered "without doubt the richest in the state" at the time (Heckendorn and Wilson, 80). The settlement on Jackass Hill, however, was never more than "a small community of homes, not a town, not even a village" (Gray, 8–13, 20). Within two years most of the miners had drifted away to more productive mining regions; the population of Tuolumne County reached a peak of over eighteen thousand in 1852, declining to eight thousand by 1870. The area nevertheless continued to yield significant amounts of gold: in January 1866, for example, the Gillis brothers struck a rich pocket that yielded up to forty dollars per pan (MacKinnon, 5, 79–80; Buckbee, 337).

412.25–30 One of my associates in this locality . . . for eighteen years he had decayed there . . . Latin and Greek sentences] None of Clemens's known acquaintances on Jackass Hill exactly fits this description, which may draw on at least two men, Dick Stoker (the model for Dick Baker in the next chapter) and Jim Gillis. In 1907 Clemens noted that Stoker had lived in his cabin for eighteen years by 1864 (he had actually lived there only fifteen years, since 1849: see the note at 416.4). Furthermore, Albert Bigelow Paine's description of Stoker as a passive, serene man who "had no world outside of the cabin and the hills, no affairs" is consistent with the portrait of this "decayed" miner (*MTB*, 1:267; AD, 26 May 1907, CU-MARK, in *MTE*, 362). While Stoker was "slenderly educated" (416.5–6), however, Gillis, in addition to having a medical degree, was reputed to know Latin and Greek (William Wright 1891).

413.6–419.28 In . . . me.] Mark Twain first published this passage in a Buffalo *Express* "Around the World" letter on 18 December 1869; he revised the earlier printing for inclusion in *Roughing It* (SLC 1869o).

416.4 Dick Baker, pocket-miner] In his Autobiographical Dictation of 26 May 1907 Clemens identified Baker as Dick Stoker, Jim Gillis's partner and cabinmate. Jacob Richard Stoker (1820–98), originally from Kentucky, left a successful business in Illinois to fight in the Mexican War. After the war, in 1849, he joined the California gold rush and went to Jackass Hill, where he remained, eking out a living as a pocket miner. Many years later, Jim Gillis's brother Steve recalled Stoker:

> Dick Stoker—dear, gentle unselfish old Dick—died over three years ago, aged 78. I am sure it will be a melancholy pleasure to Mark to know that Dick lived in comfort all his later life, sincerely loved and respected by all who knew him.

> He never left Jackass Hill. He struck a pocket years ago containing enough not only to build himself a comfortable house near his old cabin, but to last him, without work, to his painless end. He was a Mason, and was buried by the Order in Sonora. (Undated letter to A. B. Paine, quoted in *MTL*, 1:171)

Clemens always held Stoker in affection, recalling with particular pleasure his portrayal of a character in Jim Gillis's skit "The Tragedy of the Burning Shame" (AD, 26 May 1907, CU-MARK, in *MTE*, 361; Stoker monument in the Masonic Cemetery, Sonora, photograph courtesy of Margaret Sanborn; Buckbee, 331; Gillis, 170–71; SLC to James Gillis, 26 Jan 70, PH in CU-MARK, courtesy of CCamarSJ, in *MTL*, 1:170–71).

416.4 Dead-Horse Gulch] A fictional name for Jackass Gulch, adjacent to Jackass Hill.

416.16–17 I heard him talking about this animal once] Although Baker (i.e., Stoker) is represented here as the narrator, Clemens later identified Jim Gillis as the author of the story of Tom Quartz:

> Every now and then Jim would have an inspiration, and he would stand up before the great log fire, with his back to it and his hands crossed behind him, and deliver himself of an elaborate impromptu lie—a fairy tale, an extravagant romance—with Dick Stoker as the hero of it as a general thing. Jim always soberly pretended that what he was relating was strictly history, veracious history, not romance. Dick Stoker, gray-headed and good-natured, would sit smoking his pipe and listen with a gentle serenity to these monstrous fabrications and never utter a protest. . . . I used another of Jim's inventions in one of my books, the story of Jim Baker's cat, the remarkable Tom Quartz. Jim Baker was Dick Stoker, of course; Tom Quartz had never existed; there was no such cat, at least outside of Jim Gillis's imagination. (AD, 26 May 1907, CU-MARK, in *MTE*, 360–62)

Mark Twain made many changes when revising the Buffalo *Express* printing of this story, primarily in the spelling of dialect pronunciations (such as " 'n' " for "and"), which brought the monologue closer to vernacular speech. Both the *Express* and the *Roughing It* versions were preceded by a manuscript sketch entitled "Remarkable Sagacity of a Cat," probably written in June 1868 (SLC 1868f).

419.37–38 We prospected around Angel's Camp, in Calaveras County, during three weeks] Clemens was at Angel's Camp, about seven miles northwest of Jackass Hill (across the Stanislaus River, the border with Calaveras County), between 22 January and 20 February 1865. Along with Gillis and Stoker, he spent some time prospecting, and some time sitting out the rainy weather listening to the conversation of the locals at the Angel's Hotel bar. During this time he made several notebook entries recording anecdotes that he would later include in *Roughing It* (*N&J1*, 66, 76–81).

420.7 post shovels] Shovels evidently used for digging ore: see the textual note.

420.10–14 I could give the reader a vivid description of the Big Trees . . . less conscientious tourists] It is unclear whether Mark Twain is referring to the giant sequoias at the Calaveras Grove of Big Trees, about twenty miles northeast of Angel's Camp, or to the more spectacular Mariposa Grove, about thirty-five miles south of Yosemite Valley, mentioned by most travelers visiting the valley (Hart, 72, 304). He was probably familiar with typically reverent accounts of these sites in such works as Richardson's *Beyond the Mississippi* (431–35), Bowles's *Our New West* (391–94), Ludlow's *The Heart of the Continent* (421–24), and Greeley's *Overland Journey* (310–15). That he considered such accounts tiresome is suggested by an entry in his 1865–66 notebook: "Passenger volunteers account of journey to Big Trees & Yo Semite—& then Dan's old Ram" (*N&J1*, 172).

421.1–3 After a three months' absence . . . I had become too mean and lazy, now, to work on a morning paper] Clemens returned to San Francisco on 26 February 1865, after an absence of twelve weeks. He seems to have earned only a minimal income over the next several months by writing occasional items for the Virginia City *Territorial Enterprise* and sketches for the *Californian*, the *California Youths' Companion*, and the San Francisco *Dramatic Chronicle* (*L1*, 321; SLC 1865a–r).

421.4–6 I was created San Francisco correspondent of the *Enterprise*, and at the end of five months I was out of debt] Mark Twain's daily correspondence for the *Enterprise*, for which he earned one hundred dollars a month, probably did not begin until the fall: the overwhelming majority of surviving *Enterprise* items date from after 10 October 1865, while only three survive from earlier in the year. Clemens was able to write to Orion and Mollie Clemens on 19 October 1865 that he had "gone to work in dead earnest" to get out of debt (*L1*, 324). Although the *Enterprise* files for the period are no longer extant, many of Mark Twain's letters are preserved in the Yale Scrapbook (see **YSMT** in References), and many more have been found reprinted in California and Nevada newspapers and magazines (SLC 1865s–t, 1865w, 1865ff, 1866a–d, 1866f–g). Besides his daily letter to the *Enterprise*, his effort in the five months between October 1865 and March 1866 included contributions to the San Francisco *Dramatic Chronicle* for forty dollars a month, correspondence for the *Napa County Reporter*, contributions to the *Californian* and the New York *Weekly Review*, and two pieces for the New York *Saturday Press*, one of which—"Jim Smiley and His Jumping Frog"—earned him his first major success with eastern readers (*ET&S2*, 481; SLC 1865u–v, 1865x–ee, 1866e, 1866h; *L1*, 327–28).

421.9–12 I got a new berth . . . for the Sacramento *Union*, an excellent journal and liberal with employés] Clemens traveled to Sacramento on 24 February 1866 to discuss the terms of his employment with the proprietors of the Sacramento *Union:* James Anthony, Paul Morrill, and Henry W. Larkin. Charles Henry Webb, who accompanied him, later asserted that he helped Clemens obtain the assignment. On 5 March Clemens informed his mother and sister: "I start to the Sandwich Islands day after to-morrow. . . . I only decided to-day to go. . . . I am to remain there a month & ransack the islands, . . . & write twenty or thirty letters to the Sacramento *Union*—for which they pay me as much money as I would get if I staid at home" (*L1*, 333, 333–34 n. 1; SLC 1866g). He later claimed that the *Union* proprietors—the "best men who ever owned a newspaper"—generously paid him "a great deal more than they promised," but the exact amount is not known (SLC 1899, 77; *L1*, 353; see the note at 533.5–6). Clemens remained in the islands for over four months and wrote twenty-five letters for the *Union,* thirteen of which he later revised to create chapters 63–69 and 71–74 of *Roughing It.*

421.13 We sailed in the propeller Ajax, in the middle of winter] Clemens departed on 7 March 1866 aboard the California Steam Navigation Company's steamer *Ajax,* which was making its second voyage to Honolulu (*L1*, 331 n. 10, 334 n. 1).

421.17–20 Williams, and three sea-worn old whaleship captains . . . drank astonishing quantities of raw whisky] The *Ajax* passenger list does not include any "Williams," nor does this "quiet passenger" (as he is described at 426.6) appear in Mark Twain's letters to the *Union.* Mark Twain probably did not draw Williams from life, but rather created him to serve as the nemesis of "the old Admiral" (see the next note). The sea captains listed on the *Ajax*'s roster were James Smith, W. H. Phillips, and A. W. Fish, whom Mark Twain—in his first two letters to the *Union*—called Cuttle, Phelps, and Fitch. He reported that during the voyage they consumed nineteen gallons of whiskey while playing euchre and exchanging nautical banter in the ship's smoking room (*Ajax* passenger list, PH in CU-MARK; SLC 1866i–j; see also *N&J1*, 191, 196).

421.22–423.19 "the old Admiral"—a retired whaleman . . . was around] The prototype of this character was Captain James Smith (1800–77), whom Mark Twain included on a list of ideal shipmates published in January 1868, referring to him as "Admiral Jim Smith, late of Hawaiian Navy" (SLC 1868b). Smith began his long sea career at the age of twelve as a cabin boy aboard a privateer during the War of 1812. He commanded a whaleship out of New London, Connecticut, for a number of years before being connected with the earliest line of sailing packets between San Francisco and Honolulu—the "Regular Dispatch Line"—as captain of the *Yankee* and the *Comet.* Smith's death in August 1877 resulted in a well-publicized estate dispute that was not resolved in the courts until October 1879. Members of Smith's family attempted to show that "the testator was unsound in mind, and unduly influenced when he made his will," even soliciting Clemens's affidavit—based on his shipboard acquaintance with the captain—to that effect. Testimony failed to support their case, revealing Smith as "an obstinate, clear-headed, profane, hot-tempered old fellow, who swore by Andrew Jackson, Jeff Davis, the New York *Sun* and *World,* and was no more susceptible to influence than a congressman is to the grace of God" (unidentified clipping enclosed in Helen R. Fitch to SLC, 16 Sept 79, CU-MARK). A third of Smith's considerable estate was left to his Hawaiian protégé, John Kellett, who, at age sixteen, was Smith's companion aboard the *Ajax* in March 1866 (Caulkins, 643; Decker, 82; Kuykendall 1953, 17, 265 n. 40; Hartford *Courant:* "Deaths," 24 Aug 77, 2; "The Last of a Privateer's Crew," 25 Aug 77, 4; "News of the State," 7 Oct 79, 4; Honolulu *Pacific Commercial Advertiser:* "Death of Capt. James Smith," 22 Sept 77, 3; "Passengers," 24 Mar 66, 2; *Ajax* passenger list, PH in CU-MARK).

425.14–15 At his heels frisked the darling . . . terrier "Fan,"] Gladys Bellamy has pointed out the similarity between Mark Twain's portrait of the admiral and his dog and the description of General Tecumseh Brown and his beloved bullterrier, also named "Fan," in John Phoenix's "A Legend of the Tehama House" (Bellamy, 33; Derby, 254–69).

425.21–22 "The Old Guard," a secession periodical published in New York] *The Old Guard,* a New York monthly published from June 1862 to December 1870, was "the only consistently anti-Lincoln magazine published in the North during the war" (Mott, 544–46). In an 1866 notebook entry Clemens made reference to Smith's "secesh" sympathies (*N&J1,* 191).

431.1 the Islands hove in sight] The *Ajax* docked at Honolulu at 11 A.M. on Sunday, 18 March ("The Pioneer Steam Line," Honolulu *Pacific Commercial Advertiser,* 24 Mar 66, 2).

431.9–434.2 then . . . sail—] Mark Twain based this portion of the text (except for the paragraph at 432.11–433.11) on his letter in the Sacramento *Union* of 19 April 1866, revising it for inclusion in *Roughing It* (SLC 1866*l*).

431.26–27 San Francisco's pleasure grove, the "Willows,"] Clemens was well acquainted with this popular resort, located at Mission and Eighteenth streets, whose attractions included a hotel and restaurant, gardens with tables and chairs, a minstrel and variety theater, an aquarium and zoo, and facilities for bowling and dancing (*ET&S1,* 494).

432.3–4 I saw cats] On 19 May the Honolulu *Advertiser* reported the publication of Mark Twain's first letters to the *Union* and reprinted much of his description of Honolulu, commenting: "His letters abound in genuine good humor and fun, though if he would stick a little closer to facts, they would be more reliable." In particular, the passage on cats struck the *Advertiser* as apocryphal: "We half suspect he brought the cats with him," suggested the paper ("Mark Twain," Honolulu *Pacific Commercial Advertiser,* 19 May 66, 1). Soon after his arrival in Honolulu, however, Clemens wrote in his notebook, "1000[s] of cats and nary snake" (*N&J1,* 220).

435.9–17 they were rather sour that year . . . it will come off when the enamel does] Mark Twain adapted this description of tamarind tasting from a similar account, in a section entitled "Fruit," in his letter in the Sacramento *Union* of 20 April. He did not use this letter elsewhere in *Roughing It* (SLC 1866m).

436.1–441.20 In my diary . . . itself.] In fact, Mark Twain did not draw on either of his two extant Hawaiian notebooks for this chapter (notebooks 5 and 6 in *N&J1,* 91–237). Rather he based this portion of the text on his letter in the Sacramento *Union* of 21 April 1866, revising it for inclusion in *Roughing It;* he reserved a section of the letter for use in the next chapter (SLC 1866n; see the note at 444.16–448.18).

436.9 the Government Prison] Mark Twain described his visit to this "model prison of the western half of the world"—completed in 1857 on the outskirts of Honolulu—in his letter in the *Union* of 21 May, but he used none of the account in *Roughing It* (Scott, 856; SLC 1866p).

436.10 Capt. Fish . . . Capt. Phillips] See the note at 421.17–20. Clemens recorded in his notebook that both captains had been victims of the Confederate privateer *Shenandoah,* which destroyed a number of Pacific whaling vessels (*N&J1,* 113, 182).

436.15 Capt. Cook] Captain James Cook (1728–79)—English circumnavigator, explorer of the Pacific Ocean, and first European to reach the Sandwich Islands—was killed by natives on 14 February 1779 at Kealakekua Bay on the island of Hawaii. Mark Twain recounts the events surrounding his death in chapter 71 (490.39–491.24).

436.19 the American Hotel] This hotel opened for business at the beginning of March 1866 on the "premises lately occupied by the British Consul" ("American House," *Friend* 17 [1 Mar 66]: 17). Clemens, with other *Ajax* passengers, took some of his meals there, but roomed in a nearby cottage ("American House," Honolulu *Pacific Commercial Advertiser,* 3 Mar 66, 3, and 10 Mar 66, 1; *MTH,* 19–22; SLC 1866m).

437.10–438.7 Inside of five minutes I was mounted . . . plunging of the Ajax in a storm] This description of the horse "Oahu" recalls an amusing sketch by George Washington Bates about his own recalcitrant "steed" in his 1854 account of a visit to the islands, *Sandwich Island Notes,* a book Clemens had read. Bates, the perspiring rider, attempts to whip his horse into consistent motion, but "he would trot, walk, or come to a stand, just as it suited him; and when I arrived at an elevation of the road, he stood as still as a sculptured war-steed" (Bates, 127). The horse suddenly breaks into a mad gallop, before lapsing again into somnolence. "On the whole, it was a curious performance, but very far from being agreeable" (Bates, 129). Early in his Sandwich Islands trip, Clemens filled many notebook pages with references from Bates's book—without citing his source, which has now been identified for the first time (*N&J1*, 210–15). Bates's narrative, while it furnishes abundant evidence of the author's chauvinism and his disdain toward the islanders, is leavened by humor and treats frankly the discomforts and incongruities of island travel and native life. Its author remains mysterious: references in two extensive reviews of the book in the *Polynesian* suggest that Bates (also known as William Baker) was incarcerated in a New York prison sometime in 1854 or 1855, apparently for bigamy (*Polynesian:* 12 [11 Aug 55]: 53–54; 12 [1 Sept 55]: 66).

439.11–22 About a dozen cottages . . . "The King's Grove."] In his 21 April *Union* letter Mark Twain identified this place as "Waikiki . . . , once the Capital of the kingdom" (SLC 1866n). After Europeans discovered Honolulu harbor in 1793, the importance of nearby Waikiki diminished, although at the time of Clemens's visit it was still the royal summer residence. The current king was Kamehameha V (see the note at 462.4; Whitney, 26).

440.20–441.3 This ancient temple was built of rough blocks . . . Kamehameha . . . impaled their heads on the walls] Mark Twain's description of this site, located about a mile outside the village of Waikiki, and of Kamehameha's vengeful display there owes some of its details to James Jackson Jarves's *Scenes and Scenery in the Sandwich Islands* (Jarves 1844a, 59–60).

440.35–441.1 When Kamehameha . . . took full and final possession of the country] Through military triumphs and alliances between 1782 and 1810, Kamehameha (1758?–1819) gradually consolidated his power beyond his native island of Hawaii, ultimately uniting the islands and ruling as Kamehameha I. The decisive victory occurred in 1795 when, at the battle of Nuuanu on the island of Oahu, he completed the conquest of all the principal islands except Kauai, whose king did not acknowledge Kamehameha's sovereignty until 1810. For the quarter century following the battle, Kamehameha's skilled management of domestic and foreign affairs assured the stability and independence of the kingdom and established the dynasty that was to follow. Mark Twain's information about Kamehameha's victory on Oahu, here and in chapter 65, relies on Jarves's accounts in his *History of the Hawaiian Islands* and its companion volume, *Scenes and Scenery in the Sandwich Islands* (Kuykendall 1938, 32–61, 429–30; Jarves 1847, 92; Jarves 1844a, v–vi, 60).

440.36 a sort of a Napoleon] See the note at 469.34.

441.11–20 The missionaries have clothed them . . . Their work speaks for itself] In a number of published statements, Clemens reiterated his generally favorable assessment of the missionaries' role in the islands. He first listed the "benefit conferred" by them in early August 1866, in one of his Hawaiian notebooks (*N&J1*, 154; *MTH*, 128–48).

442.6–444.15 Gayly . . . business.] Mark Twain based this portion of the text on his letter in the Sacramento *Union* of 24 April 1866, revising it for inclusion in *Roughing It* (SLC 1866o). The "we" in the opening sentence of the chapter refers to the "half a dozen gentlemen and three ladies" whom he had intended to accompany (436.7–8). In revising the *Union* printing he deleted his report of catching up to his party.

442.11–12 We picked up a lot of them for mementoes] Clemens mentioned his explorations of Oahu's "ancient battle-fields & other places of interest" to his mother and sister in a letter of 3 April 1866 and added: "I have got a lot of human bones which I took from one of these battle-fields—I guess I will bring you some of them" (*L1*, 334).

443.24 the Pari] In his *Union* letter Mark Twain supplied a parenthetical explanation of the term "Pari" at this point: "pronounced *Pally;* intelligent natives claim that there is no *r* in the Kanaka alphabet" (SLC 1866o). Early writings on the Sandwich Islands used variant spellings of some sounds (such as "l/r" and "k/t"), reflecting regional differences in pronunciation. The spelling "Pari" was less common than "Pali," which became the standard form (Jarves 1847, 46; Ellis, 13–17; Charles Samuel Stewart, 95).

443.26 Mr. Jarves's excellent history] During his stay in the islands, Clemens made use of the extensive library of a Honolulu friend, Samuel Chenery Damon (1815–85), chaplain of the American Seamen's Friend Society, pastor of the Oahu Bethel Church, and publisher and editor of the *Friend*, a monthly newspaper. "I take your Jarves' History with me, because I may not be able to get it at home," Clemens confessed to his friend just before his departure for San Francisco in July; "I 'cabbage' it by the strong arm" (*L1*, 349). The copy he appropriated was almost certainly the third edition of Jarves's *History of the Hawaiian Islands*, published in Honolulu in 1847: Clemens quoted at length from this edition in two *Union* letters, one of which was used for *Roughing It* (see the notes at 469.30–470.5 and 470.11–472.43; SLC 1866x, 1866aa). His borrowing of the Jarves book was the subject of some humorous chaffing in the Hawaiian press. He finally mailed the book back to Damon in May 1867 (SLC 1867h; *MTH*, 155–63; *L1*, 349–50).

444.16–448.18 This . . . expense.] Mark Twain based this portion of the text on his letter in the Sacramento *Union* of 21 April 1866, revising it for inclusion in *Roughing It;* he used the beginning and end of this letter in the previous chapter (SLC 1866n; see the note at 436.1–441.20).

445.33 J. Smith] This may be a reference to Clemens's shipboard acquaintance Captain James Smith (see the note at 421.22–423.19), although that identification is belied by an entry of March 1866 in one of Clemens's notebooks: "No good livery horses—put em on ranch, Kanakas hire em out or ride em to death. Trick they played Wheelock by keeping their own blanket on sore-back horse" (*N&J1,* 219). A "Mr. Wheelack" had arrived in Honolulu from San Francisco on 7 January 1866 and had stayed at the Volcano House on the island of Hawaii in early March ("Passengers," *Friend* 17 [1 Feb 66]: 16; Volcano House Register, 74).

447.4 a certain Mr. L.] "Mr. L." is more fully identified in the *Union* text as "Leland" (SLC 1866n). Lewis Leland (1834–97) was the proprietor—until 1868—of San Francisco's Occidental Hotel, where Clemens made several sojourns in the mid-1860s. In 1868 Clemens named Leland as a reference, assuring Jervis Langdon, his future father-in-law, that Leland had known him "intimately for 3 or 4 years" (*L2,* 359). Clemens frequently mentioned the convivial Leland in his reporting, and recounted a humorous anecdote of Leland's January 1866 trip to Honolulu aboard the *Ajax* for his *Enterprise* readers (SLC 1866f).

447.31 Williams] The fictional Williams also figures in Mark Twain's account of the *Ajax* voyage in chapter 62 (see the note at 421.17–20). The *Union* text for the present passage, however, reads "Brown," the name Mark Twain gave to a comic figure appearing throughout the *Union* letters, first as a passenger aboard the *Ajax.* (The ship's passenger list did include a merchant named "W. H. Brown," but he returned to San Francisco on 4 April 1866 and thus could not have been the Brown of the *Union* letters, who supposedly accompanied Clemens on his excursion to the island of Hawaii in May and June.) The boisterous and vulgar Brown, who reappears in Mark Twain's 1866–67 letters to the San Francisco *Alta California,* is undoubtedly a composite creation, a comic foil incorporating elements of Clemens's own personality with those of some actual companions. In revising the *Union* letters for *Roughing It* Clemens consistently deleted passages involving Brown, or changed his name, as he did in this instance (SLC 1866n; *Ajax* passenger list, PH in CU-MARK; *N&J1,* 182 n. 6; "Passengers," *Friend* 17 [1 May 66]: 40).

449.2–6 I recognize a familiar home air . . . "When we were marching through Georgia."] Mark Twain derived this remark from his 24 April *Union* letter, in which he commented, "If it would have been all the same to General Sherman, I wish he had gone around by the way of the Gulf of Mexico" (SLC 1866o). Henry Clay Work (1832–84) wrote the lyrics and music for "Marching through Georgia" in 1865 to commemorate General Sherman's Georgia campaign of late 1864. Mark Twain had protested being "attacked, front and rear," by this immensely popular song in a letter to the *Enterprise* in late 1865 (SLC 1865w). A few months later, in one of his Hawaiian notebooks, he wrote: "I wish Sherman had marched through Alabama," and in December 1866 he included the song in a list of "the d—dest, oldest, vilest songs" (*N&J1*, 228, 262).

450.1–453.37 PASSING . . . art.] Mark Twain based this portion of the text on his letter in the Sacramento *Union* of 21 May 1866, revising it for inclusion in *Roughing It* (SLC 1866p).

450.3–451.14 The native girls . . . encircle their dusky throats with . . . vermillion-tinted blossom of the *ohia*] This description of the riding style and costume of the native girls owes much to Jarves's chapter covering Honolulu "street scenes" and "Saturday afternoon" activities in *Scenes and Scenery.* Furthermore, one of Clemens's early Hawaiian notebook entries reads "*Ohia* wreaths—crimson—& feathers" (*N&J1*, 215), referring to the following passage in Jarves's book: "Their hair is either done up after the latest fashions imitated from the foreign ladies, or is encircled with rich and expensive wreaths made from feathers. The less wealthy wear those made from the beautiful crimson blossoms of the *ohia* tree" (Jarves 1844a, 47, 53).

451.37–452.17 Poi is the chief article of food . . . it produces acrid humors] Mark Twain derived his information about poi from Jarves's *History:*

> *Poi,* the principal article of diet, was prepared from the kalo [taro] plant. The roots, after being baked under ground, were mashed on a large platter, by a heavy stone pestle, or an instrument made of lava, resembling a stirrup, and were mixed with water, until a thick paste was formed. This is sometimes eaten in a sweet state, but generally put aside until it ferments, in which condition it is preferred. It is a highly nutricious substance, though, when solely used, has a tendency to produce acrid humors. (Jarves 1847, 42)

452.36–453.1 The natives manufacture an intoxicating drink from it which . . . causes premature decrepitude] According to Jarves, the effects of awa "were very pernicious, covering the body with a white scurf, or scaliness, like the scurvy, inflaming the eyes, and causing premature decrepitude. It was also taken as a medicine" (Jarves 1847, 49). The narcotic drink was made from the root of the kava (*piper methysticum*), a shrub native to the Pacific islands, and had a bitter, unpleasant taste. Clemens again referred to it in an article entitled "The Sandwich Islands," written for the New York *Tribune* in 1873 (SLC 1873c; Pukui and Elbert, 30; Ellis, 386).

453.32–35 The demoralizing *hula-hula* was forbidden to be performed, save . . . only by permission . . . and the payment of ten dollars] The restrictions on the performance of the hula were part of the Civil Code of 1859 and resulted from legislative pressure brought by Prince Lot Kamehameha (later Kamehameha V). Clemens also referred to the ten-dollar fee in a Hawaiian notebook: "Have to take out a license ($10,) to have the Hulahula dance performed, & then if the girls dress for it in the usual manner, that is with no clothing worth mentioning, it must be conducted in strict privacy" (*N&J1*, 221).

454.3–4 It is the most universally educated race of people] In one of his Hawaiian notebooks Clemens made the following entry, based on a passage in Bates's *Sandwich Island Notes:* "* No place where *public* education so widely diffused | * Children of ten—all read & write" (*N&J1*, 210; Bates, 63).

454.11–13 contact with civilization . . . has reduced the native population . . . to *fifty-five thousand*] In a Hawaiian notebook Clemens noted: "*Certainly* were 400,000 here in Cook's time—& even in 1820" (*N&J1*, 129). Captain Cook had estimated the population to be 400,000 in 1778, but Captain George Vancouver

> some fifteen years after, puts it at a much lower figure, and intimates that Cook was misled by the multitudes that flocked to the shores whenever his ships appeared. But the fact nevertheless remains, that the natives have, since their first intercourse with foreigners, decreased at a fearful rate. (Bennett, 3)

Another estimate, probably more accurate, put the population at 142,000 in 1823; the official 1866 census figure was 58,765 (Bennett, 59).

454.16–456.6 If . . . "shoved."] Mark Twain based this portion of the text on his letter in the Sacramento *Union* of 20 April 1866, revising it for inclusion in *Roughing It.* Before reusing the material in *Roughing It* he had already reprinted it as a sketch entitled "Honored As a Curiosity in Honolulu" in *The Celebrated Jumping Frog of Calaveras County* (SLC 1866m, 1867a). Clemens also made the following related notebook entry in March–April 1866: "If you don't know a man in Hon—call him Capt & ask him how many barrels he took last season—chances are he's a whaler" (*N&J1*, 225).

457.1–458.18 I STILL quote from my journal . . . etc., etc.] Mark Twain based this portion of the text on his letter in the Sacramento *Union* of 20 June 1866, revising it for inclusion in *Roughing It.* This material is not found in either of Clemens's extant Hawaiian notebooks, but it may derive from a missing notebook that he used from mid-April to mid-June 1866 (SLC 1866v; *N&J1*, 100–101).

457.5–6 David Kalakaua (the King's Chamberlain)] Kalakaua (1836–91) held the office of chamberlain and secretary to Kamehameha V at a salary of $2,500 per year. Clemens met Kalakaua early in his stay in the islands, when, on 3 April, he was among Kalakaua's guests at a dinner in honor of James McBride, the American minister. Kalakaua was also scheduled to accompany Clemens on a visit to Iolani Palace on 4 April (see the note at 462.4). Mark Twain described Kalakaua in a *Union* letter:

> [He] is a man of fine presence, is an educated gentleman and a man of good abilities. He is approaching forty, I should judge—is thirty-five, at any rate. He is conservative, politic and calculating, makes little display, and does not talk much in the Legislature. He is a quiet, dignified, sensible man, and would do no discredit to the kingly office. (SLC 1866x)

Kalakaua, a descendant of ancient Hawaiian chiefs, became king in February 1874 after an abortive attempt to secure the throne in 1873. He reigned until his death in January 1891 in San Francisco (Honolulu *Pacific Commercial Advertiser:* "The Budget," 5 May 66, 1; "Audience at the Palace," 28 July 66, 3; *MTH,* 31; *L1,* 334; Withington, 229–34, 249, 275).

457.6 Prince William] As Kamehameha V's cousin and the grandson of a half-brother of Kamehameha I, the popular William Charles Lunalilo (1835–74) was widely recognized as the likely successor to the throne. Mark Twain noted in a *Union* letter that Lunalilo was

> of the highest blood in the kingdom—higher than the King himself, it is said. . . . Prince William is a man of fine, large build; is thirty-one years of age; is affable, gentlemanly, open, frank, manly; is as independent as a lord and has a spirit and a will like the old Conqueror himself. He is intelligent, shrewd, sensible—is a man of first rate abilities, in fact. . . . I like this man, and I like his bold independence, and his friendship for and appreciation of the American residents. (SLC 1866x)

In two articles entitled "The Sandwich Islands," published in the New York *Tribune* on 6 and 9 January 1873, Mark Twain, although acknowledging Lunalilo's excessive fondness for whiskey, urged that he be chosen as the next king. Lunalilo was elected—by popular and legislative vote—to succeed Kamehameha V in January 1873, but he reigned only briefly, until his death in February 1874 (SLC 1873b–c; *N&J1,* 124; Kuykendall 1953, 240, 242–44; Withington, 229–39).

457.6–9 The President of the Assembly, his Royal Highness M. Kekuanaoa,* . . . the King's father] Mataio Kekuanaoa (1794–1868) and his wife, the high chiefess Kinau (see the note at 458.13), were the parents of Kamehameha IV, Kamehameha V, and Princess Victoria. Kekuanaoa served as governor of Oahu from his wife's death in 1839 until 1864. In the administration of Kamehameha V, Kekuanaoa served as president of the legislature and of the Board of Education, and as *kuhina nui* (preeminent adviser and chief administrator) to the king, until the abolition of that office in 1864. Mark Twain may not have learned of Kekuanaoa's death until the fall of 1871, after this chapter had already been set in type and it was too late to insert the words "Since dead" (457n.1) into the body of the text ("Death of His Highness Mataio Kekuanaoa," Honolulu *Pacific Commercial Advertiser,* 28 Nov 68, 2; Bailey, 225–

26; Kuykendall 1938, 64; Kuykendall 1953, 107, 126; Varigny, 138, 168; W. D. Alexander, 289).

457.7–8 the Vice President (the latter a white man,)] The vice-president of the legislature was Honolulu merchant Godfrey Rhodes (1815–97), an Englishman resident in the islands since the 1840s who was known for his anti-American sentiments (Varigny, 252; Kuykendall 1953, 255; "Opening of the Legislature," Honolulu *Pacific Commercial Advertiser*, 28 Apr 66, 2).

458.2–3 the honored guest of royalty in Europe] Kekuanaoa had been one of the party that accompanied Kamehameha II on an ill-fated voyage to England in 1823–24. Both Kamehameha and his favorite queen, Kamamalu, died of the measles before they could be received by King George IV, but others of the party, including Kekuanaoa, met with him in September 1824 (Kuykendall 1938, 76–79).

458.13 his wife, who was a daughter of Kamehameha the Great] Kinau (d. 1839), whom Kekuanaoa married in October 1827, was a daughter of Kamehameha I. From June 1832 until her death she served as *kuhina nui* to Kamehameha III (Kuykendall 1938, 133–36; Bennett, 68–69).

458.21–23 a popular belief that . . . your enemy can . . . *pray you to death*] This phenomenon—and the related ability to *"die whenever they want to"* (459.21–22)—was frequently reported by early visitors to the islands (Archibald Campbell, 172–73; Charles Samuel Stewart, 202–3; Dibble 1839, 61–62, 77–78; Jarves 1847, 24–25, 99; Bates, 396–97). Clemens's interest in the subject is evidenced by an entry in one of his Hawaiian notebooks, as well as references in his Sandwich Islands lecture and in the fragments of a Sandwich Islands novel that he began in 1884 (*N&J1*, 117; SLC 1866kk, 1884a).

459.21–22 the natives are able to *lie down and die whenever they want to*] Clemens witnessed what he thought was an instance of this phenomenon while staying with Samuel G. Wilder and his family on Oahu. When the family's nursemaid died, he noted in his journal: "Her father died last week—nothing matter with the girl—just thought she was going to die" (*N&J1*, 128).

459.31 the Great Shark God] Mark Twain identified the Great Shark God as "Kauhuhu" in his 1866 piece "A Strange Dream." Kauhuhu was one of many powerful shark gods worshiped by the Hawaiians, a "fierce king shark of Maui who lives in a cave in Kipahulu and also has a home . . . on the windward side of Molokai" (SLC 1866t; Beckwith, 129).

461.14–25 a brown, stately dame . . . with nothing . . . but a "stove-pipe" hat . . . a fiery neck-tie and a striped vest] A similar description in Bates's *Sandwich Island Notes* may have inspired Mark Twain:

> When civilized habits first dawned upon them, their personal appearance was the most eccentric that can well be imagined. In coming to church on a Sunday,

one man would come clad in nothing but a coat buttoned up on his back instead of in front. The entire wardrobe of a second would be a ragged cravat, and a single strip of native cloth crossed over his loins, called a *malo;* that of a third, the *malo,* and a pair of high boots; that of a fourth, the *malo,* and a tattered palm-leaf hat that might have served some foreigner nearly a score of years; that of a fifth, a shirt, with a collar reaching his eyes and half way up the back of his head, and the *malo.* (Bates, 262)

462.4 his royal Majesty the King] Kamehameha V (1830–72), known as Lot Kamehameha, reigned from 1863 until his death. Said to resemble his grandfather Kamehameha I, he was a capable and forceful administrator. Clemens was impressed with his abilities; in his 9 January 1873 *Tribune* article he described him as a "wise sovereign" who "tried hard to do well by his people, and succeeded. There was no trivial royal nonsense about him" (SLC 1873c). Clemens intended to meet Kamehameha V at Iolani Palace on 4 April 1866. Although he visited the palace, he apparently did not see the king, since he mentioned in 1873 that he only saw him "but once, . . . attending the funeral of his sister," Princess Victoria Kamamalu (SLC 1873c; Bennett, 7; Kuykendall 1938, 27–28; Jarves 1844a, 59; Kuykendall 1953, 125–26; *L1,* 334–35).

462.4–9 with a New York detective's income of thirty . . . thousand dollars a year from the . . . "royal domain."] As Clemens correctly states, Kamehameha V had two sources of income for the period of 1866 through 1868: an annual salary of $17,500, and income from the Crown Lands amounting to about $20,000 a year (Honolulu *Pacific Commercial Advertiser:* "Hawaiian Legislature," 5 May 66, 3; "Report of the Minister of Finance to the Legislature of 1866," 5 May 66, 4).

462.9–10 two-story frame "palace."] Iolani Palace, built in 1844–45, was a large square building with wide verandas on all sides. It was set in grounds "extensive enough to accommodate a village," according to Mark Twain, and afforded a panoramic view of Honolulu (SLC 1866s). The original palace was replaced in 1879 by a much grander structure (Scott, 113).

463.3–8 his Excellency the "royal Chamberlain" . . . the Commander-in-chief of the Household Troops, whose forces . . . under a corporal in other lands] Both of these titles belonged to the same man. David Kalakaua, the king's chamberlain (see the note at 457.5–6), was also—as Mark Twain mentioned in his 6 January 1873 article in the New York *Tribune*—commander-in-chief of the Household Troops. Kalakaua, who held the rank of colonel, reportedly "took a special interest in military matters, and was fond of appearing in elaborate military uniforms. Being tall and well built, he modeled such uniforms with great distinction" (Kuykendall 1967, 13). The Household Troops, comprising one hundred native soldiers, constituted the standing army and were charged with guarding the palace, the prison, and the treasury (SLC 1873c; Zambucka 1983, 10; Honolulu *Pacific Commercial Ad-*

vertiser: "Audience at the Palace," 28 July 66, 3; "Majority Report of the Military Committee," 23 May 68, 4; "The Mutiny at the Barracks," 13 Sept 73, 2).

463.9–12 the royal Steward and the Grand Equerry in Waiting . . . the First Gentleman of the Bed-chamber] These positions were not listed in the official government budget, and may have been invented by Mark Twain to add color to his description of how the "grown folk . . . play 'empire'" (462.2–4).

463.13–464.9 his Excellency the Prime Minister, a renegade American . . . his Excellency the Imperial Minister of Finance . . . all for four thousand dollars a year and unimaginable glory] There was at this time no official position of prime minister in the Hawaiian government. The "renegade American from New Hampshire" and the "Imperial Minister of Finance" were in fact the same person—Charles Coffin Harris (1821–81), the minister of finance and Kamehameha V's closest adviser. Harris was a native of New Hampshire who settled in the Sandwich Islands in 1850, practiced law, engaged in business, and, in 1862, began an association with the government that culminated in his becoming chief justice in 1877. His salary was $4,000 in 1866. As a member of the Hawaiian Reformed Catholic Church, he was considered an enemy of the American Protestant mission. Mark Twain first expressed his violent antipathy toward Harris—after observing him during a visit to the Hawaiian legislature—in a *Union* letter published on 21 June 1866; he continued his ridicule in several subsequent newspaper letters (SLC 1866w, 1866z–aa; see also the remark about Harris's vanity at 469.20–25). In a letter of 20 December 1870 to Albert Francis Judd of Honolulu, Clemens mentioned his plan to "do up the Islands & Harris" in some form in "2 or 3" years (PH in CtY-BR, in *MTH,* 467). Beyond his scathing remarks in *Roughing It,* however, plus similar comments in his 9 January 1873 *Tribune* article, Mark Twain is not known to have written anything further about Harris ("The Late Justice Harris of Hawaii," New York *Times,* 27 July 81, 3; Honolulu *Pacific Commercial Advertiser:* "'The Budget,'" 5 May 66, 1; "Estimated Expenditures for the Two Years Ending March 31, 1870," 25 Apr 68, 3; "Death of the Chief Justice," 9 July 81, 2; "Death of the Late Chancellor," *Friend* 30 [1 Aug 81]: 69; Kuykendall 1953, 36, 96–98, 126–28, 218; *MTH,* 27–28; SLC 1867i, 1873c).

464.5–8 a million dollars of public money a year . . . the "national debt" (of a hundred and fifty thousand dollars,)] Mark Twain's figure is more than double the Sandwich Islands' actual budget. The two-year budget for 1866 to 1868 was $826,823, and for the following two years, $997,680. His figure for the national debt, however, is more accurate: in April 1866 it stood at $166,649, and in March 1870 at $112,000 (Honolulu *Pacific Commercial Advertiser:* " 'The Budget,'" 5 May 66, 1;

"Report of the Minister of Finance to the Legislature of 1866," 5 May 66, 4; "Our National Finances," 21 May 70, 2).

464.10–11 his Excellency the Minister of War, who holds sway over the royal armies] This title was Mark Twain's invention: although there was a Department of War, it had no minister. Charles de Varigny (1829–99), as minister of foreign affairs, had overall charge of the Hawaiian military, which consisted of the Household Troops and various volunteer companies. Varigny was born at Versailles, settled in the Sandwich Islands in 1855, and received his first government appointment in 1864. Mark Twain described him as a "sensible, unpretentious" man, but added: "If Varigny were as hopelessly bad as his English pronunciation, nothing but a special intervention of Providence could save him from perdition hereafter" (SLC 1866w; Varigny, 255, 258, 261; Honolulu *Pacific Commercial Advertiser:* "'The Budget,'" 5 May 66, 1; "Estimated Expenditures for the Two Years Ending March 31, 1870," 25 Apr 68, 3).

464.17–18 some venerable swivels on Punch-Bowl Hill] Puahi, or Punch-Bowl Hill, was an extinct crater half a mile behind Honolulu. According to Jarves, it "obtained its soubriquet in times not quite as temperate as the present; its shape internally is much like a bowl, being a gradual and uniform hollow" (Jarves 1844a, 23). Bates described the battery on its summit as consisting of "eleven guns, pointing different ways, at irregular distances from each other. . . . They rest on carriages in a state of rapid decay" (Bates, 100).

464.20–21 his Excellency the Minister of the Navy—a nabob who rules the "royal fleet," (a steam-tug and a sixty-ton schooner.)] There was no naval ministry; responsibility for a tugboat in Honolulu harbor, the *Pele,* fell to the minister of the interior—F. W. Hutchinson, an Englishman. The *Pele,* launched in 1856, was in service at Honolulu for thirty years. In June 1866, during Clemens's visit, it was fitted with a "small rifle of suitable caliber" so that it could be classed as a gunboat (Mifflin Thomas, 41, 221 n. 30). Nothing is known about the "sixty-ton schooner" ("'The Budget,'" Honolulu *Pacific Commercial Advertiser,* 5 May 66, 1; Varigny, 195; W. D. Alexander, 329).

464.22–28 his Grace the Lord Bishop of Honolulu . . . a cheap ready-made Bishop from England to take charge] In 1860 Kamehameha IV, motivated in part by a desire to reinforce the Hawaiian monarchy, petitioned Queen Victoria to establish a branch of the Anglican (Episcopal) church in the Sandwich Islands. Despite protests from the American missionary community, the "Hawaiian Reformed Catholic Church" was created. Thomas Nettleship Staley (1823–98), a recently consecrated English bishop, arrived in Honolulu in October 1862 to serve as its head. Within a few weeks, Staley had confirmed as members of his church Kamehameha IV and Queen Emma, as well as other high chiefs and government figures, including Robert C. Wyllie, then the minister of foreign affairs, and Charles Harris, the attorney general. Despite some initial success, Staley and his bishopric proved unpopular, rousing antagonism from the already well-established Protestant and Roman Catholic missions. He resigned in 1870. In his *Union* letters Mark Twain sided with the American Protestant missionaries against Staley, condemning his dismissal of the missionary effort and his support of "barbarous" native rituals. He described the bishop as "a weak, trivial-minded man," spiteful, pretentious, and vain (SLC 1866z, 1866x, 1866aa; Korn, 333; *N&J1*, 134–35).

464.31 his Excellency the Minister of Public Instruction] There had been no such minister since 1855. At the time of Clemens's visit, educational matters were handled by a five-member Board of Education, whose president was Mataio Kekuanaoa (see the note at 457.6–9), and an inspector general of schools, Abraham Fornander (Kuykendall 1953, 106–8).

464.32 their Excellencies the Governors of Oahu, Hawaii, etc.] The governor of Oahu was John Owen Dominis (1832–91), son of an American sea captain who had settled in the Sandwich Islands in 1837. The island of Hawaii had been governed since 1855 by the high chiefess Ruth Keelikolani (1826–83) (Gasinski, 23, 26; Scott, 60; Korn, 303).

464.35–38 their Excellencies the Envoy Extraordinary . . . of the French; her British Majesty's Minister; the Minister Resident, of the United States] The French minister was M. Desnoyers. The acting British commissioner was William L. Green, a prominent Honolulu businessman. The American minister, James McBride, was awaiting the arrival of his successor, General Edward M. McCook, appointed in March 1866. McCook did not arrive in Honolulu until 22 July, three days after Clemens's departure for San Francisco (Honolulu *Pacific Commercial Advertiser:* "Programme of the Funeral," 30 June 66, 2; "Presentation at the Palace" and "British Commissioner," 8 Sept 66, 3; "H. B. M. Acting Commissioner," 6 May 65, 2; "Passengers," 1 Dec 66, 2; Kuykendall 1953, 206, 209, 291 n. 40; *L1*, 335 n. 2, 343 n. 4).

465.3–4 whose population falls absolutely short of sixty thousand souls] The 1866 census reported a population of 62,959, of whom 58,765 were native Hawaiians (Bennett, 59; see also the note at 454.11–13).

466.2–4 the King's sister, her Royal Highness the Princess Victoria . . . had lain in state at the palace *thirty days*] Princess Victoria Kamamalu Kaahumanu (1838–66) was the sister of Kamehameha IV and Kamehameha V, and the granddaughter and last female descendant of Kamehameha I. Since her brother Kamehameha V was unmarried, Victoria was heir apparent to the Hawaiian throne. She died on 29 May 1866 and, according to native custom, her body lay in state for one month before the funeral on 30 June 1866. Clemens was touring the island of Hawaii when Victoria died, but returned to Oahu in time to witness the elaborate funeral ceremonies. He devoted three of his *Union* letters to a description of these ceremonies and to a discussion of local politics, which had been thrown into "a state of unusual stir" as a result of Victoria's untimely death (SLC 1866x, 1866z–aa; "Death of the Heir Apparent," Honolulu *Pacific Commercial Advertiser,* 2 June 66, 2).

466.15–473.3 After . . . missionaries.] Mark Twain based this portion of the text on his letter in the Sacramento *Union* for 1 August 1866, revising it for inclusion in *Roughing It* (SLC 1866aa). That letter included the text of the funeral program (466.19–468.3), probably typeset from a clipping of the Honolulu *Pacific Commercial Advertiser* for 30 June 1866 ("Programme of the Funeral," 2). The *Union* letter also included the two lengthy quotations on the death of Kamehameha from Jarves's *History:* see the notes at 469.30–470.5 and 470.11–472.43.

466.27 Governor of Oahu] John Dominis (see the note at 464.32).

467.4–5 His Lordship Louis Maigret, the Rt. Rev. Bishop . . . of the Hawaiian Islands] Louis Désiré Maigret (1804–82), who arrived in the Sandwich Islands in 1840, headed the French Roman Catholic mission there from his cathedral of Our Lady of Peace in Honolulu. A notebook entry that Clemens made in late June 1866 suggests that he visited the cathedral (*N&J1,* 118). In contrast to his critical portrait of Bishop Staley, Clemens praised Maigret as "a leader of distinguished ability" in his *Union* letter published on 30 July (SLC 1866z; Kuykendall 1938, 150–52, 341–42; Korn, 324; "Death of Bishop Maigret," *Friend* 31 [1 July 82]: 67).

467.7 His Lordship the Right Reverend Bishop of Honolulu] Bishop Staley (see the note at 464.22–28). The *Advertiser* reported that Staley "appropriated" the position next to the hearse, which custom assigned not to him but to the "officiating clergyman." The paper claimed that Staley's "bigoted conduct" provoked "an intense feeling of disgust," reporting that "he would not walk side by side with the American Protestant Missionaries, but thrust himself above them, and above the Roman Catholic Bishop, all of whom have been longer upon the Islands, and have a greater influence than he has or ever will have among the people" (Honolulu *Pacific Commercial Advertiser:* "Funeral of the Princess Victoria" and "Side by Side," 7 July 66, 3).

467.9 Her Majesty Queen Emma's Carriage] Queen Emma—Emma Naea Rooke (1836–85), the widow of Kamehameha IV, sister-in-law of Kamehameha V, granddaughter of John Young (see the note at 471.7), and great granddaughter of the younger brother of Kamehameha I—was not in this carriage and did not attend the funeral. She had sailed for England in May 1865 for an extended visit and would not return until October 1866, after spending several weeks in the United States. Gracious, kindhearted, and highly cultivated, the popular Queen Emma had been known during her reign for her pro-British feelings and her promotion of the Hawaiian Reformed Catholic Church (*N&J1*, 220; Kuykendall 1953, 35, 78, 83–98 passim, 202–5).

467.12 Her Majesty the Queen Dowager] Queen Kalama (1817–70), widow of Kamehameha III ("Death of Her Majesty the Dowager Queen Kalama," Honolulu *Pacific Commercial Advertiser*, 24 Sept 70, 2).

467.13 The King's Chancellor] Elisha Hunt Allen (1804–83) was appointed United States consul to the Sandwich Islands in 1849 and joined the Hawaiian government in 1853, serving first as minister of finance. In 1857 he was appointed chief justice and chancellor. Over the next two decades he distinguished himself in diplomatic missions for the Hawaiian government, successfully negotiating the 1876 treaty of reciprocity with the United States. After 1876 he served as Hawaiian minister in Washington, D.C.

467.15–17 His Excellency the Minister Resident of the United States. H. I. M.'s Commissioner. H. B. M.'s Acting Commissioner] These three men were identified by name in the *Advertiser*'s printed program—and in Mark Twain's *Union* letter—as "James McBride," "Mons. Desnoyers," and "W. L. Green" (see the note at 464.35–38).

467.29 Ahahui Kaahumanu] "The 'Ahahui Kaahumanu'—a benevolent society instituted (and presided over) by the late Princess for the nursing of the sick and the burial of the dead—was numerously represented. It is composed solely of native women. They were dressed in black, and wore sashes of different colors" (SLC 1866aa).

468.11 Burlingame] Anson Burlingame (see the note at 371.10–13), the United States minister to China (1861–67), arrived in Honolulu on 18 June en route to China. During his three-week stopover he developed a warm friendship with Clemens and helped him secure and conduct an interview with the survivors of the *Hornet* sea disaster—a journalistic scoop that Mark Twain reported in a *Union* letter published on 19 July (SLC 1866y; *L1*, 348 n. 1).

468.11 Gen. Van Valkenburgh] Robert Bruce Van Valkenburgh (1821–88), the recently appointed United States minister to Japan, was stopping over in Honolulu until 7 July on his way to his diplomatic post. A two-term congressman from New York State (1861–65), he had also served as a brigadier-general in the New York militia and commanded a regiment of New York volunteers at Antietam. He served in Japan until November 1869, and was later an associate justice of the Florida Supreme Court.

469.30–470.5 On . . . execrations.] Mark Twain's source for this extract was the third edition of Jarves's *History* (Jarves 1847, 105; see the note at 443.26).

469.34 not only great, but good] The first and second editions of Jarves's *History* include a passage at this point comparing Kamehameha I to Napoleon, which does not appear in the book's third edition (the one Mark Twain consulted and quoted in writing *Roughing It*): "He may be justly styled the Napoleon of the Pacific. Without the worst traits of his prototype, he possessed, according to the situation he occupied, equal military skill, as vigorous an intellect, and as keen a judgment, as his illustrious cotemporary" (Jarves 1843, 188; Jarves 1844b, 206). Mark Twain makes a similar comparison in chapter 64 (440.36), which suggests that he had seen an earlier edition of the *History*. In 1884 he owned a copy of the second edition, but he almost certainly acquired it after the publication of *Roughing It* (Jarves 1847, 105; Gribben, 1:352; *N&J1*, 104–5).

469.43–470.3 The bones of Kamehameha . . . were so carefully concealed . . . they made fish-hooks and arrows of them] Clemens recorded in his notebook in April 1866: "Kammy's bones hidden at his own request, to keep them from making fish hooks of them—a superstition that hooks made of the bones of a great Chief would concentrate the fish" (*N&J1*, 230). In "A Strange Dream," probably written in April 1866, Mark Twain recounted an imaginary trip to Kilauea crater to search for the great chief's bones, which have never been found (SLC 1866t).

470.6–10 The account . . . written by the native historians . . . is the most comprehensive document I have yet met with] Mark Twain refers to *Ka Mooolelo Hawaii*, an 1838 history of the Sandwich Islands "written by scholars at [a Hawaiian] High school, and corrected by one of the instructors" (Malo et al., 58). Most of this history appeared for the first time in translation in 1839 in the second volume of the *Hawaiian Spectator*, a quarterly review published in Honolulu from January 1838 to October 1839 ("A Catalogue of Works Relating to the Hawaiian or Sandwich Islands," *Friend* 11 [1 May 62]: 38). Mark Twain's introductory remarks are a paraphrase of Jarves's own introduction to the extract that follows: see the next note.

470.11–472.43 When . . . abuse.] Mark Twain's source for this extract was the third edition of Jarves's *History* (Jarves 1847, 105–6; see the note at 443.26). Jarves's source, in turn, was the April 1839 *Hawaiian Spectator* (Malo et al., 227–31).

470.15 Kukailimoku] This was Kamehameha I's "favorite war god," represented "by images of wicker-work, covered with red feathers, with eyes made of mother-of-pearl," and a wide gaping mouth "armed with sharks' teeth" (Jarves 1847, 29–30; W. D. Alexander, 41).

470.23 his son, Liholiho] Kamehameha I's heir, who ruled as Kamehameha II: see the note at 496.23–498.23.

471.6 Kaikioewa] A chief (d. 1839) who served as guardian of Prince Kauikeaouli (later Kamehameha III) during his minority and became governor of Kauai in 1824 (Dibble 1843, 199, 231–32; Kuykendall 1938, 118).

471.7 your foreigner] John Young (1742–1835), an English sailor who arrived in the Sandwich Islands in 1790 as boatswain of the American vessel *Eleanora.* Young—along with another English seaman, Isaac Davis (d. 1810) of the *Fair American*—was detained by Kamehameha I as a result of violence between the foreigners and the natives. The two Englishmen became trusted advisers to the king. Young served as governor of the island of Hawaii from 1802 to 1812, and through his marriage to one of the king's nieces became a member of the royal family (Kuykendall 1938, 24–25, 43–44, 54; Withington, 72–73; Scott, 887).

471.8 Kaahumanu] The favorite wife (1768?–1832) of Kamehameha I and a descendant of the chiefs of Maui. In 1819, when Kamehameha's son Liholiho became Kamehameha II, Kaahumanu assumed the position of *kuhina nui,* or chief adviser, in effect governing jointly with him. This position had been created for her by Kamehameha I, who did not want his successor to rule alone. After Liholiho's departure for England in 1823 (see the note at 496.23–498.23) Kaahumanu served as regent, continuing this role during the minority of Kamehameha III until her death. The beautiful and imperious Kaahumanu was a major force behind the overthrow of the tabu system in November 1819 (described in chapter 72, at 496.25–497.4). After 1821 she reversed her initially unfriendly attitude toward the Protestant missionaries, becoming a vigorous supporter of their educational, social, and moral reforms (Kuykendall 1938, 63–64, 67–68, 77–78, 106, 114; Bingham, 148–49, 164–65; Bradley, 141–44, 173, 190–93, 211–13; Kamakau, 306–23).

471.12 Hoapili] The chief Ulumeheihei (1767?–1840) was given the name "Hoapili," or "close adhering companion," by Kamehameha I, "from the friendship which existed between the old king and himself" (Jarves 1847, 108). It was Hoapili who successfully concealed the king's bones. He married Keopuolani and Kalakua, two of Kamehameha's widows. From 1823 until his death he served as governor of Maui (Judd, 41–42 n. 42; Jarves 1847, 119, 122).

471.23 Leleiohoku] One of Kalaimoku's sons (1826–48) (see the next note). At an early age he married Nahienaena, one of Kamehameha I's daughters, and later married the high chiefess Ruth Keelikolani. He was governor of the island of Hawaii from 1844 until his death at age twenty-two. The first part of his name, "Leleio," means "to die quickly" or suddenly, and "hoku" means "night of the full moon," a reference to Kamehameha's decease "on the night of Hoku, May (Ka'elo) 14 according to the Oahu calendar" (Kamakau, 212; Andrews, 336; Pukui and Elbert, 71; Zambucka 1977, 21).

471.24 Kalaimoku] Kamehameha I's trusted prime minister and treasurer (d. 1827), also known as Kalanimoku or Karaimoku. He adopted the name of one of his contemporaries, the great English prime minister William Pitt, and was often so addressed. He continued as prime minister in the reign of Kamehameha II (1819–24), and in the early years of the reign of Kamehameha III. During his long service, he was second in power (under the king's ultimate authority) only to Kaahumanu, the *kuhina nui* and regent (Kuykendall 1938, 53, 64, 431–32).

471n.3–6 †This . . . would certainly have been cannibalism if they had cooked him] This footnote misrepresents the view of Sandwich Islands historians. Jarves observed:

> Some doubt formerly existed, whether cannibalism ever prevailed in the group. The natives themselves manifested a degree of shame, horror and confusion, when questioned upon the subject, that led Cook and his associates, without any direct evidence of the fact, to believe in its existence; but later voyagers disputed this conclusion. The confessions of their own historians, and the general acknowledgment of the common people, have now established it beyond a doubt. (Jarves 1847, 49)

Mark Twain often treated the subject of cannibalism humorously during this period—for example, in two items about Honolulu publisher Henry Whitney, in his Sandwich Islands lecture, in the sketch "Cannibalism in the Cars," and in an 1870 Buffalo *Express* piece, "Dining with a Cannibal" (SLC 1866mm, 1870n, 884; Fatout 1976, 10; *MTH*, 144–45; SLC 1868i, 1870c).

472.12–14 Kau . . . Kohala . . . Kona] Kamehameha I died at his home, Kamakahonu, in the village of Kailua, Kona district. Kona is on the west side of the island of Hawaii, between the districts of Kohala to the north and Ka'u to the south. Kau is in the Ka'u district (Pukui, Elbert, and Mookini, 80, 91, 114).

472.39–40 Keeaumoku, Kaahumanu's brother] Keeaumoku (d. 1824), a high chief of the Maui royal line, was a trusted counselor to Kamehameha I, like his father of the same name. He served as governor of both Maui and Kauai (Kuykendall 1938, 53; Withington, 134–36; Jarves 1847, 108, 123).

473.7–15 Forty years ago . . . both sexes gave themselves up to . . . licentiousness] This paragraph summarizes a passage in Jarves's *History,* which Mark Twain quoted in full in his Sacramento *Union* letter published on 16 July 1866 (Jarves 1847, 40; SLC 1866x).

475.1–480.2 Bound . . . fruit.] Mark Twain based this portion of the text on his letter in the Sacramento *Union* of 18 August 1866, revising it for inclusion in *Roughing It* (SLC 1866bb).

475.3–5 we sailed from Honolulu . . . in the good schooner Boomerang] Clemens sailed for the island of Hawaii on Saturday, 26 May, aboard the schooner *Emeline*, and returned to Honolulu three weeks later. The *Roughing It* account somewhat skews the chronology of Clemens's Sandwich Islands sojourn. His attendance at the funeral of Princess Victoria on 30 June, described in chapter 68, actually followed his trip to Hawaii; and his trip to Maui, mentioned briefly in chapters 76 and 77, in fact preceded the Hawaii trip (*N&J1*, 101; Honolulu *Pacific Commercial Advertiser:* "Departures," 2 June 66, 2; "Passengers," 16 June 66, 2).

475.11–12 the captain and my comrade (a Mr. Billings)] The *Emeline*'s skipper was Captain Crane, not further identified. Mark Twain altered his traveling companion's name from "Brown" to "Billings" when revising his 18 August *Union* letter; see the note at 447.31 ("Departures," Honolulu *Pacific Commercial Advertiser*, 2 June 66, 2; SLC 1866bb, 1866gg).

475.30–476.1 Balaam's ass] Numbers 22:21–33.

478.2 Billings's white upturned face] In revising his 18 August *Union* letter Mark Twain deleted a passage beginning here in which he made clear that Brown/Billings was lying seasick on the deck (SLC 1866bb).

478.5–8 Hualalai . . . being only ten thousand feet high . . . Mauna Loa is said to be sixteen thousand feet high] Modern measurements give elevations of 8,276 and 13,680 feet, respectively, for Hualalai and Mauna Loa. In his 18 August *Union* letter, Mark Twain gave Mauna Loa's elevation more accurately as 14,000 feet, then apparently revised the figure upward for *Roughing It*. The sources for his rather high figures are not known for certain, but two possibilities have been identified. James D. Dana of the 1838–42 United States Exploring Expedition (see the note at 523.30–31) estimated the elevation of Hualalai as "not far from 10,000 feet" (Dana, 156), a figure echoed by Rufus Anderson in *The Hawaiian Islands: Their Progress and Condition under Missionary Labors*, a book that Clemens is known to have consulted (he quoted a passage from it, without specific attribution, in his *Union* letter published on 24 August). Captain James King, in the final volume of Cook's *Voyage to the Pacific Ocean* (1784), reported Mauna Loa to be "at least 16,020 feet high" (Cook and King, 3:103; SLC 1866bb–cc; Rufus Anderson, 128).

478.22–24 we . . . went ashore at Kailua, designing to . . . rejoin the vessel at a point some leagues distant] On 28 May Clemens, apparently accompanied by another passenger on the *Emeline*, went ashore at the village of Kailua, in the Kona district on the west shore of Hawaii. They rode overland on horseback about fifteen miles to Kealakekua Bay, south of Kailua, reboarding the *Emeline* there around midnight. The *Roughing It* account of this journey omits many details found in Mark Twain's *Union* letters published on 18, 24, and 30 August (*MTH*, 62; SLC 1866bb–cc, 1866ee).

480.3–24 At . . . required.] Mark Twain based this portion of the text on the first half of his letter in the Sacramento *Union* of 24 August 1866, revising it for inclusion in *Roughing It;* he reserved the second half for use in chapter 71 (SLC 1866cc; see the note at 489.1–491.24).

480.11–24 We passed several sugar plantations . . . no irrigation whatever is required] Mark Twain confined his remarks in *Roughing It* on the subject of the islands' sugar production to this paragraph. He made no use of his *Union* letter published on 26 September, which—possibly at the behest of the *Union*—was largely devoted to the subject. Many years later he asserted, "Circumstance and the Sacramento *Union* sent me to the Sandwich Islands for five or six months, to write up sugar. I did it; and threw in a good deal of extraneous matter that hadn't anything to do with sugar" (SLC 1910, 1866hh).

481.1 We stopped some time at one of the plantations] This may have been the Kona plantation of Thomas Lack, possibly also the place where the travelers ate the "large peaches of excellent flavor" (480.3) (*MTH*, 20, 63–64).

482.15–19 that bloody and distressful war over there in Italy . . . battle of Sadowa] In the Austro-Prussian (or Seven Weeks') War of 1866, Prussian forces decisively defeated Austrian troops on 3 July 1866 near the Bohemian town of Sadowa. In subsequent peace treaties Austria agreed to the creation of the North German Confederation under the leadership of Prince Otto von Bismarck and ceded Venetia to Italy, a Prussian ally. This Prussian success set the stage for the Franco-Prussian War of 1870–71 and the complete unification of Germany.

483.7–8 She desired me to confer with Mr. Greeley about turnips] Horace Greeley (see the note at 131.12), an enthusiastic amateur farmer at his home in Chappaqua, New York, aired his views on agriculture in speeches, books, and the columns of the New York *Tribune.* "It became the fashion for critics and fun makers to jibe at Greeley's farming efforts, and the Chappaqua wood chopper was made the butt of much merriment" (Van Deusen, 147). In 1868, in a humorous but fundamentally respectful sketch of Greeley entitled "Private Habits of Horace Greeley," Mark Twain wrote that every day before a late breakfast Greeley

> goes out into his model garden, and applies his vast store of agricultural knowledge to the amelioration of his cabbages; after which he writes an able agricul-

tural article for the instruction of American farmers, his soul cheered the while with the reflection that if cabbages were worth eleven dollars apiece his model farm would pay. (SLC 1868j)

An 1870 *Tribune* series of Greeley's essays, entitled "What I Know of Farming," was collected in a book of the same name (Greeley 1871). In mid-April 1871 Greeley gave Clemens a copy inscribed as follows: "To Mark Twain, Esq., Ed. Buffalo Express who knows even less of MY farming than does Horace Greeley. N. York" (Anderson, lot 204); a slightly different version of the inscription was quoted in "H. G. as a Joker," Buffalo *Courier*, 21 Apr 71, 1).

484.17 I could not read it readily] Greeley's hand was notoriously illegible: "No doubt the 'worm fence' handwriting was difficult for a stranger to decipher, but *Tribune* printers and proofreaders were familiar with it. Others compared it to gridirons struck by lightning" (Stoddard, 140, facsimile facing 241). The newspapers of the day frequently printed jokes about the difficulty of reading Greeley's handwriting. In May 1871, for example, the following anecdote appeared in the Boston *Post:*

Greeley wrote a letter to the Iowa Press Association, in which he said: "I have hominy, carrots and R. R. ties more than I could move with eight steers. If eels are blighted, dig them early. Any insinuation that brick ovens are dangerous to hams, gives me the horrors. GREELEY." That is, they read it so. They have since learned what he meant to say was: "I find so many cares and duties pressing upon me, that with the weight of years I feel obliged to decline nearly every invitation that takes me over a day's journey from home. Yours among them. HORACE GREELEY." ("Varieties," Buffalo *Express*, 10 May 71, 2, reprinting the Boston *Post*)

Mark Twain himself had commented on Greeley's penmanship in "Private Habits of Horace Greeley" and in a Buffalo *Express* column of 4 September 1869. He may have been further inspired by the facsimile of Greeley's hand published in Richardson's *Beyond the Mississippi* (SLC 1868j, 1869h; Richardson, 163–64). In any event, the immediate occasion for the illustration on page 485 (possibly engraved from a drawing by Mark Twain himself), and its accompanying "transcriptions," was undoubtedly a letter that Greeley wrote to Clemens on 7 May 1871, presumably in response to a letter from Clemens (now lost) thanking Greeley for the gift of his book (see the previous note). Greeley's letter is reproduced in supplement C.

489.1–491.24 At . . . retaliation.] Mark Twain based this portion of the text on the second half of his letter in the Sacramento *Union* of 24 August 1866, revising it for inclusion in *Roughing It;* he used the beginning of this letter in chapter 69 (SLC 1866cc; see the note at 480.3–24).

490.22 the great god Lono] Lono was one of the four major Hawaiian male deities. Associated with clouds and storms, he was worshiped as the god of fertility. Hawaiian tradition merges the god Lono with an ancient chief of the same name, who for a time lived at Kealakekua long before Captain Cook's arrival. Chapter 72 (495.15–496.11) contains Mark Twain's summary of Lono's legendary history (Beckwith, 31–41; Kuykendall 1938, 7–8; Kamakau, 61).

490.39–491.24 Plain unvarnished history . . . justifiable homicide . . . proportionate retaliation] Mark Twain's assessment of Captain Cook's relations with the Sandwich Islands natives was clearly influenced by Jarves's account in his *History.* "While it is not my desire to detract from the fame lawfully [Cook's] due," wrote Jarves, "yet I cannot, with his biographers, gloss over the events which occurred at the Hawaiian Islands" (Jarves 1847, 68). Jarves—in language somewhat less emphatic than Clemens's—points out Cook's intemperate and high-handed behavior, and his abuse of the deference accorded him by the worshipful Hawaiians. The foremost contemporary British accounts of Cook's actions were by James King, Cook's lieutenant, and by John Ledyard, a marine corporal on Cook's flagship, the *Resolution.* Jarves found Ledyard's account, the more critical of the two, to be substantiated by the account of native historians (Jarves 1847, 65–70; Cook and King, 3:25–82; Ledyard, 143–55; Malo et al., 64–67).

491.11–12 "He groans!—he is not a god!"] Mark Twain encountered this detail of Cook's death struggle, though not these words, in Jarves's *History,* which quotes the account of native historians. He found the remark quoted here either in Sheldon Dibble's *History of the Sandwich Islands,* where it first appeared, or in Henry T. Cheever's *Life in the Sandwich Islands* (Malo et al., 66; Jarves 1847, 68; Dibble 1843, 39; Cheever 1851b, 24).

491.13–18 His flesh was stripped from the bones and burned . . . Some of Cook's bones were . . . consigned to the deep] The natives' treatment of Cook's remains was the customary one accorded a dead king. Mark Twain probably learned most of the particulars from Jarves, who repeats and affirms the account of native historians. Jarves, however, does not report the detail about the survival of one child to be "a very old man," which can be found in Dibble's *History* and in Cheever's *Life* (Kuykendall 1938, 19; Malo, 141–43; Jarves 1847, 68–70; Dibble 1843, 39; Cheever 1851b, 24).

491.25–492.20 Near . . . innocent.] Mark Twain based this portion of the text on his letter in the Sacramento *Union* of 30 August 1866, revising it for inclusion in *Roughing It* (SLC 1866ee).

493.1–495.14 IN . . . point.] Mark Twain based this portion of the text on his letter in the Sacramento *Union* for 6 September 1866, revising it for inclusion in *Roughing It* (SLC 1866ff).

493.1–2 we went ashore and visited the ruined temple of the lost god Lono] Clemens visited the ruins of Hikiau temple, which had once housed the red-draped image of Lono. In his *Union* letter published on 6 September he noted that it was the very temple "so desecrated by Captain Cook. . . . Its low, rude walls look about as they did when he saw them, no doubt" (SLC 1866ff). Cook desecrated the temple—apparently with the acquiescence of the temple priests, who believed him to be the returned Lono—by carrying off the wooden railings and the idols of the lesser gods for use as firewood on his ship (Kamakau, 99; Kuykendall 1938, 16; Cook and King, 3:6–8, 25–26; *MTH*, 67).

493.4–10 Obookiah . . . was taken to New England . . . This resulted in the sending of missionaries there] The orphaned Henry Obookiah, also known as Opukahaia (1792?–1818), took passage—along with two other Hawaiian youths, William Kanui (see the note at 493.22–28) and Thomas Hopu—aboard the merchant ship of Captain Caleb Brintnal and arrived in New Haven, Connecticut, in 1809. There Obookiah was tutored by Edwin Welles Dwight (1789–1841) of Yale College, became a Christian, and actively encouraged the creation of a mission to the Sandwich Islands. Obookiah died of typhus at age twenty-six while a student at the newly created Foreign Mission School in Cornwall, Connecticut. His story, incorporated into Dwight's much-reprinted *Memoirs of Henry Obookiah, a Native of Owhyhee,* became a staple of missionary literature and influenced the decision to send the first missionaries to the islands in 1819 (Dwight, 3–129; Rufus Anderson, 46–48; Bradford Smith, 21–25; Bradley, 123–24; Boothby, 53–54).

493.11–12 savage who sat down on the church steps and wept because his people did not have the Bible] According to Anderson's history of missionary labors in the Sandwich Islands, Obookiah "was one day found sitting on the doorsteps of one of [the Yale College] buildings, weeping because the treasures of knowledge were open to others, but were not open to him. Mr. Edwin W. Dwight, who saw him thus, had compassion on him, and became his religious teacher" (Rufus Anderson, 46). Obookiah's own memoir makes no mention of such an encounter (Dwight, 18–20). Mark Twain's version of the story may derive from an unidentified source.

493.20–21 The other native youths made the voyage] The first missionary group, dispatched to the Sandwich Islands in October 1819, included three Hawaiian youths educated at the Foreign Mission School: William Kanui, Thomas Hopu, and John Honolii (Rufus Anderson, 46–49).

493.22–28 William Kanui, fell from grace . . . went to mining . . . was a bankrupt . . . died in Honolulu in 1864] Mark Twain learned these facts about William Kanui (1798?–1864) from an obituary notice in the February 1864 issue of the *Friend,* which he quoted and cited in the *Union* letter on which this passage is based (SLC 1866ff). Kanui lost his money in 1855, when the San Francisco bank of Page, Bacon and Company suspended operations on 22 February and closed its doors permanently on 2 May.

> [Kanui] then, being obliged to exert himself for a livelihood, opened a boot-blacking stand, and continued it for some time. But sad to relate, in his religious interests he became quite reckless, and continued for a long time in a back-slidden state. ("William Kanui Still Alive," report dated 20 June 1860 from San Francisco, *Friend* 10 [1 Feb 61]: 13)

Kanui's piety subsequently revived, and during his last years he "labored in San Francisco, and was connected with the Bethel Church of that city" ("Died," *Friend* 13 [5 Feb 64]: 16; Rufus Anderson, 48–49 n. 1; Bradford Smith, 24, 58–59, 288; San Francisco *Alta California:* "The Crisis Past," 23 Feb 55, 2; "Commercial," 3 May 55, 2).

494.21–495.14 At noon I observed a bevy of nude native young ladies . . . I will not urge this point] Mark Twain wrote this paragraph on the swimming prowess of the Hawaiians expressly for *Roughing It,* to replace a comic passage in his 6 September *Union* letter in which he claimed he "undressed and went in myself" (SLC 1866ff).

495.15–506.4 I have . . . charge.] Mark Twain based this portion of the text on his letter in the Sacramento *Union* of 22 September 1866, revising it for inclusion in *Roughing It* (SLC 1866gg).

495.17–496.7 The idol . . . was a slender, unornamented staff . . . he . . . sailed for foreign lands on a three-cornered raft] Mark Twain's description of the Lono idol and legend was apparently summarized from Jarves's *History* (Jarves 1847, 27–28).

495.25 "on the shoulder;"] That is, looking for a fight. See Scotty Briggs's description of Buck Fanshaw in chapter 47 (312.21–29).

496.5–6 he instituted games called makahiki, and ordered that they should be held in his honor] According to Jarves, Lono instituted the games to commemorate his wife's death. The makahiki season, which corresponded to the rainy months from roughly October through January, was sacred to Lono. During this time the chiefs gathered taxes and eschewed war, and on certain festival days all labor and the usual religious practices were prohibited while everyone enjoyed feasting, sports, and other recreation (Jarves 1847, 28; Malo, 186, 189–91; Kamakau, 180–81; Kuykendall 1938, 7–8; Beckwith, 33–35).

496.16 the place where the last battle was fought for idolatry] Kuamoo: see the note at 498.3–15.

496.23–498.23 his son, Liholiho, the new King . . . the gospel was planted as in a virgin soil] Mark Twain's primary source for the information in this passage was probably Jarves's *History* (Jarves 1847, 109–11). Liholiho (1797–1824) was the son of Kamehameha I and the chiefess Keopuolani. He was strictly raised by his parents and priests to prepare him for succession to the throne. His reign as Kamehameha II, from 1819 to 1824, was notable for the abolition of the tabu system, the arrival of the American missionaries, the growth of the sandalwood trade and the whaling industry, and the removal of the seat of government from Kailua to Honolulu. Liholiho shared his father's pro-British attitude, and in 1823–24 he visited England, accompanied by his wife Kamamalu and an official entourage. Kamamalu died of the measles in London in July 1824, and Liholiho followed her in death within a week. The other members of the royal party, however, were able to accomplish the king's mission—to confirm Hawaii as a protectorate of Great Britain (Kuykendall 1938, 71–81).

496.29–30 Kaahumanu had a whole mind to badger him into doing it] Liholiho was urged by two women to indulge in traditionally forbidden "free eating": Keopuolani, his mother, and Kaahumanu, his *kuhina nui* (see the note at 471.8). For some time both women had ignored certain eating tabus without suffering any ill consequences. Liholiho's decision to follow their example was all the harder because as a child he had been carefully instructed in the tabu rites of the priestly order, and because tradition held that only a chief who respected the ancient tabus, like Kamehameha I, would have a long reign (Kuykendall 1938, 67–68; Kamakau, 222–23).

496.32 Liholiho came up to Kailua as drunk as a piper] The feast at Kailua took place during the first week of November 1819, six months after the death of Kamehameha I (Kuykendall 1938, 68). According to Jarves, Kaahumanu

> sent word to the king, that upon his arrival at Kailua, she should cast aside his god. To this he made no objection, but with his retainers pushed off in canoes from the shore, and remained on the water for two days, indulging in a drunken revel. Kaahumanu despatched a double canoe for him, in which he was brought to Kailua. (Jarves 1847, 109)

498.3–15 They raised a revolt . . . idolatry and the *tabu* were dead in the land] Kamehameha II's forces, commanded by the prime minister, Kalaimoku (see the note at 471.24), met the opposing force, under Kekuokalani (or Kekuaokalani), at Kuamoo on or about 20 December 1819. Kekuokalani, an ambitious chief who clung to the traditional ways, was Liholiho's cousin, a son of Kamehameha I's brother. He was killed at Kuamoo and his forces were routed. Other minor uprisings by disaffected traditionalists were quickly put down by Liholiho's forces (Jarves 1847, 109–10; Malo et al., 337–40; W. D. Alexander, 170–71; Kuykendall 1938, 69).

498.21 The missionary ship arrived in safety shortly afterward] The first missionary party, comprising seventeen adults and their children, left Boston in the brig *Thaddeus* in October 1819 and arrived on the west coast of the island of Hawaii on 30 March 1820 (Bingham, 69; Kuykendall 1938, 102).

499.2 Honaunau] Honaunau is south of Kealakekua Bay on the western coast of the island of Hawaii.

499.21 Billings] See the note at 475.11–12.

501.25–29 the ancient City of Refuge . . . whose stone walls were twenty feet thick . . . a thousand and forty feet one way . . . seven hundred the other] The City of Refuge was built for Keawe (or Keave), a sixteenth-century chief. In 1823 William Ellis found its ruins to be 715×404 feet, with walls 15 feet thick and 12 feet high. Subsequent works about Hawaii accepted Ellis's dimensions as authoritative (Ellis, 157; Jarves 1847, 34; Cheever 1851b, 42; Rufus Anderson, 151). No source has been found for Mark Twain's figures.

503.17 How did they transport and how raise them?] This remark echoes previous descriptions of the site in the works of Ellis, Jarves, and Cheever. Cheever's description of the wall of rock apparently derived from Ellis's earlier account: "There are fragments of lava in these walls that must be of two or more tons weight each, six or eight feet above the ground, which it is difficult to imagine how Hawaiians could have raised (as they must) without machinery, by the mere force of the unassisted human hands" (Cheever 1851b, 42; Ellis, 157; Jarves 1847, 34).

503.26–504.2 a sort of coffin-shaped stone . . . When he stretched . . . on his lounge, his legs hung down over the end] This passage may have been inspired by a description written by S. S. Hill, an earlier visitor to the site:

> Our guide pointed out to us a block of hewn lava, that we judged to be about thirteen feet in length, which was preserved in remembrance of an ancient chief, who is said to have been of the length of the block when lying with outstretched arms upon its surface. If this be no exaggeration, the chief must have been of enormous dimensions indeed. (S. S. Hill, 185)

504.4–505.27 a monstrous seven-ton rock . . . a congealed cascade of lava . . . several cavernous tunnels] Similar accounts of these features have been found in works with which Mark Twain was probably familiar (Ellis, 160–63; Rufus Anderson, 151, 152).

507.1–4 WE . . . sailed down to Kau . . . Next day we bought horses and bent our way . . . toward the great volcano of Kilauea] From Kealakekua Bay the *Emeline* sailed south down the western coast of Hawaii on Wednesday, 30 May. Rough weather forced the schooner to tack far out to sea in order to round the treacherous southern point of the island. The *Emeline* was finally able to anchor at Kaalualu, a port on the southeast coast of Hawaii in the Kau district, on Friday, 1 June. Clemens rode on horseback six miles inland to the village of Waiohinu, where he purchased a mule for the forty-mile trip to Kilauea crater on the slopes of Mauna Loa, which occupied the better part of two days, 2 and 3 June (*MTH*, 69, 71–72; SLC 1866nn).

507.14 I have seen Vesuvius since] Clemens ascended Vesuvius, on the eastern shore of the Bay of Naples, in August 1867 with a party from the *Quaker City.* In his description of that ascent, in chapters 29 and 30 of *The Innocents Abroad,* he stated that "the Vesuvius of to-day is a very poor affair compared to the mighty volcano of Kilauea, in the Sandwich Islands" (SLC 1869a, 325; *L2,* 78).

507.20–21 nine hundred feet deep in some places, thirteen hundred in others . . . and *ten miles in circumference*] At the time of Clemens's visit, the crater was probably closer to four hundred feet in depth, considerably less than it had been in former years before successive lava flows raised its floor. Its circumference was accurately established in 1864 as eight and a half miles. Mark Twain could have obtained his figures on Kilauea's depth and circumference from any of several published sources, and may have been unaware that they did not reflect the configuration of the ever-changing crater in mid-1866. No source has been found giving the exact figures reported here, but Mark Twain could have derived them from Cheever's *Island World,* which described the crater as "nine to fifteen hundred feet deep, and from nine to fifteen miles in circumference," or from an article in the *Friend* for February 1866 which stated that its "depth varies from 600 to 1,200 feet. . . . The circumference by trigonometry is more than 7½ miles, while to a pedestrian it is 10 miles" (Cheever 1851a, 285; Titus Coan 1866, 10; Ellis, 226; Charles Samuel Stewart, 313–14; Hitchcock, 203–6 and plates 29–31).

508.1–512.8 By . . . hotel.] Mark Twain based this portion of the text on his letter in the Sacramento *Union* for 16 November 1866, revising it for inclusion in *Roughing It* (SLC 1866pp). It is the last section of the book to be derived from a *Union* letter.

508.1 the Volcano House] Some form of rude shelter had existed at Kilauea's northern edge for as many as forty years before Clemens's 1866 visit. Accommodations improved dramatically in March 1866 when the Volcano House, a thatched hotel capable of sleeping twenty, opened at the site. Mark Twain concluded his final Sacramento *Union* letter with a compliment for the "neat, roomy, well furnished and well kept hotel," claiming that "the surprise of finding a good hotel in such an outlandish spot startled me considerably more than the volcano did" (SLC 1866pp). He stayed at the Volcano House for about four nights, enjoying his accommodations free of charge, as he told his mother and sister in a letter of 21 June 1866 (*L1,* 343–44; Olson, 15–16, 28–31; *MTH,* 72–74, 125–27).

508.19 "pillar of fire."] Exodus 13:21.

511.22–23 many years had elapsed since any visitor had seen such a splendid display] Between the cataclysmic eruptions of 1840 and 1868,

Kilauea experienced several periods of rather intense activity, although prior to 1866 it had been relatively quiet for about ten years. Significant eruptions began on 22 May 1866 and continued into August, creating "a series of discharges all over the surface of the crater" as well as several new lava lakes in the northern portion (Brigham, 410–27; "The Volcano in Eruption Again," Honolulu *Pacific Commercial Advertiser*, 9 June 66, 3; Hitchcock, 188–206).

511.26–27 the "Record Book" at the Volcano House] It had long been the custom for visitors to Kilauea to record their impressions and sign their names in a guest book. Lodgers at the Volcano House continued this custom in the hotel's register, which eventually grew to many volumes and contains valuable scientific observations as well as effusions from a wide range of visitors, both celebrated and obscure. Clemens's own entry of 7 June 1866 burlesqued some of the other visitors' typical remarks (Olson, 67–69; Volcano House Register; SLC 1866u).

512.7 Pele's furnaces] In Hawaiian mythology, the fearsome Pele was the goddess of volcanoes. She and her family of deities made their home in Halemaumau, a large lake of molten lava in the southern portion of Kilauea crater (W. D. Alexander, 38).

513.1–525.7 THE . . . always.] Chapters 75–76—which include Mark Twain's descriptions of his descent into Kilauea crater, his tour of the island of Hawaii on horseback, and his visit to Maui—were not based on 1866 *Union* letters. It is not known for certain whether Mark Twain wrote them in late 1866 or early 1867 when preparing his never-published Sandwich Islands manuscript— or in 1871, when composing *Roughing It*.

513.1–2 a visit to the bottom of the crater] During his Sandwich Islands sojourn Mark Twain had probably read one or more of the numerous published accounts of trips into the crater, but there is no clear evidence that he drew upon any of them when later writing his own version (see Ellis, 224–36; Charles S. Stewart, 308–13; Byron, 183–90; Wilkes, 4:130–38, 181–91; Cheever 1851a, 290–309; and Hill, 256–78).

513.14 Marlette] Charles W. Marlette of Jacksonville, Illinois, had arrived in Honolulu in September 1865 and by March 1866 had visited Kilauea at least four times. Mark Twain's correct recollection of his companion's name suggests that he might have relied on his notebook for early June, which is now lost, to refresh his memory (Volcano House Register, 63, 74; "Passengers," *Friend* 14 [2 Oct 65]: 80).

516.14–15 About 1840 it rent its overburdened stomach] This eruption of Kilauea began on 30 May 1840 and continued for three weeks.

516.17–22 The stream was *five miles broad* . . . fine print could be read at midnight] Mark Twain drew the figures in this passage (as well as the remark about the fishes at 517.9) from an account by the Reverend Titus Coan, a missionary stationed at Hilo, which was first published in the *Missionary Herald* of July 1841 and widely reprinted thereafter. He also quoted parts of this account in his Sandwich Islands lecture, which he wrote upon his return to San Francisco (Titus Coan 1841; SLC 1866kk; Fatout 1976, 12).

517.10–12 The earthquakes caused some loss of human life, and a prodigious tidal wave swept inland . . . drowning a number of natives] The 1840 eruption was attended by neither loss of life nor a tidal wave. Clemens may have had in mind the devastating volcanic and seismic activity of March–April 1868, vivid reports of which (in the San Francisco newspapers) had prompted him to inform his lecture agent on 12 May that he intended to "revamp my Sandwich Islands talk & put in this superb eruption 3 weeks ago" (*L1*, 216–17). The eruption was also described by Titus Munson Coan (son of Titus Coan) in the September 1868 issue of *Harper's New Monthly Magazine:* "At the same time with the earth eruption the sea receded far below the low-water-mark. Pausing a few seconds, as if gathering its power, it leaped upon the shore in a wave forty feet high, that swept every thing before it. . . . Nearly a hundred persons were drowned" (Titus Munson Coan, 557–58).

518.1–3 We rode horseback all around the island . . . We were more than a week making the trip] Clemens left Kilauea, probably on 7 June 1866, accompanied by Edward Tasker Howard (1844?–1918), an acquaintance made at the Volcano House. "Confound that island, I had a streak of fat & a streak of lean all over it," he told his family on 21 June; "got lost several times & had to sleep in huts with the natives & live like a dog" (*L1*, 344). From the volcano Clemens and Howard headed north to Hilo on the coast, then northward to Onomea, the Waipio valley, and finally across the island to the west coast port of Kawaihae. In Hilo, Clemens later mentioned, he stayed for three days with John H. Coney, sheriff of the island. Other evidence suggests that he may also have been the guest of blustery and profane Captain Thomas Spencer, a leading citizen of Hilo and owner of an extensive ship chandlery. At Onomea, six miles north of Hilo, Clemens and Howard stayed overnight at the sugar plantation of Stafford L. Austin, whose son, Franklin H. Austin, later wrote a detailed account of that memorable visit (*MTH*, 74–79; *L1*, 346 n. 9; *N&J1*, 133 n. 74; Whitney, 73; Austin, 202–3, 250–54). Howard, a New Yorker who had lived in San Francisco since 1864, returned to New York after his Sandwich Islands trip and became a partner in Howard and Company, a Broadway jewelry and silverware firm ("Edward Tasker Howard," New York *Times*, 9 Aug 1918, 11; advertisement, New York *Times*, 3 Oct 66, 3). "I don't think an enormous deal of Howard," Clemens later admitted to a Honolulu friend, though that's nothing against *him*, of course. Tastes differ, & 200 miles muleback in company is the next best thing to a sea-voyage to bring a man's worst points to the surface. Ned & I *like* each other, but we don't *love*, & we never did. I like to talk with him, & I buy little jewelry trifles there, but we don't embrace—I would as soon think of embracing a fish, or an icicle, or any other particularly cold and unemotional thing—say a dead stranger, for instance. (SLC to Albert Francis Judd, 20 Dec 70, PH in CtY-BR, in *MTH*, 467)

518.10 the whole duty of man] An allusion to a devotional work entitled *The Whole Duty of Man* (1658), whose authors may have included Richard Allestree and Bishop John Fall. Clemens mentioned it several times in his writing, usually with comic intent (Gribben, 1:21).

520.9–10 they had never drank that fluid in their lives] While returning to San Francisco in early August 1866, Clemens reminded himself in his notebook of the horses that "don't drink" (*N&J1*, 159). Walter Frear has suggested that Clemens saw these horses not in June, after visiting Kilauea, but in May during his horseback ride from Kailua to Kealakekua Bay in the Kona district (*MTH*, 64). For a discussion of the verb form "had drank," see the textual note.

520.30–31 I mark the circumstance with a white stone] Marking something with a white stone "has been understood, from classical times[,] as an expression for commemorating any piece of good fortune or any lucky day" (Hazlitt, 2:568).

520.35–37 We returned to Honolulu, and from thence sailed to the island of Maui, and spent several weeks there] Clemens and Howard embarked from Kawaihae on the interisland steamer *Kilauea*, reaching Honolulu on 16 June. As explained in the note at 475.3–5, Clemens's trip to Maui actually preceded his trip to Hawaii. He sailed from Honolulu to Maui in mid-April (perhaps aboard the *Mary Ellen* on 17 April) and returned to Honolulu aboard the schooner *Ka Moi* on 22 May, on which day he wrote to Mollie Clemens:

I have just got back from a sea voyage—from the beautiful island of Maui. I have spent 5 weeks there, riding backwards & forwards among the sugar plantations—looking up the splendid scenery & visiting the lofty crater of Haleakala. It has been a perfect jubilee to me in the way of pleasure. I have not written a single line, & have not once thought of business, or care, or human toil or trouble or sorrow or weariness. Few such months come in a lifetime. (*L1*, 341)

Clemens limited his remarks about Maui in the Sacramento *Union* to a discussion of its sugar plantations (SLC 1866hh; Honolulu *Pacific Commercial Advertiser:* "Passengers," 16 June 66, 2; "Departures," 21 Apr 66, 2; *N&J1*, 234; *MTH*, 55).

520.38–522.1 a romantic gorge there, called the Iao Valley] Clemens would long remember the scenic Iao Valley behind the coastal village of Wailuku, where he stayed for part of his Maui visit. In his 1898 sketch "My Platonic Sweetheart," published posthumously in 1912, he described himself and his "dream-sweetheart," Agnes, "lounging up the blossomy gorge called the Iao Valley" on the "darling island" of Maui. In that Edenlike setting Agnes dies when struck by a falling arrow from the bow of a Kanaka (SLC 1912).

522.28–31 We climbed a thousand feet up . . . and next day climbed the remaining nine thousand feet] Apparently Clemens made the ascent of Haleakala shortly after 26 April, accompanied by Warren Woods Kimball (1838–74) and William Cargill Kimball (1841–90) of New York, brothers who had been his fellow passengers on the *Ajax* (*L1*, 335–36; Kimball biographical information courtesy of Rodney C. Eaton).

523.11–12 an article in which Poe treated of this singular fraud] Edgar Allan Poe, in his 1844 story "The Balloon Hoax," explained that because the extent of the horizon visible to the balloonist is many times greater than the height of the balloon car, the horizon "would appear to be *on a level* with the car. But, as the point immediately beneath him seems, and is, at a great distance below him, it seems, of course, also, at a great distance below the horizon. Hence the impression of *concavity*" (Poe, 3:1080). This high-altitude optical illusion was also mentioned in at least four works that Clemens had perused during his Sandwich Islands sojourn (Hopkins, 28; Jarves 1844a, 226; Cheever 1851b, 112; Bates, 327).

523.26 The crater of Vesuvius, as I have before remarked, is a modest pit about a thousand feet deep] In chapter 74 Mark Twain estimated the depth of Vesuvius to be only "three hundred feet" (507.17), while in *The Innocents Abroad* he had placed it at "two hundred feet" (SLC 1869a, 323).

523.30–31 Commander Wilkes, U. S. N., . . . testifies that it is *twenty-seven miles in circumference*] Commander Charles Wilkes (1798–1877) was the leader of a United States naval expedition that in 1838–42 surveyed and charted the Antarctic coast, the islands of the Pacific Ocean, and the American northwest coast. He reported in his *Narrative of the United States Exploring Expedition* (1844) that several expedition members—himself not among them—visited Haleakala in February 1841, but he made no mention of the crater's circumference. The expedition's geologist claimed in his report, published in 1849, that one of the party who visited the crater estimated its circumference to be fifteen miles. A more accurate 1869 survey established it as eighteen to twenty miles. Mark Twain's source for the figure of twenty-seven miles is unknown; he may have derived it—as well as the measurement of its depth as "two thousand five hundred feet" (523.22)—from Cheever's *Life*, which described Haleakala as "a deep, wide pit, twenty-five or thirty miles in circumference, and two or three thousand feet deep" (Cheever 1851b, 110; Wilkes, 4:251, 270–73; Dana, 228; Whitney, 50–51).

524.21 the Last Man] An allusion to the poem "The Last Man" by Thomas Campbell (1777–1844), published in 1824. Mark Twain is echoing—perhaps unconsciously—Bates's description of his emotions on the summit of Haleakala:

> I seemed to stand on the portals of another world, or to cling, solitarily and sadly, to the wrecks of this, as if it were just emerging from the grave of a deluge. . . . Like CAMPBELL'S *"Last Man,"* surveying the wrecks that old Time had flung over the lap of earth's mightiest nations, I was alone on that naked summit. (Bates, 328)

526.1 one curious character in the island of Maui] The eccentric Francis A. Oudinot (1822?–71) of Lahaina, Maui, was a native of Kentucky. At the time of his arrival in the Sandwich Islands in 1851, he listed his occupation as "jeweler." Claiming descent from Charles Nicolas Oudinot (1767–1847), the famous marshal of Napoleon's forces, he celebrated French national holidays by dressing in a resplendent French uniform and carrying a French flag. Oudinot, alone among Lahaina's American population, was known to be a Southern sympathizer during the Civil War. He also had a reputation as a spinner of yarns. Harriet Baldwin Damon, a resident of Lahaina in her youth, recalled him:

> Oudinot, well known throughout the islands as something of a farmer, had wonderful stories to recount of the marvelous growth of his plantings. With him the sugar cane grew so fast, it rustled and rattled, and with a lantern at night, he had watched the progress. All his products were magnified, nor did there ever appear to be a doubt in his mind but that his stories were accepted. With his lack of veracity, he was however most generous, and we never left his place empty handed. (Mary Charlotte Alexander, 250)

According to his obituary notice, Oudinot was a deputy sheriff at Lahaina for a number of years: "His hospitality, cheerfulness of temper and many other good qualities, caused him to be universally known on these islands and secured for him a large number of friends. Through industry and energy he has accumulated a valuable property situated in Lahaina" ("Died," Honolulu *Pacific Commercial Advertiser,* 22 July 71, 2; naturalization document of Francis A. Oudinot dated 18 June 55, Naturalization Book N:55, Hawaiian Ministry of Interior, Bureau of Immigration, H-Ar; William Ap Jones to Mr. Chapman of the Interior Ministry, 24 Aug 61, Miscellaneous File, Hawaiian Ministry of Interior, H-Ar; *MTH,* 57–58; *N&J1,* 120 n. 38).

526.11–531.22 I . . . sir."] Mark Twain first published this portion of the text as "About a Remarkable Stranger" in his "Memoranda" in the April 1871 *Galaxy* (SLC 1871b). He revised the sketch only slightly when incorporating it into *Roughing It.*

526.14–21 you ought to have seen *my* chimney . . . I had to dig it out with a pickaxe] In August 1866 Clemens wrote in one of his Hawaiian notebooks: "Chimney got choked with smoke so thick had to *dig* it out" (*N&J1,* 146).

528.26–35 *there* was lightning for you . . . my dog was a swimming behind the wagon] In late July 1866 Clemens wrote in his notebook, "Oudinot's bee & dog & lightning story—lightning came in at front door as he was just going out & drove him clear through & out at the back door" (*N&J1*, 147). Although the lightning anecdote sketched in the entry does not occur in this chapter, the listed elements (the bee, the dog, and the lightning) are nevertheless present (see the phrase "little small bee" at 530.11).

531.2–4 Markiss was found . . . dead] Oudinot was still alive when Mark Twain published his *Galaxy* sketch, but died of heart disease three months later.

532.1–3 AFTER half a year's luxurious vagrancy in the Islands, I . . . returned to San Francisco] Clemens left Honolulu aboard the *Smyrniote* on 19 July and arrived in San Francisco on 13 August. His Sandwich Islands trip, including the voyages there and back, lasted a little more than five months ("Passengers," Honolulu *Pacific Commercial Advertiser*, 21 July 66, 2).

532.4–30 lying two long weeks in a dead calm . . . trying to sit on an empty champagne bottle . . . and thread a needle] Between 24 July and 8 August the *Smyrniote* was becalmed, and so made negligible progress. Clemens's shipboard notebook entries and a letter written to his mother and sister describe certain games devised by the passengers, although not the one mentioned here (*N&J1*, 134–62; *L1*, 350–54).

532.13–14 For a whole day and part of a night we lay so close to another ship] The nearby ship was the *Comet*, which departed Honolulu for San Francisco just two and a half hours before the *Smyrniote*. Its passengers included some of Clemens's Sandwich Islands acquaintances: Mrs. Thomas Spencer and her two daughters, as well as Charles Marlette and Edward Howard (see the notes at 513.14 and 518.1–3; *N&J1*, 133; *L1*, 352; "Passengers," Honolulu *Pacific Commercial Advertiser*, 21 July 66, 2; "Passengers," San Francisco *Alta California*, 14 Aug 66, 4).

533.5–6 I was home again, in San Francisco, without means and without employment] Clemens was not in fact idle upon his return, as this remark suggests. During the seven weeks before his first public lecture in early October, he was busy with a variety of literary projects and journalistic assignments. He completed his Sandwich Islands letters to the Sacramento *Union* and, for the same newspaper, reported the horse races at the thirteenth annual fair of the California State Agricultural Society in Sacramento between 10 and 15 September (see Branch 1969). He contributed the sketch "How, for Instance?" to the New York *Weekly Review* and "Origin of Illustrious Men" to the *Californian*, and probably drafted "Forty-three Days in an Open Boat," which *Harper's Monthly* published in December. He may also have worked on a book-length manuscript based on his Sandwich Island letters, which he submitted for publication in 1867 without success. It is also unlikely that he was financially pressed during this period. According to his later recollection, the *Union* proprietors cheerfully agreed to pay him twenty dollars a week for "general correspondence" (presumably about three hundred and fifty dollars for seventeen and a half weeks), plus an extra $300 for his "grand 'scoop'" of the *Hornet* disaster (SLC 1899, 76–77; SLC 1866ii–jj, 1866qq; *L2*, 3–4, 58 n. 1).

533.7 at last a public lecture occurred to me] Clemens delivered his first lecture on 2 October 1866. He gave his first public account of the experience at a banquet held in his honor on 30 October 1869 in Pittsburgh, Pennsylvania, where he was scheduled to lecture two days later. The Pittsburgh account, widely quoted in the press, accords with the version that follows here except in a few particulars, which are identified in the notes below (*L3*, 382 n. 2; "A Feast of Humor," Buffalo *Express*, 3 Nov 69, 2, and "Mark Twain's First Lecture," San Francisco *Alta California*, 24 Nov 69, 2, both reprinting the Pittsburgh *Leader* of 31 October).

533.8–10 I showed it to several friends, but they . . . said . . . I would make a humiliating failure of it] In 1887 George E. Barnes, a proprietor of the San Francisco *Morning Call*, recalled that Clemens appeared at his office shortly after returning from the Sandwich Islands and solicited an opinion of his lecture idea, admitting that he had already been advised against it by Bret Harte, Charles Warren Stoddard, James F. Bowman, and "the rest of the fellows," who believed it would damage his "literary reputation" (Barnes, 1).

533.12–13 at last an editor . . . told me to "go ahead."] Barnes claimed that a *Call* editor (possibly meaning himself) read the manuscript of the lecture, found it "a well-constructed piece of work," and advised Clemens to go ahead with his plan (Barnes, 1). In writing this passage, however, Mark Twain probably had in mind (as Albert Bigelow Paine suggests) his friend and enthusiastic supporter John McComb (1829–96), a foreman on the San Francisco *Alta California* who would soon become its supervising editor and one of its owners (*MTB*, 1:292; *L1*, 361; *L2*, 12–13 n. 1).

533.16–18 The proprietor of the several theatres . . . said I might have his handsome new opera-house] Thomas Maguire (1820–96), originally from Ireland, was at this time San Francisco's most noted theatrical impresario. He owned the Opera House, built in the early 1850s, and the larger and more splendid Academy of Music, completed in May 1864. It was at this latter hall that Clemens delivered his first lecture. Many years later Clemens recalled Maguire's advice to "make my fortune—strike while the iron was hot—break into the lecture field!" (AD, Apr 1904, CU-MARK, in *MTA*, 1:242; Hart, 300; Lloyd, 153–54).

533.23–27 the last line of my posters . . . Doors open at 7½. The trouble will begin at 8 . . . Showmen have borrowed it frequently] Mark Twain explained in an 1867 letter to the *Alta* that he wrote his lecture announcement in the offices of the *Call.* The last line of the original text read: "Doors open at 7 o'clock. The trouble to begin at 8 o'clock" (SLC 1866*ll*). The announcement appeared in the San Francisco papers beginning on 27 September, and was distributed throughout the city as a poster. By the following year, the "trouble" phrase had been copied by performers as far away as New York City (SLC 1867g; Fatout 1960, 36–37; *MTTB,* 292 n. 2, Letter XVIII).

533.35–534.3 I went to three old friends . . . and said: . . . I would like to have you . . . help me through] One of these friends was certainly John McComb, whom Joseph Goodman described in 1881 as "the same wholesome, considerate fellow that befriended us all in early days and clacqued so conscientiously at your first lecture" (Goodman to SLC, 9 Mar 81, CU-MARK). Goodman's remark suggests that he was present as well. And according to Bailey Millard, one of Clemens's successors as local reporter on the San Francisco *Morning Call,* "Bret Harte and some of his friends" decided to "form a big claque that would insure the success of the affair" (Millard, 371; *CofC,* 10).

534.4–7 the wife of a popular citizen . . . and her husband would sit prominently in the left-hand stage-box] Amelia Ransome Neville, who attended the lecture, identified this cooperative acquaintance as Mrs. Frederick F. Low, whose husband—a former gold miner and banker—was governor of California from 1863 to 1867 (Neville, 162–63; *L1,* 373 n. 1).

534.14–16 My name's Sawyer . . . if you knew how bad I wanted to laugh, you'd give me a ticket] In April 1872 the San Francisco *Chronicle* identified Sawyer as long-time San Francisco resident William M. Slason (1831?–72), "a member of old Knickerbocker Engine Company, of a jolly, rollicking, boisterous nature, whose love for a joke was only exceeded by a fondness for rye" ("Bill Slason," 11 Apr 72, 3). At the time of Mark Twain's lecture, Slason was a driver for Wells, Fargo and Company (Langley 1865, 404; "Died," San Francisco *Call,* 9 Apr 72, 4).

534.31–32 "No sales," I said to myself] Clemens's 1869 version was probably more accurate, if less dramatic: "I went down to the theater about four o'clock in the afternoon. . . . Every seat in the house had been sold" ("Mark Twain's First Lecture," San Francisco *Alta California,* 24 Nov 69, 2).

536.23–24 as for the bludgeons, they performed like pile-drivers] Bailey Millard claimed that "although Harte tried to steer the claquers, they insisted upon applauding and laughing in the wrong places, which may or may not have been intended as a joke on Twain" (Millard, 371).

536.28–29 All the papers were kind . . . I had abundance of money] The press reviews of the lecture were uniformly favorable. The San Francisco *Dramatic Chronicle* called it "one of the greatest successes of the season" ("Academy of Music," 3 Oct 66, 3), while the *Evening Bulletin* went so far as to praise it as "one of the most interesting and amusing lectures ever given in this city" ("Local Matters," 3 Oct 66, 5). The *Call* noted that the lecture "evinced a good deal of shrewd observation on the part of the speaker, and was replete with valuable information and eloquent description, judiciously varied at intervals by telling bits of humor, which were given in the lecturer's happiest manner" ("'Mark Twain's' Lecture on the Sandwich Islands," 3 Oct 66, 3, clipping in Scrapbook 1:61, CU-MARK). The reviewer for the *Alta California* concluded, "Mark Twain has thoroughly established himself as the most piquant and humorous writer and lecturer on this coast" ("City Items," 3 Oct 66, 1, clipping in Scrapbook 1:61, CU-MARK). According to Albert Bigelow Paine, Clemens's gross returns from ticket sales were about twelve hundred dollars, of which he kept about one-third after paying his expenses and his agent (probably Denis McCarthy: see the next note; *MTB,* 1:294). On the morning after the lecture the *Dramatic Chronicle* printed the following anecdote:

> Meeting "Mark" this morning on Montgomery street, the following dialogue ensued:
> *"Mark"*—Well, what do they say about my lecture?
> *We*—Why, the envious and jealous say it was "a bilk" and a "sell."
> *"Mark"*—All right. It's a free country. Everybody has a right to his opinion, if he *is* an ass. Upon the whole, it's a pretty even thing. They have the consolation of abusing me, and I have the consolation of slapping my pocket and hearing their money jingle. They have their *opinions,* and I have their *dollars. I'm* satisfied. (" 'Mark Twain's' Consolation," 4)

537.4 I took an old personal friend along to play agent for me] The old friend was Denis E. McCarthy (1840–85), an Australian of Irish descent who went to San Francisco with his parents in 1850 and began to work in a printing shop. When Clemens joined the staff of the Virginia City *Territorial Enterprise* in 1862 McCarthy was one of its proprietors (see the note at 274.25–26). After selling his share in the *Enterprise* to Joseph Goodman in September 1865, McCarthy moved to San Francisco, expecting to augment his fortune through mining-stock investments. He also launched a short-lived weekly paper, *The Irish People.* Unfortunately, however, McCarthy "was not a success as a speculator, for within four months he had lost his last dollar," and was apparently struggling financially when Clemens needed an agent in the fall of 1866. After the lecture tour McCarthy "returned to Virginia City and engaged as foreman in what but a few months before had been his own job office" (Angel, 326). He continued at the *Enterprise* until 1869, eventually recouping his losses in the Big Bonanza boom of 1873–74 (*L1*, 361–62; "Death of D. E. McCarthy," Virginia City *Evening Chronicle*, 17 Dec 85, 2; Lingenfelter and Gash, 254).

537.5 for two or three weeks we roamed through Nevada and California] The lecture tour lasted one month. In California, Clemens spoke in Sacramento (11 October), Marysville (15 October), Grass Valley (20 October), Nevada City (23 October), Red Dog (24 October), and You Bet (25 October); then, moving on to Nevada, in Virginia City (31 October), Carson City (3 November), Washoe City (7 November), Dayton (8 November), Silver City (9 November), and Gold Hill (10 November). According to the *Enterprise*, Clemens spent a brief time "rusticating at Lake Tahoe" between his Carson City and Washoe City engagements. According to Thomas Fitch, however, Clemens was his guest at Washoe City during the interim ("Mark Twain," Virginia City *Territorial Enterprise*, 6 Nov 66, 3; Fitch, 55–56).

537.6–8 Two days before I lectured in Virginia City, two stage-coaches were robbed . . . just at dawn] Clemens lectured in Virginia City on the evening of 31 October. Between 1:00 and 2:00 A.M. on that same day two stages of the Pioneer Line, traveling together from California, were waylaid and robbed near the summit of the Geiger grade, three or four miles north of the town. The masked highwaymen—whose leader was gentlemanly and well spoken—blew open a Wells, Fargo safe containing $5,150 in gold coin and then robbed the male passengers, treating them politely and addressing some of them by name (Virginia City *Territorial Enterprise*: "Highway Robbery—Is There No Remedy for It?" 1 Nov 66, 2; "Daring Stage Robbery," 1 Nov 66, 3; "The Brigands of the Geiger," 4 Nov 66, 3).

540.17–19 this whole thing was a practical joke, and the robbers were personal friends of ours in disguise] This hoax was actually perpetrated on the night of 10 November after Mark Twain's Gold Hill lecture, ten days after his appearance in Virginia City (not the "night after instructing Virginia," as he claims at 537.17). That same night, still unaware of the joke, Clemens wrote a "Card to the Highwaymen," which was printed in the *Enterprise* the following day. There he gave a briefer and less good-humored account of the hold-up and asked the attackers to return his watch, a cherished memento of his tenure as governor of the Third House in the winter of 1863–64 (SLC 1866oo; see the note at 297.22). Of the many other accounts of the hoax, perhaps the most authoritative is Steve Gillis's, contained in a 1907 letter to Albert Bigelow Paine. Gillis claimed that he and McCarthy staged the joke to provide Clemens with a financial incentive, as well as a fresh subject, for a second Virginia City lecture, inasmuch as he had refused to "repeat himself in the same town" (Chester L. Davis 1956a, 3). They enlisted some of Clemens's Virginia City acquaintances to join them in impersonating highwaymen, among them police officer George W. Birdsall, Leslie F. Blackburn, Pat Holland, and Jimmy Eddington, who acted as the captain of the band. Clemens, however, was furious when he learned of the prank from Judge Alexander W. ("Sandy") Baldwin. He left Virginia City for San Francisco on 12 November, unmollified by the return of his stolen property and the conspirators' explanation. Paine's version of the story agrees substantially with Gillis's; another brief but straightforward sketch of the affair may be found in the journals of Alfred Doten, long associated with the Gold Hill *Evening News.* Considerably less factual are the recollections of William Gillis (who gives a different roster of participants) and the ill-natured reminiscences of Senator William M. Stewart (see the notes at 288.16–17 and 288.27–28; "Departures," Virginia City *Territorial Enterprise,* 13 Nov 66, 3; *MTB,* 1:297–302; Doten, 2:900–904 passim; Gillis, 108–16; William M. Stewart, 221–22).

542.4 When I returned to San Francisco] Clemens, apparently not incapacitated by his "troublesome disease" (541.19), delivered a revamped version of his Sandwich Islands lecture in San Francisco on 16 November, concluding it with "the only true and reliable history of the late REVOLTING HIGHWAY ROBBERY, Perpetrated upon the Lecturer, at dead of night, between the cities of Gold Hill and Virginia" (advertisement, San Francisco *Times,* 16 Nov 66, 4). He went on to lecture in San Jose (21 November), Petaluma (26 November), and Oakland (27 November). Before he left for the East, he gave one final performance in San Francisco, on 10 December (*L1,* 367 n. 4).

542.4–5 I projected a pleasure journey to Japan and thence westward around the world] In Honolulu in June 1866 Anson Burlingame, the American minister to China, urged Clemens to visit him in Peking in 1867. "I expect to do all this," Clemens wrote to his family at the time, "but I expect to go to the States first—& from China to the Paris World's Fair" (*L1,* 347–48). Clemens's intention of visiting the Orient was still alive in September 1866, when he mentioned the proposed trip in a letter to the Honolulu *Hawaiian Herald.* Soon thereafter, on 20 October, the Honolulu *Pacific Commercial Advertiser* printed a "Letter from San Francisco" that reported, "Mark Twain will probably revisit your shores en route for Japan and China, where he proposes to spend a few years traveling and writing for the Eastern press" (Ajax, 1; SLC 1866mm). Another item in the same issue added, "Verbally we hear that he is to write for the [San Francisco] *Bulletin*" ("An interesting letter . . . ," Honolulu *Pacific Commercial Advertiser,* 20 Oct 66, 3).

542.5–9 but a desire to see home again changed my mind, and I took a berth . . . to New York] By 4 December Clemens had decided against traveling directly to the Orient: "The China Mail Steamer is getting ready & everybody says I am throwing away a fortune in not going in her. I firmly believe it myself. [¶] I sail for the States in the Opposition steamer of the 15th inst, positively and without reserve" (*L1*, 369). Having accepted an assignment as a traveling correspondent for the San Francisco *Alta California,* Mark Twain was about to embark on the first leg of a journey that would eventually take him, according to the *Alta,* to "the 'Universal Exposition' at Paris, through Italy, the Mediterranean, India, China, Japan, and back to San Francisco by the China Mail Steamship line." He bid formal farewell to San Francisco and California in the concluding remarks of his 10 December lecture at Congress Hall in San Francisco. Speaking in his most exalted oratorical style, he predicted "the dawn of a radiant future" for the state: "A splendid prosperity shall descend like a glory upon the whole land!" (" 'Mark Twain's' Farewell," San Francisco *Alta California,* 15 Dec 66, 2, in Benson, 211–13). Clemens sailed on the steamer *America,* captained by Edgar Wakeman, on 15 December and arrived at San Juan del Sur, Nicaragua, on 28 December. After crossing the isthmus to San Juan del Norte (Greytown), he embarked on the steamer *San Francisco* on 1 January 1867, arriving at New York on 12 January (*N&J1*, 238–40; *L2*, 1).

542.9–11 the cholera broke out among us . . . and we buried two or three bodies at sea every day] Soon after the *San Francisco* sailed, cholera broke out among the steerage passengers. Before the vessel anchored at New York seven passengers had died from cholera and other causes. Clemens's notebook for the period and his correspondence for the *Alta* record the details of the harrowing voyage (see *N&J1*, 238–99, and *MTTB*, 11–81).

542.11 I found home a dreary place] Clemens left New York on 3 March 1867 to visit his family in St. Louis. There is little in his *Alta* correspondence to suggest that his St. Louis stay was "dreary": he told his readers that he "found it and left it the same happy, cheerful, contented old town" (SLC 1867e). A year and a half later, however, he would admit to Mary Mason Fairbanks: "There is something in my deep hatred of St. Louis that will hardly let me appear cheery even at my mother's own fireside. Nobody knows what a ghastly infliction it is on me to visit St. Louis. I am afraid I do not always disguise it, either" (*L2*, 252). During his 1867 visit, Clemens lectured several times—in St. Louis and Hannibal (Missouri), in Keokuk (Iowa), and in Quincy (Illinois)—during March and the first half of April before returning to New York (*L2*, 19 n. 2, 23 n. 1).

542.17–18 I went away and joined the famous Quaker City European Excursion] This pleasure excursion to Europe and the Holy Land was organized by members of Henry Ward Beecher's Plymouth Church in Brooklyn. The travelers embarked from New York on 8 June 1867 for a five-month cruise aboard the steamer *Quaker City*. Clemens's participation was sponsored by the *Alta*, which paid his $1,250 fare plus $500 for expenses, as an advance against fifty letters he was expected to write during the voyage. He also arranged to correspond for the New York *Tribune* and (without signature) the New York *Herald*. The excursion ultimately became the subject of his first major book, *The Innocents Abroad* (SLC 1869a; *L2*, 14–15, 23–24 n. 1, 55 n. 3, 62).

542.19 after seven years of vicissitudes] See the note at 2.24–28.

545.6–9 Joseph Smith . . . was driven from State to State . . . inscriptions with] See the notes at 107.5–10 and 107.12. Smith claimed that he acquired the metal plates and "seer" stones near his home in Manchester, New York, in 1827. He soon carried them to Harmony, Pennsylvania, where in 1828–29 he dictated his translation of them (Brodie, 37–42; Donna Hill, 73).

545.9–10 he instituted his "church" in Ohio and Brigham Young joined it] Smith founded his church on 6 April 1830 in Fayette, New York, but settled in Kirtland, Ohio, about one year later. Young converted in the fall of 1831 and was baptized in April 1832 at Mendon, New York (Arrington and Bitton, 16, 21; Arrington 1985, 16–20, 413).

545.14–16 He was made one of the Twelve Apostles . . . shortly fought his way to a higher post . . . President of the Twelve] Young was among the twelve Mormon apostles named in February 1835. On 19 January 1841, Smith reported a divine revelation that, among other things, made Young the president of the apostles, a position he had already assumed (on lesser authority) in October 1838—rather than in 1836, as Waite inaccurately asserted (Cook, 242, 251; Arrington 1985, 48, 66; Waite, 13).

545.16–19 The neighbors rose up and drove the Mormons out of Ohio, and they settled in Missouri . . . they retreated to Nauvoo, Illinois] Shortly after Smith and about two hundred followers settled in Kirtland, Ohio, where they built their first temple, he designated Jackson County in western Missouri as the Mormon "Zion," or gathering place, and many of his followers, including some from Ohio, began to settle there. Conflict with non-Mormon neighbors in 1833 forced the Jackson County Mormons, numbering over a thousand, to resettle in neighboring counties north of the Missouri River. In 1837–38 the remaining Ohio group, which included Young and Smith, joined the colony in Missouri, driven there mainly by former Mormons who were outraged at what they regarded as Smith's financial dishonesty. By 1839 the often violent antagonism of non-Mormons in Missouri had driven the Mormons to Illinois, where they settled in Nauvoo on the Mississippi (Arrington 1985, 37, 53, 61–62; Allen and Leonard, 84–88, 108–9, 128–37; Brodie, 199–207, 210).

545.19–21 built a temple which . . . achieved some celebrity] Guided by Smith's revelation, the Mormons began this temple in 1841; it was still incomplete when they left Nauvoo in 1846. Smith envisioned a building on a "magnificent scale . . . which will undoubtedly attract the attention of the great men of the earth" (Andrew, 57). It was an imposing, boxlike structure built of limestone and costing as much as eight hundred thousand dollars. It had thirty ornamental pilasters, a domed octagonal tower, and a massive, pool-sized baptismal font (Flanders, 190–91, 194–99, 207–8; Andrew, 62–76). Clemens must have been well aware of Nauvoo while growing up in the 1840s, since it was only about seventy miles upstream from his boyhood home at Hannibal, Missouri, and even closer to Keokuk, Iowa (an outfitting center for Mormon emigrants in the early 1850s), where Clemens lived in 1855–56. See also the note at 546.27–31 (*L1,* 58–59, 69; Kimball 1988, 48).

545.24–26 All the proclamations Joseph Smith could issue denouncing polygamy . . . were of no avail] See the notes at 99.27–29 and 111.22–24.

546.1–3 Brigham returned from a mission . . . Mormon newspaper . . . converts to his preaching] While directing Mormon missionaries in England in 1840–41, Young began a monthly periodical, the *Latter-day Saints' Millennial Star,* and arranged for an English edition of the Book of Mormon as well as a Mormon hymnal. The English mission recorded six thousand new members that year and oversaw the emigration to Nauvoo of some eight hundred English converts (Arrington 1985, 80–81, 84, 94–95; Waite, 13).

546.4–6 Nauvoo was invaded by the Missouri and Illinois Gentiles, and Joseph Smith killed] External antagonism and internal dissension focused increasingly on Smith himself, particularly his political ambitions and self-serving economic and theological policies. On 19 June 1844, he ordered the destruction of the office and press of the *Nauvoo Expositor,* a newspaper founded by apostates trying to reform the church, which brought matters to a climax:

> Angry crowds . . . were swarming the streets of Carthage and Warsaw [Illinois]. Missourians and Iowans were crossing the river in droves. . . . Armed bands already were threatening isolated Mormon families and driving them into Nauvoo. There was lynch talk everywhere—always in the name of justice and liberty. (Brodie, 378)

Smith was arrested on a charge of treason and then murdered by Illinois militiamen in the Carthage jail on 27 June 1844 (Brodie, 362–94; Donna Hill, 387–418).

546.6–15 A Mormon named Rigdon . . . buffetings of Satan for a thousand years] Sidney Rigdon (1793–1876) had been a prominent Baptist and Campbellite preacher for more than a decade when he joined the Mormons in 1830, shortly after the church was founded. He was a powerful influence on Smith, who, shortly after Rigdon's conversion, claimed a revelation instructing him to move, along with his own rapidly increasing following, to Kirtland, Ohio, near Rigdon's home. Kirtland remained effectively the church's headquarters until 1838. Several of Smith's revelations were addressed to Rigdon, and on one occasion the two men reported sharing a vision in which they conversed with Christ. In 1842, however, they became enemies. After Smith's death in 1844, Rigdon claimed a revelation appointing him "guardian" of the church. In August 1844 this claim was rejected by the church hierarchy and by the great majority of the Nauvoo Mormons. Young declared Rigdon's revelations to be "from the Devil," and in September he was excommunicated and "delivered over to the buffetings of satan until he repents" (Nauvoo *Times and Seasons:* "Continuation of Elder Rigdon's Trial," 5 [1 Oct 44]: 667; "Conclusion of Elder Rigdon's Trial," 5 [15 Oct 44]: 686). Mark Twain's account borrowed much from Waite's *Mormon Prophet,* even some of its wording (Waite, 14; McKiernan, 11, 41, 45–46, 68–69; Van Wagoner and Walker, 232–38).

546.16–17 They straightway elected Brigham Young President] Mark Twain apparently misinterpreted his source, who ambiguously stated that Young was immediately "elected President by an overwhelming majority" (Waite, 14). In rejecting Rigdon, the Mormons affirmed the leadership of the twelve apostles, of whom Young was already president. It was not until December 1847, more than three years later, that Young was named president of the church (Arrington 1985, 153).

546.23–25 on a bitter night in February filed . . . across the frozen Mississippi] In 1846, when the Mormons in Illinois numbered around sixteen thousand, conflicts similar to those which had driven them from Ohio and Missouri forced them to abandon Nauvoo. They first intended to leave in April, when the grass would support their livestock on the move west, but out of fear of further attack (possibly even by federal troops), they began their exodus in February, when the Mississippi was still frozen over, allowing some to cross on the ice (Arrington 1985, 125–27; Brodie, 362–63; Waite, 15).

546.25–26 their burning temple, whose sacred furniture their own hands had fired] This detail is not mentioned in Waite's account, or in any other known source, and is presumably fiction. Before departing Nauvoo the Mormons tried, but failed, to sell or lease their temple. On 9 February 1846, an accidental fire damaged a small section of the roof. The building was later vandalized but remained standing until, damaged by an arsonist's fire in 1848, it was destroyed by a cyclone in 1850 (Linn, 355–56; Rich, 4).

546.27–31 They camped . . . on the western verge of Iowa . . . and many succumbed and died . . . Two years the remnant remained there] For more than a year (until April 1847), the exiled Mormons lived in temporary camps spread out across Iowa and on either bank of the Missouri River, where it divided Iowa from Nebraska Territory. Some stayed in Iowa as long as five years before migrating to Utah (Arrington 1985, 127–29; Stegner, 209–10). In a letter to the San Francisco *Alta California* written on 19 April 1867, Mark Twain reported on a convention held by those who had remained permanently in Iowa—"a grand pow-wow at Keokuk" of the Reorganized Mormon Church under Joseph Smith III:

> It is strange how this lost tribe has kept its faith through so many years of sorrow and disaster. These are people who were scattered in tents for miles and miles along the roads through Iowa when the Mormons were driven out of Nauvoo with fire and sword, twenty-five years ago. Their heavy misfortunes appealed so movingly to the kindly instincts of the Iowa people that they rescued them from starvation, and gave them houses and food and employment, and gradually they became absorbed into the population and lost sight of—forgotten entirely, in fact, till this Convention of young Joe's called them out, and then from every unsuspected nook and cranny crept a Mormon—a Mormon who had for many a year been taken for a Baptist, or a Methodist, or some other kind of Christian. (SLC 1867f)

546.32–37 purposely choosing a land . . . *outside . . . the hated American nation* . . . the United States] Waite claimed that in 1846 Young intended "to found his theocratic monarchy" in Mexico (Waite, 16). Great Salt Lake City remained in Mexican territory from its settlement in July 1847 until the ratification of the treaty ending the Mexican War in March 1848. In choosing a place to settle, the Mormons sought primarily to escape persecution by their neighbors. Their patriotic feelings for the "American nation" were certainly eroded by the repeated failure of government to protect them from violence, but there is little evidence that the Mormons were surprised or disappointed by the results of the Mexican War (Bancroft 1882–90, 21:239–41; Arrington 1985, 128–29; Eugene E. Campbell, 201–4; Flanders, 86).

546.37–547.5 In 1849 the Mormons organized a "free and independent" government . . . but made Brigham Governor of it] Mark Twain quotes from Waite, who quoted from the preamble of the "Constitution of the State of Deseret," submitted to the constitutional convention on 18 March 1849:

> We, the people, grateful to the Supreme Being for the blessings hitherto enjoyed, and feeling our dependence on Him for a continuance of those blessings, *do ordain and establish a free and Independent Government*, by the name of *the State of Deseret;* including all the territory of the United States within the following boundaries. (Waite, 21–22)

Deseret included some two hundred and sixty-five thousand square miles, extending from the Rockies to the Pacific Coast in present-day southern California, and from present-day southeastern Oregon to southern Arizona. Waite characterized the "formation of this government for the State of Deseret" as "the first effort to throw off the yoke of the Federal Government" (Waite, 23). In fact, Deseret promptly applied to Congress for statehood. Congress instead created the (much smaller) Territory of Utah in September 1850, and President Fillmore appointed Young the territorial governor, since he had already been elected governor of the provisional state (Arrington 1985, 223–27).

547.16–19 dressed to personate the worshipped and lamented prophet Smith . . . "President Brigham Young!"] Mark Twain's source inaccurately placed this incident in Iowa in December 1847, when Young became president of the church. It actually took place in Nauvoo, at the time of Young's victory over Rigdon in August 1844 (Waite, 18–19; Arrington 1985, 114–15).

547.21–25 Within five years afterward he openly added polygamy . . . denouncing polygamy to the day of his death] See the notes at 99.27–29 and 111.22–24.

547.26–27 Now was Brigham become a second Andrew Johnson in the small beginning and steady progress of his official grandeur] At least three times in 1869 Mark Twain ridiculed President Johnson's pride in being a self-made man who rose from poverty to the highest office in the land. In "The White House Funeral," written in March, he had Johnson say, in part: "born and reared 'poor white trash,' I have clung to my native instincts, and done every small, mean thing my eager hands could find to do" (SLC 1869b). In "The Last Words of Great Men," published in September, he had Johnson say: "I have been an alderman, member of Congress, Governor, Senator, Pres——adieu, you know the rest" (SLC 1869i). And in an unpublished burlesque of Victor Hugo, "L'Homme Qui Rit," probably written about the same time, the hero, representing Johnson, becomes a clown and plays "all the characters known to the profession—Alderman, Mayor, Legislator, Congressman, Senator, Vice President, President!" (SLC 1869g).

547.30–34 President of all Mormondom, civil and ecclesiastical; . . . he proclaimed himself a God] This passage owes something to Waite's listing of Young's various *"rôles"*

> as "Governor of Utah and Superintendent of Indian Affairs;" "President of the Church, Prophet, Seer, and Revelator;" "Trustee in Trust for the Church;" "President of the Emigration Company;" "Lord of the Harem;" "Eloheim, or Head God;" and "Grand Archee of the Order of the Gods." (Waite, 20)

The final accusation was based in part on Waite's claim that Young "has encouraged a doctrine, which he dare not put in print;—no less than *to arrogate to himself the attributes of Deity*" (Waite, 174–75). Mormons believe that every man is capable of becoming a god after death, but there is no evidence that Young made any more grandiose claim for himself (Arrington 1985, 205).

547.37–548.6 Into it all faithful Mormons will be admitted . . . status advanced accordingly] In Mormon doctrine, a man's status in the afterlife is enhanced by the number of his children. There is some evidence that in early years the Mormons sanctioned the practice of proxy marriage and fatherhood, but it was never widespread (Remy and Brenchley, 2:153–56; Waite, 189, 257–58; Foster, 163–66).

548.21–22 the deathless hatred which the Mormons bear our people and our government] An exaggeration. There were Mormon separatist factions, and even nonseparatists often expressed bitterness about federal policies they regarded as punitive, but the Mormons persistently sought statehood for Utah Territory (see also the note at 546.32–37; Waite, 3–4, 23, 28–29, 51, 300; Hyde, 310, 314, 315; Remy and Brenchley, 2:248–52; Creer, 107–13).

548.23 "fed fat its ancient grudge"] *The Merchant of Venice,* act 1, scene 3.

548.26 Mormondom was for the Mormons] Young's policy from the outset was to settle Mormons as widely as possible throughout the region in order to prevent rival settlements. He encouraged Mormon self-sufficiency and discouraged commerce with non-Mormons, even at times boycotting non-Mormon businesses (O'Dea, 84–85; Arrington 1958, 248–49, 256; Arrington 1985, 169, 173).

548.26–31 The United States tried to . . . put these gentlemen in office] Based on Waite's chapter 4, "Political History Continued.—The Mormon War" (50–69), Mark Twain's capsule account of the 1857–58 hostilities between Mormons and federal troops is somewhat simplified. Some, but not all, non-Mormon territorial officials came into conflict with the community and were resisted. In the summer of 1857, President Buchanan concluded that the Mormons were in rebellion against federal authority. He appointed Alfred Cumming to replace Young as governor (see the note at 552.40–553.2), and ostensibly to secure his installation and that of other non-Mormon officials, ordered twenty-five hundred army regulars, accompanied by a civilian force of about equal size, to go to Utah. Fearing invasion and military occupation, the Mormons harassed the approaching force by occasionally destroying its supplies, but did not attack it outright. With the force present during the spring and summer of 1858, Mormons offered no resistance either to Cumming and other newly appointed officials, or to the establishment of Camp Floyd (see the note at 85.7; Furniss, 21–33, 52–61, 95–97, 109, 122–23; Creer, 90–101, 128, 149, 158–60; Arrington 1985, 251).

548.31–549.9 And after they were in office they . . . got scared and . . . left the Territory] A condensation of Waite's dramatic account of Mormon hostility toward federal appointees, who issued writs that the "people, instigated by the Mormon leaders, refused to obey." In particular, she mentioned a judge who found "his life threatened and in danger, and soon after left the Territory," and another who reportedly "died from the effects of poison, administered by the hands of a Mormon" (Waite, 31, 34, 46).

549.11–12 In 1857 Gen. Harney came very near being appointed Governor of Utah] No evidence has been found (nor does Waite assert) that Brevet Brigadier General William Selby Harney (1800–89) was considered for governor, but in May 1857 he was put in command of the troops sent to Utah with newly appointed Governor Cumming. In late August, however, long before the troops reached Utah, Harney was replaced by Colonel Albert Sidney Johnston (1803–62). Hubert H. Bancroft described Harney as "a man of much rude force of character, ambitious, and a capable officer, but otherwise ill fitted for the conduct of an expedition that needed the qualities of a diplomatist more than those of a soldier" (Bancroft 1882–90, 21:497). Harney served briefly as commander of the Department of the West, headquartered at St. Louis, but was relieved of his command in May 1861, shortly before the Clemens brothers left there for Nevada. Suspected of Southern sympathies, Harney remained inactive during the Civil War (Furniss, 63, 67, 95–96, 101).

549.13–14 Cradlebaugh Judge] In 1857 President Buchanan appointed John Cradlebaugh (1819–72) associate justice of Utah Territory, but Cradlebaugh did not arrive in Salt Lake City until November 1858. His determined efforts to try certain cases antagonized the Mormons as well as Governor Cumming, who favored conciliation. In particular, Cradlebaugh tried the men accused of perpetrating the infamous Mountain Meadows massacre (see the notes at 552.14–15, 552.40–553.2, and 553.3–4). He was reprimanded by Buchanan's attorney general for disregarding the government's "principles and rules of action," and in 1860 resisted the appointment of his replacement, claiming that his own term had not expired. He then settled in the part of western Utah which in 1861 became Nevada Territory, eventually serving as its first delegate to Congress. As a volunteer officer in the Civil War, he was seriously wounded in 1863 and returned to Nevada, where in 1864 he ran unsuccessfully for United States senator (Bancroft 1882–90, 21:500, 562 n. 36; Furniss, 97, 208; Angel, 78, 87; Marsh, 682 n. 160, 687 n. 217).

549.26–28 Congress of the United States had enacted a solemn law against polygamy . . . thirty more wives] President Lincoln signed the first antipolygamy legislation in 1862 during the Civil War, a conflict Mormon leaders thought would eventuate in the millennium and the vindication of Mormon doctrines. Active enforcement of the law was delayed until the early 1870s, first by the war itself, then by legal technicalities. After 1862 Young added three more wives (in 1863, 1865, and 1868) to the seventeen then living (Van Wagoner, 107–10; Arrington 1985, 420–21).

550.7–17 A great emigrant train from Missouri and Arkansas . . . additional grounds for lack of love for these wayfarers] In September 1857, when they were still fearful of being invaded by federal troops, a group of Mormons (abetted by Indians) attacked a wagon train at Mountain Meadows in southern Utah, killing some fifty men, forty women, and thirty-two children. The victims were members of a wagon train led by Alexander Fancher of Arkansas, which early in August had passed through Salt Lake City, where Mormons declined to resupply it. Resupply became increasingly difficult as the train traveled south through the territory, producing friction as it went: there were reports of damage to crops, water sources, and livestock, as well as injury to Indians. Some witnesses recalled that the travelers boasted of having persecuted Mormons in Missouri, and one even claimed to have the gun that had killed "Old Joe Smith." The "noted Mormon missionary" recently killed in Arkansas was also clearly pertinent: he was Parley Pratt (see the note at 103.13–14). But what Mark Twain cites as in itself a "sufficient cause for hot retaliation by the Mormon chiefs" was probably not even a contributing factor. Waite's claim that the emigrant families were "joined by some few Mormons, who were disaffected, and sought to travel under their protection," has not been confirmed (Waite, 76, 80). They were joined at Provo by a non-Mormon who had lived several months in Utah, which may explain the error (Brooks 1962, 211; Wise, 2, 270–76; Brooks 1970, 20–22, 30–57, 61–67, 78, 219–20).

550.17 this train was rich] Waite asserted that although the massacre was largely prompted by a desire for "revenge and retaliation," the "principal motive was plunder" (Waite, 80). The Fancher train was well equipped, and its members were more prosperous than typical emigrants. There were even reports that they carried a large quantity of gold coin (Wise, 10–12; Brooks 1962, 340, 372–76; Brooks 1970, 193, 199; Bancroft 1882–90, 21:545 n. 4; Carleton, 1–2, 9, 11).

550.20–21 "spoil" of an enemy . . . "delivered it into their hand?"] See, for example, Deuteronomy 2:33–36 and 3:3–7.

550.24–551.6 A "revelation" from Brigham Young . . . the mandate of Almighty God] Mark Twain quotes Waite (76, 79), adding the quotation marks around "revelation." No decisive evidence has been found to support Waite's claim regarding Young's orders. It is clear that his policies and behavior contributed to the charged atmosphere in which the crime occurred, and that he afterward collaborated in the coverup. A letter preserved in the Mormon archives indicates that he explicitly counseled against bloodshed in this instance and had no prior knowledge of the attackers' intentions. Nevertheless, John D. Lee, the high-ranking Mormon later executed for the Mountain Meadows massacre (see the note at 550.25–26), came to believe that "exterminating Captain Fancher's train of emigrants" was the "direct command of Brigham Young" (John D. Lee, 225; Brooks 1970, 61–67, 112–13, 219).

550.24 Great Grand Archee, or God] Waite identifies the "Grand Archees" as the highest ranking Mormons, who had the "power of life and death," within the "Order of the Danites," an "established institution in the Mormon Church" (Waite, 281; see the note at 85.33–34). This title has not been verified in Mormon literature, religious or secular.

550.25–26 President J. C. Haight, Bishop Higbee, and J. D. Lee (adopted son of Brigham)] These men, all deeply implicated in the Mountain Meadows massacre, were among the local leaders who shared civil, religious, and military authority in the small Mormon communities of southern Utah. Isaac Chauncey Haight (1813–86) was, at the time of the massacre, mayor of Cedar City (the town nearest the emigrants' encampment), delegate to the territorial legislature, president of the Cedar Stake of the Mormon church (the highest local religious authority), and lieutenant colonel in the local militia. In his military capacity he was the immediate superior of the men who attacked the emigrants, receiving and sending messages and orders between the men at Mountain Meadows and his own military superior in a neighboring town, but he was not present during the actual attack, first visiting the site the following morning. John Mount Higbee (1827–1904) was a counselor to Haight in the local church leadership and a major in the militia, a detachment of which he commanded in the attack at Mountain Meadows. Higbee coordinated his activities with John Doyle Lee (1812–77), who assumed responsibility for carrying out the overall plan of attack. Lee, who had been "sealed for eternity" to Young as an adopted son in 1845, was a long-time leader in southern Utah. At the time of the massacre he was a probate judge, county clerk, assessor, and local agent to the Indians. In time, the leading participants in the massacre, including these three men, went into exile outside Utah. By 1870, disapproval had grown so strong within the Mormon church that Haight and Lee were excommunicated, although no action was taken against Higbee. Haight was readmitted about four years later. Lee remained in hiding—ostracized by his church, his associates, and his neighbors—until his arrest in 1874. His first trial ended with a hung jury. He was convicted after a second trial, at which a number of his associates at Mountain Meadows testified against him, evidently having agreed to make him a scapegoat. He was taken to the site of the massacre and executed there in 1877, the only participant ever tried for the crime. Lee's autobiography, including his account of the Mountain Meadows massacre, was published posthumously (Brooks 1970, 52–55, 72–74, 76, 79, 83, 86, 110–11, 184–87, 191, 193–98, 207–12; Brooks 1962, 73, 185; Jones and Jones, 10–11, 28; Eugene E. Campbell, 170–72; John D. Lee).

551.7–552.2 A large party of Mormons . . . tricked out as Indians . . . the slaughter commenced] The emigrants were first attacked on 7 or 8 September 1857, while camped about two hundred sixty miles south of Salt Lake City at Mountain Meadows, where they planned to take an extended rest before continuing their journey to California. Eyewitness accounts of the initial attack conflict; the aggressors are described both as an Indian party of "several hundred" and as a group of Mormons disguised as Indians (John D. Lee, 226; Brooks 1970, 275). Mark Twain accepts the latter version, on the authority of Waite's quotation of the account by Cradlebaugh (see the note at 551.25–28), who interrogated the Indians in 1859 while investigating the incident. The Indians reported that the Mormons alone—"all painted"—had initiated the attack, after which the Indians joined in (Waite, 72). By 10 September a group of Mormons, over fifty strong, commanded by the local military, had gathered near the besieged emigrants. On Friday afternoon, 11 September, the emigrants were lured from their camp by the Mormons' promise of protection from the Indians. After allowing themselves to be disarmed, they were systematically murdered, the Mormons killing the men, the Indians killing the women and older children. The Mormons subsequently attempted to place full responsibility for the crime on the Indians (Brooks 1970, 67, 69–75, 101–5, 158–59, 165–66; Brooks 1962, 206–15; John D. Lee, 226–44, 379–80).

551.13–14 the sort of scurvy apologies for "Indians" which the southern part of Utah affords] Mark Twain may be echoing Cradlebaugh's remark that "the Indians in the southern part of the Territory of Utah" were unlikely to participate in a prolonged attack on the emigrants because they were "a very low, cowardly, beastly set" (Waite, 72).

551.24–25 The leaders of the timely white "deliverers" were President Haight and Bishop John D. Lee] Contrary to Cradlebaugh's assertion (quoted by Waite), Haight was not at the site, although he was a full participant in planning the massacre. Lee and a militiaman carried the white flag into the emigrants' camp and Lee negotiated the (false) terms of surrender (Waite, 73; John D. Lee, 238, 329, 334; Brooks 1970, 72–73).

551.25–28 Mr. Cradlebaugh . . . tells in a speech delivered in Congress] Cradlebaugh delivered this speech, on the "Admission of Utah as a State," in the House of Representatives on 7 February 1863. Waite quoted only a portion of it, apparently taking her text from its publication as a book (and making only minor changes in punctuation); her quotation in turn served as Mark Twain's source for the information paraphrased in the text at 551.7–25, as well as for the extract at 551.29–552.11 (Cradlebaugh, 17–19; Waite, 72–73).

552.3–5 Two only escaped . . . before they were overtaken and slaughtered] Most accounts agree that three emigrants escaped the initial attack on 7 or 8 September, but were killed subsequently. There were no adult survivors (Brooks 1970, 70–72, 97–100).

552.8–9 Seventeen individuals . . . were spared, and they were little children] The Mormons spared eighteen young children. In 1859 the territorial superintendent of Indian affairs, Jacob Forney (see the note at 553.33–34), located and took custody of seventeen of them to be returned to relatives. The remaining child apparently lived her life among the Mormons (Brooks 1970, 101–5).

552.14–15 Judge Cradlebaugh . . . proceeded to make Mormondom answer for the massacre] Cradlebaugh held court in the town of Provo in March 1859 and attempted to prosecute a number of crimes, including the Mountain Meadows massacre. The following month he traveled with a military escort to the towns nearest Mountain Meadows, where he gathered testimony about the massacre and issued writs for the arrest of thirty-eight men. None was served because those named were all in hiding. Cradlebaugh's strong judicial stance won him high regard in some quarters: when he returned to Nevada in December 1863 he was hailed as a hero, both for his war record and his actions in Utah. "His fearlessness and impartiality in the administration of justice secured him the enmity of the Mormons of Salt Lake," noted the Carson City *Independent:*

> Pistols were drawn in the Court room, and men threatened to shoot him if he persisted in his course. The stern and plain-spoken old Judge told them to "shoot and be d—d, but he intended to do his duty." Neither threats nor persuasion could swerve him one hair's breadth from what he deemed to be the path of duty. ("Judge Cradlebaugh," Sacramento *Union*, 28 Dec 63, 1, reprinting the Carson City *Independent*)

Mark Twain, who was then reporting for the Virginia City *Territorial Enterprise,* would surely have seen this article or others like it ("Ovation to Colonel Cradlebaugh," Sacramento *Union,* 4 Jan 64, 4, reprinting Carson City *Independent* of 30 December; Furniss, 214–19; Cradlebaugh, 15–16, 19–20; Waite, 70, 74; Brooks 1970, 173, 177).

552.19 "breathing threatenings and slaughter!"] Acts 9:1.

552.20 An editorial in the *Territorial Enterprise*] No example of the *Enterprise* printing is known to survive. Mark Twain's source for the extract at 552.22–35 was Waite's book, which quoted only a portion of the original (Waite, 84–85).

552.40–553.2 Cumming was the Federal Governor . . . to screen the Mormons from the demands of justice] In July 1857 Buchanan appointed Alfred Cumming (1802–73) to replace Young as territorial governor. Cumming had been mayor of Augusta, Georgia, and an Indian agent on the upper Missouri. Despite fears to the contrary (see the note at 548.26–31), Cumming was able to enter Salt Lake City in April 1858 and peaceably effect the transfer of executive power. He adopted a conciliatory approach to the Mormons, "possibly going beyond moderation to leniency" (Furniss, 208). With Lincoln's inauguration in 1861, Cumming returned to Georgia (Furniss, 96–98, 207–8; Hafen and Hafen, 286–87, 296; Bancroft 1882–90, 21:525–26; Linn, 505–7; Wise, 252–54).

553.3–4 he even went so far as to publish his protest against . . . Cradlebaugh's proceedings] On opening his court in Provo in March 1859, Cradlebaugh requested of General Johnston a military detachment to aid in securing prisoners. The presence of armed troops from Camp Floyd—in direct contact for the first time with the civilian population—quickly inflamed the Mormon community. As the situation worsened, Governor Cumming ordered the troops withdrawn, but not before their numbers in and around Provo had swelled to over eight hundred. Johnston refused the order. Cumming, indignant at the usurpation of his authority, issued a proclamation on 27 March 1859 "protesting against all movements of troops except such as accorded with his own instructions as chief executive magistrate" (Bancroft 1882–90, 21:562). The conflict was rendered moot when Cradlebaugh adjourned his court because the Mormons refused to testify, the Mormon grand jury refused to bring charges, and all the likely suspects had gone into hiding. Cumming's position was later sustained by the federal government, and Cradlebaugh was censured for using federal troops to facilitate the work of the court (Furniss, 214–19; Bancroft 1882–90, 21:561–62 n. 36).

553.11–12 "confirmations strong as proofs of Holy Writ."] *Othello,* act 3, scene 3.

553.13–38 1. The evidence of Mormons themselves . . . Indian depredations] In reproducing Waite's list, Mark Twain reordered and renumbered items 1–7, presumably to reflect his own view of their relative importance: Waite's order (expressed with Mark Twain's numbers) was 1, 5, 7, 6, 3, 4, 2. In addition, he dropped Waite's extract of Campbell's testimony from item 8 and omitted entirely the last item on her list, a lengthy excerpt from the letters and reports of Jacob Forney (Waite, 76–79).

553.14–15 Deputy U. S. Marshal Rogers] During late March and April 1859 William H. Rogers, a territorial Indian agent and acting deputy United States marshal, assisted both Jacob Forney, superintendent of Indian affairs, and Cradlebaugh in their investigation of the Mountain

Meadows massacre. On 29 February 1860 Rogers published in the Salt Lake City *Valley Tan,* an anti-Mormon newspaper, a lengthy and dispassionate "Statement" about their findings and the evidence for Mormon participation in the crime (reprinted in Brooks 1970, 265–78). Rogers assisted Forney in recovering the surviving children and joined Cradlebaugh in interviewing people claiming knowledge of the massacre. His statement included an account of a detailed confession by one Mormon who participated in the massacre and "gave Judge C. the name of 25 or 30 other men . . . who assisted" (Brooks 1970, 276). He also described conversations with Indians who attributed the massacre to Mormons acting on orders of Young. Rogers attempted to serve Cradlebaugh's writs for the arrest of Haight, Higbee, and Lee, but found that the suspects—along with a "large portion" of the male population of the area—had fled (Brooks 1970, 272; Bancroft 1882–90, 21:557 n. 23; Furniss, 210–11).

553.16–19 The failure of Brigham Young to embody any account of it . . . until several years after the occurrence] Young continued to function as superintendent of Indian affairs until his replacement arrived in June 1858 (see the note at 553.33–34). On 6 January 1858, in his official report to the commissioner of Indian affairs in Washington, D.C., Young blamed the massacre on the emigrants themselves, claiming that their poisoning of meat and water resulted in the deaths of several Indians; he quoted Lee's report to him that "about the 22nd of Sept. Capt Fanchers & Co. fell victims to the Indians wrath near Mountain Meadows." Young took the occasion to deliver a homily on the mishandling of Indian affairs and expressed the hope that future relations with the Indians would benefit from "a uniform consistent humane and conciliating course of superior acts by those who profess superior attainments" (Brooks 1970, 158–59). Several years later, in a sermon of 8 March 1863, Young also claimed that he had assured Governor Cumming of the Mormons' full cooperation with a trial before "an unprejudiced judge"—that is, someone other than Cradlebaugh—but, Young maintained, the case had remained unprosecuted "for fear the Mormons would be acquitted . . . and our enemies would thus be deprived of a favorite topic to talk about, when urging hostility against us" (Arrington 1985, 280, 480 n. 30; Morgan, 407–8).

553.23–25 The failure of the "Deseret News," . . . to notice the massacre, until several months afterward] The Salt Lake City *Deseret News,* the only newspaper published in the territory between 1850 and November 1858, made no mention of the massacre until it published an account of Cradlebaugh's proceedings in March 1859 (Bancroft 1882–90, 21:326, 715–19).

553.27 The testimony of the children saved from the massacre] Forney, in his report of August 1859 to the commissioner of Indian affairs, stated that two such children were being "detained to give evidence" (Brooks 1970, 260).

553.33–34 J. Forney, who was, in 1859, Superintendent of Indian Affairs for the Territory] Jacob Forney of Philadelphia officially succeeded Young as territorial superintendent of Indian affairs in August 1857, although he did not reach Salt Lake City until June 1858. The results of Forney's inquiry into the massacre may be found in his several official reports to the commissioner of Indian affairs in Washington, D.C., and his letter of 10 May 1859 to the Salt Lake City *Valley Tan* (reprinted in Brooks 1970, 253–65, and Cradlebaugh, 34–38, 40–42; see also Waite, 78–79). In his report of August 1859 Forney concluded that the "massacre was concocted by white men and consummated by whites and Indians. The names of many of the whites engaged in this terrible affair have already been given to the proper legal authorities" (Brooks 1970, 259; Morgan, 407–8; Furniss, 194–95).

553.36–37 The testimony of R. P. Campbell, Capt. 2d Dragoons, who was sent . . . to protect travellers] Reuben P. Campbell was a United States Army captain who commanded the detachment of troops accompanying Cradlebaugh to southern Utah in April 1859. Campbell's report to his superior officer was included in the appendix to the published text of Cradlebaugh's speech. In it he attributed the massacre to "the *Mormons* . . . assisted by such of the wretched Indians of the neighborhood as they could force or persuade to join" (Cradlebaugh, 31–32; also in Waite, 77–78; Brooks 1970, 271, 312).

554.1–2 Conrad Wiegand, of Gold Hill, Nevada] Conrad Wiegand (1830–80), a native of Pennsylvania trained as a chemist, worked at the Philadelphia mint before relocating to the Pacific Coast. During the early 1860s he was the supervising assayer at the San Francisco branch mint. (There, in July 1861, Wiegand engaged in a public controversy with a fellow employee, accusing him of assault—much as he accuses John B. Winters in the document reproduced in this appendix.) Wiegand, described by the Virginia City *Union* as "one of the best assayers in the United States," accepted a position with the Gould and Curry works near Virginia City in November 1863 ("Ex-Assayer Wiegand," San Francisco *Evening Bulletin*, 6 Nov 63, 3, reprinting the Virginia City *Union*). He opened his own assay office in Gold Hill, Nevada, in June 1865. In June 1880, in debt and suffering from nervous depression, he committed suicide. It was sometime after Clemens left Nevada in 1864 that Wiegand became familiar to Virginia City and Gold Hill residents through frequent articles in the local newspapers. The Virginia City *Territorial Enterprise* tended to view Wiegand's crusading journalism with indulgence:

> Mr. Wiegand means well. All his instincts are humane and moral. He is among the worthiest of a class of reformers, who, in the abstract, perhaps, think rightly, but who fritter away valuable lives in attempting to accomplish impossibilities.

> But while Mr. Wiegand is one of the worthiest of the class referred to, he is also one of the most impracticable. His purposes are rambling, practically aimless, and almost numberless. To-day he assaults one public vice, to-morrow another, and the next day a third. The result is that he makes no impression upon any of them, and will die without having made the world a whit better than he found it. ("Hold, Enough!" Virginia City *Territorial Enterprise*, 4 Nov 69, 2)

("The Mint Again—Wiegand's Statement," San Francisco *Alta California*, 22 July 61, 1; "Assaying at Gold Hill," Virginia City *Union*, 1 June 65, 3; "A Shocking Suicide," Virginia City *Evening Chronicle*, 14 June 80, 3; "The Suicide of Conrad Wiegand," Virginia City *Territorial Enterprise*, 16 June 80, 3.)

554.10–11 When I met Conrad, he was "Superintendent of the Gold Hill Assay Office"] Although Clemens left Nevada several months after Wiegand's arrival, the two men apparently did not meet until April 1868, when Clemens visited Wiegand's Gold Hill assay office during a lecture tour. On 28 April, in Virginia City, Wiegand presented him with a silver brick inscribed "Mark Twain—Matthew v, 41—Pilgrim," an allusion to the verse "And whosoever shall compel thee to go a mile, go with him twain." In an unpublished account, probably written shortly after his visit to Wiegand's office, Mark Twain expressed admiration for him, marveling at his honesty and evident lack of self-interest: "In his theories he is earnest & sincere, but as he tries to secure them realization in life, he should anticipate the fate of all [who] attempt such toil, isolation, persecution, and defamation [tempered] only by the respect of a few" (SLC 1868c, 13; *ET&S1*, 43).

554.12–13 he was a street preacher, too, with a mongrel religion of his own invention] In December 1867, Wiegand became rector of Virginia City's newly formed "Humanitarian Christian Society." He resigned in disgust two months later, after his fellow Humanitarians objected to his lecturing on "politico-religious" themes ("Humanitarian Christian Society Organized," Gold Hill *Evening News*, 23 Dec 67, 3; Virginia City *Territorial Enterprise:* "Politico-Religious Notice," 23 Feb 68, 3; "A Card from Conrad Wiegand," 25 Feb 68, 2; "Resignation," 27 Feb 68, 3). At that time the *Enterprise* published an editorial about Wiegand (almost certainly written by Joseph T. Goodman), coining the word "Wiegandish" to characterize his views and attempting to explain the "Humanitarian" creed of "this erratic genius." In conclusion the editorial described Wiegand as

> a slight built man, with regular and pale features that wear an indescribable expression of mildness and intellectuality, and large blue eyes that are full of fire and thought yet impress you only as singularly pure and gentle, which, together with a profusion of soft brown hair and whiskers, make up a countenance that will irresistibly recall to mind the likeness of the Savior. ("Wiegandish," Virginia City *Territorial Enterprise*, 23 Feb 68, 2)

554.14–15 Here latterly he has entered journalism] On 3 November 1869 Wiegand began circulating a prospectus for his projected newspaper, the *People's Tribune*, whose mission, the *Enterprise* inferred, would be to "show its teeth to the Bank of California, talk of the management of the Comstock mines, extend a helping hand to suffering men and lewd women, and play numerous other 'fantastic tricks before high heaven'" ("Hold, Enough!" Virginia City *Territorial Enterprise,* 4 Nov 69, 2). According to Wiegand, the paper was to be "an observer and photographist of the Beautiful and the Good—a spirit-like friend" and "a watchman for rascality in the mines and in public posts—a terrier till able to be a mastiff" (*People's Tribune* prospectus, quoted in "Dissolving Views," Gold Hill *Evening News,* 19 Jan 70, 2). The first number of the *Tribune* appeared on 13 January 1870, its masthead bearing a sweeping declaration: "Devoted to the Betterment of All Things, to the Defence of Right and to the People" (1:1). Among the specific causes espoused by the *Tribune* were women's rights, free schools, free homestead lands for the poor, and the abolition of income tax. The paper—initially eight pages, later reduced to four—cost fifty cents a year; a total of six numbers were issued, one each month through June 1870 ("The People's Tribune," Gold Hill *Evening News,* 13 Jan 70, 2; "Our Creed," *People's Tribune* 1 [June 70]: 32).

555.3–569.29 From the Territorial Enterprise, Jan. 20, 1870 . . . CONRAD WIEGAND.] This account by Wiegand appeared on the front page of the *Enterprise* of 20 January 1870, labeled as an "advertisement" and entitled "Mr. Winters' Assault on Conrad Wiegand." Wiegand reprinted the account—slightly corrected and revised—in the February number of his own *People's Tribune,* with the title given at 555.4, "A Seeming Plot for Assassination Miscarried." Mark Twain's source for the account was in fact Wiegand's reprinting in the *Tribune,* and not the *Enterprise,* as the credit line seems to imply. He could have obtained a copy of the *Tribune* from Joseph Goodman, when Goodman visited him in the spring of 1871. Indeed, it is possible that Goodman brought with him other material on the Wiegand controversy, perhaps as background for a planned book of his own, or for a joint project that remains unidentified (see the Introduction, page 841).

555.5 TO THE EDITOR OF THE ENTERPRISE] The intended addressee of Wiegand's newspaper letter has not been identified. The official editor-in-chief of the *Enterprise,* Joseph Goodman, was not in Nevada in January 1870, having left Virginia City on 1 December 1869 for a trip to Europe ("For Europe," Virginia City *Territorial Enterprise,* 2 Dec 69, 2). Nevertheless, it could have been he who "warned" (555.8) Wiegand and made "prophecies" (555.16) about the consequences of publicly opposing the Bank of California (see the next note). The acting editor, in Goodman's absence, may have been Rollin Daggett, who would take over the editorship when William Sharon bought the newspaper in 1874 (see the note at 340.8–9).

555.6–7 Months ago, when Mr. Sutro incidentally exposed mining mismanagement on the Comstock] On 20 September 1869 Adolph Sutro delivered a speech in Piper's Opera House in Virginia City, to persuade miners and other workingmen to lend their financial and political support to his tunnel project (see the notes at 360n.3–9 and 360n.12). He accused the Bank of California, which had initially backed the tunnel but was now strongly opposed to it, of having created a virtual monopoly on Comstock mining and milling operations through mortgages and unethical stock manipulations. Furthermore, he charged, this "bank ring" had fostered "ruinous and wasteful" management practices that exploited laborers, created extremely uncomfortable and unsafe working conditions, and would soon exhaust the surface lodes. He asserted that the proposed tunnel would increase safety in the mines by providing a means of escape from underground fires, such as the one that had recently killed about forty miners in the Yellow Jacket shaft. At the same time it would destroy the bank's monopoly and empower workingmen to "rule the destinies of this State" ("Speech of Adolph Sutro," Virginia City *Territorial Enterprise,* 23 Sept 69, 1, 4; Stewart and Stewart, 59–80).

555.7–8 among others roused me to protest against its continuance] Wiegand and others were persuaded by Sutro's speech to join his fight against the "banking ring." Within a few days, on 29 September, an unsigned advertisement appeared in the *Enterprise* for an 11 November meeting of Yellow Jacket stockholders, to discuss "an investigation into the affairs of the Company and a change in the management of the mine" ("Yellow Jacket Stockholders," 2). Wiegand pressed the fight in other ways as well. On 30 October the Gold Hill *Evening News* mentioned a circular he had produced attacking the Bank of California, reportedly containing "the *wildest* set of ideas" (" 'Awake!' " 2). And on 5 November the *Enterprise* announced an upcoming public meeting at which Wiegand was to deliver an address entitled "The Morals of Nevada, and the Future of the Comstock Mines" ("People's Tribune Meeting," 2).

555.26–29 On Thursday last . . . I was felled to the ground, and . . . kicked by a man] On 13 January 1870, while delivering the first issues of the *Tribune,* Wiegand was assaulted by a man named Griffith Williams, who was arrested and fined $7.50 by Judge E. C. Cook. The next day the Gold Hill *Evening News* remarked, "Mr. Wiegand rightly thinks that if that is the price set for half killing a man, $15 only would be the price for completing the job, according to Cook" ("A Dangerous Precedent," 14 Jan 70, 3; "Our Publisher Assaulted," *People's Tribune* 1 [Feb 70]: 1).

556.26–28 JOHN B. WINTERS, President of the Yellow Jacket Company, a political aspirant and a military General] Winters was the president and superintendent of the Yellow Jacket mine (see the next note) from April 1864 until November 1870. He served in the second Territorial Legislature and ran for Congress in 1864 under the first (defeated)

Nevada state constitution, and was an officer in Nevada's militia. Clemens first became friendly with Winters and his wife in 1862, while residing in Carson City. On several occasions he wrote warmly and favorably of Winters's character and tried to advance his political career, suggesting in mid-1863, for example, that he should run for territorial delegate to Congress, for the "people here know him, respect him, and have confidence in him, and he could be elected very easily" (SLC 1863k). After Winters's attack on Wiegand, the *People's Tribune* described him as a "powerful but cowardly bully, whose best title to the term of gentleman would seem to be that he is well-barbered, wears good clothes, drives a good team, and is permitted by genuine gentlemen in San Francisco to retain the Presidency or Superintendence of an important mine" ("Mr. Winters' Attack on Conrad Wiegand," *People's Tribune* 1 [Feb 70]: 13; *ET&S1*, 487, 488–89; "Report of the Territorial Adjutant-General for 1863," Virginia City *Union*, 4 Feb 64, 1; Doten 2:1109; Angel, 506).

556.27 Yellow Jacket Company] The Yellow Jacket silver mine, just south of Gold Hill, was located in May 1859 and consisted of 1,200 feet of the Comstock lode; the company was incorporated in February 1863 with a capital value of $1,200,000. In his correspondence for the San Francisco *Evening Bulletin* in December 1866, Mark Twain characterized the Yellow Jacket as the "principal mine" of the area, a formerly "shaky" operation that had been salvaged by "good management," presumably under Winters's direction (SLC 1866rr).

556.29–30 PHILIP LYNCH, Editor and proprietor of the Gold Hill *News*] Lynch (1822–72) went to the West in 1850 from Pennsylvania. He was a proprietor of the Sacramento *Index*, and then, in 1862–63, the *Placer Courier* in Forest Hill, California. He founded the Gold Hill *Evening News* in October 1863 and continued with the successful daily as publisher and editor until his death in February 1872 (Sacramento *Union:* "Died," 16 Feb 72, 5; "The Death of Philip Lynch," 17 Feb 72, 1, reprinting the Gold Hill *Evening News;* Lingenfelter and Gash, 97). Beginning in 1869, Lynch's newspaper followed the lead of the Bank of California and the major Comstock mining companies in opposing Adolph Sutro and his tunnel project. Lynch also supported John B. Winters and consistently put a good face on Yellow Jacket affairs and prospects. When the special meeting of Yellow Jacket stockholders was called, his newspaper refused to run the advertisement for it, calling it "irresponsible," and stating that the mine had "always been well conducted, and never better than under the management of its present officers" ("The Yellow Jacket S. M. Co.," Gold Hill *Evening News,* 29 Sept 69, 2).

557.23 as a stockholder in the Yellow Jacket mine] Wiegand owned thirty shares of Yellow Jacket stock ("Mr. Wiegand's Card," *People's Tribune* 1 [Feb 70]: 14).

557.26 Sharon] William Sharon (1821–85), an Ohio-born financier, had been the general agent in Virginia City for the Bank of California's Nevada branch since its establishment in November 1864; he also served as the agent for the Gold Hill office, which opened the following year. As the production of the Comstock mines declined in the latter half of the decade, Sharon lured mine owners and investors to borrow money at low interest rates and then foreclosed when they defaulted. The bank soon controlled extensive mining and milling operations—among them the Yellow Jacket mine—under the aegis of the Union Mill and Mining Company, and Sharon quickly accumulated a personal fortune (Virginia City *Union:* advertisement and "Bank of California," 17 Nov 64, 2, 3; Lord, 244–56, 263–65; Lavender 1975, 186–87; Hart, 468).

558.3 Dr. Zabriskie] C. B. Zabriskie, a physician and surgeon, had an office on Main Street in Gold Hill near Wiegand's assay office (advertisement, Gold Hill *Evening News,* 2 July 69, 2).

558.13 Sheriff Cummings] W. J. Cummings, sheriff of Storey County from November 1868 until November 1870 (Angel, 607).

560.7–8 those damnably false charges which you have preferred against me in that . . . lying sheet of yours] According to the Gold Hill *Evening News,* Winters objected to "two articles in the Tribune—the one being headed 'Hiding Ore,' and the other being the answers to 'A Miner's' communication, called 'What's the Matter with Yellow Jacket?'" (Lynch 1870a, 3). "Hiding Ore," an undated letter to the editor from "Silver Stuck," charged that Yellow Jacket officials had concealed information about the discovery of a body of good ore, asking "what right John B. Winters, or Wm. Sharon, or any one else, had to *order* a discovery of that kind to be concealed; or, *while levying assessments,* to allow that body of ore to remain untouched?" The second article—a letter to the editor dated 15 December 1869 and signed "A Miner," together with the *Tribune*'s response—accused the Yellow Jacket management of numerous illegal or highly questionable practices, summed up in the assertion that "Wm. Sharon, the Board of Trustees, or John B. Winters are indictable before the Grand Jury for offenses of omission and commission, of which, if convicted, that fact would go far to purify the atmosphere of the State" (*People's Tribune* 1 [Jan 70]: 3). The author of the editorial response is not known; Wiegand clearly implies (at 563.9–12) that he did not write it. The allegations it contained were evidently true, for the most part. Winters himself reportedly later admitted that he had done Sharon's "dirty work"—sabotaging mine equipment and adulterating the ore being mined—in order to "break the price of the stock" (Michelson, 189–90; Marye, 88–89, 92–93; Grant H. Smith, 91, 93; Bancroft 1891–92, 4:52–57). After the disastrous Yellow Jacket fire of April 1869, the company's stock—which had reached over two thousand dollars a share in the spring of 1865—plummeted, never to recover: the price was under forty dollars by October. Joseph Goodman was evidently among those who "lost heavily" on Yellow Jacket stock, claiming that the mine's indisputably rich ore "all went to feed the Union Mill and Mining Company's mills. The stockholders never got a dividend from it" (Michelson, 190; Angel, 59, 615; Kelly 1863, 18; Lord, 269–77, 426–35).

560.22–24 Months ago you put your property out of your hands . . . to escape losing it on prosecution for libel] Wiegand responded to this charge in the February number of the *People's Tribune.* He explained that in 1865 his Gold Hill assaying business appeared to be growing so rapidly that he borrowed money from the Bank of California to expand. When ore production dropped late in the year, the bank brought suit for repayment, and his assaying tools were confiscated and sold by the sheriff. The case of *Sharon* v. *Wiegand* was heard in December 1865, and Wiegand was forced to suspend business; the court accepted his bankruptcy in January 1866. Wiegand almost immediately reopened with a new co-proprietor, and began to repay his debts, although not legally obliged to do so. In the fall of 1869, when establishing the *People's Tribune,* he anticipated that he might become a target for libel suits, and "to prevent a second seizure of my tools, I *sold* them and delivered possession of the same in the presence of witnesses," since "the best security against legal plunder in the State of Nevada . . . is not to be upright, *but to be POOR*" ("Mr. Wiegand's Card," *People's Tribune* 1 [Feb 70]: 14; Gold Hill *Evening News:* " 'Awake!' " 30 Oct 69, 2; "Insolvent Notice," 2 Jan 66, 4; "For Assay," 19 Jan 66, 2; advertisement, 29 Jan 66, 2; Virginia City *Union:* "The Court Reports" and "Insolvent," 17 Dec 65, 3).

561.33 Address to the People] The title of Wiegand's *People's Tribune* prospectus, published on 3 November 1869 (see the note at 554.14–15).

563.17–18 I, a man of family, and *not* as Mr. Winters is, "alone."] Wiegand and his wife, Martha, had one daughter. Winters's wife had recently died of cancer in San Francisco, on 20 November 1869 (Virginia City *Territorial Enterprise:* "The Suicide of Conrad Wiegand," 16 June 80, 3; "Death of Conrad Wiegand," 15 June 80, 3; "Death of Mrs. John B. Winters," 21 Nov 69, 3).

563.32–33 "Surely in vain the net is spread in the sight of any bird."] Proverbs 1:17.

567.23–24 that unguarded remark of Philip Lynch convicts him of having been privy . . . to Mr. Winters' intentions] In response to Wiegand's accusation against him, Lynch wrote: "I trust, also, to be able to vindicate myself of the foul charges of 'conspiracy to murder and assassinate,' and acting in bad faith towards Mr. Wiegand in asking him into my office to have an interview with General Winters—in making which charges Mr. Wiegand has done me a gross injustice" (Lynch 1870b, 2).

569.3–4 he has . . . suffered a thoroughly garbled statement of facts to appear in the Gold Hill *News*] Wiegand refers to "A Case of Slanderous Vilification and Its Consequences," almost certainly written by Lynch. Lynch's report ignored the substance of the *Tribune*'s charges, characterizing them as "rather sweeping insinuations against the honesty and integrity of several business men in this community." The account also differed from Wiegand's in some of its particulars. For example, Lynch stated that Wiegand refused to visit Winters at the Yellow Jacket office (cf. 557.19–558.11), and he claimed that Wiegand initially agreed to sign a statement acknowledging that he had written the charges against Winters "willfully and deliberately, knowing them to be false" (cf. 561.4–10; Lynch 1870a, 3).

569.7–9 what even the Gold Hill *News* has pronounced a disgraceful affair . . . because of some telegraphic mistake in the account of it] Lynch explained in the *News:*

> We regret that this disgraceful affair occurred in the NEWS office, and it happened without any collusion whatever on the part of anybody connected with the office. The senior editor, who was the only witness of the affair, besides the parties themselves, especially feels aggrieved, as the report has been telegraphed all over the State that he was "cowhided like the devil" on Saturday! When in fact it was all a mistake. Several telegrams have been received by him to-day, from different sections, inquiring after his health, the price of raw-hides, etc., etc. (Lynch 1870a, 3)

569.15 W. C. Ralston] William C. Ralston (1826–75), son of an Ohio farmer, served as a steamboat clerk and then as the Panama City agent for a steamship company. He moved to San Francisco in 1854 and within two years became involved in banking. In 1864 he founded the Bank of California with Darius O. Mills and served as its cashier and manager until 1873, when he succeeded Mills as president. Ralston's injudicious and unauthorized investments and speculations in a vast empire of enterprises on the Comstock lode and in San Francisco led to the bank's collapse in August 1875. Forced to resign on 27 August, he drowned while swimming in San Francisco Bay later that same day. Subsequent investigations revealed that he owed the bank several million dollars (Lavender 1975, 372–79).

569.32–33 the merited castigation . . . ought to have been done in the street] Mark Twain's comment is strikingly similar to one printed in the Gold Hill *News:* "We regret, as a friend, that Winters was so delicate about the chastisement as to do it in a corner. It ought to have been done, if at all, in the street" ("An Explanation Wanted," Gold Hill *Evening News*, 1 Feb 70, 2, reprinting the Hamilton [Nev.] *White Pine News* of 29 January). As mentioned earlier, Mark Twain might have read this remark, and others equally unsympathetic to Wiegand, in Nevada newspapers supplied by Goodman (see the note at 555.3–569.29).

569.34–36 When a journalist maligns a citizen . . . he deserves to be thrashed for it] The contempt for Wiegand that Mark Twain expresses throughout this appendix and especially in this final gloss is a marked change from his earlier approval, even admiration, for him (see the note at 554.10–11). Although his friendship with Winters may have influenced his attitude, it hardly seems an adequate justification for the intensity of his scorn. It has been suggested that the Wiegand episode revived uncomfortable memories of the journalistic disputes that precipitated his departure from Virginia City in May 1864, albeit his own offense was inadvertent and prankish, and in no way comparable to Wiegand's deliberate exposé (see the notes at 378.6–8 and 379.37, and Robinson, 60–64). It has also been conjectured that Mark Twain's inability to perceive Wiegand as a "peculiar" but nevertheless "brave and prudent man, devoted to democratic rights, to journalistic confidentiality of sources, and to a free press" was in the end merely the result of his own cynicism, which caused him to believe that "Conrad Wiegand should have known better than to attack things the way they were. The strong will prosper. The rest will be thrashed" (Bridgman, 58–60).

SUPPLEMENT A

Background Material Supplied by Orion Clemens

Item 1: Orion Clemens to Mollie Clemens, 8 and 9 September 1861

When Clemens began to work on *Roughing It* in July 1870, he asked his brother Orion to help him recall the details of their stagecoach trip to Nevada Territory in July–August 1861: "Have you a memorandum of the route we took—or the names of any of the Stations we stopped at?" Orion responded by forwarding his journal of the trip, which Clemens found to be "ever so much use" in writing the overland chapters.[1] Unfortunately, this journal is no longer extant. Its contents survive, however, in a letter that Orion wrote to his wife—Mary Eleanor (Mollie) Clemens (1834–1904)—upon his arrival in Carson City: Orion copied the journal, probably in its entirety, into this letter, which is transcribed below from the original in the Mark Twain Papers (CU-MARK). Mollie, who had remained with her family in Keokuk, Iowa, joined Orion in Nevada in October 1862 with their daughter, Jennie Clemens (1855–64). The portion of the letter giving the trip itinerary is thoroughly glossed in the explanatory notes to the *Roughing It* text; notes for the remaining portion are provided below.

Carson City, Nevada Territory,
September 8, 1861.

My Dear Wife:—

Thinking you may take some interest in my journal, I copy it:

July 26.—Left St. Joseph. Started on the plains about ten miles out. The plains here are simply prairie.

July 27. Crossed the Nebraska line about 180 miles from St. Joseph. Here we saw the first Jack Rabbit. They have larger ~~legs~~ bodies, longer legs and longer ears than our rabbits.

July 28. Saw first prairie wolf, and first antelope,/, and first prairie dogs

[1] *L1*, 242 n. 1, 382–83; SLC to OC, 15 July 70, CU-MARK, in *MTL*, 1:174–75; SLC to OC, 24–31? Aug 70, *MTL*, 1:175.

and villages. Also came in sight of the long range of Sand Hills. 2 P.M. Timber of Platte in sight. 7 miles further arrived at Ft. Kearney, 296 miles from St. Joseph. The Platte is a muddy, shallow stream, full of sand bars. This was the South Platte. In places it is skirted by timber, but generally it meanders through the plains like a ribbon, without a tree or shrub on its banks.

July 29.—Saw the first Indians, 75 miles from Kearney, with Buffalo skin wigwams, the hide dressed on both sides, and put up on poles, sugar loaf shape. Here we found Buffalo robes at three to six dollars, beautifully dressed, and some of them wonderfully large. This is the Buffalo region, and robes are higher as you go further, either east or west. Saw an Indian child's grave on a scaffold about eight feet from the ground, supported by four stakes. Sand Hills and Platte river still in sight.

Tuesday, July 30. Arrived at the "Crossing" of the South Platte, alias "Overland City," alias "Julesburg," at 11 A. M., 470 miles from St. Joseph. Saw to-day first Cactus. 1:20 P. M. across the South Platte.

Wednesday, July 31.—Sunrise. Court House Rock, Chimney Rock, and Scott's Bluffs, in sight. At noon passed through Scott's Bluff's pass/, 580 miles from St. Joseph. This was the first high ground, since entering upon the plains. All was vast, prairie, until we reached Fort Kearney. Soon afterwards, we struck the barren region, and thenceforward we had a level expanse covered with sage brush, and that was the character of the growth until we arrived here, the plains being more or less elevated, or broken, but in other respects preserving the same characteristics. After we crossed the South Platte we found a great deal of cactus. When we crossed Scotts Bluff's we had been traveling in sight of the North Platte river all day. In the afternoon we found alkali water in the road, giving it a soapy appearance, and the ground in many places appearing as if whitewashed. About 6 P. M., crossed the range of Sand hills which had been stretching along our left in sight, since Sunday. We crossed this long low range near the scene of the Indian mail robbery and massacre in 1856, wherein Babbitt alone was saved, though left for dead. The whole party was killed, including some passengers. There was some treasure in the coach, which the Indians got.

Thursday, Aug. 1. Found ourselves this morning in the "Black Hills," with "Laramie Peak," looming up in large proportions. This peak is 60 miles from Fort Laramie, which we passed in the night. We took breakfast at "Horseshoe" station, forty miles from Fort Laramie, and 676 miles from St. Joseph. After dinner we climbed to the yellow pines. This afternoon passed, near La Parelle station, the little canon in which the Express rider was last night when a bullet from Indians on the side of the road passed through his coat. About 2½ hours before the station keeper at La Parelle had fired four times at one Indian. At noon we passed a Morm train 33 wagons long. They were nooning. About midnight, at a station we stopped at to change horses, a dispute arose between our conductor and four drivers who were at the Station. The conductor came to me for a pistol, but before I could hand it to him, one of the men came up and commenced cursing him. Another then came up and knocked the conductor down, cutting a bad gash in his upper lip, and telling him he would have killed him if he had had his boots on, and would ~~have~~ killed him ~~then~~ if he reported him. I had not heard the fuss before the pistol was called for, and supposed it was for the Indians, who, it was said, would be dangerous along this part of the road. The four drivers were drunk.

Friday, Aug. 2.—3 o'clock, A. M., passed over North Platte bridge, 760 miles from St. Joseph. 2 P. M., reached "Sweet water" creek, "Independence Rock," the "Devil's Gap," the "Devil's Gate," and alkali, or "Soda Lake," where the mormons shovel up the saleratus, take it to Salt Lake, and sell it for 25¢ per pound. A few days ago they took two wagon loads. Also, the "Rocky Ride," all within two or three miles of Independence Rock, which is 811 miles from St. Joseph. Passed in the night, "Cold Spring," an ice water spring, issuing near one of the Stations. Now, or at any time of the year, the men at this Station by scraping off the soil, sometimes only to the depth of six inches, can cut out pretty, clear, square blocks of ice. This "cold spring" is 36 miles from "Independence Rock," and 847 miles from St. Joseph.

Saturday, Aug. 3. Breakfast at Rock Ridge Station, 24 miles from "Cold Spring," and 871 miles from St. Joseph. A mile further on is "South Pass City" consisting of four log cabins, one of which is the post office, and one unfinished. Two miles further on saw for the first time, snow on the mountains, glittering in the sun like settings of silver. Near the summit of the South Pass appears in sight Fremont's Peak. The wind river mountains, in which we first saw snow, are about 50 miles distant. About 72 6 miles beyond the very summit of the South Pass of the Rocky mountains, is Pacific station, in Utah Territory, near the Nebraska line, where we got an excellent dinner. Near this Station are the Pacific Springs, which issue in a branch, taking up its march for the Pacific Ocean. The summit of the Rocky mountains, or the highest point of the South Pass, is 902 miles from St. Joseph.

Sunday, Aug. 4.—Crossed Green River. It is something like the Illinois, except that it is a very pretty clear river. The place we crossed was about 70 miles from the summit of the South Pass. Uinta mountains in sight, with snow on them, and portions of their summits hidden by the clouds. About 5 P. M arrived at Fort Bridger, on Black's Fork of Green river, 52 miles from the crossing of Green river, about 120 miles from the South Pass, and 1025 miles from St. Joseph.

Monday, Aug. 5.—52 miles further on, near the head of Echo Canon, were encamped 60 soldiers from Camp Floyd. Yesterday they fired upon 300 or 400 Utes, whom they supposed gathered for no good purpose. The Indians returned the fire, when the soldiers chased them four miles, took four prisoners, talked with and released them, and then talked with their chief. Echo Canon is 20 miles long, with many sandstone cliffs, (red) in curious shapes, and often rising perpendicularly 400 feet.

4 P. M., arrived on the summit of "Big mountain," 15 miles from Salt Lake City, when the most gorgeous view of mountain peaks yet encountered, burst on our sight.

Arrived at Salt Lake City at dark, and put up at the Salt Lake House,. There are about 15,000 inhabitants. The houses are scattering, mostly small frame, with large yards and plenty of trees. High mountains surround the city. On some of these perpetual snow is visible. Salt Lake City is 240 miles from the South Pass, or 1148 miles from St. Joseph.

Wednesday, Aug. 7. Bathed in the warm spring. Mountains in the morning, Southwest and East enveloped in clouds.

Thursday, Aug. 8.—Arrived at Fort Crittenden—(Camp Floyd) 8 A. M., 45 miles from Salt Lake City. Arrived at the edge of the desert, 95 miles from Salt Lake City, at 4 P. M.

Friday, Aug. 9.—Sunrise. Across the desert, 45 miles, and at the commencement of the "little Desert." 2 o'clock, across the little desert, 23 miles, and 163 miles from Salt Lake, being 68 miles across the two deserts, with only a spring at Fish Creek Station to seperate them. They are called deserts because there is no water in them. They are barren, but so is the balance of the route.

Saturday, Aug 10. Arrived in the forenoon at the entrance of "Rocky Canon," 255 miles from Salt Lake City.

Sunday, Aug 11.— Passed points declared by the driver to be the highest we had crossed. Saturday and Sunday nights were very cold, though the days were very warm.

Tuesday, Aug 13.—Arrived at Carson Sink where Carson river loses itself. It is a beautiful lake, 25 miles long by 15 wide, and 60 miles from Carson City.

Wednesday, Aug. 14,—Arrived at Carson City 580 miles from Salt Lake, or 1700 miles from St. Joseph

Carson City, N. T. Sept 9, 1861.

My Dear Wife—

I am very sorry to find from your letter of Aug. 9th that you are sick; I will accept that as your apology for not writing every week as you promised. Your description of the events going on around you are very interesting. It must be deeply exciting to you all. Even to me it comes home, very close home, when I see the names of intimate friends engaged in the battle, near both to Memphis & Keokuk, and some of them wounded. The

Walker family is singularly divided. Tarrence's[2] speech was eloquent/, though brief.

I am very glad indeed you waved your handkerchief to the soldiers in St. Louis. It was a noble impulse, and they will always remember it.

I received to-day your letter written ~~to-day~~ August 2 at Lagrange. Have you any idea what made Jennie's face become a running sore and a scab? Poor little thing, I hate to hear of her being in that condition. Tell her I love her and want her and her Ma out here very much, and I am sorry she is not well. I think Tom Bohon will do very well for Belle.[3] Give my love to Cousin Mary.[4] It gets pretty hot here about noon, but the climate is too dry for sweat. It has not rained since I have been here. I have just read the 28th chapter of Deuteronomy.

To-night I received from you the most fearful letter I ever read. When I commenced reading it I felt like I did when in Tennessee on my way to Memphis, I picked up a paper announcing Henry's death—the same stopping and stillness of the heart.[5] How thankful I was when I got through the letter, and found the dear little creature was thought by the doctor to be out of danger. Her affection for and thoughtfulness of me touches me deeply. How could we spare her? What was the matter with Jennie? What caused her convulsions?

I am sorry you had to pay out any money on the trunk. I hope, as Congress has made an appropriation for us I will soon have some money to send you. I brought my dictionary with me. I wrote from Salt Lake. Nothing keeps me from depression on account of your absence, but being busy from the time I get up till I go to bed. I do not know that I am any more attached to the Swedenborgian[6] than the Presbyterian faith.

Do they still send you the Tri-weekly Democrat/?[7] What a relief the last part of your letter was after reading the first part. I shall look for a letter every day, until Jennie gets entirely well. You have indeed passed through a terrible trial—only three hours sleep in three days. I send you

---

[2]Unidentified.

[3]Thomas B. Bohon married Susan Isabella (Belle) Stotts (b. 1837), Mollie's sister, in October 1861 (*L1*, 68–69 n. 12).

[4]Unidentified.

[5]Henry Clemens (1838–58), Orion and Samuel's younger brother, was injured in a boiler explosion on a Mississippi River steamboat on 13 June 1858 and died a week later (*L1*, 80–86, 382).

[6]Emanuel Swedenborg (1688–1772) was a Swedish scientist and mystic who claimed that direct insight into the spiritual world had revealed to him the true meaning of the Scriptures. His ideas aroused considerable interest among American intellectuals—especially the Transcendentalists—during the nineteenth century.

[7]The St. Louis *Missouri Democrat*—a Republican newspaper, despite its name. Orion was acquainted with one of its editors, William McKee (Rowell, 59; *L2*, 198 n. 1).

many kisses, and don't forget to give Jennie a great many for me. I wish you were both with me.

Good night.

Your affectionate Husband,
Orion Clemens.

Item 2: Comparative Chart of the Overland Itinerary

THE FOLLOWING CHART summarizes, in schematic form, the overland itinerary as set down in Orion Clemens's letter to his wife of 8 and 9 September 1861, and as described by Mark Twain in *Roughing It.* Its purpose is to enable the reader to determine, at a glance, the major points of similarity and difference between the two accounts. The mileage figures in the second column are either taken directly, or calculated, from Orion's letter. An arrow (→) in the "*Roughing It* narrative" column indicates that the text agrees with Orion's account, and was presumably based on it. Whenever the text specifically mentions time and/or distance, it is noted in this column. Entries in *italic type* indicate that Mark Twain used exact wording from Orion's account. Entries in **boldface type** indicate incidents mentioned in both accounts, but on different days of the journey. Entries in SMALL CAPITALS indicate incidents unique to *Roughing It.* The chart does not include incidents and anecdotes in the narrative of the book which cannot be linked to a particular time or place in the itinerary, such as the description of overland facilities in chapter 4, the anecdote of Eckert and the cat in chapter 7, or Greeley's ride in chapter 20.

Page.line	Day	Miles	Orion's letter	*Roughing It* narrative
6.4	Day 1, 26 July	0	departure from St. Joseph	→
12.18	Day 2, 27 July	180	Nebraska boundary	→ 180m
12.25	↓		first jackass rabbit	→
——	Day 3, 28 July		**first prairie dogs, cayote**	——
26.18	↓		timber of Platte, 2 P.M.	→ 2 P.M.
26.21	↓		——	CROSSING OF PLATTE, 5 P.M.
26.22	↓	296	Fort Kearny	→ 56 hours out, 300m
30.5	Day 4, 29 July	371	Indians, buffalo region	**first prairie dogs, cayote**
40.5	Day 5, 30 July	470	*Julesburg/Overland City,* 11 A.M.	→ noon, 5th day, 470m
41.11	↓		crossing of South Platte, 1:20 P.M.	→
41.27	Day 6, 31 July		——	BREAKDOWN, BEMIS & BULL, DAWN, 550M
50.2	↓		——	PONY-EXPRESS RIDER
52.8	↓	580	Scott's Bluffs Pass, noon	→
52.10	↓		*alkali water*	→
53.14	↓		*sand hills, mail robbery,* 6 P.M.	→
55.1	Day 7, 1 Aug	636	Fort Laramie, at night	→ 7th day
55.2	↓		Black Hills, Laramie Peak	→
55.7	↓	676	Horseshoe station	→ 676m
55.10	↓		La Prele ("La Parelle") station	→
55.13	↓		attack on pony rider	→
55.20	↓		attack on Indian	→
——	↓		**Mormon train, noon**	——
57.13	↓		altercation at station, midnight	→
67.14	Day 8, 2 Aug		——	BREAKFAST WITH SLADE
——	↓	760	North Platte Bridge, 3 A.M.	——
76.1	↓		——	**Mormon train, after breakfast,** 8th day, 798m
76.10	↓		——	BATH IN HORSE CREEK

76.19	↓		Sweetwater Creek, 2 P.M.	→ afternoon
76.19	↓	811	Independence Rock	→
76.23	↓		Soda Lake	→
77.3	↓	847	Cold Spring, at night	→ at night
——	Day 9, 3 Aug	871	breakfast at Rocky Ridge station	——
77.15	↓	872	South Pass City	→
78.16	↓	902	South Pass summit	→
81.38	↓	908	Pacific station	LEAF AND WATERMELON ANECDOTES
84.15	Day 10, 4 Aug	972	crossing of Green river	→ 10th day
85.4	↓	1025	Fort Bridger, 5 P.M.	→ 5 P.M., 1025m
85.7	Day 11, 5 Aug	1077	soldiers from Camp Floyd	→ 1077m
85.15	↓		Echo Cañon, 20m long	→ 20m long
85.27	↓	1133	*Big Mountain*, 4 P.M.	→ 4 P.M., 1133m
85.33	↓		——	SUPPER WITH A DESTROYING ANGEL
87.4	↓	1148	Salt Lake City, nightfall	→
89.8	Day 12, 6 Aug	——		SALT LAKE CITY SIGHTSEEING
92.19	Day 13, 7 Aug		bath in warm spring	VISIT TO BRIGHAM YOUNG
107.1	↓		——	MORMON BIBLE
120.15	↓		——	DEPARTURE, LATE EVENING
122.1	Day 14, 8 Aug	1193	Camp Floyd, 8 A.M.	→ 8 A.M., 1193–98m
122.3	↓	1243	edge of desert, 4 P.M.	→ 4 P.M., 1238–48m
122.7	Day 15, 9 Aug	1311	desert crossing, 68m across	→ 68m across
122.13	↓		Fish Springs ("Fish Creek") station	unnamed station
126.2	Day 16, 10 Aug	1403	Egan ("Rocky") Cañon, afternoon	→ 16th day, 1398m
126.6	↓		——	GOSHOOT INDIANS
130.1	Day 17, 11 Aug		highest points on trip	→ 17th day
130.6	Day 18, 12 Aug		——	REESE RIVER STATION, 18th day
130.23	Day 19, 13 Aug	1640	Carson Sink	→ 19th day
137.29	Day 20, 14 Aug	1700	Carson City	→ 20th day

Item 3: Orion Clemens to Samuel L. Clemens, 11 March 1871

On 10 March 1871 Clemens asked Orion to "torture your memory & write down in minute detail every fact & exploit in the desperado Slade's life that we heard on the Overland—& also describe his appearance & conversation as we saw him at Rocky Ridge station at breakfast" (NN-B†). Orion's response, written the following day, is transcribed below from the original in the Mark Twain Papers (CU-MARK); it provided Clemens with ideas for much of the material in chapter 10.

AGENTS WANTED FOR OVERLAND THROUGH ASIA, KNOX. UNCIVILIZED RACES, OR NATURAL HISTORY OF MAN, WOOD. INNOCENTS ABROAD, TWAIN. BEYOND THE MISSISSIPPI, FIELD, DUNGEON AND ESCAPE, PERSONAL HISTORY OF GRANT, RICHARDSON. GREAT METROPOLIS, BROWNE. THE GREAT REBELLION, HEADLEY. HISTORY OF THE BIBLE, STEBBINS. PEBBLES AND PEARLS, ABBY SAGE. ILLUSTRATED FAMILY BIBLES.

E. G. HASTINGS, PRES'T.
E. BLISS, JR., SEC'Y
F. E. BLISS, TREAS.

OFFICE AMERICAN PUBLISHING COMPANY,
149 ASYLUM STREET.

HARTFORD CONN. March 11 18 71

My Dear Bro:—

your letters of 9th & 10th just received. I showed them to Bliss, who is much pleased.

I don't think we heard of Slade till after we had left Rocky Ridge Station—the last before reaching South Pass station where ~~w~~‸ the clouds looked so low, where we saw the first snow, and where a spring with waters destined for the Atlantic stood within a man's length ‸(or within sight)‸ of another spring whose waters were about to commence a voyage to the Pacific. There was nothing then in a name to attract us to Slade, and yet I remember something of his appearance while totally forgetting all the others. Perhaps the driver's description caused the difference. We got there (to R R Station) about sun up. There were a lot of fellows, young and rough in a room adjoining that in which we sat~~. They~~ —if indeed it was not in the same room. They were ‸washing in a tin pan,‸ joking, laughing and chaffing each other, and kept it up at the table. I don't remember what they said, or anything they said, but I believe the subject was their hostelry and silly trifles. I think Slade got to the table after every body else did, and shewed good appetite for the bacon slices, &c. I think he was about your size, if any difference rather shorter and more slender. He had gray eyes, very light straight hair, no beard, and a hard, looking face seamed like a man of 60, though otherwise he did not seem over thirty. I think the sides of his face were wrinkled. His face was thin, his nose straight and ordinarily prominent—lips rather thinner than usual—otherwise nothing unusual about his mouth, except that ~~w~~ his smile was attractive and his manner pleasant. Nothing peculiar about his ~~wa~~ voice. It does not leave a pleasant recollection,—but I don't know in what respect—it was neither very fine nor very coarse. My impression is that he was a *division* agent, from Overland City to Salt Lake,—having ~~two~~ ‸*several*‸ conductors under him.~~—one each~~ The one who wanted us to lend him a pistol, I think had about two hundred miles or 240 miles of the road. Slade was *not* a conductor. He had the conductors and drivers under him. They were a wild and desperate set, and the contractors on the Butterfield line (It seems to me that was the name of the old weekly or monthly line there and when the new daily line came on that he ‸(Butterfield)‸ took his stock south and ran the southern overland route through Santa Fe,,) kept him a long time after they knew of his infernal deviltry, because he was the only man the~~y s~~ ‸conductors, drivers and station men‸ held in awe. It seems to me ‸we‸ had got down off the Rocky mountains—no, now may be it was before we reached the foot of the last ridge on this side, after all, that the driver commenced telling about Slade. I was sitting outside with the driver. I don't recollect whether you were sitting with us or inside, and I told you afterwards. Any how it was getting late, we were on level ground and hasting to make the next station, when the driver pointed out to me (or us) a corral and told us that there had been a fight there. Some spaniards were keeping the station. They were contumacious in some way and Slade brought some of his ~~drivers~~ ‸men‸ over ‸from other stations‸. The Spaniards used their ~~for~~ corral as a fortification, but Slade's party was victorious. There were several, but he killed them all. One of them had a ~~wife~~ squaw wife and two little children. Slade fastened them up in a house (or the house) and setting fire to it burned them to death, swearing none of the breed should live. There had been bad blood between him and the Spaniards some time. Once they got him fastened up in the station by fastening the door when he was in, mounting guard ~~outside,~~ and giving him half an hour to prepare for death. He entreated them to ~~pre~~ permit him to bid farewell to his wife. They finally consented that he might send for her. He dispatched a note for her by the pony express which seems to have come along about the right time. She came immediately on horseback and was allowed to enter his room. For a wonder he seems to have been caught without his arms, and that he only needed a visit from his wife to supply the deficiency, for soon after her arrival he issued with her from the station, ~~with~~ ‸having‸ a pistol in each hand, with which he defied his guards, and mounting the horse with his wife galloped away.

Once Slade had a quarrel with a huge teamster, and in ‸an‸ apparent excess of courage dared the latter to fight. Whether the teamster had got him "covered" first, or whether Slade was afraid of the result on some other account, he proposed that each should throw away his pistol and fight a fair fist fight. The teamster agreed and the pistols were flung one side; but the moment the teamster's ‸pistol‸ left his hand Slade sprang for them, ‸pistols,‸ obtained both and shot the teamster dead.

Slade had a desperate fight at Overland City with Julian a Frenchman. Slade had a pistol and the Frenchman a shot gun. He was as desperate a man as Slade, and forced the latter to retreat into a house where he took refuge behind a door which stood ajar. They shot at each other through the door, and Slade was so badly wounded about the body as that he was confined to his bed several weeks. Julian improved the opportunity to leave for the purpose of avoiding Slade's vengeance. He went to Pikes Peak and was gone about six months. He returned and was captured by Slade or his friends near one of the stations/, and bound to a tree. Then Slade cut off his ears, tantalized him, poured out invectives on him, shot his so as barely to miss him several times, and after torturing him half an hour in these ways, killed him.

I don't know how he came to leave that road, but he went to Montana, where he was worked up into hanged by a vigilance committee. I believe his offence was belonging to a gang of horse thieves and robbers, with some particular murder laid to his charge. On the scaffold he was unmanned by terror and begged piteously for life.

Charlie Kincaid[1] had a rough time on that old mail route with the Indians once. If you want it I guess Mollie will remember something about it.

I have done the best ‸I could‸ on Slade—told all I can remember—and more than I recollect distinctly or W feel entirely certain of—trusting that it would be practically near enough correct.

Lo Bliss don't think you can sell your house soon.

Love to wife and baby.

Bliss has a queer notion about things. He can work at his business all through the month and then in a day or two sit down and spin off no end of insurance articles, and if I am not down here in the office where he writing and where he can holler at me he to go after a proof or do something about the paper he thinks I aint doing any thing, and instead of hiring a girl to write on wrappers has put me at it, because, I suppose, I spent time walking to think in the fresh air, or staid at home to pol after meals to polish up what I had written where I could be uninterrupted, having writ seized the opportunity to write the rough drafts at the office while Bliss was away at New York, for when he is away the others don't bother me. I

[1]Possibly the same "Mr. Kincaid, a Salt Lake trader," who was wounded by Indians in a stagecoach attack in the 1850s. Although he received "two arrow shots as he fled," he "entirely recovered by the next year" (Root and Connelley, 77).

dispair of making him comprehend the matter, and so accept the situation, being resolved to publish nothing of any importance which has not been well considered. I feel some delicacy in speaking to him also, because if I were to object to my girlish duties ~~and~~ ~~and~~ on the ground that I wanted time to think, and then fail to produce anything valuable he ~~he~~ would consider that I had merely made a shirking excuse and was humbugging him‸.~~, hoping eventually to work into something higher.~~

He shows about the same discernment in grumbling because your portrait goes into the Aldine.[2] I laughed at him telling him you couldn't ~~and~~ propose it ‸for this paper‸ and he hadn't thought of it and the Aldine people had. ~~I'll work along here the best I can till I get my machine out,~~[3] ~~and then I shall hope for better things.~~

Your Brother,
Orion.

Knox[4] has a column for this paper he charges $10 for.
What I am at work on is the exchange list—copying from a book—perhaps 5,000 papers—to help out till first April as they are taking stock.

---

[2]Clemens's portrait appeared in *The Aldine: A Typographic Art Journal* for April 1871 (58).

[3]An invention Orion was developing, not further identified.

[4]Thomas W. Knox (1835–96), a New York *Herald* correspondent and author of *Overland through Asia*, published by the American Publishing Company in 1870.

SUPPLEMENT B

Maps

Map 1, divided into four adjoining segments, is a large-scale representation of the western United States and territories that figure in the *Roughing It* narrative. It depicts the route that Samuel Clemens and his brother Orion followed on their journey by overland-mail stagecoach from St. Joseph, Missouri, to Carson City, Nevada Territory, in July–August 1861. This route has been reliably established by studies of the overland mail and of the pony express, which often—but not always—made use of the mail-route facilities. All of the significant geographic features—both physical and cultural—mentioned in *Roughing It* and in the explanatory notes are represented on the map, in addition to other selected major features useful for orientation. The level of detail is not uniform: western Nevada Territory, for example, which contains more features of importance to the book than do other regions, appears in greater detail. The map is accurate as of July–August 1861, except for the town of Austin, Nevada, established in 1863. The representation of the travelers' daily progress is based on Orion's letter to his wife of 8 and 9 September 1861 (supplement A, item 1). Also shown are the three routes between Nevada Territory and Sacramento: the overland-mail route to Placerville, the road over Henness Pass (which Clemens traveled in May 1864), and the road over Donner Pass (which he traveled in April–May 1868).

Maps 2 and 3 represent a closer view of western Nevada Territory as of November 1861, when the Territorial Legislature established the first county boundaries: Map 2 shows the Humboldt region, which Clemens visited in the winter of 1861–62; Map 3 shows Carson City, Virginia City, and environs, plus the Esmeralda region—including Mono Lake—where he sojourned in the spring and summer of 1862 (having made a brief visit there in September 1861). Dotted lines indicate commonly traveled trails and roads. Clemens's probable route to Unionville is shown on Map 2, but the route of his return trip as far as Ragtown is not known; the map depicts the possible routes. The *Roughing It* account of his horseback trip to Aurora in April 1862 implies that he followed the stagecoach road, by way of Genoa. The route he walked on his return trip to Virginia City is not known for certain. Map 3 shows the two likeliest possibilities: the stagecoach road, and a shorter road between the Walker River and Dayton. Nothing is known about Clemens's routes to and from Lake Tahoe. On his first visit, in September 1861 (described in chapter 22), he apparently visited the north or the northeastern shore; in August 1863 he went to Glenbrook, midway along the eastern shore (see *L1*, 127 n. 5, 265 n. 3). According to his *Roughing It* account he made other trips as well. The map depicts the likeliest routes.

The following general source books defined in References were useful in preparing the maps: Angel's *History*, Browning's *Place Names of the Sierra Nevada*, Carlson's *Nevada Place Names*, Kelly's 1862 *Directory*, Mattes's *Great Platte River Road*, and Root and Connolley's *Overland Stage*. Clemens's route to the Humboldt region was established primarily from his own account of the trip in a February 1866 "San Francisco Letter" to the Virginia City *Territorial Enterprise* (SLC 1866d). Three letters (not by Clemens) to the Sacramento *Union* provided descriptions of the route: "Visit to the Humboldt Mines," 24 Sept 61, 1; "Letter from the Humboldt Mines" (signed "Wyoming"), 1 Apr 62, 4; and "Letter from the Humboldt Mines" (signed "D."), 6 May 62, 1. The remaining map sources are listed below.

American Automobile Association.

1989. *Iowa, Nebraska*. Falls Church, Va.: American Automobile Association.

1990. *Colorado, Wyoming*. Heathrow, Fla.: American Automobile Association.

1990. *Nevada, Utah*. Heathrow, Fla.: American Automobile Association.

1990. *Western States and Provinces*. Heathrow, Fla.: American Automobile Association.

Baltensperger, Bradley H. 1985. *Nebraska: A Geography*. Boulder, Colo.: Westview Press.

Bancroft, H. H. 1862. *Bancroft's Map of the Washoe Silver Region of Nevada Territory*. San Francisco: H. H. Bancroft and Co.

California State Automobile Association. 1979. *Lake Tahoe Region*. San Francisco: California State Automobile Association.

Clayton, Joshua Elliot. 1861. *Map of Esmeralda and Mono*. San Francisco: Britton and Co.

Clayton, William. 1848. *The Latter-Day Saints' Emigrants' Guide*. St. Louis: Missouri Republican. Reprint edition, edited by Stanley B. Kimball. Gerald, Mo.: Patrice Press, 1983.

Colton, J. H. 1864. *Colton's Map of the States and Territories West of the Mississippi River to the Pacific Ocean*. New York: J. H. Colton.

Coy, Owen C. 1973. *California County Boundaries*. Rev. ed. Fresno, Calif.: Valley Publishers.

DeGroot, Henry. 1863. *DeGroot's Map of Nevada Territory, Exhibiting a Portion of Southern Oregon & Eastern California*. San Francisco: Warren Holt.

Fike, Richard E., and John W. Headley. 1979. *The Pony Express Stations of Utah in Historical Perspective*. Bureau of Land Management, Utah. Cultural Resources Series, Monograph 2. Washington, D.C.: U.S. Government Printing Office.

Fink, K. W. 1935. *Map of the Pony Express Trail Beginning April 3rd. 1860 from St. Joseph Mo. and Sacramento Calif.* Kansas City, Kans.: W. R. Honnell.

Fox, Theron. 196–. *Nevada Treasure Hunters Ghost Town Guide*. San Jose, Calif.: Theron Fox.

Hunt, Thomas H. 1974. *Ghost Trails to California*. Palo Alto, Calif.: American West Publishing Company.

Kimball, Stanley B. 1988. *Historic Sites and Markers along the Mormon and Other Great Western Trails*. Urbana: University of Illinois Press.

Marcy, Randolph B. 1863. *The Prairie Traveler, A Hand-Book for Overland Expeditions*. London: Trübner and Co.

Mason, Dorothy. 1976. *The Pony Express in Nevada*. Compiled for the Nevada Bureau of Land Management. Carson City: Harrah's.

Maule, William M. 1938. *A Contribution to the Geographic and Economic History of the Carson, Walker and Mono Basins in Nevada and California*. San Francisco: California Region, Forest Service, U.S. Department of Agriculture.

National Geographic Society. 1981. *National Geographic Atlas of the World*. 5th ed. Washington, D.C.: National Geographic Society.

Nevada Emigrant Trail Marking Committee. 1975. *The Overland Emigrant Trail to California*. Reno: Nevada Historical Society.

State of Nevada. 1981. *Directory of Geographic Names in Nevada*. Prepared by State of Nevada, Department of Transportation Planning Division, Cartography and Graphics Section. 2d ed. Reno: State of Nevada.

Swackhamer, William D. 1979. *Political History of Nevada*. 7th ed. Carson City: Nevada State Printing Office.

Townley, John M. 1980. *Across Nevada with the Pony Express and Overland Stage Line*. Reno: Great Basin Studies Center.

Urbanek, Mae.

1974. *Wyoming Place Names*. 3d ed. Boulder, Colo.: Johnson Publishing Company.

1978. *Ghost Trails of Wyoming*. Boulder, Colo.: Johnson Publishing Company.

U.S. Department of the Interior. General Land Office. 1866. *Map of the State of Nevada to Accompany the Annual Report of the Commr. Genl. Land Office.* New York: Major and Knapp.

U.S. Department of the Interior. U.S. Geological Survey.

1916. *U.S. Contour Map, Polyconic Projection.*

1951. *Bucklin Reservoirs, Wyoming.* Photorevised 1981. 7.5 Minute Series (Topographic).

1951. *Carson Sink, Nevada.* 15 Minute Series (Topographic).

1951. *Graham Ranch, Wyoming.* Photorevised 1984. 7.5 Minute Series (Topographic).

1951. *Independence Rock, Wyoming.* Photorevised 1981. 7.5 Minute Series (Topographic).

1953. *Western United States 1:250,000; Delta.* Revised 1972.

1953. *Western United States 1:250,000; Tooele.* Revised 1970.

1955. *Western United States 1:250,000; Elko.* Revised 1972.

1955. *Western United States 1:250,000; Lovelock.* Revised 1970.

1956. *Aurora, Nevada-California.* 15 Minute Series (Topographic).

1956. *Toulon, Nevada.* 15 Minute Series (Topographic).

1957. *Western United States 1:250,000; Mariposa.* Revised 1970.

1957. *Western United States 1:250,000; Reno.* Revised 1971.

1957. *Western United States 1:250,000; Sacramento.* Revised 1970.

1957. *Western United States 1:250,000; Walker Lake.* Revised 1969.

1958. *Bodie, California.* 15 Minute Series (Topographic).

1958. *Trench Canyon, California-Nevada.* 15 Minute Series (Topographic).

1960. *Fairbury, Nebraska.* Photorevised 1980. 7.5 Minute Series (Topographic).

1960. *Fairbury SW, Nebraska-Kansas.* 7.5 Minute Series (Topographic).

1960. *Gladstone, Nebraska.* 7.5 Minute Series (Topographic).

1961. *Mountain Dell, Utah.* Photorevised 1975. 7.5 Minute Series (Topographic).

1963. *Fort Douglas, Utah.* Photorevised 1969 and 1975. 7.5 Minute Series (Topographic).

1966. *Hanover East, Kansas.* Photorevised 1983. 7.5 Minute Series (Topographic).

1966. *Hanover SE, Kansas.* Photorevised 1983. 7.5 Minute Series (Topographic).

1966. *Hanover SW, Kansas.* Photorevised 1983. 7.5 Minute Series (Topographic).

1966. *Hanover West, Kansas.* Photorevised 1983. 7.5 Minute Series (Topographic).

1966. *Herkimer, Kansas.* Photorevised 1983. 7.5 Minute Series (Topographic).

1966. *Marysville, Kansas.* Photorevised 1983. 7.5 Minute Series (Topographic).

1966. *Washington NE, Kansas.* 7.5 Minute Series (Topographic).

1970. *Endicott, Nebraska-Kansas.* 7.5 Minute Series (Topographic).

1978. *Lander, Wyoming.* 30×60 Minute Series (Topographic).

1979. *Bairoil, Wyoming.* 30×60 Minute Series (Topographic).

1979. *Casper, Wyoming.* 30×60 Minute Series (Topographic).

1981. *Rattlesnake Hills, Wyoming.* 30×60 Minute Series (Topographic).

1984. *South Pass, Wyoming.* 30×60 Minute Series (Topographic).

Wesley, Edgar B. 1961. *Our United States: Its History in Maps.* 2d ed. Chicago: Denoyer-Geppert Company.

Wheeler, George M. 1873. *Parts of Southern Nevada and Eastern California, Atlas Sheet No. 57; Geographical Explorations and Surveys West of the 100th Meridian.* Washington, D.C.: U.S. Government Printing Office.

Wheeler, Sessions S. 1971. *The Nevada Desert.* Caldwell, Idaho: Caxton Printers.

WPA.

1939. *Kansas: A Guide to the Sunflower State.* Compiled and written by the Federal Writers' Project of the Work Projects Administration for the State of Kansas. New York: Viking Press.

1939. *Nebraska: A Guide to the Cornhusker State.* Compiled and written by the Federal Writers' Project of the Works Progress Administration for the State of Nebraska. New York: Viking Press.

1940. *Nevada: A Guide to the Silver State.* Compiled by workers of the Writers' Program of the Work Projects Administration in the State of Nevada. Portland, Oreg.: Binfords and Mort.

1941. *Wyoming: A Guide to Its History, Highways, and People.* Compiled by workers of the Writers' Program of the Work Projects Administration in the State of Wyoming. New York: Oxford University Press.

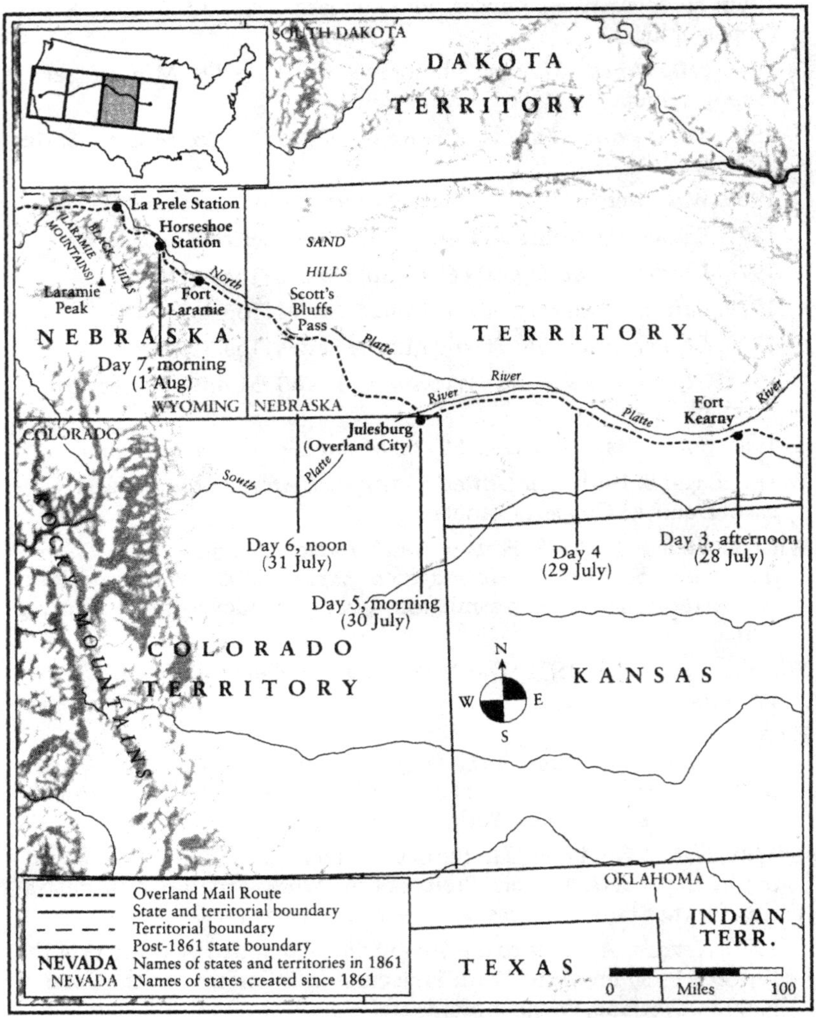

MAP 1B: Days 3–7.

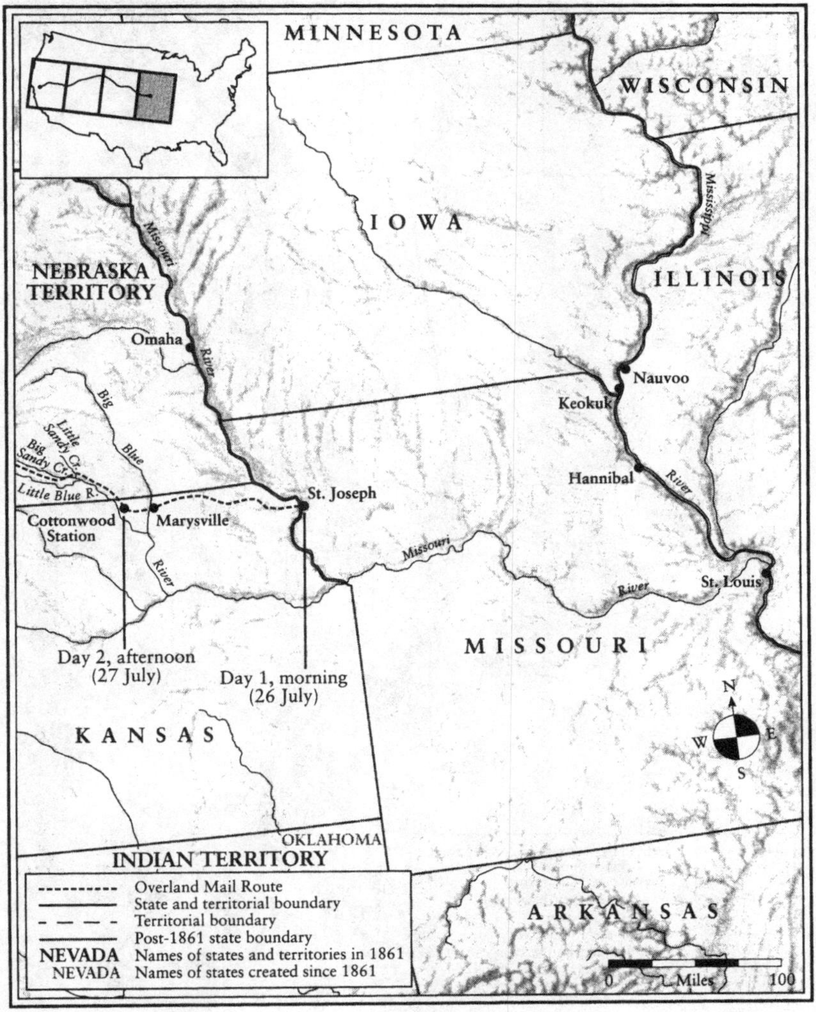

Map 1A: Days 1–2.

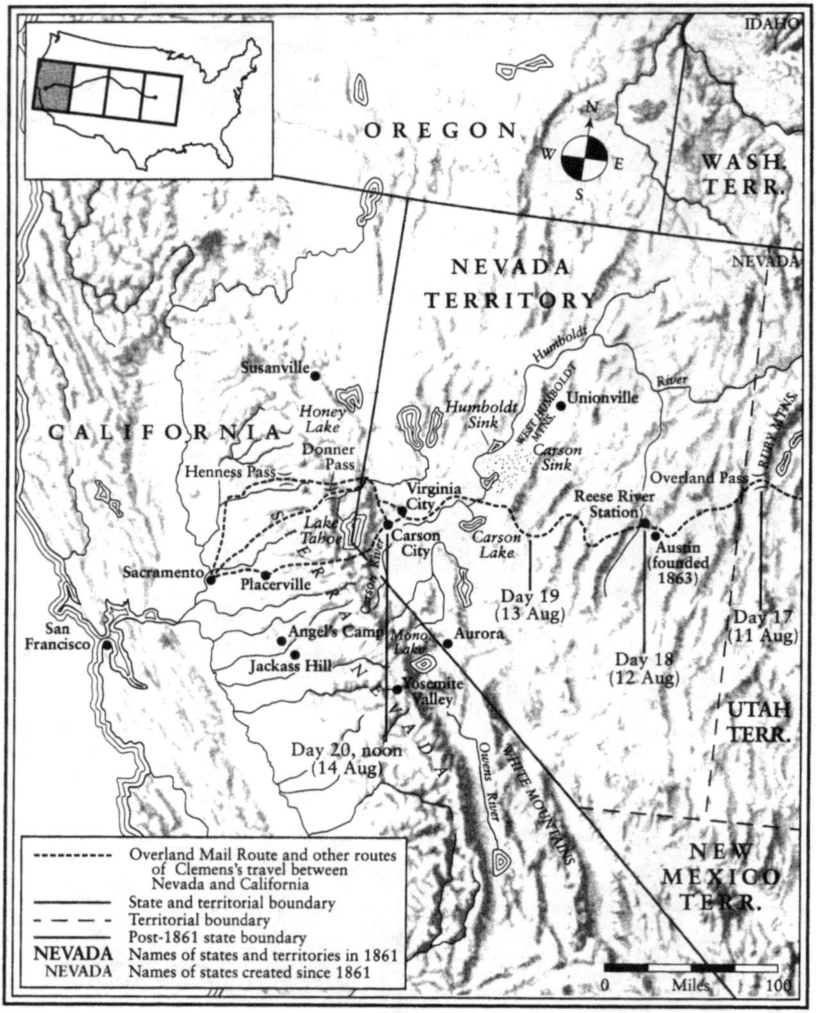

Map 1D: Days 17–20.

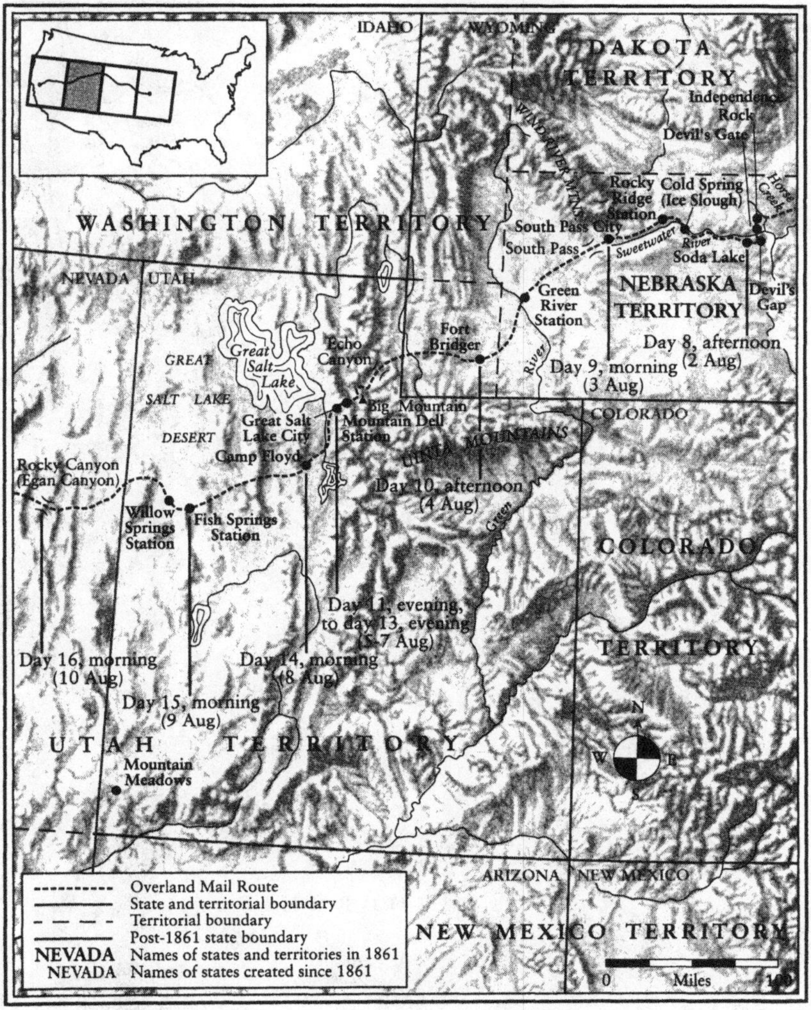

MAP 1C: Days 8–16.

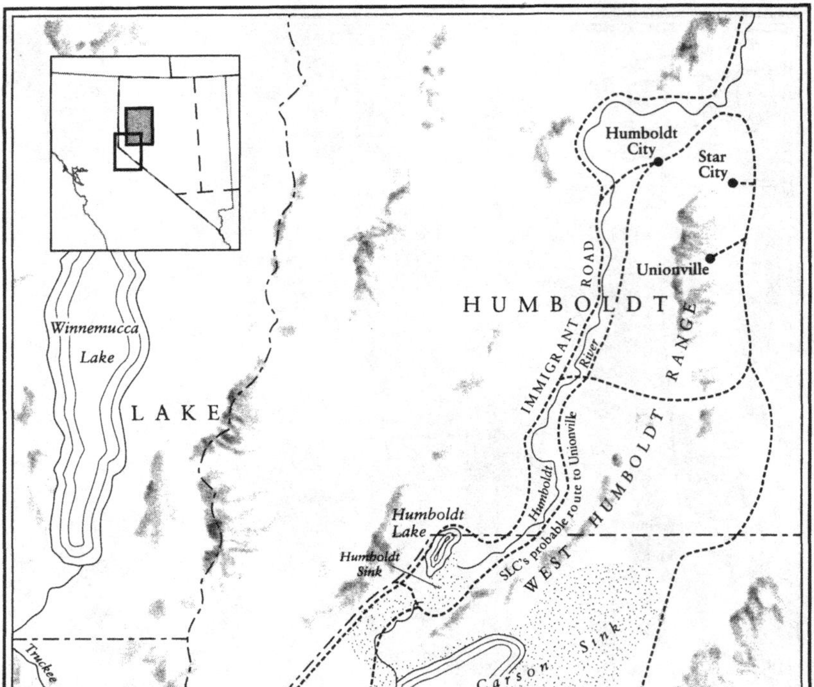

MAP 2: West central Nevada Territory, November 1861, showing the possible routes of Clemens's Humboldt trip.

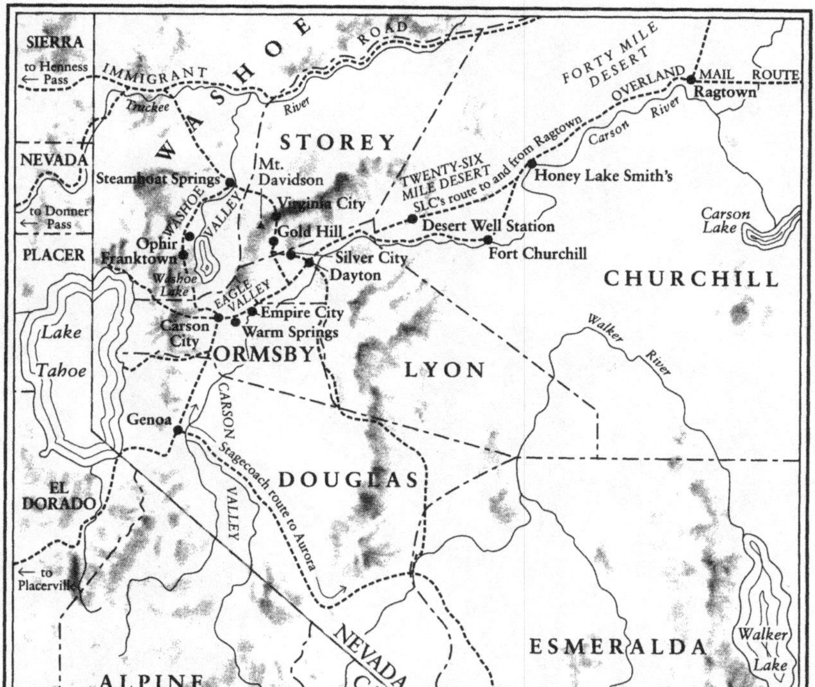

MAP 3: Southwestern Nevada Territory, November 1861, showing Virginia City, Carson City, and environs, and the Esmeralda region.

SUPPLEMENT C

Horace Greeley to Samuel L. Clemens, 7 May 1871

The letter reproduced here from the original in the Mark Twain Papers (87 percent of actual size, CU-MARK) almost certainly served as the inspiration for Mark Twain's parody of Greeley's illegible handwriting in chapter 70. A transcription of the letter is provided below. Greeley evidently wrote it in response to an acknowledgment from Clemens, to whom he had recently given a copy of his new book, *What I Know of Farming* (1871). See the notes at 483.7–8 and 484.17.

NEW-YORK TRIBUNE.
NEW YORK, May 7, 187 1.

Mark:

You are mistaken as to my criticisms on *your* farming. I never publicly made any, while you have undertaken to tell the exact cost per pint of my potatoes and cabbages, truely enough the inspiration of genius. If you will really betake yourself to farming, or even to telling what you know about it, rather than what you *don't* know about mine, I will not only refrain from disparaging criticism, but will give you my blessing.

Yours,
Horace Greeley.

Mark Twain.

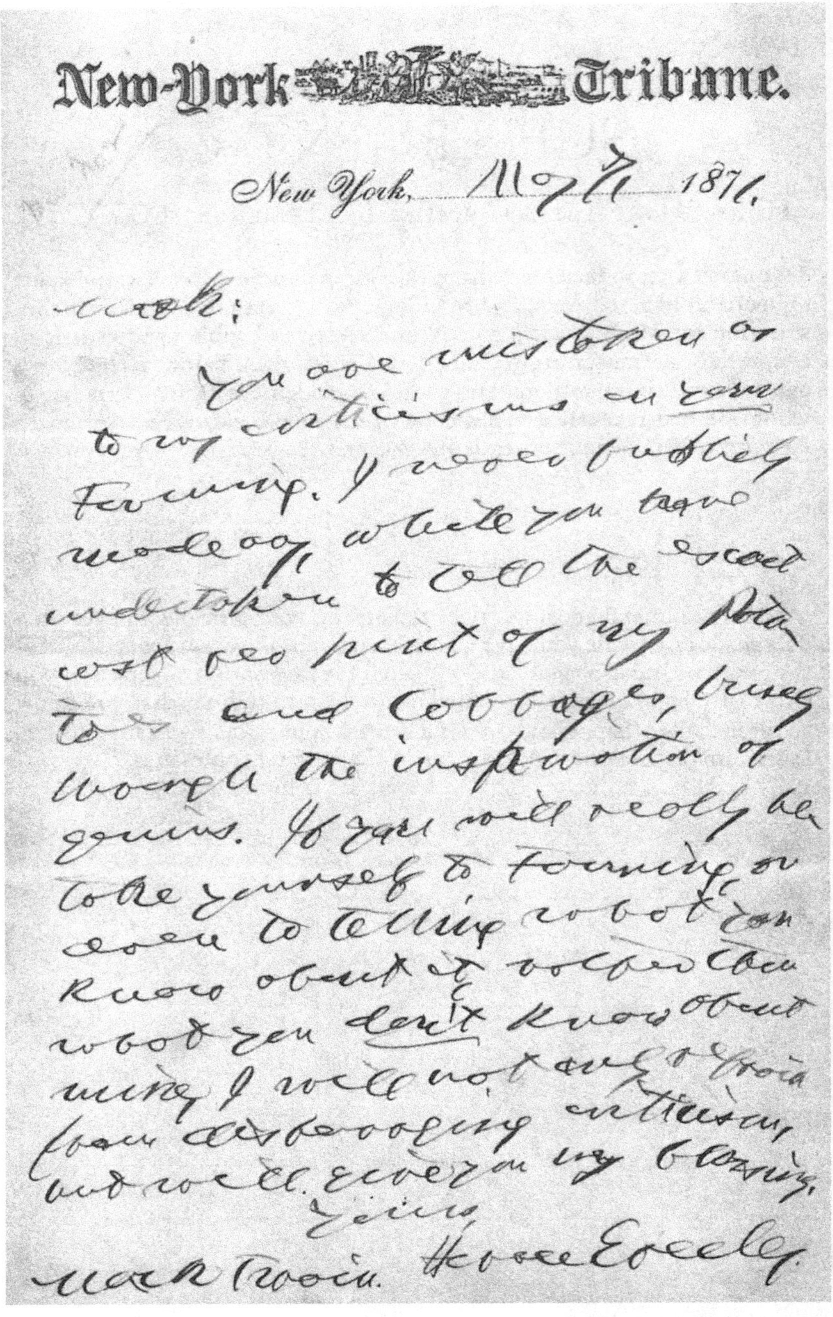

New-York Tribune.

New York, May 7th 1871.

Mark:

You are mistaken as to my criticisms on your farming. I never publicly made any, while you have undertaken to tell the exact cost per pint of my potatoes and cabbages, being through the inspiration of genius. If you will really take yourself to farming, or even to telling what you know about it, rather than what you don't know about mine, I will not only refrain from discouraging criticism, but will even give you my blessing.

Yours,

Horace Greeley.

Mark Twain.

SUPPLEMENT D

Pages Discarded from the *Roughing It* Printer's Copy

The manuscript, or printer's copy, for *Roughing It* is not known to survive; it was probably destroyed by the compositors after the book was set in type. Three pages that Clemens removed from it during the process of revision are extant, however, and are preserved in the Mark Twain Papers (CU-MARK). They are reproduced in facsimile below. The first page, drafted as part of chapter 12, contains an original, longer version of the passage about the leaf in the stream. In the final version, Clemens described the incident in two sentences: "I freighted a leaf with a mental message for the friends at home, and dropped it in the stream. But I put no stamp on it and it was held for postage somewhere" (see pages 81–82). The second discarded page contains an earlier version of the opening of chapter 18. The numbers at the top show that it was page 423 of the manuscript, and suggest that the chapter was at one time numbered "19," and then "20." The page contains a passage that does not appear in the text as finally printed (see page 122). The third discarded page demonstrates how Clemens used clippings of his earlier published work to prepare some of the *Roughing It* printer's copy. This page, numbered "968," was originally drafted as part of chapter 46. At the top Clemens pasted a clipping from the Buffalo *Express* for 8 January 1870, marking several revisions in the margin. After removing the page from his manuscript, Clemens recopied the text in the clipping onto a new page, making further changes; he rejected the paragraph at the bottom altogether (see pages 303–4). For a complete discussion of these discarded pages, and a conjectural reconstruction of the entire printer's copy, see the Introduction to the Works of Mark Twain edition of *Roughing It* (1993), pages 797–911.

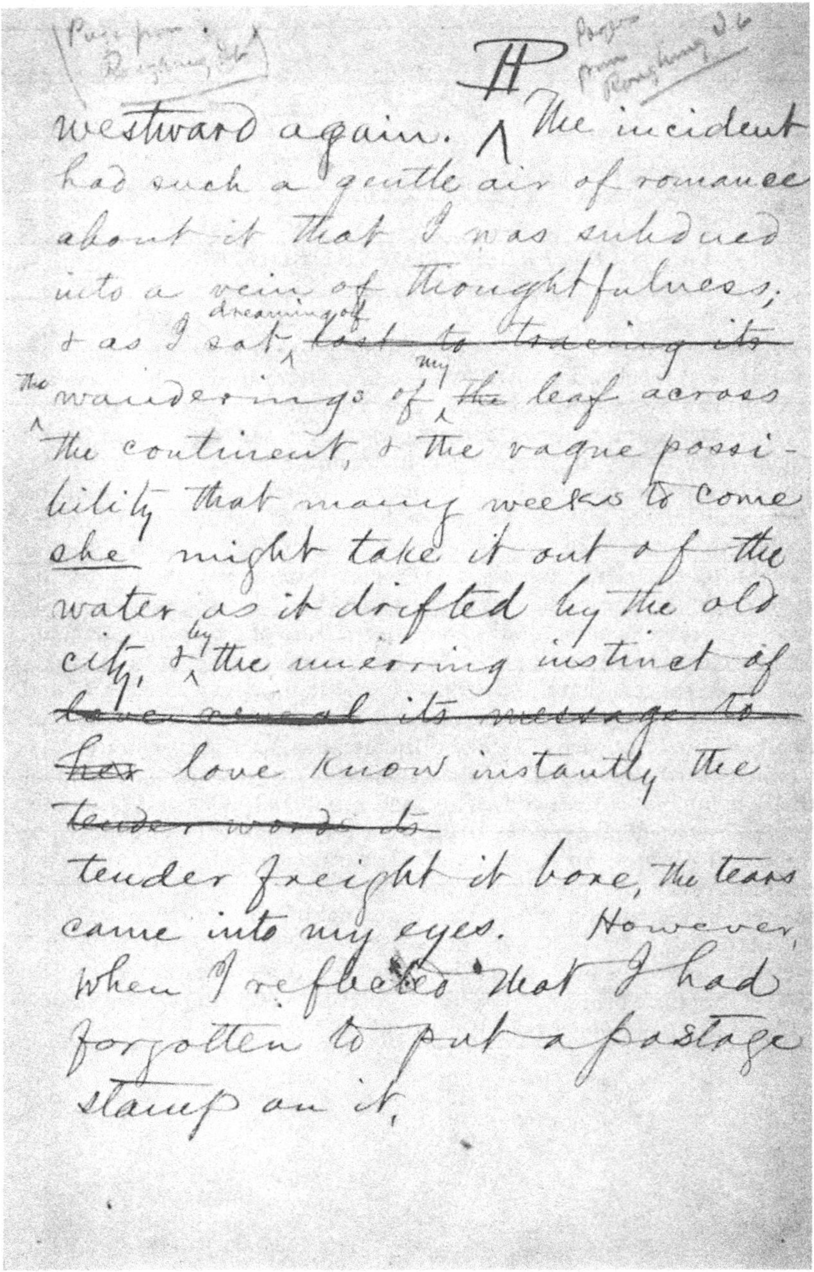

Pages from Roughing It

Pages from Roughing It

westward again. The incident
had such a gentle air of romance
about it that I was subdued
into a vein of thoughtfulness,
& as I sat, dreaming of ~~lost to tracing its~~
the wanderings of my ~~the~~ leaf across
the continent, & the vague possi-
bility that many weeks to come
she might take it out of the
water as it drifted by the old
city, & by the unerring instinct of
~~love reveal its message to~~
~~her~~ love know instantly the
~~tender words its~~
tender freight it bore, the tears
came into my eyes. However,
when I reflected that I had
forgotten to put a postage
stamp on it.

Unnumbered manuscript page, removed from what is now chapter 12. Reproduced at 87 percent of actual size, from the original in the Mark Twain Papers, The Bancroft Library (CU-MARK).

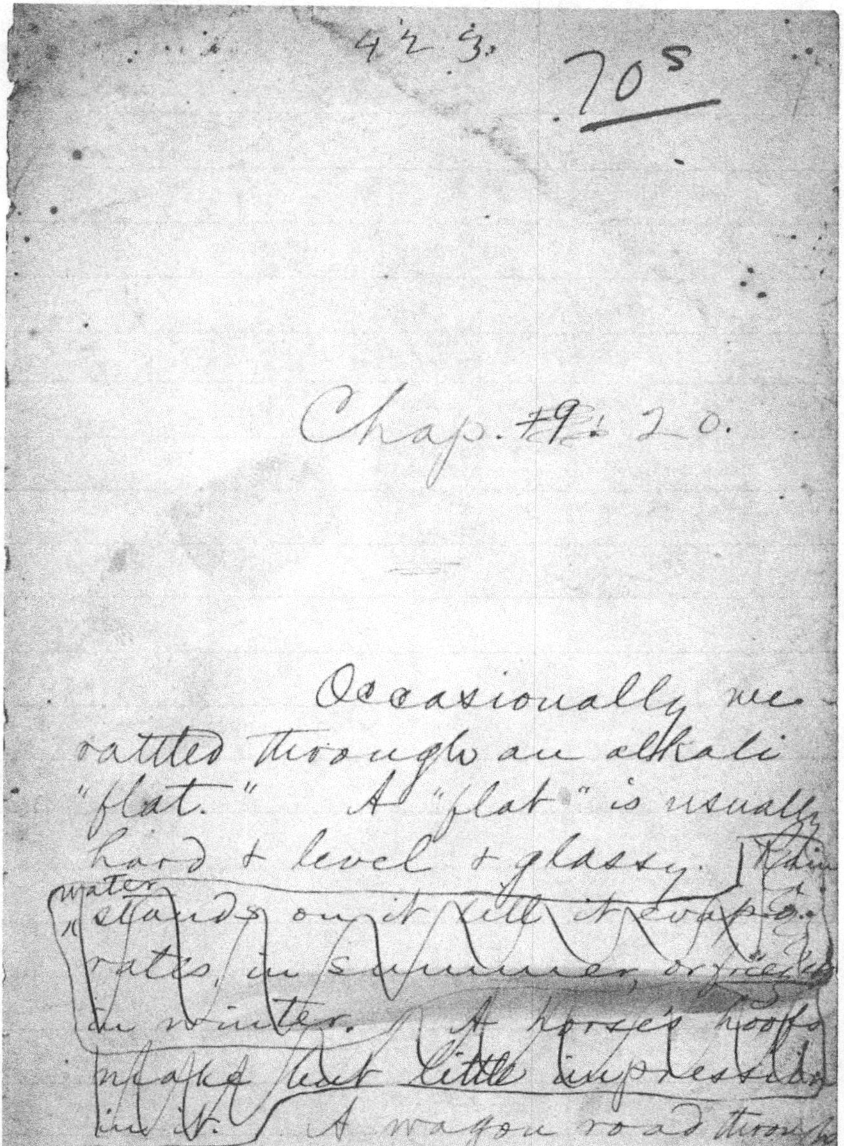
423.

705

Chap. 19 20.

Occasionally we rattled through an alkali "flat." A "flat" is usually hard & level & glassy. When water stands on it till it evaporates, in summer, or freezes in winter. A horse's hoofs make but little impression in it. A wagon road through it is generally as straight as a dart, & being hard & fre

Manuscript page numbered 423, removed from what is now chapter 18. Reproduced at 87 percent of actual size, from the original in the Mark Twain Papers, The Bancroft Library (CU-MARK).

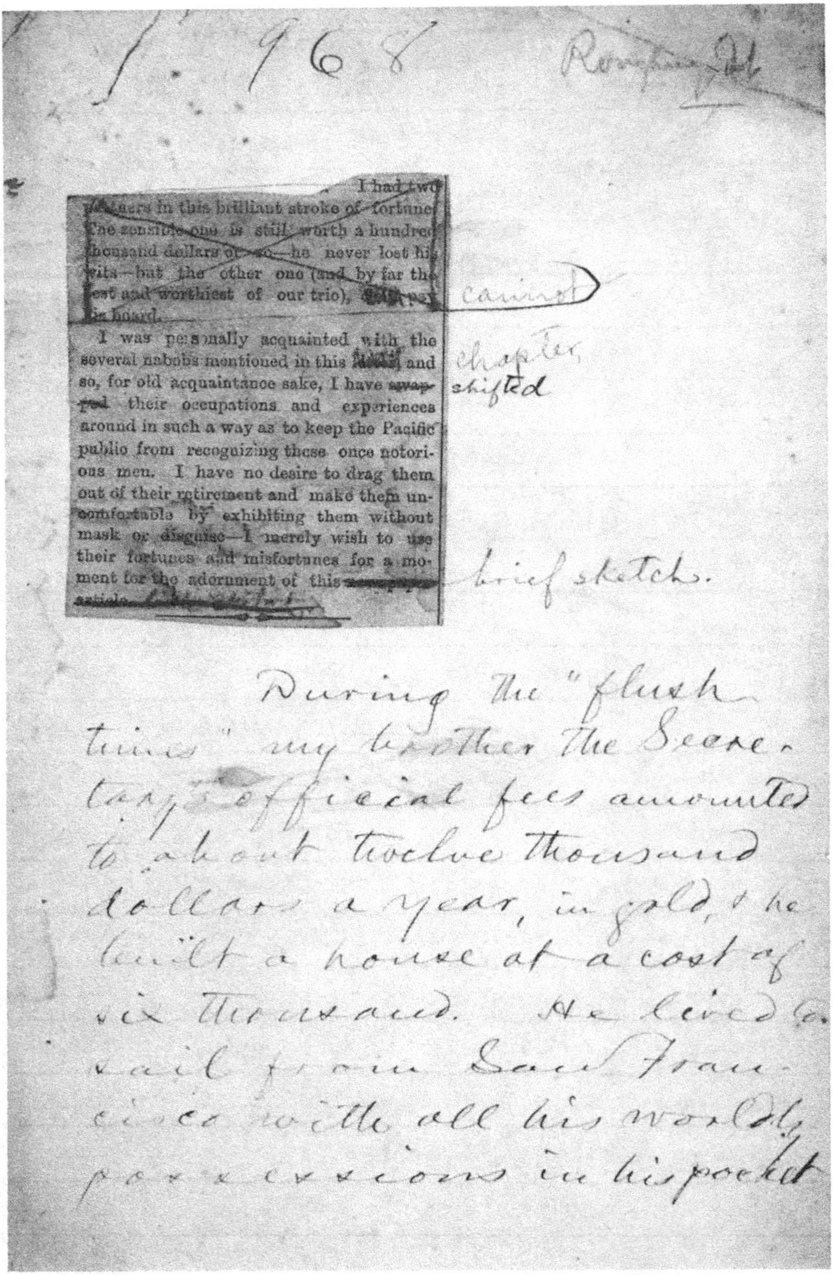

968

I had two partners in this brilliant stroke of fortune. The sensible one is still worth a hundred thousand dollars or so—he never lost his wits—but the other one (and by far the best and worthiest of our trio), cannot pay his board.

I was personally acquainted with the several nabobs mentioned in this chapter and so, for old acquaintance sake, I have shifted their occupations and experiences around in such a way as to keep the Pacific public from recognizing these once notorious men. I have no desire to drag them out of their retirement and make them uncomfortable by exhibiting them without mask or disguise—I merely wish to use their fortunes and misfortunes for a moment for the adornment of this brief sketch.

During the "flush times" my brother the Secretary's official fees amounted to about twelve thousand dollars a year, in gold, & he built a house at a cost of six thousand. He lived to sail from San Francisco with all his worldly possessions in his pocket

Manuscript page numbered 968, removed from what is now chapter 46. It contains a clipping from the Buffalo *Express* for 8 January 1870. Reproduced at 87 percent of actual size, from the original in the Mark Twain Papers, The Bancroft Library (CU-MARK).

REFERENCES

This list defines the abbreviations used in this book and provides full bibliographic information for works cited by the author's name, by the author's name and publication date, or by a short title.

AAA. 1927. *The Notable Library of Major W. Van R. Whitall of Pelham, New York.* Sale of 14–15 February. New York: American Art Association.

"Abstract of Disbursements."

1861. "Abstract of Disbursements on Account of the Legislative Assembly of the Territory of Nevada, from July 1st 1861, to November 29th 1861." In Miscellaneous Treasury Account No. 142896, Office of the First Auditor, RG 217, Records of the General Accounting Office, DNA.

1861–62. "Abstract of Disbursements on Account of the Legislative Assembly of the Territory of Nevada, from November 29th 1861 to June 30th 1862." In Miscellaneous Treasury Account No. 144986, Office of the First Auditor, RG 217, Records of the General Accounting Office, DNA.

AD. Autobiographical Dictation.

Adams, Thomas F. 1857. *Typographia; or, The Printer's Instructor: A Brief Sketch of the Origin, Rise, and Progress of the Typographic Art, with Practical Directions for Conducting Every Department in an Office, Hints to Authors, Publishers, &c.* Copyright 1845. Philadelphia: L. Johnson and Co.

Addenbrooke, Alice B. 1950. *The Mistress of the Mansion.* Palo Alto, Calif.: Pacific Books.

Ahlborn, Richard E., ed. 1980. *Man Made Mobile: Early Saddles of Western North America.* Smithsonian Studies in History and Technology, no. 39. Washington, D.C.: Smithsonian Institution Press.

Ajax [pseud.]. 1866. "Letter from San Francisco." Letter dated 24 September. Honolulu *Pacific Commercial Advertiser,* 20 October, 1.

Alexander, Mary Charlotte. 1953. *Dr. Baldwin of Lahaina.* Berkeley: Printed by Stanford University Press for Mary Charlotte Alexander.

Alexander, W. D. 1891. *A Brief History of the Hawaiian People.* New York: American Book Company.

Alexander, Thomas G., and Leonard J. Arrington. 1966. "Camp in the Sagebrush: Camp Floyd, Utah, 1858–1861." *Utah Historical Quarterly* 34 (Winter): 3–21.

Allen, James B., and Glen M. Leonard. 1976. *The Story of the Latter-day Saints.* Salt Lake City: Deseret Book Company.

AMT. 1959. *The Autobiography of Mark Twain.* Edited by Charles Neider. New York: Harper and Brothers.

Anderson Auction Company. 1911. *Catalogue of the Library and Manuscripts of Samuel L. Clemens [Mark Twain].* Part 1. Sale no. 892 (7–8 February). New York: Anderson Auction Company.

Anderson, Nels. 1942. *Desert Saints: The Mormon Frontier in Utah.* Chicago: University of Chicago Press.

Anderson, Rufus. 1864. *The Hawaiian Islands: Their Progress and Condition under Missionary Labors.* Boston: Gould and Lincoln.

Anderson, Frederick, and Edgar M. Branch, eds. 1972. *The Great Landslide Case by Mark Twain: Three Versions.* Berkeley: The Friends of The Bancroft Library.

Andrew, Laurel B. 1978. *The Early Temples of the Mormons: The Architecture of the Millennial Kingdom in the American West.* Albany: State University of New York Press.

Andrews, Lorrin. 1865. *A Dictionary of the Hawaiian Language.* Honolulu: Henry M. Whitney.

Angel, Myron, ed. 1881. *History of Nevada.* Oakland, Calif.: Thompson and West.

Annual Cyclopaedia 1873. 1877. "Hoosac Tunnel." *The American Annual Cyclopaedia and Register of Important Events of the Year 1873.* Vol. 13. New York: D. Appleton and Co.

APC. 1866–79. "Books received from the Binderies, Dec 1st *1866* to Dec 31. *1879,*" the American Publishing Company's stock ledger, NN-B.

Argentoro [pseud.]. 1863. "Letter from Washoe." Letter dated 24 October. San Francisco *Morning Call,* 28 October, 1.

Arrington, Leonard J.

1958. *Great Basin Kingdom: An Economic History of the Latter-day Saints, 1830–1900.* Cambridge: Harvard University Press.

1985. *Brigham Young: American Moses.* New York: Alfred A. Knopf.

Arrington, Leonard J., and Davis Bitton. 1979. *The Mormon Experience: A History of the Latter-day Saints.* New York: Alfred A. Knopf.

Ashbaugh, Don. 1963. *Nevada's Turbulent Yesterday: A Study in Ghost Towns.* Los Angeles: Westernlore Press.

Asser, John. 1908. *Asser's Life of King Alfred.* Translated with an introduction and notes by L. C. Jane. London: Chatto and Windus.

Austin, Franklin H. 1926. "Mark Twain Incognito—A Reminiscence." *Friend* 96 (September, October, November): 201–4, 224–29, 248–54. Partly reprinted in *MTH*, 75–79.

Ayers, James J. 1922. *Gold and Sunshine: Reminiscences of Early California.* Boston: Richard G. Badger.

Baetzhold, Howard G. 1970. *Mark Twain and John Bull: The British Connection.* Bloomington: Indiana University Press.

Bailey, Paul. 1975. *Those Kings and Queens of Old Hawaii.* Los Angeles: Westernlore Books.

BAL. 1957. *Bibliography of American Literature.* Compiled by Jacob Blanck. Vol. 2. New Haven: Yale University Press.

Bancroft, Hubert Howe.

1882–90. *History of the Pacific States of North America.* 34 vols. San Francisco: A. L. Bancroft and Co. / History Company.

1891–92. *Chronicles of the Builders of the Commonwealth.* 7 vols. San Francisco: History Company.

Barnes, George E. 1887. "Mark Twain, as He Was Known during His Stay on the Pacific Slope." San Francisco *Morning Call*, 17 April, 1.

Barrett, Don C. 1931. *The Greenbacks and Resumption of Specie Payments, 1862–1879.* Cambridge: Harvard University Press.

Barth, Gunther. 1964. *Bitter Strength: A History of the Chinese in the United States, 1850–1870.* Cambridge: Harvard University Press.

Bates, George Washington. 1854. *Sandwich Island Notes. By a Haole.* New York: Harper and Brothers.

BDUSC. 1989. *Biographical Directory of the United States Congress, 1774–1989.* Bicentennial edition. Washington, D.C.: Government Printing Office.

Beadle, J. H. 1872. Preface to *Brigham's Destroying Angel.* In Hickman, v–vii.

Beckwith, Martha. 1940. *Hawaiian Mythology.* New Haven: Yale University Press. Citations are to the 1970 reprint edition, Honolulu: University of Hawaii Press.

Beebe, Lucius. 1954. *Comstock Commotion: The Story of "The Territorial Enterprise."* Stanford: Stanford University Press.

Beebe, Lucius, and Charles Clegg. 1954. *Legends of the Comstock Lode.* Rev. ed. Stanford: Stanford University Press.

Beeton, S. O., ed. 1868. *Beeton's Dictionary of Geography: A Universal Gazetteer.* London: Ward, Lock, and Tyler.

Bellamy, Gladys Carmen. 1941. "Mark Twain's Indebtedness to John Phoenix." *American Literature* 13 (March): 29–43.

Bennett, Chauncey C. 1869. *Honolulu Directory, and Historical Sketch of the Hawaiian or Sandwich Islands.* Honolulu: C. C. Bennett.

Benson, Ivan. 1938. *Mark Twain's Western Years.* Stanford: Stanford University Press.

Berkove, Lawrence I.

1988a. "Jim Gillis: 'The Thoreau of the Sierras.'" *Mark Twain Circular* 2 (March–April): 1–2.

1988b. "Dan De Quille's Narratives of Ohio: Lorenzo Dow's Miracle." *Northwest Ohio Quarterly* 60 (Spring): 47–56.

1993. "Dan De Quille and *Roughing It:* Borrowings and Influence." *Nevada Historical Society Quarterly,* forthcoming.

Bingham, Hiram. 1855. *A Residence of Twenty-one Years in the Sandwich Islands; or, The Civil, Religious, and Political History of Those Islands.* 3d ed. Canandaigua, N.Y.: H. D. Goodwin.

Blair, Montgomery. 1861. "Report of the Postmaster General," dated 2 December. In *Message of the President of the United States to the Two Houses of Congress at the Commencement of the Second Session of the Thirty-seventh Congress.* Washington, D.C.: Government Printing Office.

Bloss, Roy S. 1959. *Pony Express—The Great Gamble.* Berkeley: Howell-North.

Book of Mormon.

1866. *The Book of Mormon: An Account Written by the Hand of Mormon, upon Plates Taken from the Plates of Nephi.* Translated by Joseph Smith, Jun. Sixth European Edition. Liverpool: Published by Brigham Young, Jun. [*Citations in the notes are to chapters and verses in this edition, followed by parenthetical citations to chapters and verses in all editions published since 1879. "1 Nephi" and "2 Nephi" refer to the "First" and "Second" books of Nephi; "3 Nephi" refers to a book listed in the table of contents as merely "Book of Nephi"; "4 Nephi" refers to another "Book of Nephi," not listed in the table of contents, which follows immediately after "3 Nephi."*]

1981. *The Book of Mormon. The Doctrine and Covenants of the Church of Jesus Christ of Latter-day Saints. The Pearl of Great Price.* Salt Lake City: Church of Jesus Christ of Latter-day Saints.

Boothby, H. E. 1919. "Up from Idolatry." *Hawaiian Almanac and Annual for 1920,* 53–78.

Bowers, Fredson. 1989. "Regularization and Normalization in Modern Critical Texts." *Studies in Bibliography* 42:79–102.

Bowles, Samuel.

1866. *Across the Continent: A Summer's Journey to the Rocky Mountains, the Mormons, and the Pacific States, with Speaker Colfax.* London: Sampson Low, Son, and Marston.

1869. *Our New West. Records of Travel between the Mississippi River and the Pacific Ocean.* Hartford: Hartford Publishing Co.

Bradley, Harold Whitman. 1942. *The American Frontier in Hawaii: The Pioneers, 1789–1843.* Stanford: Stanford University Press. Citations are to the 1968 reprint edition, Gloucester, Mass.: Peter Smith.

Branch, Edgar Marquess.

1946. "A Chronological Bibliography of the Writings of Samuel Clemens to June 8, 1867." *American Literature* 18 (May): 109–59.

1967. "'My Voice Is Still for Setchell': A Background Study of 'Jim Smiley and His Jumping Frog.'" *PMLA* 82 (December): 591–601.

1969. "Mark Twain Reports the Races in Sacramento." *Huntington Library Quarterly* 32 (February): 179–86.

1978. "'The Babes in the Wood': Artemus Ward's 'Double Health' to Mark Twain." *PMLA* 93 (October): 955–72.

1985. "Fact and Fiction in the Blind Lead Episode of *Roughing It.*" *Nevada Historical Society Quarterly* 28 (Winter): 234–48.

Brewer, William H. 1930. *Up and Down California in 1860–1864.* Edited by Francis P. Farquhar. New Haven: Yale University Press.

Bridgman, Richard. 1987. *Traveling in Mark Twain.* Berkeley, Los Angeles, London: University of California Press.

Brigham, William T. 1868. *Notes on the Volcanoes of the Hawaiian Islands.* Boston: Riverside Press.

Brodie, Fawn M. 1971. *No Man Knows My History: The Life of Joseph Smith the Mormon Prophet.* 2d ed., rev. and enl. New York: Alfred A. Knopf.

Bromer. 1992. *Selections from Our Stock to Be Featured . . . February 14, 15, 16 1992 at the Los Angeles Airport Hilton.* Los Angeles: Bromer Booksellers.

Brooks, Benjamin S. 1876. *The Chinese in California. Addressed to the Committee on Foreign Relations of the U.S. Senate.* n.p.

Brooks, Juanita.

1962. *John Doyle Lee: Zealot—Pioneer Builder—Scapegoat.* Glendale, Calif.: Arthur H. Clark Company.

1970. *The Mountain Meadows Massacre.* 3d ed. Norman: University of Oklahoma Press.

Brooks, Roger L. 1962. "A Second Possible Source for Mark Twain's 'The Aged Pilot Man.'" *Revue de littérature comparée* 36 (July–September): 451–53.

Browne, Charles Farrar [Artemus Ward, pseud.].

1862. *Artemus Ward: His Book.* New York: Carleton.

1865. *Artemus Ward: His Travels.* New York: Carleton.

Browne, J. Ross.

1860–61. "A Peep at Washoe." *Harper's New Monthly Magazine* 22 (December, January, February): 1–17, 145–62, 289–305. Reprinted in J. Ross Browne 1864, 309–436.

1864. *Crusoe's Island: A Ramble in the Footsteps of Alexander Selkirk. With Sketches of Adventure in California and Washoe.* New York: Harper and Brothers.

1865a. "Washoe Revisited." *Harper's New Monthly Magazine* 30–31 (May, June, July): 681–96, 1–12, 151–61. Reprinted in J. Ross Browne 1869, 293–392.

1865b. "A Trip to Bodie Bluff and the Dead Sea of the West." *Harper's New Monthly Magazine* 31 (August, September): 274–84, 411–19. Reprinted in J. Ross Browne 1869, 393–444.

1865c. "The Walker River Country." *Harper's New Monthly Magazine* 31 (November): 700–709. Reprinted in J. Ross Browne 1869, 445–73.

1866. "The Reese River Country." *Harper's New Monthly Magazine* 33 (June): 26–44. Reprinted in J. Ross Browne 1869, 475–535.

1868. *Report of J. Ross Browne, on the Mineral Resources of the States and Territories West of the Rocky Mountains.* San Francisco: H.H. Bancroft and Co.

1869. *Adventures in the Apache Country: A Tour through Arizona and Sonora, with Notes on the Silver Regions of Nevada.* New York: Harper and Brothers.

Browne, Junius Henri. 1872. *Sights and Sensations in Europe.* Hartford: American Publishing Company.

Browning, Peter. 1986. *Place Names of the Sierra Nevada: From Abbot to Zumwalt.* Berkeley: Wilderness Press.

Buckbee, Edna Bryan. 1935. *The Saga of Old Tuolumne.* New York: Press of the Pioneers.

Budd, Louis J., ed. 1977. "A Listing of and Selection from Newspaper and Magazine Interviews with Samuel L. Clemens, 1874–1910." *American Literary Realism* 10 (Winter): i–100.

Bunker, William M. 1879. *From Report upon the Aurora Mining District, Esmeralda Co., Nevada.* San Francisco: Barry, Baird, and Co.

Burton, Richard F. 1861. *The City of the Saints and Across the Rocky Mountains to California.* London: Longman, Green, Longman, and Roberts.

Bush, Lester E., Jr. 1981. "The Word of Wisdom in Early Nineteenth-Century Perspective." *Dialogue* 14 (Autumn): 46–65.

Byron, George Anson. 1826. *Voyage of H. M. S. Blonde to the Sandwich Islands, in the Years 1824–1825.* London: John Murray.

Callaway, Llewellyn Link. 1973. *Two True Tales of the Wild West.* Oakland: Maud Gonne Press.

Callicot, T. Carey. 1855. *Cyclopedia of Universal Geography: Being a Gazetteer of the World.* New York: A. S. Barnes and Co.

Cameron, Marguerite. 1939. *This Is the Place.* Caldwell, Idaho: Caxton Printers.

Campbell, Archibald. 1816. *A Voyage Round the World, from 1806 to 1812.* Edinburgh: Printed for Archibald Constable and Co.

Campbell, Eugene E. 1988. *Establishing Zion: The Mormon Church in the American West, 1847–1869.* Salt Lake City: Signature Books.

Canning, Ray R., and Beverly Beeton. 1977. *The Genteel Gentile: Letters of Elizabeth Cumming, 1857–1858.* Salt Lake City: Tanner Trust Fund, University of Utah Library.

Carleton, J. H. 1902. *Special Report of the Mountain Meadow Massacre, by J. H. Carleton, Brevet Major, United States Army, Captain, First Dragoons,* dated 25 May 1859. U.S. Congress, House of Representatives, 57th Congress, 1st session, volume 110, document 605.

Carlson, Helen S. 1974. *Nevada Place Names: A Geographical Dictionary.* Reno: University of Nevada Press.

Carson County Census. [1860] 1967. "Free Inhabitants in . . . Carson County." *Population Schedules of the Eighth Census of the United States, 1860. Roll 1314. Utah: Carson County.* National Archives Microfilm Publications, Microcopy no. 653. Washington, D.C.: General Services Administration.

Carter, Kate B., comp. 1952–57. *Treasures of Pioneer History.* 6 vols. Salt Lake City: Daughters of Utah Pioneers.

Caulkins, Frances Manwaring. 1895. *History of New London, Connecticut.* New London: H. D. Utley.

CCamarSJ. Estelle Doheny Collection, The Edward Laurence Doheny Memorial Library, Saint John's Seminary, Camarillo, California.

CCC. Honnold Library, Claremont, California.

Chalfant, Willie Arthur. 1928. *Outposts of Civilization.* Boston: Christopher Publishing House.

Chapel, Charles Edward. 1961. *Guns of the Old West.* New York: Coward-McCann.

Chapman, Arthur. 1932. *The Pony Express: The Record of a Romantic Adventure in Business.* New York and London: G. P. Putnam's Sons.

Cheever, Henry T.

1851a. *The Island World of the Pacific.* New York: Harper and Brothers.

1851b. *Life in the Sandwich Islands; or, The Heart of the Pacific, as It Was and Is.* New York: A. S. Barnes and Co.

Citizen [pseud.]. 1864. Letter dated 18 May, quoting the Virginia City *Territorial Enterprise* of 17 May. In "The 'Enterprise' Libel of the Ladies of Carson," Virginia City *Union,* 25, 26, and 27 May, 2. Reprinted in *L1,* 289 n. 2.

Clagett, Fred. 1990. "The Life of William H. Clagett." Paper presented on 20 April at the Pacific Northwest History Conference in Boise, Idaho. TS in CU-MARK.

Clayton, Dick. 1932? "Mark Twain and Jack Slade Entertain At Weber Stage Station in 1862." TS of six pages, an account by Dick Clayton, Coalville, Utah, retelling a narrative by Tom Rivington. U.S. Works Progress Administration, Series A, Group 3. Historical Records Survey: Utah. Transcripts of Mormon Diaries and Journals, 3–14. Manuscripts Division, DLC.

Clayton, Joshua E. 1864. "Pocket Veins." *Mining and Scientific Press* 8 (5 March): 145–46.

Clemens, Cyril. 1932. *Mark Twain the Letter Writer.* Boston: Meador Publishing Company.

Clemens, Mary Eleanor. See MEC.

Clemens, Orion. See OC.

Clemens, Samuel Langhorne. See SLC.

Coan, Titus.

1841. "Letter from Mr. Coan, Dated at Hilo, 25th Sept. 1840." *Missionary Herald* 37 (July): 283–85.

1866. "Volcanic Phenomena of the Island of Hawaii." *Friend* 17 (1 February): 9–11, 14.

1882. *Life in Hawaii: An Autobiographic Sketch of Mission Life and Labors (1835–1881).* New York: Anson D. F. Randolph and Co.

Coan, Titus Munson. 1868. "The Greatest Volcano in the World." *Harper's New Monthly Magazine* 37 (September): 553–59.

CoDR. Regis College Library, Denver, Colorado.

Cody, William F. 1879. *The Life of Hon. William F. Cody, Known as Buffalo Bill, the Famous Hunter, Scout and Guide: An Autobiography.* Hartford: Frank E. Bliss. Citations are to the 1978 reprint edition, with a foreword by Don Russell, Lincoln: University of Nebraska Press.

CofC. 1969. *Clemens of the "Call": Mark Twain in San Francisco.* Edited by Edgar M. Branch. Berkeley and Los Angeles: University of California Press.

Collins, Charles, comp. 1864–65. *Mercantile Guide and Directory for Virginia City, Gold Hill, Silver City and American City.* Virginia City: Agnew and Deffebach.

Conard, Howard L., ed. 1901. *Encyclopedia of the History of Missouri*. 6 vols. New York: Southern History Company.

Congressional Globe. 1863. "Appendix to the Congressional Globe." *Congressional Globe*, 37th Congress, 3d session. John C. Rives, comp. Washington, D.C.: Congressional Globe Office.

Conkling, Roscoe P., and Margaret B. Conkling. 1947. *The Butterfield Overland Mail, 1857–1869*. 3 vols. Glendale, Calif.: Arthur H. Clark Company.

Considine, John L.

1923a. "The Desperadoes." San Francisco *Evening Bulletin*, 20 September, Section 2, 2.

1923b. "Mark Twain." San Francisco *Evening Bulletin*, 22 September, Magazine Section, 10.

1923c. "Mark Twain Achieves Fame." San Francisco *Evening Bulletin*, 13 October, Magazine Section, 10.

Cook, James, and James King. 1784. *A Voyage to the Pacific Ocean*. 3 vols. Volumes 1 and 2 written by Captain Cook and volume 3 written by Captain King. London: G. Nicol and T. Cadell.

Cook, Lyndon W. 1981. *The Revelations of the Prophet Joseph Smith: A Historical and Biographical Commentary of the Doctrine and Covenants*. Provo, Utah: Seventy's Mission Bookstore.

Coolidge, Mary Roberts. 1909. *Chinese Immigration*. New York: Henry Holt and Co.

Copinger, Walter Arthur. 1870. *The Law of Copyright, in Works of Literature and Art*. London: Stevens and Haynes.

Cornish [pseud.]. 1860. "Washoe: Thither and Hither." San Francisco *Golden Era* 10 (15 April): 5.

Cracroft, Richard H. 1984. "'Ten Wives Is All You Need': Artemus Twain and the Mormons—Again." *Western Humanities Review* 38 (Autumn): 197–211.

Cradlebaugh, John. 1863. *Speech of Hon. John Cradlebaugh, of Nevada, on the Admission of Utah as a State. Delivered in the House of Representatives, February 7, 1863*. Washington, D.C.: L. Towers and Co.

Creer, Leland Hargrave. 1929. *Utah and the Nation*. University of Washington Publications in the Social Sciences, vol. 7. Seattle: University of Washington Press.

CSmH. Henry E. Huntington Library, San Marino, California.

CtHMTH. Mark Twain Memorial, Hartford, Connecticut.

CtHSD. Stowe-Day Memorial Library and Historical Foundation, Hartford, Connecticut.

CtY-BR. Collection of American Literature, Beinecke Rare Book and Manuscript Library, Yale University Library, New Haven, Connecticut.

CU-BANC. The Bancroft Library, University of California, Berkeley.

CU-MAPS. Map Collection, University of California, Berkeley.

CU-MARK. Mark Twain Papers, CU-BANC.

CU-NEWS. Newspaper and Microcopy Division, University of California, Berkeley.

Curry, C. F., comp. 1907. *California Blue Book or State Roster.* Sacramento: State Printing Office.

Curtis, Camphor. 1864. "The Newspapers of Virginia." Undated letter. Sacramento *Bee,* 6 January, 1.

DAB. 1928–36. *Dictionary of American Biography.* Edited by Allen Johnson and Dumas Malone. 20 vols. New York: Charles Scribner's Sons.

Daggett, Rollin M. 1893. "Daggett's Recollections," in "The Passing of a Pioneer." San Francisco *Examiner,* 22 January, 15. Reprinted as "*Enterprise* Men and Events" in Lewis, 11–16.

DAH. 1940. *Dictionary of American History.* 5 vols. New York: Charles Scribner's Sons.

Daley. Collection of Robert Daley.

Dana, James D. 1849. *Geology.* Vol. 10 of *United States Exploring Expedition. During the Years 1838, 1839, 1840, 1841, 1842. Under the Command of Charles Wilkes, U.S.N.* Philadelphia: C. Sherman.

David, Beverly R. 1986. *Mark Twain and His Illustrators: Volume I (1869–1875).* Troy, N.Y.: Whitston Publishing Company.

Davis, Chester L., Sr.

1944. "About Mark Twain's Job on the San Francisco *Call.*" *Twainian* 3 (May):4–6.

1952a. "Mark's Letters to San Francisco Call." *Twainian* 11 (January–February): 1–4.

1952b. "Mark's Letters to San Francisco Call." *Twainian* 11 (March–April): 1–4.

1956a. "Mark Twain's Highway Robbery as Told by Steve Gillis." *Twainian* 15 (January–February): 3–4.

1956b. "Letters from Steve Gillis." *Twainian* 15 (March–April): 1–3.

1956c. "Goodman's Assistance on the Biography." *Twainian* 15 (May–June): 2–4.

1956d. "Letters from Frank Fuller." *Twainian* 15 (July–August): 1–3.

Davis, Jefferson. 1856. "Report of the Secretary of War." In *Message from the President of the United States to the Two Houses of Congress, at the Commencement of the Third Session of the Thirty-fourth Congress.* Washington, D.C.: Cornelius Wendell.

Davis, Sam P., ed. 1913. *The History of Nevada.* 2 vols. Reno: Elms Publishing Company.

Davis, Winfield J. 1893. *History of Political Conventions in California, 1849–1892.* Sacramento: California State Library.

Dawson's Book Shop. 1925. *A Catalogue of Rare Books.* No. 37 (February). Los Angeles: Dawson's Book Shop.

Decker, Robert Owen. 1976. *The Whaling City: A History of New London.* Chester, Conn.: New London County Historical Society.

DeGolyer, E. 1953. Introduction to *The Vigilantes of Montana* by Thomas J. Dimsdale, 2d ed. Norman: University of Oklahoma Press.

DeGroot, Henry.

1860. *Sketches of the Washoe Silver Mines.* San Francisco: Hutchings and Rosenfield. Citations are to the 1961 reprint edition, Morrison, Ill.: Karl Yost.

1863. *DeGroot's Map of Nevada Territory, Exhibiting a Portion of Southern Oregon & Eastern California.* San Francisco: Warren Holt.

1876a. "Comstock Papers. No. 2." *Mining and Scientific Press* 33 (29 July): 80.

1876b. "Comstock Papers. No. 5." *Mining and Scientific Press* 33 (2 September): 160.

Delaney, Wesley A. 1948. "The Truth about That Humboldt Trip as Told by Gus Oliver to A. B. Paine." *Twainian* 7 (May–June): 1–3.

Denny, William R. 1867. "*Quaker City* and Holy Land Journal." TS of 273 pages, Manuscripts Department, ViU, PH in CU-MARK.

Denton, Lynn W. 1971–72. "Mark Twain and the American Indian." *Mark Twain Journal* 16 (Winter): 1–3.

Derby, George H. [John Phoenix, pseud.].

1856. *Phoenixiana; or, Sketches and Burlesques.* New York: D. Appleton and Co.

1865. *The Squibob Papers.* New York: Carleton.

De Vinne, Theodore Low. 1901. *Correct Composition: A Treatise on Spelling, Abbreviations, the Compounding and Division of Words, the Proper Use of Figures and Numerals, Italic and Capital Letters, Notes, etc. with Observations on Punctuation and Proof-Reading.* New York: Century Company.

Dibble, Sheldon.

1839. *History and General Views of the Sandwich Islands' Mission.* New York: Taylor and Dodd.

1843. *A History of the Sandwich Islands.* Lahainaluna: Press of the Mission Seminary.

Dilke, Charles Wentworth. 1868. *Greater Britain: A Record of Travel in English-Speaking Countries during 1866 and 1867.* 2 vols. London: Macmillan and Co.

Dimsdale, Thomas J. 1866. *The Vigilantes of Montana, or Popular Justice in the Rocky Mountains. Being a Correct and Impartial Narrative of the Chase, Trial, Capture and Execution of Henry Plummer's Road Agent Band, Together with Accounts of the Lives and Crimes of Many of the Robbers and Desperadoes, the Whole Being Interspersed with Sketches of Life in the Mining Camps of the "Far West;" Forming the Only Reliable Work on the Subject Ever Offered the Public.* Virginia City, Montana Territory: Montana Post Press.

DLC. United States Library of Congress, Washington, D.C.

DNA. United States National Archives and Records Service, National Archives Library, Washington, D.C.

DNB. 1921–22. *The Dictionary of National Biography.* Edited by Sir Leslie Stephen and Sir Sidney Lee. 22 vols. London: Oxford University Press.

Doctor, The [pseud.].

1862a. "Notes of a Trip to the Humboldt Mines, Nevada Territory." Letter dated 28 September. San Francisco *Alta California*, 2 October, 1.

1862b. "Notes of a Trip to the Humboldt Mines, Nevada Territory.—No. 2." San Francisco *Alta California*, 4 October, 2.

Doctrine and Covenants. 1954. *The Doctrine and Covenants, Containing Revelations Given to Joseph Smith, Jr., the Prophet.* With an introduction and historical and exegetical notes by Hyrum M. Smith and Janne M. Sjodahl. Rev. ed. Salt Lake City: Deseret Book Company.

Dorson, Richard M. 1946. *Jonathan Draws the Long Bow.* Cambridge: Harvard University Press.

Doten, Alfred. 1973. *The Journals of Alfred Doten, 1849–1903.* Edited by Walter Van Tilburg Clark. 3 vols. Reno: University of Nevada Press.

Drury, Wells. 1936. *An Editor on the Comstock Lode.* New York: Farrar and Rinehart.

Dwight, Edwin Welles. 1819. *Memoirs of Henry Obookiah, a Native of Owhyhee, and a Member of the Foreign Mission School; Who Died at Cornwall, Conn. Feb 17, 1818, Aged 26 Years.* New Haven: Nathan Whiting.

Dwyer, Richard A., and Richard E. Lingenfelter. 1984. *Lying on the Eastern Slope: James Townsend's Comic Journalism on the Mining Frontier.* Miami: Florida International University Press.

Edwards, William B. 1953. *The Story of Colt's Revolver; the Biography of Col. Samuel Colt.* Harrisburg, Pa.: Stackpole Company.

Edwords, Clarence E. 1914. *Bohemian San Francisco: Its Restaurants and Their Most Famous Recipes. The Elegant Art of Dining.* San Francisco: Paul Elder and Co.

Elliott, Russell R. 1983. *Servant of Power: A Political Biography of Senator William M. Stewart.* Nevada Studies in History and Political Science No. 18. Reno: University of Nevada Press.

Ellis, William. 1827. *Narrative of a Tour through Hawaii, or Owhyhee.* 3d ed. London: H. Fisher, Son, and P. Jackson.

Esshom, Frank. 1913. *Pioneers and Prominent Men of Utah.* Salt Lake City: Utah Pioneers Book Publishing Company.

ET&S1. 1979. *Early Tales & Sketches, Volume 1 (1851–1864).* Edited by Edgar Marquess Branch and Robert H. Hirst, with the assistance of Harriet Elinor Smith. The Works of Mark Twain. Berkeley, Los Angeles, London: University of California Press.

ET&S2. 1981. *Early Tales & Sketches, Volume 2 (1864–1865).* Edited by Edgar Marquess Branch and Robert H. Hirst, with the assistance of Harriet Elinor Smith. The Works of Mark Twain. Berkeley, Los Angeles, London: University of California Press.

ET&S3. Forthcoming. *Early Tales & Sketches, Volume 3 (1866–1868).* Edited by Edgar Marquess Branch and Richard Bucci, with the assistance of Harriet Elinor Smith. The Works of Mark Twain. Berkeley, Los Angeles, London: University of California Press.

ET&S4. Forthcoming. *Early Tales & Sketches, Volume 4 (1869–1870).* Edited by Edgar Marquess Branch and Robert H. Hirst. The Works of Mark Twain. Berkeley, Los Angeles, London: University of California Press.

ET&S5. Forthcoming. *Early Tales & Sketches, Volume 5 (1870–1871).* Edited by Edgar Marquess Branch and Robert H. Hirst. The Works of Mark Twain. Berkeley, Los Angeles, London: University of California Press.

Evans, Albert S. 1870. *Our Sister Republic: A Gala Trip through Tropical Mexico in 1869–70.* Hartford: Columbian Book Company.

Fatout, Paul.

1960. *Mark Twain on the Lecture Circuit.* Bloomington: Indiana University Press.

1964. *Mark Twain in Virginia City.* Bloomington: Indiana University Press.

1976. *Mark Twain Speaking.* Iowa City: University of Iowa Press.

Fife, Austin, and Alta Fife. 1956. *Saints of Sage & Saddle: Folklore among the Mormons.* Bloomington: Indiana University Press.

Fike, Richard E., and John W. Headley. 1979. *The Pony Express Stations of Utah in Historical Perspective.* Bureau of Land Management, Utah. Cultural Resources Series, Monograph 2. Washington, D.C.: Government Printing Office.

Fitch, Thomas. 1978. *Western Carpetbagger: The Extraordinary Memoirs of "Senator" Thomas Fitch.* Edited by Eric N. Moody. Reno: University of Nevada Press.

Flanders, Robert Bruce. 1965. *Nauvoo: Kingdom on the Mississippi.* Urbana: University of Illinois Press.

Fletcher, Robert H., ed. 1898. *The Annals of the Bohemian Club from Its Beginning, in the Year Eighteen Hundred and Seventy-two, to Eighteen Hundred and Eighty,* vol. 1. San Francisco: Hicks-Judd Company.

FM. 1972. *Mark Twain's Fables of Man.* Edited with an introduction by John S. Tuckey. Text established by Kenneth M. Sanderson and Bernard L. Stein. Series editor, Frederick Anderson. The Mark Twain Papers. Berkeley, Los Angeles, London: University of California Press.

Ford, Darius R.

1870a. "Around the World. Letter Number IX. The Pacific." Letter dated 19 November 1869, signed "D. R. F." Buffalo *Express,* 12 February, 2.

1870b. "Around the World. Letter Number X. Japan." Letter dated 17 and 24 January, signed "D. R. F." Buffalo *Express,* 5 March, 2.

Foster, Lawrence. 1981. *Religion and Sexuality: Three American Communal Experiments of the Nineteenth Century.* New York and Oxford: Oxford University Press.

Fowler, H. W. 1965. *A Dictionary of Modern English Usage.* 2d ed., revised by Sir Ernest Gowers. New York and London: Oxford University Press.

Fox, Theron. 196–. *Nevada Treasure Hunters Ghost Town Guide.* San Jose, Calif.: Theron Fox.

Frederick, J. V. 1940. *Ben Holladay, the Stagecoach King.* Glendale, Calif.: Arthur H. Clark Company.

Fried, Martin B. 1951. "The Composition, Sources, and Popularity of Mark Twain's *Roughing It.*" Ph.D. diss., University of Chicago.

Fulton, Robert. 1914. "Glimpses of the Mother Lode." *Bookman* 39 (March): 49–57.

Furniss, Norman F. 1960. *The Mormon Conflict, 1850–1859.* New Haven: Yale University Press.

Gaines, David. 1981. *Mono Lake Guidebook.* Lee Vining, Calif.: Kutsavi Books.

Gamble, James. 1881. "Wiring a Continent." *The Californian: A Western Monthly Magazine* 3 (June): 556–63.

Gasinski, T. Z. 1976. "Captain John Dominis and His Son Governor John Owen Dominis: Hawaii's Croatian Connection." *Journal of Croatian Studies* 17:14–46.

Gianella, Vincent P. 1960. "The Site of Williams Station, Nevada." *Nevada Historical Society Quarterly* 3 (October–December): 5–10.

Gillis, William R. 1930. *Gold Rush Days with Mark Twain.* New York: Albert and Charles Boni.

Glasscock, Carl Burgess. 1931. *The Big Bonanza.* Indianapolis: Bobbs-Merrill Company.

Goodman, Joseph T.

1872. "Greeley and Hank Monk." Virginia City *Territorial Enterprise,* 24 July, 2.

1891. "Taming a Terror." San Francisco *Chronicle,* 27 December, 1–2.

1892a. "A Battle-Born State." San Francisco *Chronicle,* 14 February, 1.

1892b. "How Tom Peasley Died." San Francisco *Chronicle,* 21 February, 1.

Goodwin, Charles C. 1913. *As I Remember Them.* Salt Lake City: Salt Lake Commercial Club.

Gould, Alva. 1877. "An Historical sketch of Alva Goulds life since the 22nd March 1849." Carson City, Nevada. MS notebook of twenty pages, dictated, dated 29 January at Carson City, CU-BANC.

Gowans, Fred R., and Eugene E. Campbell. 1975. *Fort Bridger: Island in the Wilderness.* Provo, Utah: Brigham Young University Press.

Graham, J. B. 1915. *Handset Reminiscences: Recollections of an Old-Time Printer and Journalist.* Salt Lake City: Century Printing Company.

Graham, J. H. 1878. *Revised Ordinances of the City of Virginia, County of Storey, State of Nevada.* Virginia City: Enterprise Steam Printing House.

Gray, Harriet Helman. 1939. "A Story of Jackass Hill." TS of seventy-four pages, CU-BANC.

Greeley, Horace.

1860. *An Overland Journey, from New York to San Francisco, in the Summer of 1859.* New York: C. M. Saxton, Barker and Co.

1868. *Recollections of a Busy Life.* New York: J. B. Ford and Co.

1871. *What I Know of Farming.* New York: G. W. Carleton.

Green, Nelson Winch. 1870. *Mormonism: Its Rise, Progress, and Present Condition.* Hartford: Belknap and Bliss.

Greever, William S. 1963. *The Bonanza West: The Story of the Western Mining Rushes, 1848–1900.* Norman: University of Oklahoma Press.

Gribben, Alan. 1980. *Mark Twain's Library: A Reconstruction.* 2 vols. Boston: G. K. Hall and Co.

Gudde, Erwin G. 1962. *California Place Names: The Origin and Etymology of Current Geographical Names.* 2d ed., rev. and enl. Berkeley and Los Angeles: University of California Press.

Gunn. Collection of Mr. and Mrs. Robert M. Gunn.

Hafen, LeRoy R. 1926. *The Overland Mail 1849–1869, Promoter of Settlement, Precursor of Railroads.* Cleveland: Arthur H. Clark. Reissued in facsimile as *The Overland Mail* in 1976 by Quarterman Publications of Lawrence, Massachusetts.

Hafen, LeRoy R., and Ann W. Hafen, eds. 1958. *The Utah Expedition, 1857–1858.* Glendale, Calif.: Arthur H. Clark Company.

Hale, Richard Walden. 1930. *Sir Richard F. Burton: A Footnote to History.* Boston: Richard Walden Hale.

Hamilton, Sinclair. 1958. *Early American Book Illustrators and Wood Engravers, 1670–1870.* Princeton, N.J.: Princeton University Library.

Hanks, Sidney Alvarus, and Ephraim K. Hanks. 1948. *Scouting for the Mormons on the Great Frontier.* Salt Lake City: Deseret News Press.

H-Ar. Hawaii State Archives, Iolani Palace Grounds, Honolulu.

Harris, Helen L. 1975. "Mark Twain's Response to the Native American." *American Literature* 46 (January): 495–505.

Hart, James D. 1987. *A Companion to California.* New edition, rev. and enl. Berkeley, Los Angeles, London: University of California Press.

Harvey, Paul, ed. 1967. *The Oxford Companion to English Literature.* 4th ed., revised by Dorothy Eagle. Oxford: Clarendon Press, Oxford University Press.

Hay, John M.

1870a. "Little-Breeches." New York *Tribune,* 19 November, 5. Reprinted in the Buffalo *Express,* 22 November, 2.

1870b [*attributed*]. "The Western School." New York *Tribune,* 27 December, 4. Reprinted as "The Western Literati. Who They Are—What They Have Done. Their Future" in the Buffalo *Express,* 29 December, 1.

1871. "Jim Bludso (of the Prairie Belle)." New York *Tribune,* 5 January, 5. Reprinted in the Buffalo *Express,* 7 January, 2.

Hazlitt, W. Carew. 1905. *Faiths and Folklore: A Dictionary of National Beliefs, Superstitions and Popular Customs, Past and Current, with Their Classical and Foreign Analogues, Described and Illustrated.* 2 vols. London: Reeves and Turner.

Heckendorn, John, and W. A. Wilson, comps. 1856. *Miners and Business Men's Directory for the Year Commencing January 1st, 1856. Embracing a General Directory of the Citizens of Tuolumne, and Portions of Calaveras, Stanislaus and San Joaquin Counties.* Columbia, Calif.: Columbia *Clipper.*

Hermann, Ruth. 1981. *Virginia City, Nevada, Revisited.* Sparks, Nev.: Falcon Hill Press.

HF. 1988. *Adventures of Huckleberry Finn.* Edited by Walter Blair and Victor Fischer, with the assistance of Dahlia Armon and Harriet Elinor Smith. The Works of Mark Twain. Berkeley, Los Angeles, London: University of California Press.

HHR. 1969. *Mark Twain's Correspondence with Henry Huttleston Rogers, 1893–1909.* Edited with an Introduction by Lewis Leary. Berkeley and Los Angeles: University of California Press.

Hickman, Bill. 1872. *Brigham's Destroying Angel: Being the Life, Confession, and Startling Disclosures of the Notorious Bill Hickman, the Danite Chief of Utah.* Edited by J. H. Beadle. New York: George A. Crofutt.

Hill, Donna. 1977. *Joseph Smith: The First Mormon.* Garden City, N.Y.: Doubleday and Co.

Hill, Hamlin.

1962. "Mark Twain's Quarrels with Elisha Bliss." *American Literature* 33 (January): 442–56.

1964. *Mark Twain and Elisha Bliss.* Columbia: University of Missouri Press.

1981. Introduction to *Roughing It.* New York: Penguin Books.

Hill, S. S. 1856. *Travels in the Sandwich and Society Islands.* London: Chapman and Hall.

Hilton, Hope A. 1988. *"Wild Bill" Hickman and the Mormon Frontier.* Salt Lake City: Signature Books.

Hingston, Edward P. 1871. *The Genial Showman: Being Reminiscences of the Life of Artemus Ward and Pictures of a Showman's Career in the Western World.* London: John Camden Hotten. First published in 1870 in two volumes.

Hirst, Robert H. 1975. "The Making of *The Innocents Abroad:* 1867–1872." Ph.D. diss., University of California, Berkeley.

Hitchcock, Charles H. 1909. *Hawaii and Its Volcanoes.* Honolulu: Hawaiian Gazette Company.

Hodge, Frederick Webb, ed. 1912. *Handbook of American Indians North of Mexico.* Smithsonian Institution Bureau of American Ethnology Bulletin no. 30. 2 parts. Washington, D.C.: Government Printing Office.

Hodges, A. D., Jr. 1890. *Amalgamation at the Comstock Lode, Nevada: A Historical Sketch of Milling Operations at Washoe, and an Account of the Treatment of Tailings at the Lyon Mill, Dayton.* San Francisco: Author's Edition.

Hopkins, Manley. 1862. *Hawaii: The Past, Present, and Future of Its Island-Kingdom.* London: Longman, Green, Longman, and Roberts.

Horner, Charles F. 1926. *The Life of James Redpath and the Development of the Modern Lyceum.* New York: Barse and Hopkins.

Houck, Louis. 1908. *A History of Missouri from the Earliest Explorations and Settlements until the Admission of the State into the Union.* 3 vols. Chicago: R. R. Donnelley and Sons Company.

House of the Lord. 1897. *House of the Lord: Historical and Descriptive Sketch of the Salt Lake Temple.* Salt Lake City: George Q. Cannon and Sons Company.

Howard, G. M. 1976. "Men, Motives, and Misunderstandings: A New Look at the Morrisite War of 1862." *Utah Historical Quarterly* 44 (Spring): 112–32.

Howells, William Dean. 1872. "Recent Literature." *Atlantic Monthly* 29 (June): 754–55.

Hoy, William. 1942. *The Chinese Six Companies.* San Francisco: Chinese Consolidated Benevolent Association.

HU. Thomas Hale Hamilton Library, University of Hawaii at Manoa, Honolulu.

Hunter, Louis C. 1949. *Steamboats on the Western Rivers: An Economic and Technological History.* Cambridge: Harvard University Press.

Hyde, John. 1857. *Mormonism: Its Leaders and Designs.* New York: W. P. Fetridge and Co.

IaHi. State Historical Society of Iowa, Iowa City.

IC. Chicago Public Library, Chicago, Illinois.

Inds. 1989. *Huck Finn and Tom Sawyer among the Indians, and Other Unfinished Stories.* Foreword and notes by Dahlia Armon and Walter Blair. Texts established by Dahlia Armon, Paul Baender, Walter Blair, William M. Gibson, and Franklin R. Rogers. The Mark Twain Library. Berkeley, Los Angeles, London: University of California Press.

IU. University of Illinois, Urbana.

James, George Wharton. 1911. "How Mark Twain Was Made." *National Magazine* (February): 525–37.

Jarves, James Jackson.

1843. *History of the Hawaiian or Sandwich Islands.* London: Edward Moxon.

1844a. *Scenes and Scenery in the Sandwich Islands, and a Trip through Central America.* London: Edward Moxon.

1844b. *History of the Hawaiian or Sandwich Islands.* 2d ed. Boston: James Munroe and Co.

1847. *History of the Hawaiian Islands.* 3d ed. Honolulu: Charles Edwin Hitchcock.

Jenson, Andrew. 1901–36. *Latter-day Saint Biographical Encyclopedia.* 4 vols. Salt Lake City: Andrew Jenson History Company.

JI2. Iwaki Meisei University, Iwaki, Fukushima, Japan.

JLC. Jane Lampton Clemens.

Johnson, Merle. 1935. *A Bibliography of the Works of Mark Twain.* New York: Harper and Brothers.

Jones, Evelyn K., and York F. Jones. 1986. *Mayors of Cedar City.* Cedar City: Southern Utah State College.

Jorkins [pseud.]. 1868. "Jorkins at Washington." Letter dated 18 February. San Francisco *Evening Bulletin,* 14 March, 5.

Journal. 1862. *Journal of the Council of the First Legislative Assembly of the Territory of Nevada.* San Francisco: Valentine and Co.

Judd, Laura Fish. 1966. *Honolulu: Sketches of Life in the Hawaiian Islands from 1828 to 1861.* Edited by Dale L. Morgan. Chicago: R. R. Donnelley and Sons Company. First published in 1880.

Kamakau, Samuel M. 1961. *Ruling Chiefs of Hawaii.* Honolulu: The Kamehameha Schools Press.

Kelly, J. Wells, comp.

1862. *First Directory of Nevada Territory.* San Francisco: Valentine and Co.

1863. *Second Directory of Nevada Territory.* San Francisco: Valentine and Co.

Kimball, Stanley B.

1981. *Heber C. Kimball: Mormon Patriarch and Pioneer.* Urbana: University of Illinois Press.

1988. *Historic Sites and Markers along the Mormon and Other Great Western Trails.* Urbana: University of Illinois Press.

King, Moses, ed. 1893. *King's Handbook of New York City: An Outline History and Description of the American Metropolis.* 2d ed. Boston: Moses King.

Knight, William H., ed.

1863. *Hand-Book Almanac for the Pacific States: An Official Register, and Business Directory.* San Francisco: H. H. Bancroft and Co.

1864. *Hand-Book Almanac for the Pacific States: An Official Register and Business Directory.* San Francisco: H. H. Bancroft and Co.

Knox, Thomas W. 1870. *Overland through Asia.* Hartford: American Publishing Company.

Kolb, Harold J., Jr. 1984. "Mark Twain and the Myth of the West." In *The Mythologizing of Mark Twain,* edited by Sara deSaussure Davis and Philip D. Beidler. University: University of Alabama Press.

Korn, Alfons L. 1958. *The Victorian Visitors.* Honolulu: University of Hawaii Press.

Koundakjian. Collection of Theodore Koundakjian.

Kouwenhoven, John A. 1953. *The Columbia Historical Portrait of New York.* New York: Doubleday and Co.

Küstel, Guido. 1863. *Nevada and California Processes of Silver and Gold Extraction.* San Francisco: Frank D. Carlton.

Kuykendall, Ralph S.

1938. *The Hawaiian Kingdom, 1778–1854: Foundation and Transformation.* Honolulu: University of Hawaii.

1953. *The Hawaiian Kingdom, 1854–1874: Twenty Critical Years.* Honolulu: University of Hawaii Press.

1967. *The Hawaiian Kingdom, 1874–1893: The Kalakaua Dynasty.* Honolulu: University of Hawaii Press.

L1. 1988. *Mark Twain's Letters, Volume 1: 1853–1866.* Edited by Edgar Marquess Branch, Michael B. Frank, Kenneth M. Sanderson, Harriet Elinor Smith, Lin Salamo, and Richard Bucci. Berkeley, Los Angeles, London: University of California Press.

L2. 1990. *Mark Twain's Letters, Volume 2: 1867–1868.* Edited by Harriet Elinor Smith, Richard Bucci, and Lin Salamo. Berkeley, Los Angeles, London: University of California Press.

L3. 1992. *Mark Twain's Letters, Volume 3: 1869.* Edited by Victor Fischer, Michael B. Frank, and Dahlia Armon. Berkeley, Los Angeles, London: University of California Press.

L4. 1995. *Mark Twain's Letters, Volume 4: 1870–1871.* Edited by Victor Fischer and Michael B. Frank. Berkeley, Los Angeles, London: University of California Press.

L5. Forthcoming. *Mark Twain's Letters, Volume 5: 1872–1873.* Edited by Lin Salamo and Harriet Elinor Smith. Berkeley, Los Angeles, London: University of California Press.

Lamb, George W. 1863. "Gold Hill Mining District, N. T." San Francisco *Evening Bulletin,* 29 December, 2.

Lang, Herbert O. 1882. *A History of Tuolumne County, California.* San Francisco: B. F. Alley.

Langford, Nathaniel Pitt. 1890. *Vigilante Days and Ways; The Pioneers of the Rockies; The Makers and Making of Montana, Idaho, Oregon, Washington, and Wyoming.* 2 vols. Boston: J. G. Cupples Company.

Langley, Henry G., comp.

1859. *The San Francisco Directory for the Year Commencing June, 1859.* San Francisco: Valentine and Co.

1860. *The San Francisco Directory for the Year Commencing July, 1860.* San Francisco: Valentine and Co.

1861. *The San Francisco Directory for the Year Commencing September, 1861.* San Francisco: Valentine and Co.

1862. *The San Francisco Directory for the Year Commencing September, 1862.* San Francisco: Valentine and Co.

1863. *The San Francisco Directory for the Year Commencing October, 1863.* San Francisco: Towne and Bacon.

1864. *The San Francisco Directory for the Year Commencing October, 1864.* San Francisco: Towne and Bacon.

1865. *The San Francisco Directory for the Year Commencing December, 1865.* San Francisco: Towne and Bacon.

1867. *The San Francisco Directory for the Year Commencing September, 1867.* San Francisco: Henry G. Langley.

Lavender, David. 1975. *Nothing Seemed Impossible: William C. Ralston and Early San Francisco.* Palo Alto, Calif.: American West Publishing Company.

1983. *Fort Laramie and the Changing Frontier.* Washington, D.C.: U.S. Department of the Interior.

Laws.

1862. *Laws of the Territory of Nevada, Passed at the First Regular Session of the Legislative Assembly.* San Francisco: Valentine and Co.

1863. *Laws of the Territory of Nevada, Passed at the Second Regular Session of the Legislative Assembly.* Virginia City: J. T. Goodman and Co.

1864. *Laws of the Territory of Nevada, Passed at the Third Regular Session of the Legislative Assembly.* Virginia City: John Church and Co.

Lean, Vincent Stuckey. 1902. *Lean's Collectanea: Proverbs (English & Foreign), Folk Lore, and Superstitions, Also Compilations towards Dictionaries of Proverbial Phrases and Words, Old and Disused.* 4 vols. Bristol, England: J. W. Arrowsmith.

Ledyard, John. 1963. *John Ledyard's Journal of Captain Cook's Last Voyage.* Edited by James Kenneth Munford. Corvallis: Oregon State University Press, 1963. Ledyard's journal first published in 1783.

Lee, John D. 1877. *Mormonism Unveiled; or, The Life and Confessions of the Late Mormon Bishop, John D. Lee; (Written by Himself).* St. Louis: Bryan, Brand and Co.

Lee, L. L. 1974. "Mark Twain's Assayer: Some Other Versions." *Markham Review* 4 (May): 47–48.

Leonowens, Anna Harriette. 1871. *The English Governess at the Siamese Court.* Boston: Osgood and Co.

Letters of Application. [1861–69] 1970. *Letters of Application and Recommendation During the Administrations of Abraham Lincoln and Andrew Johnson, 1861–1869.* National Archives Microfilm Publications, Microcopy no. M650, Roll 10. Washington, D.C.: National Archives and Records Service, General Services Administration.

Levison, Jacob B. 1933. *Memories for My Family.* San Francisco: John Henry Nash.

Levy, Lester S. 1967. *Grace Notes in American History: Popular Sheet Music from 1820 to 1900.* Norman: University of Oklahoma Press.

Lewis, Oscar. 1971. *The Life and Times of the Virginia City "Territorial Enterprise": Being Reminiscences of Five Distinguished Comstock Journalists.* Ashland, Oreg.: Lewis Osborne.

Lex. 1963. *A Mark Twain Lexicon.* By Robert L. Ramsay and Frances G. Emberson. New York: Russell and Russell.

Liljegren, S. B. 1945. "The Revolt against Romanticism in American Literature as Evidenced in the Works of S. L. Clemens." *Essays and Studies on American Language and Literature* 1:9–60.

Lillard, Richard G. 1943. "Evolution of the 'Washoe Zephyr.'" *American Speech* 18 (December): 257–60.

Lillard, Richard G., and Mary V. Hood. 1973. *Hank Monk and Horace Greeley: An Enduring Episode in Western History.* Georgetown, Calif.: Wilmac Press.

Lingenfelter, Richard E., Richard A. Dwyer, and David Cohen, comps. and eds. 1968. *Songs of the American West.* Berkeley and Los Angeles: University of California Press.

Lingenfelter, Richard E., and Karen Rix Gash. 1984. *The Newspapers of Nevada: A History and Bibliography, 1854–1979.* Reno: University of Nevada Press.

Linn, William Alexander. 1963. *The Story of the Mormons, from the Date of Their Origin to the Year 1901.* First published in 1902. New York: Russell and Russell.

Litten, Jane. 1962. "Old Poheoheo's Ghost." *Hawaii Historical Review* 1 (October): 6–8.

LLMT. 1949. *The Love Letters of Mark Twain.* Edited by Dixon Wecter. New York: Harper and Brothers.

Lloyd, B. E. 1876. *Lights and Shades in San Francisco.* San Francisco: A. L. Bancroft and Co.

Logan, Olive. 1870. "Does It Pay to Visit Yo Semite?" *Galaxy* 10 (October): 498–509.

Loomis, Noel M. 1968. *Wells Fargo.* New York: Clarkson N. Potter.

Lorch, Fred W.

1929. "Orion Clemens." *Palimpsest* 10 (October): 353–88.

1945. "Mark Twain's Early Views on Western Indians." *Twainian* 4 (April): 1–2.

1966. *The Trouble Begins at Eight: Mark Twain's Lecture Tours.* Ames: Iowa State University Press.

Lord, Eliot. 1883. *Comstock Mining and Miners.* Washington, D.C.: Government Printing Office. Citations are to the 1959 reprint edition, introduction by David F. Myrick, Berkeley: Howell-North Books.

Ludlow, Fitz Hugh. 1870. *The Heart of the Continent: A Record of Travel Across the Plains and in Oregon.* New York: Hurd and Houghton.

Lyman, George D. 1934. *The Saga of the Comstock Lode: Boom Days in Virginia City.* New York: Charles Scribner's Sons.

Lynch, Philip.

1870a. "A Case of Slanderous Vilification and Its Consequences." Gold Hill *News,* 17 January, 3.

1870b. "An Explanation Wanted." Gold Hill *News,* 1 February, 2.

McClelland, Robert. 1857. "Report of the Secretary of the Interior." In *Executive Documents Printed by Order of the House of Representatives, during the Third Session of the Thirty-fourth Congress, 1856–'57.* 13 vols. Washington, D.C.: Cornelius Wendell.

McClernan, John B. 1977. *Slade's Wells Fargo Colt (Historical Notes).* Hicksville, N.Y.: Exposition Press.

McCue, Robert J. 1981. "Did the Word of Wisdom Become a Commandment in 1851?" *Dialogue* 14 (Autumn): 66–77.

M'Culloch, J. M. 1859. *A Manual of English Grammar, Philosophical and Practical.* 18th ed. Edinburgh: Oliver and Boyd.

McGrath, Roger D. 1984. *Gunfighters, Highwaymen & Vigilantes: Violence on the Frontier.* Berkeley, Los Angeles, London: University of California Press.

McGrew, William K. [McGrooge, pseud.]. 1865. "A Sheik on the Move." San Francisco *Morning Call,* 29 October, 3.

McHenry, Roy C., and Walter F. Roper. 1945. *Smith & Wesson Hand Guns.* Huntington, W.Va.: Standard Publications.

Mack, Effie Mona.

1936. *Nevada: A History of the State from the Earliest Times through the Civil War.* Glendale, Calif.: Arthur H. Clark Company.

1947. *Mark Twain in Nevada.* New York: Charles Scribner's Sons.

1961a. "James Warren Nye: A Biography." *Nevada Historical Society Quarterly* 4 (July–December): 9–59.

1961b. "Orion Clemens, 1825–1897: A Biography." *Nevada Historical Society Quarterly* 4 (July–December): 61–108.

MacKellar, Thomas. 1885. *The American Printer: A Manual of Typography.* 15th ed., rev. and enl. Philadelphia: MacKellar, Smiths and Jordan. Citations are to the 1977 reprint edition, Nevada City, Calif.: Harold A. Berliner.

McKiernan, F. Mark. 1971. *The Voice of One Crying in the Wilderness: Sidney Rigdon, Religious Reformer, 1793–1876.* Lawrence, Kans.: Coronado Press.

MacKinnon, Richard Malcolm. 1967. "The Historical Geography of Settlement in the Foothills of Tuolumne County, California." Master's thesis, University of California, Berkeley.

McNutt, James C. 1978. "Mark Twain and the American Indian: Earthly Realism and Heavenly Idealism." *American Indian Quarterly* 4 (August): 223–42.

Malo, David. 1903. *Hawaiian Antiquities.* Translated from the Hawaiian by Dr. N. B. Emerson. Honolulu: Hawaiian Gazette Company.

Malo, David, et al. 1839. "Ka Mooolelo Hawaii." *Hawaiian Spectator* 2 (January, April, July): 58–77, 211–31, 334–40.

Marsh, Andrew J. 1972. *Letters from Nevada Territory, 1861–1862.* Edited by William C. Miller, Russell W. McDonald, and Ann Rollins. Reno: Legislative Counsel Bureau, State of Nevada.

Marsh, Andrew J., Samuel L. Clemens, and Amos Bowman. 1972. *Reports of the 1863 Constitutional Convention of the Territory of Nevada.* Edited by William C. Miller, Eleanore Bushnell, Russell W. McDonald, and Ann Rollins. Reno: Legislative Counsel Bureau, State of Nevada.

Marshall, George M. 1864. "Our Traveler's Letters." Letter dated 3 July. Virginia City *Union,* 7 July, 1.

Marye, George Thomas, Jr. 1923. *From '49 to '83 in California and Nevada.* San Francisco: A. M. Robertson.

Mason, Dorothy. 1976. *The Pony Express in Nevada.* Compiled for the Nevada Bureau of Land Management. Carson City: Harrah's.

Mathews, Mitford M. 1951. *A Dictionary of Americanisms on Historical Principles.* 2 vols. Chicago: University of Chicago Press.

Mattes, Merrill J. 1969. *The Great Platte River Road: The Covered Wagon Mainline via Fort Kearny to Fort Laramie.* Lincoln: Nebraska State Historical Society.

Maule, William M. 1938. *A Contribution to the Geographic and Economic History of the Carson, Walker and Mono Basins in Nevada and California.* San Francisco: California Region, Forest Service, U.S. Department of Agriculture.

MB. Boston Public Library and Eastern Massachusetts Regional Public Library, Boston.

MBAt. Boston Athenaeum, Boston, Massachusetts.

MEC (Mary E. [Mollie] Clemens). 1862–66. "Mrs. Orion Clemens. 'Journal.' For 1862." Location unknown, PH of MS in CU-MARK. Partly printed in Lorch 1929, 357–59.

MH-H. Houghton Library, Harvard University, Cambridge, Massachusetts.

Michelson, Miriam. 1934. *The Wonderlode of Silver and Gold.* Boston: Stratford Company.

MiD. Detroit Public Library, Detroit, Michigan.

Millard, Bailey. 1910. "Mark Twain in San Francisco." *Bookman* 31 (June): 369–73.

Miller, William C. 1973. "Samuel L. and Orion Clemens vs. Mark Twain and His Biographers (1861–1862)." *Mark Twain Journal* 16 (Summer): 1–9.

Mining Laws. 1863. *Mining Laws of Esmeralda District, Mono County, California.* San Francisco: Towne and Bacon.

Mitchell, Wesley C. 1903. *A History of the Greenbacks.* Chicago: University of Chicago Press.

Mono County Archives. Mono County Archives, County Courthouse, Bridgeport, California.

Moody, Eric N.

1977. "Another Last Word on the Weekly Occidental." *Mark Twain Journal* 18 (Summer): 11–13.

1978. Foreword to *Western Carpetbagger: The Extraordinary Memoirs of "Senator" Thomas Fitch.* In Fitch, vii–x.

Moody, Ralph. 1967. *Stagecoach West.* New York: Thomas Y. Crowell Company.

Morgan, Dale L. 1948. "The Administration of Indian Affairs in Utah, 1851–1858." *Pacific Historical Review* 17 (November): 383–409.

Morton, Charles Ledyard. 1890. *Political Americanisms: A Glossary of Terms and Phrases Current at Different Periods in American Politics.* New York: Longmans, Green, and Co.

MoSW. Washington University, St. Louis, Missouri.

Mott, Frank Luther. 1938. *A History of American Magazines, 1850–1865.* Cambridge: Harvard University Press.

Moulton, Louise Chandler. 1872. "Literary Notes." New York *Tribune,* 10 June, 6.

MS. Manuscript.

MTA. 1924. *Mark Twain's Autobiography.* Edited by Albert Bigelow Paine. 2 vols. New York: Harper and Brothers.

MTB. 1912. *Mark Twain: A Biography.* By Albert Bigelow Paine. 3 vols. New York: Harper and Brothers. [*Volume numbers in citations are to this edition; page numbers are the same in all editions.*]

MTBus. 1946. *Mark Twain, Business Man.* Edited by Samuel Charles Webster. Boston: Little, Brown and Co.

MTE. 1940. *Mark Twain in Eruption.* Edited by Bernard DeVoto. New York: Harper and Brothers.

MTEnt. 1957. *Mark Twain of the "Enterprise."* Edited by Henry Nash Smith, with the assistance of Frederick Anderson. Berkeley and Los Angeles: University of California Press.

MTH. 1947. *Mark Twain and Hawaii.* By Walter Francis Frear. Chicago: Lakeside Press.

MtHi. Montana Historical Society, Helena.

MTHL. 1960. *Mark Twain–Howells Letters.* Edited by Henry Nash Smith and William M. Gibson, with the assistance of Frederick Anderson. 2 vols. Cambridge: Belknap Press of Harvard University Press.

MTL. 1917. *Mark Twain's Letters.* Edited by Albert Bigelow Paine. 2 vols. New York: Harper and Brothers.

MTLP. 1967. *Mark Twain's Letters to His Publishers, 1867–1894.* Edited by Hamlin Hill. The Mark Twain Papers. Berkeley and Los Angeles: University of California Press.

MTMF. 1949. *Mark Twain to Mrs. Fairbanks.* Edited by Dixon Wecter. San Marino, Calif.: Huntington Library.

MTS. 1923. *Mark Twain's Speeches.* With an introduction by Albert Bigelow Paine and an appreciation by William Dean Howells. New York: Harper and Brothers.

MTTB. 1940. *Mark Twain's Travels with Mr. Brown.* Edited by Franklin Walker and G. Ezra Dane. New York: Alfred A. Knopf.

N&J1. 1975. *Mark Twain's Notebooks & Journals, Volume I (1855–1873).* Edited by Frederick Anderson, Michael B. Frank, and Kenneth M. Sanderson. The Mark Twain Papers. Berkeley, Los Angeles, London: University of California Press.

NBu. Buffalo and Erie County Public Library, Buffalo, New York.

NBuU-PO. Poetry Library, State University of New York at Buffalo.

Neff, Andrew Love. 1940. *History of Utah 1847 to 1869.* Salt Lake City: Deseret News Press.

Neville, Amelia Ransome. 1932. *The Fantastic City: Memoirs of the Social and Romantic Life of Old San Francisco.* Boston: Houghton Mifflin Company, Riverside Press.

Newman, Mary Richardson [May Wentworth, pseud.], ed. 1867. *Poetry of the Pacific: Selections and Original Poems from the Poets of the Pacific States.* San Francisco: Pacific Publishing Company.

NhD. Dartmouth College, Hanover, New Hampshire.

NHyF. General Services Administration National Archives and Record Service, Franklin D. Roosevelt Library, Hyde Park, New York.

NN. The New York Public Library, Astor, Lenox and Tilden Foundations, New York City.

NN-B. Henry W. and Albert A. Berg Collection, NN.

Nomad [pseud.]. 1862. "Letter from Humboldt, N. T." Letter dated 17 September. Sacramento *Union*, 23 September, 1.

NPV. Jean Webster McKinney Family Papers, Francis Fitz Randolph Rare Book Room, Vassar College Library, Poughkeepsie, New York.

NRU. University of Rochester, Rochester, New York.

Nv-Ar. Nevada State Library and Archives, Division of Archives and Records, Carson City.

NvHi. Nevada State Historical Society, Reno.

NvU. University of Nevada Reno.

NvU-NSP. Nevada State Papers, NvU.

Nye-Starr, Kate. 1888. *A Self-Sustaining Woman; or, The Experience of Seventy-two Years.* Chicago: Illinois Printing and Binding Company.

OC (Orion Clemens). 1861. "From Nevada Territory." Letter dated 19 August, signed "Carson." St. Louis *Missouri Democrat*, 16 September, 1, clipping in Scrapbook 1:40, CU-MARK. Reprinted in Rogers 1961, 47–49.

OC. Cincinnati Public Library, Cincinnati, Ohio.

OClRC. Rowfant Club, Cleveland, Ohio.

OClWHi. Western Reserve Historical Society, Cleveland, Ohio.

ODaU. Collection of Victor and Irene Murr Jacobs, Roesch Library, University of Dayton, Dayton, Ohio.

O'Dea, Thomas F. 1957. *The Mormons.* Chicago: University of Chicago Press.

Odell, George C. D. 1927–49. *Annals of the New York Stage.* 15 vols. New York: Columbia University Press.

O'Donnell, Sheryl. 1963–64. Notes for chapters 7–11 of *Roughing It* in "Notes toward an Annotated Edition of *Roughing It* by the Members of the English 400 Class, Fall 1963–64." Unpublished paper, John Carroll University, Cleveland, Ohio. Courtesy of John Melton.

OED. 1989. *The Oxford English Dictionary.* 2d ed. Prepared by J. A. Simpson and E. S. C. Weiner. Oxford: Clarendon Press.

"Official Correspondence." 1861–64. Official letters sent by Secretary Orion Clemens, Nv-Ar.

Ogden, Richard L. [Podgers, pseud.]. 1866. "Podgers' Letter from New York." Letter dated 10 December 1865. San Francisco *Alta California,* 10 January, 1.

Ohles, John F., ed. 1978. *Biographical Dictionary of American Educators.* 3 vols. Westport, Conn.: Greenwood Press.

OLC. Olivia (Livy) Langdon Clemens.

Olson, Gunder Einer. 1944. *The Story of the Volcano House.* 3d ed. Hilo, Hawaii: Hilo Tribune Herald.

Paher, Stanley W. 1970. *Nevada Ghost Towns & Mining Camps.* Berkeley: Howell-North Books.

PAM. Pamela Ann Moffett.

Parker, Hershel. 1973. "Regularizing Accidentals: The Latest Form of Heresy." *Proof* 3:1–20.

Pasko, Wesley Washington. 1894. *American Dictionary of Printing and Bookmaking.* New York: Howard Lockwood and Co. Citations are to the 1967 reprint edition, Detroit: Gale Research Company.

Paul, Almarin B. [Cosmos, pseud.]. 1864. "Affairs in Washoe." Letter dated 21 May. San Francisco *Evening Bulletin,* 25 May, 1.

PBL. Robert B. Honeyman Collection, Linderman Library, Lehigh University, Bethlehem, Pennsylvania.

PH. Photocopy.

Phillips, Michael J. 1920. "Mark Twain's Partner." *Saturday Evening Post* 193 (11 September): 22–23, 69–70, 73–74.

Poe, Edgar Allan. 1978. *Collected Works of Edgar Allan Poe.* Edited by Thomas Ollive Mabbott. 3 vols. Cambridge: Harvard University Press.

Presbrey, Frank. 1929. *The History and Development of Advertising.* Garden City, N.Y.: Doubleday, Doran and Co. Citations are to the 1968 reprint edition, New York: Greenwood Press.

Pukui, Mary Kawena, and Samuel H. Elbert. 1971. *Hawaiian Dictionary.* Honolulu: University of Hawaii Press.

Pukui, Mary Kawena, Samuel H. Elbert, and Esther T. Mookini. 1974. *Place Names of Hawaii.* Rev. and enl. ed. Honolulu: University Press of Hawaii.

Putnam, C. A. V. 1898. "Dan De Quille and Mark Twain: Reminiscences by an Old Associate Editor of Virginia City, Nevada." Salt Lake City *Tribune,* 25 April, 3.

Quartz [pseud.]. 1863. "Letter from Nevada Territory." Letter dated 1 February. San Francisco *Alta California,* 8 February, 1.

Rabb, Kate Milnor, ed. 1907. *The Wit and Humor of America.* 5 vols. Indianapolis: Bobbs-Merrill Company.

Rambler [pseud.].

1862. "Mining Prospects as Represented." Letter dated 12 September. San Francisco *Alta California,* 17 September, 1.

1863. "Letter from Nevada Territory." Letter dated 28 June. San Francisco *Alta California,* 11 July, 1.

Ransome, Frederick Leslie. 1909. *Notes on Some Mining Districts in Humboldt County, Nevada.* United States Geological Survey Bulletin no. 414. Washington, D.C.: Government Printing Office.

Rawls, James J., ed. 1980. *Dan De Quille of the Big Bonanza.* San Francisco: Book Club of California.

Reade, Alfred Arthur, ed. 1883. *Study and Stimulants; or, The Use of Intoxicants and Narcotics in Relation to Intellectual Life.* Manchester, England: Abel Heywood and Son.

Reade, Charles. 1859. *Love Me Little, Love Me Long.* New York: Harper and Brothers.

Reid, James D. 1886. *The Telegraph in America and Morse Memorial.* New York: John Polhemus.

Remy, Jules, and Julius Brenchley. 1861. *A Journey to Great-Salt-Lake City.* 2 vols. London: W. Jeffs.

Reports. 1868. *Reports of Cases Determined in the Supreme Court of the State of California,* vol. 4. San Francisco: Sumner Whitney.

RI 1972. 1972. *Roughing It.* Introduction and explanatory notes by Franklin R. Rogers. Text established and textual notes by Paul Baender. The Works of Mark Twain. Berkeley, Los Angeles, London: University of California Press.

Rice, Harvey. 1870. *Letters from the Pacific Slope; or, First Impressions.* New York: D. Appleton and Co.

Rich, Russell R. 1972. *Ensign to the Nations: A History of the Church from 1846 to the Present.* Provo, Utah: Brigham Young University Publications.

Richardson, Albert Deane. 1869. *Beyond the Mississippi: From the Great River to the Great Ocean.* 2d ed., rev. and enl. Hartford: American Publishing Company. First published in 1867.

Ringwalt, J. Luther, ed. 1871. *American Encyclopædia of Printing.* Philadelphia: Menamin and Ringwalt.

Ripley, George. 1873. "New Publications." New York *Tribune,* 31 January, 6.

Robinson, Forrest G. 1980. "Seeing the Elephant: Some Perspectives on Mark Twain's *Roughing It.*" *American Studies* 21 (Fall): 43–64.

Rodecape, Lois Foster. 1942. "Tom Maguire, Napoleon of the Stage." *California Historical Society Quarterly* 21 (March): 39–74.

Rogers, Franklin R.

1957. "Washoe's First Literary Journal." *California Historical Society Quarterly* 36 (December): 365–70.

1960. *Mark Twain's Burlesque Patterns.* Dallas: Southern Methodist University Press.

1961. *The Pattern for Mark Twain's Roughing It: Letters from Nevada by Samuel and Orion Clemens, 1861–1862.* Berkeley and Los Angeles: University of California Press.

Root, Frank A., and William Elsey Connelley. 1901. *The Overland Stage to California.* Topeka, Kans.: Published by the Authors. Citations are to the 1970 reprint edition, Glorieta, N.Mex.: Rio Grande Press.

Roper, Gordon. 1966. "Mark Twain and His Canadian Publishers: A Second Look." *Papers of the Bibliographical Society of Canada* 5:30–89.

Rowell, George P. 1869. *Geo. P. Rowell & Co's American Newspaper Directory.* New York: George P. Rowell and Co.

Rowlette, Robert. 1973. "'Mark Ward on Artemus Twain': Twain's Literary Debt to Ward." *American Literary Realism* 6 (Winter): 13–25.

RPB-JH. John Hay Library of Rare Books and Special Collections, Brown University, Providence, Rhode Island.

Rusling, James F. 1875. *Across America: or, The Great West and the Pacific Coast.* New York: Sheldon and Co.

Russell, Israel C. 1889. *Quaternary History of Mono Valley, California.* Washington, D.C.: Government Printing Office.

Sage Brush [pseud.]. 1864. "Humboldt Correspondence." Letter dated 11 February. Undated clipping from the Oroville (Calif.) *Union Record,* Bancroft Scraps, Set W (Nevada Mining), 94:1:208–9, CU-BANC.

Sahab [pseud.]. 1863. "The Esmeralda Region." Letter dated 24 January. San Francisco *Evening Bulletin,* 3 February, 1.

S&B. 1967. *Mark Twain's Satires & Burlesques.* Edited by Franklin R. Rogers. Berkeley and Los Angeles: University of California Press.

Sandburg, Carl. 1927. *The American Songbag.* New York: Harcourt, Brace and Co.

Sandmeyer, Elmer Clarence. 1939. *The Anti-Chinese Movement in California.* Urbana: University of Illinois Press.

Sanger, George P., ed. 1871. *The Statutes at Large and Proclamations of the United States of America, from December 1869 to March 1871, and Treaties and Postal Conventions.* Boston: Little, Brown, and Co.

Schindler, Harold. 1983. *Orrin Porter Rockwell: Man of God, Son of Thunder.* 2d ed. Salt Lake City: University of Utah Press.

Scott, Edward B. 1968. *The Saga of the Sandwich Islands.* Crystal Bay, Nev.: Sierra-Tahoe Publishing Company.

Sheldon, Addison E. 1930. "Old Fort Kearny," an appendix to Lillian M. Willman, "The History of Fort Kearny." *Publications of the Nebraska State Historical Society* 21: 211–318.

Shinn, Charles Howard. 1896. *The Story of the Mine, as Illustrated by the Great Comstock Lode of Nevada.* New York: D. Appleton and Co.

Shuck, Oscar T., ed. 1870. *Representative and Leading Men of the Pacific.* San Francisco: Bacon and Co.

Shuck, Oscar T., et al., eds. 1875. *Sketches of Leading and Representative Men of San Francisco.* London: London and New York Publishing Company.

Simmons, A. J. 1861. "The Humboldt Mines." Sacramento *Union,* 15 November, 1.

Singer, Isidore, ed. 1901–6. *The Jewish Encyclopedia.* 12 vols. New York and London: Funk and Wagnalls Company.

SLC (Samuel Langhorne Clemens).

1861. "Nevada Correspondence." Letter dated 26 October. Keokuk *Gate City,* 20 November, 2. Reprinted in *L1,* 136–40.

1862a. "Model Letter from Nevada." Letter dated 30 January. Keokuk *Gate City,* 6 March, 4. Reprinted in *L1,* 146–52.

1862b. Letter dated 20 March. Keokuk *Gate City,* 25 June, 1. Reprinted in *L1,* 174–80.

1862c [*attributed*]. Letter dated 13 July, in "Late from Washoe." Sacramento *Union,* 22 July, 2, reprinting the Virginia City *Territorial Enterprise* of 20 July.

1862d [*attributed*]. "A Gale." Oroville (Calif.) *Butte Record,* 11 October, 2, reprinting the Virginia City *Territorial Enterprise* of 1 October. Reprinted in *ET&S1,* 389.

1862e [*attributed*]. "The Indian Troubles on the Overland Route." Marysville (Calif.) *Appeal,* 5 October, reprinting the Virginia City *Territorial Enterprise* of 1 October. Reprinted in *ET&S1,* 390–91.

1862f [*attributed*]. ["More Indian Troubles."] Marysville (Calif.) *Appeal,* 5 October, reprinting the Virginia City *Territorial Enterprise* of 1 October. Reprinted in *ET&S1,* 391.

1862g. "The Spanish Mine." Oroville (Calif.) *Butte Record,* 1 November, 1, reprinting the Virginia City *Territorial Enterprise* of unknown date, probably late October. Reprinted in *ET&S1,* 160–66.

1862h. "Letter from Carson." Virginia City *Territorial Enterprise,* 12 December, clipping in Scrapbook 1:60, CU-MARK. Reprinted in *MTEnt,* 38–41.

1862i [*attributed*]. "Particulars of the Assassination of Jack Williams." San Francisco *Morning Call,* 14 December, 2, reprinting the Virginia City *Territorial Enterprise* of 10–12 December.

1862j [*attributed*]. "Blown Down." Virginia City *Territorial Enterprise,* 30 or 31 December, clipping in Scrapbook 4:14, CU-MARK. Reprinted in *ET&S1,* 393–94.

1863a. "The Spanish." Undated clipping from the Virginia City *Territorial Enterprise* (probably 12 or 22 February), Grant Smith Papers, carton 3, box 4, CU-BANC. Reprinted in *ET&S1,* 167–68.

1863b. "Silver Bars—How Assayed." Stockton (Calif.) *Independent,* 26 February, 1, reprinting the Virginia City *Territorial Enterprise* of 17–22 February. Reprinted in *ET&S1,* 210–14.

1863c. "City Marshal Perry." Rabb, 5:1809–13, reprinting the Virginia City *Territorial Enterprise* of 4 March. Reprinted in *ET&S1,* 233–38.

1863d. "Frightful Accident to Dan De Quille." San Francisco *Golden Era* 12 (1 May): 5, reprinting the Virginia City *Territorial Enterprise* of 20 April. Reprinted in *ET&S1,* 357–61.

1863e. "'Mark Twain's' Letter." Letter dated 5 July. San Francisco *Morning Call,* 9 July, 1. Reprinted in *ET&S1,* 254–58.

1863f. "'Mark Twain's' Letter." Letter dated 12 July. San Francisco *Morning Call,* 15 July, 1. Reprinted in Chester L. Davis 1952a, 2–3.

1863g. "'Mark Twain's' Letter." Letter dated 16 July. San Francisco *Morning Call,* 18 July, 1. Reprinted in Chester L. Davis 1952a, 3.

1863h [*attributed*]. "Particulars of the Recent 'Cave' of the Mexican and Ophir Mines." San Francisco *Evening Bulletin,* 21 July, 1, reprinting the Virginia City *Territorial Enterprise* of 16 July.

1863i. "'Mark Twain's' Letter." Letter dated 19 July. San Francisco *Morning Call,* 23 July, 1. Reprinted in Chester L. Davis 1952a, 3–4.

1863j [*attributed*]. Extracts published in *Mining and Scientific Press* 6 (27 July): 1, reprinting the Virginia City *Territorial Enterprise* of 14–17 July.

1863k. "'Mark Twain's' Letter." Letter dated 2 August. San Francisco *Morning Call,* 6 August, 1. Partly reprinted in Chester L. Davis 1944, 5.

1863*l.* "'Mark Twain's' Letter." Letter dated 8 August. San Francisco *Morning Call,* 13 August, 1. Reprinted in Chester L. Davis 1952b, 3.

1863m. "Letter from Mark Twain." Letter dated "Tuesday Afternoon" [18 August]. Virginia City *Territorial Enterprise,* 19 August, clipping in Scrapbook 2:62, CU-MARK. Reprinted in *MTEnt,* 66–70.

1863n [*attributed*]. "Ye Bulletin Cyphereth." Virginia City *Territorial Enterprise,* 27 August, clipping in Scrapbook 2:70, CU-MARK. Reprinted in *ET&S1,* 414–17.

1863o. "The Virginia City Fire." Dispatch dated 28 August. San Francisco *Morning Call,* 29 August. Reprinted in *CofC,* 287.

1863p. "'Mark Twain's' Letter." Letter dated 20 August. San Francisco *Morning Call,* 30 August, Supplement, 1. Reprinted in *ET&S1,* 277–83.

1863q. "Jack McNabb Shooting Policeman." Dispatch dated 2 September. San Francisco *Morning Call,* 3 September, 1. Reprinted in *CofC,* 287.

1863r. "Bigler *vs.* Tahoe." San Francisco *Golden Era* 11 (13 September): 3, reprinting the Virginia City *Territorial Enterprise* of 4–5 September. Reprinted in *ET&S1,* 288–90.

1863s. "How to Cure a Cold." San Francisco *Golden Era* 11 (20 September): 8. Reprinted in *ET&S1,* 296–303.

1863t. "Mark Twain—More of Him." San Francisco *Golden Era* 11 (27 September): 3, reprinting (with an addition) the Virginia City *Territorial Enterprise* of 21–24 June. Reprinted in *ET&S1,* 304–12.

1863u. "The Lick House Ball." San Francisco *Golden Era* 11 (27 September): 4. Reprinted in *ET&S1,* 313–19.

1863v. "The Great Prize Fight." San Francisco *Golden Era* 11 (11 October): 8. Reprinted in Walker 1938, 24–31.

1863w. "First Annual Fair of the Washoe Agricultural, Mining and Mechanical Society." Letter dated 19 October. Virginia City *Territorial Enterprise,* 20 October, clipping in Scrapbook 2:99–101, CU-MARK. Partly reprinted in *MTEnt,* 80–86.

1863x [*attributed*]. Letter from Dayton, written between November 1863 and February 1864. Glasscock, 122–23, reprinting the Virginia City *Territorial Enterprise* of unknown date, sometime between November 1863 and March 1864. Reprinted in *ET&S1,* 418–19.

1863y. "Letter from Mark Twain." Letter dated 12 December. Virginia City *Territorial Enterprise,* 15 December, clipping in Scrapbook 3:42–43, CU-MARK. Reprinted in *MTEnt,* 95–100.

1864a. "Doings in Nevada." Letter dated 4 January. New York *Sunday Mercury,* 7 February, 3. Reprinted in *MTEnt,* 121–26.

1864b. "Legislative Proceedings. . . . House—Thirty-first Day." Virginia City *Territorial Enterprise,* 12 February, clipping in Scrapbook 3:106, CU-MARK. Partly reprinted in *MTEnt,* 154–55.

1864c. "Letter from Mark Twain." Letter dated "Monday" [25 April]. Virginia City *Territorial Enterprise,* 28 April, clipping in Scrapbook 3:144, CU-MARK. Reprinted in *MTEnt,* 178–82.

1864d [*attributed*]. "Grand Austin Sanitary Flour-Sack Progress through Storey and Lyon Counties." San Francisco *Evening Bulletin,* 19 May, 5, reprinting the Virginia City *Territorial Enterprise* of 17 May.

1864e [*attributed*]. "Travels and Fortunes of the Great Austin Sack of Flour." San Francisco *Evening Bulletin,* 20 May, 1, incorporating a report from the Virginia City *Territorial Enterprise* of 18 May.

1864f. "Washoe.—'Information Wanted.'" San Francisco *Golden Era* 12 (22 May): 5, reprinting the Virginia City *Territorial Enterprise* of 1–14 May. Reprinted in *ET&S1,* 365–71.

1864g [*attributed*]. "Anticipating the Gridley Flour-Sack History." San Francisco *Evening Bulletin,* 26 May, 2, reprinting the Virginia City *Territorial Enterprise* of unknown date, probably mid-May.

1864h. "'Mark Twain' in the Metropolis." San Francisco *Golden Era* 12 (26 June): 3, reprinting the Virginia City *Territorial Enterprise* of 17–23 June. Reprinted in *ET&S2,* 9–12.

1864i. "The Evidence in the Case of Smith *vs.* Jones." San Francisco *Golden Era* 12 (26 June): 4. Reprinted in *ET&S2,* 13–21.

1864j. "Early Rising, As Regards Excursions to the Cliff House." San Francisco *Golden Era* 12 (3 July): 4. Reprinted in *ET&S2,* 22–30.

1864k [*attributed*]. "Stocks Down." San Francisco *Morning Call,* 28 July, 3.

1864*l* [*attributed*]. "What Goes with the Money?" San Francisco *Morning Call,* 19 August, 2. Reprinted in *ET&S2,* 454–55.

1864m. "The New Chinese Temple." San Francisco *Morning Call,* 19 August, 3. Reprinted in *ET&S2,* 38–43, and in *CofC,* 77–80.

1864n [*attributed*]. "Suit against a Mining Superintendent." San Francisco *Morning Call,* 20 August, 2, clipping in Scrapbook 5:41, CU-MARK.

1864o. "The Chinese Temple." San Francisco *Morning Call,* 21 August, 1. Reprinted in *ET&S2,* 44, and in *CofC,* 81.

1864p. "The New Chinese Temple." San Francisco *Morning Call,* 23 August, 3. Reprinted in *ET&S2,* 45–46, and in *CofC,* 81–83.

1864q. "Supernatural Impudence." San Francisco *Morning Call,* 24 August, 2. Reprinted in *ET&S2,* 47–48, and in *CofC,* 84.

1864r [*attributed*]. "The Californian." San Francisco *Morning Call,* 4 September, 3. Reprinted in *ET&S2,* 470.

1864s [*attributed*]. "Answer in a Mining Company's Suit." San Francisco *Morning Call,* 28 September, 1.

1864t. "A Notable Conundrum." *Californian* 1 (1 October): 9. Reprinted in *ET&S2,* 66–71.

1864u. "Concerning the Answer to That Conundrum." *Californian* 1 (8 October): 1. Reprinted in *ET&S2,* 72–78.

1864v. "Still Further Concerning That Conundrum." *Californian* 1 (15 October): 1. Reprinted in *ET&S2,* 79–85.

1864w. "Whereas." *Californian* 1 (22 October): 1. Reprinted in *ET&S2,* 86–93.

1864x. "A Touching Story of George Washington's Boyhood." *Californian* 1 (29 October): 1. Reprinted in *ET&S2, 94–99.*

1864y. "Daniel in the Lion's Den—and Out Again All Right." *Californian* 1 (5 November): 9. Reprinted in *ET&S2,* 100–107.

1864z. "The Killing of Julius Cæsar 'Localized.'" *Californian* 1 (12 November): 1. Reprinted in *ET&S2,* 108–15.

1864aa. "A Full and Reliable Account of the Extraordinary Meteoric Shower of Last Saturday Night." *Californian* 1 (19 November): 9. Reprinted in *ET&S2,* 116–24.

1864bb. "Lucretia Smith's Soldier." *Californian* 2 (3 December): 9. Reprinted in *ET&S2,* 125–33.

1865a. "An Unbiased Criticism." *Californian* 2 (18 March): 8–9. Reprinted in *ET&S2,* 134–43.

1865b. "San Francisco's New Toy." San Francisco *Morning Call,* 16 May, 1, reprinting the Virginia City *Territorial Enterprise* of unknown date, sometime after 6 April.

1865c. "Important Correspondence." *Californian* 2 (6 May): 9. Reprinted in *ET&S2,* 144–56.

1865d. "Further of Mr. Mark Twain's Important Correspondence." *Californian* 2 (13 May): 9. Reprinted in *ET&S2,* 157–62.

1865e. "How I Went to the Great Race Between Lodi and Norfolk." *Californian* 3 (27 May): 9. Reprinted in *ET&S2,* 163–68.

1865f. "A Voice for Setchell." *Californian* 3 (27 May): 9. Reprinted in *ET&S2,* 169–73.

1865g. "Advice for Good Little Boys." San Francisco *California Youths' Companion* 2 (3 June): 213. Reprinted in *ET&S2,* 240–42 (misdated 1 July).

1865h. "Answers to Correspondents." *Californian* 3 (3 June): 4. Reprinted in *ET&S2,* 174–80.

1865i. "Answers to Correspondents." *Californian* 3 (10 June): 9. Reprinted in *ET&S2,* 181–86.

1865j. "Answers to Correspondents." *Californian* 3 (17 June): 4–5. Reprinted in *ET&S2,* 187–96.

1865k. "Enthusiastic Eloquence." San Francisco *Dramatic Chronicle,* 23 June, 2. Reprinted in *ET&S2,* 233–35.

1865*l*. "Advice for Good Little Girls." San Francisco *California Youths' Companion* 2 (24 June): 237. Reprinted in *ET&S2,* 243–45 (misdated 1 or 8 July).

1865m. "Answers to Correspondents." *Californian* 3 (24 June): 4–5. Reprinted in *ET&S2*, 197–207.

1865n. "Just 'One More Unfortunate.'" Downieville (Calif.) *Mountain Messenger*, 1 July, reprinting the Virginia City *Territorial Enterprise* of 27–30 June. Reprinted in *ET&S2*, 236–39.

1865o. "Answers to Correspondents." *Californian* 3 (1 July): 4–5. Reprinted in *ET&S2*, 208–18.

1865p. "Mark Twain on the Colored Man." San Francisco *Golden Era* 13 (23 July): 2, reprinting the Virginia City *Territorial Enterprise* of 7–19 July. Reprinted in *ET&S2*, 246–49.

1865q. "Answers to Correspondents." *Californian* 3 (8 July): 4–5. Reprinted in *ET&S2*, 219–32.

1865r. "The Facts." *Californian* 3 (26 August): 5. Reprinted in *ET&S2*, 250–61.

1865s. "The Cruel Earthquake." Gold Hill *News*, 13 October, 2, reprinting the Virginia City *Territorial Enterprise* of 10–11 October. Reprinted in *ET&S2*, 289–93.

1865t. "Popper Defieth Ye Earthquake." Virginia City *Territorial Enterprise*, 15–31 October, clipping in **YSMT**, 38A–39. Reprinted in *ET&S2*, 294–96.

1865u. "Earthquake Almanac." San Francisco *Dramatic Chronicle*, 17 October, 3. Reprinted in *ET&S2*, 297–99.

1865v. "Real Estate *versus* Imaginary Possessions, Poetically Considered." *Californian* 3 (28 October): 5. Reprinted in *ET&S3*.

1865w. "'Mark Twain' On the Ballad Infliction." *Californian* 3 (4 November): 7, reprinting the *Territorial Enterprise* of 28 October–2 November. Reprinted in Benson, 194–95, and in *ET&S3*.

1865x. "San Francisco Correspondence." Letter dated 8 November. Napa (Calif.) *Napa County Reporter*, 11 November, 2. Reprinted in *ET&S3*.

1865y. "Jim Smiley and His Jumping Frog." New York *Saturday Press* 4 (18 November): 248–49. Reprinted in *ET&S2*, 282–88.

1865z. "'Mark Twain' on the Launch of the Steamer 'Capital.'" *Californian* 3 (18 November): 9. Reprinted in *ET&S2*, 359–66.

1865aa. "The Great Earthquake in San Francisco." New York *Weekly Review* 16 (25 November): 5. Reprinted in *ET&S2*, 300–310.

1865bb. "Mark Twain's Letters. Number 1." Letter dated 23 November. Napa (Calif.) *Napa County Reporter*, 25 November, 2. Reprinted partly in *ET&S2*, 371–75, and partly in *ET&S3*.

1865cc. "Mark Twain's Letters." Letter dated 30 November. Napa (Calif.) *Napa County Reporter*, 2 December, 2. Reprinted partly in *ET&S2*, 380–84, and partly in *ET&S3*.

1865dd. "The Christmas Fireside." *Californian* 4 (23 December): 4. Reprinted in *ET&S2*, 405–10.

1865ee. "Enigma." *Californian* 4 (23 December): 4. Reprinted in *ET&S2*, 411–12.

1865ff. "San Francisco Letter." Letter dated 23 December. Virginia City *Territorial Enterprise*, 26–28 December, clipping in YS**MT**, 55–56. Reprinted partly in *ET&S2*, 413–15, and partly in *ET&S3*.

1866a. "San Francisco Letter." Letter dated 29 December 1865. Virginia City *Territorial Enterprise*, 3 January. Reprinted in *ET&S3*.

1866b. "Romance in Real Life." Redwood City *San Mateo County Gazette*, 6 January, 1, reprinting the Virginia City *Territorial Enterprise* of 2–4 January. Reprinted in *ET&S3*.

1866c. "San Francisco Letter." Letter dated 28 January. Virginia City *Territorial Enterprise*, 30–31 January. Reprinted in *ET&S3*.

1866d. "San Francisco Letter." Letter dated 12 February. Virginia City *Territorial Enterprise*, 15–16 February. Reprinted in *ET&S3*.

1866e. "An Open Letter to the American People." New York *Weekly Review* 17 (17 February): 1. Reprinted in *ET&S3*.

1866f. "San Francisco Letter." Letter dated 23 February. Virginia City *Territorial Enterprise*, 25–28 February, clipping in YS**MT**, 42–42A. Reprinted in *ET&S3*.

1866g. "Letter from Mark Twain." Letter dated 25 February. Virginia City *Territorial Enterprise*, 27 February–1 March, clipping in YS**MT**, 39. Reprinted in *ET&S3*.

1866h. "The Mysterious Bottle of Whiskey." New York *Saturday Press* 5 (3 March): 3. Reprinted in *ET&S3*.

1866i. "San Francisco to Sandwich Islands—No. 1." Letter dated 18 March. Sacramento *Union*, 16 April, 5, clippings in Scrapbook 6:107–8 and Scrapbook 7:37, CU-MARK. Reprinted in *MTH*, 262–64.

1866j. "San Francisco to Sandwich Islands—No. 2." Letter dated 19 March. Sacramento *Union*, 17 April, 2, clippings in Scrapbook 6:108 and Scrapbook 7:37–39, CU-MARK. Reprinted in *MTH*, 265–69.

1866k. "San Francisco to Sandwich Islands—No. 3." Letter dated March. Sacramento *Union*, 18 April, 2, clippings in Scrapbook 6:109 and Scrapbook 7:39–41, CU-MARK. Reprinted in *MTH*, 270–73.

1866*l*. "Scenes in Honolulu—No. 4." Letter dated March. Sacramento *Union*, 19 April, 2, clippings in Scrapbook 6:109–10 and Scrapbook 7:41–43, CU-MARK. Reprinted in *MTH*, 274–78.

1866m. "Scenes in Honolulu—No. 5." Letter dated March. Sacramento *Union*, 20 April, 2, clippings in Scrapbook 6:110–11 and Scrapbook 7:43, CU-MARK. Reprinted in *MTH*, 279–83; partially reprinted in *ET&S3*.

1866n. "Scenes in Honolulu—No. 6." Letter dated March. Sacramento *Union,* 21 April, 3, clippings in Scrapbook 6:111–12 and Scrapbook 7:43–47, CU-MARK. Reprinted in *MTH,* 284–90.

1866o. "Scenes in Honolulu—No. 7." Letter dated March. Sacramento *Union,* 24 April, 4, clipping in Scrapbook 6:112–13, CU-MARK. Reprinted in *MTH,* 291–95.

1866p. "Scenes in Honolulu—No. 8." Letter dated April. Sacramento *Union,* 21 May, 3. Reprinted in *MTH,* 296–301.

1866q. "Scenes in Honolulu—No. 9." Letter dated April. Sacramento *Union,* 22 May, 3, clipping in Scrapbook 6:113–14, CU-MARK. Reprinted in *MTH,* 302–7.

1866r. "Scenes in Honolulu—No. 10." Letter dated April. Sacramento *Union,* 23 May, 3, clipping in Scrapbook 6:114–15, CU-MARK. Reprinted in *MTH,* 308–12.

1866s. "Scenes in Honolulu—No. 11." Letter dated April. Sacramento *Union,* 24 May, 3, clipping in Scrapbook 6:115–16, CU-MARK. Reprinted in *MTH,* 313–17.

1866t. "A Strange Dream." *Saturday Press* 5 (2 June): 1–2. Reprinted in *ET&S3.*

1866u. ["At the Volcano."] Entry dated 7 June in the Volcano House Register (q.v.). The two leaves containing the entry (pp. 75–78) were removed from the book sometime after 1912 and are now lost, but its text survives in two transcriptions. Published in *MTH,* 126–27, and in *ET&S3.*

1866v. "Scenes in Honolulu—No. 12." Letter dated 23 May. Sacramento *Union,* 20 June, 1, clipping in Scrapbook 6:116–17, CU-MARK. Reprinted in *MTH,* 318–22.

1866w. "Scenes in Honolulu—No. 13." Letter dated 23 May. Sacramento *Union,* 21 June, 3, clipping in Scrapbook 6:117–18, CU-MARK. Reprinted in *MTH,* 323–27.

1866x. "Scenes in Honolulu—No. 13." Letter dated 22 June, number 14 in the sequence. Sacramento *Union,* 16 July, 3, clipping in Scrapbook 6:118–19, CU-MARK. Reprinted in *MTH,* 328–34.

1866y. "Letter from Honolulu." Letter dated 25 June, number 15 in the sequence. Sacramento *Union,* 19 July, 1, clipping in Scrapbook 6:119–21, CU-MARK. Reprinted in *MTH,* 335–47.

1866z. "Scenes in Honolulu—No. 14." Letter dated 30 June, number 16 in the sequence. Sacramento *Union,* 30 July, 1, clipping in Scrapbook 6:121–22, CU-MARK. Reprinted in *MTH,* 348–55.

1866aa. "Scenes in Honolulu—No. 15." Letter dated 1 July, number 17 in the sequence. Sacramento *Union,* 1 August, 1, clipping in Scrapbook 6:122–23, CU-MARK. Reprinted in *MTH,* 356–64.

1866bb. "Letter from Honolulu." Letter dated July, number 18 in the sequence. Sacramento *Union,* 18 August, 1. Reprinted in *MTH,* 365–71.

1866cc. "From the Sandwich Islands." Letter dated July, number 19 in the sequence. Sacramento *Union,* 24 August, 3. Reprinted in *MTH,* 372–78.

1866dd. ["The Moral Phenomenon."] *Californian* 5 (25 August): 9. Reprinted in *ET&S3.*

1866ee. "From the Sandwich Islands." Letter dated 1866, number 20 in the sequence. Sacramento *Union,* 30 August, 3. Reprinted in *MTH,* 379–83.

1866ff. "From the Sandwich Islands." Letter dated July, number 21 in the sequence. Sacramento *Union,* 6 September, 3. Reprinted in *MTH,* 384–90.

1866gg. "From the Sandwich Islands." Letter dated July, number 22 in the sequence. Sacramento *Union,* 22 September, 1. Reprinted in *MTH,* 391–97.

1866hh. "From the Sandwich Islands." Letter dated 10 September, number 23 in the sequence. Sacramento *Union,* 26 September, 1. Reprinted in *MTH,* 398–407.

1866ii. "How, For Instance?" New York *Weekly Review* 17 (29 September): 1. Reprinted in *ET&S3.*

1866jj. "Origin of Illustrious Men." *Californian* 5 (29 September): 8. Reprinted in *ET&S3.*

1866kk. MS of sixty-six pages, a draft of the Sandwich Islands lecture, together with related fragmentary notes or drafts, Daley. Mark Twain first delivered this lecture on 2 October in San Francisco. Partly published in *MTS,* 7–20.

1866*ll.* Advertisement, San Francisco *Dramatic Chronicle,* 2 October, 3. Reprinted in *MTB,* 1:292.

1866mm. "An Epistle from Mark Twain." Letter dated 24 September. Honolulu *Hawaiian Herald,* 17 October, 1. Reprinted in *MTH,* 460–61, and in *ET&S3.*

1866nn. "From the Sandwich Islands." Letter dated June, number 24 in the sequence. Sacramento *Union,* 25 October, 1. Reprinted in *MTH,* 408–15.

1866oo. "Card to the Highwaymen." Virginia City *Territorial Enterprise,* 11 November, 3. Reprinted in *ET&S3.*

1866pp. "Letter from Honolulu." Letter dated 3 June, number 25 in the sequence. Sacramento *Union,* 16 November, 1. Reprinted in *MTH,* 416–20.

1866qq. "Forty-three Days in an Open Boat." *Harper's New Monthly Magazine* 34 (December): 104–13.

1866rr. "Mark Twain's Interior Notes—No. 2." San Francisco *Evening Bulletin*, 6 December, 1. Reprinted in Benson, 204–7, and in *ET&S3*.

1867a. *The Celebrated Jumping Frog of Calaveras County, And other Sketches*. Edited by John Paul. New York: C. H. Webb.

1867b. "Letter from 'Mark Twain.' Number 2." Letter dated 20 December 1866 on "Steamer 'Columbia.'" San Francisco *Alta California*, 22 February, 1. Reprinted in *MTTB*, 20–27.

1867c. "Letter from 'Mark Twain.' Number 3." Letter dated 23 December 1866. San Francisco *Alta California*, 24 February, 1. Reprinted in *MTTB*, 28–33.

1867d. "Letter from 'Mark Twain.' Number IV." Letter dated "Christmas Eve" 1866. San Francisco *Alta California*, 15 March, 1. Reprinted in *MTTB*, 34–45.

1867e. "Letter from 'Mark Twain.' [No. 14.]" Letter dated 16 April. San Francisco *Alta California*, 26 May, 1. Reprinted in *MTTB*, 141–48.

1867f. "Letter from 'Mark Twain.' [No. 15.]" Letter dated 19 April. San Francisco *Alta California*, 2 June, 1. Reprinted in part in *MTTB*, 149–58.

1867g. "Letter from 'Mark Twain.' [No. 18.]" Letter dated 18 May. San Francisco *Alta California*, 23 June, 1. Reprinted in part in *MTTB*, 180–91.

1867h. "Letter from 'Mark Twain.' [No. 20.]" Letter dated 20 May. San Francisco *Alta California*, 7 July, 1. Reprinted in *MTTB*, 202–13.

1867i. "Letter from 'Mark Twain.' [No. 22.]" Letter dated 26 May. San Francisco *Alta California*, 21 July, 1. Reprinted in *MTTB*, 226–37.

1867j. "Letter from 'Mark Twain.' [No. 25.]" Letter dated 5 June. San Francisco *Alta California*, 11 August, 1. Reprinted in *MTTB*, 259–69.

1867k. "The Holy Land Excursion. Letter from 'Mark Twain.' [Number Twenty-eight.]" Letter dated 12 September. San Francisco *Alta California*, 4 December, 1. Reprinted in *TIA*, 183–88.

1868a. "Mark Twain's Letters from Washington. Number II." Letter dated 16 December 1867. Virginia City *Territorial Enterprise*, 7 January, no page, PH in Willard S. Morse Collection, CtY-BR.

1868b. "Letter from 'Mark Twain.' Home Again." Letter dated 20 November 1867. San Francisco *Alta California*, 8 January, 1. Reprinted in *TIA*, 309–13.

1868c. "Assaying in Nevada." Incomplete MS of nineteen pages, written sometime in May, catalogued as A3, NPV. Bracketed words within quotations were supplied by a twelve-page typed transcript containing readings no longer visible in the MS, also catalogued as A3, NPV.

1868d. "I Rise to a Question of Privilege." MS of fifteen pages, written ca. 18–23 May for the San Francisco *News Letter and California Advertiser,* although left unpublished, a discussion of reverence versus ridicule, catalogued as A15, NPV. Published in *ET&S3.*

1868e. "Letter from Mark Twain." Letter dated 2 May. Chicago *Republican,* 31 May, 2.

1868f. "Remarkable Sagacity of a Cat." MS of four pages, probably written in June, catalogued as A4, NPV. Published in *ET&S3.*

1868g. "The Treaty with China." New York *Tribune,* 4 August, 1–2.

1868h. "Letter from Mark Twain." Letter dated 17 August. Chicago *Republican,* 23 August, 2.

1868i. "Cannibalism in the Cars." *Broadway: A London Magazine* (November): 189–94. Reprinted in *ET&S3.*

1868j. "Private Habits of Horace Greeley." *Spirit of the Times* 19 (7 November): 192.

1869a. *The Innocents Abroad; or, The New Pilgrims' Progress.* Hartford: American Publishing Company.

1869b. "The White House Funeral." Written on 7 March for the New York *Tribune,* but not then published. First published in *L3,* 458–66. One sheet of *Tribune* galley proof, CU-MARK.

1869c. "Scenery." MS of eleven pages, written in late June or early July as part of a lecture on "Curiosities of California," CU-MARK. Published in Wecter 1948, 13–17, and *ET&S4.*

1869d. "People and Things." Buffalo *Express,* 18 August, 2.

1869e. "A Day at Niagara." Buffalo *Express,* 21 August, 1. Reprinted in *ET&S4.*

1869f. "People and Things." Buffalo *Express,* 24 August, 2.

1869g. "L'Homme Qui Rit." MS of twenty-two pages, written ca. September, CU-MARK. Published in *S&B,* 40–48.

1869h. "People and Things." Buffalo *Express,* 4 September, 2.

1869i. "The Last Words of Great Men." Buffalo *Express,* 11 September, 1. Reprinted in *ET&S4.*

1869j. Letter dated 11 October to the California Pioneers, in "The California Pioneers." New York *Tribune,* 14 October, 5. Reprinted in *L3,* 370–74.

1869k. "Around the World. Letter No. One." Letter dated 10 October. Buffalo *Express,* 16 October, 1. Reprinted in *ET&S4.*

1869*l*. "Around the World. Letter No. 2. Adventures in Hayti." Letter dated 5 October. Buffalo *Express,* 30 October, 1. Reprinted in *ET&S4.*

1869m. "Around the World. Letter No. 3. California—Continued." Undated letter. Buffalo *Express,* 13 November, 1. Reprinted in *ET&S4.*

1869n. "Around the World. Letter Number 4. California—Continued." Undated letter. Buffalo *Express,* 11 December, 2. Reprinted in *ET&S4.*

1869o. "Around the World. Letter Number 5. California—Continued." Undated letter. Buffalo *Express,* 18 December, 2. Reprinted in *ET&S4.*

1870a. "Around the World. Letter Number 6. 'Early Days' in Nevada." Undated letter. Buffalo *Express,* 8 January, 2–3. Reprinted in *ET&S4.*

1870b. "Around the World. Letter Number 7. Pacific Coast—Concluded." Undated letter. Buffalo *Express,* 22 January, 2. Reprinted in *ET&S4.*

1870c. "Around the World. Letter Number 8. Dining with a Cannibal." Letter dated 20 November 1869. Buffalo *Express,* 29 January, 2. Reprinted in *ET&S4.*

[For "Around the World" letters 9 and 10 see Ford, Darius R.]

1870d. "A Big Thing." Buffalo *Express,* 12 March, 2. Reprinted in *ET&S4.*

1870e. "The Facts in the Great Land Slide Case." Buffalo *Express,* 2 April, 2. Reprinted in *ET&S4.*

1870f. "Disgraceful Persecution of a Boy." *Galaxy* 9 (May): 722–24. Reprinted in *ET&S4.*

1870g. Untitled MS of seven pages, written ca. 14 May–8 June, labeled "Chinese Labor &c" by Albert Bigelow Paine, CU-MARK. Published in Wecter 1948, 24–26.

1870h. "A Couple of Sad Experiences." *Galaxy* 9 (June): 858–61. Reprinted in *ET&S4.*

1870i. "John Chinaman in New York." *Galaxy* 10 (September): 426. Reprinted in *ET&S5.*

1870j. "The Noble Red Man." *Galaxy* 10 (September): 426–29. Reprinted in *ET&S5.*

1870k. "Science vs. Luck." *Galaxy* 10 (October): 574–75. Reprinted in *ET&S5.*

1870*l.* "Goldsmith's Friend Abroad Again." *Galaxy* 10 (October, November): 569–71, 727–31. Reprinted in *ET&S5.*

1870m. "Riley—Newspaper Correspondent." *Galaxy* 10 (November): 726–27. Reprinted in *ET&S5.*

1870n. "Favors from Correspondents." *Galaxy* 10 (December): 883–85.

1870o. "The Famous Sanitary Flour Sack." Letter dated 11 December signed "S. L. C." New York *Tribune,* 13 December, 5.

1871a. "Goldsmith's Friend Abroad Again." *Galaxy* 11 (January): 156–58. Reprinted in *ET&S5.*

1871b. "About a Remarkable Stranger. Being a Sandwich Island Reminiscence." *Galaxy* 11 (April): 616–18.

1871c. "The Old-Time Pony Express of the Great Plains." *American Publisher* 1 (May): 4.

1873a. Untitled play fragment, MS of twenty pages, a dramatization of the "Arkansas" incident in chapter 31 of *Roughing It,* CU-MARK.

1873b. "The Sandwich Islands." Letter dated 3 January. New York *Tribune,* 6 January, 4–5. Reprinted in *MTH,* 489–94.

1873c. "The Sandwich Islands." Letter dated 6 January. New York *Tribune,* 9 January, 4–5. Reprinted in *MTH,* 494–500.

1878. "Some Random Notes of an Idle Excursion." In *Punch, Brothers, Punch! and Other Sketches.* New York: Slote, Woodman and Co. First published in 1877–78 in the *Atlantic Monthly* 40 (October): 443–47; 40 (November): 586–92; 40 (December): 718–24; 41 (January): 12–19.

1884a. MS fragments, totaling eighteen pages, of an unfinished Sandwich Islands novel, CU-MARK.

1884b. "Huck Finn and Tom Sawyer among the Indians." MS originally of 228 pages, written beginning in July, primarily in MiD (some of the MS is at other institutions, some is missing: see *Inds,* 372). Published in *Inds,* 33–81.

1885. "The Private History of a Campaign That Failed." *Century Magazine* 31 (December): 193–204.

1897. "Villagers of 1840–3." MS of forty-three pages, CU-MARK. Published in *Inds,* 93–108.

1897–98. "My Autobiography. [Random Extracts from it.]" MS of seventy-five pages, CU-MARK. Published, with omissions, as "Early Days" in *MTA,* 1:81–115.

1899. "My Début as a Literary Person." *Century Magazine* 59 (November): 76–88.

1903. *"AS REGARDS THE COMPANY'S BENEVOLENCES."* TS of four pages, CU-MARK. Published in *HHR,* 533–34.

1905. "Joan of Arc. Address at the Dinner of the Society of Illustrators, Given at the Aldine Association Club, December 22, 1905." *MTS,* 269–75.

1905–6. "The Refuge of the Derelicts." MS of 307 pages, CU-MARK. Published in *FM,* 157–248.

1909. *Extract from Captain Stormfield's Visit to Heaven.* New York: Harper and Brothers. First published in 1907–8 in *Harper's Monthly Magazine* 116 (December): 42–49; 116 (January): 266–76.

1910. "The Turning Point of My Life." *Harper's Bazar* 44 (February): 118–19.

1912. "My Platonic Sweetheart." *Harper's Monthly Magazine* 126 (December): 14–20. Partly reprinted in *MTH,* 480–82.

1982. *The Adventures of Tom Sawyer by Mark Twain: A Facsimile of the Author's Holograph Manuscript.* Introduction by Paul Baender. 2 vols. Frederick, Md., and Washington, D.C.: University Publications of America and Georgetown University Library.

Smith, Benjamin E., ed. 1895. *The Century Cyclopedia of Names.* 2d ed. New York: Century Company.

Smith, Bradford. 1956. *Yankees in Paradise: The New England Impact on Hawaii.* Philadelphia: J. B. Lippincott Company.

Smith, Elizabeth H. 1965. "Reuel Colt Gridley." *Tales of the Paradise Ridge* 6 (June): 11–18.

Smith, Grant H. 1943. *The History of the Comstock Lode, 1850–1920.* University of Nevada Bulletin, Geology and Mining Series No. 37. Reno: Nevada State Bureau of Mines and the Mackay School of Mines.

Smith, Henry Nash.

1959. Introduction to *Roughing It.* New York: Harper and Brothers.

1962. *Mark Twain: The Development of a Writer.* Cambridge: Belknap Press of Harvard University Press.

Smith, Joseph. 1904. *History of the Church of Jesus Christ of Latter-day Saints. Period I. History of Joseph Smith, the Prophet by Himself.* 7 vols. Introduction and Notes by B. H. Roberts. Salt Lake City: Deseret News.

State Historical Society of Colorado. 1972. *Point of Interest.* Denver: State Historical Society of Colorado.

Statutes.

1852. *The Statutes of California, Passed at the Third Session of the Legislature.* San Francisco: G. K. Fitch and V. E. Geiger and Co., State Printers.

1866. *The Statutes of California, Passed at the Sixteenth Session of the Legislature, 1865–6.* Sacramento: O. M. Clayes, State Printer.

1870. *The Statutes of California, Passed at the Eighteenth Session of the Legislature, 1869–70.* Sacramento: D. W. Gelwicks, State Printer.

1876. *The Statutes of California, Passed at the Twenty-first Session of the Legislature, 1875–6.* Sacramento: State Printing Office.

1878. *The Statutes of California, Passed at the Twenty-second Session of the Legislature, 1877–8.* San Francisco: A. L. Bancroft and Co.

Stegner, Wallace. 1964. *The Gathering of Zion: The Story of the Mormon Trail.* New York: McGraw-Hill Book Company. Citations are to the 1981 reprint edition, Salt Lake City and Chicago: Westwater Press.

Steinbrink, Jeffrey. 1991. *Getting to Be Mark Twain.* Berkeley, Los Angeles, Oxford: University of California Press.

Stevenson, Burton, comp. 1948. *The Home Book of Proverbs, Maxims and Familiar Phrases.* New York: Macmillan Company.

Stewart, A. A., comp. 1912. *The Printer's Dictionary of Technical Terms.* Boston: School of Printing, North End Union.

Stewart, Charles Samuel. 1839. *A Residence in the Sandwich Islands.* 5th ed. Boston: Weeks, Jordan and Co.

Stewart, George R.

1937. *John Phoenix, Esq., the Veritable Squibob: A Life of Captain George H. Derby, U.S.A.* New York: Henry Holt and Co. Citations are to the 1969 reprint edition, New York: Da Capo Press.

1968. "Travelers by 'Overland.'" *American West* 5 (July): 4–12, 61.

Stewart, William M. 1908. *Reminiscences of Senator William M. Stewart of Nevada.* Edited by George Rothwell Brown. New York: Neale Publishing Company.

Stewart, Robert E., and Mary Frances Stewart. 1962. *Adolph Sutro: A Biography.* Berkeley: Howell-North Books.

Stillé, Charles J. 1866. *History of the United States Sanitary Commission.* Philadelphia: J. B. Lippincott and Co.

Stoddard, Henry Luther. 1946. *Horace Greeley: Printer, Editor, Crusader.* New York: G. P. Putnam's Sons.

Storey County Archives. Storey County Archives, County Courthouse, Virginia City, Nevada.

Sutro, Adolph. 1868. *The Mineral Resources of the United States, and the Importance and Necessity of Inaugurating a Rational System of Mining, with Special Reference to the Comstock Lode and the Sutro Tunnel, in Nevada.* Baltimore: John Murphy and Co.

Sutro, Theodore. 1887. *The Sutro Tunnel Company and the Sutro Tunnel: Property, Income, Prospects, and Pending Litigation.* New York: J. J. Little and Co.

Tanselle, G. Thomas. 1975. "Problems and Accomplishments in the Editing of the Novel." *Studies in the Novel* 7 (Fall): 323–60.

Taylor, Bayard. 1862. *At Home and Abroad: A Sketch-book of Life, Scenery and Men.* 2d series. New York: G. P. Putnam.

"Territorial Letters Received." 1861–64. Letters received from Secretary Orion Clemens, in "Letters Received from Territorial Officials." Office of the First Comptroller of the Treasury Department, RG 217, Records of the General Accounting Office, DNA.

"Territorial Letters Sent." 1861–69. Letters sent to Secretary Orion Clemens, in "Letters Sent Relating to Territorial Expenses." Office of the First Comptroller of the Treasury Department, RG 217, Records of the General Accounting Office, DNA.

Territorial Papers. 1942. *State Department Territorial Papers, Nevada Series, Vol. 1: May 13, 1861–October 31, 1864.* File Microcopies of Records in the National Archives, Microcopy no. 13, roll 1. Washington, D.C.: National Archives.

Thayer, William Roscoe, ed. 1915. *The Life and Letters of John Hay.* 2 vols. Boston: Houghton Mifflin Company.

Thomas, Frank J. 1964. *Mark Twain Roughed It Here.* Los Angeles: Tenfingers Press.

Thomas, Mifflin. 1983. *Schooner from Windward: Two Centuries of Hawaiian Interisland Shipping.* Honolulu: University of Hawaii Press.

Thompson, Robert Luther. 1947. *Wiring a Continent: The History of the Telegraph Industry in the United States, 1832–1866.* Princeton, N.J.: Princeton University Press.

Thrapp, Dan L. 1988. *Encyclopedia of Frontier Biography.* 3 vols. Glendale, Calif.: Arthur H. Clark Company.

TIA. 1958. *Traveling with the Innocents Abroad: Mark Twain's Original Reports from Europe and the Holy Land.* Edited by Daniel Morley McKeithan. Norman: University of Oklahoma Press.

Tinkham, George H. 1921. *History of Stanislaus County, California.* Los Angeles: Historic Record Company.

Toby, B. B. 1872. "'Mark Twain.' Biographical Sketch of the Great Humorist. Carefully Compiled from Imaginary Notes by B. B. Toby." San Francisco *Morning Call,* 28 April, 1.

Townley, John M. 1980. *Across Nevada with the Pony Express and Overland Stage Line.* Reno: Great Basin Studies Center.

Tribute. 1883. *A Tribute to the Memory of Reuel Colt Gridley. Compiled and published for the purpose of raising money to aid in building a monument to his memory, and establishing a fund for his family. Stockton, California, April 9, 1883.* San Francisco: A. L. Bancroft.

TS. 1980. *The Adventures of Tom Sawyer; Tom Sawyer Abroad; Tom Sawyer, Detective.* Edited by John C. Gerber, Paul Baender, and Terry Firkins. The Works of Mark Twain. Berkeley, Los Angeles, London: University of California Press.

TxU. Harry Ransom Humanities Research Center, University of Texas, Austin.

Urbanek, Mae.

1974. *Wyoming Place Names.* 3d ed. Boulder, Colo.: Johnson Publishing Company.

1978. *Ghost Trails of Wyoming.* Boulder, Colo.: Johnson Publishing Company.

Van Deusen, Glyndon G. 1953. *Horace Greeley: Nineteenth-Century Crusader.* Philadelphia: University of Pennsylvania Press.

Van Sickle, Henry. 1883. "Utah Desperadoes." MS of thirteen pages, dictated at Genoa, Nevada, CU-BANC.

Van Wagoner, Richard S. 1989. *Mormon Polygamy: A History.* 2d ed. Salt Lake City: Signature Books.

Van Wagoner, Richard S., and Steven C. Walker. 1982. *A Book of Mormons.* Salt Lake City: Signature Books.

Varigny, Charles de. 1981. *Fourteen Years in the Sandwich Islands, 1855–1868.* Translated by Alfons L. Korn. Honolulu: University Press of Hawaii and the Hawaiian Historical Society. Modern translation of *Quatorze ans aux îles Sandwich,* first published in 1874.

Veni, Vidi [pseud.].

1862a. "Mono County Correspondence." Letter dated 3 July. Sacramento *Bee,* 12 July, 3.

1862b. "Esmeralda Correspondence." Letter dated 28 July. Sacramento *Bee,* 1 August, 1.

Vi. Virginia State Library, Richmond.

ViU. Clifton Waller Barrett Library, Alderman Library, University of Virginia, Charlottesville.

Volcano House Register. 1866. Register of visitors to the Volcano House in 1866, pp. 63–85 of volume 1. The leaves containing the entries made between 25 April and 18 July, including Clemens's entry of 7 June, are now missing: see SLC 1866u. Original at the Volcano House, Hawaii Volcanoes National Park, Hawaii; PH in HU.

Waite, Mrs. Catharine V. 1868. *The Mormon Prophet and His Harem; or, An Authentic History of Brigham Young, His Numerous Wives and Children.* 5th ed., rev. and enl. Chicago: J. S. Goodman and Co.

Walker, Franklin.

1938. *The Washoe Giant in San Francisco.* San Francisco: George Fields.

1969. *San Francisco's Literary Frontier.* Rev. ed. Seattle: University of Washington Press.

Warner, Charles Dudley. 1872 [*attributed*]. "'Roughing It.' Mark Twain's New Book." Hartford *Courant,* 18 March, 1.

Watson, Margaret G. 1964. *Silver Theatre: Amusements of the Mining Frontier in Early Nevada, 1850 to 1864.* Glendale, Calif.: Arthur H. Clark Company.

Webb, Charles Henry [John Paul and Inigo, pseuds.].

1865a. "Local Matters: An Afternoon of Blood." San Francisco *Evening Bulletin,* 8 July, 5.

1865b. "Letter from San Francisco." Letter dated 12 July. Sacramento *Union,* 14 July, 2.

Webster, Noah.

1847. *American Dictionary of the English Language.* New York: Hurst and Co.

1870. *A Dictionary of the English Language.* Rev. and enl. by Chauncey A. Goodrich and Thomas Heber Orr. 2 vols. Glasgow: William Mackenzie.

1934. *Webster's New International Dictionary of the English Language.* 2d ed. Springfield, Mass.: G. and C. Merriam Company.

Wecter, Dixon.

1948. *Mark Twain in Three Moods.* San Marino, Calif.: Friends of the Huntington Library.

1952. *Sam Clemens of Hannibal.* Boston: Houghton Mifflin Company, Riverside Press.

Wedertz, Frank S. 1978. *Mono Diggings.* Bishop, Calif.: Chalfant Press.

Weisenburger, Francis Phelps. 1965. *Idol of the West: The Fabulous Career of Rollin Mallory Daggett.* Syracuse, N.Y.: Syracuse University Press.

Wells, Evelyn.

1921a. "The Silver Sixties." Chapter 5 in "The Silver Sixties: Tom Fitch's Story of California-Nevada Comstock Days," San Francisco *Call and Post,* 1 April, 15.

1921b. "Fighters of Old Days." Chapter 14 in "The Silver Sixties: Tom Fitch's Story of California-Nevada Comstock Days," San Francisco *Call and Post,* 12 April, 13.

West, George P. 1924. "Bret Harte's 'Roaring Camp' Still Producing." San Francisco *Call and Post,* 24 May, 13, 18.

Wharton, Don. 1948. "Why We Brush Our Teeth." *Reader's Digest* 53 (July): 139–42.

Wheat, Carl I. 1929. "'California's Bantam Cock'—The Journals of Charles E. De Long, 1854–1863 (Continued)." *California Historical Society Quarterly* 8 (December): 337–63.

Whitney, Henry M. 1875. *The Hawaiian Guide Book.* Honolulu: Henry M. Whitney.

Wilkes, Charles. 1844. *Narrative of the United States Exploring Expedition. During the Years 1838, 1839, 1840, 1841, 1842.* 5 vols. Philadelphia: C. Sherman.

Williams, George, III. 1986. *Mark Twain: His Adventures at Aurora and Mono Lake.* Riverside, Calif.: Tree By the River Publishing.

Wise, William. 1976. *Massacre at Mountain Meadows: An American Legend and a Monumental Crime.* New York: Thomas Y. Crowell Company.

Withington, Antoinette. 1953. *The Golden Cloak.* Honolulu: Hawaiiana Press.

Wood, John George. 1870. *The Uncivilized Races, or Natural History of Man; Being a Complete Account of the Manners and Customs, and the*

Physical, Social and Religious Condition and Characteristics, of the Uncivilized Races of Men, throughout the Entire World. 2 vols. Hartford: American Publishing Company.

Wood, Richard Coke. 1949. *Tales of Old Calaveras.* Angels, Calif.: Calaveras Californian.

Worcester, Joseph E., comp. 1863. *Dictionary of the English Language.* Boston: Brewer and Tileston.

Work, James C. 1979. "The Julesburg of Mark Twain's Roughing It." *Mark Twain Journal* 19 (Summer): 24.

WPA. 1941. *Wyoming: A Guide to Its History, Highways, and People.* Compiled by workers of the Writers' Program of the Work Projects Administration in the State of Wyoming. New York: Oxford University Press.

Wright, James W. A. 1960. *The Cement Hunters: Lost Gold Mine of the High Sierra.* Edited by Richard E. Lingenfelter. Los Angeles: Glen Dawson.

Wright, William [Dan De Quille, pseud.].

1864 [*attributed*]. "New Mining District." Sacramento *Union,* 10 May, 3, reprinting the Virginia City *Territorial Enterprise* of 7 May.

1876. *The Big Bonanza.* Hartford: American Publishing Company. Citations are to the 1947 reprint edition, introduction by Oscar Lewis, New York: Alfred A. Knopf.

1891. "The Thoreau of the Sierras." Salt Lake City *Tribune,* 19 July. Reprinted in Berkove 1988a, 2.

1893a. "The *Territorial Enterprise* . . . ," in "The Passing of a Pioneer," San Francisco *Examiner,* 22 January, 15. Reprinted as "The Story of the *Enterprise*" in Lewis, 5–10.

1893b. "Salad Days of Mark Twain." San Francisco *Examiner,* 19 March, 13–14. Reprinted in Lewis, 37–52.

1893c. "Reporting with Mark Twain." *Californian Illustrated Magazine* 4 (July): 170–78.

WU. Memorial Library, University of Wisconsin, Madison.

Young, Brigham. 1861. "Office Journal." Brigham Young Collection, Archives Division, Church Historical Department, The Church of Jesus Christ of Latter-day Saints, Salt Lake City, Utah.

YSMT. Yale Scrapbook, Willard S. Morse Collection, CtY-BR. [*Clemens used this scrapbook to collect clippings of his articles dating from December 1863 to October 1866, many of which he revised in the margins. The scrapbook was the source for roughly half of the pieces in SLC 1867a: see* ET&S1, *506–42.*]

Zambucka, Kristin.
1977. *The High Chiefess Ruth Keelikolani.* Honolulu: Mana Publishing Company.
1983. *Kalakaua: Hawaii's Last King.* Honolulu: Mana Publishing Company.

NOTE ON THE TEXT

The text of *Roughing It* reprinted here is identical in every respect with the text of that work published by the University of California Press in 1993 as Volume 2 in the Works of Mark Twain. (That 1993 edition superseded the 1972 Iowa-California edition by Franklin R. Rogers and Paul Baender.) The 1993 edition was edited from the original documents by Harriet Elinor Smith and Edgar Marquess Branch, in collaboration with associate editors Lin Salamo and Robert Pack Browning, and with assistance from still other members of the Mark Twain Project in The Bancroft Library at the University of California, Berkeley. The editors established the text in accord with the standards of the Center for Scholarly Editions (CSE) of the Modern Language Association. The 1993 Works edition is a CSE "approved edition"; this Mark Twain Library edition reprints the CSE "approved text," lacking only the technical apparatus and the introduction, with its full statement of editorial procedures. All editorial work was supported by a generous grant from the L. J. Skaggs and Mary C. Skaggs Foundation, and by outright and matching grants from the National Endowment for the Humanities, an independent federal agency.

Mark Twain's original manuscript for *Roughing It*—the document from which the illustrators and typesetters worked to produce the first American edition in February 1872—has not been found, probably because the publisher discarded it once he thought the text was safely in type. The author's manuscript therefore cannot serve (as it does for almost every other book by Mark Twain) as the documentary basis for the text, permitting the editors to identify and correct errors imposed on it by the typesetters and proofreaders of the first edition. Nor can authorial corrections be drawn from any subsequent edition of *Roughing It,* since Mark Twain never corrected or revised the text he first published, either for the "simultaneous" English edition (set from late proofs of the American) or for the 1899 Autograph Edition (the second American), or for any other edition published in his lifetime. The plates of the first American edition continued in use for at least twenty-five separate impressions, until at least 1903, and although a few errors and deliberate alterations gradually appeared in them, none was authorized by Mark Twain.

Under such circumstances, the earliest state of the first American edition would ordinarily be the sole authority for the text of *Roughing It.* But the editors have been able to recover, or reconstruct, many significant details of the author's missing manuscript. These range from a highly detailed chronology of its growth and revision over eighteen months of composition and production, to such things as the specific method Clemens used to prepare parts of his narrative which he had previously published in various journals, from the Buffalo *Express* to the Sacramento *Union*. It is clear, for example, that in most such cases he relied on an actual clipping of the original printing, pasting it to blank sheets and revising it, both on the clipping itself and in the margin (see the example from an early stage of the manuscript, illustrated on page 800). With few exceptions, these earlier printings were set directly from copy in Mark Twain's handwriting, and are available independently of the lost *Roughing It* manuscript. The same method, generally speaking, was used for printed texts written by others, from which Mark Twain wanted to quote: *The Book of Mormon*, for instance, or Catharine V. Waite's *The Mormon Prophet and His Harem*. So in addition to the first American edition, there are literally dozens of authoritative texts for different parts of *Roughing It*. Whenever the punctuation, spelling, or (occasionally) wording of these earlier printings is judged *more* authorial than the first edition set from them, the earlier reading has been adopted. On the other hand, whenever Mark Twain's deliberate changes to these clippings are evident in the first American edition, those changes are adopted and the decision recorded in the 1993 edition. This method permits a more complete recovery of the author's spelling and punctuation (or that of his sources) than relying solely on the first edition would. (In addition, it creates in the list of editorial choices published in the 1993 edition a detailed record of exactly how Mark Twain is thought to have revised these parts of his text.)

The critical text necessarily includes all of the illustrations that appeared in the first American edition (these were not reproduced in any other lifetime edition, and only occasional facsimiles of the first edition have since included them). But from the very beginning of composition in August 1870, Mark Twain expected his book to be extensively illustrated, and throughout its composition and production he rarely missed an opportunity to remind his publisher, Elisha Bliss, of the importance he attached to the illustrations. On 4 September 1870, for instance, he wrote Bliss: "During past week have written first four chapters of the book, & I tell you the 'Innocents Abroad['] will have to get up early to beat it. It will be a book that will jump right strait into a continental celebrity the first month it is issued. Now I want it illustrated lavishly. We shall sell 90,000 copies the first 12 months. I haven't even a shadow of a doubt of that. I see the capabilities of my subject."

Mark Twain also exerted some influence on who was chosen to draw the illustrations: True W. Williams, Edward F. Mullen, and Roswell Morse Shurtleff. Mark Twain had previously tried to secure Mullen as the illustrator for his *(Burlesque) Autobiography* (1871), and also for the book of sketches that was planned to follow *Roughing It.* True Williams, who became the principal illustrator of *Roughing It,* had previously delighted him with his drawings for *The Innocents Abroad* (1869), and would go on to contribute drawings to *The Gilded Age* (1873), *Mark Twain's Sketches, New and Old* (1875), *The Adventures of Tom Sawyer* (1876), and *A Tramp Abroad* (1880).

Clemens's brother, Orion, working as an editor for Bliss, helped to cull and criticize the artists' drawings before they were engraved ("I told Frank to take the tree out of Carson and put the auctioneer on the horse," Orion wrote his brother on 4 July 1871). And although Mark Twain's specific influence on the selection of drawings is not well documented, he clearly attended closely to the illustrations as they appeared in proof, for he twice altered his text in order to refer to, or comment on, individual drawings (see pages 289 and 370). And although Mark Twain later quarreled with Bliss about the quality of the paper and engravings used for *Roughing It,* there is no reason to suppose that he thought anything but highly of the drawings themselves.

The present text is, therefore, as close as we are likely to come to a reliable, fully authorial text of Mark Twain's second book—at least unless or until the original manuscript is found to survive. The text apart, what Mark Twain wrote is here supplied with contextual annotation (including notes and maps) of unprecedented thoroughness and detail. For a much more detailed and documented account of the composition and production of *Roughing It,* the reader is likewise referred to the Introduction by Harriet Elinor Smith in the 1993 edition (pages 797–911), from which the present note is wholly derived.

Robert H. Hirst

August 1995 *General Editor, Mark Twain Project*

THE MARK TWAIN PAPERS series publishes Mark Twain's private papers—his letters, notebooks, unpublished literary works, and autobiography. All volumes in the series are fully annotated scholarly editions that have been inspected and approved by the MLA's Committee on Scholarly Editions (CSE). For a full list of books please visit http://www.ucpress.edu/books/series/mtp.php

THE WORKS OF MARK TWAIN series publishes authoritative, critical editions of Mark Twain's published works. Based on original manuscripts or first printings, they attempt to repair the textual damage done by the author's original typists, typesetters, and proofreaders; and they restore all of the original illustrations. Each volume is fully annotated and has been approved by the CSE. For a full list of books please visit http://www.ucpress.edu/books/series/mtw.php

THE MARK TWAIN LIBRARY series reprints texts from the Papers and Works for students and the general reader. Issued in both paperback and cloth, volumes in the Library always include the original illustrations and explanatory notes, while omitting the textual apparatus and scholarly introduction. The series will eventually include all of Mark Twain's best work. For a full list of books please visit http://www.ucpress.edu/books/series/mtl.php

THE JUMPING FROGS series brings neglected Mark Twain treasures—stories, tall tales, novels, travelogues, plays, imaginative journalism, speeches, sketches, satires, burlesques, and much more—to readers. Each volume has its own distinctive design and illustrations and is presented by editors selected from Mark Twain's greatest enthusiasts. For a full list of books please visit http://www.ucpress.edu/books/series/jf.php

MARK TWAIN PROJECT ONLINE offers unfettered, intuitive access to reliable texts, accurate and exhaustive notes, and the most recently discovered letters and documents. Its ultimate purpose is to produce a digital critical edition, fully annotated, of everything Mark Twain wrote. MTPO was launched in 2007 by the Mark Twain Papers and Project of The Bancroft Library, the California Digital Library, and the University of California Press. For more information please visit http://www.marktwainproject.org/

www.ingramcontent.com/pod-product-compliance
Lightning Source LLC
LaVergne TN
LVHW090428230725
816804LV00022B/760
* 9 7 8 0 5 2 0 2 6 8 1 7 3 *